The Promise

The Promise

KRISTEN ASHLEY

Dedication and Acknowledgement

When I needed to understand how someone would recover from a gunshot wound, I asked my cousin (a nurse), Laura Foster Giannini.

She gave it all to me, from the nitty-gritty to the good stuff, like when someone could again have sex…in her words the "gentle, non-violent Rock Chick" kind.

Since I'm acknowledging Laura's help, I'll just sally forth and dedicate this book to her.

Not as an afterthought. Oh no.

Because Laura is, was, and always will be one of the single coolest people I know. She's funny. She's generous. She's crazy. She's loyal. She's beautiful. She's classy.

She's everything I wanted to be growing up, even knowing if I managed it I'd always be a poor imitation.

So this book is for you, Laura. As is my love.

Always.

Author's Note

As ever, I have my grand schemes when writing a series.

But sometimes, my characters have different plans.

In my head, the way Benny and Frankie's story would go after saying goodbye to them in *At Peace* was much different than what they gave me. In my head, it worked within the flow of the series.

In reality, Benny and Frankie had their own story to tell. Try as I might to bend them to my will, they simply wouldn't let me.

And they were right, seeing as I got to do a whole bunch of fun stuff I wouldn't have been able to if I'd made their story what *I* wanted it to be.

So I hope it is no spoiler to share that this is somewhat of a rewind. I won't mention more.

But there are bonuses to that rewind.

I just hope you agree.

One

Takin' the Fight Outta You

"*Y*ou ready?"

"Yep."

"Called a taxi?"

"Yep."

"Let's go."

With effort, I heaved myself off the hospital bed, twisted and aimed my ass at the wheelchair Cindy was holding still for me. I could feel my mouth get tight at the pain, but other than that, I didn't let it show (I hoped).

I settled in, but the pain didn't entirely subside. Luckily, Cindy handed me my bag that I put on my lap, then she gave me a big envelope filled with some papers. I had to concentrate on taking hold of all that so I didn't get to concentrate on the pain.

The pain, incidentally, was the result of a gunshot wound.

It was surprising that a gunshot wound only bought me a week and a half in the hospital. Apparently, according to Cindy and the other nurses, I was a fast healer.

I didn't feel like a fast healer.

I felt like shit.

But I wanted to get out of that fucking hospital. The bed wasn't comfortable. The place was freaking noisy so I wasn't sleeping well. And it didn't help that the shot I took was to the middle so I had to sleep on my back.

1

I never slept on my back. I snored when I slept on my back. Women didn't snore. I knew this wasn't a reality; women snored. But for me, as a woman, *I* was not going to be a woman who snored. So, although I used to sleep on my back all the time, I trained myself to sleep on my stomach or side so I wouldn't snore.

Yes, I did this, even though I hadn't had a man in my bed in seven years. Seven.

Still, I didn't snore. Even in my own company.

The final, most important reason to get out of that fucking hospital was because I had more company in that hospital than I'd had to my apartment for the last seven years. Sal. Sal's boys. Sal's wife, Gina.

And worst of all, the Bianchis. The freaking Bianchis wouldn't leave me alone. Vinnie Senior, Theresa, even fucking Manny.

Then, of course, there was Benny.

If I was honest, Benny was the real reason I was happy to escape that hospital.

I'd been avoiding the Bianchis for a week and a half by pretending I was asleep and that was even more exhausting than not sleeping. My door would open and it didn't matter what I was doing. Watching TV. Reading a book. Flipping through a magazine. Talking on the phone. I'd instantly feign sleep, even disconnecting a phone call to do it.

Of course, I'd stop doing this if it was Sal, one of his guys, his wife, or one of my friends.

I wouldn't if it was a Bianchi.

But yesterday, Benny got fed up with this.

He had, on more than one occasion the last week and a half, said right in my ear, his lips so close to my skin I could nearly feel them, "Babe, open your eyes. I know you're fakin'."

Usually, he would do this and wait. But not for long.

I knew Benito Bianchi. I knew all the Bianchis. They were not patient by nature. And Benny was a male Bianchi so his span of patience was akin to the attention of a gnat. Therefore, I could wait him out, no sweat.

And I did. Successfully. For a week and a half.

Yesterday, though, I knew Benny was done. This was because he didn't whisper in my ear that he knew I was faking.

Oh no.

Instead, he scooched my ass right over and stretched out in bed beside me, shoving an arm under me, wrapping it around and tucking me close. He then grabbed the remote from my hospital table and turned on a fucking baseball game.

I lay next to him biting my tongue (figuratively, seeing as if I let my mouth move, I could no longer fake sleeping), wanting to remind him of the fact that I'd been shot and perhaps he shouldn't scrunch in my hospital bed with me.

Admittedly, this didn't feel awful. He'd been gentle about it and it sucked to discover that Ben could be gentle physically. I didn't need to know that about him, as in I *really* didn't need to know that about him seeing as he was my dead boyfriend's brother, he was Italian American, and last, he was hot in the sense that Death Valley was hot. He so topped the scale on hotness, he reinvented the scale. I was already perving on him, and he was my dead boyfriend's brother, so this made it wrong to perv on him, as in *wrong*.

So I didn't need to know he was gentle.

But he was. Which sucked.

And made him even hotter.

In the end, he was so gentle and so warm and so hard—in that good way men's bodies could be hard (or, that *other* good way)—and all that was so comfortable to feel tucked up close, I genuinely fell asleep.

I had a feeling I snored.

That was the bad news.

The good news was he was gone when I woke up.

The other good news was I hoped the snoring turned him off. No one liked someone who snored.

You might put up with it if you loved them, but Benny didn't love me and I was going to make sure that remained the case.

Now I was getting the hell out of there. Not because it was my choice, but I sure as hell wasn't saying no.

Cindy started wheeling me to the door and she did this speaking.

"There are some scripts in that envelope. You get home, you got someone to go to the pharmacy for you?"

Yes. I did. I could call on anyone in the Bianchi family (primarily Ben) and they'd go to the pharmacy for me. They'd also take me home, tuck me into bed, clean my house, fill my fridge, and then stay awhile, cooking for me and keeping me company.

They had a breach to heal. I took a bullet for one of their own. They considered me family once, and when a Bianchi considers you family and a rift forms and they want to patch it, they'll go all out to do it. Hence the Bianchi visits I'd faked sleeping through.

But I took their shit for years. I did it because I loved them. I did it because I loved Vinnie Junior. I did it because they lost a son and a brother and they had to pile their pain on somebody, and seeing as I loved them, I let that be me.

Then I took a bullet for them.

Enough.

I also had Sal. Sal would do anything for me. His business killed my man. He owed me and he was the kind of man who felt markers like that never went fulfilled.

He was also a Mafia crime boss. So, as much as I loved him, I didn't want to go there.

I also had friends. I used to have more—prior to my dead boyfriend deciding on a career path that meant he became a made man in the mob— but I still had a few.

I wasn't going to go there either. I didn't pretend to sleep when they stopped by, but even before I had the spectacular idea to stick my nose in a situation that got me shot, I was making moves to get on with my life. I'd been treading water in Chicago for too long; seven years after Vinnie died. It was time to be done with it. Start over. I was thirty-four years old. I'd wasted seven years. I shouldn't waste any more.

Who I could not call was any of my own flesh and blood. I loved them. I really did. But the drama they brought with them wasn't worth it. I'd been shot. People lived their whole lives not only never getting shot, but also not getting shot *at*.

My family still could out-drama a gunshot wound. This would be no challenge to them.

So I didn't need that either.

"Sure," I answered Cindy as she wheeled me down the hall.

"You got painkiller scripts in there," she told me, heading toward the elevators. "Now, you know I saw what happened to you on the TV. You went all out, bein' a hero, helpin' to save that woman from that psycho guy. You use those pills when you need them, stop when you don't. Be a shame you went from hero to junkie."

Cindy spoke truth.

Cindy was also an African American nurse who worked in that suburban hospital just outside Chicago, but she used to work at a hospital deep in the city. Over the last week and a half, I'd learned that Cindy had seen a lot and most of it was not good.

I'd also learned that Cindy didn't beat around the bush.

"I'll do my best not to become a junkie," I assured her as she hit the elevator button.

"Follow the doctor's orders. Read 'em good," she ordered. "Get your booty out of bed and get around. But don't overdo it. You hear?" she finished as the elevator binged.

"I hear," I muttered.

She wheeled me in the elevator and expertly wheeled me around to face forward.

"This has not been real fun," I told the doors but did it speaking to Cindy. "But I'm gonna miss you and the girls."

Weirdly, this was true. It was likely I'd never forget getting shot or the ensuing weeks where I had to battle the pain, struggle to recover, and do this with a Bianchi onslaught in full swing. But the nurses in that hospital were the best. I couldn't say this with any authority; I'd never had a hospital stay before. But they were so good I couldn't imagine better.

"Yeah, we're gonna miss you too," she replied. "Mostly we'll miss tryin' to figure out what is *up* with you doin' the Sleepin' Beauty act when that boy comes callin'."

Apparently they were also attentive. And to more than just my health.

I pressed my lips together.

"What *is* up with that?" Cindy prompted.

"Uh…" I non-responded as the elevator doors binged again and started to open.

"That boy came every day to see me," she started as she began to push me out of the elevators, "I'd be on the phone with my stylist *like a shot*. I'd have my hair done. My nails done. My toenails done. And I'd be in a negligee."

I tamped down visions of me in a negligee reclining in a hospital bed, which were too ridiculous to fathom, even for me (and there was very little too ridiculous to fathom about me), and I thought about Gina.

Gina had brought me some new nightgowns and a robe to wear during my hospital stay. They were pretty in a cute way that was *very* Gina and *so* not me.

I was about flash and impact all the time. I could put on the glitz just going down to the lobby to get my mail.

But when it came to bed wear, the less material the better. And if there was material, I liked it to leave as little to the imagination as possible (yes, even if I was sleeping just with me).

As cute as the ones Gina brought were, they were also appropriate for a hospital stay, thus no flash, no impact, and lots of material.

I'd opted to wear hospital gowns.

They were ugly, shapeless, and no one could get ideas about a woman in a hospital gown.

And I had a feeling Benny was getting ideas.

Cindy started wheeling me toward the exit doors and she did this still talking.

"So the girls, we've been talkin' about that since he brought you in covered in your blood. Now, I didn't see that part, but it's made the rounds *big time*. Hot guy. Hot girl. GSW. Blood. Drama. Resulting television crews. That happens."

I was sure it did.

But it was time to put a stop to this.

"He's my dead boyfriend's brother."

"Ah," she uttered knowingly, still wheeling. Her voice had gone from no-nonsense nosy to soft with nurse concern when she went on, "Sorry to hear about your loss, hon. When'd he die?"

"Seven years ago."

She stopped wheeling.

"Uh…what?"

I twisted my neck to look up at her to see her staring down at me.

"Vinnie died seven years ago."

"And you're fakin' sleepin' when his hottie brother comes a-callin' because of why?"

"Because Benny, the hottie brother, wants to talk," I told her.

"About what?" she asked.

I had no clue.

But with the way he traced my lower lip with his thumb when he told me we were going to talk...With the way he picked me up off the forest floor and sprinted to his SUV with me in his arms after I was shot...With the way he caught my pass years ago when I was drunk after Vinnie died and stupidly, crazily, sluttily threw myself at him...

Well, with all that, I was thinking all this attention wasn't about remembrance of sisterly love, what with the lip-tracing and tongues-tangling parts being included.

"I don't know," I shared with Cindy.

Her brows shot up. "And you faked sleepin' and didn't find out?"

"Yep."

Her head tipped to the side and she deduced, "'Cause no boy who looks like that comes to the hospital every day for a girl who looks like you 'cause he's keepin' an eye on his seven-years-dead brother's girlfriend."

Indication that Cindy not only had seen it all, but she understood it.

"Something like that," I conceded.

"Everything like that," she returned.

She was right, but I didn't confirm that fact.

"You're not into him?" she asked, and I felt my eyes get wide.

"He's Benny," I said in response, figuring that said it all.

"He sure is," she agreed, knowing it said it all because she'd seen him, repeatedly (though, once would do it).

"But he's my dead boyfriend's brother."

"Girl," she started, wheeling me toward the doors again, "God doesn't care who you let in there, just as long as the feelin's are honest when you let him in."

I looked to my bag on my knees. "It's my understanding God *does* care who you let *in there*."

"Sure enough," she replied. "But that's not the *there* I'm talkin' about. The *there* I'm talkin' about is your heart."

I was not going to get into this with my soon-to-be-ex nurse while she wheeled me to the taxi that would take me home after my hospital stay, so I pressed my lips together again.

I unpressed them when I felt her stutter step behind me and the wheelchair jerked slightly with her movement.

I also looked up when this happened.

And what I saw was Benny Bianchi in a white t-shirt that hugged his muscular torso in a way that made you jealous of that tee. He also had on faded jeans that fit loose in a way that only hinted at the power in those long legs (not to mention the power behind that package), making you want to get acquainted with both…*intimately*. He was leaning against his Explorer right outside the doors.

He had his arms crossed on his chest and shades over his dark brown eyes, but I knew those eyes were on me.

He was waiting on me.

Not parked illegally outside a hospital to come for a visit.

Waiting on me to be released.

"Uh…Cindy," I muttered, eyes glued to Ben. "Did someone at the nurse's station share with Benny when I'd be released?"

"He may have made that inquiry," she evaded.

"And was it answered?" I asked, though the evidence it was was pushing away from his Explorer. It was then I knew why Cindy was wheeling me to the doors and not a nurse's assistant or an orderly. She didn't want to miss this or miss reporting back to the girls.

"Mm," Cindy mumbled her evasion this time.

I couldn't get pissed at this. Not because it wasn't worthy of being pissed at, but because Benny was moving in our direction, we were moving in his, and all my attention was taken in concentrating on watching him move.

He moved well. He looked good. He was tall. He worked on his body and this work was extremely successful. He had a lot of thick, messy black hair. And he had a face that was movie-star handsome in a way that, without a doubt, launched a million wedding fantasies, even from women who just caught a glimpse of him walking down the street.

My eyes remained locked on him as the doors swished open and we trundled through at the exact same time Benny arrived at our location.

I opened my mouth to say something but didn't get a word out because Ben grabbed my bag from my lap and thrust it Cindy's way with a murmured, "Could you hold that, darlin'?"

Cindy took it and I again opened my mouth to say something and, again, didn't get a word out because Ben bent, shoved a hand under my knees, one around my waist, and lifted me into his arms.

But gently.

There was pain, but it was minimal. Mostly because it came with his strength and warmth and the smell of his aftershave.

Shit!

I said something then. It was loud, but it was lame.

And what it was was, "Ben!"

He didn't even look at me. He turned to Cindy and said, "I'll take that now." She must have given my bag to him because he immediately went on, "Thanks, beautiful. You've been great. Got it from here."

After delivering that, he turned and started walking to his SUV.

I glared around his shoulder at Cindy.

Cindy stood with hands on the handles of the wheelchair and grinned at me.

"I'm canceling that big bouquet of flowers and three-layers-deep box of Fannie May I ordered for the nurse's station!" I yelled.

She pulled her phone out of her scrubs, lifted it, and I knew she took a picture while Benny opened the back door to his SUV in order to toss my bag in, because she called, "That's okay. I'll share this shot with the girls." She looked from her phone to me. "This'll be all the thanks we need."

I had more to say to my now ex-nurse Cindy, but I lost sight of her and couldn't retort when Benny deposited me (gently, God!) into the front passenger seat.

I turned my glare to him.

"You aren't taking me home," I declared.

"You're right. I'm not," he replied, attention on the seatbelt.

He wasn't?

"I *am* in your truck, Ben," I pointed out.

His eyes came to mine and I was glad he had his shades on because he had beautiful eyes. Amazing. A rich dark brown that could dance with laughter and warm with feeling, both having the capacity to melt your heart.

Unfortunately, his eyes also looked good hidden behind his silver wire-rimmed shades.

"I'm not takin' you home. I'm takin' you to *my* home," he clarified.

I blinked. I stared. I totally forgot about how cool his sunglasses looked. Then I lost my mind.

"I'm not goin' to your house!" I shouted.

"Yeah, you are," he replied, attention back to the seatbelt he was pulling around me, shoulder strap yanked way out to clear my head.

This was thoughtful. I didn't need that strap pressing against my body. It would kill.

I ignored his thoughtfulness and declared, "I'm goin' to my house."

"Nope. You aren't."

"I ordered a taxi," I told him.

"Found him. Gave him a twenty. Sent him on his way."

He was leaning in to latch the seatbelt, and since he was that close, I got a good whiff of his aftershave. I also got a good view of the back of his head with his thick, black, wavy hair.

It was hair you'd run your fingers through just because. Any occasion granted you, you'd take it.

If you were standing close and talking.

If you were lying around, tangled up together, watching TV.

If you were kissing.

I closed my eyes.

God really, *really* hated me.

I opened my eyes. "You can't send the taxi away. I gave them my credit card. They're gonna charge me anyway."

I heard the belt click and he adjusted his position so he was facing me. He was still leaning into the cab of the truck. He was still close. And I could still smell his aftershave.

It was spicy.

Yes, God hated me.

"I'll reimburse you," he said.

"Benny, this is not cool," I snapped. "I've just been shot. I don't need this."

"You were shot a week and a half ago, babe. And if you felt shit, you wouldn't be able to mouth off."

I clamped my mouth shut.

Ben grinned.

My clit pulsed.

Yes. God so totally hated me. He was punishing me. Doing it on earth before He sent me to the fiery depths of hell.

Ben moved out of the cab and slammed my door.

It was at this point that I could make a break for it. Then again, I didn't think the awkward, painful strolls I'd been taking around the hospital corridors had prepared me to make a desperate dash from lean, fit Benito Bianchi. Hell, if I was in perfect shape, I still couldn't execute a desperate dash from Benny Bianchi.

So I didn't make a desperate dash. I glared at him through the windshield as he rounded the hood of his Explorer and I kept glaring at him as he pulled his long body into the driver's seat. Committed to this act, I continued to do it as he switched on the ignition and guided the truck away from the curb.

It was then I noticed he didn't put on his seatbelt.

"It's law to wear your seatbelt in Illinois, Benny," I shared snippily.

He didn't glance at me, kept negotiating the rounding drive out of the hospital, but reached for his seatbelt and clicked it in place.

Well, hell. He took direction. Even snippy direction.

I didn't need to know that either.

He pulled out onto the street.

"Can you explain why you're kidnapping me?" I requested to know.

"Kidnapping you?" he asked the road.

"I *am* in your truck against my volition," I pointed out.

"Right." He grinned. I saw it and my mouth went dry. "Then I guess I'm kidnapping you," he finished good-naturedly.

It was unfortunate that it was highly likely I'd rip my gunshot wound open if I attempted to scratch his eyes out. Furthermore, I didn't want to survive genuinely getting kidnapped by a madman, running through a forest, ending up shot, only to get in a car accident mere minutes after being released from the hospital.

Therefore, I decided not to do that and instead kept questioning.

"Now that we have that down, can you explain why?"

"'Cause you're not gonna convalesce under the watchful eye of a mob kingpin."

"I was heading home, Ben," I shared.

"And you don't think Sal wouldn't have his ass, Gina's, and every Chicago mob wife and girlfriend up in your shit, catering to your every whim?" he returned. "You're family and you took a bullet for family. He was your godfather. Now he's your *fairy* godfather."

Pure Benny.

"I wouldn't let Sal hear you refer to him as my fairy anything," I advised.

"I don't give a fuck what Sal hears me say about him."

It was not surprising that the Bianchis, who owned a family pizzeria and had nothing to do with the *Cosa Nostra*, weren't all fired up when Vinnie Junior decided to cast his lot with his uncle Sal. They were less fired up about it when he got whacked during a war Sal found himself in.

There weren't a lot of people who would disrespect a Mafia boss.

The Bianchis were the exception. And Benny, who loved his brother, loved his mother and father, sister, and other brother, hated to lose Vinnie Junior. He also hated to watch his family suffer that same loss. Therefore, he took that disrespect to extremes.

It scared the crap out of me.

If you knew Salvatore Giglia like I knew him, you would think he was the kindest-hearted man you'd ever met.

But he absolutely was not.

Therefore, my voice was lower when I noted, "You need to be careful about Sal, Ben."

He glanced at me before looking back to the road while asking, "What? You think he'll take another son from my father?"

At the reference to Vinnie Junior, I decided I was done talking.

"He would not do that shit," Benny went on.

No. Sal wouldn't. He respected Vinnie Senior. He might not eat any shit in his life at all. None.

But he'd eat Benny's shit because of what happened to Vinnie Junior and because he respected Vinnie Junior's father.

This was surprising. In Sal's world, he figured he'd won respect from everyone—save cops, the FBI, and IRS agents—so he demanded it.

But he didn't mingle at family reunions with cops and FBI agents.

And he ate shit from the Bianchi family.

Particularly Benny.

"Anyway, babe, he's not here," Ben finished.

Luckily, this was true.

I decided to keep not talking.

This was because there was nothing to say to his comment. It was also because I had a new strategy.

Silence. Preserve my energy. Get to Benny's house and ask him to go to the pharmacy for me. Wave him happily away. Call a taxi. Get the fuck out of there.

And not to my home. I'd go to a hotel.

The Drake. I'd always wanted to stay at The Drake and now was my shot.

One last hurrah.

I had a new job in Indianapolis. They'd been pretty cool about the whole me-getting-shot-and-having-to-delay-starting-work-for-them thing. Mostly because I'd been on TV (or my picture had) and they thought I was a hero rather than a crazy bitch on a mission who nearly got herself killed.

So I'd check into The Drake. Live it up for a few days. Get out. Pack up. Go.

Sal would be able to find me.

Ben, probably not.

After a few days, I would feel better and have more fight in me should Benny *still* not get the hint.

Then I'd be gone.

Benny drove. I watched the city start to engulf us as we left the suburb where I'd been hospitalized and entered the urban area of Chicago.

I tried not to look at it, but it was all around me.

My city.

I'd been born there. I loved it there. I loved The Wrigley Building. I loved Sears Tower. I loved Marshall Field's (when it was Marshall Field's). I loved the lakefront. I loved The Berghoff (which, thankfully, was still The Berghoff). I loved Fannie May meltaways and pixies. I loved the ivy on the walls of the outfield at Wrigley Field. I loved the Bears, even when they were losing. I loved the Cubs because they were always losing.

And I loved Vinnie's Pizzeria. The smell of the place. The feel of the place. The pictures on the walls. The memories.

But I hadn't stepped foot in Vinnie's in seven years because I wasn't welcome.

And it was time for new horizons.

So it was goodbye Chicago and hello new horizons.

"You're quiet."

That was Benny.

I wasn't even looking at him and I got warm just hearing his voice. It was deep and easy. The kind of voice that could talk you out of being in a snit because something went bad at work. The kind of voice that could make your heart get tight as you listened to him talk to a little kid. The kind of voice that would make you feel at peace with the world before you closed your eyes to sleep after he whispered goodnight in your ear.

I looked out the side window.

"Frankie?" Benny called.

"I'm tired," I said to the window. That wasn't entirely true, but luckily my voice sounded like it was.

"Babe," he replied softly.

Damn. Now his voice was deep and easy and *soft*.

God *so totally* hated me.

I felt his finger slide along the outside of my thigh and I closed my eyes tight.

Totally. Hated. *Me*.

"We'll get you home, get you to bed, get some decent food in you, turn on the TV, and you can rest."

Now was my time and I wasn't going to waste it. "I'm not gonna fight it, Ben, 'cause I can't. We'll fight tomorrow. But I need some prescriptions filled, and quick."

"Ma's comin' over. She'll get you fed and I'll go out and get your meds."

My head whipped around at the word "over" and I stared at him in scared-as-shit disbelief. "Theresa's comin' over?"

He glanced at me, then back at the road. "Yeah, babe. She didn't fall for your sleep fake either, but she gave you that play. Now she wants to kick in. Make sure you're all right."

"I can't face Theresa."

Ben's eyes came to me again and stayed on me a shade longer than they should have, seeing as he was driving. Then he looked back at the road. "Frankie, *cara*, she wants—"

"I can't face Theresa."

His hand came out and folded around mine. "*Cara*—"

I didn't fight his hand holding mine. I had another fight I needed to focus on. "I can't, Ben. Call her. Tell her not to come."

He squeezed my hand. "Baby, it's—"

I squeezed his hand. "Ben." I leaned his way. "*Please.*"

He did another longer-than-safe glance at me, then he gave me another squeeze before he let me go. He shifted forward in his seat, dug his cell out of his back pocket, and I held my breath.

His thumb moved on the screen and he put it to his ear.

I took a breath, because it was needed for survival, and I held it again.

"Ma, yeah. Listen, Frankie's with me. She's good. She's cool. She's comin' home with me, but she needs 'til tomorrow for you. Can you give that to her?"

Tomorrow. I'd bought time. I was golden.

"Thanks, Ma."

Yes, I was golden.

I did not grin. I heaved a sigh of relief. This was not a victory. I was genuinely freaked about seeing Theresa. I loved her. I missed her. And there was something about the loss of her that cut deeper than any of the Bianchis, save Benny, but I was not going to go there. And, of course, Vinnie, who had no choice but to leave me, except the one he should have made before he hooked his star to Sal.

My ma was the shit. She was hilarious. She was the best wingman a girl could have, be it at a bar or a church. No joke, even at fifty-three, she could rack 'em up and pin 'em down for you, and I knew this because she not only picked Vinnie for me, she scored both my sisters' husbands for them, not to mention four of her own. She drank like a sailor, cursed like a sailor, and I wasn't certain, but evidence pointed to the fact that she'd entertained most of the boys who'd been through the Naval Station for the last three decades (plus). I knew this because my father was one of them.

She was any girl's best friend.

The problem with that was that she'd been my "best friend" since I was two.

A girl needed a mother.

And Theresa Bianchi was that for me.

And then she wasn't.

I'd waited for twenty-one years to get that for me.

And then it was gone.

"You got a day, darlin'," Benny said quietly. "A day to prepare. You gotta face her, but more, Francesca, you gotta let her face you."

"Fine," I told the window.

"Fine?" Ben repeated on a question.

"Yeah."

"Shit," he muttered. "No lip. You *are* tired."

"I'll have my strength back after a nap and we'll fight about it then," I lied, because we wouldn't. I'd be at The Drake while Ben was losing his mind in his empty house.

"You're on." He was still muttering, but he had humor in his deep and easy voice now.

Humor from Benny was a killer. He had a great smile. He had a better laugh. And I'd already mentioned how fabulous his eyes were when they were dancing with humor.

He also had a great face. It was more than just drop-dead handsome. It was expressive. Benny Bianchi was not a man who held back emotion. He let it hang out. And there was no time it didn't look good.

But when he was in a good mood, smiling and laughing, that was the best. I used to go for it—his smiles, his laughter. I used to *work* for it. Even when Vinnie was alive.

That was how great Benny was when he was laughing.

It was worth the work.

Suddenly, I decided a nap at that precise moment was the way to go. The problem was, when I rested my head on the window, it kept bumping against the glass, which was not conducive to sleep.

So I sat back in the seat and closed my eyes.

Two seconds into this, Benny whispered, "Shoot that fucker again for takin' the fight outta you."

At the low rumble of his words, which said he *really* meant them, I closed my eyes tighter.

He'd shot the man who shot me. His shot was not the kill shot. But he'd shot him.

"Can we not talk about that?" I whispered back.

"Drill him full of holes for takin' the fight outta you."

I felt the wet behind my eyes and said nothing.

He took my hand again and I didn't pull away again. In my effort at holding back the tears, I just didn't have it in me.

"We'll get you fightin' fit again, baby," he promised me, deep and easy.

We would, but that being the royal "we."

I didn't share that.

I took in a deep breath and let it out.

Benny held my hand and he did this a long time. In fact, he did it until he had to let it go to hit the garage door opener on his visor. I opened my eyes when he let me go and I watched him do it. Then I watched him pull into his garage.

Time to instigate Operation Drake.

I did well, even allowing Ben to lift me out of the vehicle and carry me into his house and up the stairs.

My plan fell apart when he carried me into his bedroom.

It went up in smoke when he bent to lay me on his bed.

As he was removing his arms, I caught hold of his wrist.

His eyes came to mine.

He now had his glasses shoved into his hair. No man could shove his glasses up into his hair and look that hot. But Benny could.

God…so…freaking…*totally hated me.*

"Why am I in your bedroom?" I asked.

"'Cause you need a nap."

"I can nap in one of the other bedrooms."

He grinned.

Torture!

"Babe, got shit in my second bedroom," he shared. "Packed with it. Can barely move, there's so much shit in there."

"How do you have so much shit?" I pressed. "You're a single guy. Single guys don't accumulate shit."

"I'm the commissioner of the Little League."

I stared at him.

Please do not tell me that Benito Bianchi, in a volunteer capacity during the summers, hung on his free time with a bunch of baseball-playing little boys.

But I knew this could be true. First, Vinnie's Pizzeria sponsored a Little League team every year and had for the last thirty years. Second, Vinnie Junior, Benny, and Manny had all played Little League, then went on to play high school baseball (Vinnie, catcher; Benny, first base; Manny, pitcher). And third, that was something Ben would do because he was a decent guy.

"Season ended, storage space costs when we could use the money for things for the boys, so all their shit is now packed in my second bedroom," he finished.

"Then put me in your third bedroom."

"That's my office."

This surprised me. "You have an office?"

Another grin. Another indication I was not God's favorite person. Then, "No. It's the place where Pop's old desk is collectin' dust. Carm's old computer is collectin' dust with it. And the rest of the space is packed with the rest of the Little League shit."

"Okay," I said slowly. "Then I can nap on your couch."

His face got hard. "You ain't sleepin' on my couch."

"Ben—"

"You're recovering from a gunshot wound."

"I know that."

"So you're not sleepin' on my couch."

"For God's sake, it won't kill me."

He ended that particular conversation with, "Non-negotiable."

It was at that point I wondered why I was fighting him. Sure, lying in Benny's bed in Benny's house, which had the unusual but unbelievably appealing scent of his spicy aftershave mixed with pizza dough clinging to the air, was a thrill I wished I did not have. But he was going to the pharmacy soon and that thrill would be short-lived.

So I shut up.

Ben looked at my mouth.

I swallowed.

Then Benny lifted away and moved around the bed.

He took something from the nightstand opposite and tossed it on the bed beside me. "Ma's already been here fillin' the fridge and sortin' shit. She bought you those."

I stared at the magazines lying beside me on the bed.

There were a bunch of them and Theresa didn't mess around. They were all the good ones: juicy, like *People* and *Us,* and slick, like *Vogue* and *Marie Claire.*

Theresa *so* knew me.

I swallowed again just as a remote bounced on the magazines.

"TV," Ben stated and I looked up at him. "Got HBO. Got Showtime. It's a smart TV. Universal remote. Just hit the screen to get to the smart TV and you can get Netflix. Should keep you occupied 'til you nod off while I'm at the drugstore."

I looked in the direction of the TV and saw it was at least a sixty-incher.

What human being needed a sixty-inch TV in their bedroom?

This made me wonder what size TV he had in his living room.

As I was wondering this, Benny was rounding the bed again. "Like I said, Ma's stocked the fridge, but while I'm out, you want me to pick up anything?"

If I knew Theresa, there would not be one thing anyone on the block needed that would be lacking in Benny's fridge.

However, this was a golden opportunity to buy more time.

Especially if I sent him to more than just the drugstore.

"Tapioca pudding," I declared.

He stopped at my side of the bed and looked down at me. "Say again?"

"Tapioca pudding. Not the snack-pack size. The big tub."

He stared at me.

I scrambled to think of more shit he could buy.

"And a trashy romance novel. I don't care which one, but the less the guy on the cover is wearing, the better. Tattoos are a plus. Leather is another plus. And if there's an indication that he's a shifter, buy the whole series."

"I am not buyin' books with pictures of guys with no clothes on them," Benny said, deep and *not* easy.

It was worth a shot.

I gave up on that and reeled it off. "Fanta Grape. Diet. Chocolate-covered cashews. Cookies from D'Amato's. And a Lincoln's sub wouldn't go amiss."

His eyes had narrowed at my mention of D'Amato's, as it would seeing as they were pizza competition to Vinnie's.

He let that slide, though, and instead noted, "Babe, Lincoln's is in Hobart."

"Yeah? So?"

"Francesca, I'm not drivin' forty minutes to fuckin' Indiana to buy you a sub."

"We have to have dinner," I pointed out.

"Yeah. So later I'm goin' in to Vinnie's to make you a pie."

My heart squeezed.

I'd heard through the grapevine that Benny had succumbed to Vinnie Senior's pressure and learned the sacred Bianchi art of making a pizza pie. A friend of mine even shared that Vinnie had put up a new sign for the restaurant, changing it from *Vinnie's Pizzeria* to *Vinnie and Benny's Pizzeria*.

Since learning Benny had taken over the kitchen at Vinnie's, I'd wanted one of his pies. Ma always said, a guy who cooked was a keeper (advice she did not take herself). What Ma would say if she'd ever met one was that if you found a guy who cooked and looked like Benny, you should consider surgical attachment.

Of course, I hadn't allowed myself go to Vinnie's and have one of Benny's pies. This was because I would have been run out on a rail if I'd tried.

I stopped thinking about Benny making a pizza and said, "Okay, subs tomorrow night then."

He tipped his head back and looked at the ceiling.

I needed to move this along so I stated, "I think that's all."

He looked at me. "You sure?"

He was being sarcastic.

I didn't call him on that and just nodded.

His eyes narrowed again.

I attempted to look innocent.

Eventually, he muttered, "Fuck. Be back," and bent to take the envelope with my prescriptions out of my hand before he started to make a move to the door.

This was a problem, seeing as he carried me in but didn't carry my bag in. My purse was in my bag and I'd need that to order a taxi.

"Ben, could you bring my bag in before you go?" I called to his departing back.

He turned and leveled his eyes on me. "No. I can't. 'Cause your shit is in that bag, including your wallet and phone. Got a cell, don't need a house phone. So you got any bright ideas to take off, you can't call a taxi, you can't pay a taxi, and you sure as fuck can't walk anywhere you could get a taxi. But don't matter. I'm hittin' old lady Zambino across the street and tellin' her to keep an eye out. You know she'll be glued to the window, I ask. And she'll call me, she sees you attemptin' a getaway. I'll also be hittin' Tony next door. He'll keep an eye out back. So you got a bright idea, *cara*, get rid of it. 'Cause your ass is in that bed until you have a sit-down with Ma, let Pop say his words to make amends, and you and me got a meetin' of the minds about the future."

That was when I felt *my* eyes narrow, even as what he said made my heart beat funny.

"So, what you're saying is, you actually *have* kidnapped me."

"You wanna look at it that way, go ahead. Don't give a fuck. You took a bullet to the belly, babe. Didn't hit your gut, but it did damage, so I gave you a week and a half to pull your shit. Now I'm done with that."

"I think I've noticed that since you've kidnapped me," I returned.

"Do you want your pudding and fuckin' grape soda?" he asked.

21

"Yes, because that'll give me something to throw at you," I answered.

"Okay, both those are off my shoppin' list," he shot back. "Do you want your pain meds?"

I snapped my mouth shut because the pain was nagging. I could ignore it while plotting my escape or arguing with Benny. When neither was an option open to me, I had a feeling I couldn't.

He watched me snap my mouth shut, hesitated only a moment, and then strode back to the bed.

He, however, didn't hesitate to lean in and wrap a hand around the side of my neck and dip his face so close, I could see those eyes now warm and gentle in a way my heart really wanted to melt. I just wouldn't let it.

"You're crazy-brave, babe," he said quietly. "You proved that a week and a half ago. You're crazy-beautiful and I 'spect you been that way all your life. You're crazy-funny. You're crazy-sweet. But you're just plain crazy if you think you can do what you did for this family, be the way you were with me that night before they took Cal and Vi, and think I'm lettin' you move to fuckin' Indianapolis without us havin' a conversation. You know what this is. That's why you're freakin' and hidin'. I know what this is. That's why I'm not lettin' this shit go." His fingers squeezed and he got even closer. "We're talkin'. You don't like that, I don't give a fuck. Seven years I been fuckin' up. Right now, that shit ends."

And with that, he pulled me to him (but gently, God!), kissed my forehead, let me go, and before I could say a word, he disappeared out the door.

I stared at it, feeling his words gather in my belly, and the way they did, I liked the feeling.

Then I glared at it, wishing I had something to throw, even if he was long gone and I wouldn't hit him.

The only things I had were magazines and a remote, and if I threw any of them, I'd have to haul myself out of bed and go get them.

So, instead, I took the only option open to me.

I snatched up Ben's universal remote, pointed it at the TV, and commenced fucking with all of his settings so it would take him at least an hour to sort that shit out.

Done with that, I filled his Netflix favorites queue with programs that would make Homeland Security put him on a watch list.

While I waited for his return, I selected the most non-Benny television show Netflix had to offer (*Dr. Who*, precisely), let it play in the background, and flipped through my *People*.

While doing so, I fell dead asleep.

Genuinely.

Two

SHAKESPEARE

I woke up feeling a t-shirt-covered chest under my cheek and hand, an arm angled down my back, hand resting on my hip, and I heard baseball on the TV.

I opened my eyes and saw I was right, white tee stretched across a broad chest, a chest my hand was resting on.

I instantly rolled to my back. The arm around me let me, but the tee came with me and then Benny was up on an elbow in the bed, forearm under me, upper body looming over me. Now I could see tee spread across a broad chest *and* shoulders, a handsome face with the beginnings of a sexy five o'clock shadow, tousled dark hair, and gentle dark brown eyes.

"Sleep good?" he asked quietly.

"Why are you in bed with me?" I asked back, not quietly.

One side of his lips hitched up slightly and he repeated, "Sleep good?"

I decided to dispense with the back and forth and snapped, "Yes," then did my own repeating. "Why are you in bed with me?"

"Watchin' the game," he replied.

"Don't you have a TV in your living room?"

"I do, but got home, started up here to check on you, heard somethin' that freaked me out. Thought you were takin' a chainsaw to my bed. Got in here, saw it was you out and snorin'."

I closed my eyes.

I opened them when Ben kept speaking.

"Looked at the TV, *heard* the TV, knew it was fucked up. Babe, you messed with my contrast?"

I fought my smirk by glaring at him.

He ignored my glare and continued, "A man's TV has gotta be the way he wants it to be. So I decided to sort that shit without delay. Took a while so I figured I should be comfortable doing it, and bein' comfortable meant movin' you so you'd stop makin' that God-awful noise."

I said not a word, but what I thought was that my TV ploy was an epic fail.

Benny did say a word, more than one. "Jesus, Frankie, you even fucked with the receiver."

"No one has surround sound in their bedroom, Ben," I informed him.

"I do," he informed me.

"Why?" I asked.

He leaned slightly toward me and I tensed because Benny close was bad. Benny *very* close was *very* bad.

"Tell me this, *cara*," he started. "Why does a woman ask 'why' about shit a man does? I'm not askin' just to ask. I honestly wanna know the answer to that. He does what he does. If it doesn't hurt anybody, why does there have to be a 'why?'"

It was more than a little annoying that he had a point.

"We want to understand you," I explained.

"Half the shit any woman I know does I do not get. Not even a little bit. And I do not care that I don't get it. She does what she does. She doesn't get in my face doin' it, who gives a fuck?"

"So you're sayin' you don't give a fuck about how women think?" I asked.

"I'm sayin' I don't *need* to know how you think," he replied.

"Is this why you're thirty-five and single?" I went on snottily.

"No," he returned immediately. "I'm thirty-five and single because I am not gonna settle for somethin' that doesn't feel right, doesn't feel good, doesn't bring me joy, doesn't have my back, doesn't know how to cook, keep house, listen, laugh, make *me* laugh, give great head, or ask me why I do shit."

"I'm not sure that woman exists," I shared, and something changed in his eyes that I could probably read if I tried. But I didn't try.

"I'll find her," he replied.

"I'm thinkin' you won't," I told him, no longer being a bitch. I really didn't think he would. The giving-great-head part especially. It was my experience, both personally and anecdotally, that most women found that a chore. It had to be done occasionally, but you went through the motions to do it.

He leaned in even closer. "Then I'll train her."

I felt my eyes get squinty. "We're not dogs, Ben."

"A woman gets in a relationship, you're tellin' me she doesn't do her thing to train her man?" he shot back.

She did. Absolutely. She started building her lesson plans the day after a first good date.

On that thought, I decided a change in subject was in order so I brought us back to priority one.

"So you fixed your TV. Why were you still in bed with me?"

"You felt good. I like you close. And when you aren't sawin' logs, you're makin' cute little noises, like little whimpers that I like hearin' nearly as much as I like you close."

Suddenly, we were catapulted into dangerous territory, and that dangerous territory was that what he said was making me feel warm inside.

"Benny," I whispered, but said no more.

Benny didn't need me to. He had plenty to say.

"Seven years, fucked around. I knew. I figure you knew. Told you before I left, not fuckin' around anymore. Playin' it straight. You asked, I gave it to you straight."

I decided not to ask Benny Bianchi another question *in my life*, which meant I fell silent.

Benny held my silence for long moments before he asked, "You hungry?"

I was, so I said, "Yep."

His eyes changed again, they grew warm with concern, and he went on quietly, "You got pain?"

I absolutely did.

I didn't answer verbally. I nodded.

The skin around his mouth tightened momentarily before he muttered, "Right."

Then he moved. Carefully extricating his arm from under me, he rolled off the bed and immediately shoved his hand in his back pocket. He pulled his phone out, then nabbed the remote from the nightstand and shoved it in his pocket, taking away any further opportunities of TV revenge.

Since he did this, he clearly didn't know I considered the first try spectacularly unsuccessful. I wasn't all that smart, but I was smart enough not to repeat an ineffective maneuver.

He started walking toward the door with his thumb moving over the screen of his phone.

He was out the door when I heard him say, "Man? That pie I made? Put it in the oven and have someone bring it over when it's done. Breadsticks. Salad. Yeah?"

I heard no more as I figured either Manny agreed to what his big brother ordered and/or Benny was going down the stairs.

I moved a hand to rest just above the bandages at my midriff and stared at the ceiling.

I wanted to think about the fact that I was soon going to experience a pizza pie created at the hands of Benny Bianchi. This thought was too titillating, so I couldn't think of it and opened my mind to find something else to think about.

Seeing as I was lying in Benny's bed, where my mind took me was to the fact that, growing up, the Bianchis went to the same church as my family. I used to watch them, even as a little girl. All six of them.

I watched them because I liked what I saw.

Ma, being a crazy, rowdy, trouble-making, fun-loving, adventure-seeking slut (the last part was not nice, but it was true and she'd say the same damn thing with crazy, rowdy, fun-loving, pride), weirdly did not miss church on Sunday.

"Gotta wash away the sin, my precious girl, so you can sin again," she'd tell me frequently on a flashy smile.

Watching the Bianchis, and having years to do it, truth be told I'd had my eye on Ben way before I even thought about Vinnie. Vinnie was five years older than me, so back in the day he was out of my league.

Ben was not. He was one year older than me. I went to school with him and every girl in school had their eye on Benito Bianchi.

Way back then, Ma had her eye on Benny too. For me. She used to don a tube top and a pair of short shorts, put hot rollers in her hair, tease it out to extremes, spray it so it barely moved (in other words, her normal routine), and then drag my ass to his baseball games.

Even though Benny was not hard to look at, and back then (and now) he had that *thing*—that thing the cool boys had that set them apart and made you want them so much it was like an ache—I avoided Ma's many and varied plans to throw me in his path.

This was because he played the field, even in high school, and I wasn't talking about baseball. Stealing bases in all the ways that could be implied was definitely a specialty of Benny's. By his junior year, he'd gone through all the available, easy girls in our school and had started to concentrate on casting lures more widely.

Even in high school, I knew I didn't want to get involved with a boy like that, no matter how cute he was. No matter that he had that *thing*. No matter that I'd secretly watch him and wish so hard he had that *thing* in a one-girl type of way (instead of an any-girl-who-would-give-it-up type of way) and ache for him to be mine.

And even in high school, I knew why the unbeatable lure of Benny Bianchi was beatable for me.

My half-Italian, half-Irish father had a kid—my brother, Dino—from some chick he knocked up before he knocked up my mother with me.

Enzo Concetti, my dad, was hot (still). He was rough. He was crazy. He was adventure-seeking. And he got a kick out of my ma. So after he knocked her up, he took her ball and chain and they enjoyed themselves immensely for the next five years. I knew this because Ma squeezed out both my sisters, Catarina and Natalia, and my baby brother, Enzo Junior, in that time.

Unfortunately, as time went by with marriage and family in the mix, neither Dad nor Ma stopped being crazy or thinking life was about having a really fucking great time as often as you could get it, and if life didn't give it to you, you made it. The drag of a family and a spouse was just that, a drag.

So things went as they were bound to go when my parents were faced with something like responsibility, which, no getting away from it (though they tried), kids were. It got ugly and my parents weren't about ugly. They also weren't about fixing things that were broken, even if those things were important. And, being how they were, they didn't let it stay ugly for long before they bailed.

Dad never got remarried. Dad spent the next decades doing what he liked most: having a great time. Dad was currently fifty-six and living with his latest piece, who was four years older than me.

Ma did get remarried, three more times. All of them had been to good guys that I liked. All of them had failed because those guys were good guys who eventually wanted to settle down, or who were settled and thought they could have fun with Ma for a while and then settle her down. When they failed, they bailed. Or, more to the point, *she* bailed or made it so they had no choice but to do the same. She was currently living in Florida and had a rock on her finger, setting up plans to get hitched to number five.

This was obviously not conducive to a stable childhood home. Ma and Dad got along, yucked it up when they were together, and it was not unusual in times when they both were unattached (or even times when they were) when we woke up to Ma at Dad's house or Dad at Ma's, seeing as they frequently hooked up for a trip down memory lane.

During all this, they did not have a formal custody agreement.

Well, actually, they did. They just didn't adhere to it. They went with their flow. Therefore, we were bounced from one to the other, to aunts, uncles, grandparents, boyfriends, girlfriends, wherever they were or whenever they needed to be quit of us, all of this at random. When we got older, we just went wherever we wanted. They didn't really care, as long as we eventually came home breathing.

Through this, I'd developed a deep jealousy I never told a single soul about toward my brother Dino. His mom got her shit together, got married to a stand-up guy, gave Dino a brother and sister, a lot of love, a solid family, and a good home.

So by the time I hit high school, I knew that was what I wanted. I didn't want a guy out for a good time with the mission to get laid and drunk as often as he could, participating in the parking lot fist fights and bar brawls that came along the way.

I wanted a solid family. I wanted to be part of building a good home. After that, I wanted to spend my energy making it stay good.

How that led me to Vinnie, I had no idea, except for the fact that Ma's eye eventually turned to him for me.

And Vinnie was a Bianchi.

Vinnie was good-looking. Vinnie was loud. Vinnie was the life of any party. Vinnie never met anyone he didn't like. That was, unless you rubbed him the wrong way. Then he didn't have any problem letting you know you did and acting on it if he felt that kind of attention was deserved.

Vinnie had one life plan: to live large. He just didn't know how to get that.

So he saw a good thing—the thriving success of his father's restaurant—and tried to convince Vinnie Senior into franchising the pizzeria, telling his father it would make them millionaires.

That didn't go over too good. Vinnie Senior was vehemently against it, feeling Vinnie's Pizzeria was about quality and tradition, both of which would no doubt get lost in an attempt at nationwide franchising. Vinnie Senior went so far as to be disappointed (openly) that his son didn't get that and would even suggest franchising.

In order to show his father, Vinnie Junior washed his hands of the pizzeria and opened his own sandwich business. He had no idea what he was doing, even though I told him he should learn before he dumped his time and limited money into that kind of thing. In the end, unsurprisingly, it failed.

A dozen other schemes, all half-baked, either died an ugly death or never left the starting gate.

Enter Sal and his business, something that Vinnie took to with scary ease, something I should have read as what it was when it happened.

Through all this, the Bianchis cast their eyes to me as the woman behind the man pushing Vinnie to do stupid shit in order to hand her the world. They didn't judge outright. They didn't say shit. But as time went on, I felt the blame I didn't deserve.

I didn't say a word.

I didn't say a word because I loved their pizzeria. I loved what it represented. The solidity of their family. Their history. Their loyalty. Their teasing. Their warmth with each other. Their spice when one of them would get pissed, but it was okay because it was based in love and loyalty and it felt good to be around, rather than shaky and dysfunctional.

So I held on when I knew I should've let go. I held on thinking that Vinnie would eventually get his head out of his ass and give me what I wanted. I held on because I loved being a part of the Bianchis, something I always wanted.

And I held on because I loved Vinnie. He was loud and loved life and I understood that. I'd lived it with my parents. I felt comfortable there, even though I knew it was dangerous.

I held on.

Then there was nothing to hold on to.

I was too young to recognize I'd found my father.

I also had no clue at the time that I'd picked the wrong brother. I had no clue I'd be forced to watch from up close, and then afar, as Benny started to settle down.

First, he quit his job in construction and went to work at the pizzeria. This meant he stopped carousing at night because he was working at night.

After that, he bought that house.

A row house in the middle of the row, built up from the sidewalk. Front stoop. Back stoop. Nonexistent front yard. Backyard big enough to play catch in and house a two-car garage and another spot for family parking. There were four bedrooms in all the other houses, but Benny's was three, with a converted master bath. Living room/dining room up front. Kitchen, den, utility room in the back. Small powder room downstairs. Family bathroom upstairs.

It was settled—had been there over a century and the surrounding inhabitants were mostly Italian American families whose relatives had lived in that 'hood for generations and weren't going to give it up.

Once he got the house, he got rid of his muscle car and bought an SUV.

And he eventually took over the pizzeria from his old man.

He still fucked everything that moved, but I paid attention to the talk. I knew some of the women he took to his bed. I knew exactly when it went from being about getting off to being about finding the right one.

Sure, he would have his times that were just about getting laid.

But Benny started to move down the path that I knew was leading him to find someone who would help him build a solid family and create a good home.

Vinnie never did that. Vinnie had no interest in that path. He only was interested in his path, however murky, and he dragged me along with him.

The problem was, I let him.

On this thought, I sensed movement and cast my eyes down my body to see Ben walking in. He was carrying a pint glass filled with ice and purple liquid in one hand, a little pharmacy pill bottle in the other.

I pushed up to sitting as Benny hit my side of the bed. He put the stuff on the nightstand and leaned into me in order to arrange pillows behind my back. When he was done, I scooted up the bed to rest on the pillows and Ben went to the bottle.

I had the glass by the time he handed me the pill.

I took the medicine and decided not to argue when Ben sat his ass, hip to mine, on the bed.

"Pizza's comin'," he stated.

"Okay," I replied, putting the glass on the nightstand.

"Read your doctor's notes," he told me and I looked his way.

That was none of his business and he knew it.

I decided not to share that that irked me, and just how much, and stayed silent.

"Wants you to make a checkup appointment next week. I'll get Ma on that."

I did not want Theresa "on that." I was quite capable of making a phone call to set an appointment with my own freaking doctor.

I decided not to give him that information either.

"He wants you movin' around. Not much at first, but he wants you active."

"Okay," I repeated.

"And he says for a few days you can't shower without someone close."

Again, we were in dangerous territory. Dangerous for Benny because he was not going to go there. He could kidnap me (because he did). He could put me in his bed (because he did).

But he wasn't getting anywhere near me in a shower.

"If you think—" I started.

"I don't," he cut me off. "But I want Ma around when you do it. I have a friend whose woman had surgery. They weren't livin' together then and she's independent, thinks she can do it all. She decided to take a shower by herself. But when she took off the bandage and saw that shit, she freaked and passed out. Hit her head on the tub. Gave herself a concussion and another hospital stay. So you let Ma help you out and you let her dress your wound. You don't want that, you got a girl, I'll let you call her. You don't let Ma do it or make a call, not fuckin' with you, Francesca, you'll shower with me in this room, the door open, and I'll dress your wound."

I was about to serve the attitude when it hit me this was an excellent idea.

If I called one of my friends, I could enlist her in helping me escape.

"I'll phone a friend," I told him, but I forced it to sound annoyed so he wouldn't cotton on to my game.

"Good," he muttered.

"Did you buy my tapioca?" I asked.

His eyes lit with humor, and when they did, I remembered how very much I liked that in a way that made me wonder, if I had a different kind of life—in other words, I'd made smarter decisions in the life I had—if I would ever get used to that. Watching Benny Bianchi's eyes light with humor. Feeling that light shine on me, making me warm all over, even on the inside. If that would ever become commonplace.

But I'd never have that life.

Still, I knew if I had it, if Ben and I had a year together or fifty of them, I'd go for that light. I'd work for it. I'd do it every day for fifty years.

And I'd never get used to the warmth it would give me.

"Yeah," he answered.

"A trashy novel?" I pushed.

More humor in his eyes and a, "Fuck no."

"Benny, TV and magazines aren't gonna get me very far."

"Seein' as you got my company tonight, Ma *and* me tomorrow, not to mention one of your girls comin' over to help you shower, you'll be good. After tomorrow, I'll send Ma out to buy you some smut. That'll mean she'll do it after goin' to church and lightin' a candle in aid of your soul, but she'll do it."

She would. There was a breach to heal. She'd frown on my smut, but she'd buy it for me.

"I was kinda hopin' that tonight you'd bring me pizza, leave me alone, and go watch the game downstairs," I noted.

"You'd be hopin' wrong since your ass is walkin' down the stairs to have dinner with me at the kitchen table so you can get some exercise in. After that, we're watchin' whatever we watch up here together, in my bed, 'cause I know you. I know you're fuckin' crazy. I know a bullet to the belly will not stop you from crawlin' out the window. So my ass isn't on that couch downstairs until you fall asleep."

He intended to sleep on the couch.

This made me feel relief.

It also made me feel a niggle of gloom.

I'd been alone a long time. Living alone. Sleeping alone. Keeping myself to myself.

I knew Ben was dangerous and I knew prolonged exposure to him would increase that danger significantly.

That didn't change the fact that he was not hard to look at, it was not a hardship to watch him move, I got a kick out of squabbling with him, and it far from sucked waking up with my cheek to his chest, his arm wrapped around me, the feel and smell of him everywhere.

Obviously, I not only didn't share this, I didn't let these thoughts show.

Instead, I mumbled, "Whatever. Until you release me from captivity, I'll go through the motions to avoid the hassle."

"You've never gone through the motions to avoid hassle," he returned. "You've gone through the motions to deflect attention so you can carry out whatever scheme you're hatchin'."

I focused on him. I did it intently and with some annoyance I didn't bother to hide because it *was* annoying that he knew I was plotting.

He grinned at my reaction and kept talking.

"Like I said, bein' straight up, Frankie. You should know I'm not fallin' for your shit. So whatever girl you got lined up to help you make your getaway, get that shit out of your head. Old lady Zambino saw what you did on TV. She knows you took one for family and she's all over keepin' you safe and settled, recuperatin' at my house. Probably half a second after my chat with her, enlisting her officially in the cause, she was on her phone with that bowlin' posse of hers and, swear to God, I saw one of those women in her Chrysler, cruisin' the alley when I got home. You're stuck. Give in to that and this'll go a whole lot smoother."

Old lady Zambino lived across the street from Benny. Old lady Zambino was Italian. Old lady Zambino was nosy. And if she knew anyone referred to her as "old lady Zambino," she would hire a hit on them.

She was in her eighties, but she looked like she was in her fifties. She had peachy-red hair she wore up in a puffy 'do fastened at the back through curls. She was trim and fit. She wore jeans, nice blouses, and high heels. She had weekly manicures done to her talons and was never without one of her signature nail polishes: gold or wine red in the winter (scarlet red for the Christmas season); silver or fuchsia in the summer (pale pink for Easter). Her face was always made up perfectly, and she was the poster child for a good skincare regime because she had wrinkles, just not many of them.

She power walked daily and she did this in sporty athletic gear that many would say she should leave to the twentysomethings, but she worked that shit like no other.

She also played with a team of old lady bowlers in three different leagues and they took that shit seriously. If there was a senior ladies tour, she'd be the champion. Her famed ball was a marbled black with hot pink, gold, and silver veins, and she carted her ass and that twelve-pounder from alley to alley without effort and with a great deal of determination.

If she and her bowling buddies intended to keep me at Benny's, they'd succeed.

In other words, it was time for me to act on the fly and hatch a different scheme.

So I did it.

"Does it bother you in the slightest that *I* don't want to be here? That *I* don't want this talk you wanna have? That *I* don't wanna let Theresa have a sit-down with me? That *I* don't want your dad to say his words to make amends? *I* just want to get on with my life after seven not-very-great years, and before that, six years with Vinnie that I realized too late weren't real great, all of that ending with me running through the forest with a woman I did not know, and a grand finale of blood and bullets and a fair amount of gore, which, luckily, wasn't *all* mine. But watchin' Cal blow a hole in that man's head was not fun, even though I hate that man and I'm glad he's rottin' in hell."

"Frankie—"

I shook my head. "No, Ben. I'd really like to get in your truck and for you to take me home, then leave me alone. I think I made the leavin'-me-alone part pretty clear the night I got shot because I told you that, straight up. Then I made it clear a more subtle way, hopin' you'd get it, fakin' sleepin' every time you or one of your family showed at the hospital. Now you're bein' straight, I'll be straight right back. I do not want what you want. I want to be left alone."

I should have known by the look on his face that I liked way too much that what would come next would be a blow, but I stupidly didn't brace.

So when he whispered, "But…you're family, baby," it was a blow.

Because it was the wrong thing to say.

It hurt. Too much.

Emotional pain was far worse than a gunshot wound and I was in the position to know.

I'd wanted that…once. I got it…once.

Then they took it away.

"Family doesn't turn their back on family for seven years, *especially* doin' that shit when one of their own loses the man in her bed."

I saw his flinch. He tried to hide it, but I saw it.

He recovered from my hit and his voice was gentle (and thus beautiful) when he asked, "So you know what family does, *cara*?"

"Uh…yeah," I snapped. "I know what family does."

"Then where's your ma?"

I clamped my mouth shut.

"Where's Enzo Senior?" he went on.

I glared at him.

"Where's Nat, Cat, Enzo Junior? Talked to Cindy and the girls at the nurse's station. Not a visit. Not from one of them."

"Ma's in Florida," I reminded him.

"Babe, you were *shot*. The only excuse she can give not to be at your bedside after that kind of shit happens is she's on the fuckin' moon and NASA declared there's no safe reentry without burnin' up."

"You know Ninette is not the bedside-vigil type of mom," I reminded him.

"I know not one of those folks you count as blood is the bedside-vigil, takin'-care-of-their-girl type *at all*. That is not family, Frankie, and it proves my point. You don't know family. You did, you'd know that shit is not right. Fuck, your dad, Nat, and Cat all still live in the city and they didn't haul their asses to the hospital to see you."

"Nat works nights," I pointed out. "She has to sleep during the day."

"She works as a cocktail waitress," Benny returned. "She's not an ER doc who takes the night shift and has to get her shuteye in 'cause, if she doesn't, she could make a mistake the next day that might cost someone their life."

He'd been annoying me.

Now he was pissing me off.

"Why are we talking about this?" I hissed.

"Because, for some fool reason, you're denyin' yourself somethin' you want." He shook his head. "No, somethin' you *need*. Somethin' I'm handin' you and you refuse to reach out and take it."

"What I'm tryin' to get through that thick head of yours is I *don't* want it, Benny. I definitely don't *need* it. I want to move *beyond* it."

"That's a straight-up lie," he shot back.

"It is not." My voice was rising.

Suddenly, his face was in my face and all I could smell was his after-shave, all I could see were his eyes. "So you're sayin' I kissed you right now, you would not want that?"

I stopped breathing.

The slightly good thing about that was now I had confirmation about what Ben's talk would be about. I had guessed, now I knew.

That was the slightly good thing.

Slightly.

"I'm your brother's girlfriend," I reminded him.

"You *were* Vinnie's girlfriend," he retorted immediately. "Now you're just Frankie."

"If you don't think he's always gonna be between us—the history of bad blood your family clung to for seven years and the shit they laid on my shoulders for years before that isn't gonna be between me and them—you're cracked."

"I think we give this a go, we'll both get to the point where we remember we loved Vinnie and that'll be all there is about Vinnie. Gettin' to that, there'll be shit we hit that'll be awkward and uncomfortable, but we'll power through it and get there in the end."

"You're so sure?" I asked snidely.

"Yeah," he answered firmly.

"And how are you so sure, Ben? Hunh? Tell me that."

"'Cause if I didn't waste seven fuckin' years, that would be where we were now if I had finally pulled my finger outta my ass and made my move on you then. Instead of sittin' on this bed arguin' with you about where we should be goin', I'd be doin' somethin' else to you in this bed while our kids were at Ma's house, tearin' it up."

His words hit me so hard in a way that felt dangerously good, I sucked in a painful breath. But Benny was not done.

"'Cept I did it back then, we'd have to live with Vinnie knowin' I stole his woman. Until he got whacked, that is."

The word, "What?" came out of me in a gush of breath.

"Francesca, you givin' me a week and a half to think on all this shit, things got clear. And what got clear was that the minute Vinnie became a made man, you lost him. I lost him. My family lost him. He stopped bein' ours and he became Sal's. Say it didn't end in his bein' dead. Do you think Ma would let that kind of man sit at her table for Christmas dinner?" He shook his head again. "No fuckin' way. Ma and Pop are stubborn. They were holdin' on to hope. But it was slippin' and he was cruisin' straight to bein' disowned, dead to them in a different way, and you know it."

I did. Vinnie Senior and Theresa were gearing up to let him go. I knew it then. I felt it. It hurt. Vinnie felt it. It killed. There were a lot of things family forgave, looked beyond, got used to, sucked it up for, and they could shift the blame to me for a lot of shit.

But he'd been made in the Mafia. The things he was doing were going to get harder and harder to blame on me. The things he was doing were all on him. He knew it and they were figuring it out.

And once you were made in the mob, you never got out.

There was no turning back.

For him.

For me, now, that was another matter.

And Benny immediately got into that matter.

"And I know you. You would not let him plant babies in you, not go out and do the shit he did for Sal, come to you with blood on his hands after puttin' drugs on the street or shakin' people down or whatever the fuck they do, and let him put a baby inside you. I know that, Frankie. He was livin' on borrowed time in more ways than the one that got him and we both know it."

"So you were gonna move on his woman?" I asked.

"Why do you think I was so fuckin' pissed when you made that move on me after we put him in the ground?" he asked back. "You stole my show, babe. And you did it too fuckin' quick. I was not ready, you were not ready, and I got pissed. Too pissed. Held a grudge. Pissed away time. Now we're here."

"I didn't make a move," I reminded him sharply. "*You* kissed *me*."

"You made a move, Frankie," he said with rigidity.

I did.

Fuck.

I did.

"This is insane," I snapped, because it fucking well was!

He got even closer. "This is real and you fuckin' know it."

"I do not," I bit out.

"You so fuckin' do," he returned. "I get where you are. I was there for seven years. Denyin' where I was at and where I wanted you to be. Holdin' guilt about all a' that. How I felt and what I wanted before he died. How I felt and the same thing I wanted after he was gone. You see the woman you want bleedin' from a gunshot wound on a forest floor, she survives that shit and gives you a week and a half, Frankie, that's plenty of time to pull your head outta your ass. I did it on my own. Now you're gonna do it, and if you don't, I'm right here and I'm gonna do it for you."

"You are *not*!" My voice was beginning to rise as my heartbeat was beginning to escalate. "Primarily because there's nothing to pull my head outta my ass about."

"You need me to kiss you?"

"No!" I shouted, my voice now loud and my breathing now harsh.

"Shakespeare," he clipped, and my head jerked.

"What?" I rapped out.

"What'd he say about protesting?"

I felt my eyes go squinty again.

"You got it all figured out, don't you, Benny?" I asked sarcastically.

"Bet you five hundred dollars I kiss you, in about five seconds you'd have it figured out too."

No way in hell I was taking that bet.

"Gambling is a sin," I hissed.

"Yeah, so you go to Vegas every year to catch the shows?"

My eyes got squintier.

"Five hundred bucks, Frankie."

"I'm recovering from a major bodily trauma, Ben."

"Read your doctor's notes, babe. Said nothin' about you not kissin'. Told you to refrain from intercourse, so we'll save that for later."

I clenched my teeth, even as I felt my nipples tingle.

God, I wanted to slap him.

I also wanted him to kiss me.

And I couldn't even think of intercourse with Benny, not with him that close. Hell, not *ever*.

"Not gonna take the bet?" he taunted, moving an inch closer.

"Fuck off, Ben."

He grinned.

Then he repeated, "Shakespeare."

"Whatever," I muttered, pressing back into the pillows and sliding my eyes away.

"My win," he said softly. "You're off your game. Figure you'll get yours in when you get stronger so I gotta get in as many as I can now."

I slid my eyes back and informed him, "You're taking advantage of an injured woman."

"Yep," he replied easily.

I glared.

We heard the doorbell ring.

Ben pushed up from the bed, sauntered to the door, and ordered, "Ass downstairs, babe. Time for pie."

I did not get my ass downstairs.

I stared at the door and I did it for a long time after he disappeared. I did it wondering if what just happened actually happened. After that, I did it trying to figure out if I could pretend that what just happened didn't happen. Eventually, I figured out I couldn't.

Then I realized there was a pizza pie downstairs created by Ben.

Not to mention Benny himself was downstairs.

And as much as it sucked (and it sucked huge), I couldn't stop myself from swinging my legs over the side of the bed, making my way to the door, and doing it more excited than was healthy, all in order to taste Benny's pie.

And do it with Ben.

⌒

I woke enough to feel Benny slide my hair off my neck and then slide his finger along my jaw.

I also felt how nice that was.

Behind my closed eyes, the dim light penetrating went out.

Finally, I felt his presence leave the room.

He didn't close the door.

I opened my eyes to the dark.

Score one for Benny before dinner. Score one for me during and after. This was because I managed to hold on to the silent treatment throughout both (mostly).

The silent treatment was not a weapon in my female arsenal. My mother came from German, Polish, and French stock, probably with a few more things thrown in.

But my father was half Italian, and considering how he was, I was, and all the other fruit of his loins were, Italian blood was clearly dominant.

This meant I was hotheaded, low on patience, and had a flair for drama.

So managing the silent treatment, going so far as not even moaning when I took my first bite of Benny's deep-dish pie (it had been a long time so maybe I was wrong, but in that moment, I would swear it was better than Vinnie's), was a feat.

A Bianchi pie, I'd been told by Vinnie Bianchi Senior himself in better times, had no single secret ingredient. It wasn't the dough. It wasn't the sauce. It wasn't the cheese.

It was all of that.

All of it was homemade except the cheese, which was not grated and dashed around. It was sliced off a ball of buffalo mozzarella and laid on to melt its mild, smooth, milky goodness into tangy red sauce that leaned a bit to the spicy side, and pan-style or hand-tossed crust that made you know there was a God and He was Italian.

I could do a hand-tossed pie and be happy.

But I was from Chicago.

It was all about the pan.

And no one did better pan pizza than Vinnie's Pizzeria. Sure, there were some who could extol the virtues of Uno's and Due's.

They were wrong.

Vinnie's was the best.

Now Benny's was the best.

I didn't share with him my overwhelming approval of his culinary skills with a Chicago-style pan pizza pie.

I just ate it and kept my mouth shut.

After Benny was done eating, but I wasn't, he left the table and went out to his garage. He came back with my phone.

He set it on the table beside me and said, "Phone a friend."

I glared at him. He grinned at me. I snatched up my phone and he sat down to watch me call my friend Asheeka.

Asheeka was a woman I worked with who I'd met after the Vinnie debacle. We became friends and she became acquainted with my story.

With experience, I found it was better with those who learned after the fact that I could have been on a reality show of Chicago's mob wives and girlfriends. This was because I could attempt to convince them I was beyond it and on my way to becoming a better person who made smarter choices.

Seeing as I made no choices outside of what I'd wear that day, living my life quiet, without a man, this turned true.

Asheeka had come to visit me twice in the hospital and she was all over coming in the morning to be around when I showered. She was a little concerned about the staying-at-Benny's part of that scenario, but she got from the tone of my voice that I couldn't talk about it at that moment and she let it go.

This was one of the reasons I'd called Asheeka. She was very sweet, very generous, very funny, and she could take a hint like no girlfriend I'd ever had. She could read an eye gesture or a hair flip at twenty paces. She was the master and, therefore, didn't press about me being at Benny's because she knew I needed her to leave it alone.

She also knew I'd give it all to her in the morning.

After the call, Benny confiscated my phone.

I let him, sat at the table and watched him do the dishes, wishing I wasn't watching Benny do the dishes because I didn't need to know he could be gentle, he could take direction, he could make amazing pizza, *and* he could do the dishes. He was like a man out of a dream except for the fact that I could get up, wrap my arms around him, kiss his neck and then kiss other parts of him, and men you made up in your dreams obviously didn't afford those opportunities.

As I thought this while watching him do the dishes, close to him finishing up, he decreed, "You get a pass tonight 'cause you had a big day. Tomorrow, your ass is at my side helpin'."

The idea of doing dishes with Benny was bizarrely alluring.

So I quit thinking about it.

Benny finished the dishes and ordered me upstairs. I went because I was exhausted and that was the only place he'd let me lie down. I didn't need another altercation with him. I wasn't doing too good with those. I needed a chance to regroup.

He came upstairs with my bag, dumped it on the floor by the door to the bathroom, and kept issuing orders.

"Get ready for bed, *cara*."

He then left.

I went to my bag with more hope than realism and, upon perusal, found my hopes dashed.

The nightgowns and robe Gina got me were there. The panties and the toiletries my friend Jamie went to my apartment to get where there. My purse, with my wallet and phone, wasn't.

I got ready for bed, then I got in the bed, pulling the covers up to my neck.

Ben joined me ten minutes later.

He produced the remote and asked what I wanted to watch. Committed to the silent treatment and satisfied with my performance thus far, I said nothing.

Ben asked again.

I still said nothing.

He found a game.

I continued to say nothing, just lay there, eyes to the TV, mind wondering how drama found me even when I lived quiet.

It was at that point I remembered I'd heard that Daniel Hart was on a rampage with Cal in his sights.

Joe Callahan, known to all but his woman as Cal (his woman called him Joe), was Benny's cousin. He was an awesome guy, a good (albeit distant) friend of mine who had been tight with Vinnie Junior and the entire Bianchi family, mostly because they were family but for a lot of other reasons besides.

And Daniel Hart was the man who waged war against Salvatore Giglia, the man whose war meant Vinnie was no longer breathing.

When I got word things could go bad for Cal, I warned Benny. Directly after that, as I was wont to do, I got a wild hair, acted on that wild hair, drove to fucking Indiana to have Cal's and his new woman, Violet's, back, did something stupid, and ended up getting shot by none other than the man who ordered the hit on my boyfriend.

So that was how drama followed me.

I went searching for it.

Shortly after this uncomfortable realization, I carefully curled on my side in order to sleep and do it not snoring. Shortly after that, I fell asleep.

Now was now.

I was in Benny Bianchi's house, alone in Benny Bianchi's bed, and Benny had thrown down. I knew where he stood. I knew what he wanted. I knew where his head was at.

And I knew I'd never go there.

Not because I didn't want to. I was going to hell for it, but Benny was not wrong and neither was Shakespeare. This particular lady doth protest too much.

In the dark in Benny's bed, I couldn't go there.

I had to go where I needed to go.

And that was to formulate a new plan.

I knew I didn't have it in me to fight the good fight—that fight being my normal fight, all about drama, hysterics, shouting, and eventually getting my way.

I had to wait it out and fight the slow, calculated fight—that fight being about quiet and giving in early to get what I needed in the end.

So I would have to see Theresa, let her mother me, give her the forgiveness she needed and should have. The same with Vinnie.

And in the meantime, I had to find some way to get Benny to let go of his idea that there was a future for us.

There wasn't.

He was a good guy. Decent. Strong. Loyal. He went into the family business not only because his father wanted him to—it meant something to his dad and he respected his dad—but because Benny was all about family and that was what you did. He ran the Little League. He bought a house and started a search for a good woman with whom he could make a solid family and build a good home.

He deserved to find that good woman.

She just was not me.

But I had to find a way to convince Benny of that.

And I would do it. Because I was a quarter Italian, which meant I wasn't only hotheaded, impatient, and dramatic, I was also crazy-stubborn.

And I would do it because Benny should have a good woman.

Which meant he had no business being with me.

Three

Sweet and Spicy

"*Francesca*, baby, wake up."

Benny's voice—deep, easy, and sweet—was at my ear, his mouth so close I could feel his lips whisper there.

My eyes fluttered open and I immediately felt the pain. To alleviate it, I shifted from my side to my back. Benny, sitting on the bed next to me and leaned onto a hand on my other side, shifted to accommodate me. As I untwisted to lie flat on my back, I made the mental note that being a woman who snored was better than waking with this kind of pain.

Still half asleep, I was unable to hide it and I knew it when Benny murmured, "Brought you coffee. Your girl's downstairs. She just showed. I'll send her up with some water and a pill."

I focused on him to see his hair a sexy mess from sleep, his eyes warm and somnolent, his white tee on.

Asheeka had woken him. Asheeka had gotten a load of all of that opening the door. Therefore, even if the option of enlisting Asheeka in an escape plan was still open, she probably wouldn't take it, seeing as she knew I was currently occupying all that was Benny's bed. Thus, she would not lift a finger to help me escape due to the fact she'd think I was insane for wanting to.

"You need help gettin' out of bed and to the bathroom?" Benny asked, and it was then I knew I *really* wasn't hiding the pain because I also felt stiff, like my body would break if I moved it another inch, and I didn't want to try.

It was this way in the mornings. It got better as I got more lucid, moved around a bit, warmed up, and, most importantly, got some drugs in me.

I was looking forward to the time when I didn't wake up this way. It was getting better. But it was also taking its fucking time.

"I—" I started to refuse, not only because this was Benny and I wanted to make it clear I didn't need or want his help, but because I would do the same if it was anyone.

It was a pride thing. It was stupid. But it was me.

Benny knew I was going to refuse and didn't allow me to do it. He shifted again, wrapping an arm around my waist, carefully moving me with him. He exited the bed, sliding me out from under the covers as he did it.

As for me, as he did it, I winced outright, not having it in me to attempt to hide it.

I ended up with my feet on the floor and my side pressed close to Benny's, his arm around my waist, his other hand coming out to settle on my hip. He was holding my weight and steadying me at the same time.

"I'd carry you to the bathroom, *cara*, but you gotta get used to doin' this on your own," he said gently.

I looked up at him and nodded because he was right. I would be alone soon enough and I had to get used to it, in a variety of ways.

He nodded back, his lips tipping up, his eyes warming. Then he moved us toward the bathroom. He got me in and to the basin and kept hold of me until I put my hand to the counter. Even then, his hold only loosened. He didn't let me go.

"You good?"

I kept my eyes to my hand on the counter. "Yep."

"Francesca."

I lifted my eyes to his.

The instant I did, he lifted his hand to rest it light on my jaw and leaned in. Brushing his lips against my cheekbone, when they left it, his thumb shifted and brushed across the touch as if he wanted to seal it there.

And as it was sealing there for what I knew would be eternity, I completely forgot about the pain.

"I'll send your girl up."

"Okay," I whispered.

He didn't move. Just held my eyes as I looked into his and held my breath.

Then his thumb shifted again, gliding along the edge of my lower lip. I felt my toes curl, my fingers curl, and last, a curl in my belly that had nothing to do with pain.

"She's sweet in the morning," he murmured.

Oh God. He was totally going for it. He was taking advantage. He was getting his licks in before the bell even rang.

"Ben—"

"Sweet and spicy. What more could a man want?"

Oh God.

Before I could get another word in, his thumb did another brush of my lip, his arm around me gave me a squeeze, and then he let me go and walked out of the room.

~

I stood at the basin in Benny's bathroom in a pair of undies and a bra, my new bandage that Asheeka taped on me covering my skin several inches under my breasts, slightly to the right.

I had my roller brush in hand and was blasting a thick lock of dark hair with heat from Benny's hair dryer.

I did not allow myself to consider why Benny had a hair dryer.

I didn't do this because I knew why Benny had a hair dryer.

The first part of what I knew was that it wasn't for Benny's personal use. Asheeka had amused herself (and me) by calling out an inventory of Benny's bathroom cabinets while I showered. We learned he had product for his hair.

This was not surprising. With all that hair, he'd need something to rule it. Though, I was slightly surprised (as was Asheeka) he used a designer brand that cost a whack and could only be bought at upscale salons. That didn't seem very Benny.

But the hair dryer wasn't for Benny. He probably put that gel in when his hair was wet, did a slapdash job when he did it, and didn't give a fuck mostly because he simply didn't give a fuck and partly because, no matter how half-assed he did it, he had such great hair, it was just going to look good.

I didn't think of Benny standing in front of his bathroom mirror, probably inattentively running his long, strong fingers through his hair by rote and doing this with nothing but a towel wrapped around his waist.

No, I absolutely didn't think about that.

I thought that it was certain a lot of women had been through that bedroom and, thus, in that bathroom. One either had left that hair dryer (this was the greater possibility), or he'd bought one as an act of consideration for all the women who'd been through that bathroom and needed one (this wasn't very likely).

I was thinking with some irritability about using another woman's hair dryer, and I was doing this in an attempt not to think about the fact that I was doing my hair. If I allowed my mind to go there (which I unfortunately did), I would tell myself it was me (something else I did).

I was out of the hospital. It was time to get back to me and I was a girl who did my hair. I did it big. I used beaucoup products. I put creams in for heat protection, oils in for frizz prevention, mousse in for lift and volume, spray in for hold. I teased. I flipped. I fiddled. I could work on one curl for ten minutes to make it lie right.

But I was not...absolutely *not*...doing this because Ben Bianchi had seen me for a week and a half looking like shit, and now I had my opportunity to look decent.

Even Jamie knew how important this was to me, thus, when she brought my packed bag to the hospital, she'd included all my products, my teasing comb, and my roller brush.

Alas, she'd failed with the makeup, only bringing my moisturizer, powder, one single shade of blush (when I had at least twelve in my makeup drawer at home), and mascara.

When I did the makeup part earlier, I'd had to make do.

What I wouldn't do was make do with the single tube of lip gloss (by Asheeka's report, shade: "Berry Promising") that was rolling around in Ben's drawer with black barbers' combs, Band-Aids that, for some reason, had found themselves box-less, nail clippers, used razors that should have been dropped in the trash, not in that drawer, random pills that found themselves out of the bottle, and the like.

That lip gloss was definitely not Benny's.

Later, in a moment of alone time, I'd do what my doctor ordered: get some exercise, walk to the bathroom, grab that lip gloss, walk to the bedroom, and throw it out the window.

I turned off the hair dryer, put it on the basin, and used the roller brush to fiddle with the lock I was currently drying.

"This pains me to say, babe," Asheeka started, sitting on the toilet seat and watching me. "Seein' as that boy looks like that boy looks, but I've got three older brothers. My brothers have got their own brothers. By the look of the biceps on that man downstairs, not to mention other stuff on that man downstairs, he could hold his own. Ten black men show up at his door to get the woman he's holdin' captive out of his house, I'm thinkin' that won't go down too great for him."

Asheeka was tall, big of chest, and abundant of booty, with short, straightened, styled-to-the-teeth hair, and eyes that made you wish she'd find a man and have babies because children needed to see that kindness directed at them from birth to the last glance she gave them on her deathbed.

She also called work that morning to say she'd be late since she was taking care of me. When she was not calling down the inventory of Benny's bathroom, she was reminding me my soon-to-be-ex boss would not mind if she was a half an hour late, or three hours late, due to the fact she was seeing to me.

This was because he liked Asheeka. This was also because he loved me.

I knew he loved me partially because he wanted to get in my pants.

Mostly he loved me because I was the top salesperson on his sales force. When I put in my resignation, I thought he was going to cry.

I understood this. I was a hot commodity. I could sell. It was a gift. I had the knack. Even I had to admit that.

It started when I got my first job in sales at age twenty selling cars. The man who hired me did it as a joke. He wanted to watch me try to sell cars and he wanted to make fun of me with his boys when I failed.

What he didn't get, as many car salesmen didn't, was that there were some women who actually knew cars, and one of those women was me.

Another thing he didn't get was that there were other women who bought cars on their own without a man attached to their hip and speaking for the both of them. Those women wanted someone they could trust, someone they could relate to, someone they didn't think would screw them, and that was also me.

What he also didn't get was that I was not hard on the eyes, I was not above flirting my ass off to make a sale, and ninety-eight-point-seven percent of the male population thought with their dicks.

So I killed.

But I didn't stay at that job long, mostly because he was an asshole. Even though I'd shown him and wanted a goodly amount of time to crow about it and hit the top of the sales board month after month and crow about that to the good ole boys he employed, no one likes to spend time with an asshole. When another dealership made an offer, I took it.

Then I sold a car to a man who owned a huge office supply business who recognized my skills and he hired me away. I was later poached by my current boss who sold hospital supplies.

Since then, I'd had headhunters come to me frequently to try to lure me away.

I'd stayed for stupid reasons, holding on to a life that didn't want me.

But I also stayed for good reasons. I liked my job, made better than good money, had great clients, a boss who wanted in my pants but, even so, respected me, and nearly all my co-workers were friends.

Two months ago a pharmaceutical company in Indianapolis approached and made me an offer I couldn't refuse. Even though I had no pharmaceutical sales experience, I had hospital sales experience so I knew the drill and a number of the players. I'd be heading up my own team and my base salary would be nearly double my current salary. The area my team and I were going to cover was vast, which meant travel—an idea I liked.

The escape hatch opened, I decided to slide through.

But I was going to miss my boss, my clients, my co-workers, and especially Asheeka.

I prepared my hair in the brush for another blast of heat, aimed my eyes on Asheeka in the mirror, and told her, "You do that, old lady Zambino will come outta her house with her bowling ball. She might be eighty-two, but she's got mad skills with that ball. So I'm not sure it'll go too great for your brothers and *their* brothers."

After delivering that, I blasted my hair with heat.

When I was done and moving on to new territory, Asheeka said, "I'm worried about you."

She said this, I knew, because, while she was taping the clean bandage to me, I told her about what Benny was up to. Since then, she'd been biding her time, likely looking for when she'd have my undivided attention. As that was not happening and she actually did have to go to work eventually, she was winging it.

I turned my eyes from my hair to her and assured her, "I'm gonna be okay."

"Boy like that can be persuasive," she replied.

I knew that and was scared shitless of it.

"I'll be okay," I repeated.

"Honey." She leaned toward me, putting her elbows on her knees, but her eyes didn't leave mine in the mirror. "My next question should come with wine and relaxing music after we've had facials and our hair done, but I gotta throw it out there. And that question would be, why *wouldn't* you want him to persuade you?"

I pressed my lips together and blasted the curl with heat.

When I switched off the dryer, Asheeka kept at me. "Avoidance? From Frankie Concetti? The girl who lets it all hang out?"

"He's my dead boyfriend's brother," I said for the millionth time in less than two days. Though, this time, it was telling her something she knew already.

She nodded. "I see why you wouldn't wanna go there. I totally see that. But I saw that boy down there, and when I say that, I'm not only talkin' about the fact that he looks good enough to eat. It's that he was sweet but firm when he told me I had to look out for you. Not fall for any of your shit when you tried to convince me you could do somethin' on your own that I didn't think it smart that you be doin'. And that I needed to get that pill down you 'cause you're prideful and stubborn and tryin' to hide the pain." She paused, didn't release my eyes in the mirror, and finished, "He cares, Frankie. A lot."

"That's not the point," I told her.

"What *is* the point?" she asked.

"The point is, it's just not right," I explained.

"That's not the point 'cause that's bull-hockey."

I fiddled with my curl and blasted it with more heat because I didn't want to be talking about this *again*.

When I was done, Asheeka got right back in there. "You're holdin' a grudge."

I looked back at her in the mirror. "Uh...*yeah*."

She shook her head. "Only God can judge him and his family for the way they treated you. Here, on earth, the right thing to do is forgive. Harder to forget and that'll mess with you, honey. That's your cross to bear and that's the whole thing about forgiveness. They gave you that cross and it's you who has to bear it at the same time findin' a way to forgive. That's the reason forgiveness is divine. 'Cause someone wrongs us, we live with that wrong right alongside them, but it's us who has to find the strength to let them off the hook. If they work for it, ask for it, only you have the power to offer it to them so their soul can be less heavy. And the right thing to do is use that power."

"I am. I've already decided that. That's why I'm not taking you up on the offer to rally your brothers. I'm gonna let them heal the breach," I shared before I ended it. "Then I'm gone."

She stared at me in the mirror.

I went back to my hair.

My arms were tired, I had a nagging ache that prolonged standing and moving was beating through the medication, and I knew I should give up on my hair.

But I didn't.

Asheeka said no more. Just when I got down to sliding my fingers coated with elixir through my hair and putting another coat of mascara on, she walked into the bedroom and came back with a fresh nightgown.

I pulled it on over my undies and saw it was really cute. The one I'd chosen last night was kind of a caftan—flowy and comfortable, but full coverage.

This one had a high-low hem, the front of which hit me several inches below the knees, the back dip went nearly to my ankles. The neckline plunged to an empire waist, with gathering at the bodice and waistline that drew attention to the cleavage. And last, it was a bright coral color that looked great with my hair.

You could see the turquoise lace of my bra at the neckline but…whatever. It wouldn't be the first time I showed hints of a bra, including to Ben and Theresa.

"Cute nightie," Asheeka observed, giving it a once-over.

"Gina. She has an eye for cute," I told her.

"Sexy-cute," she told me.

I looked into the mirror. The cleavage was sexy. The material was semi-shiny and clingy.

Jeez, it was sexy-cute. Who knew Gina had that in her?

"I'm thinkin' you're good for now and need to take a load off," Asheeka said.

I turned to her and took the hint.

She needed to go.

"Sorry, babe, my mind's all over the place. You gotta go."

"Happy to stay as long as you want, but yeah. There are syringes to sell and we're one girl down in sellin' 'em."

I grinned.

She shifted out of the way and swung an arm toward the door.

I took her invitation and headed that way. Once in the bedroom, I didn't waste time taking a load off, stretching out on the bed, pillows tucked behind me, upper body resting back.

That was a lot better.

"You want me to come tonight, company and a buffer?" Asheeka asked and I looked up at her.

I would love that. It was sweet as all get-out and would help a lot.

But she was late for work for me and I'd need her to come around to Benny's for at least a couple more days. I didn't need to suck all her time and goodness. I was not a fan of owing markers, and with me moving away, I wouldn't have many opportunities for her to call them.

"I'll be okay," I answered.

"You keep sayin' that, and I know you want me to believe it, but gotta say, honey, not sure that I do."

I gave her a face and she returned a grin. Then she bent down, grabbed my hand, and gave it a squeeze.

"You need me, you know how to get me."

"Yeah, babe. I do. And I appreciate it like you wouldn't believe. Thank you," I replied.

That got me another squeeze and a smile before she let me go and walked out.

"Later!" I called as she did.

"Later, girl!" she called back.

When she was gone, I looked to the nightstand to see if Ben left the remote.

He did not.

Something about that made me want to giggle out loud.

Perhaps my TV ploy *did* work.

I was reaching for *Vogue* when Benny walked in. I watched him do this. I also watched him come to a dead stop five feet in, eyes on me.

"I attacked my hair this morning," I declared. "That's a feat that's difficult to conquer on the best of days, so, warden, if you intend to force me to walk down to the commissary for breakfast, I'm gonna have to starve until lunch."

Ben said nothing.

I kept talking. "If you bring me something to eat and more coffee, I'll be nice to you for fifteen minutes."

Ben still didn't speak.

So I allowed, "Okay, twenty."

Benny planted his hands on his hips but said not a word.

I went on, "And you can bring the remote back. Last night, I saw the Entenmann's coffeecake on your counter. For a slice, I won't fuck with your TV all day."

"Told you, you can't have sex. Doctor's orders."

I felt my head jerk in surprise at his words before I asked, "What?"

"Babe, you want me to fuck you, you give me big hair, a hint of a bra I'll wanna see covering your tits before I'll wanna take it off, and skin."

My stomach tightened and not in a bad way.

But...

Was he crazy?

"*What?*" I asked, louder this time.

"Actually, you want me to fuck you, you gotta breathe. You want me to fuck you immediately, you give me that hair, a hint of bra, and show some skin."

I narrowed my eyes. "What is up with you?"

"You play games with all that," he flicked a hand in my direction, "you get repercussions."

"Benny, what…the hell…are you talkin' about?" I demanded to know.

"Hair, bra, nightie, skin," was his absurd (and repetitive) answer.

"Gina bought me this nightie, Ben," I informed him. "It's like a dress."

"It's clingy and shows skin," he informed me.

"It's one of the only choices I have, seein' as you didn't take me home so I'd have different choices," I retorted.

"Then I'll set Ma on hittin' your house to get you different choices."

This would be a wasted chore as the nighties I had at home were way clingier and showed a whole lot more skin.

Therefore, I advised, "Actually, if you can't control your base instincts, you should send her to the granny section of Macy's."

He got my drift and I knew it when his jaw got hard. "You doin' that shit to fuck with me?"

"Fuck with you how?"

"Bein' a tease, babe. A tease recovering from a fuckin' GSW, which means I can't teach you the lesson you should get for bein' a tease."

I felt my blood start to get hot and this time it was in a bad way.

"What, in all that I've done and said in the last week and a half, would give you the impression I'd tease you, Benny Bianchi?" I snapped.

"You, lyin' in my bed, dressed like that, lookin' like that."

"I did my hair and put on a nightgown!" Now I was shouting.

"Precisely," he returned.

"Are we really having this conversation?" I asked sarcastically, as well as still loudly.

"You got a robe?" he asked back.

Oh shit. I did.

Since I did, I glared.

Benny read my glare, dropped his hands from his hips, stalked to my bag, and dug through it, yanking out my robe.

He then stalked to the bed and dropped it in my lap, whereupon he announced, "Ma's on her way over."

I closed my eyes and forgot to be pissed because panic was gathering around my heart.

"She's gonna be cool with you, Frankie," Benny stated.

That was what I was panicked about. She was going to be cool. Sweet. Kind. Motherly. All this while feeling badly because she'd been in the wrong and something extreme happened that brought that to light. And her feeling badly would make me feel badly. Then I'd have to accept all the goodness of her, knowing I'd have to give it up again, my choice this time.

The bed depressed and my eyes flew open to see Benny sitting on it, again hip to hip.

"Can you give me a hint why this is so difficult for you, babe?" he asked, sounding less peeved.

"Which part?" I asked.

"Any of it," he answered.

"No," I finally answered his question.

"You're not gonna let me in there, even a little bit." He stated this as a fact, but I decided to take it as a statement that needed affirmation.

"No, I'm not," I agreed.

"Then I'm gonna hafta dig in there."

I drew in a breath.

Benny digging in there.

God seriously freaking hated me.

It was time to put my plan in motion so I did.

"Your family blamed me. They turned their back on me. I loved you all. That hurt. Things have changed. I get that. But they changed while I was recovering from getting shot, Ben. *You* need to get that. I'll be cool with Theresa. I'll sit down with Vinnie Senior. And after I get through that, you and me'll talk. But you gotta cut me some slack. This isn't easy on you. Think how it feels for me."

He leaned closer and didn't look or sound peeved at all when he asked, "Was that hard?"

It was.

Absolutely.

And as time went on, it would get harder until it eventually killed. But I'd lived through bad. I could live through worse.

Or, at least, I hoped so.

"Uh, yeah, Benny. That was hard. That's the point."

He bent in, leaning onto a hand in the bed on the opposite side of me as he took my hand in his free one, lifting it to hold it to his tight upper abs.

There it was. It happened right away. My hand on Benny's tight abs that I'd never really get to explore. It got worse.

"You got nothin' but good comin' your way, Frankie, I can promise you that," he said softly.

He was wrong. I never had nothing but good coming my way. If I got good, I lost it. That was my life. I'd learned to live with it. I didn't like it, but I had no choice.

I didn't share that. If he hadn't figured that out for himself, I wasn't going to enlighten him.

He squeezed my hand and pressed it tighter to his abs. "You open yourself up, you could find it'll be the best you ever had."

I didn't know what he was promising, but I had a feeling it had a variety of nuances. I also had a feeling he was right—about *all* of those nuances.

The problem was, *he* should find the best he'd ever have, and he couldn't get that from me.

"Can we stop talking now?" I requested.

His eyes got soft, but his lips said, "Yeah. About that. I'm gonna go get you some coffeecake, but before that, I'm gonna tell you how this is gonna go down."

I had a feeling I knew what "this" was and, admittedly, I was grateful he had a plan. This would likely come as an order, which would be annoying, but I needed to be prepared and I'd take whatever I could get.

"When she gets here, I'll bring Ma up. She'll do what she's gotta do and I'll be here with you in the beginning. Then I gotta get to the restaurant. Got paperwork to do and Pop's takin' my back at nights while you're here. He does things his way. I do things my way. Obviously I like my way better. He fucks up my kitchen, I'll deal. He fucks up my system in the office, that will not go good. So I gotta see to shit. Ma will stay. I'll be back as soon as I can."

This was a good plan, the best part being I'd get a break from Benny during it. I'd take dealing with Theresa over Benny any day.

"Gotcha. But just sayin', if you need to be at the restaurant at night, I'll be good here alone."

"You'll be here alone and schemin'. So that shit's not gonna happen."

To preserve the precarious mellow mood I had going, I decided not to reply.

"So, you're down with that plan?" he pressed.

"Do I have a choice?" I asked.

"No," he answered.

"Then yes, I'm down with that plan."

He smiled at me.

I allowed myself a nanosecond to long for a life where I could be lying in a sweet nightie in Benny Bianchi's bed with him sitting close, holding my hand against his taut abs, smiling at me, and what I would be free to do in that pleasant happenstance, before I shut that shit down.

"Bring the remote with my cake," I ordered.

"Back to spicy," he muttered, still smiling.

He liked spicy. If I was playing it smart, I wouldn't give him spicy.

But I was Francesca Angelica Concetti. That just wasn't in me.

"I was under the impression I'm here to finish recuperating, Benny. I can't do that if you starve me to death."

I felt those tight abs shaking with his silent laughter and I liked that feeling a whole lot. Too much.

Dangerously much.

Then he gave my hand a squeeze, let it go, and pushed up from the bed, muttering, "At your service."

I should have let it go, I really should have. But I didn't because it was just…not…me.

"I will note at this juncture that if I was in my own apartment, which doesn't have steps and is a lot smaller, I could get my own coffeecake."

"You're right," he replied, not looking at me and walking toward the door. "But you probably wouldn't have coffeecake."

"No, I would have Gina makin' me ciabatta toast with homemade ciabatta, which, incidentally, she'd deliver to me in bed without the hassle."

"Then lucky you're here," he returned, walking through the door. "Entenmann's cheese coffeecake with crumble is better, even than Gina's ciabatta."

There it was. I should have kept my mouth shut.

Because he was right.

I lay in Benny's bed, eyes glued to the TV, plate in my hand with a slice of coffeecake the size of which, coupled with last night's dinner, proved irrefutably that Ben didn't intend to starve me.

I did this as Benny took a shower.

I was good, resting, eating, a fresh cup o' joe sitting on the nightstand and a huge slice of fresh Entenmann's in hand, but I was wishing for pain. Pain would take my mind off Benny in the shower.

Fortunately, the shower turned off.

Unfortunately, this conjured images of Ben standing at his sink in nothing but a towel, running his hands through his hair.

I was reconsidering Asheeka's offer of her brothers and *their* brothers coming to my rescue when Ben, with excellent timing, exited the bathroom.

Looking his way, I found I was right. He gelled as a necessary afterthought to tame all that thick, unruly hair. It was wet and an attempt had been made, just not a very good one, which left it wet, messy, and hot. This meant it would dry messy and *hot*.

He was wearing another white tee but different jeans—more faded and there was a worn white patch that was nearly threadbare at his crotch.

My mouth got dry.

The doorbell rang.

Theresa was there.

My mouth suddenly filled with saliva.

Ben's eyes came to me. "You're good," he said quietly.

"Unh-hunh," I mumbled disbelievingly.

"You think I'd let anything harm you?"

Oh God. More dangerous territory.

A man, any man, said that to a woman, he dug his way in there, straight into your heart. A man who looked like Ben said it, that hole he was digging went deep. A man who looked like Ben said it and meant it, he got in so deep, he'd never get out.

"Ben—"

"You think she would, even before you took a hit?"

I didn't reply.

"You're good, *cara*," he whispered, then moved to the door.

I hastily set my plate aside and took a sip of coffee.

After putting the mug back on the nightstand, I didn't know what to do with my hands or eyes.

I didn't figure it out before Benny appeared in the door again.

He came through and on his heels came Theresa.

Later, I would process the fact that Ben positioned himself in the room halfway between me and his mother. I would also process the fact that he did this as a show of support for both of us. He took no sides. What he was saying was, if this started to turn bad, he was in the position to deal, for either one of us.

It was a good thing for a son to do. It was a good thing for a woman's man to do.

At that moment, though, I only had eyes for Theresa, who looked unsure of herself, and that look cut straight to the bone.

Theresa Bianchi had a husband, four children, three grandchildren, and ran the front of a very busy, very popular restaurant for forty years. She wasn't unsure about anything. There was not an occasion when she didn't know what to do.

Except one like this one.

She stopped three feet in the room and I watched as she struggled with how to place her body, what to do with her hands. She even visibly struggled with holding my gaze.

Watching it and unable to stand it, I blurted, "Thanks for the magazines."

Her head twitched and her body got tight.

"And the coffeecake." I threw out a hand to the nightstand.

Her eyes went there.

"There's leftover," I said, explaining the remaining cake quickly, "because Ben cut a slice for Refrigerator Perry, not a woman who's been subsisting on IVs, then Jell-O, making her stomach the size of a golf ball."

"You did all right with the pie last night, *cara*," Benny put in, and I looked at him.

He was grinning, happy, relieved, and his eyes on me were proud.

He was a man who could easily take a girl's breath away.

Standing there, looking at me like that, he'd never been more breathtaking.

"It was a Bianchi pie," I returned and said no more for that said it all.

Ben's grin got bigger.

Theresa made a noise and we both looked back to her.

She was fighting tears and I knew she'd win just because that was who she was, so I shut up and gave her time.

I was right. She won.

And when she did it, she lifted her chin slightly, took two more steps into the room, and declared, "That coffeecake was for sweet tooth snackin'. Not breakfast." She looked to her son. "You didn't make Frankie bacon and eggs?"

"She asked for coffeecake," Benny replied.

"Tomorrow she gets bacon and eggs," Theresa decreed.

"Tomorrow she gets what she got today, which is whatever the fuck she wants," Benny shot back, and this was killing me because I liked his words, but more, I liked watching his banter with his mom.

I missed it and it hurt to have it back because I wasn't going to be able to keep it.

Theresa crossed her arms on her chest and set her expression straight to severe.

"I am uncertain why you, your father, and your brother feel the need to include the f-word in every other sentence."

At this point, Ben looked at me. "And there it is, *tesorina*. A woman askin' a man 'why' when the answer doesn't mean shit."

I couldn't hold it back.

I grinned at him.

The instant I did, I wished I'd held it back because his face changed in a way I wanted to remember for the rest of my life.

"The s-word is not much better, Benito Bianchi," his mother snapped, but Benny didn't look from me.

Instead, he came at me, bent in, grabbed me behind my head, and pulled me gently to him until I felt his lips on my hair.

He let me back and I tipped my head to catch his eyes.

"I'll get to the restaurant so I can be back quick," he said quietly.

"All right," I agreed.

He gave me a smile and his hand cupping the back of my head gave me a squeeze before he let me go, straightened, and strode to the door.

"Are we done talking?" his mother asked his back.

"Yep," he answered his mother by way of the hall.

She turned an exasperated look to me.

I grinned at her too and, again, wished I'd held it back.

Because *her* face took on a look I wanted to remember for the rest of my life.

"Later, Ma!" Benny yelled and, thankfully, the spell was broken.

"'Bye, Benny!" she shouted back, then looked at me. "Now, Frankie, is there anything I can get you before I call your doctor to make your checkup appointment?"

I shouldn't have done it.

But I did it.

I looked into her eyes and, again, I smiled.

⟋⟍⟋

On his way home from the restaurant, Benny's cell rang.

He leaned forward, pulled it out of his pocket, checked the screen, and took the call.

"Yo," he greeted.

"She at your place?" Cal asked, and Benny shook his head at the windshield.

"Yep."

"She spittin' fire?" Cal went on.

"Occasionally."

"Recuperating," Cal guessed as to the reason it was only occasionally.

"Yep."

"You'll get it when she heals."

He fucking hoped so. "Yep."

"Vi wants a visit and the girls wanna meet her," Cal told him.

Ben's cousin's woman had two daughters, Kate and Keira. Gorgeous. Sweet. Just like Violet. So Benny was not surprised by this request. He also wasn't surprised by the fact that it wasn't exactly voiced as a request. That was Cal.

"She just got through the reunion with Ma. Pop's chompin' at the bit. And she's still got considerable pain, *cugino*. Doesn't get 'round too good. Give us a few days."

"You got until the weekend."

At that, Benny grinned at the windshield.

Pure Cal.

"Just to say, man, it's Friday so it *is* the weekend, or near on it."

"I'll rephrase. You got until Sunday."

Suddenly, Benny wasn't finding this amusing and he didn't hesitate to get into why.

"You comin' up to let your woman commune with Francesca, or are you comin' up to make sure I'm not fuckin' that shit up?"

"Two birds," Cal replied.

Yes, he was no longer finding this amusing.

"Reminder, Cal, you let your life stay fucked for nearly two decades and it was only Vi pullin' your head outta your ass that bought you what you got today."

"Yeah, so, I learned. Now I'm makin' sure a man who means somethin' to me doesn't waste as much time or more, and worse, lets the woman who should be in his bed waste her life waitin' for him to pull his head outta his ass."

Definitely not finding this amusing.

"I got this," Benny said low.

"And I'm gonna give my woman time with the woman who kept her company during a serious-as-shit situation, let my girls meet the woman who kept their mother company and kept her alive, and rejoice in the fact that you got the other shit under control."

Benny decided to shut this down. "We done talkin'?"

"Yep."

"See you Sunday."

Cal might have said something, but Benny didn't hear it. He'd disconnected.

He parked in his garage and was walking up his back walk when he saw his mother come out the back door and down the stoop.

"Where you goin'?" he asked, his body tensing, hoping like fuck she wasn't escaping because things went shit with Frankie.

"Frankie's," she answered, bustling to him, eyes to the massive handbag over her shoulder that she was digging into. She yanked out a sheet of paper and stopped just short of slamming into him, which was why he'd stopped one step earlier. She waved the sheet of paper at him. "I got a list. She needs to get back to normal, not be wanderin' around in nightgowns. Gonna pick up some stuff."

That he would allow. Frankie wandering around his house and lying on his bed in nightgowns was not conducive to him having patience through the delicate operation he was attempting. As was evidenced by his ludicrous overreaction to seeing her—all her hair, that body of hers, and her flawless skin—in his bed hours before.

"Right," he said to his mother. "Her purse is in my truck."

"Okay, *caro*," she muttered, leaning up distractedly to kiss his cheek before she was bustling toward his garage.

"Ma," he called. She stopped and turned back. "All good with you two?"

He watched her face get soft and she nodded.

Thank fuck. She wanted that and Frankie gave it to her.

That said a lot about Frankie. He couldn't say he was in her shoes he'd ever give that shit to anyone. They'd treated her like garbage, all of them, Benny especially, with Theresa not far behind. If it was him, he'd hold on to it until the day they died and then he'd spit on their grave.

It was good to know Frankie wasn't going to put his folks through that. Fuck, it was just good to know she was the kind of woman who had that kind of forgiveness in her.

The tough stuff over, Benny got to the good stuff. "Cal and Vi are comin' up on Sunday, bringin' the girls."

He watched then as his mother's face lit with joy and Benny smiled at her.

After years of Cal's distance that he took while he was nursing wounds most men would never recover from, having him back was good for his ma, his pop, him.

Having Frankie would be icing, a thick, rich layer of it.

But, hope to God he succeeded in talking Frankie around to his way of thinking, Benny would be the one who'd get to eat it.

He watched his ma smile back.

The family all back together, healthy, happy, and growing with the addition of Vi and her girls. The only thing his mother ever wanted in her life she was going to get and Ben liked to see her get it.

"Good news," she said.

"Yeah," he replied.

Her smile got bigger. She waved and, again, started bustling away.

Benny moved to his house.

Frankie was not in the kitchen and he didn't bother searching downstairs. He went upstairs and straight to his bedroom.

When he hit it, though, she wasn't there. The bathroom door was open and he couldn't see the whole of it, but he also couldn't imagine her being in it for any purpose where she didn't close the door.

He turned and looked down the hall, stopping when he saw the bathroom door open, as usual, one of the bedroom doors closed, as usual, and the other one open, not as usual.

He moved to the room he called his office, but it was just another room where he and members of his family dumped shit.

When he bought the house, it was four bedrooms. All the occupants of the bedrooms, when he filled them up one day, would need to share that hall bath.

This meant the only thing he changed was converting the smallest bedroom, which was the size of a big closet, to a master bath.

He'd liked doing it. It reminded him of working construction, something he also liked doing. Building things. Using his hands, his body, seeing something form from his work. He also liked working days, having nights off to go out and throw back a few, shoot the shit with the guys, watch a game, pick up a woman who had promise, see how that panned out.

Working in the kitchen at the restaurant was hot and it was a pain in the ass dealing with the kids who worked with him. Kids who were more worried if the girl they texted would text back in a way that meant they'd soon get laid than getting the pies out of the oven or not burning the meatballs.

He'd often catch himself in that kitchen and wonder what the fuck he was doing there, working his ass off, killer hours, all of them so busy half the time he was on autopilot to get it done.

Then he'd get a whiff of the sauce his pop taught him how to make, sauce his grandmother taught his father how to make (and so on), and it was fucking crazy, totally insane, but he'd know why he was there. Not only that, he'd know there was no other place for him.

That was where he was meant to be.

These thoughts came to him as he walked down the hall and stopped in the doorway of his office, seeing Frankie sitting in his pop's huge, old desk chair with its cracked leather. She was staring at the computer on the desk that she'd turned on.

He leaned a shoulder against the jamb and noted, "Not connected to the Internet, babe, so can't send your SOS that way."

She jumped at his voice and he tensed when she did, thinking random, jerky movements like that in her state were not good.

But he didn't see the pain tighten her mouth or her eyes wince. Her head just shot to him. She looked him up and down and ended with his eyes.

"Ben, black screen and green cursor?" she asked.

"Told you it was Carm's old computer," he reminded her.

"From when?" she returned. "The second grade?"

He grinned and crossed his arms on his chest, but he didn't reply. He just stood there, liking watching Francesca Concetti and all her hair, wearing a robe, sitting in his father's old chair, giving him lip.

When he didn't speak, she did.

"Is there any reason to keep this?" she asked on a flip of her hand to the computer.

"Nope."

"Do you use it?" she pushed.

"Nope."

"Not to play Asteroids or Space Invader?" she kept at him.

He grinned at her sass but repeated, "Nope."

"So why're you keepin' it?"

He had no clue, outside of the fact that he never went into that room so it didn't matter if it was there or not.

"That's another 'why,' Frankie."

She ignored that and kept pushing, "Do you have another computer?"

"Nope," he said again and watched her light brown eyes with their fans of thick, curling lashes, get wide.

"You don't?"

"Nope," he said yet again.

"How do you get email?" she asked.

"Don't have email."

Her eyes got wider.

He'd thought a lot of things about Francesca in the past, too many of them wrong—back in the day, most of them wrong for different reasons—but none of them were that she was cute.

But she was sitting right there, all kinds of cute.

"You don't have email?" she pressed, sounding slightly breathy with disbelief in a way that made him wonder what other ways he could make her sound like that.

"Don't need it."

"Even for work?"

"I make pizza, Frankie. Why would I need email to make pizza?"

She swiveled the chair to face him, which was not good. It wasn't bad because he could see her fantastic, long-ass legs. It was just that he liked what he saw, but he couldn't do shit about it, which he didn't like.

"I don't know," she started, attitude leaking into her words, the good kind, the kind that was about hot and spicy and Frankie. "To take pizza orders?"

"Folks can come in and give their order."

"They could also email it in or, say, phone it in."

"Restaurant never had a number that was listed and we've done all right."

She said nothing to that because she knew it to be true. There was a line every night, no exception, and usually the wait was at least an hour long.

As much as he enjoyed standing there, seeing her in his father's chair, having a good view of her legs and that hair, it was time to shut it down.

And he spoke the words why.

"You good with sittin' up, *cara*?" he asked quietly.

"I have to get used to it," was her not great answer.

"You don't have to do it today."

"I'm okay," she told him.

"Come to bed," he replied and watched it move over her face. He couldn't get a lock on what it was, but since he brought her home the day before, he'd seen a number of expressions move over her face he couldn't get a lock on.

Some of them he sensed were good, like the one she just gave him.

The others he sensed were not good. So not good they were bad.

"Come on, baby," he urged when she didn't move.

She seemed to force herself out of whatever thoughts she was having and swiveled to the computer, saying, "I gotta turn this off."

At that, Benny walked into the room, bent to the outlet, and yanked the computer plug out.

He straightened, looked at her, and said, "Now it's off. Let's go."

Her mouth moved like she was fighting a smile before she pressed her hands into the arms of the chair and carefully folded out.

Ben didn't like seeing her move like that. She was always a bundle of energy. Electric. Francesca Concetti saw no reason to walk up stairs when she could jog up them or, more frequently, skip. Frankie Concetti went to the gym. She did spin classes, Pilates, Zumba. Frankie Concetti didn't cook; she *cooked*, swaying around the kitchen while she did it. Even sitting down or lazing around, she seemed charged. Mostly because you knew when she got up, it wouldn't just be getting up. It would be bursting.

Not like she just got out of his father's chair.

Seeing that energy shut down made him want to relive that day in the woods and do it over. In other words, not aim at Daniel Hart's middle, where he shot Frankie and where Benny shot him. But instead, aim higher, like Cal did, and take the motherfucker's head clean off.

He stopped thinking this when Frankie started moving. He moved after her, following her to his room. She went to his bed and climbed up on the covers.

He headed to the other side and angled in beside her.

She immediately started, "Ben—"

"Quiet," he ordered, twisting and leaning across her, to which she pressed herself into the pillows to keep well away, a move that made him grin to himself.

He nabbed the remote, laid back, flicked on the TV, then multitasked, maneuvering through the guide as he shoved an arm under her and maneuvered her closer.

"Ben!" she snapped.

"You rest on your back and fall asleep, you'll snore and I won't be able to hear the TV. Tucked up to me, you don't snore," he told the TV as explanation to the protest he didn't let her voice.

"Then I'll rest on my side *not* tucked up to you and I won't snore. But if I did, you wouldn't hear me anyway because you'll be downstairs watching TV."

He ignored that, found there was nothing on they both might like, and hit the buttons to get to Netflix.

"Benny," she prompted, putting minor pressure on his stomach to push away.

He looked down at her. "Quiet and settle."

She gave him squinty eyes. "I'll be quiet and settle when you aren't in bed with me."

"We gonna have this conversation every time I'm in bed with you? That is, until you come to terms with the fact I'm gonna be in bed with you a lot?"

Her eyes got squintier and she didn't hesitate with her response. "No, since that day is never gonna happen and *this* day and the ones close to it, you're gonna stop climbin' into bed with me."

"No, I'm not."

"Yes, you are."

"You do know I'm in this for the long haul." She opened her mouth to speak, but he kept going. "And, just sayin', I get a kick out of it. It makes my dick twitch in a way I like, squabblin' with you, that attitude of yours. So, baby, you gotta know, I'm happy with you keepin' on with that for as long as you like."

That did it. She clamped her mouth shut.

He looked back at the TV and smiled.

Then he asked, "You seen *The Expendables 2*?"

She said nothing.

Back to the silent treatment.

He could work with that too, seeing as he hadn't seen that movie, had been meaning to, and Francesca shutting her trap meant he could see to that. So he hit the button to fire up the movie.

He felt her attitude clog the air in the room as the movie started to roll and he kept feeling it until she fell asleep.

When she did, he curled her closer.

He did this because he liked her closer.

He also did it because, when he did, he could hear those sexy-as-fuck noises she made when she was sleeping a fuckuva lot better.

They didn't come often.

But when they did, Benny liked every one.

Four

Until Monday

The doorbell rang and Benny's eyes opened.

He instantly felt the kinks in his body from sleeping on the couch.

He moved when he slept, which was why he'd bought a king-sized bed the instant he moved out of his parents' house, five months after he graduated high school. He'd had a tiny apartment and that bed took up nearly the whole bedroom, but he didn't give a fuck. At his folks' house, he'd had a twin and that shit was torture with the way Benny slept.

He forced himself to sitting and reached out to grab his jeans. He got up, stretching to get the kinks out, tugged them on, and nabbed his tee on the way to the door.

Frankie was out by nine the night before, so even though the kitchen took last orders at nine thirty, he went in to take over from Pop in order to supervise closing. He also went in to talk any of his kids down from quitting, seeing as his father was a drill sergeant in the kitchen and his kids weren't used to that shit. This meant he didn't get home until near on midnight.

He'd done the same the night before.

He was used to the late nights.

He was not used to that fucking couch.

He just hoped he could sort things with Frankie in a way so he wouldn't have to get used to it.

He was pulling down his shirt at his stomach when he looked through the window at the top of the door and saw Frankie's girl out there.

He unlocked it, opened it, and greeted, "Hey."

"Hey," she greeted back, her eyes traveling the length of him, catching on his crotch and staying there too long. They jerked up and he could swear he saw pink tinge the chocolate skin of her cheeks.

Used to that from women (without the blush, and the blush was cute), he bit back a grin and stepped out of the way, inviting her inside nonverbally but saying, "I'll go wake her. Then I'll make coffee and bring you both a cup."

She was in by the time he was done speaking, so she turned to him, offering, "I'll make coffee."

He gave her a nod. "Have at it. Kitchen's in the back. Make yourself at home."

She dipped her chin and made a move to the back hall.

Benny closed the door and made his own move to the stairs.

"Uh…Benny?" she called when he had a foot on the first step.

He stopped and looked at her standing halfway down the hall. "Yeah?"

Her eyes went to the ceiling, then to him. "Figure you're the kind who isn't real big on interference, but…" She jerked her head toward the ceiling. "You know what you're doin' with her?"

She was right. He wasn't the kind who was big on interference. Further, he didn't know her and he was *really* not the kind who was big on interference from someone he didn't know.

What he did know was that she was up early on a Saturday to come and hang when her girl was taking a shower. Same with her bein' late to work the day before. So he didn't know her, but he respected that.

He also knew from her question that Frankie had shared.

Not surprising. Women did that and that was a big part of what he didn't understand about them. Why they would talk to their girls about their men in an attempt to understand their men when their girls were fucking *girls* and couldn't begin to understand how a man's mind worked, he did not get. Or, more to the point, get the concept that a man's mind didn't work at shit. Most men did what they did and that was it.

Trying to explain that to a woman was like slamming your head repeatedly into a wall.

But since Frankie shared and this woman had Frankie's back, he was forced to do what he normally would not do with respect to the last.

"I know what I'm doin'," he assured her.

"Frankie's not right," she told him.

"Yeah," he agreed quietly. "She just got shot. That shit'll shake you."

"That's not why she's not right."

He knew she was not wrong.

But he didn't agree with her. He just stated, "I'm seein' to her," in a way he hoped didn't invite further discourse but didn't do it in a way where he came off sounding like a dick.

She held his eyes, and while she did, he had to give her more respect. This coming from the fact that it was clear she gave more than a passing shit about Frankie and he already knew she did that just from her going out of her way to take care of their girl.

So he gave her more.

"I have not done right by her. I'm rectifyin' that."

She nodded and he had a feeling she wanted to say more, but she didn't. Her ending their conversation indicated she was showing him respect, and with that, he respected her more.

She moved back to the kitchen.

Benny moved up the stairs.

When he hit his bedroom, he saw Frankie on her back, covers resting at her hips, one leg slightly hitched at the side under the sheets, one hand resting low on her belly, her other arm cocked on the bed at her side, her mass of dark hair everywhere.

Beauty sleeping alone in his bed.

Fuck.

She was not snoring, which was surprising.

Another surprise, he hated snoring. His pop snored and did it so loud it filled their house at night growing up. That shit would wake Benny, and hearing it constant, he wouldn't be able to get back to sleep.

Frankie doing it, for some insane reason, he thought was cute.

But now she wasn't.

He sat on the bed above her hitched leg, bent low, and whispered in her ear, "Frankie, baby, wake up. Your girl's here."

He lifted up and saw her eyes flutter open, still not believing those lashes were that thick and curly without aid of makeup. He'd discovered this impossibility when she was in the hospital. He'd liked it and wondered if that was a dominant trait, say, one she'd give to her daughters.

But right then, her eyes open, he saw that she seemed disoriented and the pain instantly tightened her mouth, which, in turn, made him tighten his.

With no warning, she did an ab curl to lift up and he heard her mew of discomfort. When he did, he moved quickly. Getting off the bed, then carefully shoving his arms under her, he lifted her and put her to her feet. Keeping an arm around her waist, he held her close to his side and lifted his other hand to her jaw.

She tipped hazy eyes to his and he looked into them with more than a little concern because she should be getting better day to day. Instead, she seemed far more out of it this morning than she was yesterday.

"You okay?" he asked.

"Yeah," she muttered.

"Sure?" he pushed.

She held his eyes, hers remaining hazy, but she nodded.

"Bathroom?"

"Yeah," she agreed.

He dropped his hand at her jaw and guided her to the bathroom. Just like the day before, he didn't loosen his hold until she had a steadying hand on the counter.

"You seem fuzzy today," he observed as, just like the day before, she stared at her hand on the counter with zero focus.

When he spoke, she tilted her head back to look at him. "I'll shake it off, baby."

His gut tightened.

Definitely fuzzy. She'd called him "baby."

And Benny liked it, so he grinned at her, gave her a squeeze, and dropped his mouth to touch it to hers. Not her cheek this time. She had to get used to taking his mouth and she might as well start now.

Her eyes were still hazy when he lifted his head and looked down at her, at the same time lifting his hand to her jaw so he could brush his thumb over the soft skin of her full lower lip.

"Coffee, a pill, and your girl, comin' up," he said.

"Okay, Ben," she murmured.

Looking in her eyes that were no less hazy but also crazy-beautiful, he whispered, "Sweet."

Something moved through her gaze he didn't quite get, but it was the good kind of something. So he left her with whatever thought was working behind that look and headed out of the bathroom.

Asheeka was filling a glass with water when Benny hit the kitchen.

She looked to him when he got there. "Coffee's brewin'. Not quite done."

"I'll bring up some mugs when it is," he told her. "How do you take yours?"

"Milk, one sugar," she said, grabbing the pill bottle on the counter and making to move out. "She good?"

"Hazier this morning. Keep an eye."

Her mouth twisted like she wanted to smile but wouldn't let herself. She nodded and headed out.

Benny moved to the counter, put his back to it, and rested his hips against it. He watched her walk out of the kitchen, then watched where he last saw her when she was gone, settling in and listening.

Less than five minutes and the shower went on.

He grinned slow.

Then he took in his kitchen, and as he did it, the reason he bought this house came to him.

It had been in a time when he knew he needed to quit dicking around with his life and start living it. Not living it just to work to make money, buy shit, go out and have a good time, and get laid. Living it with meaning.

He grew up knowing that Vinnie would take over the restaurant from Pop. Since he had no intention of seeing to the front of the house, his life was his own.

Then he actually grew up and Vinnie twisted that notion, going his own way—that way being the wrong way—and Benny knew his younger brother Manny did not have what it took to run the kitchen for the long haul. Manny being social and liking flash clothes, the front of the house was where he worked. But the kitchen took something else, and with Vinnie out, Benny had to step up.

This was not an edict and it was not an expectation, not from Pop, not from Ma. They made it known they wanted the restaurant to remain in the family, but they didn't lean on any of their kids to make this so.

But the home they provided through hard work, and the love they gave that they showed was never hard work, meant it meant something to them and it meant something to their kids.

Which meant Benny didn't want to do it, but with Vinnie out, he had to make a choice and there was only one right one.

It wasn't a hardship. If he didn't fuck that shit, taking over the restaurant, he knew his life would be comfortable and he could give that to his family like Ma and Pop gave it to him.

So he made the right choice.

That thought in his head, his eyes drifted to the calendar tacked to the wall. It was three years old, arrested in time on the month of April.

Seeing it, it came to him that he didn't think on his future much. He just knew, whatever he did, he wanted to give the kind of comfort his ma and pop gave to him to his family. A big one. At least three, maybe four kids. The house always full, loud, comings and goings, a calendar on the wall in the kitchen like his ma kept that was completely marked up. Little League practices and games. Dance recitals. Parent-teacher conferences. Barbeques, sleepovers, and birthday parties. The woman he'd eventually claim keeping the schedule, pinning him down to sign a birthday card to one of their kids' cousins, a text coming to remind him she was picking their girl up from dance so he had to get their boys from the baseball diamond.

Until that moment, he didn't realize that that was the only dream he had for his future. All he had to do was find his way to put money in the bank to make sure his family had what they needed. But the goal was to treat them more than occasionally to what they wanted. Not to mention, have times when he could afford to pile them in a car or on a plane to go see his sister, Carm, in California. Or take them to a beach where the kids could play in the sand and he could fuck his woman with the sounds of the surf coming through the window.

Wanting that—only that—he did not get where his brother went wrong. With the way they grew up, he couldn't wrap his head around why the fuck anyone would want more.

Since Frankie got shot, he'd had to come to painful terms with why he'd been such a dick to her and then make a plan to sort that out.

But in that time, he had not given headspace to figuring out why Vinnie threw his life away.

Frankie, so fucking gorgeous, absolutely perfect…it was easy to go there. To twist it so it came down to her, Vinnie doing everything he could to give her everything she wanted in order to keep her. But Frankie never gave any indication she wanted anything but love and a solid life that she was right there, happy to help create.

So it was Vinnie who'd had something to prove.

Benny just did not get what there was to prove. Their pop was not a pushover, but he was not a driven man, driving his kids along with him. Their ma was definitely not a pushover, but she gave no indication she had great expectations, outside of hoping her sons wouldn't knock up some girl too early or come home from carousing after the blood dried on their clothes so it was harder to get the stains out.

Both his folks just wanted their kids to be happy, however that came about.

Kids were kids to them. They had no choice but to mature and, if they were smart, learn along the way. His folks could and did provide support, advice, and, on occasion, showed disappointment in order to nudge their children to learn the right things, but neither of them did this with a thundering hand.

So Benny didn't get it. He didn't get his brother having that growing up, then getting what was right then naked in Benny's shower, and fucking up so fucking huge and losing it all so fucking early.

And the shit of it was, he knew he'd never get it. That would always be a question mark in his life that his mind would go to in order to pick at it, find an answer, erase that mark—a mark that would never go away.

Vinnie left him with that. He left his folks with that. And he left Frankie with that. Wondering why he was like he was. But worse, wondering if there was something one of them could have done to stop it.

He couldn't deny this pissed him off. What he'd quit denying was that he was pissed at his dead brother, not the woman upstairs. It was not comfortable having that feeling about a brother he loved who could no longer make explanations or amends. That wound was arrested in time, gapping, sore, bloody, no way to heal it. And it was arguable, but Benny thought that might be worse than Vinnie turning to the dark side, working for Sal, and losing his life in a violent way doing it.

On that thought, he heard the coffeemaker beep that it was done. He had the mugs ready by the time the shower went off. He delivered them, setting them on the nightstand, then rapped on the bathroom door with his knuckles to communicate that fact. He came down the stairs and was walking back into the kitchen at the same time his parents walked in the back door.

"*Caro*," his mother greeted, coming direct to him, giving him a distracted kiss on the cheek, then moving straight to the coffeepot.

"Ben," his father greeted, looking not at Benny but at the ceiling.

Apparently, Vinnie Senior was done waiting to sort things out with Francesca. Eyeing him, Benny thought his father might be done waiting, but he wasn't looking forward to it.

"She's just out of the shower, Pop," he told his old man, and Vinnie Senior's eyes came to him. "That means you got at least an hour and forty-five minutes while she does her hair to get some coffee and come to terms with the fact that she's Frankie. She never changed and she's not gonna make you work for it."

"I told him that," his ma put in. "He's decided to worry."

Vinnie Senior directed a dark look to his wife, then he changed the subject by directing an order at her. "Coffee, woman."

She turned to him, pot in hand, two mugs already on the counter in front of her. "You know, just like every time the last forty-one years I've been near a coffeepot, I already got your mug ready. And just like every time the last forty-one years you tell me to get you coffee instead of asking for it, I want to throw your mug at you. Now, after hearing that for forty-one years, I'm wonderin' why I held back."

"You do because, for forty-one years, you have not once filled up your gas tank. You take the good, Theresa, you gotta take the bad."

"You fill up my tank maybe once a week. *Maybe.* I fill up your coffee mug more than once a day. I'm beginning to see this doesn't balance out," his ma returned.

Jesus. They'd been there two minutes and they were already at it.

"Right," Benny cut in. "You wanna bicker, do it after *I* get a cup of coffee."

At that, Theresa's eyes went right to her son. "*Caro,* you've had no coffee?"

"Pot just got done. I just got done deliverin' it to the women upstairs. So, no."

His mother's face softened when he mentioned doing something for Frankie. What his mother didn't do was move out of the way of the coffee-pot or pull down another mug.

So he moved into her to get his own mug.

"I got it, I got it," she mumbled, shooing him away before stating, "I take it you haven't made Frankie her eggs and bacon."

At this, Benny hoped like fuck that he could sort shit out with Frankie, and soon. Then he hoped like fuck what he figured they could have was what both of them wanted. And at that moment, he hoped this so that kitchen would cease to be his kitchen and, instead, it would be Frankie's. That way she could battle it out for supremacy with his mother and Benny could quit doing that shit.

"Ma, you know Frankie likes sweet in the morning," he reminded her.

"Then I'll make pancakes," his mother replied.

Benny looked to his father.

His father had his mug and was seating himself at Benny's kitchen table. He also caught his son's eyes and shrugged. Then he took a sip of coffee and leaned back in his seat, one leg stretched out, like he owned the fucking table and the house it was in.

No help there and it wasn't worth the hassle to take it any further. Frankie would eat Theresa's pancakes, even if she preferred coffeecake or wanted to switch it up and have him haul his ass to a donut shop.

"*Caffè, mio figlio,*" his ma murmured.

Benny looked to her and saw her extending a mug.

He took it and went to the table.

His mother went to the fridge.

He was downing the last of the cup, listening to the hair dryer upstairs going on and off (and on and repeat), hoping that meant Frankie had shaken off her daze. At the same time, he was hoping his mother brought her clothes that would cover her up, like turtlenecks and massive sweatshirts, when the doorbell rang.

His mother turned to face the kitchen door, his father's eyes came to him, and Benny got out of his chair.

He wasn't expecting company, but Frankie was in his house. Word would be making the rounds.

Manny had his own amends to make, but Manny would no way be there that early. Manny had settled on a woman, they'd been together over a year, and Ma was biting her lip that they'd moved in together two months ago with no ring on Sela's finger.

Sela was a good woman. Benny liked her. And Man came to work with a content look on his face that said he liked what he left at home. So Ben knew he liked his time at home, especially if a man was getting what Man obviously was getting…and liking, the mornings.

Sal would come in the morning. So would Gina. Sal's boys knew better than to show at Benny's door, morning or anytime. But the big man and his wife would do whatever the fuck they wanted.

For Frankie, he'd have to eat that shit and he would. Once. Then he'd have words with her, and if she intended to keep Sal and his wife in her life, she'd do that well away from him.

But Ben found halfway down the hall to the door that he wouldn't be eating that particular shit that morning.

He'd be eating other shit.

He knew this when a vaguely familiar female voice shouted from outside the door, "Yeah! Fuck you too! And kiss all this goodbye *forever*, asshole!"

He wasn't sure, he hadn't been around the woman in years, but he was thinking that was Nat, Frankie's sister.

Closing in on the door and seeing her head through the window, he saw he was right.

Fuck.

Frankie did not need this shit. More, he didn't need it. She was not his favorite person normally. Having to keep his shit together after her sister spent a week and a half in a hospital bed and the bitch did not even send flowers was not something he had the patience to do maybe ever, but definitely not then.

He opened the door, positioned himself firmly in it, and got an eyeful of her jumping up and down, giving the finger to a beat-up Dodge Stratus racing down the street.

He also got an eyeful of her short, tight, black knit skirt, which was a centimeter away from giving a crotch shot, and skintight tank with material so thin, he could easily see the lace of her bra. With this, for some fucked reason, she was wearing a lightweight but bulky scarf wrapped around her neck. Silver and gold was profuse at ears, fingers, and wrists. She smelled like she'd just walked through one of those bitches at the mall who offered sprays of perfume and choked the air with it for reasons he never got. And he only had her profile, but he could see she'd taken Ninette's heavy-handed makeup lessons to extremes.

Even way back when, when he was at school with the Concettis, it was like Frankie was not one of them. She knew how to trick herself out, absolutely. But the sisters dressed like whores from age twelve up and Frankie never did that shit.

She could do big hair, she did, and she did it well, as evidenced yesterday. She could show skin, but she did it with style and class that made it appealing, not cheap. And she liked her makeup, but as heavy as she could go with it, it never crossed that line from class to trash.

Ninette led that brigade, teaching her daughters lessons no girl should learn. Frankie was the only one opposed to them. The other two sucked that shit in and turned that shit out, not only in look, but in deed.

He'd never liked them, Nat *or* Cat, and not because they dressed like trash. Because they acted like it.

The brothers were a different story. He'd briefly met her brother Dino, and he knew Enzo Junior well.

Dino seemed an upright guy, affectionate with his little sister, pleasant to be around.

Enzo was a fucking crazy man, but he adored Frankie and didn't have much time for the other two, so Benny had always liked him.

Now, with her showing out of the blue, he knew he'd be reminded why he wasn't Nat's biggest fan.

He just did not know she was bringing her A game.

When the Stratus screeched around the corner at the end of the block, she turned to him. Just like he wasn't even fucking there, she picked up one of the three massive duffels sitting on his stoop and heaved it right by his legs into his foyer.

Oh no.

Fuck no.

"*Yo!*" he barked, and her eyes snapped to his.

"Hey, Ben," she greeted. Either not processing or ignoring his tone, she twisted and snatched up another duffel, dropping the strap on her shoulder and then shouldering her way right into his goddamned house.

She had to be joking.

"Get the last one, would you, big man?" she ordered, then stopped in the foyer and shouted up the stairs, "Frankie!"

She was. She was absolutely joking.

He turned to her, leaving her bag outside and the door open, and bit out, "Have you lost your mind?"

She drooped a shoulder, the duffel thudded on the floor, and she looked to him. "Heard Frankie was crashing here. Just scraped off my douchebag of a husband so I need to crash at her place." She finished this outrageousness with even more outrageousness, "I could use a ride when I get her keys."

"You've lost your mind," he whispered, and he whispered because, if he didn't, he'd shout.

"Say what?" she asked.

When she asked that, he knew she wasn't ignoring what she couldn't possibly miss: that Benny did not want her or her shit in his home. No, she was in her own world and she didn't give a shit he didn't want to occupy that world. And he sure as fuck didn't want it landing in his foyer.

So he decided to give her that information.

"You are not here," he told her, then explained, "And by that I mean, get your ass out."

Her eyes narrowed and it was not sexy-cute and full of attitude the way her big sister did it, mainly because he'd never liked the bitch. She was rough in a way there was no smooth. She was loud, she was obnoxious, and with this shit, she'd proved she could take selfish to extremes.

"You don't wanna give me a ride, that's cool, but keep your pants on, asshole. I just need Frankie's keys," she snapped.

Benny felt his body get tight, which was good. That meant it'd make it hard to move.

He didn't have the same problem with his mouth. "You're tellin' me you shouldered your way in my home, I haven't seen you in fuckin' years, and you're callin' me an asshole?"

"You just told me to get out," she shot back.

"It's my house. I can do that shit when someone who isn't welcome is in it," he returned.

He knew Theresa and Vinnie Senior were in the back hall.

Unfortunately, on his words, Francesca entered the space by walking slowly down the stairs.

Further to that misfortune, she was wearing a light pink baby-doll tee that was tight at her tits and a light gray pair of those loose but clingy draw-string yoga pants women wore that showed no skin but gave it all away in a way every man liked if his dick worked and he wasn't into guys.

So no turtleneck or sweatshirt.

Fuck.

Her eyes were on her sister and her mouth was moving to ask, "What's goin' on?"

Nat looked up at her sister, and before Ben could say a word, she announced, "Just got shot of the douche, soon to be formerly known as my husband. Need a place to crash. Heard you were here, which means your place is empty, so I'm gonna crash there. I need your keys, and quick, 'cause Benny's decided to be a dick and I've had a bad morning. I don't need that shit."

Benny was pissed. Absolutely.

But he instantly had another problem on his hands.

This was that he knew, with the way Frankie's face changed, his house was about to turn into a Concetti war zone. He'd seen it, more than once, but had been removed from it. Vinnie had to put up with that shit and that was one thing in all that was Frankie that he did not envy his brother.

But now, the woman on his stairs was not one hundred percent and she had no business throwing down with her sister. Not the way the Concetti women threw down.

Therefore, he made a move to the stairs just as Frankie replied, "First, you think of *askin'* to crash at my place?"

To this, Nat retorted, "I don't need hassle from you either."

Frankie made her way down the rest of the stairs and stopped on the last step where Benny was standing at the bottom, barring her from going further, thinking distance was key in this scenario.

She ignored her sister and kept with her list. "Second, you come to Ben's and call him a dick right to his face, right in his damned house?"

"Think I called him a dick to you, not to his face," Nat fired back. "He just happened to be standin' there."

Frankie ignored that too.

"Third, you show at Ben's house, layin' your shit at my feet and *his* door, when I can't take a fucking shower by myself, doctor's orders, 'cause I got a hole in me?"

Her voice was getting louder, so Benny murmured a soothing, "Frankie," that he knew no way in hell would soothe her.

"Babe—" Nat started, a change coming over her face. What Frankie said, by some miracle, got in there.

But for Frankie, it was too little, too late. "No. *Fuck* no," Frankie hissed. "Get your shit and get gone."

"Got no place to go, sis. Need you to help me out," Nat told her.

"Why?" Frankie returned immediately. "'Cause you screwed around on Davey again, he found out again, and I'm up on the rotation when he kicked your ass out and you need somewhere to wait it out until he loses his mind and takes your cheatin' ass back?"

Nat's face, which had gone soft with guilt at Frankie's earlier comment, went hard in a shot. "I'm not discussin' my marital woes with you in front of the fuckin' Bianchis and whoever that bitch is." She jerked her chin toward the stairs.

Benny looked that way to see Asheeka three steps up. When he did, he also saw Asheeka didn't take kindly to being called a bitch.

Fuck.

He had to wade in. Immediately. The Concettis were bad enough. He didn't need the unknown Asheeka throwing her hat into the ring.

"This is what's gonna happen," Benny stated, eyes back to Nat. "I'm gonna call a cab and give you some cake so you can put yourself up in a hotel for a coupla days while you sort your shit."

Frankie instantly fucked with his plan by declaring, "You absolutely are *not* doin' *any* of that shit, Benny Bianchi. And *you*," he saw her finger jab out toward her sister in his peripheral vision, "do not *ever* call one of my sisters of the heart a *bitch*."

He cut his eyes to her face. "Babe, just let me deal with this quick so we can get you some breakfast."

"And there it is. Rumor is flyin' and here's the proof," Nat put in with a full-on bitch voice that Benny should have reacted to quicker and would not know until later that he would pay the price in a variety of painful ways when he didn't. "Francesca Concetti, always wantin' an in on that pizzeria and the cash it makes, has grasped on to another Bianchi cock to get it. Hat's off to you, babe. Never thought after you killed the first, you'd get a shot at the next."

Ben stood stone-still, afraid to move, because he knew precisely what he'd do if he did. He stayed motionless as he felt the emotion beating down from Frankie and he fought back the urge to do violence against a female.

His father, with more years to learn control, moved.

He did this to walk into the foyer. He grabbed a duffel, took it to the door, and sent it flying. He put some heft behind his toss because it didn't hit the top of the stoop; it hit the sidewalk.

"Hey! What the fuck! I got fragile shit in that!" Nat shouted.

Vinnie Senior didn't hesitate. He did the same with the other one.

"*What the fuck!*" Nat screeched.

Done with the bags, Vinnie Senior stood, hand on the door, leveled his eyes on Natalia, and said one word.

"Out."

She was too stupid to take that one word, or read the look on his pop's face that said the smart move was not to earn more. She straight-up prompted more with "Fuck you, old man."

That was when Benny moved.

He only stopped when he felt his mother wrap her fingers around his forearm and she did this tight.

"One warning, Natalia," Vinnie said low. "You go or I put you out, and I will be puttin' my hand on you to put you out. You give me lip or problems when I put my hand on you, you'll be makin' a big mistake 'cause my son is holdin' back and you do not wanna force him to let go. Now, you go and you do not come back to this house, and you have not one thing to do with your sister unless she reaches out to you. Are you hearin' me?"

"Let me get this straight," Nat started, crossing her arms on her chest. "The Bianchis pissed all over my sister for years, she gets shot savin' one of your women you actually give a shit about, unlike Frankie, and you all see the error of your ways and crawl up her ass. Is that right?"

"Yeah, that's right, Natalia," Vinnie Senior replied. "And perhaps you should see this as a lesson in family. You mess up, you fess up. Make amends. And if you can do that bein' there for someone you care about in her time of need, all the better. Somethin' my son tells me you didn't do, her lyin' in a hospital bed for days without a visit from her sister."

"Not that it's any of your business, but I work nights so I gotta sleep days," she returned.

"That is not an excuse and you stand there sayin' those words knowin' it," Vinnie Senior replied.

Nat opened her mouth to speak, but Benny had gotten a lock on it.

That said, he was also done.

"Pop, get her out before I do it," he warned.

Nat's eyes shot to him just as Vinnie moved to her and he saw she was at least smart enough to read his look and know her time was up.

This was why she yelled, "Shit! Fuck! I got no place to go and no money to get there!"

"Not my problem," Benny told her.

She looked to her sister. "Frankie, seriously—"

"I did not kill Vinnie."

This was unexpected. It was also whispered. And it sounded tortured. Hearing it, everyone in that space went still except Ben, who looked to Francesca at the same time he moved up, crowding her on the step.

Her eyes stayed glued to her sister. "That you would say that to me, even *think* that about me...you're dead to me."

Fuck.

"Frankie, babe—" Nat started.

"Dead," she whispered, turned, and rushed up the steps.

Benny cut his eyes to his father and ordered a growled, "Get her the fuck out, Pop. *Now.*"

Then he turned and took the steps two at a time, following Frankie.

He hit his bedroom to see Frankie pacing, face pale, visibly deep breathing. He was concerned about her state of mind, but he was downright worried when he saw she had her hand resting where her wound was.

Uncertain about getting physical when she was so clearly agitated, he called, "Baby, come here."

Her eyes moved to him. She opened her mouth to say something but closed it before she got a word out.

He still caught the look in her eye and it was one he again couldn't read. This one was bad.

"Francesca, come here," he repeated.

"I need alone time," she stated, her voice dead, her feet still moving her around the room in a twitchy way he did not like.

"*Cara*, you don't need that," he told her. "You need more coffee, breakfast, and to sit down at the kitchen table with people who give a shit about you."

"Everything okay?"

This came from the door where Asheeka was standing, eyes on Frankie.

They moved to Benny when he said, "Got this, darlin'. Be down in a minute."

She bit her lip, looked to her girl, hesitated indecisively, then nodded in a way that Benny knew she didn't like doing it. After that, she disappeared.

Frankie paced throughout this.

Benny approached, gently pulled her in his arms, and put a stop to it.

She didn't put her arms around him, nor did she remove her hand from her middle.

"You got pain?" he asked.

"I was premature in upping my doctor-ordered exercise to a dramatic dash up a flight of stairs," she answered.

Fucking Nat.

"Right. Then I'll carry you downstairs, you'll lie on the couch, eat Ma's pancakes, visit with people who give a shit about you, and after they're gone, you can give me what's right now fuckin' with your head."

Her gaze moved to his and he could easily read what was in it before she hid it.

Panic.

He didn't get that, but he did get he had to conquer it. Not later.

Now.

So he drew her cautiously closer. "Frankie?"

She looked to his shoulder. "You're right. Pancakes would be good."

"Francesca."

Her eyes lifted to his and they were carefully blank.

Oh yeah, he had to conquer that.

Now.

"Maybe we should talk right now about what happened downstairs," he suggested.

"Vinnie's here. I should talk to him."

"He's not goin' anywhere."

She shook her head, her eyes drifting away, but he got them back by giving her a light squeeze.

"She's Nat," she surprised him by whispering the second she caught his eye. "She's been married to Davey for five years, with him for three before that, and I know of four times she's stepped out on him. There's probably more. And he's a good guy. If she's not screwing around on him, and he's not pissed and tryin' to save face by puttin' her out when everyone knows he's gonna take her back, he treats her like gold. They don't have it great, but they're not starving. They got a decent place. But bottom line, he loves her. What more does she need? What's she lookin' for?"

Her words so closely followed his earlier train of thought about his brother, Benny found it disturbing. At the same time, it stirred something deep in his gut, which was a place he felt a variety of things stir when it came to Frankie.

But this one went deeper.

Frankie kept talking.

"I know she learned that shit from my parents, thinkin' it's okay to have your fun however it comes and the people around you who love you will put up with your shit or bail, and if they bail, it's no skin off your nose. You just keep on findin' your fun and you don't think a thought about the people who love you that you're hurting in the meantime."

"Babe—" he started, but she was on a roll and she wasn't ready to quit.

"And she's my sister and that scene played out in front of your folks who don't get that. They've been together for decades and they have been because they know what's important. And they made Carm, who's been tied to her man for twelve years and wouldn't even think about lookin' at another guy. Hell, the four years she was with him before they got married, she wouldn't do it."

Benny was just disturbed at hearing her talk about his sister and her man and the time they'd been together, and how at the beginning of that time Frankie was not a part of their lives.

But she wasn't done.

"She'll never grow out of that shit. She'll never wake up. She brought her shit to your door, it got ugly, but in six months or two years or whenever she fucks up again, she will not hesitate to do it again. Who does that?"

"Francesc—"

"My family," she answered her own question. "They do that shit. Cat's almost as bad but in her own unique way. And right now, Enzo has two women who both say they're pregnant with his kid. They live in two different states and he's currently shacked up with *another* woman who luckily *isn't* knocked up...*yet*. And he's only twenty-eight."

"Can I talk?" he asked when she fell momentarily silent.

"What's there to say?" she asked back. "That was embarrassing."

His brows drew together. "How was that embarrassing?"

"Ben," she threw a hand out, "that happened in your house, in front of you, your folks. She even called Asheeka a bitch and she's never even *met* Asheeka."

"Yeah, that happened and she did that. *She* did. Nat. That doesn't reflect on you."

"She's blood."

"And Vinnie's my blood. Does him bein' in the mob reflect on me? My family?" he returned and knew he scored when she clamped her mouth shut. "No. I think we all learned the hard way not to take that on or pile that shit on someone who doesn't deserve it." He gave her a careful squeeze. "So don't take that on."

She turned her head to the side.

"Francesca," he drew her closer, "do not take that shit on."

She kept her gaze aimed to the side.

"Baby, put your arms around me and look at me."

She remained unmoving.

"Francesca, *cara*, put your arms around me and *look at me*."

He watched and felt her heave a sigh, and being Frankie, she didn't do what she was told. But at least she lifted both hands, rested them on his chest, and gave him her eyes. It wasn't what he wanted, but it was something.

"Do not take that shit on," he whispered.

He saw it again, something moving over her face, shifting in her eyes. This was bigger, weighty. He thought she was going to say something, give it to him, explain it, and he felt her body tensing as if she was going to share the weight, let it go.

But she relaxed and said, "I'm hungry."

Benny had to admit, he was disappointed. But she'd opened up before closing down and he felt it wise at that juncture to take what she gave freely and not push for more.

So he asked, "You good?"

"Yes," she lied immediately.

"You aren't," he replied. "But you are full of shit."

Fire danced in her eyes as they started to narrow.

That made him feel better.

"We'll talk more when we don't have a house full of people," he told her.

"An alternate and slightly more enjoyable plan than talking about my family or *anything* you might want to talk about when you don't have a house full of people, you tear my fingernails out by their roots."

He grinned and pulled her as close as he felt safe. "You do know you just get it over with, give in to it, let me in, you could get to the good parts."

He knew she was done when she shut it down. "I'm too hungry to have this conversation."

"Too hungry, maybe. Too chicken, definitely."

Her eyes narrowed again, right to squinty, and Benny had to bite back laughter.

Fuck, as hard as she could be, she was easy.

"I'm not chicken. I'm hungry."

"Total chicken."

"Am not."

"Absolutely are."

Her eyes went to slits. "You make clucking noises, I'm kicking you in the shin."

He let himself smile as he asked, "You gonna suck it up and talk to me later?"

"We'll talk tomorrow."

"Chicken," he teased.

"Am not!" she snapped, getting louder, and that was when he let himself laugh, he just did it silently.

When he quit laughing, he reminded her of something he told her the night before, "Cal, Vi, and the girls'll be here tomorrow."

"Shit. Right," she muttered.

"Right then. Plan," he stated, and she focused on him. "You got today with Ma and Pop. You got tomorrow with Cal and his girls. Monday, you're feelin' up to it, we'll go out to dinner. Neutral ground for you. Change of scenery. We'll talk where you'll feel safe."

She stiffened in his arms. "Are you talking a date?"

"Yeah," he answered.

She stiffened more. "Ben—"

He dipped his face to hers and he was straight-up serious when he said, "Honest to God, all I've done to you, what you know you mean to me, do you think in a million years I'd make anything tough on you?"

She closed her eyes.

"I wouldn't," he answered his own question.

She opened her eyes.

"I get you're scared and I know why. But if I didn't have somethin' to offer that I'm gonna bust my balls to make good, somethin' I know in my gut you want, same as me, this would be goin' a whole lot differently. I haven't earned it, baby. I don't even fuckin' deserve it. But I gotta ask you to trust me anyway."

"Okay," she whispered, straight up, right there, no hesitation.

Jesus. That felt good.

He couldn't let that feeling settle.

He somehow got her where he wanted her, he had to press his advantage.

So he asked, "Monday?"

She pressed her lips together and nodded.

Thank fuck.

He knew he'd be pushing it to kiss her, as bad as he wanted that mouth.

It killed, but he didn't kiss her.

He still gave himself a taste of her by dipping his head further and touching his lips to hers.

He lifted it and said, "Pancakes."

She relaxed in his arms and nodded.

He let her loose only to bend and lift her in his arms.

Then he took her downstairs so she could have pancakes.

An hour and a half later, while Theresa was in the kitchen doing dishes, Frankie was lying flat out on the couch, her mass of hair spread on the armrest where her head was resting, smiling huge at something Vinnie said to be funny.

He'd been right. She didn't make his pop work for it. Not even for a second. And she did this two seconds after Benny had put her on that couch and she asked his pop if he minded getting her a "cup of joe," like she did the same the day before and the day before that.

His father had grinned, openly showing his relief, then shocked the shit out of him and his ma by getting it for her.

It was while Frankie was smiling at Vinnie Senior that Asheeka made a move to leave.

Benny waited until the goodbyes were said, hand squeezes were given to Frankie, hugs to Vinnie, then he stood and murmured, "Walk you out."

Frankie gave him a look.

Asheeka gave Frankie a look before she moved her look to Benny.

But Benny held her eyes, and with nothing for it, she moved to the door, him following, her calling her goodbye to Theresa on her way out.

He walked with her to a flash black Land Rover parked at the curb.

"Sales are good," he noted, eyes on her truck.

"I'm not complaining," she replied, feet firm on the sidewalk.

He moved his gaze to her. "Got anything for me to go on in there?" he asked straight up. He had no time to beat around the bush, no inclination, and no skills with that shit.

She crossed her arms on her chest and studied him.

He read her as quiet, a little shy, but not dumb.

With what she said next, he'd learn he was right about the last, and she could get beyond the first two.

"You do know with that question, you're askin' me to break the sacred sister trust."

"I know."

"Don't know you, but she's my girl."

"Know that too."

She fell into studying him again.

He didn't have time for that either.

"You don't know me so I'll tell you. I get I'm puttin' you on the spot, and I mean no offense when I also tell you I don't give a fuck because the reason I'm doin' it is important."

She didn't study him after that.

She said, "You know that commercial where the guy wakes up in half a bed, eats outta half a bowl of cereal, and sits on half a couch?"

He heard her. He got her. He lifted his chin to communicate that and tell her to get on with it.

She got on with it. "That's our Frankie. Livin' half a life. Doin' it by choice. Now, way I see it, before, it was penance. Punishing herself for somethin' that was not her fault. You all pullin' out the stops to say she needs to let that go, I still see Frankie goin' to sleep in half a bed and watchin' her shows on half a couch."

Yeah.

He heard her. He got her. And what she said made him uneasy.

"Why?" he asked.

"I read you right with the way you're positionin' yourself to be in her life, that's the part *you* gotta figure out, sort it out, then show me you can fill her full of life. I'll tell you, you do that, you'll have my gratitude 'cause I've known her years and she can fake it real good. But you watch. You listen. She laughs half a laugh, even as she's tryin' to convince you it comes full. And every breath she takes is half a breath. Nobody can live like that, half breathing. And no person like Frankie Concetti should."

Benny felt his mouth get tight as his eyes moved to his house.

He then felt Asheeka get close and his gaze went back to her.

"It's not your brother," she said quietly. "She'll use that as a shield to hold you back." She shook her head. "It's not him, though. It's deeper. It's why she *chose* him when, no offense, but the woman you and I know could have had more." She held his gaze and whispered, "Think about that."

She said nothing more and moved to the driver's side of her vehicle.

Ben watched her pull out and his eyes remained on the road long after she was gone.

But his mind was on Frankie.

And his thoughts were troubled.

Because, suddenly, he couldn't figure out if back in the day, when she was with Vinnie, if she was electric.

Or if she was desperate.

And he wondered, even back then, if every breath she took was half a breath.

By the time he made a move to his house, he had no answers.

All he knew was he had to find them.

Hours later, when everyone was long gone, Benny rested his back against pillows shoved up on the headboard of his bed, Frankie doing the same beside him. After thirty minutes of watching television, which was after ten minutes of Frankie bickering with him about why he was stretched out beside her and not downstairs on the couch, she declared, "I need you to take me home tomorrow."

He turned eyes from the TV to her. "Why?"

"'Cause your ma brought me loungewear. I'm meeting Vi's girls. I need better than loungewear."

He turned his eyes back to the TV. "I think they know you were shot so I'd guess they won't expect you in a ball gown."

"I don't want a ball gown. I don't even *own* a ball gown. I want a nice dress."

"I think they know you were shot," he repeated to the TV. "So I'd guess they won't expect you to be in a nice dress."

"Do you have pressing matters to attend to tomorrow before they get here?" she asked.

"Nope," he answered, feeling her attitude beginning to fill the room and fighting back a smile.

"So you aren't making pizza for the governor?" she went on.

"Not that I know of," he replied.

"Then it isn't that your schedule is full that you can't take me to my apartment to get a nice dress."

He didn't turn his eyes to her on that. He turned his whole torso to her and got her gaze when he did.

"You own a dress that won't make my dick get hard?"

Her eyes got squinty, but her mouth stayed closed.

"Can I take that as a no?" he pushed.

"FYI, women don't like it when men talk like that, Benny Bianchi."

"Bullshit, Francesca Concetti. They fuckin' love that shit."

"Wrong," she snapped.

"After our talk on Monday, when you come to your senses, I'll give you more of that when I'm in the position to test the results of my theory."

She straightened on her pillows. "Seriously?"

"Absolutely."

"When I've come to my senses," she stated.

"Yep," he replied.

"Do you *try* to piss me off?" she asked, and he grinned.

"You haven't got that?"

"Why?" Her voice was pitching higher.

"You pissed is cute. It's hot. And, just sayin', it makes me hard."

"Are you hard right now?"

"Be my pleasure, you wanna check."

Abruptly, she leaned forward, pulled a pillow from behind her, swung it around, and slapped it against his chest.

Then she found it no longer in her hands and her body no longer up on pillows but on its back down the bed, her side pinned by his front and his face in hers.

"Do not move like that," he growled, and she stared up at him, eyes wide, as he did.

"Benny."

"I'm all for a pillow fight in three weeks when your stitches have dissolved, you don't wake dazed and fightin' pain, and I don't have a heart attack every time you do somethin' jerky or abrupt."

"Ben—"

"You need to see to yourself, Francesca. You don't, like I just demonstrated, I will."

He watched it pass through her eyes. That good something he was getting meant he'd said or done something she liked, but she wasn't going to give it to him straight out, and he felt her body relax against his.

"You got me?" he asked.

"Yeah," she answered.

"You hurt yourself just now?" he pressed.

"No, Ben. It's actually been a good day," she told him.

"You woke rough," he told her.

"I know. It was weird. But I rallied faster."

"It worried me."

He watched her entire face soften to a look that made beauty indescribable before she said, "Nat's brand of good morning notwithstanding, it's the best day I've had since it happened."

"You good with Pop?"

"Yeah, Benny."

"Good."

She was silent a moment before she asked, "You done being a hotheaded, protective, Italian guy?"

"I'm never done with that."

At that, he felt her body melt against his and she whispered, "Ben," but said no more.

He wasn't done talking. Not with her body partly under his, her eyes on his, her hair all over his bed.

He had something to say.

So he said it.

"I wanna kiss you."

Her body tensed, and not the bad way. The fucking good one. But she said nothing.

"You got until Monday," he informed her.

She drew her lower lip between her teeth, and fuck, he wanted to kiss her even more.

Instead, carefully, gently, he rolled, taking her with him and pulling her up so he was again on his back on the pillows and she was tucked to his side, head to his chest.

Once he got her in place, it was Frankie who snaked her arm around his gut.

Progress. Fucking finally.

He aimed his eyes at the TV but said, "You wanna wear somethin' nice for Vi and her girls, I'll take you to your place in the morning."

"Thanks, Benny," she said softly, pressing closer to him.

He slid his fingers from her hip up her side, over her shoulder blade, and into her hair. Once there, he used his thumb to curl a lock around his finger again and again.

He felt her sigh and he knew it was half a sigh.

He also knew she was giving him more, but she was still holding back.

For now, he'd give her that play.

She had until Monday.

Five

DRAWER IN THE BATHROOM

I stood at the door of my own apartment while Benny inserted the key. At least he shoved open the door and stepped back for me to go in first.

"Thanks," I snapped.

He grinned.

I rolled my eyes, walked into my apartment, and instantly felt weird.

I'd moved into that place six months after Vinnie died, leaving the semi-deluxe condo Vinnie put us in when he started to make decent money with Sal. Sal told me he'd cover the rent on my old place, but I said no because I thought that was weird. Anyway, it would pinch, but I could afford it on my own.

The real reason I left the condo was because I couldn't be in our place anymore. It had memories of Vinnie everywhere. Sometimes I could swear even the smell of him would hit me, making it all come back, pain so immense I couldn't breathe.

I was so desperate to get out I'd signed the lease on the first place I looked at. It wasn't a great place, but it was in a good neighborhood. You walked into the dining area from the corridor. Kitchen off to the side. Living room off the dining area. A balcony off that with views of the city. Down a hall, two bedrooms, both with balconies to that view. Guest bath in the hall. The master had a bath and walk-in closet. A big utility closet for a washer and dryer, and storage in the hall.

It was everything I needed.

It just had no personality.

Well, it did when I'd done it up, made it a place I liked coming home to, a place I liked to spend time in, mostly because I spent a lot of time in it.

But bare bones, it had no personality.

Now, it was almost back to that, seeing as it was weird walking into my place because I hadn't been there in weeks. It was also weird walking into it because a lot of it had been boxed up in preparation to move. Nothing on the walls. Ready to be void.

Shaking off the weird, I looked to Benny to see he was throwing the door closed behind him, but his eyes were on the boxes stacked three deep, resting against the dining area wall.

He didn't look happy.

"I'll just be a minute," I told him, and his gaze cut to me.

"Grab what you wanna wear to dinner tomorrow while you're at it," he ordered.

I gave him a look to tell him how I felt about him ordering me around and then I stomped down the hall to *show* him how I felt about him ordering me around. I did the last without looking at him, because when I gave him the look, he stopped looking ticked and started grinning.

Once in my walk-in closet, I slapped hangers across the rail, looking for a dress that wouldn't make Benny hard (knowing this was a fruitless endeavor; I was me, I was about impact, and apparently, he *really* liked me *and* my impact) and wondering why I agreed to have dinner with him.

I wondered, but I knew.

He was being persuasive in the way only Ben could be, which was bound to be successful.

In other words, he was fighting his own good fight and he was a lot better at it.

A date with Benny.

I couldn't say no.

I wanted to. I even fought it. But I caved.

I also wanted to make my boundaries clear by not lying in bed with him and watching TV.

But did I manage that?

No.

Instead, I not only lay in bed with him, I lay *cuddled* in bed with him, Benny playing with my hair, which felt so nice I couldn't describe how nice it felt. I even eventually fell asleep against him watching TV, Benny playing with my hair.

The good fight was not working, being quiet, giving in to get my way in the end. Because giving in meant being around Benny who was showing he was a lot more than gentle, could take direction, do the dishes, and make a great pizza.

He was protective. He was honest. He had control. I mean, seriously, what went down with Nat? It was a miracle he kept hold of his shit through that. I'd been in my own tizzy, but I'd watched him and I knew what it took for him to do that. It took a lot. He still kept his shit.

And my usual fight of being loud and full of attitude didn't work either because Ben thought it was "cute."

I was screwed.

And I knew just how screwed I was when I found the exact dress I was going to wear to dinner with Benny tomorrow night. And then I found and grabbed the shoes.

A dangerous dress.

Straight-up treacherous shoes.

I still grabbed them, carefully folded the dress, and put it and the shoe-box in my wheelie overnight bag.

I also grabbed other shit that did not say, "Back off, Benny Bianchi," but said, "Do you mind if I have a drawer in your bathroom?"

God, I was on such rocky ground, it was like experiencing an earthquake.

I just couldn't find it in me to fight my way to solid ground.

Making matters worse, I grabbed a dress for that day that was out of necessity, since I really didn't have anything that wasn't about flash and impact and I had no choice.

But that didn't mean it wasn't one of my choices that had more impact than most. It was just more subtle.

I was totally insane and totally going to hell.

Knowing this didn't mean I didn't move to my bathroom to change.

Asheeka had been over that morning and Asheeka had done the whole shower thing.

This was, of course, after Ben woke me, got me to the bathroom, was sweet, gentle, and gave me a lip touch.

The good news about this was that finally I'd woken up with less pain. It was there, but it wasn't as bad.

I always woke up a little hazy, even before I'd been shot, and I kept the haze for a while. But today, it was better, more like my normal hazy. I knew it and I knew it made Benny feel relief, not only because he showed it with grins and lip touches, but he'd told me flat-out.

Asheeka took off to get to church and Benny put me in his SUV.

But he didn't take me directly to my place. He took me directly to Glazed and Infused where he bought two dozen donuts.

This was not just for Cal, Vi, and the girls.

This was because Ben knew I loved donuts. My sweet tooth knew no time restrictions so it reared its ugly head in the mornings (and the rest of the day).

He was fighting the good fight and he was *so* much better at it.

He also bought two coffees and opened the box the minute we got back into his SUV.

I wasn't proud of it, and I was trying to forget I did it (even though it happened less than half an hour ago), but I ate three of those donuts on the way to my apartment.

What was done was done.

Now I was doing worse.

It was September but still warm, so I'd grabbed an oversized, royal-blue tee tunic dress with three-quarter sleeves and a short skirt that fit tight. The top was blousy and fell off my shoulder, the waist cinched in so the tunic top could flow slightly over the skintight skirt. It was the kind of dress that made a girl feel good wearing it because she knew a man might get hard seeing her in it.

I was no longer on dangerous ground.

I was playing with fire.

The problem with this was that I liked Vi, I loved Cal, and I was looking forward to seeing them both when I wasn't running for my life or bleeding (near) to death. I was also looking forward to meeting Vi's daughters, seeing the family Cal found himself after years of drifting through life when shit went down in his that was too painful to even think about, and that shit didn't even happen to me.

And I was Francesca Concetti. So I wasn't going to do it in jeans or yoga pants.

This was the least sexy thing I had that wasn't one of my business outfits (and those had short, tight skirts too).

There was nothing for it.

Even with the mental war I'd waged over the dress, I didn't consider not strapping on the stiletto-heeled bronze sandals.

This was because, unless I was working out, I didn't do flats. *Ever.* Not with jeans (of which I only owned two pairs and wore them rarely). Not with shorts (all of which were the dressy kind; my brand of casual was also about flash and impact). Certainly not with a dress.

I might have been shot, but a lot worse would have to happen to me before I'd consider giving up my heels.

Strangely, straightening from the bed after putting on my shoes, with my hair big, makeup on, in a dress that looked hot but was comfortable, and my usual heels, I felt better than I had in weeks.

Finally, I felt me.

I closed my suitcase, put its wheels to the carpet, and rolled it out, walking down the hall with more pep in my step than I'd had in ages, calling, "Okay, done with that. And I saw we're running out of Fanta Grape, so on the way home, we should stop by…"

I trailed off and stopped dead when I hit the living room/dining room area and saw Ben in the corner of the living room, standing by a set of shelves that I had not yet packed.

He turned to me and then he stopped dead, but I didn't really notice it because I saw what was in his hand: a heavy, expensive, beautiful glass frame that I knew contained an eight-by-ten photo of me with the Bianchis at Christmastime years before.

We were all in front of the tree. Carm was home with her husband and kids so we were all scrunched together to fit in the frame. Manny, Theresa, and Carm's husband, Ken, were even kneeling in order to fit us all in.

Everyone was smiling so big, it wasn't hard to read every one of us was laughing.

And we were.

The thing about that picture was, Vinnie Junior had claimed Carm's little toddler girl and was holding her in his arms, her little girl leg tucked to his chest, her little girl hand to his throat, his arms holding her safe and tight to his tall body.

This left me free.

And I remembered that Christmas. I remembered taking that photo. I remembered that it seemed entirely natural that Benny and I would find each other, and we did. I could not say if I was the one to make the move, or he was, it was that natural. We just gravitated to each other.

So in that photo, everyone scrunched together, I had my front tucked to the side of Benny's front, my arms tight around his middle, head on his shoulder. He had one arm around my waist, the other arm tight around my shoulders, and you could even see his fingers at my top, squeezing in.

If anyone looked at that picture who didn't know, they would easily think I was Benny's, not Vinnie's. Carm and Vinnie Senior were between us. I was nowhere near Vinnie.

But I was tucked tight to Benny.

That was the only photo of Vinnie I kept out on display. A photo that included all of the Bianchis.

And I kept it out on the shelves in my living room that stood beside my TV.

This meant I saw that photo every day.

My eyes flew to Benny's and I started, "I—"

I didn't get another word out.

If I had it in me to guess, I still would not have been able to guess what I would read in his expression when he saw that picture.

But when I looked at his face, I knew he wasn't thinking about the picture.

And I let go of the handle of my bag and was able to retreat three steps when he set the picture aside and rushed me, acting on what he was thinking.

It was only three steps because he caught me, turned me, and I had no choice but to press against the wall because his body wasn't giving me one.

I looked up to see his face right there, a look in his eyes that made my stomach dip in a way I'd never felt *in my life*.

"Ben—"

His hands came to me, one at my hip, the other at the side of my neck, and he cut me off to ask, "Are you serious right now?"

"I—"

His voice was a growl that made my knees get weak when he stated, "'Cause I'm serious right now."

Suddenly, I *loved* that he was serious, even though I wasn't entirely certain what he was even talking about.

"Baby," I whispered and I had no fucking clue why.

"Yeah," he whispered back, his fingers on both hands digging in, his face getting closer. "You're serious right now."

That was when he kissed me.

No lip touch this time. He *kissed* me. Fingers digging in, mouth opening up, tongue thrusting inside, *kissed me*.

I didn't make that first protest. Not even one.

No.

I tasted the hot, sweet magnificence of Benito Bianchi, felt his hands on me, smelled his aftershave. My hands lifted to his neck and slid up, diving into his thick, fantastic hair, and I held him to me.

When I did, Benny tangled his tongue with mine in a delicious way that made my toes curl in my sandals. He slid one hand in my hair, the other one over my ass to cup it, hauling me into him.

I pressed closer.

Benny kissed me harder.

God, he felt good. He tasted good.

I hadn't had a kiss since the last one Benny gave me.

I was drunk then, but I still remember it was good.

This one was better. Much better. Too much better. Too dangerous.

Too amazing.

I had to have more.

So I pressed closer and whimpered that need into his mouth.

This had the unfortunate result of Benny breaking the kiss, his hand moving from my ass so he could wrap his arm around my waist, his other hand gliding down to wrap around the side of my neck again. He dropped his forehead to mine.

"Jesus, shit," he muttered, and I opened my eyes to see his closed.

God, he was beautiful—close, far, eyes closed, annoying me, being gentle with me, being protective of me, after kissing me.

Always.

I slid my hands down to where I could press my palms in the muscle of his neck under his ears, but I kept my fingers in that fabulous hair.

His eyes opened.

More beauty.

"I hurt you?"

And more beauty.

"No," I whispered.

"That dress, baby," he whispered back as explanation for the kiss.

"It's the least sexy one I have."

His eyes closed again and he repeated, "Jesus, shit."

Seeing as I'd lost my mind with that kiss right then, I wanted to smile. I felt it fighting inside to get loose. And I wanted this because it felt so *fucking* good to know all I had to do was put on a hot dress and I could make Benito Bianchi lose control.

It wasn't a healthy thought. It wasn't even rational, considering my frame of mind about all things Benny and me.

But I had it.

I beat it back, but just barely.

"You said you wouldn't kiss me until Monday," I reminded him, and his eyes opened.

"I didn't know that on Sunday I'd get that dress."

"I really don't do jeans," I shared.

"Just sayin', *tesorina*, I'll wanna kiss you, even if you're in jeans."

"I'm getting that sense," I muttered, my gaze drifting to his lips.

"Baby," he called, and I again focused on his eyes. "That picture."

With those two words, I was torn painfully out of my happy just-been-kissed-by-Benny-Bianchi zone and thrown into my usual zone. A zone I didn't like much normally, but hated right then.

I dropped my chin and pressed my forehead to his chest, saying, "Don't."

"You were mine, even when you were his."

He was right. It was whacked. It didn't even make sense.

But I'd always loved Benny. We were tight. We got along. Of all Vinnie's family, I was closest with Benny. It made me happy being around him.

I was Vinnie's, but with each passing week as Vinnie did stupid shit, I was also drifting away.

And I was Benny's. Then when we lost Vinnie, I fucked up and he pushed me away.

I closed my eyes tight and slid my hands down to his chest, curling my fingers in his tee.

"I gotta say this." He was speaking into my hair.

"I'm not ready."

His fingers at my neck gave me a squeeze. "This has to be said, *cara*. I get you're vulnerable right now. That kiss came as a surprise...to both of us... but what I gotta say isn't about that."

"What do you gotta say?"

"I'm pissed at him."

That was such a surprise, I tipped my head back and looked into his eyes. "What?"

"Vinnie. I'm pissed at him. Spent years pissed at you so I wouldn't feel the way I feel right now about my brother. I look at that picture..." He shook his head. "What came back raw, after seein' it clear what I did to you, why I did it, so I wouldn't feel how I'm feelin' about him right now...I look at that picture and I'm fuckin' pissed he didn't feel what I felt when we took that photo, Christmas, family, laughin', and know he had everything in his life he needed."

I let his tee go and my hands slid right back up to curl around his neck, hating every word he said, at the same time, but for a different reason, loving them.

And he was sharing. Honest. Putting it right out there.

It was my experience not a lot of men shared—not about their feelings, certainly not what was behind those feelings. Vinnie hadn't. He bottled everything up. He never talked to me about important shit, which meant I never understood when he did stupid shit.

Benny sharing touched me...deep.

Digging in there...deeper.

"Ben," I whispered.

"Should have my ass kicked, not givin' this emotion to him at the time. But I didn't. So, not only did it mean I fucked up and hurt you, it feels like I lost him all over again."

I held on tighter and got up on my toes to get close and kept whispering when I said, "Honey. Stop."

"How?" he asked.

I didn't have a clue.

"I don't know," I admitted. "But there's no purpose to you being pissed, Benny. He's gone. You can't change anything."

"I know that, babe, and it doesn't help."

"Then how's this?" I went on. "*You* get it. *You* get what's in that picture is everything in life you need. And Vinnie making that lesson clear, you'll never forget it. It sucks how he gave you that lesson, Ben, but at least he gave you something and you cannot deny it was important."

He held my eyes as his hand at my waist slid up and he started idly stroking my side.

It felt nice. Casual. Natural. *Benny.*

And the ground under my feet continued to rock.

I just didn't care.

"She's sweet, spicy, and smart," he muttered, his lips tipping up slightly, his words and the lip tip telling me he was letting go of the heavy.

I gave a slight shrug.

"That was a great Christmas," he said quietly.

"Yeah," I agreed just as quietly.

"Miss those cookies you make, the ones with the dough around the Hershey's Kisses."

"Chocolate-filled snowballs."

"Yeah."

Yeah.

Oh yeah.

I knew he liked them. I knew this because, if he heard word I was making them, he was over, sitting on a stool at the bar, shooting the shit with me while I made them. And he'd also eat them warm, the second I finished rolling them in powdered sugar and putting them in the tin.

And I knew right then this was why I made them every year.

Two batches.

Sometimes three.

I was *so* going to hell.

"We're connected," he pointed out the obvious.

"I know."

"I want us more connected, baby."

"I know," I repeated softly.

"Can you kiss me like that and then think you can convince me you don't wanna go there with me?"

I closed my eyes and dropped my chin again to put my forehead to his chest.

Benny kept at me.

"I know I'm pushin', *cara*, but seriously."

"Can we talk about it at dinner tomorrow?"

He was silent and he was that way awhile.

So I breathed a sigh of relief when he gave me a squeeze and said, "Yeah."

I tipped my head back and, again, slid my hands down to his chest. "They'll be here soon and we need Fanta."

"Babe, they're comin' up from Brownsburg with two teenage girls. Teenagers don't get out of bed on a Sunday at the crack of dawn and it's a four-hour drive. They won't be here until noon, earliest. We got an hour and a half, at least."

I felt my brows draw together. "Cal didn't text you to let you know when they'd left?"

My question made him smile huge. It was white. It was gorgeous. And it made his eyes warm with humor in that way I liked so much.

Witnessing that up close and personal for the first time, I had no choice but to wrap my arms around his middle and hold on.

"I'm not sure Cal does the text thing, Frankie. More, I'm not sure it's humanly possible for Cal to check in with anybody about any of his activities."

"He'll have to learn. He has a woman in his life."

His smile stayed white and gorgeous, and even as I felt the ground quake beneath me, I kept right on enjoying it up close and personal.

"Strike that," he stated. "I'm not sure it's humanly possible for Cal to check in with anybody about any of his activities unless that anybody is in his bed and he likes what she gives him there."

My eyes drifted to his ear. "This is probably true."

Ben gave me a squeeze and regained my attention.

"You got everything you need in that bag?" he asked.

"Yep," I answered.

"Now's the time to stock up, babe. We're here."

"I'm stocked up."

"Right," he said, then bent in and went deep. I held my breath and kept holding it when he brushed his lips against my neck.

I also kept holding on because I had to in order to stay standing.

Then I had to let him go because he let me go. He moved away but caught my hand, the handle of my bag, and he pulled me to the door, rolling my bag with us, saying, "We get home, I'll clean out a drawer in the bathroom."

My eyes hit the ceiling.

Lord, I hope you're paying attention, I silently prayed. *That was Benny's idea.*

Ben kept speaking.

"And in the dresser in the bedroom."

My hand spasmed in his.

He ignored it and pulled me out the door.

⌣⟶

Likely speeding up my trip to hell, an hour and a half later, I was curled on my side on Benny's couch, head to his thigh. Benny was sitting on the couch, feet up on the coffee table, eyes to a game on the TV.

Incidentally, a TV that was eighty inches.

Eighty.

The thing was so huge, it took up nearly the whole side wall of his living room.

And the surround sound rivaled those found in cinemas.

Even so, Theresa could be heard over the surround sound, banging around in the kitchen.

I had learned when I was with Vinnie that Theresa didn't do this because she was making a point that she wanted you to get off your ass and help her. She didn't. She wanted you nowhere near her when she was cooking or cleaning up after. She wanted no disruptions or distractions because only she could do whatever she was doing in a way she liked. If you tried to help, it only messed with her mojo and put her in a bad mood.

Theresa in a bad mood was not good.

So, even if I hadn't been shot in a forest a couple of weeks earlier and Theresa was banging around in the kitchen, I would have stayed in the living room.

Though how I got in my current position, I was still hoping God was paying attention because I didn't put me in it. Benny did. And when I'd protested, he muttered, "Quiet."

I didn't think it was the right thing to do, lying with my head on his thigh, not ever. But with his parents in his house, and after I had participated fully in the kiss he laid on me, definitely not then.

I also didn't think it was the right thing to do to get into an argument about it with his parents in the house.

This was something we'd come home to an hour ago. They were in the kitchen as we came through the back door—Vinnie sitting at the table drinking a cup of joe, Theresa bustling around a bevy of grocery bags on the table, bags whose contents I had no idea where she would put, seeing as Benny's fridge was decidedly full.

Vinnie had fallen on the donuts like he didn't have the huge-ass breakfast I knew Theresa cooked him before they went to church.

Theresa had shooed us out nearly the minute we got in the door and definitely the second Benny dumped the donut boxes on the counter.

Not long after, I found myself lounging with Benny on the couch.

In the end, his jeans were soft, his thigh was hard, so I told myself I was being polite and I'd give Benny hell later.

But in reality, it was just that I liked where I was.

"Ben, your ma wants to know where your casserole dish is," Vinnie Senior said, and I shifted my eyes to the side of the couch (but did not lift my head from Benny's thigh) to see Ben's father come to a stop there.

"I don't have a casserole dish," Benny answered.

Vinnie looked in the direction of the door that led to the foyer, muttering, "That's not gonna go over too good."

"She wanted to cook, she should have brought over what she needed," Benny noted. "I was gonna get takeout barbeque."

Vinnie's eyes sliced back to his son and he hissed, "Jesus, don't let her hear you say that shit."

"Why?" Benny asked.

"'Cause family's gonna come callin'. Boy, you know you don't serve takeout barbeque to family comin' callin'."

"I'm a single guy, Pop. They're lucky I thought about feeding them at all," Benny returned, and I couldn't hold it back, my body started shaking with suppressed giggles.

Feeling it, Benny's hand that was resting on my waist gave me a squeeze.

"Go in the kitchen and help her find somethin' she can use to assemble the lasagna," Vinnie ordered.

"Pop, I don't own anything she can use to assemble the lasagna," Benny replied.

"Then get your ass to the store and *buy* something she can use to assemble the lasagna," Vinnie kept ordering.

"That shit is just not gonna happen," Ben growled.

My body started shaking harder.

"Vinnie!" Theresa shouted from the kitchen. "I got the noodles laid out! Where's my dish?"

"Ben doesn't have one!" Vinnie shouted back.

"*What?*" Theresa yelled in a borderline screech. "I got the noodles laid out! What am I supposed to do with noodles and sauce and cheese and no dish?"

I lifted a hand, curled it around Benny's thigh, tucked my face in it, and snorted.

"Jesus, shit, I'll go to the store," Benny mumbled testily. I felt his thigh muscles tense in preparation to get up, even as I felt his hand glide to the back of my neck to nonverbally tell me he was getting up.

I lifted my head and looked up at him, grinning.

He was not grinning.

"It's good you're amused, babe, but this shit is not funny," he stated right when the doorbell went.

I turned my head and aimed my eyes over the back of the couch.

"*They're here!*" Theresa shrieked from the kitchen.

I lost purchase on Benny's thigh, then I lost purchase on the couch when Benny lifted me up and set me on my sandals.

We turned and I saw Vinnie was already at the door, huge smile on his face, opening it.

Ben took my hand and started us toward the door when Theresa showed, arms up in the air, mouth shouting, "Happy day!"

I heard, "Uncle Vinnie! Aunt Theresa!" shouted back in teenage girls' voices, but I couldn't see them.

Ben and I made it to the foyer and waited in it for a full three minutes while Theresa pushed out to the stoop and grabbed everyone's face, jerking their head back and forth to give them kisses before they were allowed to come in to get handshakes (Cal) or hugs (Vi and the girls) from Vinnie.

I watched as Cal took his kisses from Theresa like he'd rather wrestle an alligator. But Vi gave her kisses back and a hug, and Vi's gorgeous daughters acted like Theresa's signature dramatic welcome was a delight the like they'd never experienced.

The girls hit the foyer and practically bowled Cal and their mother over to rush Benny, shouting, "Benny!"

He let me go just in time to get hit by them both. He went back on a foot, steadied, and put his arms around them, murmuring something I didn't catch because I was completely drawn in by the scene.

This was because something about it didn't strike me right. It was beautiful watching Ben give affection to Vi's gorgeous girls. Downright dazzling.

But I was under the impression that Vi and Cal were relatively new, so I wondered how the girls were so tight with everyone so quickly.

"Hey." I heard.

I turned my head to see Vi close and I completely forgot about watching the dazzling display of Benny Bianchi giving affection to two young girls.

"Hey," I replied, looking into Violet's eyes.

I didn't think about it, her visit, except to look forward to seeing her, like she was a close gal pal who lived a few hours away, and thus, we didn't have cocktails every Friday night but instead had to make plans for special occasions.

Looking into her eyes right then, seeing her in normal circumstances for the first time ever, it hit me that the last time I saw her, Daniel Hart was pointing a gun to her head. The entire time I'd made her acquaintance, our lives were in danger or we were running for them.

Together.

She did not let me separate from her when it probably would have been prudent.

And I did not let her separate from me when it probably would have been prudent.

We'd stuck together.

And we'd made it through.

Looking at her beautiful face in the foyer of Ben's home, I felt it happening, my face crumbling, as I watched it happen to her. And then we were in each other's arms, holding close, so fucking tight, my face shoved in her neck, hers in mine.

"I'm sorry," I cried into her neck, my voice thick and clogged, muffled by her hair.

"No, I'm sorry," she cried into mine, her voice the same.

"I'm an idiot," I told her, holding tight and still crying.

"I'm a dork," she told me, holding tight and also still crying.

"No, you aren't," I blubbered.

"You aren't either," she blubbered back.

"Jesus." I heard Cal mutter.

"Shut up, Joe," Violet snapped but did it in my neck, not moving a centimeter away from me.

We just held on.

For my part, I held on because she felt good. She felt alive.

And we'd made it through.

Suddenly, Vi's body jerked and she asked, "Am I hurting you?"

I lifted my head, she lifted hers, and we caught each other's eyes.

"I'm fine," I whispered.

"I'm glad," she whispered back, and I knew she meant she was glad I was fine in more ways than just enduring her hug.

I smiled at her. She smiled back.

Seeing it, I felt my face start crumbling again, but I beat it back and gave her a shake. "You fine?" I asked.

"Absolutely," she answered, then asked, "You wanna meet my girls?"

"Absolutely," I answered.

Her smile came back and she kept hold of me with one arm but turned us toward her daughters. I swiped my hand on my face as I saw one girl was hanging on Cal. The other one was hanging on Benny. Both had eyes to their mother and me and both sets of eyes were wet.

"Katy, Keirry, come here and meet Frankie," she urged.

They moved forward cautiously, undoubtedly knowing I was convalescing.

I threw out my free arm and they came a lot faster, but they didn't knock me back to a foot.

What I figured was the older one, Kate, got there first. Vi let me go so she could give me a light hug and say close to my ear, "Cool to meet you."

When she would've let go, I held tighter and said, "Same here, honey."

She turned her head, looked into my eyes, and her lip quivered, but she held it together and smiled.

I let her go and Keira came forward.

Her hug was just as light, but I knew things were going to go bad when she said in my ear, "Thanks for taking care of Momalicious."

Then her arms spasmed and I knew she'd lost it.

I tightened my arms around her and my eyes moved to Benny, who was watching us with a warm intensity that would have taken my breath away if Keira was letting me breathe.

I tore my eyes from Ben, turned my head, and whispered in her ear, "My pleasure, baby."

Keira's body bucked with her sob.

Kate slid in beside her mom and I heard her whimper. So I caught her eyes and grinned at her.

She, again, held it together and grinned back.

Suddenly, Cal was there, hand wrapped around the back of Keira's neck, and he asked in a gentle, quiet voice I'd never heard from him in my life, "You wanna let me in there, Keirry?"

His voice was so beautiful, if Keira was letting me breathe, again, it would have made me stop.

She let go abruptly, almost like she was embarrassed, nodding and wiping her face.

Vi claimed her and Cal claimed me. He didn't hold on tight, but he did communicate a lot with his hug and I felt myself begin to lose it again.

I took in a shuddering breath and held it together as Cal leaned away, looked down at me, and asked in a voice meant only for me, "You good?"

I knew what he meant.

"I'm thinkin' I need to get off my feet," I answered because all that hugging felt great, but at the same time, it didn't feel real great against my wound.

Then Cal, Vinnie Junior's best friend in the world, did something weird.

He let me go but did it leaving a hand in the small of my back whereupon he gently, immediately, and *firmly* pushed me direct to Benny as he said low, "She's gotta take a load off."

That was when Benny claimed me, arm around my waist, turning me to the living room and moving us in, saying, "Let's get settled."

Company followed, but I couldn't see how they did because Benny deposited me in the corner of the couch and instantly bent in, one hand to the seat beside me, one hand to the armrest, his face an inch away.

"You need a pill?" he asked.

"No, I'm gonna tough it out. It might get better when I'm not bawlin'."

His head went back a bit, his eyes moved over my face, and he said, "Right. You need somethin', you tell Pop or Ma."

I nodded.

"Now, I gotta go to the store and get a fuckin' casserole dish."

I felt my lips quirk before I nodded again.

He watched my lips quirk before he looked back into my eyes, grinned, and winked.

Then he was gone.

But his grin and wink remained and I found I didn't have to tough out the pain.

A grin and wink from Benny Bianchi was the best medicine a girl could have.

"School is awesome, the best part about it being Jasper Layne."

It was after lasagna, which Theresa served at Benny's dining room table after spending nearly the entire time the lasagna cooked in his dining room, shifting what looked like three years of discarded junk mail from the top of the table and attacking the old-fashioned, definitely hand-me-down eight-seater with Pledge.

We were in the living room. Vi, obviously not knowing she should leave Theresa alone, was in the kitchen with Benny's mother, helping her do the dishes.

I was back on the couch, sitting up again but not in the corner. Benny was in the corner and I was tucked to his side, his arm around me. Kate was down the sofa from us. Vinnie Senior was in Ben's recliner. Cal was in an armchair. Keira was on the floor and she was the one who was talking.

I was surreptitiously watching Cal, who was not surreptitiously watching Benny and me tucked into the side of the couch. He had a small smile playing at his mouth, the warm light of humor in his eyes, but with both of these, he also had a knowing look on his face.

And I did not get that. He and Vinnie Junior were the same age, close as brothers. He'd tried to talk Vinnie out of working with Sal but was one of the few who intended to take Vinnie as he came. That was how tight they were. He didn't like that Vinnie was on Sal's crew, but he didn't intend to lose him because of it.

So the way Benny was holding me, which was not with brotherly affection, I would have thought would anger Cal, or at the very least perturb him.

It obviously didn't.

He obviously liked it.

Which was strange.

Stranger, Vinnie Senior had no reaction to it either.

This was making me uncomfortable, and with all that was going on in my head, not to mention having company, I didn't have the time to sort out why.

"Jasper Layne is hot, no doubt about that, but he's also a dawg."

That came from Kate, and the instant it did, Cal stopped grinning knowingly at Benny's foot, which he'd tangled with mine in an intimate way that felt nice but I knew I should not allow (though I did, bent on earning my first-class ticket straight to hell), and his attention cut to Kate.

"He is not," Keira snapped.

"Total player," Kate declared.

"He is not!" Keira's voice was rising.

"Keirry, he's had three girlfriends already and we've been in school, like, a month," Kate told her.

I quit surreptitiously watching and started openly watching, and also openly grinning (huge), as a dark, protective dad look moved over Cal's face.

He loved Violet. I knew that when he pulled out all the stops and made a miracle happen when he found us in the middle of nowhere in a forest and took a man's life to save hers.

He also loved her girls.

And I loved that.

"So, he's lookin' for the right one," Keira shot back.

"He's lookin' for somethin'," Kate muttered.

"No Jasper Layne," Cal decreed, and I watched Keira jerk her gaze to Cal.

"Joe!" she cried.

"No Jasper Layne," he repeated.

I felt Benny give me a squeeze and I looked at him to see him smiling big at his cousin.

My attention went back to the scene when Keira exclaimed, "He's cute!"

"He's off-limits," Cal proclaimed.

"Joe!" she repeated loudly.

Cal scowled at her. Then I stopped grinning at him and started staring at him when I saw it begin.

I couldn't believe it might happen.

Then it happened.

He caved.

"How old is he?" Cal asked.

"He's a sophomore," Keira answered—Keira, incidentally, being a freshman.

"You wait until you're older, he's older, then we'll see."

I watched Keira study her "Joe." Then I watched her face get soft and her eyes light. It was then I knew she knew she had the big, rough man who was Joe Callahan wrapped around her finger.

That had to be why she said much calmer and definitely sweeter, "Okay, Joe."

"You do know this is hilarious," Benny put in at that point.

"Shut it," Cal growled.

Ben chuckled, I giggled, and Vinnie Senior laughed outright.

Cal's face took on another dark look, this one annoyed, so I quit giggling and looked at Keira. "Sometimes, those are the best ones," I shared my womanly wisdom.

"What are the best ones?" she asked me.

"The wild ones. You let them get it out of their system and you get them when they're tame. That can be the best," I told her, and Benny's arm got tight, but this time it didn't loosen.

"Tame doesn't sound fun," Keira noted.

Cal sighed audibly and I smiled, but only so I wouldn't laugh.

Cal had his hands full with this one and I thought that was hilarious.

"It's not *tame* tame, it's the good kind of tame," I explained. She looked confused, so I went on, "I'm just sayin', listen to Cal. You might not get it 'cause you're young, but you'll learn. And he's tryin' to make sure when you learn, it isn't the hard way."

"Right," Keira whispered, eyeing me, eyeing Cal, and sucking my womanly wisdom in like a sponge.

"So," Kate said, and I looked to her. "It's like Joe bein' the Lone Wolf, and Mawdy and us gettin' in there, and he's still hot and cool, but he's got us."

"Something like that," I replied, smiling back at her.

"The Lone Wolf?" Benny asked.

"Shut it," Cal growled.

I giggled again.

"What are we talking about?" Theresa asked, and I looked over the back of the couch to see her and Violet joining us.

"Something we're not talkin' about anymore," Cal answered.

I gave Vi a big smile as Kate exited the couch to go sit on the floor with her sister so Theresa could sit in the corner. Violet scrunched next to me.

The minute she did, she grabbed my hand and held on.

I rested our hands on my thigh and held on tighter.

"I made cannoli and Benny bought enough donuts for an army. Anyone in the mood for something sweet?" Theresa asked.

"Me!" Keira cried.

"Totally!" Kate exclaimed, already getting back to her feet.

Theresa, barely just sitting down, got back up. "Let's go make coffee and get something sweet."

"I could use some coffee and somethin' sweet," Vinnie Senior muttered, hefting himself out of the recliner and following them.

"Ben, a word," Cal said.

I felt Benny tense against me. I looked at him to see he was giving a hard look to his cousin. Then he looked to me and that look softened.

"Be back, *cara*," he said quietly.

"Right," I replied.

He carefully shifted from beside me and got to his feet.

The men left and I looked to Vi.

"Do you know what that's about?" I asked.

Violet was looking over the couch, watching the men depart, but at my question her eyes came to me. "Joe obviously has something on his mind. Unfortunately, he hasn't shared with me what it is."

I looked over the couch and saw that whatever it was took them out to the front stoop. In other words, where no one could listen in.

I turned my gaze back to Violet. "Is everything cool?"

She nodded. "Police found the carnage Hart left in his lake house. He shot you. Both Joe and Benny's guns were registered. The cops were in the know we'd been kidnapped, and they knew all about Hart and his obsession with me. So, to end, they didn't press charges against Joe for blowin' a hole in his head. And, obviously you know, the same with Benny for shooting him in the stomach."

I knew all that. Sal had explained it to me in the hospital.

So I clarified, "No, what I mean is, you, the girls, the drama." I leaned closer. "They're beautiful, Vi," I said softly. "So sweet. Amazing. But they seem—"

She gave my hand a squeeze. "They lost their dad, their uncle, and almost me and Joe to Daniel Hart. They latch on to family, having lost all that. Joe and I are keepin' an eye on it, but I reckon it's better they latch on to love rather than acting out."

"You'd be right about that," I replied.

She tipped her head to the side as she lifted her eyebrows up. "You and Benny?"

"Long story," I muttered, and she grinned.

"You two look good together."

I caught her eyes direct. "I looked good together with his brother too."

She held my gaze for long seconds before she asked cautiously, "Do you like him?"

"He's the commissioner of the local Little League."

Her lips twitched and she murmured, "You like him."

"He's also my dead boyfriend's brother," I noted for the fucking gazillionth time in three days.

She assessed my face and remarked, "I'm sensing you don't wanna talk about this."

"Since Ben made it clear what he was thinking about this, it's pretty much the only thing I think about, we talk about, and I talk about with other people. So yeah, I could use a break."

Violet nodded. "Right. So you ever need to talk it through with someone who'll just listen, or you ever need to talk *anything* through with someone who'll just listen, or you ever just want to shoot the breeze, you call me. Okay?"

That was so nice, I grinned at her, declaring, "I just knew you were the shit."

She grinned back and replied, "I knew you were the shit when you jimmied up that window so we could escape."

I shrugged. "Figured Hart was shooting people in the other room, it was time for us to take a stroll."

She started giggling and through it said, "You were *so* right."

I started giggling too and we did this for a while until we both sobered, our eyes glued to each other's, our hands clutching tight.

"You're up, talking, you look gorgeous, but are you sleeping? Dealing? Healing?" Vi asked in a whisper.

"One good thing about Benny throwing down with me is that I haven't really had a chance to have a proper freak out about that whole thing with Hart. But we're here, he's not, so it all worked out in the end."

"Yeah," she agreed.

"You?" I asked.

"I have Joe," she answered, and I smiled. She had Cal. Cal had her. And obviously, that was all she needed.

"You're good for him," I told her.

"He's good for me," she told me.

Excellent response.

"He loves your girls," I told her.

"They adore him," she told me.

Another excellent response.

"Thanks for making him happy," I whispered.

"That, honey, is not a hardship," she whispered back.

We smiled at each other again. Then, being women, and thus prone to do crazy shit for no reason whatsoever, we burst out laughing.

Hours later, when everyone was gone, I walked out of the bathroom in another one of Gina's sexy-cute nightgowns to see Benny with bare feet, in his t-shirt and jeans, stretched out on the bed.

His eyes came to me, dropped to my body, and he muttered, "Jesus."

That made me feel awesome and irked me at the same time.

"You could avoid the torture by watchin' TV downstairs," I remarked.

His eyes lifted to mine. "I could."

That was all he said.

I sighed, went to the robe at the foot of the bed, shrugged it on, tied the belt, and climbed into bed.

Benny was in that bed and I should be throwing a conniption about it, but I needed to climb in. It had been a big day with lots of hugging, moving around, and sitting up. It felt good to do it. It felt better I made it through. It wasn't too much too soon, but that didn't mean I didn't need to take a load off.

I turned my eyes to the TV to see Benny scrolling through the guide like a man would stand in front of a refrigerator—that was, not paying a whole lot of attention, not knowing what he wanted, not liking what he saw, and willing to do it for the next half an hour, thinking something would magically appear that would ease a craving.

"What'd you talk about with Cal?" I asked.

"He wanted to make sure you were good," Ben answered, eyes to the TV.

"He could have asked me," I pointed out, eyes to Ben.

"He didn't. He asked me," Ben told me what I already knew.

"Did this require you being on the front stoop where no one could hear?" I pushed.

"Yep, since it happened on the front stoop where no one could hear," Ben stated, and that didn't feel awesome. It just irked me.

"Benny!" I snapped, and he looked at me.

"Ask what you wanna ask, baby," he said gently, reading me and knowing I was beating around the bush.

So I quit beating around the bush.

"Cal doesn't seem to have a problem with the idea of you and me," I noted.

"He doesn't, since he's told me, repeatedly, after that shit went down with Hart, to get my head outta my ass and sort out you and me."

My mouth dropped open.

I snapped it shut to declare, "There isn't a 'you and me.'"

His eyes did a sweep of me in his bed, they came to rest on mine, and he said quietly, "Babe."

Shit.

"We're talkin' about this tomorrow," he reminded me. "Right now, I can tell you had a big day and you need to kick back."

He wasn't wrong about that. What he was was attentive, noticing it.

Another good thing about Benny.

"Come here," he ordered.

"I'm good here," I said, turning my eyes to the TV.

"Frankie, come here," he repeated.

I looked to him. "I'm good here, Benny."

"Babe," he stated firmly, but said no more.

"I'm comfy."

"Come here," he said yet again.

"Ben, I'm fine where I am."

"Come here."

My eyes narrowed. "Seriously?"

"Francesca, come...*here.*"

"Are you gonna repeat it until I do it?" I snapped.

"Yes," he replied.

"You're annoying," I told him.

"Come here."

"Now you're *more* annoying."

"Come here."

I glared at him as I informed him, "I really wanna hit you with a pillow right now."

"Come here."

"Benny!" I shouted.

Then I was no longer reclining on my side of the bed.

I was tucked tight to Benny's side on his side of the bed.

It felt good. Natural. Right.

I clenched my teeth.

Then I unclenched them to say, "You're totally freaking annoying."

"And you're all kinds of cute."

I clenched my teeth again.

Ben settled on some television show set in a prison.

"I don't watch prison shows," I declared.

Ben said nothing but didn't change the channel.

"Or war shows," I went on inanely.

Ben didn't move and the channel remained the same.

"Ben, find something else," I ordered.

"Please?" he said that one word as a demand.

I tipped my head from its place on his chest to glare at him.

He grinned at me.

Then he offered me the remote.

Yes, Benny Bianchi, a man who was all man *handed me the remote.*

To the TV!

Yet another good thing about Benny.

Tentatively, like the woman I was, a woman who was entering previously uncharted territory and needing to do it cautiously, I took it.

Even more tentatively, I found a cooking show I liked.

Benny said not a word and I marveled as he lay there watching a cooking show with me, not saying a word.

And again, he showed me another good thing.

The problem with that was that I was thinking, when it came to Benito Bianchi, it was all a good thing.

Six

LOVE IS NEVER WRONG

"Thanks, babe, and again, don't worry about comin' tomorrow."

It was the next morning. I was standing at Benny's door, Asheeka out on the stoop. I was showered, ready to face the day, and letting her off shower duty.

"You sure?" she asked.

"I was good yesterday, better today," I reminded her.

"Yeah," she said. "Still, you need me, just call."

My Asheeka. So awesome.

"What I need to do is buy you tickets to Usher the next time he's in Chicago."

Her eyes went huge. "Girl, you know it would *not* be good, that boy and me in the same building, even if that building is a stadium."

What I knew was that Asheeka had a thing for a baby face. And a bigger thing for a man who could move.

"Right. In order to avoid Usher taking a restraining order out on you, I'll find something else," I told her.

This time her eyes went sweet before she replied, "I know it'd be a fool waste of time, tryin' to talk you outta doin' something. But I'm also gonna make it clear, you don't have to do anything."

"I do," I returned.

"I know," she whispered.

My Asheeka. So *awesome.*

I refrained from hugging her because that would probably make me cry and I'd just done my makeup.

She grinned at me. "You keep me in the know about what's happenin' with all that," she ordered, jerking her chin to the hall behind me, meaning Benny.

"I get my phone back, I will," I promised.

She kept grinning and said, "Later, babe."

"Later, Asheeka."

She aimed her eyes beyond me and shouted, "'Bye, Benny!"

"Later!" Ben's deep voice shouted back from where he was in the kitchen.

She let out a little chuckle, shook her head once and I watched her walk down to her Land Rover and get in. I closed the door when she was pulling out.

I turned, looked down the hall, straightened my shoulders, and walked that way.

Benny and I had to have a chat. One where I communicated some important things, he listened, and I got *my* way for a change.

This I'd decided in the shower.

This, I decided right then, was happening now.

I walked down the hall, turned into the kitchen, took two steps in, stopped, and planted my hands on my hips.

And there I saw that Ben was on a mission. I knew this because he had a donut clamped in his teeth, a travel mug in his hand, he was shoving his phone in his back pocket, and his car keys were sitting on the counter in front of where he was standing. His hair was wet because he'd showered in the hall bathroom. I'd heard him when I was getting ready.

"Ben," I called.

He looked my way and finished with his phone, lifted his hand to the donut, took a bite, and said through a full mouth, "Yeah?"

"We gotta talk," I told him.

He chewed and swallowed. "Yeah," he agreed readily. "Ma's got somethin' on with Father Frances this morning, so while you were upstairs, I talked with Mrs. Zambino. She's takin' you to the alley today. League play. She says she and her girls'll keep you company. I gotta get to the restaurant and do some shit. I'll meet you back here."

I knew my eyes were squinty when I declared, "I'm not goin' to the bowling alley with old lady Zambino and her cronies."

"Yeah, you are," Ben replied before he took another bite of donut.

I shook my head so I wouldn't get distracted from *my* mission, and stated, "Benny, we need to talk about what *I* wanna talk about."

"Can't. She'll be here in five minutes and I gotta go. One of our suppliers is gonna be at the restaurant in twenty. I made the order. His shit is good, but he's known to jack his clients around, so I gotta inspect it when it gets there so he doesn't jack us around."

Although normally I would find it fascinating, the inner workings of a popular pizzeria and how a supplier might "jack you around," right then, I couldn't get distracted by that either.

"I want my phone," I announced, and Benny focused on me.

"Babe—" he started quietly.

"No," I cut him off. "We have plans tonight. I made you that promise, I'm keeping that promise. I won't take off. But I'm out of the hospital and I have a life. Friends who are probably wondering about me. A job I quit, where my notice period ended up as sick leave, but I have strings to tie up there, clients to contact. I also have a new job. They know I experienced a traumatic event, but now they probably think I've fallen off the face of the earth. I gotta check in, and to do it, I need my phone. I'd rather make my calls here. But, so as not to court the wrath of old lady Zambino, who probably now is excited about her opportunity to show off her skills at the lanes, I'll make my calls from the bowling alley."

Benny looked decidedly unhappy when I started talking about my new job.

But he shocked the shit out of me when he said, "It's in the truck. I'll go get it."

"Really?" I asked, my voice breathy due to the fact I was shocked as shit he gave in and did it so easily.

He stopped looking unhappy and looked something else entirely when he said gently, "Yeah, honey." He put the donut in his teeth again, nabbed his keys, pushed them in his pocket, came to me, then took the donut out of his mouth before he wrapped his fingers around my hip and bent to me, going deep where he touched his mouth to my neck. He lifted to look in my eyes and whispered, "Be back."

"Okay," I whispered too.

He shoved the last of the donut in his mouth, disappeared out the door, and I stood there thinking how easy that was.

Maybe I should have asked for my phone the day before.

Or the day before that.

I was still thinking on this when Ben came back in with my purse. He didn't bring it to me. He took it to the table, dumped it there, then he came to me.

He got close, and for some reason, I didn't brace. I didn't pull away. I didn't move a muscle.

This meant that when he lifted a hand to curl it around the side of my neck and dipped his head, I was an open target.

It also meant that when the lip touch I was expecting became something else—his mouth opened, mine opened with it, and he was able to sweep his tongue inside—I was able to taste the miraculous flavor of donut and Benny.

My stomach dipped again.

Almost before it began, his lips and tongue were gone. Then his fingers were digging in my neck, his were eyes looking into mine, and he whispered, "Later, baby."

"Later," I whispered too.

His eyes smiled. His fingers squeezed. Then he let me go and moved out the door.

I stood in his kitchen, staring at the door, knowing that could be my life.

Ben, off to the restaurant to make sure some supplier didn't jack him around after giving my neck a squeeze, me a sweep of his tongue that left the taste of him in my mouth, and I'd watch him go out the door after a "Later, baby," which meant I'd get him back.

And I stood in Benny's kitchen, staring at the door, knowing I wanted that life. Knowing I wanted it so bad, it was an ache. Knowing I'd wanted it since I was a little girl. Knowing I wanted it even more thinking I could have it with Benny.

But the pain came when I remembered I'd never have it.

On that thought, I heard the front door open and Mrs. Zambino shouting, "Francesca Concetti! Shake a leg! We gotta pick up Phyllis and I don't wanna be late!"

I took in a deep breath.

Then I went to my purse, made sure my charger was in there because, Lord knew, after days with no charging I'd be screwed, and I did this shouting, "Coming, Mrs. Zambino!"

I sat in my chair at the alley and watched Mrs. Zambino make her approach and let her ball fly. The ball spun down the lane quickly, listing to one side, then *crack!* She hit the pin so hard, it slammed across the lane and she got the split.

I jumped out of my chair, arms up, mind ignoring the not-insignificant ping of pain that hit my wound, and shouted, *"Go Zambino!"*

As she and all her posse did when someone got a strike or spare, which was frequently, she turned and instantly started shaking her ass, hands lifted in front of her in jazz hands position, forearms swaying, mouth chanting, "Wowee, wowee, wowee."

Her posse were all doing the same dance and chant as she moved through them, giving double high fives.

She came to me and her look of joy turned severe.

"Francesca, sit down," she snapped.

"You rock," I told her.

"I know," she replied. "Now sit down. I do not need the entire Bianchi family blaming me for you having a setback due to my stellar performance at the bowling alley."

I sat but kept my head tipped back and did it grinning at her.

She dropped gracefully into the seat next to me as I declared, "I'm taking up bowling as soon as I'm fully recovered so I can be you when I grow up."

Her eyes did a scan of my head before she decreed, "You'll need to learn to tame your hair and use blush as an accent rather than a war stripe if you wish that to become so."

"I'm sorry, I'm still riding the high of your split," I told her. "Even you being mean and cranky is not going to pollute that high."

Her mouth twisted in an effort not to allow me to see her smile.

"I saw that!" I declared, lifting a hand and pointing a finger at her mouth.

She shooed my hand away and stood up, moving toward the seating area at the back of the alley, calling, "Give me my Pepsi-Cola, Loretta."

As any bowling minion would do, Loretta handed over the queen's drink.

I turned my eyes to the alley, still grinning, as my phone in my hand rang.

I had managed to get a call in to my old boss and assure him I'd be taking care of business. I'd also managed to get a call in to my new boss to let him know I was still alive and planning on being down in Indianapolis to take the job as soon as I was able. Finally, I had managed to text a number of friends to let them know I was good.

Then I got sucked in by the bowling.

I lifted my phone, looked down at it, and saw a number I didn't recognize. Since it could be something important about a work thing (old or new), I took the call and put it to my ear.

"This is Frankie Concetti."

"Babe."

It was Benny.

My stomach dipped again, a major whoosh and he hadn't even kissed me.

"Having a good time?" he asked.

"Mrs. Zambino just nailed the split," I shared.

"Impressive," he murmured, humor in his deep and easy voice.

God, he was killing me.

"Supplier didn't jack us around," he told me. "Got what I needed to get done done, so I can come and get you."

"No," I told him. "I wanna stay 'til the bitter end. Zambino's posse is kicking ass and taking names, but they do this dance and chant every time they get a strike or spare. I wanna see how they rub it in when they beat the shit outta their opponents."

His voice was full of laughter this time when he said, "So the answer to my earlier question is, yeah. You're havin' a good time."

I didn't confirm that because I didn't want to admit to it for a variety of reasons.

He knew one of those reasons because he muttered, "Crazy-stubborn." Whatever.

"Get your calls made?" he asked.

"If I say yes, when I get home, are you gonna confiscate my phone again?"

"No."

"Then yeah."

That just got me his laughter.

I sighed and listened to it, enjoying every second.

He quit doing it, and the minute he did, he tore me out of the uncertain world I was letting myself live in and catapulted me into the pit of hell I'd been courting since that day, weeks after Vinnie died, when Ben and I got drunk and I made a crazy, stupid, inebriated, slut move on him.

"Made a reservation at Giuseppe's. Seven."

Hearing his words, I sucked in a painful breath.

Giuseppe's was like Vinnie's Pizzeria. You had to know it was there to know it was there. It was a neighborhood hangout and they liked it that way. That didn't mean they didn't accept whatever business came their way and the growth that came with that. They just were about doing what they did and doing it well, focusing solely on that and rewarding those who understood the meaning of word of mouth.

It was garden level off an alley. They had no parking. They had no listing in the phonebook. You could show up and hope you got a table, or you could be lucky enough to have Giuseppe's granddaughter, Elena, who now ran the restaurant, give you her phone number so you could make a reservation.

I had no idea with the prevalence of the Internet if social media cottoned on and she had a Yelp listing that had seven thousand five-star reviews. Though, their listing probably only had three thousand five hundred reviews, seeing as half the people who knew about Giuseppe's wanted to keep it a secret in hopes that when they went there, they could get a table. But it was so awesome the other half wouldn't be able to keep their traps shut about it.

This was because it was Italian dining at its finest. The restaurant was dark. The tables small. The décor mostly rich reds. The mood romantic. You went there for Valentine's Day. You went there to ask your woman to marry you. You went there to tell your man you were carrying his child. You did not take your children there, not ever, but you passed the knowledge of that restaurant on to them like a treasured family secret, so one day, they'd ask their women to marry them there or tell their man they were having his baby there.

It was the perfect place for a first date if the guy *really* liked you and didn't mind you knowing it. It was the kind of place where a guy took you on a first date, you sat across from him, and you instantly decided to spend the rest of your life with him.

But for me, it was a disaster.

Vinnie had taken me to White Castle on our first date. He thought that was funny, and being young and into him, I'd thought it was the same, with the addition of goofy and sweet.

Benny was taking me to Giuseppe's. He was not playing games.

"Frankie?" Ben called.

I looked at my lap and started deep breathing.

"Honey, you there?" Ben asked.

"I…uh, yeah," I pushed out. "I'm here."

"You okay?"

"Yeah. Fine."

"You good for Giuseppe's?"

No. Never. Never, ever, *ever.*

"Sounds awesome," I told him.

He was silent before he said, "You're not okay."

"When Mrs. Zambino got her split, I jumped up and had some pain. I'm still kind of recovering."

I felt guilt for telling him this because, even though the first part was true, the second part was a lie and that was the part that would make him worry.

"Jesus, that must have been some split," Benny muttered.

"It was." At least that was the truth.

"Take it easy, baby. We got a big night."

Yes, we did.

Because this ended tonight.

"Yeah," I said.

"I'll let you go. You're enjoyin' yourself. Don't want you to miss the action."

More good from Benny.

I closed my eyes but said, "Yeah. See you later."

"Later, *cara*."

I listened to him disconnect, feeling the disconnection of our phone call like a physical thing, foreshadowing of things to come, and that ache in me deepened.

I had approximately a second to feel this before I felt a hand wrap strong under my jaw and my chin was tipped up.

I opened my eyes and looked into the dark brown ones of Mrs. Zambino.

"You went white as a sheet," she said quietly, the rolling of the balls and crashing of the pins sounding all around us.

I didn't reply.

She held my jaw in her hand and peered deep in my eyes.

Then she asked, "That Benito on the phone?"

"Yes," I whispered.

She nodded once and didn't take her hand from my jaw as she said, "You got an old woman livin' across the street. You need wisdom, Francesca Concetti, you make your way over. I'll give it to you."

Then she let me go and went to the ball return.

I swallowed before I took in an unsteady breath.

I needed wisdom, anyone needed wisdom.

But no way I was walking across the street to get Mrs. Zambino's version of it.

Needless to say, the rest of my time with old lady Zambino and her crew was not as enjoyable as the start of it was.

When it was over, she dropped Phyllis first and then pointed her Caddy toward home. She had chatted with Phyllis, but when we were alone, the car was deathly quiet as it glided through the streets of Chicago in the neighborhood I called home growing up.

Which brought to mind that Benny bought a house in our 'hood.

Family man, staying close, relishing history.

God didn't hate me. He despised me.

She stopped outside Benny's house, the car idling, and I turned to her. "Thanks for lookin' out for me, Mrs. Zambino."

She stared intently in my eyes and nodded.

I turned to the door, put my hand on the handle, and mumbled, "See you later."

I didn't get the door open.

I turned back when Mrs. Zambino wrapped her silver-tipped, taloned fingers around my knee.

I caught her eyes and she launched right in, speaking softly.

"My Alonzo, rest his soul…" She did the sign of the holy cross with her free hand and kept speaking, "God tested him, givin' him three girls. A house with him and four women. Then all his girls had nothin' but girls. House full a' women, my babies were around. Did his head in."

She stopped talking and I said nothing because I didn't know where this was going.

"He loved every minute of it," she whispered.

The forlorn tone of her voice made my breath catch and reminded me that Al Zambino died only two years ago.

She kept going.

"My Al used to say that if he was a younger man, he'd make Enzo Concetti see sense—all the beauty he created, all that beauty he neglected."

And that made my breath turn harsh.

"'Nothin' more precious,' Al would say, 'than your baby girl.'"

"Mrs. Zambino," I whispered.

"Broke his heart knowin' you and your sisters looked in the mirror and saw what your father taught you to see. Not what's there. What a good man who was a good father would teach you to see."

My breath still harsh, my heart started pumping fast.

"I—"

I stopped talking when, suddenly, her hand darted out and she grasped hold of my jaw again, jerking it her way, firm but gentle.

"You're a good girl, Frankie Concetti," she declared.

I felt tears sting my eyes.

"Good girls earn good things." She let my jaw go, her eyes going beyond me toward Benny's house, then coming back to me. "Let yourself have good things."

"It's not right," I told her quietly.

"Know one thing on God's beautiful earth, and that is," she leaned into me, "love is *never* wrong."

I shook my head.

She held my gaze. "You find yourself open to accepting wisdom, Francesca, got an old lady across the street who'll give you some."

I pressed my lips together.

Her eyes again went beyond me before they came back. "Benny's waitin'."

I turned my head and looked up to Benny's house to see him standing on his stoop, arms crossed on his chest, uniform of tee and jeans on, but this time his tee was navy.

I looked back to Mrs. Zambino. "Thanks for today."

"More league play tomorrow, you feel like another day of bein' dazzled."

I grinned at her.

She stared pointedly at my door.

I got out and barely had the door closed when her Caddy started cruising down the street on its way for her to park it in her garage off the alley.

Benny watched me make my way to him and didn't move until I was one step away.

But he only dropped his arms to plant his hands on his hips as I joined him at the top of his stoop.

"What was that about?" he asked, his eyes flicking to the road before coming back to me.

I stared up at him. He was tall. He was beautiful. He was a good son. A good brother. A good guy. He'd be a good husband and an amazing father.

I wanted a shot at that.

I couldn't have it.

"We need to talk," I announced.

His eyes narrowed on my face and I watched them take in what was there and process it. I knew it when his entire face gentled.

Oh yes. I wanted a shot at that.

"Baby—" he started.

"Now," I cut him off.

He studied me for long seconds before he nodded, moved to the door, and threw it open for me.

I walked in, went directly to the living room, and tossed my purse on the couch.

As I was doing that, I heard the door closing, and when I looked that way, Ben was in the room with me.

I had to do this now. I had to get this out.

Then I had to get gone.

"I loved your brother," I declared, and his body jerked to a halt, his eyes leveling on me, his sudden intensity filling the room.

"I know that," he said slowly.

"No, Ben, I *loved* your brother," I stressed.

"I know that, Frankie," he replied.

"When I was with him, I did not think of you this way," I shared, lifting a hand and waving it between him and me. "Not ever."

"Okay," he said as a prompt when I quit talking.

"When he died, it broke me."

He closed his eyes on a wince, opened them, and focused on me again.

"I know, baby," he said quietly.

"It broke me because I loved him. It broke me because I missed him. It broke me because I wasn't the kind of woman who was strong enough to stop him from throwing his life away."

Ben's voice was still quiet but firm when he stated, "You are not responsible for Vinnie's death."

"No?" I asked.

"No," he answered.

"You sure you don't think that?" I pushed.

Understanding flowed through his face. He took a step toward me but stopped and said, "I deserved that."

I shook my head. "I'm not punishing you, Ben, honestly. I believe you when you say you don't think that anymore. But, just to say, I still do."

"Frankie, Vinnie bought what happened to him."

"A woman is supposed to have her man's back," I retorted.

"Not when her man turns his back on his woman," he returned.

His words hit me like a bullet (and I knew that feeling) and I clamped my mouth shut.

"He did that shit to you and you know it," Benny stated.

I looked to the side.

"He did that shit to you, you knew it, and you were done with it," Benny went on.

I looked to him.

"Weren't you?" he pushed.

"Yes," I whispered, then admitted my horrible secret, "I was giving up on him."

This time Ben shook his head. "*Cara*, he took away everything so there wasn't anything to give up."

His words hit me again, hard, and I drew in a sharp breath like I'd sustained a blow.

"You got a point with this talk?" he asked.

"This is between us," I explained. "It always will be."

"How?" Benny asked before he reminded me, "He's dead."

"I loved your brother, Benny," I repeated.

"Yeah. You did. He was lovable. He was a good guy. He loved you too. Fuckin' besotted. I was glad my brother had that. Then I was fuckin' pissed he shit all over it."

And still more goodness from Benny.

I couldn't take it.

"This can never work between us," I declared.

"Why?" he asked.

"Because people will see us at Giuseppe's and they'll think, 'There she is, Frankie Concetti. Dating her dead boyfriend's brother. Latching on to another Bianchi.'"

"Anyone thinks that shit can kiss your ass, and while they're at it, they can kiss mine."

He had an answer for everything, but I was losing it, so I leaned in and shouted, "It isn't right!"

He leaned forward too, his voice rising, and threw out both arms as he asked, "What about the last four days hasn't been right, Frankie? Tell me.

What hasn't been right? You gigglin' at Pop bein' Pop and me bein' me? You sharin' words of wisdom with one of Cal's girls? You in my bed handin' me shit I like, then cuddlin' up to me to watch TV? You eatin' my pie and lovin' every fuckin' bite? You sittin' at the kitchen table havin' lunch with my ma? Pop havin' your back when your bitch of a sister comes callin'? What about any of that isn't right?"

That was when I lost it.

"I don't want you to ever think I'm with you for any reason other than you're Benny!" I yelled. "Not ever, Ben. *Not ever.* You don't deserve that. You don't deserve ever to think something like that!"

As I was yelling, his torso jerked back, even as his chin did it into his neck.

When I was done yelling, he whispered, "What the fuck?"

"You're right," I snapped, throwing out a hand. "I came onto you after Vinnie died. You kissed me, but I made the first move."

"I know that, baby," he replied, still whispering.

"It was a slutty thing to do."

"You were drunk."

"It was slutty."

"Francesca, you were plastered, outta your mind, totally blotto. So was I. You lost your man, I lost my brother, you're a woman, I'm a guy, and shit happened *seven years ago.* It wasn't right. We both fucked up. We both knew it. And now it's over."

"That's it?" I clipped.

"That's it," he returned immediately.

"And you don't think I'm a slut."

His body went solid and my heart squeezed hard.

"You think I'm a slut," I whispered.

"No," he bit out.

"You do. I can read it, Benny Bianchi. It's written all over you."

"Babe—"

I shook my head, looking toward the door, demanding, "Take me home."

"Babe—"

I looked to him and shrieked, *"Take me home, Benny!"*

"Frankie, baby. Fuck. I know Vinnie took your virginity."

I took two steps back and stared.

He watched my feet move and his eyes cut to my face. "Yeah. This would be the awkward, uncomfortable shit we'll be needin' to get through." He lifted a hand, tore it through his fabulous hair, looking to the side and finishing on a mutter, "All a' this shit."

"Vinnie told you that?" I whispered, and Benny looked back to me.

"Yeah," he ground out.

"Oh my God," I breathed.

"Loved him. He was a good guy until he turned bad. But he had a big fuckin' mouth."

"Oh my God," I repeated.

I wanted to die. I wanted to rewind to the forest and not make it out.

Vinnie talked about me, as in *about me*.

To Benny!

"Frankie—"

"How much do you know?" I asked.

"Babe—"

I leaned toward him. "*How much do you know, Benny Bianchi?*"

He answered in a way that seemed he was forcing the words to come out, "I know I got some work to do to get you to enjoy goin' down on me."

I looked to the ceiling and cried, "Oh my God!"

"Babe, come here."

I looked to him and shook my head. "No. Take me home."

"Frankie, come here."

"This is humiliating," I hissed.

"What this is, is me tellin' you I know you're not a slut. You weren't then, you could never be. It isn't in you, babe. Fuck, you were twenty-one when you gave it up the first time and you haven't had a man since."

"How do you know that?" I snapped.

"Babe, *I was into you*. I'm *still into you*. I never stopped *bein' into you*. I paid attention."

Even though I liked that, a whole lot, I was too mortified to allow that good feeling to penetrate so I just glared at him.

"I'm right, aren't I?" he pushed.

I just kept glaring at him.

"I'm right," he muttered.

"Take me home," I demanded.

"Frankie—"

"Honestly," I bit out. "Do you think we can get beyond *this*? You knowin' your brother was the only one?"

"It didn't even occur to me when I had my hand on your ass and my tongue in your mouth yesterday. And do not go where you're goin', Frankie, because Vinnie didn't cross your mind either."

I shut my mouth that I'd opened in order to retort in precisely the way Benny knew I would because Vinnie didn't. He didn't cross my mind. Not until Benny started talking about him.

That was all about Benny and what Benny was doing to me.

"All right then, how about this?" I threw out. "I'm not a big fan of blowjobs."

"Then, no offense to my dead brother, he didn't teach you right."

I threw up my hands. "Do you not find this entire conversation bizarre?"

"Babe, seriously, I get you naked, I'll get you to the point where you latch on and be so into what you're doin', you'll come before I can pull you off and bury myself inside you."

"*Arrrrr!*" I screamed, mostly because, all of sudden, I had an overwhelming desire to give Benny a blowjob.

Crazy!

Just as suddenly, I was in his arms.

I jerked my body, but his arms went tight.

"Calm," he growled.

I went still and glared up at him.

"You are not a slut." He kept growling.

I kept glaring up at him.

"And I don't give a fuck what anyone thinks about us if they see us together. They judge, they gotta answer to God for that, not me *or* you."

I just kept glaring at him.

Benny withstood it for some time before he asked, "You have lunch?"

"Old lady Zambino treated her entire crew to Coney dogs from the concession stand in celebration of their resounding win."

"Too bad. I was gonna haul our asses to Lincoln's for a sub."

At this offer, my shoulders went straight and I shared, "I'm still peckish."

"A sub on top of a Coney dog is gonna fuck with your Giuseppe's experience."

"Nothing fucks with a Giuseppe's experience."

Benny grinned.

Then he asked, "You done freakin' out?"

I absolutely was not.

This realization made me slump in his arms.

I aimed my eyes at his shoulder, saying, "All of this is weird."

"Yeah," he agreed, and I looked back to him. "It's weird. It's awkward. It sucks. It reminds me I shoulda asked you out when I wanted to ask you out my senior year but didn't because it was known wide you didn't put out. But now we're here. We'll get past it. And at least it's at a time when I'm sure I can convince you to put out and give you a whole lot better than I could have when I was seventeen."

I blinked at him.

Then I asked breathily, "You wanted to ask me out when we were in high school?"

"Babe, you're crazy-beautiful and got great tits, great legs, a great ass, and an unbelievable smile, and you had all a' that back then too. So yeah. Fuck yeah. Every guy in high school wanted a piece of you."

Oh my God.

I'd had three dates in high school.

Three!

And none of them good.

I felt my brows draw together. "Then why didn't they ask me?"

"Because, Frankie, baby, you didn't put out."

It was then I felt my blood start to get hot.

"Was that the only prerequisite for a girl to get a date?"

"Pretty much. Outside of her needin' to be hot. But you had that."

"That's disgusting," I hissed.

"Frankie," he said, and my name rumbled with the laughter that was shaking his body against mine. "That was eighteen years ago, in a time when I thought with my dick."

My brows shot up. "You don't anymore?"

"Okay, it was in a time when I thought with my dick ninety-nine percent of the time, rather than now, when I think with my dick only fifty percent of the time, or anytime I'm around you."

"That's disgusting too."

"It was meant to be a compliment."

"It failed."

"Babe," he said, his arms giving me a squeeze. "You are not shitting me that you don't like the idea of me bein' all about my dick and where I wanna put it when I'm with you."

I was looking forward to a time when I could throw something at him without tearing open my wound when he pissed me off.

Like when he was right and he went about being right in a crude way that I found annoyingly arousing.

"I think I need a nap," I declared.

His arms got super tight when he burst out laughing.

I watched, up close and personal, and hated myself for enjoying every second.

His laughter died down to chuckles, his hand at my side moved to stroke me there, and he again focused on me to ask, "Right. Now, are you done freakin' out?"

I stopped being pissed. I stopped being anything.

But one thing.

And I shared with Benny what that was.

"This scares me, Ben."

He dipped his head so his face was an inch from mine and replied, "I get that, honey."

"I don't know how to get over that," I admitted.

"You wanna get over it?" he asked.

That was a loaded question I was not going to answer out loud so I kept my mouth shut.

"Okay, I'll give you that play, *cara*," Benny said when I did. "But, just sayin', you makin' your previous statement already gives me my answer."

And, again, he was right.

"So," he continued, "how 'bout this? Stick with me."

I shook my head. "I'm moving to Indianapolis."

At that, he shook his head. "Day to day, babe, not future. Not anything but the next day, fuck, the next minute, each minute into the next. Stick with me while we work it out. If it goes wrong, it does. If I can't guide you through, I'll eat that. But, I'll warn you, I'll be breakin' my back to make sure neither of those happen."

God, more goodness coming from Benny.

"There are a lot of obstacles," I pointed out.

"Francesca, no one ever got a gold medal for sittin' on their ass and doin' nothin'. You work at somethin', you work at it hard, you believe in it, you want it, you go after it, you get it, *that's* when you get your prize."

Now wisdom coming from Benny.

I couldn't take it so I dropped my chin to rest my forehead against his chest.

The hand he was using to stroke my side curled around and his other hand slid up to wrap around the back of my neck as he asked into my hair, "You really need a nap?"

"Were you really gonna take me to Lincoln's?"

"Yeah."

"Then I don't need a nap."

His hand at the back of my neck gave me a squeeze so I lifted my head.

When I did, Benny, who I was learning did not waste opportunities, dipped his and took my mouth. He got tongue action. It was more than a sweep this time. It was a deep drink.

I loved it. Every second. And I ended it with my arms wrapped around him.

"Stick with me?" he whispered, his lips still against mine.

"Yeah."

I felt his mouth smile.

I closed my eyes.

Then I felt his mouth touch my forehead.

After that, he let me go, grabbed my hand, pulled me toward the door, and said, "Let's go get subs."

Seven

Minute by Minute

*A*t six forty that night, I stood in Benny's bathroom, staring at myself in the mirror.

My hair was bigger than its normal big, by a lot.

My makeup was deeper, smokier, hotter.

My dress was black with a silver shimmer. In the front, it covered me from throat to mid-thigh, including long sleeves.

But it was skintight. *Everywhere.*

And there was no back. None. From the small to my shoulder blades, all bare.

It was a dress that demanded a woman not wear underwear. A bra was an impossibility, but I'd bested the challenge of the panties, finding a sheer black thong that was only noticeable if the dress shifted in a particular way. So under the dress, I had on nothing but that thong.

But on the outside, I'd included chunky drop earrings that nearly brushed my shoulders and a thick rhinestone bracelet over the gathers formed by the material at one of my wrists. On the other hand, I had a ring at my middle finger, on which delicate, shimmering chains were attached that dangled up the back of my hand to another bracelet linked around my wrist.

And on my feet were silver sandals that had a platform, a four-and-a-half-inch heel that was thin as a pencil, a slim wraparound strap at my ankle, and two slender straps over my toes.

I needed a manicure and a pedicure.

Other than that, top to toe, I was all I could be for a first date.

The bummer was that I was also a little tired. The day, the conversation with Benny, the trip to Lincoln's and back, and my efforts in the bathroom took it out of me.

But I was not going to miss that night.

I'd made Benny a promise. Stick with him. Minute by minute.

I was going to keep it.

I didn't know if it was right.

I did know that day we threw a lot of garbage out there and none of it fazed Ben, not in the slightest.

I also knew that pretty much everybody—from Cindy the nurse, who had no real idea of the history, to Cal, who totally did, to Theresa and Vinnie, who were intimately involved, to old lady Zambino, a not-so-casual observer—didn't think it was wrong.

It was only me who did.

So I was going to stick with Benny, take this minute by minute and ride it out, God help me.

Which meant, even though I was tired and a bit achy, I was tricked out to extremes in order to go to arguably the most romantic restaurant in Chicago with Benny Bianchi.

I turned to the door, opened it, switched off the light, walked out, and stopped dead.

This was because Ben had his neck bent forward, his side to me, and he was shrugging on the jacket of a black suit. Shrugging it on over a shirt so deep blue it was midnight, that had subtle dark gray, deep burgundy, and navy stripes. His hair was partially tamed, and once he got the jacket settled, the ends brushed the collar.

My stomach dipped and my mouth went dry.

His eyes came to me and he went completely still.

Then those eyes got dark in a way that made my legs start trembling and my clit pulse.

I braced for him to rush me.

He didn't. We just stood there staring at each other. Benny's look was carnal. I had a feeling mine was the same.

After this lasted awhile, Ben whispered, "Crazy-beautiful."

My heart squeezed, and when it did, it felt fucking *good*.

"Always were," he went on quietly.

I forced myself to find my voice, but when the words came out, they sounded husky. "You look good too."

Some of the dark went out of his eyes as sweet settled in and he ordered, "Come here, Frankie."

For once, I did as I was told and walked to him.

The instant I got close, he pulled me gently into his arms, holding me loosely, and dipped his head to touch his mouth to mine.

When he lifted it, he asked, "You ready to go?"

I nodded.

He grinned, gave me a light squeeze, then let me go. He did the rounds to turn the lights off on the nightstands, then came to me and took my hand. He held it all the way down to the kitchen and only dropped it when he nabbed his cell off the counter and tucked it into the inside pocket of his jacket.

We were at the door when he asked, "You want your purse?"

I looked up at him. "It doesn't go with my outfit and I didn't think to grab one when I was at my place."

"You need me to carry anything for you?"

I went silent and stared up at him, wondering if he was for real.

It was strange and unsettling to compare him to his brother, but even so, the fact remained that Vinnie not only never offered to carry anything for me, there were times he bitched when I asked.

Though, it was more. As my experience with men was limited, my girl-friends had reported the same thing.

"Babe?" he prompted.

Again in unchartered female territory, I cautiously answered, "My lip gloss."

His eyes dropped to my dress and he asked with more than mild incredulity, "You got it on you?"

I shook my head. "I left it in the bathroom."

"I'll get it," he muttered and moved that way.

"Ben, you wanna know which one to grab?" I called to his back.

He turned and looked at me. "Babe, you think I don't have that shade committed to memory, you'd be thinkin' wrong."

My heart squeezed again.

Ben disappeared.

He returned, got close, and waved the tube of lip gloss at me. "This it?"

He was a miracle man.

"Yep."

He shoved it in his inside jacket pocket and asked, "Anything else?"

"Nope."

He grinned, grabbed my hand, and pulled me out the door.

We were in his truck on our way to Giuseppe's when something occurred to me.

"Do you know where my car is?"

"What?"

I turned to look at him. "I left my car in front of Daniel Hart's house."

"Yeah, right. Manny went to get it."

I stared at him. "What?"

"Man," Ben stated. "Police gave us your purse at the hospital, told us where your car was and that it was okay to move it. Gave Man your keys, he took it to your pad. It's parked in the spot with your apartment number on it in the parking garage."

That was nice.

"Said you need a tune up," Ben continued. "Sweet ride, babe, 280Z with a T-top. But you gotta take care of it." He made a turn and finished on a mutter, "I'll get it in my garage, get under the hood."

"You don't have to do that," I told him, turning to face forward. "Got a guy who specializes. With things crazy because of the new job and the move, I haven't gotten it to him. I was gonna do that before I went to Indy."

"I'll do it," Benny said.

"He specializes, Ben," I replied.

"Know my way around a Z, Frankie."

I shut my mouth because I knew he did. Not because he'd owned one, but because he'd had a girlfriend once who owned one.

This brought me to remember something I forgot that I'd always thought was sweet about Benny, actually about all the Bianchis. When he'd had her, he'd taken care of that car for her. Vinnie had done the same for me. You had a Bianchi man, mechanics and oil change shops were a memory.

I also remembered more.

I remembered that she'd lasted longer than any of the other women Benny was with, over two years. It was when I was with Vinnie so I knew her. Her name was Connie. She was very beautiful and very sweet. The whole family was hoping it would go somewhere, including me.

It didn't and Vinnie, as Benny told it true, had a big mouth, so I knew why it didn't.

She was *too* sweet. A pushover.

"My brother's a man who needs a challenge, babe," Vinnie had said. "A woman's gotta stir his blood in more ways than one. You dig?"

At the time, I didn't dig. I'd liked Connie and I'd thought Benny was crazy for letting her go.

I knew now Connie would come right there when Benny demanded it. And I knew now that might be okay, for a while. Then it would bore him stupid.

These thoughts made me feel warm and weird at the same time.

I didn't know if it was right, if it would make me feel less weird or more, or make Benny feel weird at all, but I still asked, "How is Connie?"

"Married to Tommy Lasco. Two kids, another on the way. They moved to Calumet City three years ago," he stated indifferently.

As he was talking, my eyes got big and I turned to him again. "Tommy Lasco?"

"Yep."

"Oh my God," I breathed.

"Yep," Benny agreed.

Tommy Lasco was a bully in school who turned into an asshole out of it. He was good-looking, not as good-looking as any of the Bianchis, including Manny. Vinnie and Benny were strikingly handsome in a way that caught your attention and did not let go. Manny was hot and had it going on, but he was not quite that.

But being an asshole always made a man less attractive.

I turned my head and told the windshield, "I don't like that for her."

"She's happy."

Again, I looked at him. "You're sure?"

150

I saw his shoulders shrug. "They fit. Makes no sense to me, but he loves her. Treats her like gold. He's a massive dick to everybody else, no exception, but thinks the world of her, their kids. Somehow, she saw her way past the dick he was to the guy he could be with her, and somehow, he found his way not to be a dick to her."

At least that was something.

I looked back to the road, murmuring, "How did I not hear of this?"

"They live quiet. She likes it like that. He gives it to her."

Another shocker about Tommy Lasco. He was the kind of asshole who liked to spread his asshole-ness around, loud and proud.

"That's nice," I remarked.

"Yep," Benny agreed.

I rubbed my lips together, thinking about it, then I went for it. "Does that make you feel weird? You guys were together for a while."

"Nope," Benny replied immediately. "Glad she's happy. She wasn't for me. I burned her bad and that sucked. Didn't like doin' it to her 'cause she was sweet, but she wasn't for me. Sayin' that, she found what she needed in the end and nothin' to feel about that but happy for her that she got what she needed."

He did burn her bad. She was devastated when Ben broke it off.

But it was coming clear that shit happened, and when it was done, Benny put it behind him. He did that firm and he moved on, leaving it there and not looking back.

And this was something to consider.

Ben made a turn and we were on the street that led to the alley that held Giuseppe's.

"Gonna drop you at the door, honey," he said. "May have to park at a distance and don't want you walkin' that."

And more good from Benny.

"Okay," I said softly. "But I need a refresh of lip gloss."

He dug into his jacket and handed me the tube. I flipped down the visor and did my swiping as Ben made the turn into the alley. I flipped the visor up, watched as Ben drove down the alley, and I saw it.

Two scrolled, wrought-iron railings coming up from a short stairwell that led to the bowels of the building. A sign dimly lit by two arched lights over it that said only *Giuseppe's*. Planters attached to the brick of the building from street level all the way up and over the recessed door to the restaurant, dripping with flowers and greenery, same with two tall, attractive planters on either side of the railings. Deep-seated benches on each side of the door beyond the planters where people could sit and wait for tables or go out and have a smoke and not stand around loitering. The benches were lit with more of the arched lights, two for each bench.

Total class.

Ben stopped and put the Explorer in neutral. I had my door open, but he was at it before I could get a foot to the running board.

I didn't ever get a foot to the running board. Hands at my hips, he lifted me out of the SUV and put me on my feet. Without me asking him, he slipped my lip gloss from my fingers and tucked it in his jacket. And after that, even though the steps were four feet away, he led me there, hand in hand.

He stopped me at the top and I looked up at him.

"Be back," he said, then dipped his head and touched his mouth to my freshly glossed one with no apparent aversion to this fact. I watched him saunter back to his truck with his thumb at his lips, rubbing away my gloss. Something strange but not unwelcome shifted inside me at the casual way he did this. Then I watched him slam the passenger side door he left open, round the hood, angle in, and drive away.

I kept my eyes to the alley for a while before I turned and looked down the steps.

Vinnie had never taken me there.

In the early days, before it got exclusive with Vinnie, I'd had a date with a guy who took me there.

The instant Vinnie found out some guy had taken me there, he pressed for exclusive. He knew what it meant when a guy took a woman to Giuseppe's.

Why he never took me there himself, I would never know.

But right then, I couldn't go in. Not alone. Instead, I moved to a bench, sat and waited for Benny.

It didn't take long for him to show, and when he strolled into the dim light, I saw his eyes narrowed on me.

I gained my feet and he was right there.

"Why didn't you go in?" he asked.

"Waitin' for you," I answered.

He studied me a second before he took my hand and, without a word, led me to the steps.

Then we were in. Music playing so soft you could barely hear it. A faint hum of conversation that made you think every patron was whispering. Muted noises of silverware clinking on china or crystal tinkling against glass. Candlelight on the tables and in some sconces on the walls. A fresh, extraordinary, but understated bouquet of roses at the hostess station.

Love in the air.

Its silken feel glided down my throat as Ben stopped us at the hostess station and Elena appeared before us. She wore a trim, black sheath dress that skimmed her knees and a pair of delicate, black slingbacks with peekaboo toes, her hair pulled back in a soft updo.

"Frankie and Benny," she said quietly, her lips curved up in a slight smile, her hands held out low to her sides.

Elena was ten years older than me, maybe a bit more. I knew her not because I'd eaten at her restaurant only once, but because she went to the same church as my family, she lived in the 'hood so I saw her around, and even having her own eatery, she'd come to Vinnie's Pizzeria more than once (because everyone in the 'hood had been to Vinnie's more than once).

She was like her restaurant, like her father was before her and, if rumor served, her grandfather was before him.

Pure elegance.

She came to me first. Grabbing my hands, she leaned in and touched one cheek to mine, then she moved to touch the other one before she kept hold of my hands and shifted away to catch my eyes.

"You're well?" she asked.

"Yeah," I answered.

"So brave," she said softly.

She'd heard. This wasn't a surprise. She was from the 'hood. Not to mention, it was on TV.

"Thanks," I replied.

She squeezed my hands before she let me go and turned to Benny, giving him the same treatment but without the hand-holding. Instead, she let her hand rest lightly on his upper arm.

She moved from Benny and said, "Let's get you to your table."

Not waiting for us to respond, she started to glide through the restaurant. Ben put his hand to the skin at the small of my back and guided me after her.

With the shortness of time when Benny made the reservation, I was surprised that Elena led us to a premier spot—a corner table, even quieter and more private than any of the other tables due to a strategically placed planter. She stood to the side, smiling with approval as Ben proved further how awesome he could be when he shifted around me to pull back my chair.

I sat. He scooched me in, rounded the table, then he sat.

Elena moved in and floated a hand low across the table, saying, "Someone will bring your menus shortly. If you require anything, just ask." She dipped her chin and finished, "*Buon appetito.*"

With that, she glided away.

I watched her do it, saying, "She's the shit."

I heard Benny chuckle as he agreed, "Yeah."

I looked to him. "You been here before?"

"Yep, Ma and Pop's thirty-fifth wedding anniversary. They hired out the back room. And brought a couple of women here."

"Oh," I murmured as a young woman in a fabulous but refined black dress swooped in and handed Ben and me our tall, leather-bound menus.

We said thanks and she'd barely moved away when a waiter wearing a white shirt, black tie, black trousers, and a pristine, long, white apron arrived with a pedestal bucket of Champagne he placed on the floor behind Benny's chair.

"Compliments of Elena," he murmured. He put two flutes on the table, popped the cork, and expertly poured. "I'll be back for your order or to answer any questions you may have," he stated while shoving the bottle back in the ice, then he drifted away.

The Champagne was a surprise. Then again, it wasn't every day a girl from the 'hood survived a kidnapping and being shot, this making the news, and a couple of weeks later goes out with the man who rescued her.

All of us surviving that situation was worthy of celebration. It was very like Elena to think the same and do something about it.

I reached to my flute but saw Ben's fingers close on the stem before I got near it.

He took it away and I looked to him.

"When was your last pill?" he asked.

"This morning," I answered.

"You gonna need one to get through the night?"

The pain was nagging, and from experience, I knew it was likely to get worse. So the answer to that was yes.

Therefore, I gave him that answer.

"Yes."

"Frankie, read the leaflet that came with your meds. No alcohol."

I blinked. "But I'm at Giuseppe's."

"Yeah. And I'll bring you back and you can drink all the Champagne you want then. Now, you be safe."

I made a grab for my glass, saying, "I'm sure it'll be all right."

Ben pulled back the glass, saying, "I'm not, so you're gonna be safe."

I focused on him. "Ben, just a glass."

"Francesca, no."

It was then I glared at him and declared, "Already this is not a fun date."

This did not perturb him in the slightest and I knew that when he stated, "It'll be less fun you have a seizure or go to sleep and don't wake up or start gettin' sick, or whatever the reason is they put on that leaflet you shouldn't drink while on those pills."

"It's probably not that dramatic."

"Babe, you've been shot. Against all that's holy in a Chicago that is not the bootlegging, roaring twenties, your man decided to become a wise guy and ended up whacked. Your brother is about to go bankrupt due to the child support he'll be payin', or his story will be a made-for-TV movie when all those bitches he's tagging or recently tagged lose their minds and turn on him and or each other. You're a drama magnet. You wanna flirt with that, proves you're the nut I know you to be. But you aren't gonna do it on my watch."

"How is it that you can make being rational and protective so incredibly annoying?" I asked on a snap, and he grinned.

"It's a gift."

I rolled my eyes.

Benny took a sip from *my* Champagne glass.

I snapped my menu open and proceeded to study it with the intention of memorizing every word, even if it took me all night.

Unfortunately, it would be rude to make the waiter keep coming back to the table to ask if we were ready to order. So the first time he showed, I ordered the fried calamari, the spinach salad, and the lobster risotto, the last being the most expensive thing on the menu.

I ended my order with, "Later, don't trouble yourself with offering us a look at the dessert tray. Just bring it."

He bowed his head to me and looked to Benny, who placed his own order and ended it with, "Your bartender got it in him to make a virgin Bellini?"

I pressed my lips together because I loved Bellinis. They were my favorite. Benny obviously remembered and it was sweet that he did.

"I'm sure he does," the waiter replied.

"Right, then bring my girl one and be certain she doesn't have an empty glass."

The waiter nodded, took his menu to add to the one he'd divested me of, and swept away.

Ben looked at me. "Good to know Lincoln's didn't shave the edge off that appetite."

I grabbed my napkin, snapped it out to my side, and put it on my lap.

Benny continued as I did so, "Also good to know I'll need to give myself a raise so I can take you out occasionally and be able to afford it."

I crossed my legs under the table and moved a hand in order to arrange my cutlery so it was meticulously positioned around the plate sitting in front of me, even though it was already meticulously positioned.

"Francesca," he called.

I cut my eyes to him. "What?"

"I'd buy you a plate piled high with sapphires and be happy sittin' across from you as you picked through them, even if you were doin' it pissed at me for being rational and protective."

My stomach dropped, my heart squeezed, and I leaned into him to hiss, "Stop bein' awesome."

He threw his head back and laughed, showing me he didn't intend to stop being awesome because he looked good *and* sounded good doing it.

When he was down to chuckling, his hand darted across the table and closed around mine. Twisting, he forced his fingers to lace through mine and rested our hands on the table.

Once he'd accomplished that, he looked into my eyes and stated, "Been waitin' years for this, baby. Thanks for makin' it worth the wait."

"You're still bein' awesome," I informed him.

"Yeah, and it's cute as fuck that annoys you."

"Now you're bein' awesome *and* insane," I shared.

His head cocked slightly to the side. "A man likes what he likes. I'm a man who likes you and your attitude."

"Whatever," I muttered, even though I liked that he liked that and I liked it a lot.

"What makes you happy?" he asked suddenly, and I felt my body jolt at the question, not just because it was sudden, but because it was unexpectedly weighty.

"What?"

"What makes you happy? What do you want outta life?"

"I…" I started, then changed what I was going to say. "Why do you ask?"

"'Cause I wanna know if it's in me to give it to you."

God.

Benny.

"Ben," I whispered.

"I want kids. Three, four. Boys and girls, but however they come, doesn't matter to me," he put out there. "That's it. I'm good at the restaurant. Comfortable with the money I got in the bank. I get the kids, eventually gotta buy a bigger house. And told you the woman I wanted. So there it is. That's what I want outta life. That's what would make me happy."

He gave me that. No coaxing, no bullshit, no games, no holding shit back, waiting to see where I was and if I fit.

What he wanted was simple.

And beautiful.

When I said nothing, he pushed, "You want kids?"

"Yeah," I replied.

"How many?"

"Don't really care, but more than one."

His fingers tightened in mine for a moment before he went on, "You like your work?"

"Yeah."

"Wanna keep it or be a stay-at-home mom?"

"I don't know. I figure I'll know when the first kid comes."

"Yeah," he said.

"Do you want your kids' ma to be stay-at-home?" I asked.

"Want her to be happy," he answered. "So don't give a fuck just as long as she gets that. Whatever way it turns out, we'll deal."

More awesome.

"I'm moving to Indianapolis, Benny," I blurted, my hand tensing in his. "I have to. I—"

His hand gave mine a light jerk. "That's not the next minute, baby."

I shut my mouth.

"That's on your mind, I'll say this," he went on. "You want that prize, you gotta work for it. And if there are obstacles in your way, you deal with them when you hit them. You find a way. We wanna work at this, we'll find a way."

It was a big obstacle to face.

In light of that, it was also the perfect thing to say.

"Okay," I said softly.

His thumb moved, stroking the side of my hand, and he asked, "You good with our talk earlier?"

"Mostly," I answered.

"Which part are you not good with?"

"All the parts that are still awkward and uncomfortable," I told him, meaning the whole of it.

His head cocked to the side again. "Vinnie bring you here?"

I shook my head.

"I brought Connie here."

My breath stuttered and I stared into his eyes.

"You have a past, I have a past," Benny stated. "You loved a man. I had a woman who meant something to me. That was then, Frankie, this is now. It's just that your man was my brother. We can make that an issue or we can decide to let it go."

"It's easy for you to let it go?" I asked.

"No, but not because he had you. Not because you were in my life in a different way and I had to watch you love him and lose him. Because he didn't do right by you and that pisses me off. That said, I figure that'll eventually fade too."

"You wanted to go out with me in high school," I noted, not even knowing why I did it, but Ben must have known because his thumb stopped stroking and his fingers got tight in mine again.

"Loved my brother, thought you were the shit, you were with him, didn't let my mind go there. Last couple of weeks, I let my mind go there. I held no jealousy at the time. That doesn't mean when it started with you two it wasn't a blow because I fucked that up back in the day. You were around and available and I didn't do shit for years about it and Vinnie got in there because I was dickin' around. But when you were with him, that went away because it had to. Bottom line now, it brings me no joy you lost what you lost when you lost him. That doesn't change the fact that I'm glad I got my shot. I could feel guilt about that, but that's not on either of us. That's on Vinnie. And in the end, it's just the way it is."

"But you said you were thinkin' of makin' a move on me when I was *with* Vinnie," I pointed out.

He nodded once. "Could have guilt about that too, but that isn't on me either. He made his choices and he was my brother, but I knew you deserved better. It got to the point where shit was not right with you two and it wasn't gonna get better. So it got to the point where I started to realize I wanted to give it to you."

I looked away, but his hand shaking mine made me look back and he kept going.

"You were not with Vinnie but some other asshole who didn't do right by you, I woulda done the same thing. I woulda moved in. Some might say that would be a dick move, brother or not, but I don't give a fuck. I would not have any guilt about that either. It's the same fuckin' thing, except that asshole happened to be my brother. Take Vinnie out of the equation, Frankie, and you end up with a man who treats you right, that is not wrong. You could spit fire or talk at me for a year and you wouldn't convince me it was."

"Do your parents understand what this is?" I asked in a voice that was barely a whisper.

"Yes," he answered in a voice that was not.

"And they're okay with it?" Now my voice was quiet but squeaky.

"They got more years than us. They know you're a good woman. They want you to be happy. And they sure as fuck want me to be happy. They've done enough judging when it was not their place and the judgments they cast were fucked. They learned, honey. It is not lost on them that life is life and the goal is to gather as much happiness as you can while you're livin' it. Things mighta gone differently if I made a move while my brother was alive. They mighta frowned on that. Then again, they knew in their guts he was doin' you wrong so they might not. We'll never know. Right now, there is no one to hurt in this scenario 'cause the one who woulda got hurt is dead."

"You have all the answers," I noted, but not in a sarcastic way. It was just that he *did* have all the answers, answers to difficult issues I thought had none at all.

"That's because there are answers to be had."

"Why do those answers come easy for you?"

"Because I'm not makin' them hard."

I felt my brows knit. "Do you think that's what I'm doing?"

"I think you loved my brother and you think you're betrayin' his memory by lettin' yourself have what you want, goin' there with me. But his memory is a memory, baby. There is nothin' to betray. It boils down to a decision you make about what *you* want. And I know I'm hammerin' this point home, but it's a point that's there for me to hammer. That is, he betrayed you before he got taken from this world. So my question is, why, when he's gone, would you keep the faith?"

"You're very angry at him," I whispered, not having a good feeling about what Ben was making plain and not having that good feeling for a variety of reasons.

"Yeah. 'Cause I loved him and I'm pissed he's dead. I'm pissed why he's dead. I'm pissed at myself for what I did to you after he died. I'm pissed at what he did to you and my folks and my family before he died. I gotta work through that and I will. But don't twist that shit in your head to make what I want from you to be about that. I knew a girl in high school who was sweet and spicy and I pissed away my chance with her back then because I was young and stupid. Years later, after I learned not to be stupid, I got my shot, so I'm takin' it. Vinnie just happens to be what happened to you in between. It sucks because it makes it harder for you, but that's what it is to me. He made this complicated. But that's it. Now it's just you and me."

Listening to him, letting all he was saying sink in, I felt my breath escalating, but in a way where it felt I was finally getting oxygen after ages where I wasn't able to breathe.

"You're saying all the right things." I said this as a defensive accusation because I wanted to breathe; I'd just been living without oxygen so long I didn't trust it.

"No, I'm not. I'm sayin' things that are right."

Instantly, his words forced a giggle to burst out of me that I couldn't hold back.

Benny was grinning at me when he asked, "That's funny?"

"It was the right thing to say," I explained, grinning at him back.

Taking in my grin, suddenly, he tugged my hand across the table and I watched in utter fascination as his dark head bent over it, then felt the utter exquisiteness of his lips brushing my fingers.

He kept tight hold of my hand, even as his eyes lifted to mine.

"Coupla weeks ago, you trailin' me back to Chicago, you pulled off to follow Vi, I felt fear, baby. Came out as anger, but it was fear that cut right down to the bone. Sal told me they got you, it carved out my insides. Couldn't think, 'cause I knew if I did, I'd think of wastin' my time, not sortin' shit out with you. Hit that forest, saw you on the ground draggin' yourself through those leaves. Only thing that stopped me unloading my clip in that motherfucker was Vi shoutin', and you looked in my eyes and mouthed her words, makin' a fuckin' joke. Pure fuckin' Frankie. I have never loved a woman, not in my life, not like that. Honest to Christ, you're crazy-beautiful and I was into you, but I don't know where that emotion came from. I just know that whatever that is I felt that day meant something and that something is huge. So I wanna know the good parts of feelin' that. All I'm askin' is for you to let me."

I stared into his eyes, words clogged in my throat, thoughts crowding my head, feelings gathering around my heart, but before I could get a word out, in a quiet, deferential voice, our waiter said, "My apologies. The lady's Bellini."

With a practiced hand, even though Benny and I were both leaned into the table, he set it by my place setting and whisked himself away.

But both Benny and I had shifted slightly back to let him in, and as he whisked himself away, Ben stared at his back like he wished he had a knife he could throw at it.

"Ben," I called.

He looked at me.

"Minute by minute, honey," I whispered.

He closed his eyes, his hand still in mine squeezed hard, and I lost his face when he again dropped his head, lifting my hand, and touched his lips to my fingers.

Through this, I clenched my teeth, held his hand and fought back tears.

He put our hands to the table, gave me his beautiful eyes, and whispered back, "Minute by minute, baby."

⁓

Three and a half hours later, I came out of the bathroom to find Benny in the bed, eyes to the TV. As he'd been in a suit, in order to lounge, he'd changed into pair of gray, blue, and red plaid pajama bottoms with which he'd paired a white tee that fit loose at his belly, snug at his chest.

I bit my lip and headed to the bed.

"Pill's on the nightstand, honey," he muttered to the TV.

"Thanks," I muttered to the covers I was pulling back.

I slid in, turned, saw the pill Ben brought up for me next to a glass of water he also brought up for me, and I took it, feeling warm and good, and it was pure insanity, but I also felt happy.

I settled in beside him but down in the bed, head on the pillows, because I was exhausted. I didn't even have it in me to sit upright.

After the heavy, dinner went great. The food was phenomenal. Benny and I chatted and bantered and laughed and fell into what we used to have in a natural way, except it was what it used to be when we were friends, plus a whole lot more.

I was full and content (though, I would have been more content if I'd had a glass of Champagne) and we were both silent on the way home, but silent with Benny holding my hand against his thigh the entire way.

When we got in the kitchen, he turned me to hold me loosely in his arms, bent in, touched his mouth to mine, and said, "Go on up. I'll be up in a minute."

I did not argue this. I went up.

Now was now.

I would have preferred my first date with Benny Bianchi, where I'd begun to let go of what I was using to force a wedge between us, to end in a hot makeout session. But from his words after his short kiss, I knew I'd be ending it likely cuddled in bed with him watching TV.

I'd take that.

After that day, I couldn't take more.

And the good that was becoming awesome of all things Benny meant he likely knew that so he wasn't going to make me.

"Babe, do me a favor?" he asked, eyes still aimed at the TV.

"Yeah?" I prompted when he said no more.

"Next time I take you out, a time when you won't have a hole in you that's healing, wear that dress."

My lips curled up, but I said nothing.

He kept going.

"And I'm sure they're sweet, but you got my permission to lose the panties."

Of course, Benny Bianchi had the skills to spot the panties.

At that, I smiled inside but verbally muttered, "Whatever."

He ignored my "whatever" and went on, "The shoes you can wear every day for the rest of your life and I'd be a happy man."

Perhaps those shoes weren't treacherous.

Perhaps they were miraculous.

I couldn't hold back the smile at that, but I forced it to be small and trained it to the TV.

Five minutes later, when a commercial came on, Benny turned to me. He leaned in, lifting a hand to cup my jaw, and brought his face close to mine.

I looked into his eyes and held my breath.

"It'd make me happy right now I don't have to sleep on that couch," he said quietly.

I knew what he was saying.

It was too fast. Way too fast.

But after dinner that night, I didn't care.

"So don't," I said quietly back. Though my voice may have been quiet, my heart was racing.

His eyes got soft, his face got closer, then his mouth was on mine. I only got a tongue sweep, but it was a tasty tongue sweep I liked a whole lot before he pulled away.

Benny, not wasting an opportunity *or* time, shifted to slide under the covers. Then he shoved an arm under me and shifted me to cuddle into his side.

I slid my arm along his flat belly.

"Your checkup tomorrow is at ten," he reminded me.

"Yeah," I confirmed. I remembered.

"I'll take you."

"Okay."

"I'll also call Manny. After I bring you home, he and I'll go get your Z so I can see to it."

"All right."

"Gotta get back in the kitchen, Frankie. You wanna call a friend to hang with you tomorrow night while I work?"

"That'll be nice."

He gave me a squeeze. "Right."

After he finished squeezing me, his hand drifted up and into my hair. Then he started twirling a lock around his finger.

I don't know why I did it, except that I wanted to do it and I didn't get much of what I wanted, and a lot of what I wanted was right then stretched out beside me.

So I did it.

I turned my head and kissed his tee over his pec.

When I did, his fingers stopped playing with my hair and I felt his ab muscles get tight under my arm.

But when I settled my cheek back to his chest, his fingers started back up again and his body relaxed beside me.

"Nice night, honey. Thank you," I told the TV.

"Yeah, baby."

I gave him a squeeze and relaxed beside him, wondering if this was how it felt. If this was how it felt to get what you wanted for a lifetime. Have it stretched out beside you. The promise of it there all night so you'd wake up to it in the morning. The promise of it going to work the next day with you knowing it was coming back. A promise that would stay a promise—beautiful, forever there, beckoning, even as minute by minute it was being fulfilled, leaving you taking your last breath on earth knowing you lived a life filled with beauty.

If it was, it was weirdly serene.

You'd think something that magnificent would be about fireworks.

But if this was it, it wasn't.

It was quiet, tranquil, comfortable.

Beauty.

Eight

You Grew Up

I felt arms tighten on me and the haze of sleep lifted, slightly. When it did, I felt a whole lot more, and that whole lot more consisted of my body pressed snug against the hard frame of Benny's, the warmth of our cocoon of covers, and the safety both created.

It was a strange feeling.

But I liked it.

I tilted my head back, opening my eyes, and I saw Benny.

Half asleep, my belly still did a dip.

"Hey," he whispered, his voice deep, easy and gruff, and right on the heels of the last one, my belly did another dip.

"Hey," I replied.

"How you feelin'?" he asked.

Groggily, I did a mental scan and found that either Benny's bed with his body in it was a miracle elixir, or the lateness with which I took the pill meant it hadn't worn off yet, because I felt *awesome.*

"Good," I answered.

"Good," he murmured, and I tensed when he lifted his head and buried his face in my neck.

The tenseness lasted a millisecond before I felt his lips at my neck and my body melted into his, even as my hands slid from his chest, one pushing under his body, which he shifted to accommodate me so I could wrap both my arms around him.

"Gonna get up." His voice rumbled against my skin.

"I'm gonna snooze," I replied.

"Mm." The soft noise he made rolled along my neck, causing a shiver to glide down my spine and my hands to move along the intriguing ridges and flats of his back.

His mouth glided up my neck and I felt his tongue touch the hinge of my jaw.

I closed my eyes and dipped my hands lower, going under his tee and shifting up so I could feel those ridges and flats skin against skin.

That was better, by a whole lot. His skin was warm and soft, the ridges and flats fascinating.

When my touch came unhindered, one of Benny's hands slid to my ass and cupped it.

I pressed my lips together to suppress my own "mm."

Even so, his mouth came to my ear and he whispered, "Like your touch, baby, but like it too much. This's gotta end now."

I felt disappointment slide through me as his hand gave my ass a squeeze before it drifted up to the hollow of my back and he lifted his head away from my ear. I opened my eyes and his caught mine.

"Doctor gives the go-ahead, we're all over that," he told me quietly. "He doesn't, we'll wait. Findin' the wait's worth it, so know when we get there, it'll still be worth it."

Still sleepy and slightly turned on, my hands encountering Benny's skin for the first time, I didn't have it in me not to blurt out, "You're even awesome in the morning."

He grinned, his eyes warm, sexy, and full of promise when he said, "I'm awesome all the time, babe."

At his arrogance, I kept all the goodness of the last three minutes but still narrowed my eyes at him.

"Seriously?" I asked.

"Fuck yeah," he answered, still grinning.

Before I could retort, he dipped his head, touched his mouth to mine, and pulled back.

"You snooze. I'm gonna hop in the shower. You're not up, I'll wake you when you gotta start getting ready."

After delivering that, he gave me another mouth touch, let me go, and rolled out of bed.

But as he did all that, I thought there was no way I would be able to snooze with a naked Benny in the shower just a room away.

Still, I snuggled up under the covers. Cautiously curling my knees closer to my belly and still feeling no pain, I settled in, closed my eyes, and listened for the shower.

I felt a slow smile spread on my lips when it came.

The smile died when my mind moved to other thoughts.

I had not woken in a man's arms in over seven years and the last man's arms I woke in were Vinnie's.

Vinnie, like Benny, was a cuddler, even in sleep. He liked contact. He showed affection whenever he could—awake, asleep, physically, verbally, even going so far as to let me know he was thinking of me when he was going about his day. I knew this when I'd come home to flowers. Or a little sweet nothing gift. Or even a card that had a hokey love message. Vinnie would write in the card, making fun of it, but we both knew he meant those words and that's what made it sweet.

When he started to work for Sal, when he became whatever it was they were before they became a made man, those little gestures started dwindling. Not the physical affection. The verbal affection, the gifts and the cards.

Apparently, a wise guy in training (and definitely those out of it) didn't do sweet things for his woman. Apparently, a wise guy showed no weakness, even for his woman. Apparently, a wise guy considered doing thoughtful things for the woman he loved a weakness, when the woman he loved thought it was the opposite.

Knowing he had that in him, guessing why he took it away from me, the crack that had formed in our relationship when I tried to talk him out of approaching his father about franchising (and he didn't listen)...

The crack that cut deeper each time he did something reckless that I tried to explain was just that (and he didn't listen)...

The crack that split between us further when he took up with Sal...

It tore us apart.

I just wouldn't admit to it or give up.

I knew that now, forced to come to terms with it in Vinnie's brother's bed.

And lying in that bed after having a hint of Benny Bianchi's good morning for the first time, a hint that was sweet and sexy, a hint that I knew could only get bigger and better, the thing that hit me was that it wouldn't matter whose bed I was in. I would think back to what I'd had and how it went bad. I would make the comparisons. Unless I continued to live my life as I was the seven years before I was shot, which I didn't intend to do, I would find a man and as I adjusted to a new person in my life, those thoughts were bound to drift through my head. In order to get healthy mentally and get on with my life, I would eventually have to come to terms with it.

Vinnie was dead. I was alive. He made his choices, I talked to him (and yelled at him) until I was blue in the face to try to get him to make different ones.

He didn't.

Now he was gone.

But I was not.

And now I was moving on and, in doing so, finding another man.

That man just happened to be his brother.

That was it. That was where life led me. If I let it and quit fighting it, it could be as simple as that.

For Benny, it was that simple.

And for Benny, I could find my way to making it that simple.

On that thought, my eyes drifted closed as the sounds of the shower came from the next room.

By the time the water went off, I was snoozing.

I sat next to Ben as he did the parallel parking thing in front of my apartment complex.

I did this pressing my lips together, and I was pressing my lips together because I was also watching Manny and a woman get out of a red Chevy Tahoe in front of us.

It was after my doctor's appointment where the doc pronounced my improvement "gratifying" and reiterated what he'd told me in the hospital: that the stitches inside were "absorbable" and would dissolve on their own, and the "glue" on the outside was used for cosmetic purposes so my scarring would hopefully be minimal. He then ordered me to titrate the pain meds by only taking them if I *really* needed them and gave me the go-ahead for "slightly more strenuous activity and light exercise."

I didn't have the guts to ask if this included sexual intercourse because I was trying not to think of having sex with Benny.

I wanted it. That was without a doubt.

But I'd had one lover and that lover shared things with Benny, so he knew things about me. Therefore, if I let my mind go there, I'd probably freak out. So I didn't let my mind go there.

Now we were at my apartment to get my Z and I had another obstacle to face, and that was Manny, the last member of the Bianchi family who spent the last seven years firmly in the camp of Not My Biggest Fan. Unlike Benny (who had reason, considering what I did when I threw myself at him) and Theresa (who I could get, her not wanting to have bad thoughts about her son), Manny wasn't ugly about it. He'd just cut me out of his life.

I'd been tight with him. Not like with Ben, but we were close. And like losing all the Bianchis, that hurt.

Carmella, their sister, didn't do any of that. She was the second oldest and she'd started her grown-up life early, getting married and popping out kids. Doing this, and being a girl, she matured a lot quicker. She saw how things were with Vinnie Junior and she was the first one to phone him and tell him, if he cast his lot with Sal, she'd put up with him when she came home, but outside of that, he was dead to her.

Then he cast his lot with Sal and he was dead to her.

She never blamed me. She knew what it was. So I never lost her.

It wasn't like we chatted on the phone daily. But, then again, we didn't do that shit when Vinnie was alive. But she sent me Christmas and birthday cards, the occasional email update, and I did the same with her.

I knew by the sheepish, hesitant look on Manny's face as he peered into Benny's SUV that he wasn't looking forward to facing me.

It turned out not to be too hard to let any of the Bianchis off the hook. The thing was, it just kept bringing it back when I was already struggling to move on.

Benny parked and I managed to hop out on my own, even in a pair of high-heeled, platform pumps. I tugged my jacket tighter around me, seeing as we'd hit October, and just that morning, Indian summer said *sayonara*.

Benny met me on the sidewalk and took my hand in a firm grip as he moved us toward Manny and his woman.

I decided to get it over with quickly and called, "Hey," on a big smile when we were ten feet away.

Manny blinked in surprise and I saw his woman's head twitch.

This made me focus on her.

When I did, I noted she was pretty and petite, not a surprise with Manny. He liked them small but rounded, always did. She had dark hair that had a lot of curl, pretty blue eyes, and was wearing much the same as me in a way that told me it wasn't her normal uniform—platform heels, jacket, sweater, and jeans.

I also saw she seemed tense and I liked that. Not because she was tense, but because she obviously knew what was going down and, equally obviously, was anxious for her man.

In other words, I had to let her off the hook too.

So when we got close, I tugged my hand from Benny's, moved right in, and gave Manny a hug.

It took him a second, but then his arms closed around me loosely.

They felt good there and there it was. It was done. Standing in Manny's arms, I was officially back in the fold of the Bianchi family.

This made my voice husky when I said in his ear, "Thanks for gettin' my car from Hart's." Then I gave him a squeeze, leaned back and gave him a big smile.

He stared at me a second, surprise in his dark eyes, before he said quietly, "No problem, Frankie. Glad I could do somethin'."

I kept smiling at him as I pulled away and shoved a hand toward his woman. "Hey, I'm Frankie."

"Uh, Sela," she replied, taking my hand, her eyes darting between Manny and me. I knew she didn't want to be rude by not looking at me, but she wanted to take the pulse of her guy.

Yes, I liked her.

To afford her that opportunity, I quickly said, "Nice to meet you," aiming my smile her way. Then I gave her hand a squeeze, let it go, and looked up to Ben.

"Can we go up real quick so I can grab my laptop and some other shit?"

He was smiling down at me, his eyes warm and happy, his approval of how I'd handled that clear on his face, and his lips moved to say, "Anything you want, honey."

I shot him a grin, then looked around the group. "We get this done, maybe we can all go to lunch."

Manny grinned slowly at me. Sela stared at me and shifted closer to Manny.

Benny slid an arm around my shoulders and tucked me tight to his side, muttering, "Sounds like a plan."

"Right, I'm hungry, let's go," I said, moving toward the building, wrapping an arm around Benny, and taking him with me.

I got two steps in before Manny rounded us at the back and stopped us by grabbing my hand.

I looked to him.

He spoke.

"I gotta say—"

"Don't," I whispered, curling my fingers tight around his. "Don't. It's over. Over for everybody. Just let it be over, Manny. Yeah?"

He held my gaze as his hand squeezed mine hard before he said, "Yeah, Frankie."

I gave him another smile. He gave me one and let me go.

Benny moved me to the building.

I'd punched in the security code to open the door. We were in the lobby and he kept walking me to the elevators, but he did it dipping his head so he had my ear.

"You know you're the shit, right?" he said there.

My chest warmed, my lips curled up, and I pulled my head back so he would lift his. When he did I caught his eyes. "Fuck yeah."

He pulled me closer and did it laughing.

⌒

"Fuck it," I muttered, leaning forward and putting my laptop on Benny's coffee table.

I heaved myself out of his couch and moved through the house. Destination: garage, where Benny was working on my Z.

Obviously, we collected the Z. We also had a quick bite with Manny and Sela. Man, like his brother, didn't waste the opportunity my quick forgiveness afforded him. He slid back into the Manny of old, teasing, giving me shit, making a lot of jokes, and generally acting like the annoying little brother you adored for reasons that made no sense, mostly because you adored him because he was annoying.

Sela thawed when she saw I wasn't going to bust Manny's chops, not even in a passive-aggressive way, and I was surprised to find she was sweet, kind of in the way Connie was sweet. Apparently, unlike his brother, Manny didn't want a challenge. He wanted a woman to come there when she was told. Watching them together, I was glad he found what he wanted and a good one at that.

On my way to the garage, I ignored my jacket that I'd slung on the back of one of Benny's kitchen table chairs. I was thinking I wouldn't be out in the chill too long, thus I wouldn't need one. So I walked out, down the stoop and the cement pathway, and I hit the garage. I opened the side door and heard the music, though I'd heard it before I even opened the door. Metallica's "Wherever I May Roam."

Another urge to smile hit me. There wasn't a lot of music I didn't like, but there was no denying I was a metal girl down to my soul. Ben was all about metal too. I knew this from high school. I'd liked it since then, and right at that moment, I liked the idea that if it happened for us, if this worked, there would probably not be a time when we'd fight about what was playing on the stereo.

I moved between his SUV and my Z, which was backed into the garage, and found him under the hood.

There were things a man could do that were normal things to him that he would have no idea would give a private happy flutter to girls like me.

Working under the hood of a car was one of them.

I controlled the flutter and called, "Hey."

He lifted up from what he was doing and rested his forearms on the filthy blanket he had draped over the side of the car. His hands were greasy, he held some tool in one of them, he turned his eyes to me, and the flutter became harder to control.

"You need a jacket," was his greeting.

"I'm not gonna be out here that long," I shared.

"You need a jacket," he repeated.

Suddenly, the flutter became a whole lot easier to control.

"Or I *wasn't* gonna be out here that long. Since you obviously need to make a point Benny-style, I might be out here a year."

His eyes smiled as his mouth muttered, "Benny-style."

I amused him.

That made me happy and mildly ticked—a contradiction of emotions that I was finding Benny was skilled at evoking.

"I will point out you're in a t-shirt," I stated for reasons that were beyond me, since it was chilly and I didn't need to start squabbling with Benny. That'd mean I'd be out there a lot longer than I expected, which would make him right about me needing a jacket.

"I'm a guy."

At his words, I blinked, then stared, forgetting about getting to the point, mostly because he was annoying, and when he was, I had all the time in the world to squabble.

"A woman needs a jacket, but a guy is immune to cold?" I asked.

"No. *My* woman needs a jacket 'cause I don't want her uncomfortable or to catch a cold. I don't give a shit about other women. They can run around when it's fifty degrees and do it naked for all I care. But *you* need a jacket."

"There you go, making protective annoying again."

His lips quirked. "Told you it was a gift."

I lifted my brows. "Do you think if I threw down a challenge, and the person who fails to get in the last word loses, that we'd be out here an eternity?"

"Probably."

"Let's not do that," I suggested.

"I'd be up for it, if you went in and put on a jacket."

Now I wasn't happy, I was just ticked.

That was why I tipped my head back to look at the garage door rolled up on the rail and cried, "*Arrrr!*"

"Babe," he called.

I looked back to him.

"Let's get to the part about why you're out here," he suggested.

I took in a deep breath and asked, "You need a drink or something?"

He grinned and answered, "Nope."

I nodded. Offer to do something nice for him while he was doing something nice for me extended and declined. Now it was time to move on to why I was really out there.

"Your Wi-Fi password isn't working."

He looked perplexed for a second before he asked, "What?"

"Your Wi-Fi password isn't working. I'm trying to get my laptop connected so I can check my email. The password you gave me to do that isn't working."

"You type it in right?"

"Seein' as I typed it in forty-five thousand times, I'm guessin' one of those times I got it right."

"Forty-five thousand?" he asked, eyebrows going up right along with the tips of his lips. "I been out here for twenty minutes, babe. You must type fast."

I rolled my eyes before rolling them back to him and saying, "Ben, if I can get on my email, I can sort some shit out, do some work, get back into the swing of things, feel like my life is back in my control. I can do that on my phone, but it'd be a whole lot easier on my laptop. It'd help out if you could scan your brain to let me know if you gave me the correct password."

"Honestly, I have no clue," he replied. "Only got Internet for the TVs and set that up at least a year ago. But the password I gave you is what I remember the password to the router bein'."

Since his password was 13579000BB, although this would be hard to forget, and although I put in one less 0, two more 0s, and left out the 0s altogether, something was not right.

"Did you write it down somewhere?" I asked.

"Yep," he answered.

"Where?"

"No clue about that either," he said on a grin.

I looked down to my car, then back to him, beginning to feel the chill seep through my thin sweater. I needed to get this done before I shivered noticeably, giving Ben the opportunity to pounce right on that, something to be avoided.

"Okay, well, you're already doin' somethin' for me so I'll just ask when you're done, you do somethin' else for me and find wherever you wrote down that password."

"Sure."

"Thanks," I muttered, making a move to leave.

"Babe?" he called, and I looked back at him.

"What?"

"Come here," he ordered, still leaning into his arms on the side of my car.

"What, Ben?"

"Come here."

"As you yourself pointed out, it's cold. So just tell me…what?"

"Come here."

I screwed up my eyes. "Seriously?"

He grinned.

"*What*, Ben?" I asked.

"Francesca, come…here."

"Oh, all right," I snapped and stomped around the car, stopping close. "What?" I asked shortly when I got there.

"Come here," he repeated, having not moved anything but his neck in order to be able to look up at me.

"I *am* here, Ben," I pointed out.

"No, baby, you aren't. You're there and the here I want before you go back into the house is for you to be *here* so you can give me your mouth."

That caused a flutter along with a dip and my chest warming all at once.

But I was me, so it was full of attitude when I leaned into him and pressed my mouth to his.

I intended only a lip brush, but without him even moving his hands, he kept me there by touching his tongue to my lips. Naturally, the promise of that was too much not to go after, so my lips opened and his tongue swept inside. I liked that so much my body reacted and I had to put my hand to his side to steady myself.

He released my mouth and said softly, "I'll finish up here soon and find your password."

"Thanks, honey," I whispered, his kiss—the way he demanded it, the way he took it, leaning casually into my car but still managing to be all about me, something I thought was hot—causing all my attitude to leak out of me.

I was still close so I only saw his eyes smile. Therefore, it was likely he only saw mine smile too.

I lifted away and Ben turned back to my car.

I walked to the house thinking that I'd spent weeks freaking out about this, the idea of Ben and me. Torturing myself about it. Wanting it and finding every excuse not to give it to myself.

But having it—the ease of it, the naturalness of it, the excitement of it—now I was wondering why.

⌒

I stood in the hall of Benny's house, watching him in the dining room and *feeling* him in the dining room.

It was the feel of him that had me rooted to the spot.

And the weird part of that was that the feel of him was calm, quiet.

Benny.

He'd come in from the garage forty-five minutes earlier, washed his hands, and went directly in search of wherever he wrote down the password.

This began the deep state of shock I was currently experiencing.

This was because it had been at least an hour after I'd gone out to the garage to ask for it. Yet he came back, remembered, and started looking right away without me even raising my eyebrows to give him a hint there was something I'd asked him to do and I wanted him to do it.

Then he couldn't find it.

It wasn't anywhere in his "office," not the desk, not in the mess of papers shoved, what appeared to be randomly, in an expanding file. Not even in the piles that were definitely randomly piled against one wall.

He then went to the kitchen where he had not one but three drawers that were shoved full of junk that included bits of paper, stubs of bills, even envelopes that should have been thrown out.

It wasn't there either.

Now he was sorting through the shit in the dining room to find it, so much of it that it might take a year to go through all of it.

I had offered to help, but he told me he remembered what it looked like and I probably wouldn't be able to spot it, even if I had it in my hand.

And I was in a deep state of shock because Benny was a Bianchi. I'd known him for years and this was not him. This was not any of the Bianchis. Not even Theresa.

The reason why it wasn't was because he was not pissed. He wasn't even acting annoyed, frustrated, or the slightest bit impatient.

He'd been searching for a slip of paper with a bunch of digits written on it for forty-five minutes. A slip of paper he, personally, didn't give a shit about. It was a slip of paper that would help me. He probably wouldn't need to use it unless his router got screwed up, which if it hadn't after a year and he used it only for his TV, probably wouldn't.

I expected him to give up, tell me to suck it up and use my phone or haul my ass to an Internet café. I even expected him to blow, taking the frustration of his seriously lacking filing system out on me.

He didn't do either.

He just kept looking.

I could not process this.

I couldn't because Vinnie Junior would have looked for fifteen minutes and given up. He'd be apologetic, but he'd move on and it would be me that would search for whatever was needed.

Vinnie Senior would tell Theresa to look for it, even if she didn't know what she was looking for. But while she was looking, she'd keep asking him if this was it or that was it, which would force him to start looking. And then he'd finally blow his stack, not at anyone, but it would blow all the same, because *he* hadn't put an important piece of information in a place he could find it.

And seven years ago, Ben was like his father.

Now he was not.

"Fuck, here it is." I heard him mutter, and my focus went to him in the dining room.

He was moving to me with a piece of paper in his hand. He got to me, handed it to me, and immediately wrapped his hand around the side of my neck, bending in to kiss me as I stood completely motionless, still in shock.

He kissed the top of my head, let me go, and said as he moved to the stairs, "Check that, honey. I gotta get my shit sorted and get to the restaurant but wanna make sure you're covered before I go." I pivoted so I was standing facing the stairs. I saw him stop five up and look down at me. "If it's still fucked up, I'll go over to Tony's. I can see his system on mine and he'll probably be cool with you tappin' into that."

I felt my lips part.

Ben turned and jogged up the rest of the stairs.

I stared up the stairs, looked down at the paper in my hand, then back up the stairs.

He was late.

He looked for that piece of paper and he did it until he was late.

He also didn't really have to look for it for me if neighbor Tony would let me use his Wi-Fi.

But he did it.

Patiently.

For me.

I didn't know what to do with this and I knew why.

It wasn't just Vinnie Junior. It wasn't Vinnie Senior. It wasn't about how Benny used to be.

It was my dad, who could be mellow but who could also have a short fuse. He never would have spent forty-five minutes looking for something, even if it was important, even if it was my dad who lost it.

If he couldn't find it in five minutes, he'd shout, "You need it, find it your-fuckin'-self," and stalk away.

And I knew this because, needless to say, in the way he lived his life, there were a lot of important things that were lost. He had kids and a lot of women who needed those important things, asked for them, he couldn't find them, and he lost his mind because he lived his life the way he did and he didn't want anything dragging on it.

Like keeping track of important things.

Like his women and kids.

Thinking on my dad and the way he used to be (and probably still was), Benny's behavior was so difficult to process, I was standing where he left me when he came back down the stairs. Of course, it appeared he only changed from his grease-stained tee to a new one, which probably took him about two minutes, but still.

Seeing as I hadn't moved, when Ben made it to me, his expression was set firm at concerned.

He lifted a hand, again curled it around the side of my neck, and he asked, "Babe, you okay?"

I looked right into his eyes and stated, "You searched forty-five minutes to find a password for me, makin' yourself late, doin' that shit for me."

A new expression moved over his face and his fingers dug in lightly when he replied, "I see I scored with that, so it's a hit to share that I did it so you can get on your laptop, but I also did it 'cause it'd suck the router went down or some shit, and I'd need it to get my TVs back online and didn't know the password. So I also did it for me."

He gave that to me straight-up honestly, not milking something he did for himself to score a point with me.

Yet another expression shifted over his features as he watched whatever expression shift over mine before he murmured, "See I scored with that too."

"You grew up, Benny Bianchi," I whispered, and that was when soft and sweet took over his expression, even as his hand at my neck pulled me closer.

"Way you made things easy on Manny today, more proof added to a pile you've been givin' me that you did too, Frankie Concetti," he whispered back.

"Yeah, but I like the way you did it."

At that, he gave me surprised satisfaction before his eyes went dark in a way that made my heart race. His hand at my neck pulled me even closer, this time while his head bent to mine.

Then he kissed me. Not a sweep of the tongue, not a hot makeout session where I ended up pressed to a wall. But it was deep, it was wet, it was long, and it was amazing.

He lifted his head and looked into my eyes. "Would kill to take that further, but I gotta get to work."

Yes.

He grew up.

And I liked the way he did.

"You got someone comin' to keep you company?" he asked.

"Yeah. My girl, Jamie."

"Good. You two need dinner, call my cell. I'll send one of the kids with a pie or some rigatoni casserole or whatever."

The Bianchi rigatoni casserole. Second best to a Bianchi pizza pie, and there were some who (wrongly) would argue it was better.

Jamie needed some of that.

So did I.

"Thanks, Ben," I whispered.

"Anytime, baby," he whispered back.

It was me who went up to my toes to touch my mouth to his.

When I rocked back to my heels, he was grinning.

I returned it.

He took that in, his eyes dropping to my mouth to do it, before they came back to mine and he remarked, "I take it you didn't test the password."

I shook my head.

His hand swayed me slightly toward the living room when he ordered, "Get on that, honey. I gotta go, but if I gotta talk to Tony, I *gotta go*."

"Right," I murmured and broke from his hold to go to the living room.

The password written on the paper was one digit off the one Benny gave to me. It didn't end in BB but in BAB, all of his initials. Benito Alessandro Bianchi.

And it worked.

I felt arms tighten around me and the haze of sleep lifted, slightly.

When it did, I felt a whole lot more, that being Benny's body shifting into mine as he shifted mine to his.

I tilted my head back, opening my eyes, and through the dark I saw Benny.

Half asleep, my belly still did a dip.

"Go back to sleep, baby," he whispered.

"The night good?" I muttered sleepily.

"The usual insane. Now it's over. Go back to sleep."

"Thanks for sending the casserole. Jamie loved it," I told him, my voice fading.

"You need food anytime, I'll feed you. Now go back to sleep, honey."

I dipped my chin, pressed my face into his throat, and mumbled, "Okay, Benny."

He gave me a squeeze.

I moved to drape an arm over his waist and I gave him one back.

Then I did as told and went back to sleep.

Nine

YOU AREN'T EASY

My hands on the steering wheel of my Z, I was aiming her toward Vinnie and Benny's Pizzeria.

And I was freaking out.

It was the first time I was behind the wheel of my car since I'd driven it to Hart's house, following the car Hart's goons had Vi in.

But that wasn't the reason I was freaking out.

It had been three days since the first day Benny and me tried on the idea of Benny and me to see how it fit.

Since it fit really well, the last three days had been good.

I was definitely healing. I was getting around more, getting exhausted less, and the pain had gone from occasionally sharp and sometimes aching to randomly nagging.

This meant that I'd managed to get a lot done the last three days. Cleaning up my email and making arrangements with my clients to move them to new representatives. Gabbing with friends to let them know I was good and getting caught up with them.

And the last two mornings I went out with Mrs. Zambino on her power walks, which she took the "power" out of in deference to me, but still, the walks felt good. Getting out, moving, getting fresh air in my lungs, and getting a kick out of Mrs. Zambino, who was good company in a crotchety, know-it-all, old lady kind of way.

And the night before, I'd treated Asheeka to one of Benny's pies at the pizzeria—another obstacle conquered, the first time I'd been there since we lost Vinnie. I'd asked Benny for Sela's number and called her, asking her to join us, and she'd said yes.

The only weird part was seeing the sign with Benny's name on it, and the weird part about that was that seeing it felt good. Like I was proud of him and what he was doing but also proud to be the woman who was with him, walking into a restaurant that had his name over the door. Something tangible. Real. Benny didn't create that pizzeria, but I knew he took over the kitchen what was now years ago and it had lost none of its popularity. Therefore, it was Benny who kept it going.

No, kept it thriving.

So I was proud of him and proud to have a man who could do that want to be with me. And that pride came with a strange sense of peace.

It would have been easy to twist that, to think back to my time with Vinnie, who made all the wrong moves in life and paid for it in an ugly way in the end.

But I didn't twist it. I walked with the girls into that restaurant with my head held high, knowing my man would wow them with his pie, and knowing if I kept my shit together and didn't twist things that didn't need to be twisted, the real wow behind that man was all for me.

The girls and I'd had fun, and with Benny working in the kitchen and not playing watchdog over me, I'd been able to down a couple of glasses of Chianti, which didn't suck.

Man, who worked the front of the house—sometimes with Theresa, sometimes she'd take the night off—came to our table often, mostly because Sela was there. It was cute how they'd been together for a while and he still took as much time as he could get with her.

Vinnie Senior, like Theresa, had "retired," but the retirement part was a loose interpretation of the word. Ben told me he came around, stuck his nose in, even worked in the kitchen, helping Ben, or came in so he could have the night off. But he mostly left it to Benny.

Theresa, not one to kick back at night and watch games or cop shows (or kick back *at all*), had also retired loosely. This meant her form of retirement was still showing at the restaurant more than occasionally to work.

Theresa wasn't on last night, but with his girl there, Man found his times to come to our table to entertain us.

Ben had also showed once to give me a kiss, the girls a welcome, and to ask Asheeka if she enjoyed the pie.

Asheeka had.

In fact, she told me, after eating the pie (and the fresh breadsticks, and partaking of her portion of the big salad with banana peppers, olives, home-made croutons, and a healthy dusting of freshly shaved parmesan cheese in a light oil-based dressing) that I didn't owe her for shower duty. My marker was paid.

I got that. The food was that good, and the warm and welcoming feel of the red-and-white-checkered-tablecloth-table-filled room, with pictures of family mounted all over the walls, couldn't be beat.

Still, I was going to do something more for her. I had to. I was me.

I'd woken up four mornings in a row in Benny's arms to soft "heys," nuzzles, and warm arm squeezes, but Benny didn't push it any further. We kissed, often. No hot and heavy makeout sessions, but he frequently laid one on me, either claiming my mouth in a sweet kiss, brushing his lips against mine, or taking his time to make it deeper, but there was no pressure. No pushing.

With other displays of affection, like hand-holding, turning me in his arms every once in a while just to give me a hug and touch his mouth to my neck, I had the feeling he was giving me the chance to get used to him. It wasn't about making certain I was fit and healthy. It was about making certain I was *fit* and *healthy*, mentally. Ready to go there with him, take the next step.

It was like we were living together, but Benny was still giving me the dating-to-get-to-know-you-better part of the relationship and that was pure Benny. Thoughtful. Generous. Sweet.

Awesome.

So it had been a good three days.

No, outside of my own issues that messed up the first part, it had been a good *nine* days, made good by Benny from the beginning.

Minute by minute was working.

Fabulously.

Or it had been.

Until ten minutes earlier.

Now I was worried the minute-by-minute business was going to fail and do it miserably.

This was on my mind when I hit the alley behind the pizzeria and parked next to Benny's Explorer, the only car in a lot that was used only by employees.

It was relatively early. The pizzeria didn't open for lunch, dinner only. They started taking walk-ins at 4:30 for orders of takeaway, but didn't start seating until five.

But Ben had gone in because he had sauce to make. I'd learned in the last three days that he had kids who could make the croutons, whip up the homemade Caesar dressing they used, toss the salads, prepare the home-made pasta, assemble the casseroles, and roll the meatballs.

But the sauce and the pizza dough were made only by Vinnie or Benny.

I parked and got out, walking swiftly to the back door. I prayed it was open because I needed to get to Benny and not do it after pounding on the door, hoping he'd hear me. I tried the door, and for once, my prayers were answered.

I walked in and saw what I'd seen the hundreds of times I'd entered the pizzeria through the kitchen's back in the days when I was with Vinnie. Stacked up in the space around the door were used kegs. Empty crates that had held vegetables. Discarded boxes.

There was a door to an employee washroom to one side, to the other, a big room lined in stainless steel shelves that held everything the pizzeria needed, from durum flour to toilet paper.

Down the hall I went, passing two more doors; one side, the door to what was now Benny's office, the other side, a stainless steel door that led into a walk-in fridge.

I was curious to see how Benny had claimed Vinnie's office, but I was on a mission fueled by a freak-out so I kept going, past the last door, which was a walk-in freezer, then I was in the kitchen.

Stainless steel worktable down the middle with a shelf unit that had heating lights where they put prepared plates or pies. Three spindles hanging where they clipped orders. Utensils on hooks. More stainless steel tables around the walls. Big sinks. A back area where more sinks and the industrial dishwashers were. Stainless steel cabinets mounted on the walls that held plates, bowls, glasses. Lower cabinets that held pots, pans, skillets, trays, and drawers with cutlery. Smaller wire shelving under the wall cabinets that gave easy access to herbs and spices. Massive pizza ovens and three enormous restaurant-quality stoves.

Benny's domain. His kingdom. Where he worked to pay his mortgage and did it in a way that his twenty-five employees could pay their rent.

I stopped just in the kitchen, suddenly not thinking of my problem but, instead, thinking of what could be the crushing weight of being the driving force behind a business where people depended on you to do a large variety of things right on a day-to-day basis. From scheduling correctly, to not over- or under-purchasing tomatoes, to making certain wait staff was trained right, to ensuring every pizza pie and breadstick went out with equal quality, making the dinner an experience to remember and leaving the patron always wanting to come back for more.

With these thoughts coming to me, I turned my eyes to the left to see Ben in his white t-shirt and jeans, standing at one of the stoves, stirring what was in one of two humongous pots there.

The air was filled with the mouth-watering smell of garlic mixed with a subtle hint of fresh cut herbs, and I saw big cutting boards on the worktable behind Benny that had the residue of green on one, the juice and seeds of tomatoes on another.

"Babe."

He spoke and my eyes went to him.

When they did, his gaze moved over my face, his head cocked to the side, and he immediately moved to me, saying, "Jesus, what happened?"

"You know minute by minute?" I asked. He came to a stop a foot away, holding my gaze and nodding slowly. "Well, the next minute is gonna be a lot harder than the last bazillion of them," I declared.

"Talk to me," he demanded.

"You're working," I replied.

His head jerked slightly in surprise at my words and he said, "Yeah, I am, and you're here because you're freaked so now I'm not. Now, I'm standin' here waitin' for you to talk to me."

I shook my head. "What I mean is, you're working. This is me. I'm freaking and you're working and I should be good, have a mind to that, keep my shit together, and wait to discuss this with you at a time when you can focus on it, not at a time when you might burn the sauce."

I watched his face set to firm before he said, "Sauce cooks for-fuckin'-ever and is in no danger of burnin'. But I wouldn't give a shit if it burned. You got somethin' on your mind, you talk to me and I'll listen, even if it takes five hours. I can make more sauce."

God.

Benny.

"What I'm sayin' is," I kept at it, thinking it imperative he heed my warning, "I'm about drama. That's me and you need to know that. I tried to talk myself out of comin' here. I knew you'd be working and it wasn't cool that I interrupted you. That lasted about thirty seconds. Something's bugging me, I'll suck you in just to rant about what's buggin' me, but mostly, I'll lay it on you because I want you to fix it for me."

"Right then, Frankie, maybe it'd be good if you get to the rantin' part so I can get to the part where I fix it for you."

God.

Benny.

"This isn't going to be ranting, per se, just so you know," I clarified. "This is just gonna be freaking. Ranting is bad, but in some cases, Frankie-style freaking is worse."

"Babe," he said slowly, his voice getting lower, his own warning. "Talk to me."

"I just got off the phone with my new employer," I declared.

His body tightened and his eyes focused intently on mine.

He knew what was freaking me.

"They've given me until tomorrow to give them a definitive start date."

I watched his chest expand with the deep breath he pulled in, then he erased the short distance we had between us, getting in my space and doing it more by lifting his hands to curl them around either side of my neck.

He dipped his head so his face was closer to mine and he said quietly, "Okay, baby. This isn't a surprise. We knew this was coming. They weren't gonna wait forever. Now they're done waiting."

I nodded.

They certainly were. They weren't assholes about it, but they'd gone through a hiring process and those cost some cake. I was supposed to be in my new office in Indianapolis on Monday. They knew I wouldn't be there then, but no one could put up with an indefinite delay. I'd been understandably cagey about my new start date because I'd never been shot or known anyone who had (who survived it). I had no clue how long it would take for me to get back to good, or good enough, to start a new job after moving to a different state.

The doctor had given me guidance on that but did so with the warning that I hadn't only sustained a GSW, which was extreme enough, but the circumstances around that were also extreme. So I not only needed time for my body to heal, I also needed to sort out my head.

Thus, the cageyness, because I knew that I didn't only have all that to deal with, but also the Bianchis.

Now was now. I was getting around better, the pain was fading, and all was well with the Bianchis, primarily the most important one who was right then standing in my space, his hands on me.

It was *well*, as in it was *awesome*, and I could do minute by minute when I was experiencing awesome.

But when something big was encroaching on that awesome, I couldn't deal.

"I'm like this," I whispered after these thoughts coursed through my brain.

"What?" Ben asked.

"Sometimes I can't deal," I admitted. "I've been looking out for myself for a long time, a really long time, longer than losing Vinnie, and I'm good at it. But that doesn't mean sometimes I can't deal."

"Frankie, honey, there are times when anyone can't deal."

This confused me because Benny was "anyone," and from my experience of late (not to mention even before), I'd not known a time when he couldn't deal.

So I asked, "When are the times you can't deal?"

His mouth stayed closed but his jaw flexed.

I watched it, knew that meant he could always deal, and whispered, "Right."

"Okay, how 'bout this?" he started. "When my brother pisses away his life and hurts the people I love most in the world, I can't deal, as evidenced by the fact that I blamed that shit on a good woman and did it in an ugly way that lasted seven years."

Oh, right. Well, there was *that* time Benny couldn't deal.

"That was a doozy," I murmured, and he grinned.

"Yeah. So there are times when anyone can't deal."

I nodded again, feeling slightly better.

Benny spoke again and I felt not-so-slightly worse.

"You give up the lease on your apartment?"

I again nodded.

"Got a place down in Indy?" he went on.

"The company was putting me up in an executive apartment for October, which is still part of my offer. But yes, I went down and scouted a place and my apartment will be open on November first. The movers are all sorted to come, get my stuff, and bring it down the first weekend in November."

"Right," he muttered, his fingers digging lightly into my neck.

He didn't like this.

I didn't like this.

I just *knew* minute by minute wasn't going to work.

"Ben," I said, his name coming out shaky.

His face got a smidgen closer so that he was the only thing I could see.

"You gotta go, baby. You got a job. You got a contract with that lease. You got responsibilities. You gotta go."

I pressed my lips together, feeling the sting in my eyes, the tightness gathering around my heart, because he was right and I didn't know what that meant for us.

I tried us on and we fit. You tried something on that fit and felt great, you bought it. You did not put it back on the rack and move on.

"But Indianapolis isn't the moon," Benny continued. "It's four hours away. We got phones. We got cars. We got somethin' worth workin' on, gettin' past difficult shit, findin' a way. You feel up to it, you give them a start date. I'll take time off, follow you down so you have your car, and I'll have what's bound to be your fifteen suitcases in my SUV."

That made me smile, but my smile, too, was shaky.

Benny carried on, "I'll stay with you a couple of days, make sure you're settled, arrange things to come down again when your furniture gets there, help you move in."

I licked my lips and nodded, feeling the heaviness move out of me and lightness ease in because Benny was making it better.

He kept right on doing that. "You got a new job, a lot to get used to, but somethin' else you gotta do in between me takin' you down there and comin' back is you comin' up to see me."

"Okay," I said softly.

"When are you gonna start?" he asked.

"I, well, would prefer to feel closer to one hundred percent and I still have stuff to pack to get ready for the movers. So, not next week. The, uh, Monday after."

"Right," Ben said, sounding businesslike. "I'll sort shit with Pop and Manny."

I stared at him for a moment before I whispered, "You make all this sound easy."

"That's because this is important to me so I'm determined not to make it hard."

At that, I fell forward so my forehead hit his chest.

When I did, his hands moved. One to wrap around the back of my neck, one slid up into my hair to cup the back of my head.

And into the top of my hair, he murmured, "See, back to minute by minute. Easy."

Easy.

Right.

God, Benny.

"We're startin' out and I got a new job in Indy I cannot leave, a lease on an apartment that pins me there for at least a year anyway, and you've got all this." I threw a hand out to indicate the kitchen, even though I didn't move my forehead from his chest. "Which means you can *never* leave."

"That's not the next minute, Frankie," he reminded me.

I jerked my head back so he was forced to snap his up and his hands were forced to move, and they did, coming to rest just under my jaw.

"We *have* to think about it, Benny," I declared, my voice rising.

"Why?"

"Why?" I repeated but didn't allow him to respond. "Because it's out there, waiting to strike, and we should plan for when it does."

"Why?" he asked again, and I felt my eyes get squinty.

"Because, just like this, even though we knew it was coming, it *came* and now we have to *deal* and we should plan on how we're gonna *deal.*"

"Here's the drama," he muttered, lips moving like he was battling a grin.

Wrong thing to say.

And grinning?

Uh…*no.*

So no, the wax and wane of my freak out waxed, I snapped and shouted, "Benny!"

That was when his face changed, his eyes changed, the bearing of his body changed, *everything* changed, and I pulled in a breath and held it as he stated, "Honest to Christ, Frankie, you think I'd wait since high school to get my shot at makin' you mine and then I'd let a four-hour drive and a fuckin' year lease beat me?"

My breath came out in a whoosh, but this time it was Benny who didn't let me answer.

"No. I won't. Puttin' this out there, Frankie, in the end, Connie was practically livin' with me. That's how I burned her. She thought she was in there. But I woke up to her knowin' I'd come home to a house she cleaned, dinner in the oven, her breakin' her back to make everything easy on me when that's *my* job."

This particular piece of beauty made me suck in a hissed breath.

But he didn't quit talking.

"Was a time I didn't think on shit like that. Back then what I thought was, for some reason, she didn't make me happy. Simple. She just didn't make me happy so I ended it. But the time I didn't think on shit leaked into the dirt of a forest three weeks ago, Frankie. So I thought on it, and havin' you in my house, in my bed the last week, it was about me seein' to your Z. Me makin' sure you got the Wi-Fi to do your shit on your computer. Me listenin' to you bitch when you come back from a walk with old lady Zambino. Doin' it with a gleam in your eye, tellin' me you're bitchin', but you loved every minute she walked with you and busted your chops. So it boils down to this, I don't want easy, Frankie. I had my shot at that. I wanna work at gettin' the sweet, enjoyin' my time with the spicy along the way, 'cause the sweet's a fuckuva lot sweeter when you gotta earn it."

"Ben," I whispered but didn't get out another word because he wasn't done.

"Babe, you cannot plan life. You can pull out all the stops to plan for everything and life will find a way to fuck with those plans, sock you in the gut, send you scrambling. Through that, you either have the balls not to back down and the strength to know what's important and hold the fuck on with everything you got, or you don't have that and you give up 'cause you're weak. Know two things for certain, I'm not fuckin' weak and you aren't either."

He stopped talking and I said nothing because I had no freaking clue what to say.

So he kept going.

"Countin' it down, we've had one date, haven't fucked you yet, and we been livin' with each other for nine days. That time good for you?"

"Yes," I whispered.

"Yeah, it's been good for me too. Good enough I know it's important, and I already *knew* it was important, so I'm gonna hold the fuck on with everything I got and I'm takin' you with me, Frankie."

"Okay," I said quietly.

"So yeah, it's gonna suck," he stated. "I'd rather live a life knowin' you were bringin' your girls into my restaurant to throw back some Chianti and eat one of my pies. I'd rather the immediate future came with you gettin' to know Sela better because Man may be takin' his time, but he's gonna put a ring on her finger. You're already family, which means you're in a spot where you two can become sisters like no other women can be, and your two sisters are seriously fuckin' lacking so you could use a good one. I wanna get into bed beside you at night and know I'm wakin' up to you in the morning. But right now, I can't get what I want. I just know what I want. I've waited for years. I'm not doin' fuckin' cartwheels knowin' I gotta wait more, but I'll *deal*. I just gotta know, are you with me?"

I knew what to say to that.

"Yes, I'm with you, Benny."

He stared at me.

Then he said, "Fuck, gotta stir the sauce."

For some reason, this made me want to giggle, but I beat it back and just nodded.

He bent and gave me a quick, slightly annoyed but still sweet kiss on the forehead, took his hands from me, and went to the pots that were more aptly described as vats on the stove.

He stirred.

I approached, stopping just short of the stove to rest my hip against the stainless steel counter.

"I'm a pain in the ass," I told him, and his eyes cut immediately to me.

"That'd be the part where you aren't easy."

God.

God.

Benny.

I took in a breath and released it, and with it, I released a lot of garbage. Something I was not really good at doing on my own. Garbage I'd lived with because I'd never had anyone to help me deal, which meant I buried a lot of garbage and lived with it for a long freaking time polluting me. And something that Benny seemed remarkably skilled at guiding me into getting clean.

Releasing that, I released everything and was back in the minute with Benny.

Being there, I muttered, "Sauce smells good."

"That's 'cause it's not good, it's fuckin' amazing."

I didn't beat back the giggle at that. I let it loose, and when I did, even more garbage got released, making me feel it.

It wasn't just clean.

It was also the sweet Benny gave me.

I felt it more when, still giggling, his arm shot out and wrapped around my waist. He pulled me his way so my front was tucked to his side and I was watching from close as he stirred the sauce, the sweet, spicy scent enveloping me.

I slid my arms around him and rested my cheek against his chest.

"You good now?" he asked quietly, still stirring the sauce.

"Yeah," I answered, also quietly.

"We got a plan for the next bazillion minutes?" he went on, and I smiled against his chest.

"Yeah."

He kept stirring, even as I felt his lips touch the top of my hair, and he continued stirring and holding me when they were gone.

And I stood in the curve of Benny Bianchi's arm, watching his hand holding a long-handled wooden spoon, moving it through a rich, thick red sauce, with its miniscule bits of cream-colored minced garlic and dark green bits of a secret mix of fresh herbs going round and round, the goodness of it filling the air.

Another promise.

Feeling that, it hit me that I found myself—me, Francesca Concetti, having lived thirty-four years with not a lot of great, fleeting moments of happiness, and never much to look forward to—standing in the kitchen of a pizzeria in the curve of the arm of a handsome, good, decent man, living a life full of promise.

The promise of Benny.

So I pressed closer, held on tighter, and took in a deep breath, letting the goodness in the air get right in there so it could settle in sweet.

And when I did, Ben tucked me even closer, held on, and stirred the sauce.

I should have held on tighter.

I should have let that sweet settle deeper.

I didn't.

Ten

COME BACK TO ME

I felt arms tighten on me and the haze of sleep lifted, slightly.
When it did, I felt my body pressed snug against the hard frame of Benny's, the warmth of our cocoon of covers, and the safety both created.

I tilted my head back, opening my eyes, and I saw Benny.

Half asleep, my belly still did a dip.

As always.

"Hey," he whispered, his morning voice that beautiful mixture of deep, easy, and gruff.

"Hey," I replied.

"How you feelin'?" he asked.

"Good," I answered.

He lifted his head and buried his face in my neck, where he asked, "No, baby, *how you feelin'?*"

At first, still in the haze of sleep, I didn't get it.

Then the way Benny's hands were moving over the material of my nightgown on my back hit me. That wasn't a lazy first-thing-in-the-morning caress.

It was something else entirely.

And if that didn't do it, Ben gliding his tongue the length of my neck to the back of my ear, causing a shiver to glide over my skin, would have done it.

And if *that* didn't do it, Ben shoving his knee between my legs, forcing me to hook my leg over his thigh, would have done it.

Suddenly, a germ of weirdness attached tight, making my stomach clutch and panic grip me because I knew what he wanted. I knew he was done waiting. I knew it was time.

But I'd had one lover and it had been a *long* time. I wanted Ben to have what he wanted the way he wanted, but most of all, I wanted him to love it when he got it.

Not to mention everything was riding on this.

Everything.

Just as suddenly as the panic clutched my belly, when his hand slid over my ass at the same time his teeth nipped the skin at the back of my ear, it released and the shiver took hold, making me tremble in his arms.

"Frankie?" he prompted in my ear.

I turned my head and drew in his scent before I brushed my lips against his neck and whispered, "I'm feelin' good, baby."

Ben ran his nose along my jaw as he dipped his hand under the hem of my nightie and I felt the warmth of it, skin against skin, at the hollow of my back.

His eyes caught mine. "Got an idea about how I can make the next few minutes real fuckin' great, honey."

I hoped it took longer than a few minutes, though I didn't share this.

I said, "Let's see what they can bring."

I saw his eyes smile.

Then mine were closed because his head slanted and he was kissing me.

It was like being back against the wall in my apartment, all hands, mouths, tongue, and need, except I was lying on Benny's bed pressed tight to him, which was a whole lot better.

But as he took from my mouth, he also pushed his hips into mine. I felt something even better and I wanted it even more.

So I slid my hands down his tee, under, up, and in, taking his warmth and strength in through my fingers.

It felt good, good enough to push my hips against his and he liked that. He liked it a whole lot. I knew it when he growled into my mouth, pushed his hips into mine, and rolled me so I was on my back and he was on me.

And even *better.*

"Please, fuck, tell me you can take that," he rumbled against my lips.

"Oh yeah," I breathed against his.

That was all he needed. His mouth took mine and this kiss wasn't a replay of the one against the wall. It was deeper, hotter, *searing.*

God, Benny could kiss.

He would prove he could do other things too when his hand slid up my side, in, and he palmed my breast.

My clit pulsed, my back arched, and I broke the kiss to whisper, "Benny."

He didn't reply. He curled his fingers into the cup of the nightgown and pulled it down, then he palmed my naked breast and the difference was a nuance, but that nuance was astounding.

"Benny." My whisper this time was sharper.

My stomach dropped when Ben slid partially off me, and I opened my eyes to watch his head bend just as his fingers closed around my nipple, rolled, then pulled.

A mew slid up my throat as I felt wet gather between my legs, those legs tangling as best I could get them with Benny's, and his gaze cut back to my face.

At the look on his, his eyes saturated with hungry heat, I held my breath.

He again rolled, then pulled my nipple and my breath came out of me in a soft gust.

He did it again, my eyes went hooded and my hips surged up.

He did it again and I started panting.

"Jesus, baby, am I gonna make you come just teasin' your tit?" he murmured, his voice mildly disbelieving, mildly awed, and totally turned on.

I tried to open my eyes but was not very successful.

Luckily, I was more successful in pulling my hands out of his shirt, then sliding them up his back and into his hair. I put pressure on and learned Ben didn't need words.

I knew it when his mouth touched mine, where he said, "All right, Frankie, anything you need."

Oh, I needed it all right, and Benny was as good as his word because he immediately trailed his mouth down my neck, my chest, it closed over my nipple, and he drew it in.

Deep.

A moan slid out of my throat, my fingers tightened against his scalp, and he drew deeper. Then he rolled my nipple with his tongue, before he muttered against it, "Fuck yeah," then down went the other cup of my nightgown and Benny moved to it.

I was arching into him, winding my leg around his thigh, clutching my fingers in his thick hair, my stomach muscles tightening with anticipatory glee as his hand drifted over it, his destination one I wanted him to get to, and fast, when we both froze solid as we heard Theresa shouting from downstairs, "Benny! Frankie! You here?"

I didn't move a muscle, but Ben did. Lifting his head and twisting his neck, he aimed his gaze at the door. I didn't have a full view of his face, not even close, but what I saw of it was the heat of desire battling with the heat of fury.

"Ben! Francesca! Are you here?" Theresa shouted from closer. She had to be on the stairs.

That was when Ben moved.

Yanking up the cups of my nightgown while grinding out, "You gotta be fuckin' shittin' me." He looked to me and clipped, "Do not move." After that, he rolled from the bed, found his feet, and prowled out the door, slamming it behind him.

I lay in the bed, still frozen, staring at the closed door.

I heard Ben bite out, "Jesus, Ma, seriously?" and it bolted through me. Vicious. Hateful. Destructive.

Panic. Desperation.

Sheer terror.

It was irrational. I knew it. But even knowing it, I was powerless to beat it.

It forced me to roll off the bed, run to the closet, and pull out one of the four suitcases I had at Benny's.

I then ran to the bathroom. Hearing the murmurs but not listening, I opened the suitcase on the floor and took everything that was mine that I could see. I dumped it in, not even looking if it made it where it was supposed to go.

I opened the drawer Benny gave me and emptied it.

I then dashed to the shower and threw open the door, stepping in. I accidentally grabbed Ben's shampoo and instantly thrust it back in the recessed shelf, as if touching it burned me.

I snatched up my shampoo, my conditioner, then turned and went completely still when the bathroom I'd been using for over a week came into my consciousness with a clarity that was frightening.

His house was old. Old enough I knew that bathroom as new.

I also knew that Ben was not the kind of man who hired people to put in his bathroom.

He did it.

And he did it with a variety of things on his mind.

Big shower cubicle, big enough for two, all glass except the tiled walls. They were a white matte that was very attractive but not with a bent to personal taste. They were the kind of tile a number of people would like having.

Resale.

Resale in preparation for trading up, going bigger, building a home for your growing family.

My breath went ragged.

Separate tub, big, deep, oval, with just this side of an extravagant faucet with a handheld shower attachment sitting on top.

The kind of tub a woman who liked to take baths could fill with bubbles and sink into to melt away the cares of the day.

Ben didn't take baths. No way. I didn't know this as fact from experience, just as I knew it as fact.

Double basin. Two medicine cabinets. Room between the sinks so you'd never get crowded. Full, well-made cabinets underneath. Plenty of space for makeup, toiletries, first aid supplies, ibuprofen—whatever you needed, but far more space than a man would need.

Shelves built into the wall so you could display nice towels, if you wanted. Or put bathroom-style knickknacks, if that was your thing.

It wasn't Benny's thing. Towels that could use replacing were shoved in with only a passing try at folding them. Nothing else.

He'd put in that bathroom for the woman he would find to put into that house.

And he'd put in that bathroom with a mind to the buyers who would eventually take that house off his hands when the rest of the bedrooms were filled with babies.

Benny Bianchi didn't do minute by minute.

Benny Bianchi had it all planned.

I came unstuck and, in a panic, moved out of the shower when I heard Benny say in the bedroom, "Had a word. Ma's...Frankie?"

I said nothing. I dumped the bottles in the suitcase and they made a thud.

"Babe, she's gone and she won't..."

The words were closer and I knew why. I also knew why he trailed off.

Because he was in the doorway.

"Frankie, what the fuck?"

"I gotta go," I mumbled, bending double, ass in the air, fingers curling around the edge of my suitcase to drag it out of the room.

I felt hands curl around my hips and I snapped upright, whirling and tripping when I took two steps back.

My eyes hit Ben's face and it was no less expressive than always. Concern. Confusion.

"Careful, baby," he said softly.

"I gotta go," I replied.

"Something happened," he noted, his voice still soft. Soft, deep, and easy.

Killing me.

"I gotta go."

"What happened, honey?"

"I gotta go."

"What happened, Frankie?"

Everything I was holding together for the last nine days, the last seven years, the last thirty-four, came flying apart. I leaned in and shrieked, "*I gotta go, Benny!*"

He flinched at my tone but didn't move, and his voice was no less soft when he said, "Talk to me, *tesorina*."

"I can't do this," I declared.

"Why?" he asked carefully.

"I don't wanna lose you."

More confusion slid through his features. He glanced back into the bedroom, eyes aimed at his bed, then he looked to me.

"How does what we were doin' translate to you losin' me?"

I ignored that question and started babbling. "I lost you. I lost Vinnie and I did something stupid and I lost you. I can't lose you again. Not you. Not Theresa. Not Vinnie Senior. Not Manny. I can't do this because I can't lose you."

"Honey, we're not goin' anywhere."

"You could," I returned.

"We're not," he shot back.

"You could, though," I snapped. "This could go bad." I lifted a hand and jerked it back and forth with agitation, indicating him and me. "This could go bad and I'd lose you all again."

"It's not gonna go bad, Frankie."

"Promise?"

It wasn't a plea.

It was a dare.

And Benny was too good. Too honest. Too decent. Too *awesome* to make a promise he couldn't keep.

But he was also too Benny, so he was gentle and cautious when he replied slowly, "I can't tell the future, baby."

I shook my head in short, frantic shakes. "No. You can't. I can't either. And I can't take the risk. I got shot and that was good. It was good, Benny," I repeated when his face grew dark. "It brought all of you back to me. And I know what you want. It burns, it *kills*, because I like what you want. I want to give it to you. I want to have it for me. But I can't risk losing *more*. We have to go back to the way we were before. You can't promise me this won't go bad, but you *can* promise me we can keep *that* kind of good."

"The way we were before?" he asked.

"You, me, friends, family."

I felt it slice clean into my heart, the new look on his face when he whispered, "You wanna be friends?"

But I didn't delay in whispering back, this time definitely a plea, "Please give me that, Benny."

He studied me for a moment, his expression beyond unhappy, and I let him, my chest rising and falling rapidly, my bleeding heart still finding a way to beat hard.

Then he said, "There's somethin' not right here, Frankie, and we gotta get to the bottom of that."

He was right.

And that was not happening.

"Benny—" I started, but he cut me off.

"If you can't do that yourself, you gotta let me in there so I can dig whatever is eatin' at you out of you, baby."

"I'm falling in love with you."

Everything went still.

Silent and still.

Benny. Me. The air around us.

Dead still.

Then Ben wasn't still. His expression changed again and he gave me beauty—pure, undiluted beauty—as his face warmed, his eyes went sweet, and he took a step toward me.

My hand shot up and I shouted, "Don't come near me!"

"Baby, you lost a man and you—"

"No!" I yelled. "You think you understand but you don't. It isn't about losing Vinnie. It isn't about me not bein' strong enough to try again. It's about *you*. It's about the man who would come over to my house and shoot the shit with me, teasin' me and makin' me laugh while he ate my Christmas cookies. It's about findin' you and snuggling close for a Christmas picture, feelin' warm and safe, family all around me. This could be good, what we could have—amazing, awesome, *the best*. And it could go bad. And then all that's gone for me. You're all I have. You're all I ever had. And when I say that, I mean you and I mean your family."

"You gotta have it in you to try," he returned.

I shook my head. "Don't you get it, Ben? I don't have *anything* in me."

His look turned cautious when he said quietly, "I don't get that, honey."

"If you don't, you haven't been paying very close attention."

His back shot straight. "There's a lot to you, Francesca."

"There's nothing to me, Benny."

He held my eyes, a firmness entering his jaw that was more than a little scary, and he said slowly, "You are very wrong."

"Yeah?" I fired back. "You think that? Okay, then what happens when the day comes you find out I'm right?"

He continued to hold my eyes, staring into them with a focus that felt like he was unraveling me. Then he took a visible breath, lifted his hand, schooled his features, and urged, "We need to calm down and talk about this somewhere not in the bathroom."

"I need to go."

"That's the last thing you need."

On his words, it happened, so I guess he did unravel me.

Tears hit my eyes so fast, I had no hope of choking them back.

But they were the silent ones. The ones that said it all without a lot of sobbing and moaning. The ones that came from that well you held deep and only came out when the something you were crying about meant everything.

"I want you always to think the way you think about me now, Benny," I told him quietly.

"Why would you ever think I'd think differently, honey?" he asked me, also quietly.

"Because I'm me."

"Baby, we need to get outta this fuckin' bathroom and—"

He shut up when I begged, "Please let me go."

"You cannot seriously be askin' me to do that."

"Please, Ben, let me go."

"And you cannot seriously think I'm gonna say yes."

The tears kept coming, but I said nothing.

Ben did. "Come here, Frankie."

God.

Benny.

The tears came faster.

"Baby, come here."

"I want you to have the woman who deserves this bathroom, Benny."

At my words, something hit him. His look turned ravaged and it was difficult to witness as he whispered, "Jesus, come here."

"I want you to have what you deserve, honey, and it's not me."

"Fuck it, I'm—" he gritted out as he made a move to me.

I took another step back, jerked my hand at him, and shook my head. "I'm leaving, Benny. And, honest to God, I'll fight you if you don't let me."

He stopped dead and looked into my eyes.

I felt the last tear fall as I held his gaze.

We stared at each other a long time.

Benny broke it.

"Don't do this to us."

"I do, don't hate me."

"Don't do this, Frankie."

"If I do, be pissed. Then come back. I need you to come back to me, Benny."

"You do this to us, not gonna be able to get to that place, Frankie."

I felt saliva fill my mouth at that possibility, but I swallowed it down and nodded.

"You okay with that?" he asked, his face a mask of wounded incredulity.

I was not. I was absolutely not okay with that.

But it was better to take the cut, make it surgical, move on, and carry on living without Benny and his family as I'd learned to be able to do before but do it far away, where people's talk and my own memories couldn't make it torture for me.

"I'm guessin' I'm gonna have to be," I answered.

I watched in horror and an extraordinary amount of pain as his body went rigid, along with every muscle in his face.

Then he came at me so fast, I didn't have a chance to move a muscle and found my head held in his hands, his face an inch from mine.

"You need this, I'll give it to you. You need to come back, this is a promise I *can* keep, Frankie, I will not make you work for it." He moved in even closer and whispered, "But please, fuck, take this time to dig out whatever is fucked to shit inside you. And if you find you can't, I don't give a fuck. I'll do the diggin'. Just *come back to me.*"

He finished that, pulled me up, slammed his mouth down on mine, and kissed me hard and closed mouthed.

A kiss that was like a brand.

A kiss that was definitely a promise.

A kiss that hurt because of the feelings it beat into me.

And a kiss that lasted not nearly long enough before Ben let me go, turned, and walked away from me.

Eleven

THE BIRDS HAD A MERRY CHRISTMAS

Benny came in his back door, shook the cold off, as well as the snow, and dumped his workout bag on the kitchen table, tossing his keys there next.

He had to get showered, dressed, and to the restaurant. He turned on his way to do that when his cell in his bag rang.

He turned back, zipped open his bag, dug it out, and looked at the screen.

He took the call and put it to his ear, moving back to the door, greeting, "Hey, Ma."

"Hey there, Benny. You remember Carm, Ken, and the kids are flyin' in tomorrow?"

He jogged up the stairs, saying, "I remember, Ma."

"Dinner tomorrow night at the pizzeria. Manny knows to have the table ready."

"Yeah."

"Be sure to find time to come out and say hi, yes?"

He gritted his teeth as he walked down the hall, wondering why his mother would think in a million years he'd forget his sister, who he hadn't seen in over a year, was flying in with her entire family to be there for a week over Christmas and he wouldn't come out when they were at the restaurant and say hi.

But he didn't ask her that question.

He said, "I'll be sure."

"You sure you won't sleep on the couch Christmas Eve?"

He walked into the bathroom and straight to the shower to turn it on and get it hot, so when he was done with this ridiculous call, he could waste no time getting ready.

"I live ten minutes away from you," he reminded her. "I can come first thing in the morning and not have to sleep on your couch."

"Kids get up early on Christmas Day," she snapped.

"Then I'll get up and come over early," he returned.

"They get up *really* early."

"Then I'll come over *really* early."

"Benny—"

"Ma," he cut her off. "We've had this conversation." He paused for emphasis. "*Twice.* I'm not sleepin' on the couch. I don't get there at the crack of dawn when Carm's kids get up and go ballistic, I'll be there five minutes after the crack of dawn, yeah?"

He heard her sigh before she said, "All right, Benny."

"Now, I just got back from the gym. Gotta shower and get to the restaurant."

"Okay, *caro*, see you tomorrow night."

"Right."

"Bye, Benny."

"Later, Ma."

He disconnected, tossed the phone on the sink, took off his clothes, dropped them to the floor, and stepped in the shower.

Ten minutes later, hair wet, tee, jeans, and boots on, he was downstairs at his hall closet, reaching in to yank out his leather jacket, when the doorbell rang.

He took in an annoyed breath and moved to the door, seeing his neighbor Tony standing outside.

He unlocked it, opened it, and saw Tony had a brown paper-wrapped box.

"Postman came, bud. Left this with me," Tony said, holding the box out to Benny.

Ben took it and muttered, "Thanks, man."

"Not a problem," Tony replied, then lifted a hand and mumbled, "Later," before he jogged down the steps and made his way next door to his own house.

Benny closed the door, locked it, turned, and was moving back down the hall when he looked at the box, saw the postmark, and stopped dead.

Indianapolis.

"Fuck," he whispered, forcing himself to come unstuck and move back to the closet.

Juggling the box, he grabbed his coat, closed the door, and headed to the kitchen, thinking whatever it was could be from Vi. She, Cal, and the kids were in Florida, but she could have sent it before she left. And it was something a woman like Vi would do, sending a Christmas gift to a guy who would not send any in return, even a card.

But if it was from Vi, it would not be postmarked Indy unless she was in the city doing errands and happened by a post office, which was unlikely.

So he knew who it was from.

And he knew he should at the very least set it aside, but the better choice was dump it in the trash.

He did not do either.

He should have picked one, most definitely the last one.

Instead, he opened the fucker and pulled out a square tin decorated in a red, green, and gold Christmas plaid. It had a small card attached to the top with a circular gold foil sticker.

It said, *Benny.*

He set the tin down, ripped the card off, and opened it, sliding out a Christmas card with a snowman on it, decorated in way too much fucking glitter, with the words HAPPY HOLIDAYS! printed on it.

He opened it.

Inside it said, *Merry Christmas, Benny. Enjoy and have a happy one. Love, Frankie.*

He clenched his teeth, and that was when he should have taken the tin and card to the trash.

He didn't.

He opened the tin and the sweet, nutty smell of doughy goodness wafted out as he saw a massive mound of Frankie's chocolate-filled, powdered-sugar-rolled Christmas cookies sitting in it.

Fuck. The thing came through the mail, and still, there was a hint of condensation on the lid, which meant she'd packed them warm and sent them immediately.

He stared at the cookies, remembering one more time, in a line of way too much remembering, that she was trying.

She had a game going where she phoned when she knew he wouldn't answer, primarily when he was at the restaurant, and her voicemail would say, "Just checkin' in. Oh, it's Frankie," like he didn't have caller ID or wouldn't know her voice in the dark with a dozen other voices yammering at him, this happening fifteen years from now.

Or she'd say, "Just callin' to let you know things are good. Like my job. Thinkin' of gettin' a dog. Hope you're good. If you want, call me."

Or she'd say, "Hey, Ben. Thought of you, had a minute, thought I'd call. You wanna chat, you know my number."

He didn't fucking call.

Nearly three months ago, he'd walked out of his bathroom, put on a tee, jeans, and boots, and walked out of his house. When he came home, it was empty.

No Frankie.

She didn't come back.

She phoned.

But she left his house, left town…and she didn't come back.

She wanted him in her life.

She wanted to be friends.

She wanted to stay in her fucked-up world with her fucked-up head making fucked-up decisions and living a fucked-up life.

And she could stay there.

He didn't need that shit.

He stared at the cookies, thinking he also sure as fuck didn't need her cookies.

But he kept staring at them.

I'm falling in love with you.

Those words assaulted his brain one more time, in a line of way too much remembering, and it was one time too many.

Twisting his torso, with a brutal arm slice, he sent the tin sailing across the room. It slammed with a loud metallic sound against the wall and cookies flew everywhere, landing and exploding in powdered-sugar puffs, the dough breaking and crumbling, exposing chocolate kisses.

Ben didn't look at it.

He shrugged on his jacket, nabbed his keys, and his boots crunched into the cookies as he walked out the door.

The next day, he swept that shit out his back door, sending it flying down the stoop and into his yard.

He threw the tin right in his bin at the back of the house, along with the card.

And the birds had a Merry Christmas.

Twelve

HEALING THE BREACH

I paced my hotel room, phone in hand, biting my lip, freaking out, not knowing what to do.

I knew what I *wanted* to do.

But I didn't know what I *should* do.

It was early March and I was in Chicago on a business trip.

My business done, I was in my hotel room, pre-going out to dinner by myself, but it was the dinner hour.

Benny would be working.

I'd quit phoning him in January. I did this because he'd never called back.

I tried to keep him. He just wouldn't let me.

That was his play and I had no choice but to give it to him. I'd burned him badly. I did it because I was fucked up and had no idea how to get unfucked up. I just knew I didn't want Benny to put up with my fucked-upped-ness, even if I couldn't convince him he didn't need any part of that.

I knew I'd made the right decision, but it hurt. It hurt not to have him that way, or *any* way, and it hurt to hurt him, but it was still right.

This time, I didn't lose the rest of them. Theresa phoned and gabbed at me like I was still living with Benny and all was well. She never even mentioned it.

This was big-time shocking. I thought she was far more of a meddler than that, not to mention I knew from experience she could hold a mean grudge. But she didn't breathe a word. She did say that Vinnie Senior said hi, or that he told her to tell me I needed to get back to Chicago and come by for dinner. So I knew Vinnie Senior was moving on without holding a grudge too, just doing it through Theresa.

Manny was a guy so he didn't expend a lot of effort to keep in touch, but Sela did, thus, I knew Man wasn't pissed at me. No way Sela would keep in touch if Manny was angry at me. Since she did, I knew that Manny gave her an engagement ring on Valentine's Day. I also knew she said yes. And direct from Theresa, I knew she (that "she" referring to Sela, as well as Theresa) was ecstatic. It was going to be a full mass, I was going to be invited, and Theresa was planning on wearing a hat to the wedding.

This seemed weird to me, the rift cracking right back open between Benny and me and his family ignoring the breach.

But it was working. I loved having them back, so I wasn't asking, nor was I complaining.

What I was doing was pacing, doing it knowing I shouldn't make the call. Ben was pissed. I shouldn't push him. I should let him stay pissed until he found a good woman, claimed her, built a home and family, and finally came to realize I did him a favor.

I turned my mind swiftly from that train of thought. Even knowing I was right, I couldn't go there. When he found her, I'd find it in me to let him back in when he allowed it. I'd find a way to like her, even though I'd hate it. I'd find a way to take him the limited way he could give himself to me.

I'd find a way.

Which meant I should leave things be.

I knew it.

Still, I stopped pacing, bent my head, and lifted my phone. My thumb flew over the screen fast in order that my brain wouldn't catch up and stop me.

I saw his name.

One last touch and I'd made the call.

I should disconnect.

I didn't.

I put the phone to my ear.

I listened to it ring and closed my eyes.

I kept them closed when I heard his deep, easy voice saying the only words I'd heard him say the last five months: "Ben's voicemail, leave a message."

I heard the beep, opened my eyes, and starting blathering.

"Ben? Frankie. Listen, I know it's been a while since I've called, but I'm in Chicago. Staying at The Belvedere. Business. But, uh…business is done for the day and I'm about to go out to dinner." I sucked in breath and kept rambling. "I thought, maybe…well, I don't think you would, but I still thought I'd call…see if you wanted to meet for a drink. We can talk. I don't know, maybe work things out. I know you're at work but after. I'll wait. I'll be in the bar at the hotel. If you wanna drop by, drinks are on me."

Drinks are on me?

Oh God, I shouldn't have made the call.

It was time to wind it up.

"That's, well…it." I closed my eyes and stupidly whispered, "I hope you come, Benny."

I hit the button to disconnect and wished I'd never connected. I also wished I could erase the message. I further wished I could rewind my life back to high school and put out so at least I'd have a week or two of dating Benny.

But I couldn't do any of that so I did what I could do.

I went to dinner alone.

Then I went to the bar at the hotel and had a drink. One drink turned into two, then three. Closing in on midnight, plenty of time after the pizzeria shut down for Ben to get to me, I left the circling men who'd either tried to come on to me or who'd drank and tried to get up the courage to come on to me—easy target, lone woman in a hotel bar, drinking.

I went up to my room and kept my phone close.

An hour slid by before I gave up.

I put on my nightie, brushed my teeth, washed my face, moisturized, slid into bed, and turned out the lights.

I rolled to my side and settled in.

When I felt the single tear hit the side of the bridge of my nose and slide down, falling off and salting my lip, I touched my tongue to it. Then I reached out, hugged the unused pillow to me, and closed my eyes. It took a while, a long while, longer than normal, but I guessed you eventually got used to your heart perpetually breaking.

So eventually I found sleep.

I jolted awake when I heard a loud knock on the door.

I lifted up to a forearm in the dark, blinked away residual sleep, and the knocking stopped.

I listened.

Nothing.

Did I dream it?

The answer came when the knocking resumed—three firm, loud pounds.

I twisted, switched on the bedside lamp, and threw off the covers. I got to my feet and moved quickly to the door.

I looked out the peephole and stopped breathing.

Ben, head bent, and from what I could tell, both hands up. He was leaning into them, resting on the door.

This killed me. The man could be hot just leaning.

As I watched, he pulled back, then I jumped back when three more pounds came at the door.

Without thinking, not knowing what time it was, not considering the fact I was wearing nothing but a lilac nightie that was made of near-sheer, stretchy material in the body, had cups made of delicate, rosy-pink lace, the same lace skimming the just-over-the-booty hem, I unlatched the door and threw it open.

Ben's head jerked when I did and I remembered to breathe, only to suck in more and stop doing it again.

We stared at each other.

It was me who pulled it together first, and this was only enough to say, "Benny."

That unlocked his frame and he pushed in, through me, forcing me back two steps. I took two more when he grabbed the door, threw it closed, and flipped the security latch closed.

Oh God, I wasn't sure how to take that.

On a new kind of rocky ground with Benny, tentatively I greeted, "Hey."

His eyes narrowed in a scary way when he asked, "Seriously?"

I pressed my lips together.

I unpressed them when his entire face went scary, this being when his eyes did a slow scan of me in my nightie.

"How did you know my room number?"

His eyes cut back to mine. "Brett Rizzoli is night shift maintenance. I called him. He got it for me."

I was surprised Brett Rizzoli had a job, seeing as he spent his high school years, and a number after them, on a mission of scoring the best weed in order to smoke it.

"What time is it?" I asked.

"Late," Ben answered.

"Ben—"

He cut me off with, "Serious as fuck, Frankie...*cookies*?"

I snapped my mouth shut because I knew what he was talking about and my what-I'd-hoped-would-be-thoughtful gesture didn't seem so thoughtful anymore. It seemed stupid, even callous.

"You're pissed," I noted inanely.

"Uh, *yeah*," he agreed sarcastically.

"I'm sorry," I whispered.

"You didn't come back to me," he clipped.

I clenched my teeth.

"Waited, Francesca. You didn't fuckin' come back to me. Then you send me fuckin' *cookies*?"

I felt my heart hammering in my chest as I stared at Benny.

Pissed off, small drops of wet in his hair, which told me it was raining or snowing, more wet on his leather jacket, tall, built...*beautiful*.

Benny.

Taking in all that was him, feeling his angry vibe filling the air and pressing into me, there was no thought. There was nothing.

There was only action.

And that action was me rushing the four feet that separated us and throwing myself in Benny's arms.

The next action was to drive my fingers into his hair, tilt his head down, then me going up on my toes so I could slam his mouth on mine.

And the next was me touching my tongue to his lips.

The next actions were all Benny's.

I was up, legs around his hips, his hands at my ass and his tongue in my mouth. He was walking and turning. Then we were down, Ben sitting on the end of the bed, me straddling him.

We did all this kissing, tongues sparring, heads shifting one way and then back, both of us drinking deep, hard, wet, *desperate*.

His hands went up my nightie and straight down into my panties.

God, they felt good there.

I whimpered into his mouth but didn't break the connection as I moved my hands to his jacket and shoved it down his shoulders.

I lost his touch when he tore off his jacket. I vaguely heard it land on the floor with a soft *flunf*, and this was vague because most of my attention was centered on his hands back in my panties.

As much as I liked having them back, I wanted more.

I pulled his tee up at the back, breaking the kiss to demand, "Shirt off, baby."

I no sooner had the words out when Ben's hands went to the hem of the tee. He tore it up and it was gone.

I saw bare chest and shoulders, and it was an amazing chest and shoulders, then I saw nothing as Benny shoved his fingers into my hair, tilted my head down, and took my mouth with his.

Finding myself in the miraculous position of being wrapped around a shirtless Ben who was kissing me, I didn't waste the opportunity. I rolled my hips into his hard crotch, running my hand down his chest, down his abs, liking what it encountered a whole lot, but I had a premier destination in mind. I twisted my hand, flattened it, and rubbed it hard over his jeans.

"*Fuck*," he groaned in my mouth.

"Now," I whispered into his.

His brows shot up over dark, heated eyes. "Now?"

I pressed my hand deep. "Now, baby."

He said not another word. He shifted slightly to the side and I went for his belt. He had his wallet open while I undid the buttons on his jeans. I caught a glimpse of the fact that Benny Bianchi didn't carry a condom with him, he carried a string of three, but I didn't let that penetrate. I had a mission, and that mission was pressing my hand into his boxers and finally getting what I'd been craving for far too long.

It wasn't difficult to find. It was big. It was hard. And it was all mine.

I pulled his cock free of his jeans and found it was also beautiful.

I stroked.

Ben growled.

His noise made my hips jerk and my eyes went to his.

"Hurry," I begged.

"Gotta unlatch, baby," he whispered.

I didn't want to, but I unlatched.

Ben had the condom out already (thank God) and rolled it on while I watched, squirming in his lap.

He barely had it to the base before I shoved his hand away and grabbed on. I used the fingers of my other hand to shift my undies aside, then took the tip of his cock and rocked my hips against it, sliding it against me.

Ben's hands came to my hips, fingers digging in, and he rumbled, "Fuckin' hell, baby."

I looked into his eyes. "I want it, Benny."

He looked into my eyes. "Then take it, Frankie."

I rammed down, filling myself with Benny.

Oh God.

Perfect.

When I took him, Ben's hands dragged up, fingers digging deep into my flesh, pulling my nightie up my back.

But he didn't take it off. This was because I was riding him and doing it fast, hard, driving down, grinding, and I had to hold on to stay steady. He shoved one hand up through my nightgown, cupped the back of my head, and pulled it down so he could have my mouth.

I gave it to him, letting Benny take my mouth in a brutal, devouring kiss while I took his cock.

I felt his other hand slide around, in, and down, then his thumb was at my clit.

He put on pressure and rolled.

Benny inside me, Benny all around me. Almost eight years without any goodness but what I could give myself, now finally having it and it being Benny. The instant his thumb rolled, my head shot back and I cried out, sharp and hard, as my orgasm powered through me.

Still coming, Ben pulled me off him, flipped me to my back, ripped my panties down my legs, hauled me up the bed, covered me, and drilled back inside.

"Yes," I breathed, still climaxing.

Ben thrust, his hips tilted to the side, his hand gliding over my ass, down the back of my thigh to lift one knee high.

"Yes," I repeated on a gasp, opening my eyes to see him up on a forearm, pounding in, staring down at me.

"Crazy-beautiful," he whispered.

Oh God.

Benny.

I had one arm trapped under his body, so I curled the forearm around his lower back and held him as best as I could while I lifted my other hand and trailed it down the new, unfamiliar, but awesomely fabulous ridges and flats of his chest and abs.

I lifted my hips so he could get more, I could get more, and he thrust in, started grinding, and bit out, "Fuck yeah, Frankie."

"What do you need?" I whispered.

"Got it," he grunted.

God.

My Benny.

I wrapped the leg he had mostly pinned to the bed with his weight around his thigh and moved my hips in tandem with his, letting my fingers drift over the definition of his abs, looking into his eyes, feeling the glory of Benny Bianchi repeatedly filling me.

He yanked up my leg, powered so deep, it felt like he touched my womb. My neck arched and I breathed, "That's it, baby, fuck me."

At that, he threw my leg around his back, his hand gliding up the front of my thigh, my side, in, it rubbed hard over the material covering my breast, the drag over my tightened nipple forcing a moan to glide out of my throat. Then his hand moved down and his thumb was again at my clit.

My head righted and I moaned, "That's it, Benny."

"It fuckin' is. Get there, Frankie," he growled.

Our hips moved, Ben pressed and rolled, then pressed deeper and rolled harder as his hips rammed into mine and my breath caught.

"Benny."

"Close, *cara*, get there," he groaned.

Too late.

I was there. Digging my fingers into his back, clutching him with my legs, my other hand shooting up to curl around the side of his neck and hold tight, my back arched off the bed and it again shot through me.

I felt Ben thrust deep through it, his thumb moving from my clit to clamp around the back of my thigh. I just had it together enough to open my eyes when he started bucking, his breaths coming rhythmic and harsh. When I did, I saw his head dipped down and felt his hand gripping my thigh tight, the harsh breaths turning into the hard grunts of his release.

His bucking slowed, gentled, until he slid in, released my thigh, lifted his head, caught my eyes, and lowered his body to mine.

"Well, uh…how's that for healing the breach?"

That came from me. Right out of my mouth. I heard it and I couldn't believe it.

Benny couldn't either. I knew this when he blinked. Then he stared.

Then his head went back and he burst out laughing.

It was at this inopportune moment that all that I'd just done hit me in the way of the sane, rational person I wanted always to be (but rarely was) rather than the insane, crazy slut I'd just acted like, which seemed to happen a lot around Benny.

I knew Ben felt the tightness that came into my body because his head snapped back down, and when his eyes caught mine, there was zero humor in them.

"Oh no, *cara*, *fuck* no," he growled. "You are not pullin' away from me now and not just 'cause I got you pinned to the bed with my dick still hard inside you."

"I threw myself at you again," I whispered, sounding horrified, and my voice started rising when I finished, "This time *literally*."

"Yeah, you did, thank fuck."

It was me who blinked that time before I asked, "You're not mad?"

His head jerked, his eyes narrowed, and his voice was disbelieving. "Babe, been wantin' to be right here," he ground his hips into mine and my legs tensed around him when he did, "for a long fuckin' time. I'm here," he pressed in between my legs again, "and I like it. Why the fuck would I be mad?"

I didn't want to bring it up, but I couldn't get around the fact that I had to bring it up, and the only way I could think in that moment to communicate it was to say softly, "Cookies."

I knew Ben didn't want me to bring it up either when the dark, scary look passed over his face.

"That was a fucked-up play, Frankie," he said quietly.

He said it quietly.

He didn't get mean. He didn't get pissed. He didn't get sarcastic.

He pointed it out and did it quietly.

God, my Benny.

"I didn't want to lose you," I told him.

"Well, just sayin', the way not to do that was the play you made fifteen minutes ago. Though, for future reference, I got your ass to tap in my bed, in my kitchen you can make all the cookies you want."

Even though I knew I was on rocky ground, I couldn't help it. At his words, automatically, I screwed my eyes up and glared at him. "My ass to tap?"

The dark, scary look left and the light of humor came back when he said, "Yeah. You're there for me to eat and fuck whenever I want, I'm not gonna be pissed you're makin' me cookies."

My stomach dipped at the thought of Benny going down on me (much less fucking me again).

However, that was not what I shared.

"I can now officially report that women do not like it when men talk like that, Ben."

He moved his face close and whispered, "Then why, when I said it, did your pussy clench tight around my dick?"

I was pretty sure it did that, and I was pretty sure because, along with the belly dip, I felt other more pleasant sensations elsewhere.

As much as I enjoyed bantering with Benny, enjoyed it even more in our current position—Benny heavy and warm on me after having sex with him for the first time, sex that included two orgasms—this was not the time to banter.

This was the time to freak out.

And being me, I commenced in doing that.

"Ben, I'm not sure what we just did was smart."

His expression turned guarded and he asked, "Why?"

"Well, I'm pretty certain you didn't miss this, considering the drama I perpetrated in your bathroom five months ago with you in attendance, but I'm kind of fucked up."

"No, babe, I didn't miss it," he replied immediately but did it softly. "But you missed something. Something really fuckin' important."

I was fucked up so I had a strong idea that I missed a lot of things that were really fucking important.

At that moment, however, I needed to know which one he was referring to.

"What'd I miss?" I asked.

"The part about how I don't want easy."

My stomach clutched, my limbs clenched around him, and I stared up into his eyes.

"You walked away from me, shut me out and walked out of my house, and that was not cool," he said quietly. "But I'm sensin' you needed to do that, and my sense is right because you did it, knowin' you'd fuck me and knowin' you'd fuck *you* doin' it."

I pressed my lips together, partly because there was no response to that, but mostly because he told me I'd fucked him, not in the good way, and I hated that I'd hurt him.

But he was right. I did it knowing I was doing it. To him and to me.

"And, Frankie," he went on, "you did that and you did other shit since, but you do not want to be my friend. You have not been phonin' me and makin' me cookies because you want me in your life like that. You've been phonin' me and making me cookies because you want me in your life like *this*."

He emphasized his last words by, again, pressing his hips into mine, as well as momentarily giving me more of his body weight.

"I do. I told you that," I reminded him. "I also told you I'm not right for you."

"Babe, how about you let me decide what's right for me," Benny stated.

At that, I blinked again.

Ben kept talking.

"Seein' as you're fucked up, I suppose you can take what just happened between us, what you just gave me, what you just threw at me, *literally*, and twist it or deny it or bury it so that you can walk away from it, even though it was unbelievably fuckin' hot and proves not only that we both want this, we're really fuckin' good at it."

He could say that again.

"I'm just gonna tell you now," he continued. "I let you have that play five months ago because I was hopin' you'd get your head straight and come back to me. I'm takin' this," he again gave me more of his weight before he took it away, "as you comin' back to me. Now, what you gotta get is that I will not allow you to walk away from me again."

My breath started to come faster as I lay under him and stared up into his eyes.

Ben kept going.

"I'll make that clear. When I say I won't allow that to happen, I'm not talkin' about me not lettin' go again. Right now, Francesca, you gotta decide. Are we gonna work this out and see where this can go? Or is this a fucked-up play you instigated with zero control and you have every intention of carryin' on with that, jackin' me around, you're cognizant of doin' that or not, but you got no intention of puttin' in the work to sort yourself out, sort *us* out, and give us a shot?"

Pure Benny, not beating around the bush *or* wasting any time.

My chest was working hard at allowing me to breathe as my heart beat fast in my chest. Both of these, coupled with the fear coursing through my system, didn't allow me to reply.

When I didn't, Benny's hand found mine. He laced our fingers and pulled our hands up to press them against the side of his chest, saying softly, "Baby, simple yes or no. With what we just shared, you meant to share it with me or not, did you come back to me?"

"Yes."

It was one word, one syllable, it sounded strangled and just as terrified as I felt.

Terrified for me and terrified of what I might eventually do to Benny.

That one word was selfish. It wasn't right.

But it was true.

At my word, clearly not knowing all my thoughts, Ben closed his eyes as relief swept through his features, then he dropped his forehead to mine.

I closed mine too.

God, I hoped I hadn't just fucked up huge.

I opened my eyes when he lifted a breath away and, again, looked at me.

"How long you in Chicago?"

"I have more meetings tomorrow with docs, introducing them to me, as well as a new member of my team who's three years older than me—a guy who has been in the pharmaceutical business for ten years when I've been in it for five months. So tomorrow I'll also be furthering my endeavors to convince him I know what I'm doing and he has to respect that 'cause I'm his boss. I leave the day after."

"The day after is a Friday."

"Yeah."

"So you don't leave on Friday. You leave on Sunday. Tomorrow mornin', you pack your shit, and when I go home, I'll take it with me. You're done with your meetings and convincing this asshole he's gotta respect you, you come to me."

I go to him.

That didn't make me feel terrified.

That made me feel warm and safe and happy.

But *that* made me feel terrified.

"You with me?" Ben prompted when I didn't say anything.

"Yeah, Benny," I whispered.

"While you're here, we'll talk, we'll fuck, we'll sort things out and make a plan. And, heads up, Frankie, we'll be fuckin' a lot 'cause I only had you once, but we clearly already got that down. And my guess is, we fuck enough, shit will sort itself out."

"That *would* be your guess," I mumbled, and he grinned.

"One good thing about the five-month lag, baby. You're fully recovered so I didn't have to hold back and could ride you hard. Better, *you* could ride *me* and do it *really* hard."

Another belly dip, which, in turn, made me glare at him.

Unfortunately, Ben kept speaking.

"Personal best, gettin' a woman to come that fast...*twice*."

"Um...I'll just point out the first time was due to *my* activities."

The grin came back.

"Bullshit, baby. You were workin' hard to find it, but you didn't get it until you got my thumb."

That was true.

And annoying.

I shut my mouth and kept glaring.

Benny's grin turned to a smile.

The smile faded as his gaze roamed my face and finally came back to my eyes.

When his caught mine, he whispered, "Leave it to my Frankie. When she does somethin', even when she doesn't intend to do it, she goes big."

He sounded like he liked that.

Then again, we were where we were after what we'd just done so that wasn't a surprise.

Still, I liked that he liked that about me. I also liked that he let me off the hook so easily. Of course, the sex was great and an awesome motivator to get a man to let you off the hook. But I'd fucked up huge, and still, he opened it up for me and gave me another shot without making me work for it at all.

Then again, back in the bathroom, he told me if I came back, he wouldn't make me work for it.

And he was true to his promise.

I still was not certain what the hell I was doing. Worse, I was worried that eventually I wouldn't do right by Benny.

But I just couldn't seem to stop myself.

"It's late, Ben," I reminded him quietly.

"Yeah," he replied, slid down, kissed my shoulder, and rolled to the side. He allowed himself an eye sweep of my body before they came back to my face. "Like the nightie, Frankie."

"Thanks," I whispered.

Ben grasped a hip, rolling me to my side, and he pulled the covers over me. Only then did he exit the bed.

I watched him from the back adjusting his jeans on the way to the bathroom. More aptly, I watched the muscles of his back move as he made his way to the bathroom.

Mere minutes later, I watched him, wearing nothing but white boxers, sauntering back to the bed.

The light went out before he slid in beside me. The instant he was in, he pulled me in his arms.

I closed my eyes and did it hard.

I'd missed this. I'd spent months, every night, every single one, wondering what the hell was the matter with me that I ran away from it. Wanting it back. Wanting it forever.

Now, having *really* had all of Benny, I wasn't sure I'd ever be able to give it up.

Even if I made it so that Benny wanted to give up on me.

"I'm scared as shit," I said into his throat, pressing my face there.

"Know that, Frankie."

"I don't know how to get over it."

"Know that too."

"I don't wanna fuck you over again."

"So don't."

"It's not that easy," I whispered.

His hands moved over my back, and he dipped his chin so when he said, "I know that too, honey," it was in my hair. "I also know we are not gonna beat whatever is fuckin' you up tonight. Wrestled with whether or not to come here for hours, couldn't beat back the urge, and now I'm glad I didn't. But it's three o'clock in the morning. You got work tomorrow. So now, you sleep. Tomorrow, we'll set about figuring out how to beat it."

I took in a rough breath and let it out, saying, "Okay, Benny."

"Now go to sleep."

"Okay, honey."

I snuggled closer, pressing my hands to his chest and turning my head to press my cheek against his collarbone.

His arms around me got tight.

I closed my eyes, and apparently the miracle of Benny (not to mention two orgasms) was enough to quiet all the shit in my head clamoring to be heard that I was scared to face. My body relaxed and I started to drift to sleep.

I stopped when Ben's arms gave me a squeeze and he murmured, "Fuckin' thrilled you healed the breach, baby."

So Benny to give me that, straight-up honest.

"I hope you stay that way," I murmured back.

"Eyes on the prize, Frankie," he whispered.

The prize.

Having Benny.

The best prize there was.

"Right, Ben," I whispered back. "Eyes on the prize."

He shifted me closer, tangled a heavy leg in mine, and slid a hand up to play with the ends of my hair.

I settled in, took a deep breath, let his fingers moving in my hair relax me, and it didn't take long before I found sleep.

⟨⟩

The alarm on my phone sounded, and directly after, Ben sounded.

"Fuck," he groaned, rolling and taking me with him. I felt him reach and he must have grabbed my phone and touched a thumb to it to turn off the alarm because it stopped.

I was blinking but saw the light of my phone and knew Benny must have been looking at it too when he muttered, "Christ, is it six already?"

With probably four hours of sleep, my first thoughts should have been about how I was going to get through an important day of meetings and communing with one of my reps, who'd made it clear the day before he wasn't all that hot about working under me.

But those were not my thoughts.

My thoughts were how good it felt to wake up to Benny in nothing but boxers, me with no panties, after two orgasms, and making the whacked decision to come back to him.

I came back into the room mentally when I heard the phone clatter back on the nightstand, then I was on my back, Ben mostly on me because he rolled us into that position.

"You gotta get up?" he asked.

"It takes me an hour and a half to get ready and I have an eight o'clock breakfast meeting with my rep," I answered.

"So that's a yeah."

"That's a yeah," I confirmed, sounding as disappointed as I felt.

I felt a whole lot less disappointed when Ben shifted to bury his face in my neck, where he said, "Right, you get ready. I'm gonna snooze."

I rounded him with my arms and offered, "You can snooze all you want. I'll do the checkout thing, arrange a wakeup call so you have plenty of time to get up and on your way, and I'll put out the 'do not disturb' sign so they don't bother you in the meantime."

He pulled his face out of my neck to look into my eyes through the dark and say, "That's a plan."

I grinned at him, also through the dark.

Then I said, "I gotta hit it, honey."

I reached up to touch my mouth to his but left it at that because I knew I wouldn't be getting up at all if I went for more. But as I began to pull from his arms, they tightened around me.

I looked back toward his face.

"Gotta say this," he muttered, and I felt my stomach tighten because he didn't sound like he wanted to say whatever it was he had to say. "I laid it out last night," he went on. "But need to make it clear, will only make it clear this once, 'cause by tonight, I'll know and it'll be done."

My stomach didn't loosen as I asked, "What'll be done?"

He gathered me closer when he answered, "You burned me once, baby. I didn't like it. Not at all. If it wasn't you doin' it, there would be no second chance. Since it's you, I'm givin' you a second chance. You don't show tonight, it'll be done. And we're talking *done*, *cara*. I will not answer the phone. I will not come callin' when you're in town for business. You come to Man's wedding, you won't exist for me. That kind of done. You don't show at my place tonight, you commit to that future 'cause there's no goin' back."

I was deep breathing in order to hold back the panic and, focused on that, I didn't respond.

So Benny prompted, "You understand that, baby?"

"I understand," I forced out.

"All right," he murmured, sliding a hand up into my hair, cupping the back of head, and pulling me to him.

His kiss was not a lip touch. It was harder, closed mouthed, and a whole lot nicer.

But he was Benny and all the awesomeness that entailed. He knew I had responsibilities.

So he broke the kiss but touched his lips to mine once more before he whispered, "Now haul your ass outta this bed. I got sleep to catch up on."

"Okay, Ben."

He gave me a squeeze. I gave him one back, then I hauled my ass out of the bed.

Since starting my job, I'd been traveling a lot, seeing as my territory was half the continental United States, so I had a system. When I got to my hotel room, I always unpacked. Made myself at home. Made sure everything was where I needed it to be when I might need it because I was working with reps and doctors, and schedules could get fucked. I didn't want to be digging through my suitcase to find my three-tiered jewelry bag in order to locate the right earrings when I should be out the door to make a meeting.

This had the added benefit of enabling me to get ready relatively quietly (nothing I could do about the hair dryer), behind closed doors in the bathroom, only coming out to sort through the closet in the light of dawn to pick one of my business outfits and shoes.

When I did, I saw Ben on his side in the bed, one hand shoved under the pillow, one arm thrown wide, covers down to his lat, hair a mess, locks having fallen over his forehead.

I did not think in the shower. I did not process what I'd done or what I was doing. I didn't begin the Herculean task of trying to understand my panic or what I did to Ben five months ago.

I got ready.

But staring at him in the bed, my mind jumbled, turning, twisting, so much rushing through it at once it was like when you picked up a book and put your thumb tight to the edge of the pages and let loose, the entire book flying across your vision in seconds. But through that, you had to find one line. You had to.

Your life depended on it.

I got to the end of the book, turned to the closet, and grabbed my dress and shoes. I took them to the bathroom, put them on, accessorized, re-sprayed my hair, and spritzed with perfume.

Done with that, as quietly as I could, I packed up the bathroom. Going out to grab my suitcase, I carried it in the bathroom and went back out to grab my clothes. I took those in. I packed. And not using the rollers because it would be noisy, I carried it back out and set it by the door.

I walked to the bed, again taking in all that was Benny Bianchi lying in it, and nabbed my phone. I walked back to the closet to get my blazer. I grabbed it, shrugged it on, pulled my hair out of the collar, then got my light trench from where I'd thrown it on a chair, my purse, the keycard, and my computer bag. I walked to the door, put out the Do Not Disturb sign, and walked down the hall toward the elevators in order to go to the registration desk to check out.

In other words, when that book flipped in front of me, I'd found my line.

⟨⟩

I went to Ben's name on my phone and hit the button to connect.

I put the phone to my ear and waited. It rang several times, and I knew it did this because Ben's jeans were in the bathroom. It also went to voicemail.

Too far away to hear.

I should have thought to put his phone on the nightstand.

I didn't think of that so I disconnected, searched for the hotel on Safari, found it, and connected.

"The Belvedere, how can we help you today?"

"Can you ring me up to room four thirteen?"

"Of course. One moment."

I heard nothing. Then I heard clicks. Finally I heard rings.

"'Lo?" Ben's drowsy voice said.

"It's your friendly wake-up call," I stated chirpily. "Time to get your ass out of bed and out of that room or I'll have to pay for an extra day."

"Baby." Now his voice was drowsy and amused.

I liked the drowsy and amused so I went for more.

"Of course, I wouldn't be paying for it, my company would, but momma don't play that way with her employers."

I only had amused—rumbling, deep amused—when he asked, "Momma don't play that way?"

"Yep," I answered.

"Baby, there are a lotta things you are, but street is not one of them."

"I can totally do street."

"You could, if your dad was not Italian but African American. That not bein' the case, you cannot."

"Are we gonna squabble about whether I can do street or not?" I asked.

"No, seein' as I gotta get my ass outta this bed before your company has to pay the extra day you won't be usin' this room, so we don't have time since that'll take a year."

"Right then, to finish that particular discussion, I can *so* do street."

"Whatever," he muttered, but it still rumbled with amusement.

"Okay, I gotta get to a meeting."

"*Cara.*"

At his sudden change in tone, I stopped dead, standing in the hallway of a medical office building.

"What?" I whispered.

"Bag packed, by the door."

My heart tripped, but my mouth spewed attitude. "Well, I'm not trustin' *you* to pack for me. You'd totally fuck it up."

"There is no way to fuck up packing, Frankie. You toss the shit in, close the case. It zips, you've succeeded."

"Ben, just the idea of tossing my stuff in a suitcase without folding or strategizing placement gives me the heebie-jeebies."

"Then it's good you packed."

"I know."

"No, Francesca." His voice was deep and not easy, but low and heavy with meaning. "It's *good you packed.*"

My voice was not easy, but quiet and also heavy with meaning when I replied, "I know."

He was silent a second, maybe letting that sink in, before he asked, "You got a guesstimate when you're gonna be at my place?"

"With the way my day is planned, maybe I should come to the restaurant, get the keys, go to your place, and see you when you're off."

This I had thought about in the last several hours since leaving Benny. These were not good thoughts, primarily because everyone likely knew I'd bailed on him, and although his family seemed to be playing Switzerland with that, others might not. And when it came to the pizzeria, those others could be there.

They were also not good thoughts because Benny worked late and I wanted to see him, but I also needed sleep.

Maybe I'd nap while he was at the restaurant.

"Uh…honey, you came back to me. I'm not workin' tonight," Benny said, cutting into my thoughts.

"You're callin' in Vinnie Senior?" I asked, not certain how I felt about that either because it would mean there would be little delay in the Bianchis knowing I was back.

"No. Manny can cover the kitchen for a day or two. He does it sometimes when I got a day off and he doesn't fuck up my kitchen when he does it. Long haul, though, Man doesn't have it in him. It's gotta be Pop."

I found that interesting.

I didn't have the time to find out why that was interesting.

I only had the time to say, "All right."

"I'll give Man a call, get to the restaurant, make sure everything's sorted for him. So, again, when am I gonna see you?"

"Around six."

"Right. Then see you around six."

Suddenly, I felt extremely happy and couldn't keep it out of the "Yeah" I gave to him.

"Yeah." He gave it back to me.

I drew in a steadying breath.

"Later, Benny."

"Later, Frankie."

I disconnected and looked down the hall to where Trey, my rep, was standing, head bent to his phone, thumb moving over it, expression set to annoyed.

And I thought, *Fuck him.* I was good at my job, even if the learning curve meant that for four months, my downtime was spent with my nose in patient information leaflets, company brochures, past sales reports, and team evaluations.

He was going to have to suck it up.

I was there to stay.

Or, at least for the next minute.

The one after that, we'd see.

Thirteen

KID FRIENDLY

I had butterflies at the same time I was experiencing pleasantly unpleasant (or unpleasantly pleasant) flashbacks as I parked in front of Benny's house.

I sucked in a breath, grabbed my purse and computer, and exited my rental car.

When I did, as if she had a sixth sense, I saw Mrs. Zambino standing out on her stoop, high-heeled boots on, hair up, arms crossed on her chest that was covered in a sweater I was pretty certain I saw a celebrity wearing in last week's issue of *Us* magazine.

She wore it better.

She was staring at me, a severe look on her face.

Well, there you go. Benny's family was Switzerland, but Mrs. Zambino was pissed at me.

I ignored that, juggled my bags, waved enthusiastically, and called, "Hey there, Mrs. Zambino!"

Her body jerked in a peeved way, then she turned and stomped into her house.

I made a mental note I had work to do with Mrs. Zambino and turned toward Benny's.

I was at the top of the stoop when the door opened.

Then I wasn't at the top of the stoop, seeing as Benny's arm flashed out, hooked me around the waist, and yanked me inside.

The door slammed shut about a second before I slammed against the wall of Ben's foyer, pinned there by Benny.

"Couch or bed?" he asked, his eyes an inch from mine, and a throb pulsed between my legs.

"Wh-what?" I asked back, following, but not able to process what was happening quickly enough to make an appropriate response.

"Bed," he rumbled, his eyes dropping to my mouth. "Room to move. We'll break in the couch when I'm focused."

When he was focused?

What did that mean?

I had no chance to ask. My purse and computer bag were on the floor, my hand was in Benny's, and he was dragging me toward the stairs.

When we hit the stairs, I still had no chance to talk, since I had to concentrate on where my feet were taking me so I didn't slam face-first into a stair.

After that, I had to concentrate on not tripping down the hall.

Then I had to concentrate on staying upright when Ben whirled me to face him, my back to the foot of the bed, and he pulled my trench *with* blazer down my arms and tossed them aside.

Only then did I slam my hands on my hips as I glared into his eyes and snapped, "Well, hello, Benny Bianchi."

His reply was to plant his hand on my chest and shove.

I let out a small scream and hit the bed on my back.

Benny hit me.

Then his mouth hit mine.

And then he was kissing me.

It finally filtered through my brain that this was hot, *all* of it. He was kissing me and I liked the way he tasted. So I wound my arms around him and kissed him back.

If I had time to think about it that day (which I didn't), I would have thought the first time was about uncontrolled emotion, need, and the fact I hadn't been laid in over seven years. I was getting laid by Benny Bianchi, all of this explaining why it went so fast, burned so bright, and felt so good.

But luckily, I didn't have time to think about it. Because if I did, I would have started fretting about when it would go slower and I'd have plenty of time to sink right into my head like I had with Vinnie. Wondering if I was doing something right. Wondering if he liked something I was doing, if I was exciting him, or if he was just hard, ready, and going through the motions so he could get inside me and finish things.

If I'd had time to think about it, it would have embedded itself in my head so it would be all about if I was doing it right, out of practice, or never really had the skill in the first place, and if Benny liked what I was doing.

I didn't have the time to think about it that day, and I *really* didn't have the time to think of it in that moment.

This was because Benny was action man. I should have known, considering he rarely missed opportunities.

Me in his bed without stitches in me, he wasn't missing this one.

It was about hands and mouths and noises. Touch and taste. The scent of his aftershave. The titillating sound of him pulling the zipper down at the back of my dress. His hands moving in to glide skin against skin along my sides. The taste of his neck. The feel of his hardness against my thigh, my belly, my hip. The silky caress of the lining of my dress as he yanked it over my head. His tongue at my nipple over my bra. The feel of his hair in my hands. The excitement of him tearing my panties down my legs.

And then it happened.

He spread my legs, rolled between, and put his mouth to me.

Already ignited through sensory exploration, the feel of him against me made me combust.

I dug my heels into the bed to drive myself further into his mouth, but did this for a nanosecond before he swung my legs over his shoulders.

It was then I dug my heels in his back. He growled against my sex and it didn't hit me I was still wearing spiked heels. It also didn't hit me that it was not a growl of pain but something else entirely.

He feasted on me, then his mouth closed around my clit, sucked hard, and he thrust two fingers inside.

"*God*," I cried out, doing a full body arch, driving my hips deeper to Ben's mouth.

I had been beyond excited, but the climax that slammed through me at what Benny was giving me was a surprise.

More of a surprise, Ben pushed it. He sucked, he finger-fucked me, and I dug my heels in his back, straining for more, moaning and whimpering.

He pulled his fingers out, dragged his tongue through my wetness, and I shuddered against him only to feel him pull away from me.

I opened my eyes, closed my legs, lifted my head, found him standing at the foot of the bed, and I whispered, "No."

"Not leavin' you, baby," Ben whispered back before he tore off his tee and went for his jeans.

At seeing that, I moved.

I was up on my knees in the bed wearing nothing but lace-topped thigh highs, spike-heeled pumps, and my bra by the time Ben was naked. His dark, hot eyes roamed all over me, his lips rumbling, "Jesus," and he moved back to me.

His arms closed around me, mine closed around him, and he fell forward, taking me back.

I wrapped my legs around him as he reached to his nightstand.

He gave me his mouth, even as he angled his hips away, kissing me, and please, God, rolling on a condom at the same time.

Suddenly, I felt the tip of his cock glide through my wetness, and just as suddenly, he was inside.

And again, I had Benny.

"Yes," I breathed in his mouth.

"Fuck yes," Ben groaned against mine and took my mouth again in a deep, wet kiss as he pounded inside me.

It lasted awhile. It felt awesome for that while. Ben alternately kissed me or moved his mouth to play at my neck for that while. And if I could think of anything but all that Benny was making me feel, I wouldn't have been able to say which I liked better (though, probably kissing).

But I knew he was ready and he wanted me there with him when his hand went between us, thumb to my clit, and he coaxed me right where he wanted me to be.

It didn't take a lot of coaxing.

My limbs spasmed around him and my cry drove down his throat as he took me over the edge.

I held tight and enjoyed the ride as, a couple minutes later, Ben joined me.

He stayed deep and I felt his ragged breaths turn smooth against my neck as his hands, slow and gentle, roamed over me, shoving under me, anywhere he could get to me.

Finally, his lips trailed up my neck to my mouth where he brushed mine, he locked eyes with me, and finally, ending the festivities in a sweet, tender way I'd remember for the rest of my life, he skimmed the tip of my nose with his and I saw his eyes start smiling.

"Hello, Frankie."

It was his turn to see my eyes smile when I replied, "Hello, Benny."

"You wear thigh highs every day?" he asked, and my brows drew together at the strange question.

"Yes."

"Lace tops?"

"Mostly."

He looked to the pillow above my head and muttered, "Fuck me."

This confused me.

"Is that bad?" I asked.

He looked back at me. "How many doctors and reps you got who are guys?"

"Um…" I mumbled as answer, which was all I had to do. He got me.

"Right," he murmured.

"They can't see them, Benny," I pointed out.

"They can, Frankie."

That was when my eyes went squinty. "They can't."

"Okay, maybe not, but they can sense them."

Seriously?

"No they can't!" I snapped.

"Your legs, your ass, you in a dress, they absolutely can. And if they can't, then they're hopin' you're in thigh highs, and trust me, you are inspiration for good visualization, even if a man doesn't normally have that skill."

Although that was a compliment, the thought of the people I worked with visualizing anything about me, I couldn't go there. So I didn't.

"Okay, they can. Then…so?" I gave in to move on.

This time his brows went up. "So?"

"Yeah. So?"

"Babe, you get what's goin' on here, yeah?"

Suddenly, I couldn't breathe, so it sounded winded and a little unsure when I said, "Yeah."

"This is you and me, and that means *only* you for me and *only* me for you. That means you're mine and just fuckin' *me*. That means, me bein' full-blood Italian, not a big fan of you off meetin' with guys who are thinkin' about you in a bra, panties, thigh highs, and your heels."

All uncertainty left me and, again, my eyes got squinty. "I can't quit my job because men think with their dicks."

"You can wear slacks," he returned. "And nix the heels and buy some flats." He paused before he finished, "Ugly ones."

"I'm not wearin' ugly shoes!" I said loudly.

"Okay, then buy some not-ugly flats."

"I'm not wearin' flats. Or slacks," I declared.

He stared at me a moment before he repeated, "Fuck me."

"Can we stop talking about this so you can feed me?" I asked, then added, "I'm hungry."

His expression shifted from sex-satisfied with the addition of aggravated, to sex-satisfied with the addition of warm affection before he asked, "What you want?"

I wanted one of Benny's pies. What I didn't want was him to have to go to the restaurant to make one.

Nevertheless, to make a choice, I needed more information. "What are my choices?"

"Barbeque chicken sandwiches or anything that delivers."

"I take it your ma's provisions ran out."

His face gentled so his words wouldn't sting when he replied, "Yeah, baby. Five months, that was gonna happen."

His gentle face was awesome.

But his words still stung.

"I'm an idiot," I blurted on a whisper.

Ben heaved a sigh, pulled out, and rolled to his back, moving me with him. When he had me on top, he lifted his hands and gathered my hair, holding it away from my face on either side of my head, and he looked into my eyes.

"Sucks, but apparently, fuckin' you again didn't sort all our shit."

"Apparently not," I muttered, my eyes drifting to his ear.

"Baby."

My eyes drifted back.

"Let's start with the easy shit. You want barbeque or you wanna order something?"

Starting with the easy shit was a good idea.

Still, I had to ask. "What kind of barbeque?"

"Jack Daniel's ready-made."

I felt my eyes get big.

"Oh my God, that shit is the bomb," I breathed.

He grinned and murmured, "Barbeque it is."

"Yeah," I agreed.

"Right, then get off me, baby. I gotta get rid of this condom and feed my girl."

I rolled off and Ben rolled off with me.

I then watched his ass, something I'd never seen unhindered, as he sauntered to the bathroom.

After enjoying that show and allowing myself a moment to enjoy the memory of that show when he disappeared, I spied my suitcase against the wall and moved.

I found my panties on the floor, nabbed them, kicked off my shoes, pulled the undies up, and discarded my thigh highs. I had my suitcase open on the floor and was kneeling by it, digging through my limited business travel selection when I saw Benny's bare feet and the hems of his faded jeans on the floor next to my case.

I looked up (and up and *up*) encountering denim-clad thighs, a package I'd unwrapped and knew intimately that the treat inside was thrilling, bare abs, chest, and shoulders—their lines, ridges, and flats covered in smooth olive skin—and finally his handsome face pointed down to me.

"You need somethin' to wear?" he asked.

"I didn't pack lounge-around-Ben's-house gear," I answered, and his lips quirked.

"Right. Next time, remedy that," he ordered and moved to his dresser. He opened a drawer, pulled out a faded red tee, turned, and tossed it to me.

I yanked it on and it had barely fallen over my ass before he had my hand in his and was pulling us out the door.

We hit the kitchen and Ben got out the meat. He nuked it while I got plates and put out the buns. Ben opened himself a beer and grabbed a bottle of wine. I grabbed a glass for my wine (one, incidentally, that I was pretty certain he stole from the pizzeria). He poured, then he moved to the meat, divided it between the buns, put a slice of Swiss cheese on it, and nuked it again until the cheese was melted.

It smelled divine and looked better.

Best of all, the entirety of this took about five minutes.

"Livin' room," he stated as a command and went on doing it. "Grab my plate. Come back and get the drinks. I'll get the other shit."

I would find, sitting in the corner of his couch, plate in hand, wine on the coffee table in front of me, "the other shit" consisted of Ben bringing out a jar of dill pickle slices and seven bags of chips.

Seven.

Something new to learn about Benny Bianchi. He apparently *seriously* liked snack foods.

I stared at the chips and noted Doritos Cool Ranch, Doritos Nacho Cheese, Jays Mesquite BBQ, Jays Sour Cream and Onion, Cheetos Puffs, Fritos Honey BBQ, and a tube of Pringles Cheddar Cheese.

Feeling like sticking with the theme, I carefully rolled forward on my knees, balancing my plate in hand, and reached for Jays Mesquite.

"Catch up," Benny said as I sat back.

I put my plate on my lap, unrolled the top of the open chip bag, and looked to him. "Sorry, honey?"

He didn't repeat himself.

He asked, "You get a dog?"

My heart squeezed because with his question he told me that, even though he didn't answer my voicemails, he'd listened to them.

I liked that.

"No," I answered. "Had a problem with my apartment. Well..." I hesitated, "actually about seven thousand of them. Then I had a problem with how they didn't seem to give a shit that I did when the shower didn't drain, even after three days, and the garbage disposal didn't dispose, it preserved, but not very well. After that went on awhile, I told them to go fuck themselves. One of our reps moved on to a job out of state and she was stuck in a lease. So I took over her lease." I grinned at him, chip in hand halfway to my mouth. "Get this. My new pad is in Brownsburg." I popped the chip in my mouth and chewed.

"No shit?" he asked, his brows up, his eyes smiling.

I shook my head. "No shit. Moved in two weeks ago. Vi and Cal are havin' me over next week for dinner."

"Then you know she's expecting," Benny noted, sandwich in hand, and after he said what he said, he bit in and half the meat hit his plate.

We needed forks.

And maybe knives.

Definitely napkins.

I shot him a happy smile at this news and answered him as I shifted out of the couch. "Yeah. She told me." I put my plate on the coffee table, saying, "Gonna get forks and napkins."

"No napkins, babe. Paper towel."

Yeah. Right. He was a guy. Of course he wouldn't buy napkins.

I came back, handed him his fork and knife and portion of paper towel, and had just settled back with plate in hand and chips at the ready when he asked, "Your old landlord give you shit for jumpin' your lease?"

It was then I was seeing that I shouldn't have started with that.

I put my plate on my lap and began carving into my sandwich.

"Frankie?"

I lifted a bite and put it in my mouth.

So good.

"Francesca."

At my full name and the way he said it, I looked to him.

"They gave you shit," he stated as a fact he now knew from the look on my face. Then his expression turned scary. "They still givin' you shit?"

I chewed, swallowed, and mumbled, "Uh…no."

"Cut their losses," he guessed.

I looked back down at my plate.

He didn't like my avoidance tactic and I knew this when he grinded out, "Frankie."

I looked to him and said quickly, "I called Sal."

His face went straight into a scowl and he demanded, "Tell me you did not."

"Not to...uh, *lean* on them or anything. To see if one of his attorneys might put the fear of God into them. That, well...worked."

"Putting the fear of God into them *is* leanin' on them, Frankie," Benny informed me.

I made no comment.

The scowl didn't shift as Ben asked, "Have you lost your mind?"

That was a loaded question.

"Babe," he clipped out when I didn't answer immediately.

"They were jacking with my credit, Benny," I said in my defense.

"So you got a mob lawyer to threaten them?"

I tipped my head to the side as my nonverbal "yes."

"You do not get into Sal for markers," Ben said low.

"Sal said it was a freebie."

"That man keeps track of every-fuckin'-thing and you know it. You do not get into him for markers. You do not get into him for *anything*. And if I had my choice, you would not have one fuckin' thing to do with him."

"He's family, Benny," I reminded him quietly, because he was, in Ben's case, actually blood.

"He's a sociopath, Frankie," he returned.

That probably couldn't be argued.

Though he *was* a charming one.

I decided not to give that opinion to Benny.

I went back to my food, suggesting, "Maybe we shouldn't talk about Sal."

"Oh, we'll be talkin' about Sal," Ben told me, and I looked back to him, chip in hand. "Just not now. He's not top priority."

Suddenly, I wanted to talk about Sal.

"Don't look freaked," Benny said, now gentle, and I focused on him to see his tone was written on his face. "We're gonna eat. We're gonna catch up. We're gonna enjoy this. We can get into the heavy shit later."

"I vote for next February," I muttered to the chip bag.

"You're still with me then, baby, I'd give you that," Benny told me.

I looked back to him hopefully.

"But, just sayin'," he went on, "that might not be healthy."

And my hopes were dashed.

"Now, just eat, honey," he urged. "And tell me if you like your new job. Tell me about your new place. And I'll tell you how Chicago survived the earthquake that was Ma when Manny gave Sela the diamond she wanted from Tiffany's and not Aunt Mary's heirloom ring, which, even me, as a guy who knows fuck all about jewelry, knows is butt-ugly."

I giggled at Benny.

Then I popped my chip into my mouth.

After that, I told him about my job, my new place, and listened to him talk about his family.

⸻

"I travel for work," I declared.

It was after dinner and after the minimal cleanup, the most taxing part being hauling all the chips back to the kitchen. Ben and I were back on the couch but arranged very differently.

That would be, me on my back and Ben on me.

Once he got me in this position, I'd decided I'd live, breathe, sleep and eat in it, if I could.

"I get that, you livin' in Brownsburg and bein' here," Ben said on a grin, his hands, as they'd been doing since he got me on my back, were roaming.

"What I'm sayin' is, I'm usually out of town at least once every two weeks. I'm rackin' up frequent flier miles."

That ratcheted the grin up to a smile.

He got me.

I lost his smile when he dropped his head so his lips could hit my neck, where he murmured, "Sounds promising."

"Yeah," I said quietly, deciding I didn't like my hands resting on his back over his tee.

I dipped them low, then up and got skin.

Better.

"What's on for tomorrow?" he asked my neck.

"Two meetings," I told his ear. "Then I was supposed to fly back. But my secretary already got me on a Sunday flight."

"Excellent," he muttered.

I stopped talking when his roaming hand roamed over my ass.

But my mind froze when he whispered against my skin, "What freaked you?"

I knew what he was asking and I was freaking right then because I didn't have an answer.

He lifted his head and looked down at me. "What freaked you that day in the bathroom, baby?"

"I don't know," I whispered.

His head tipped to the side as his hand moved from my ass, up my side, and in to curl around my neck, where his thumb started stroking my jaw.

Once he had his soothing touch on me, he asked, "No clue?"

"Theresa came," I said quietly.

His mouth went hard.

I tightened my arms around him. "Don't blame her."

"No way she should walk into my house like that, she knows I got a woman in it or not. That said, she knew I had a woman in it."

"It's not her fault," I pushed.

"Okay, maybe not," he gave in slightly. "But that's not the point. I'm a thirty-five-year-old man, and my ma lets herself in, shouts up the stairs she's climbin', when I got my woman hot for me in my bed and the bedroom door is open? That shit's whacked, starting at the lettin' herself in part."

It kind of was.

It was also not-so-kind-of Theresa.

"She won't do that again," Ben declared.

"I bet not," I muttered.

"What about her showin' tripped you?" he asked.

I shook my head. "I don't know. Maybe it was just…just…" I searched for it and found something. The problem was, I wasn't sure if it was *the* thing. "It was just that we were taking the next step, a big step. Theresa showed, reminding me what I'd lost and got back, and I freaked. As in,

Frankie-style freaked, making a huge deal out of it and doin' stupid shit that hurts people."

His focus got weirdly acute and his voice got weirdly cautious when he asked, "When's the last time you Frankie-style freaked like that?"

"I do it all the time," I told him. "You know that."

"No, babe. When's the last time you Frankie-style freaked, doin' it and hurting people?"

I shut my mouth and thought about it.

"When, Frankie?" he pushed.

I opened my mouth. "I...I guess I don't know."

"Was there ever a time?" he asked.

Was there?

I thought about that too.

"I don't know," I admitted.

"Why'd you say that, then?"

Why did I?

Oh my God.

I stared into his eyes and whispered, "I don't know."

"Yeah," he whispered back.

"You're the only family I ever had, Benny," I said, still whispering. "The only good one. The only real one. I lost you once. All of you. I just...panicked. And it was panic, honey. I wasn't freaking. I was freaking and I was *freaked.*"

"Saw that," he told me. "Even fuckin' felt it."

"Oh God," I breathed. "I'm so sorry."

"I am too, but not sorry about seein' it or feelin' it. Sorry that you wouldn't even try to get a handle on it so I could see if I could get you through it."

To that, I said nothing.

Benny did.

"That comes up again, Frankie, need you to plant it somewhere where it'll grow, where you can get to it so you can find your way to gettin' a handle on it, at least so I can see to you."

"What if I can't do that?" I asked hesitantly.

"I don't know, *cara*. That's why you gotta do what you gotta do to plant that deep."

I decided to visualize, meditate, get crystals and talismans—whatever I had to do to plant that deep so I didn't fuck us up again. Not to mention so I didn't feel that panic again because it was not fun. And last, so I didn't make Benny feel it.

His thumb gliding over my lips took me out of my thoughts, and I focused on him again just as he said gently, "You know, you're not your ma."

I closed my eyes.

"Babe, even before you hooked up with Vinnie, it was like you weren't part of that family," he continued. "Everyone said it."

I opened my eyes.

"Enzo Junior's the shit because the man is funny," Ben told me. "He can hold his drink. He's got a sixth sense when it comes to locating fine tail. And he'd drop everything if you needed him to have your back. But I know one of the things he'd drop is his woman, even if she was in the middle of her own shit, doin' that so he could take his brother's back. He's a player. He's in his late twenties and still says stupid shit when he sees a fat girl, which makes him a dick. And he's the best of that crew you call family."

"There's Dino," I told him.

"Dino's an anomaly, proof that you weren't switched at the hospital 'cause he shares your blood and he's a good guy. But he's a good guy because he got outta the mess you were bounced around in growin' up. You're you because of a miracle."

His words made my breath catch as I stared into his eyes. "You think that?"

"Fuck yeah," he replied. "Word is, Nat's back with Davey, and she's since hooked up with two other guys who are not Davey, he just doesn't know about them yet. She's also lost her job and found another since we last saw her, and the word about that is, she's dancing."

Oh fuck. That wasn't good. That meant Nat, money, a lot of men, and not very many clothes.

Poor Davey.

"Cat has dropped off the face of the earth, which could mean anything," Ben carried on. "Your ma, I don't know and I don't care. And in the time I was with you after you got out of the hospital, and our time earlier on this couch catchin' up, you didn't say a word about your dad and he lives fifteen fuckin' minutes away. You fucked me over and sent me cookies. You make meetings on time and think about how to make an employee respect you. Your outfit today, babe...sexy, *way* too fuckin' sexy...but admittedly, it was also don't-fuck-with-me business. Sounds of it, you live in an upscale apartment building. You travel for your work in a way that they put you up in fancy hotels. Your future includes raises, promotions, the possibility of gettin' a dog, but only the kind I want, and findin' some way to do all that and circle back to a life with me. You are not them. You are nothin' like them. You grew up fucked and you still grew up smart, strong, capable, funny, and loving. So yeah. Fuck yeah. That's a miracle."

That was all too much, too beautiful, I couldn't take it. I couldn't even believe it.

I certainly couldn't comment on it.

But my voice was husky when I asked, "What kind of dog do you want?"

He gave me that play, but he did it with his eyes gentling, along with his voice, showing me he knew I needed to make it when he said, "Kid friendly."

Kid friendly.

God, he was killing me.

"A pug?" I asked, and the gentle look vanished.

"No fuckin' way."

"They're cute, sweet, snorty, *and* friendly."

"Any dog that is even partially a permanent fixture in my life has to be at least five times bigger than a cat, and when I say that, I mean a *big* cat."

"That's the only rule?"

"That, and it has to be a Labrador, a golden retriever, a German shepherd, a boxer, or a bulldog."

My heart thumped with joy in my chest as my lips said, "Oh my God, Benny, we need a bulldog named Churchill."

I got the gentle look back and it came directly on the heels of the word "we," but I couldn't wallow in it because he stated, "We are not namin' a bulldog Churchill. We get a bulldog, he's named Gus."

I screwed up my face. "That's a boring name."

He ignored that. "Lab, Charlie. Golden, Honey. Shepherd, Attila. Boxer, Bruno."

Jeez, he had it all figured out.

"Those are all boring names, Benny," I decreed, though Attila was kind of cool.

"You pick the dog, I pick the name," he offered.

I shook my head. "No, you pick the dog, I pick the name."

"Deal," he said instantly.

Shit!

"No, wait, I wanna pick the dog!" I cried.

His lips turned up and he shook his head. "We had a deal."

"We didn't shake on it."

Something changed in his face and I liked the change.

It also changed in his voice.

"Is that our gig? We make a deal, we shake on it?" he asked, his face getting closer to me.

"Yes," I declared firmly.

His head veered at the last moment and his hand at my neck tightened as his face disappeared on the other side.

"We'll shake on it later," he said against my skin, then his mouth opened over it and I felt his tongue start gliding.

"Okay," I agreed, suddenly breathless.

"Take your panties off, baby."

"Okay," I wheezed, totally breathless, shifting my hands to get my thumbs in the sides of my panties, thinking I was about to learn the meaning of what Ben said earlier about focus.

In short order, I found I was right.

I also found I liked Benny's focus.

Definitely.

⟋

"Ben."

"Yeah."

"*Ben*."

"Fuck yeah."

I drove down on his cock and ground in, coming hard. Ben was sitting up while I rode him so my arms were tight around his shoulders.

I was finding with Ben, once I got there, he needed power. So he flipped me and gave me the power. His hips beat into mine, his face in my neck, one forearm in the bed, the other hand at my ass, tipping me up to take him deeper.

I slid both my hands to his ass and clenched in, holding on and coaxing at the same time.

He didn't need my coaxing. It was Saturday night. He'd come home from the restaurant, woke me, felt energetic, and this was the culmination of a lot of hard work from Benny *and* me.

He drove deep and grunted his release against my neck, his hand at my ass clasping tight, fingers digging deep.

He didn't give himself the chance to come down before he rolled us, still connected, so I was resting on top of him. Once there, he heaved a deep breath and kept his hand at my ass while he wrapped the other arm tight along my lower back.

I nuzzled my face in his neck and sighed.

Friday had been good. Ben took another night off work to be with me. *So* Benny, he took me out to dinner and a movie. Date night. Not Giuseppe's, but it was still sweet.

That day, Saturday, we slept in. We lazed. We talked in whispers. We made love. Then Ben went to the restaurant and I camped out on his couch, watching TV, relaxing, trying to get to a place where I could accept the promise of a life that was what Benny seemed to be offering me.

Easy.

We'd agreed that my return would not be shared officially with the family (though it was certain Mrs. Zambino had been on her phone, so it was in no doubt this had happened unofficially) until I was ready.

I had a feeling Ben agreed to this to make certain my return took. But I didn't ask. He wasn't being cautious; he was all in. But I didn't suspect my departure with Ben in close proximity of at least Theresa didn't garner him some headaches. I could see him not wanting to court that again just in case I freaked, did something stupid, fucked up, and bailed.

"It gets too much, baby, you have my permission to give up on me."

I said that against his neck. I didn't think it before it came out. But what I'd been thinking before just made it come out.

When it did, Ben's grip on me tightened momentarily before he rolled us again. He slid out while he did, but he ended full-out on top of me.

It was dark. When he came home and woke me to make love with me, he didn't bother with a light.

Still, from moonlight and streetlight coming in through the windows, I could see the angles of his handsome face. I just couldn't read them.

"Where'd that come from?" he asked softly.

"I don't know," I answered in a whisper.

"Where'd that come from, Frankie?" he repeated.

I slid my arms around him and held tight, feeling a curl of fear in my belly.

"I don't know, honey."

"It came from somewhere," he noted.

"I know."

"How do we get to that place so we can dig that out?"

"I don't know."

He went silent and I did too, holding tight to him, looking into his shadowed face.

Finally, he spoke, deep, easy, quiet, and sweet.

But what he said was scary.

"Okay, *cara*, I'll be givin' you a bunch of 'I don't knows.' But then, for you, for me, for us, I'll get to a place where I can't give you them anymore. I cannot dig blind. You gotta show me where to put the shovel. And that's gotta come from you, Frankie."

"I know."

And I did know. I just didn't know how to find that place, and I didn't want to get to the place where Ben got sick of me not knowing.

"So locate where you want me to put that shovel, baby," he urged. "And while you're searchin, do it knowin' I'm at your side. That means, you need to talk, I'm here. You need to freak, I'm still here. Bottom line, *I'm here.*"

On the heels of his words, I felt the fear evaporate. I slid my hand up his back and into his hair, asking, "How'd you learn to be so awesome?"

"I got my eyes to the prize, honey."

I slid my hand to his cheek, lifted up, and put my mouth to his.

Ben slanted his head and took it.

The kiss was deep, sweet, and easy.

When it was done, Ben shifted to kiss my neck and rolled off the bed. He went to the bathroom and came back to me.

Naked, he tangled us together and murmured, "Sleep."

I cuddled closer and closed my eyes.

"'Night, Benny."

"'Night, Frankie."

I snuggled deep and fell asleep.

⁓

"This sucks," I declared, standing in Benny's arms outside the security lines at O'Hare.

"Yep," Ben agreed.

"I wish they still let non-fliers through security so I could look out the window on the plane and see you standing inside, watching me. You could put your hand to the glass and I could put mine to the window, and we could have one final moment that happens half an hour from now, and in between we can share a coffee."

Ben's lips tipped slightly up before he noted, "We're not in a romantic movie."

"That makes it better since it's real," I returned.

Ben ignored me and continued, "And I wouldn't do that shit."

My brows shot up. "Even for me?"

"It's corny. I'm not corny."

"It's a moment."

"I got one final moment with you, it won't be with my hand on glass. It'll be with my tongue in your mouth and my hand on your ass."

I glared, even as I felt a spasm between my legs.

Ben grinned and dipped his head closer, muttering, "Bet now you're wet."

I glared harder because he was right.

Ben grinned bigger because he knew he was right, then he dipped his head even closer and took a Benny-style final moment—hand on my ass in O'Hare and everything.

I didn't mind. I liked it. I wouldn't admit it out loud, but it was *way* better than my idea.

He broke the kiss and ordered, "Call me when you get in."

"Okay."

"I'll talk to Man, schedule back-to-back nights so I can take a trip down."

"Okay."

"Check your schedule and sort a time when you dip into those frequent flier miles."

My arms around his shoulders, I gave him a squeeze, smiling up at him and trying not to laugh since we'd been through this already.

Then I said, "*Okay*, Benny."

His face changed. I liked the change just as I hated it because it told me how much he was going to miss me, mirroring my same feelings.

"Fuckin' thrilled you healed the breach, Frankie."

"Me too, Benny."

His eyes warmed even further.

Then he bent his head, touched his mouth to mine, and said there, "Go, baby."

I pressed my lips together, nodded, gave him another squeeze, and let him go.

Eight times through security, I looked back, waved, made faces, and blew kisses.

Every time I looked back, Ben was standing there, arms crossed on his chest, grinning at me.

The last time I looked back, I was through security and heading toward the concourse.

And Ben was still standing there, grinning at me.

Fourteen

AND FAST

For the three thousandth time that evening, I heard a car, went to my window, and looked out.

Three thousand was the golden number. I knew this when I saw the car outside was Benny's Explorer.

This meant I ran to the door of my apartment, threw it open and dashed out, racing straight to Ben, who'd managed in that time to angle out of his SUV.

I didn't slow. I hit him on the fly, arms wrapped around his neck, legs around his hips. He went back on a foot on impact, but I only vaguely noticed. This was because I bent my head and laid a wet one on him.

One arm around my back, one under my ass, he let me.

In order to breathe, I eventually had to lift my head.

But when I did, I smiled big down at him and said, "Hey, baby. Welcome to Brownsburg."

He smiled back, gave me a squeeze, and replied, "Think it's safe to say you're happy to see me."

"Two weeks is too long," I returned.

"Yeah," he said, still smiling. "Now, do I gotta carry you in and haul my ass back out here to get my shit, or are you gonna let go so I can take one trip?"

"I suppose I'll let go," I told him.

I said it, but I didn't let go.

Ben waited.

I held on and kept grinning at him.

After this went on awhile, Ben started laughing but hefted me up a smidge, his signal he was done with my game.

It was then it hit me he'd been on the road for hours so I should get him inside, get him a beer, and get him fed. Once I got all that accomplished, I'd get something else out of him, and not out on the street.

I loosened my limbs and he put me on my feet. But he immediately grabbed my hand and used it to adjust my position in order to open the back door of his truck. He nabbed his bag, slammed the door, and moved with me to my opened apartment door.

He did this looking around, and we were on the curvy path that led to my place when he looked down at me and noted, "This place is the shit, babe."

It was. The Brendal apartment complex in Brownsburg. Steep rent, but the landscaping was amazing. It was kept clean, had security, was gated, had top-of-the-line everything, and each floor plan for each unit was different, but differently awesome.

I had a two-bedroom floor-level unit. It was designed and landscaped so the front was shaded and mostly hidden, the entryway to the door was an alcove shrouded in ivy and tucked under the upstairs apartment. The inside had views from its windows at the dining/kitchen area to the pool, the bedrooms to some now-fallow cornfields, and the living room led into a not insubstantial courtyard that had plenty of space for a couple lounge chairs and a two-seater patio table, which I'd arranged around my own personal two-tiered fountain.

I loved it. It was awesome. Removed from the town proper, thus quiet, but close to all its amenities, a nearly straight shot to work, and well kept. It was the best apartment I'd ever had.

"Wait until you see the courtyard," I told Benny.

He looked down at me before he used my hand to shove me through my front door.

I pulled free as he closed the door, dropped his bag, and looked around.

I took two steps in, turned, and asked him, "Beer before tour, or tour before beer?"

Ben quit taking in the open space that consisted of a curved living/dining/kitchen area and his eyes came to me.

Not looking, he tossed his keys on the little tile-topped table I had by the door and replied, "Tour."

"Okay."

"Of the bedroom," he went on, and a tremble ran along my inner thighs.

Apparently, the drive down hadn't tuckered Benny out.

"Okay," I whispered.

"*Immediately*," Ben finished.

I stared into his eyes.

Then I turned and walked quickly to my bedroom.

Ben followed me.

Some time later, wearing Benny's tee, I hit the bedroom with two fresh cold ones in my hands and saw Ben in my bed, sheet to his waist, back to my headboard, chest bare, eyes lazy and on me.

I wanted to stop, take a moment to memorize that or, better yet, go get my camera and take a picture. However, that would delay me joining him.

So instead, I climbed into bed using only my knees, moved to straddle him, and the instant I got in position, he cocked his knees, semi-cocooning me in the awesomeness that was Benny.

Way better than a picture.

I handed him his beer and put mine to my lips, sucking it back.

When I tipped my head down, Ben asked, "You gonna get me drunk or are you gonna feed me?"

I tilted my head to the side and asked back, "You hungry?"

"Made me do all the work, *cara*," he remarked, and I felt my eyes begin to go squinty.

"It was only ten minutes ago, Ben, so the memory is fresh that you didn't *let* me do any of the work."

"You didn't fight that too hard."

He was right.

Still, I glared at him.

He grinned at me, put a hand to my waist, and slid it back and up my spine at the same time forcing me closer to him.

"Like your bed," he murmured when he got me where he wanted me.

"That's too bad. You continue being a jerk, you'll be sleeping on the couch."

His eyes lit with humor at a threat he knew was empty. He ignored that threat and went on, "Your place is the shit."

"I know."

"Missed you, Frankie," he whispered, and at his words I dropped forward, forehead landing on his collarbone.

"Missed you too, honey," I said there.

He wrapped his arm tight around my back and asked, "Now, you gonna feed me?"

I lifted up again and looked at him. "Of course I am, but, pointing out, *I* didn't buy ready-made barbeque. *I* put dinner in the crockpot before I went to work this morning and it's been cooking all day."

"Good news, but are you gonna keep bragging about it, or am I gonna actually get the chance to eat it?"

I ignored him this time and shared, "Out of season, but chocolate-filled snowballs for dessert."

His body froze under mine, his eyes flared, and he stared at me.

Oh no. Was that too soon? A mistake? Was that reminder going to make him pissed at me?

I had my answer in under a second, that answer meaning my beer bottle met his on my nightstand, I was on my back in my bed, Ben on top of me, and he was kissing me.

When he was done, he looked into my eyes and said, "I get dessert first."

I smiled.

⌒⟶

"The next one's gonna be a boy."

This was proclaimed over dinner at Vi and Cal's table the next evening, and it was proclaimed by Cal after Vi shared they were having a girl and they were naming her after Cal's sadly departed mom, Angela.

"I haven't even given you this one yet," Vi snapped.

I pressed my lips together in order to hold my tongue, a tongue that wanted to advise Cal that teasing his seven-months-pregnant fiancée was probably not the way to go.

Cal totally ignored her and stated, "It's not, then the next one after that will be."

Vi's eyes got huge.

"I want all sisters," Keira declared unwisely at this juncture. "My friend Heather has two brothers and their rooms *smell*. Like...*crazy*."

"Joe needs a boy so he's not totally outnumbered," Kate chimed in.

"He's got me," Keira told her sister.

"You aren't a boy," Kate pointed out.

"So?" Keira returned, and not letting her sister get another word in, she carried on, "With this one bein' a girl, that means Mom will have to pop out, like...*three more* for Joe not to be outnumbered."

"Works for me," Cal muttered before shoving seafood risotto in his mouth.

"Joe!" Vi practically yelled.

Cal looked to his woman and swallowed before saying, "Well, it does."

"Can we please end this discussion of Violet, otherwise known as the one-woman baby-making factory?"

Cal gave her a look that eloquently said that baby making required two, which fortunately the girls missed since they were giggling at what their mother had said.

But it was then I felt something coming from my side. I looked there to see Ben leaned back, arms resting casually on the arms of his chair, his eyes on his cousin, his face holding another expression I wished I had a camera to capture for eternity.

He was happy for Cal. Openly. He was happy that after the nightmare Cal had lived that forced him to live half a life, it ended with this. A beautiful, kind woman, pregnant with his child, opposite him at the end of the table. Two gorgeous girls, who acted like Cal hadn't been sitting there for eight months but he'd been doing it for eight years, and they liked it. A lovely home, a fabulous meal on the table.

Happiness.

Goodness.

Everywhere.

I reached out a hand and curled it around Ben's thigh and he aimed that look at me.

I leaned toward him and he read my lean. This meant he met me halfway and touched his mouth to mine.

When we pulled away and turned back to our plates, Keira, who'd obviously witnessed the PDA, asked Cal, "It's been months. Can I make my move on Jasper Layne now?"

Cal leveled his eyes on his girl and said, "No."

"Joe!" she cried.

"No," he repeated.

"He's only had one girlfriend the last *three months,*" Keira informed Cal, sharing plainly how into this Jasper Layne she was and, thus, how closely she paid attention.

"Yeah? He still with her?" Cal asked.

"Um...no," Keira muttered.

"And how long was he with her?" Cal pushed.

"About a week," Kate put in, and Keira cut her eyes at Kate, giving her the look any little sister gave her big sister for ratting her out.

"Then, no," Joe said firmly.

Keira slumped in her seat.

"Keira?" I called, and her eyes came to me. "Good things come to those who wait."

After I said that, Ben slid an arm along the back of my chair. Keira watched this, eyes darting between Ben, me, and his arm on the back of my chair. The devastation lifted and she smiled. Then she resumed eating.

It was then that I caught a glimpse of Cal looking at Benny with much the same look as Ben had been giving him earlier. Not as open, not as out there, but the contentment in his eyes was easy to read.

This meant what he read in Ben was that Benny was happy.

And the reason he was was because of me.

When I saw that, I felt a warmth spreading, starting from my belly.

I looked back down at my plate of the phenomenal risotto that Vi made, which Cal had told us would be the "best shit we ever tasted."

He was wrong. Benny's pies were better.

Still, it was amazing.

So I resumed eating.

⟡

"This sucks," I whispered late afternoon the next day.

"Yep," Ben whispered back.

"My turn next," I reminded him.

"Yep," Ben agreed.

"I'll get on that immediately."

"Good, baby," Ben replied. "Now kiss me."

I looked into his eyes before I rolled up on my toes and kissed him.

Ben kissed me back.

Then I had to let him go so he could get in his SUV. As he was doing that, starting up and pulling out, I made my way back to the sidewalk in front of my apartment.

I stood there and waved as he pulled away.

And I kept standing there, though not waving, until I couldn't see his truck anymore.

Only then did I repeat in a whisper, "This sucks," and walked into my empty apartment.

⟡

The next day, I swiftly made my way to my office, got there, closed the door behind me, sat behind my desk, and snatched up my cell.

I found him easily. He was all over my RECENTS.

I hit GO and put the phone to my ear.

"*Cara*," Ben answered.

"Guess what?" I asked.

"Tell me," he ordered.

"Well, I have a bunch of travel coming up the next three weeks. But after that, I just talked with my boss, and he said he couldn't see why I could occasionally work from my place in Brownsburg but couldn't work from your house in Chicago."

"No shit?" Ben asked.

"No shit," I answered.

"Excellent, baby," he said, deep, easy, and happy.

I clicked on my computer, bringing up my schedule, talking into the phone, "Looks like…" I paused, doing a scan. "I could drive up Friday night after I get back from Atlanta, just under three weeks from today. And I can stay…" I clicked, scanned, and told him, "at least until the next Thursday. I have a meeting in the office on Friday, but I can ask if they can conference call me in. That'll give us a whole week." When I finished, my voice had pitched higher with excitement.

"When do you get back from Atlanta?" Ben asked.

"Flight lands at 7:45."

"At night?"

"Yep."

"Drive up on Saturday," Ben commanded.

I sat back in my chair and blinked. "Why?"

"You land at 7:45, you aren't on the road until well after eight at least, and you're a woman alone on the road at night until late."

"I can hack it."

"Bet you can, but you aren't."

"Benny."

"Frankie," he said low and in a tone I'd never heard from him.

Hearing it then, I stared unseeing out the window that made up the wall of my office and listened closely as Ben kept going.

"You give me attitude over shit like this, I'm not gonna think it's your normal cute. I'm gonna find it frustrating. Because straight up, this means somethin' to me. You can take care of yourself, but there are assholes out there who…wouldn't matter how good you were at it…they'd be better at doin' the shit they do. You gotta stop to hit a bathroom. You get a flat tire. Whatever. You're vulnerable, even though you think you got your shit tight. The freaks come out at night, Frankie, and no freak is gonna get to my baby. I wanna see you as soon as I can see you, but I'd rather it not be after I've worried for hours that you'll get to me in one piece. So come in the morning, yeah?"

After he quit speaking, I sat frozen in my seat.

Night after night, hell, day after day, growing up from age twelve to when I got the hell out, I could be anywhere with anyone doing anything and neither of my parents cared. My sisters didn't care. My brother didn't care.

As for me, I was the big sis, got in my siblings' faces and kept track of them. I knew where they were all the time, and sometimes, I even went out to check they weren't lying to me (they often lied to me, which meant, when I'd find them, I had to go bat-shit crazy in front of their friends—so they quit lying to me).

But no one worried about where *I* was. No one worried about how *I* got there. No one worried about *me getting there safe.*

I loved him for it, but Vinnie knew I could handle myself. He knew the kind of woman I was and the one I was aiming at being. He could be macho and protective, but mostly, he let me be me. He didn't even try it, probably because he didn't want me to go bat-shit crazy.

Benny didn't care if I went bat-shit crazy.

Benny wanted me to be safe and get to him healthy. Benny cared where I was, where I was going, and how I got there.

Right then, experiencing that for the first time in my thirty-four years of life, my throat felt scratchy and my eyes felt prickly, and I had to put everything into keeping it together so I wouldn't start crying at work.

"Frankie," Ben said softly when I didn't say anything. "Don't be pissed, baby."

"Hush, Benny," I whispered, my voice croaky. "I'm figuring out one of my 'I don't knows.'"

He grew silent.

I closed my eyes and pulled in a deep breath.

After giving me time, Ben prompted, "You gonna share that with me?"

I opened my eyes. "Yeah, honey, but I'm at work and things are kind of crazy. Huge schedule and I'm everywhere the next three weeks. And it's one of those things that I wanna share with you when I have you with me. But I will say it's good, you bein' the first person in my life who gives a shit that I get where I'm goin' and do it safe."

He grew silent again, but this time, the silence was loaded. Loaded with warmth. Loaded with goodness. All of this beating into me after pinging off cell phone towers over hundreds of miles.

When his silence lasted, I called, "Benny?"

"Hush, baby, I'm tryin' to figure out if I'm more happy that I gave you that or more pissed that you'd never had it."

"Well, I'm happy," I told him.

"Good," he replied quietly.

I pulled in a deep breath to keep my emotions under control while Ben kept speaking.

"Now is one of those times when a day away from you seems way too fuckin' long, and before that, a day away from you was way too fuckin' long. Three weeks is gonna kill," he told me.

"I'm a phone call away, honey."

"Yeah, and that sucks, 'cause that phone call won't hit you at the market and end with you askin' me what I want for dinner."

"You work through dinner," I pointed out.

He had a smile in his voice when he returned, "Shut up, Frankie."

I had a smile in mine when I said, "I gotta get back to work, honey."

"Right. Talk to you later."

"Absolutely. 'Bye, Ben."

"'Bye, baby."

We disconnected and I gave myself the pleasure of feeling the goodness of all of that, including coming to my epiphany. The goodness of the last part wasn't coming to understand I'd never had anyone who gave that kind of shit about me. It was coming to that understanding when I had someone who did.

That goodness ended when my attention was taken by Travis Berger walking into the Director of Research and Development's office.

Travis was the Executive Vice President of Operations. I liked him. He was driven and aggressive and built like a pit bull. But he'd also taken me out to lunch on my first day at work, took his time to get to know me, told me in a way that felt genuine they were happy to have me on their team, and shared how brave he thought I was about the whole kidnapping/getting shot thing. In other words, generally folding me in the arms of Wyler Pharmaceuticals.

But now he looked ticked as in *ticked.*

I couldn't say I knew him very well. He was around but I was not, and he was five steps above me—me as Manager of Eastern Sales, reporting to the Assistant Director of US Sales, who reported to the Director of Sales who, in turn, reported to the Assistant VP of Sales and Marketing, who reported to the Vice President, who reported to Travis Berger.

I did know he was young. I'd never known a man in his position at his age. Our company was massive and multinational, employees numbering in the thousands, and he was in his late forties.

I did know that when I wasn't on the road, I burned the night oil when I started because I had a lot to do, a lot to learn, and a lot to prove, and I never went home when he wasn't sitting at his desk behind his own (much wider) wall of glass.

He was not always affable. From what I could tell, that just wasn't his nature. But he seemed one of those quiet, watchful types who didn't miss a trick, controlled his emotions, and would have no problem telling you that you'd fucked up, but he'd do it quietly.

So him looking ticked surprised me.

My phone ringing in my hand took me out of those thoughts, and the name of my Chicago rep on my screen put me into less reflective ones and more annoyed ones.

But I made the big bucks; I had to take the shit along with it.

So I didn't have time to think about how much I was falling in love with the process of falling in love with Benny Bianchi. I didn't think about what it might mean that the Executive Vice President of our company was walking around ticked.

I took the call.

⌒⌒

"Hey, baby."

"Things got crazy, traffic primarily, not to mention a rental car agent who was way too freaking chatty to a woman who needed to catch a plane, and now the marshal on my flight is eyeing me like he's gonna tackle me and force me to put my phone in flight mode. So it sucks, but I got on this plane by the seat of my pants and I gotta say 'hey' and 'later.' I'll call you when I land," I said to Benny after his greeting.

Over the past three weeks, this had become our gig. He worked when I was not working. I worked when he was. This meant brief snatches of conversation when I had time at work and phone calls on weekends, if we were lucky.

But Ben knew my travel schedule because he demanded to know it.

Of course, thus ensued me explaining to him that if he had email, I could easily email my schedule to him rather than reciting it over the phone while he wrote it down. He replied that he didn't get to hear my voice through an email so he'd take the cramp in his hand so he could listen to me talk.

I quit giving him shit after that.

Now Benny expected me to phone when I boarded before takeoff and phone again when I landed. He didn't mind me phoning again when I got home or to my hotel, but he didn't have the schedule memorized to that point or his phone on him so he could take my call, even if he was making a pie. Which he always did when he knew I was hitting a flight and when he knew when the wheels would hit land.

I loved this.

I loved it because I loved connecting with Benny any way I could. I loved it because Benny wanted it. I loved it because when he demanded it, I knew he was demanding it because I'd opened the floodgates to him doing something like that when I told him I was glad he gave a shit that I was safe. I loved it that he had been holding it back to spring on me when we were more solid, and doing that with a mind to the woman he knew me to be.

Last, I loved the fact that I was falling in love from (mostly) afar with Benny Bianchi.

I was doing it so fast, from my previous experience after Ben took me home from the hospital, I knew if it wasn't from afar, it would happen a lot quicker.

Maybe instantly.

"You've spotted the marshal?" Ben asked, taking me from my thoughts.

"Yep. He's hot." I felt unhappy vibes from Ben over the phone, which made me smile but they also made me say, "You're hotter, obviously."

"A save, but not a good one."

"Whatever," I muttered.

"Call me when you get home," he ordered.

"You got it, *capo*."

"And call me before you leave in the morning."

"You're on my speed dial."

"And bring that nightie, the purple one with the pink at the tits. I'm feeling nostalgic."

That order caused a lovely ripple and me to hiss into my phone, "Ben, don't turn me on when I'm fifteen minutes away from thirty thousand feet."

He didn't miss a beat as he replied, "First chance we got, vacation, plane ride, mile-high club."

God!

Benny.

"Are you listening to me?" I snapped.

His voice was nothing but sweet when he whispered, "Get home safe, Frankie."

I huffed out a breath, not enjoying his increasingly utilized tactic of quelling my attitude by bringing out all the awesomeness of Benny. Even so, I had not yet figured out recourse other than to have my attitude quelled.

Falling in love with Benny was knocking me off my game.

Whatever.

"I will, honey," I told him. "And I'll call."

"Right. Later, *cara*."

"Later, Benny."

He disconnected.

I eyed the hot guy, who perhaps only in my fertile imagination was the air marshal, and put my phone into flight mode.

⌐

I parked my Z in the space off the alley at the back of Benny's place.

I grabbed my big suitcase out of the back, dropped it to its rollers, extended the handle, and barely cleared the back of my car before Ben was there.

Then I was pressed against the side of my car, Ben pressed into me, one hand at my ass, one hand curved around my side at my breast, thumb stroking *this close* to ground zero, tongue in my mouth.

When he lifted his head (and after my eyes fluttered open), he said, "Welcome home, Frankie."

I pressed deeper into him and smiled.

Ben smiled back, let me go, grabbed the handle of my case in one hand, my hand in his other, and he dragged us both up and into his house.

Ben left my bag in the kitchen and kept dragging me up to his bedroom.

But not before I saw it.

Right there, out in the open, for anyone to see.

A white sheet of paper, on the top in bold script, FRANCESCA, and on the bottom in slashed scribbles, dates and times.

My schedule.

On Ben's fridge.

Yes.

I was falling in love with Benny.

And fast.

⌒⟶

I felt Ben get close to my back.

The good part about this was that he lifted up the hem of his tee that I was wearing and cupped my ass over my panties when he did it.

The bad part was him looking over my shoulder at what I was doing at his kitchen counter and promptly asking, "Tuna casserole? Seriously?"

I twisted my neck to look up at him and pointed out, "Your cupboards were bare, Benny. I had two options. Tuna casserole or lasagna made out of chicken and cream of mushroom soup."

He'd moved his eyes from the casserole I was assembling to me as I spoke, and when I was done, he started.

"Drawer's full of delivery menus."

"And my life is full of eating out, room service, getting home late and doing it with takeout in my car. I wanna cook," I replied.

Ben's face got soft as I spoke and he muttered on a squeeze of my ass, "Whatever you want, baby." Then he moved away, stating, "We'll go to the market tomorrow."

"Works for me," I told the casserole.

It was after spending all day in bed with Benny.

Not true. He got up and made us sandwiches while I snoozed, since I'd gotten in my car at six in the morning, hightailed my ass up to Chicago, and, upon arrival, got laid thoroughly and energetically by Benny Bianchi. He came back to his bedroom with two sandwiches filled with salami, turkey, and provolone, covered in mayo and Dijon.

He also came up with three bags of chips.

Benny and his chips.

I loved that.

Now we'd surfaced. It was the dinner hour. Ben had arranged for the night off, so it was him and me.

And I was cooking.

I quit grating cheddar cheese into a bowl and opened the tub of Pringles. Then I poured the remains of the tub into the cheese.

"Pringles?" Ben asked, and I twisted my neck to see him lounging in nothing but his jeans at his kitchen table, beer in hand, eyes on me.

Benny Bianchi, lord of the manor, watching his woman cooking.

Why was that so hot?

"Pringles," I replied, then turned back and grabbed the metal spoon to start stirring and scrunching. "We aren't having tuna casserole. We're having cheesy, crunchy, Pringle-topped tuna casserole *à la* Frankie."

"I'da known about the crunchy top, I wouldn't've bitched."

I looked over my shoulder to see if he was giving me shit and grinned at him when I noted he was serious.

A man who appreciated a crunchy-topped tuna casserole.

I liked that.

The insanity in that was, I was thinking about tuna casserole, which meant I had officially entered woman-falling-in-love zone, a zone that made women crazy.

Since I was already crazy, this was a dangerous place for me to be.

As if reading my thoughts about being crazy, Ben said, "Three weeks."

At first, I didn't get him, so I looked back to what I was doing and asked, "What?"

"The answer to your 'I don't know.'"

That was when I got him.

I stopped smushing the Pringles and cheese and, spoon in hand, turned to Benny and asked, "Can we talk about that when the casserole is in the oven?"

"You get I'm into you?" he asked back crazily.

I thought about the four orgasms I'd had that day and answered slowly, "Uh...yeah."

"Okay, you get that. Do you get that I'm *into you*?"

My breathing stopped coming easy.

Still, I managed to get out, "Yes, Benny."

"Right. So you get that, then you'll get that you came to an understanding about yourself that was meaningful. I'm into you, so whatever that was means something to me too. I gave you time to give it to me. I can give you another ten minutes, babe, what I'm askin' is that you don't make me."

What he was saying was that when I freaked out on him, we nearly lost what we were enjoying right then, the hours before, and even apart, the weeks before that. I had no reason to give him that explained what I did to tear us apart. I hit upon part of that reason. And he needed that reason in order to have some hope that I was working on it so I wouldn't do it again.

I'd made him wait.

He was done waiting.

Getting all that, I was powerless not to blurt, "No one gave a shit about where I was or what I did growin' up."

"That part I got, and in gettin' it, realized I pretty much knew it already," Ben replied.

I drew in a breath and turned back to the Pringles.

I went back to smushing but did it speaking.

"It was my life. I didn't really think about it until you said that to me over the phone."

"Okay," he said when I stopped speaking. "Now, where does that lead you, *cara*?"

"It leads me to the fact that I don't have the training to be good at this."

"Good at what?"

"Anything," I whispered to the bowl, then saw the pot with the noodles was near to boiling over, so I went to the stove and turned it down.

On my way back, I ran into Benny.

His hands came to my hips and I tipped my head back to look at him.

"You know that's whacked, right?" he asked softly.

"Rationally, maybe. Crazy-Frankie, which is who I happen to be, no way."

"Rewind," he stated. "You found a man you fell in love with, shacked up with, and stood beside, even when he decided to get involved with the mob."

I pressed my lips together.

Benny kept going.

"Through that, though, you lived clean. You stood beside him all the same."

I unpressed my lips to remind him, "I already admitted to you I was givin' up on Vinnie."

"And that's a bad thing?" he returned.

"Do we have to go through this again?"

"I don't know, do we?"

"She bailed," I declared, and Ben's brows drew together.

"Come again?"

"Ma. She bailed," I told him. "Repeatedly. On Dad. On her other husbands. Boyfriends. It wasn't the same, but it was in a prolonged way, a *very* prolonged way, bailin' on her kids."

"Keep goin'," he urged.

"Same with Dad. Women in, women out."

"And?"

"No connections. No roots. Nothin' to drag them down."

"I'm tryin', honey, but I'm not followin'."

"That's what I learned. That's how I was raised. That's what I know."

"Fuck," he whispered, getting it.

"Yeah," I replied.

He put it out there verbally, "So that's why you're kickin' your own ass, thinkin' before he was killed of givin' up on Vinnie."

"I didn't want to be like them."

"And you think you'll do the same to me?"

I shook my head but said, "I don't know. Maybe."

"You need to reason that out, honey."

I didn't know what he meant, so I asked, "What?"

"First, your folks, they were shit parents. I know they're yours, babe, but evidence suggests they're straight-up shit human beings."

"Ben—" I started, but he was not done and he talked over me.

"Heard from your ma or your dad since you got out of the hospital?"

"Well, Ma phoned to ask me to her wedding."

His mouth got tight but he still managed to say, "Classic."

"It's who she is," I informed him.

"Yeah, and the fuck of it is, you got no choice but to accept that. You can cut her out or you can take her as she comes. She was my ma, she'd have seen the back of me a long fuckin' time ago. What does that say about you, Frankie?"

His words penetrated, they did it deep, and I went completely still.

Ben, eyes on me, hands on me, caught it.

That was why he said, "Right."

"Oh my God," I whispered, something fluttering in my chest.

"Right," he repeated. "Nat fucks up, she comes to you. Your ma gets hitched a-fuckin'-gain, she invites you to the wedding. Heard from Enzo Junior?"

"He calls. Not often, but regularly," I said quietly.

Benny nodded once, shortly. "Yeah, pours his shit on you. His life's a fuckin' mess, but you do not tell him to sort his shit out. You do not tell your mother she shit all over you growin' up and you don't wanna watch her marry another schmuck whose heart she's gonna crush. You don't do any of that shit 'cause you're Frankie. You stick."

All he was saying struck so deep, I had to lift my hands and curl them around his wrists to stay steady.

But Ben didn't stop talking.

"You know, babe, it is not okay for a woman to live thirty-four years without one person in her life givin' a shit. I was workin' through my shit with Vinnie, seein' as I had no choice. The man's dead and I gotta let it go. But heard that and got pissed at him all over again."

"He knew I could take care of myself. It was respect, him giving that to me," I explained.

"Bullshit," Ben bit out. "I get you get that I can take care of myself. I know how to drive a car so I can get places safe. Someone gets in my space, I can handle the situation. But it still would feel good you showed you were happy I got home safe, even if I went to the fuckin' grocery store. You do that no matter it's dick or pussy, if you care about somebody. That said, a man has a woman, he sees to that woman. He doesn't leave her to see to herself. It's not disrespect to do that. It's disrespect the other way around."

I stopped breathing.

Ben kept going.

"Pissed at your parents for doin' that to you. Pissed at Vinnie for doin' that to you. Contrary to that, I'm glad I got to give it to you, because you gettin' it now means you'll appreciate it. It also means I don't have to put up with your shit when I do what I gotta do to look after you."

That thing in my chest stopped fluttering.

"You've got a good roll going here, honey, don't fuck it up," I warned.

"Impossible," he shot back instantly. "You're into me. You're Frankie. I could treat you like shit and you'd stand by me. But lucky for you, I have zero intention of doin' that."

That flutter came back and it wasn't a flutter anymore.

It was shaking me to the core from the inside.

I held on to his wrists and stared into his eyes and knew in that instant exactly why I was falling so fast for Benny Bianchi.

Because he had zero intention of treating me like shit and every intention of caring about me.

"See I scored with that," he said softly, staring right back at me.

"Big time," I replied softly too.

"You're worried about hurting me," he kept talking softly. "Doin' the shit you grew up watchin' your parents do."

I nodded uncertainly. "I think so."

"So, in order to protect me, you instigated a self-fulfilling prophecy."

I just kept nodding.

He lifted his hands and mine went with them, even as he cupped my jaw and bent close so his face was all I could see.

"Baby, let that shit go." His fingers dug in. "It's *not in you.*"

"What if it is?" My voice sounded tortured.

"How could that be?" he asked gently.

"It's who I am."

"If it was, think about it, Francesca, when would you have left Vinnie?"

I didn't answer, just held on to his wrists at my jaw and stared in his eyes, knowing it would have been early.

After the franchise idea crashed and burned, possibly.

After the sandwich shop tanked, probably.

The minute he started things up with Sal.

Definitely.

"You got it good. You got someone who looks after you, you got someone who gives a shit. Livin' the way you lived, losin' shit you didn't even know you should have, do you *ever* think you'd leave?" he pushed.

"No," I breathed.

"No," Ben agreed.

I kept holding on, staring into his eyes while I said, "I think the noodles are gonna turn mushy, Benny."

"I don't give a fuck, Frankie."

"I also think I need tequila with dinner," I went on.

"Lucky for you, cupboards are bare, but I got that."

"You're the shit, Benny Bianchi," I whispered and watched him close his eyes.

Then I felt his hands pull me to him. He kissed my forehead before he moved me back and again looked at me.

"You gonna let me give you good?" he whispered back.

God.

Benny.

"Yes."

"You gonna freak and bail on me?"

"No."

His fingers dug in again as he said, "That's my Frankie."

I wanted to, I really did, but I couldn't stop them. The tears hit my eyes, one dropping and sliding down my cheek.

Ben saw it, pulled me by my jaw into his chest, and let go only to wrap his arms tight around me.

I did the same to him.

Another tear slid down, but I held tight to Ben and got control.

While I did, Ben held tight to me.

Minutes later, he moved to put his lips to my hair and said there, "I'll get the noodles, babe. You deal with the rest."

"Right," I agreed.

"You good?" he asked.

I was better than I'd ever been, in the arms of Benny Bianchi.

"Yep."

"Good," he murmured, then kissed the top of my head, let me go, and went to the noodles on the stove.

I turned to the counter and dealt with the rest.

The next day, Ben and I went to the market.

We got napkins.

Fifteen

CRAZY

I was hustling out of the staff kitchen on my way to my office with my clean coffee cup because it was Friday and no one wanted to come back to the office on Monday seeing the dried remains of last week's coffee in their mug.

Even though it was barely four o'clock, the place was nearly deserted. It was May, summer was coming on strong, and people were way past cabin fever. They wanted out and about and to make as much of the weekend as possible.

I was one of the last in the office, because even though I'd been there seven months, I wasn't the kind of person to slow down. I had numbers to reach, but I never looked at numbers to reach as numbers to reach. I looked at them as numbers whose asses needed kicked. I was guiding my reps to kicking that ass, and even though Ben was right then at my apartment, having called ten minutes ago to tell me he'd arrived, I wanted to make sure it was all good at work before I left. I hadn't seen him since I spent the week with him two weeks ago. He was down for a long weekend, leaving on Tuesday, and I was taking Monday off.

So I had to have my ducks in a row so I could be all about Ben and not have work encroach on that.

I'd already packed up so when I got to my office, I put down my mug, grabbed my purse and my computer bag, nabbed my keys and cell off my desk, and hightailed it out the door.

I was walking by Randy Bierman's door (he was the Director of Research and Development) and saw he was the only one left in the office. He was mostly turned in his chair to look outside, phone to his ear.

In all the time I'd been there, I still didn't know what to make of Randy, seeing as most of the time he was kind of a dick. He treated his assistant like shit, was cranky nearly every day, and he was intensely secretive. Always behind closed doors. Rushing to his office the instant his cell phone rang. Shutting the blinds on the window wall to his office, like we all could read lips or had superhuman hearing.

The guy was research and development at a pharmaceutical company, so secretive was part of the job description. But on my first day, I'd signed a nondisclosure agreement that was twelve freaking pages long, and I was management, as was everyone on our floor. I had stock options. I liked getting my salary. I liked the zeroes at the end of that salary. I'd hardly screw that pooch, nor would anyone on that floor. Especially since, if we did, we'd be memorizing the inside of a courtroom and selling a kidney to afford our attorneys because Wyler would sue us until we were living in a box on the street.

Still, a girl had to make an effort and I worked with the guy.

So I stopped by his door and was about to knock, just to give him a wave as a nonverbal goodbye, when I heard him speak.

"I don't give a fuck. It's the last time, no more. You come at me again, you will force my hand, and how you force it, you will not like. Are you understanding me?"

He didn't sound happy, and the words were definitely not happy, so I did not knock. I backed away and headed to the elevators, thinking maybe I should give up on Randy. Nothing Randy did gave any indication he was anything other than what he seemed to be.

A dick.

And it was my experience that dicks weren't worth the time, even (and maybe especially) when you worked with them.

I gratefully left that behind and was in my car, happy to be heading home. A home that was a kickass apartment that had a courtyard with patio furniture I could finally use. A home in which a hot guy I was coming to love (okay, I was mostly there already) was waiting for me, and after two weeks of phone calls with him, we had three unadulterated days together.

These were my blissful thoughts when my phone rang.

I'd tossed my cell on my purse in the seat beside me, but my Bluetooth was in the vinyl around my stick shift.

I snatched it up, put it in my ear, and hit Go.

"You've reached Francesca Concetti," I greeted.

"Frankie, *amata*."

Sal.

"Hey, Sal."

"You're well?" he asked.

"Yep. You?"

"Things are good," he answered.

"Gina?"

"Gina, not so good."

I felt my neck get tight.

I knew I shouldn't. Ben was right, Sal was probably a sociopath. But I still liked him.

I could easily blame him for Vinnie's death, but he didn't twist Vinnie's arm to make Vinnie work for him. He didn't say no to Vinnie joining his crew, but still, that was all on Vinnie.

And when Vinnie was working for Sal, before, and definitely after, Sal and his wife, Gina, were good to me. Take out the Mafia part and they would have been the parents I would have wanted to have.

I'd never say it to Vinnie Senior and Theresa, because they'd lose their minds and probably never speak to me again, but Sal and Gina were a lot like them.

Sal was a little more intense, rougher around sharp edges that were covered in a veneer of refinement that came with money and power. Gina was a little quieter than Theresa, but she found ways to do what she had to do as an Italian woman, mother, and grandmother, which consisted of meddling, getting her way, and controlling her family.

Sal did not like me and look after me just because Vinnie died and he felt that was his duty. He cared about me. Genuinely. The same with Gina.

Seeing as he was a crime boss and she was his spouse, the smart thing to do after Vinnie died would have been to extricate myself from their lives to the point it was just about Christmas cards, eventually losing their address and stopping even that.

But I was me. Frankie.

And apparently, even when I should, I didn't bail.

This thought would have made me smile, but I didn't smile because I was worried about Gina.

"Something's wrong?" I asked cautiously.

"Yeah, *amata*, somethin's wrong. She's got a lotta love for her Frankie. She hears her girl has moved to Indy but comes home to Chicago frequently and she doesn't get a call? She doesn't get an offer to meet for coffee? Her girl doesn't come over and sit at our table?"

Shit.

I drew in a deep breath and shared quietly, "Sal, honey, you probably know, but I'm seeing Benny Bianchi."

"I know, *cara*, and good for you. Good for him. It's about time that boy pulled his head outta his ass."

I blinked at the road.

Sal kept going.

"Now he's shoved it right back in. He finally got you where he's been wantin' you and where are you? In Indy. He's in Chicago. *Amata*, what is that?"

"I had a job to take in Indy, Sal."

"And he's got a pizzeria that makes more money than Tiffany's, Francesca."

"What does that mean?" I asked, slowing for a stoplight.

I heard him expel an exasperated breath, then explain like I wasn't the brightest bulb in the box, "It isn't like you gotta work."

Oh. That was what it meant.

"That's not the kind of woman I am, Sal."

"Benny got his head outta his ass...*again*...he'd have words with you and make you that kind of woman."

I reminded myself he was a mob boss—a mob boss who loved me, but a mob boss who very likely did a variety of pretty scary things to people who pissed him off.

Therefore, I didn't turn my full attitude on him when I said, "Love you, Sal. You know it. And no disrespect. But the fifties were a really long time ago."

"I'll give you that, Frankie, but you couldn't get a job in Chicago?"

"This isn't a job, Sal, it's a career. And you don't jack people around like that or you'll find your career gets real short real fast," I informed him as the light turned green and I hit the gas.

He was silent as I shifted to second, then into third and moved toward the next light, hoping it would stay green.

Finally, Sal spoke again.

"Benny and you, this mean not-so-good things for my Gina?"

I knew what he meant. He knew Ben detested him. Ben might not detest Gina, but Gina came with Sal so he had nothing to do with her by extension. Me with Benny—a Benny who might not demand that I keep his house while he's out making pizzas, but still was a man who was *all* man, not to mention Italian American man—meant that he could very well, by extension, demand I had nothing to do with either of them.

Sal was asking for Gina.

But Sal loved me, so Sal was also asking for Sal.

I thought that was sweet and it was precisely why they hadn't fallen off my Christmas list in eight years.

"We haven't really worked that out yet," I said to Sal.

"I see," Sal murmured.

"Though, I will say, I'll be at your table again, but I'm sure you won't be surprised to know that Benny won't be with me. You know you and Gina mean the world to me, but Ben and I are working this out long-distance, and when we have time together, it's been all about taking that time to be together. That means I lost track. But next time I'm up, I'll make certain to take some time with you and Gina."

I approached my turn and hit my turn signal as Sal replied, "That'd make Gina happy, *amata.*"

His voice said that would make Sal happy too.

Another five years on my Christmas list.

At least.

"Okay, Sal. Tell her I said 'hey' and I miss her."

"Will do, Frankie. *Addio, mia bella*."

"*Ciao*, Sal."

I hit the button on my Bluetooth to disconnect and tried to decide if I should share that call with Benny.

I was driving through The Brendal by the time I decided I would, but maybe I'd do it Monday.

Or on the phone on Tuesday.

I was swinging into my spot next to Ben's Explorer, again feeling happy at the same time perplexed as I saw my other guest spot taken up by a shiny blue Chrysler sedan with Illinois plates, when my cell rang again.

I was seconds away from Benny, however, so I decided the call could wait.

The caller obviously decided the same thing because my phone only rang twice before it stopped ringing.

I was out of my Z and fighting back the urge to skip (or run) to my front door when the door opened and Ben prowled out.

Tee, jeans, running shoes.

Top-to-toe yummy.

I decided on running but didn't get that first stride in because the look on Ben's hard face stopped me. If that didn't do it, him lifting a hand palm toward me did.

I met him on the sidewalk at the end of the path to my door.

"Called you just as you hit your space," he announced and immediately kept announcing, "Five minutes ago, you got company."

I looked back at the car in my guest spot that I'd never seen before, then up at Benny and I heard it.

"*Frankie!*"

Loud. Jovial. Nothing ever got him down because he wouldn't let it.

I knew that voice.

Enzo Concetti, Senior.

My father.

"Shit," I whispered, not tearing my eyes from Benny.

"Your dad," Ben confirmed what I already knew. "I wanted to slam the door in his face but couldn't. Decided to call but you showed."

"Fuck," I got out before Dad descended.

Regardless of the fact I had a purse and computer bag, which would make any embrace awkward, he wrapped his arms around my waist, picked me up, and shook me.

"My baby girl!" he shouted.

I couldn't move my hands so I just looked down at him and greeted, "Hey, Dad."

"Heya, gorgeous." He grinned up at me, then dropped me to my heels, let me go, turned, and clapped Ben hard on the shoulder, leaving his hand there and squeezing. "Girl, you scored yourself the good Bianchi."

Ben's face turned to granite.

As for me, my insides shriveled up.

Dad seemed not to notice Ben's response, or the unbelievable inappropriateness of his words, and squeezed Ben's shoulder, swaying it forward and back while saying, "No offense to the dead or that other one, uh...Manny."

I watched as, slowly, Ben looked down to the hand on his shoulder before he turned his eyes to me.

This forced me to jerk out of my horrified stupor and cry, sounding desperate and therefore loud, "Let's take this inside."

Dad, who gave Ben one more sway while I held my breath, hoping Benny wouldn't blow before Dad let him go, said, "Excellent idea."

Thankfully, Dad let Ben go, but regretfully, he did it in order to move toward my front door.

I caught Benny's eyes, giving him a nonverbal, yet still screaming, *I'm so sorry.*

Ben reached out and took my computer bag, then with his free hand, grabbed my hand and started me up the path my father was already taking.

"How'd you find me, Dad?" I called to his back, shifting the handle of my purse to my shoulder.

He stopped, turned, and smiled at me.

In that glance, I saw what I'd known a lifetime. I got a lot of him—dark hair that was shiny and lustrous (even without product), light brown, almond-shaped eyes with lashes I never had to curl because they were naturally curly, good bone structure.

Dad was tall, though, and I wasn't, not really. And I got Ma's curves and her light skin.

Looking at him now, well past his prime, he looked better than most men in their prime could ever hope to look. Vital. Strong. Handsome.

"Was it a secret?" he asked on a big smile, sharing it was all the same to him, if it was or wasn't. He didn't give a shit. If I didn't want to see him, he was coming anyway.

I knew this because he did.

But actually, it was a secret. He was one of the many reasons I escaped Chicago. So it was not great news he found me in Brownsburg.

Before I could answer, he went on, turning back to the door, "Enzo Junior."

At that moment, I decided that once I found a way to get rid of Dad, calmed Benny down, fed him, and had sex with him, I was heading straight out to the drugstore to buy a big, fat, red Sharpie. I would then go home and use it, crossing my brother's name off my Christmas list.

"Babe," Ben said low and with a weird hint, not of anger...of warning.

I didn't like the idea of what amounted to a *further* warning, especially when the bad news had already picked me up and shook me not a minute before.

Still, I looked up from watching Dad disappear into my apartment to catch Ben's eyes.

The instant I did, he said, "Not a lotta time, *cara*, but brace. He's not alone, and you get in there, don't figure you're gonna be happy."

What did that mean?

I had no chance to ask.

We were at the door.

Luckily, I braced. Further to that fortune, Ben tightened his hand in mine, and for once, he moved into my house before me.

This gave me a view to what was inside so I had a moment to process it, the kick it dealt to my stomach, and partially recover before I had to face it.

Standing among the calm, muted blue, green, and purple colors of my furniture, and the feng shui hand I had at decorating that was uncluttered and reflected the subdued tones of my furniture in harmony with my personality (or what I wanted my personality to be, which was far from subdued), stood my father's woman.

I didn't remember her name because I'd only met her twice. Once when Dad stopped at my apartment in Chicago when she was with him. He'd dragged her up, but he was only there because, "Baby, your daddy's seriously gotta pee." He did his business while she and I made awkward conversation. Then he came out, gave me a kiss, and they took off to wherever Dad preferred to be without him even telling me her name.

The second time, Enzo was in town and we were all together—Nat, Davey, Cat, her husband, Art, Enzo, and the girl he was dating at the time (who he also broke up with during that trip, making the trip home less than enjoyable...freaking Enzo).

Of course, this dissolved into pandemonium when Cat said something that set off Nat. They started fighting, loud and foul-mouthed. Enzo tried to play peacemaker and got sucked in, so he got loud and foul-mouthed. Dad lost his mind because we were "embarrassing" him in front of his woman, and he kicked us all out, even me, and I wasn't doing anything.

That had been at least a year ago. Maybe two.

But in the end, I'd long since learned not to remember their names. They came, they went. When I was younger, I would latch on, hoping one would have staying power and maybe give me what I didn't know at the time I'd needed. Most of the time, they were pretty cool and a few of them were very loving, sometimes genuinely, sometimes doing it thinking they could get to Dad's heart through his kids.

They never stuck, though, and after a little girl gets heartbroken repeatedly at losing woman after woman who drifted through her life, she learned.

I learned.

So I didn't remember this one's name.

Dad got older, but his women's ages stayed the same. The problem was, he had age, experience, and although not much maturity, he had some. His women usually didn't, at least the last part, so he got bored of them easily.

This one had lasted a lot longer than most.

And I was seeing she was probably going to last even longer (though this was not a guarantee) because she was obviously very pregnant.

My brother had two women who were imminently going to give him children, as well as lawsuits for child support.

And my father's next child would be aunt or uncle to someone who was their same age.

Now.

Seriously.

What the fuck was up with *that*?

I didn't realize I'd frozen just beyond my small foyer until I felt Ben's hand give mine a squeeze.

When it did, I looked from the woman standing in my living room to my father.

"Tell me this is a fucking joke," I demanded.

"Frankie," Ben said softly beside me.

I felt him get close, but I didn't tear my eyes away from my father.

"Francesca," Dad clipped, the jovial, nothing-gets-him-down-because-he-wouldn't-let-it look evaporating and anger replacing it.

I looked quickly to the woman, who I noted distractedly was very attractive, but she had also turned very pale. "No offense to you. You're probably awesome. But…" I looked back to Dad. "Are you fucking serious?"

"We came down to share our good news with you personally, spread the joy, and this is what we get?" Dad asked back sharply.

I, again, quickly looked at the woman and repeated, "Again, no offense to you…" My eyes returned to my father. "But, just sayin', next time, spread the joy over the phone."

Dad planted his hands on his hips and returned, "I do not believe you're actin' this way."

"You don't?" I asked, leaning back and pulling my hand from Ben's so I could throw both up. Then I lifted one and pressed a finger to my face. "Well, let me see…why would I react this way when you've gotten a woman pregnant?" I threw my hand out and finished sarcastically, "Oh, I know! You're bringin' a kid into this world, and you're the kind of man who had another kid who got shot and you," I leaned toward him, screaming, "*did not even go see her in the hospital!*"

I heard the door close behind me, meaning Ben closed it, but he got back to me quickly and I knew this when I felt his arm hook around my waist. He pulled me back a foot and then positioned in front of me, slightly to my side.

I was totally pissed way the hell off, but still, him doing that…

God.

Seriously.

Benny.

"You got shot?" the woman asked, her voice sounding dismayed, and I looked around Benny to her.

"Yeah, it was on the news," I shared.

"I don't watch the news," she said quietly, her eyes going to Dad. "Did you know this, Enzo?"

"Yeah, he did, since my ma called him the night it happened," Ben put in but didn't allow further reaction to this news. Being the awesomeness of Benny, he immediately moved to end our brief scene. "Now, congratulations on your news. Wish the best for you," he said to the woman, then turned to Dad and went on, "But this didn't go too good and you got a long drive ahead of you, so I'm thinkin' we should cut this here before it deteriorates."

Ben's rational suggestion was ignored while the woman stared at my dad and my dad, who read her stare, stated, "Sweetheart, that happened to Frankie around the time you told me you were havin' my baby."

"And I told you I was havin' your baby and you seemed pretty excited, Enzo, but you didn't take me on a six-month-long celebration cruise with no phones, Internet, or Morse code machines," she snapped back, and I felt my body jerk and my eyes get big.

None of Dad's women ever spoke to him like that.

Not a one.

Except maybe my ma.

"Chrissy, sweetheart, I didn't want anything to—" Dad started.

"Do not utter another word, Enzo Concetti," she hissed, leaning toward him. Then her eyes cut to me, and Ben crowded me, even as I pressed into the side of his back at the look in her eyes. "Are you okay?" she asked, then tossed a hand my way. "I mean, after the shooting."

"Uh…yeah. It was ages ago."

"Was it random?" she bit out.

"Um…no. I was kidnapped by a crime lord and taken to a lakeside community. I escaped and ran for my life through the forest with another lady. The crime lord caught up with us and shot me. Then Ben," I made a lame gesture in the air beside me to indicate Benny, "and his cousin, Cal, the boyfriend of the lady I was with, shot him. Seein' as Cal shot him in the head, he didn't survive. Though, Ben shot him in the gut, where the guy shot me, and I can attest that, even if that was all he'd had, he wouldn't have been doin' very well for a while. Luckily, though, he's dead, and I don't say that because I'm a bad person. I say that because he was a crazy person and he shot me."

When I was done rambling, her narrowed eyes slowly cut to my father.

"She was kidnapped *and* shot?" she asked.

"Chrissy—"

"Did you know about the kidnapping?" Chrissy demanded.

Dad didn't say a word, but he looked uncomfortable.

Ben said a word, though, and it was, "Yep."

Chrissy looked fit to be tied for a good long time. While I reached out a hand to catch Benny's, trying to breathe in the air clogged by a pregnant woman's fury, I fought back the desire to laugh. Hard.

Finally, she looked to me, and the further fury on her face made me press closer to Benny.

Then it faded clean away and she whispered, "I'm sorry."

I stared at her wondering if that just happened.

Ben was not quite as dumbfounded.

I knew this when he stated, "You don't have to be. You didn't know. You aren't blood." Ben jerked his head Dad's way. "But he should be."

"I—" Dad began.

"*Shut it,*" Benny suddenly barked with such ferocity, my whole body jerked. "You do not get to do this. I didn't know where Francesca would be at when I let you in, but now I know. So now I'm gonna tell you, this is the last time you perpetrate a scene like this with Frankie. You were not a good father. You are not a good man. You're selfish and stupid, thinkin' for however many years you been on this earth primarily with your dick. Your girl laid in a hospital bed after draggin' her bleedin' body through leaves, and that was *after* she ran for her life, and you got the fuckin' *balls* to show at her house unannounced and drop a bomb on her, not even sayin' word fuckin' one about what she went through without the support of her goddamned family?"

Ben shook his head, his eyes pinning Dad to the spot across the room, and he kept going.

"No. Frankie will put up with that shit because she's a good woman, a good daughter. She's Frankie. But I'm her man and I'm tellin' you right now, I *won't.*"

Dad squared his shoulders and declared, "Maybe we should leave."

"Good idea," Ben shot back, shifting immediately, taking me with him so we were no longer barring the door.

It was then that Dad did what Dad did when anything threatened to drag him down.

He escaped the situation immediately.

And in this instance, that meant him not looking at a single soul—not even the woman carrying his child, standing right there, not the daughter he'd come to see—and walking right out the door.

"This was a very bad idea and I'm so sorry," Chrissy said quietly, moving to follow him.

"Again, not your place to apologize," Ben said.

She nodded to him and would have only given me an embarrassed glance and a chin dip to say goodbye, but I didn't let her.

As she passed me, I grabbed her hand.

She stopped and looked at me.

"Am I havin' a brother or sister?"

Hope flared in her eyes and I got further ticked at my father, because seeing it, I knew she'd wanted this to go a whole lot better than it did. I also knew giving her child family was important. So I knew if I ever got to know her, I'd probably like her.

"Sister," she answered.

I smiled. It was small but I gave her that and whispered, "You probably need to go, but call Enzo Junior. Get my number. Keep in touch."

Bright filled her eyes and she whispered back, "I thought this would be a happy surprise. I never would have come with Enzo if I'd known—"

I cut her off with my hand tightening around hers. "I'm sorry for you it wasn't. But I do wish you the best bringin' my little sister into the world."

She nodded and squeezed my hand back, saying softly, "Thanks, Francesca. And I'll call your brother. Get your number."

287

"Good," I replied. "Now make him be safe driving you two home," I ordered, dipping my head to her belly.

She grinned at me, no bright in her eyes this time, nodded again, and hurried out the door.

The instant it closed, Ben stated, "Pure fuckin' Frankie."

I looked his way. "What?"

"Your best bet is to steer clear of that situation, which is right now not good with the forecast of gettin' real fuckin' messy, and you tell her to keep in touch."

"She's carrying my baby sister," I returned.

"Yeah. Pure fuckin' Frankie."

It was then I processed the look on his face.

So I smiled.

Ben didn't smile.

He ordered, "Come here, Francesca."

Our happy reunion delayed by a crazy one, unusually, I immediately did what I was told.

⌒

"Frankie, *tesorina*, stop."

I closed my eyes, slid Benny out of my mouth, and took my time looking up at him.

It was after the scene with Dad, time for the good reunion after the bad, and things hadn't started great.

And that was all on me.

It might have been being wound up by Dad's visit and his news. It could also be what he'd said about me scoring the good Bianchi.

But it was mostly about me thinking that it was high time I saw to something I hadn't seen to since Benny and I got physical.

He frequently went down on me to spectacular results every single time.

Either due to unconsciously avoiding it or the fact that Ben guided things in bed (completely), I'd never returned the favor.

Now, I was.

And I was tense, in my head, knowing he knew from Vinnie that I wasn't good at it, worried he was thinking the same thing, and trying too hard.

I opened my eyes and looked his way and there it was. I wasn't good at it. Ben's face did not look at all like the dark hunger I was used to seeing when we were naked.

"Come here, baby."

I didn't want to go there.

I wanted to grab my phone and run to the bathroom, lock myself in, and exist on pizza and Chinese deliveries through the window until I knew Benny was gone and he'd made the decision never to see me again.

"Frankie, come here," Ben repeated.

I still didn't move, because I was frozen with humiliation.

I'd been embarrassed a lot in my life.

Like when I was seven and my mother wore that black, slinky, wrap-around dress to church that had so much cleavage, it almost showed nipple, and Father Patrick's eyes nearly bugged out of his head when he came out to give mass. Not to mention, when he gave it, his face was tight and I knew he was displeased with my mother and the fact that all the men were paying more attention to her breasts than his sermon.

Also the many times my father would run into someone he didn't get along with too well, and it wouldn't matter where we were—at a Cubs' game, at a Burger King—he couldn't ignore it. He'd say something smartass and the guy would return it and it was never pretty. He'd even once goaded a man who was with his wife and kids and didn't want to be drawn in. But Dad didn't stand down until the man had no choice but to call him out.

That one ended bloody, for both men, and not only had Dad done that in front of his kids without thought, he'd pushed that man into doing the same in front of his.

But even with all that, and worse, I was never more embarrassed than I was right then.

This, of course, made me freeze, perpetuating my embarrassment seeing as I was on all fours close to Benny's cock, staring at him, unmoving.

"Fuck," Ben muttered, did an ab curl, grabbed me under my arms, and hauled me up his body.

He rolled and covered me.

"I think I need to go to the bathroom," I whispered, staring into his eyes probably like a deer in a road stared at the light coming its way.

"No you don't. You need to talk to me. What's fuckin' with your head?"

My gaze drifted to his ear.

His hand lifted to my jaw and he ordered, "Frankie, look at me."

I looked at him.

"What's in your head?" he asked.

"I'm not good at that," I admitted.

"Why?" he asked, and I blinked at his absurd question.

If I knew why, I'd be a whole lot better at it.

"Why?" I repeated, not knowing what else to say.

"Yeah, why?"

"Uh...I think you need to give the reasons for that, Benny," I pointed out the obvious, but even doing it, that didn't mean at that moment I *wanted* him to give me the reasons for it.

He shook his head but said (scarily), "You want that, I will, honey. But for now, I wanna know how you go hot and give it your all, lose control at a kiss, but get tense when you're goin' down on me."

"I know you know I'm not good at it," I explained.

"Okay. Is there more?"

"Isn't that enough?"

Something moved over his face I didn't get before he asked, "That shit with your dad eatin' you?"

I nodded.

"Anything else?" he pushed.

My voice sounded as horrified as I felt when I reminded him, "He said I'd scored 'the good Bianchi.'"

"Think it's been proved conclusively that your dad's an asshole, babe," Benny replied.

"That comment was more asshole than your garden-variety asshole, Benny," I noted.

"Think it's been proved your dad's more asshole than your garden-variety asshole, Frankie," Ben returned.

"You looked pissed," I told him.

"I wasn't pissed at what he said. He said it and I saw your reaction, and *that* made me pissed. I also knew what was waitin' for you inside. He followed me out so I didn't have my shot at warnin' you, which made me more pissed. Not to mention, the fuckwad had his hand on me."

He did.

"I'm sorry, Benny," I said quietly.

"Why the women in his life apologize for him is beyond me. *He's* the asshole, not you."

"He's my dad."

"He's not. He's the man whose seed made you. I got a good dad, babe. I know the difference."

I stared at him, his profound words hitting me.

I was not my father. I did not behave like him. I did not live like him. He helped create me, but now…

Well, now, I was *me*.

And it was beginning to seep in that I'd been me a long time.

As in…always.

And that was huge.

As huge as it was, naked in bed with Ben after giving him a terrible blowjob that was so bad, Ben felt the need to halt the festivities and have a chat, I didn't share this latest epiphany.

Instead, I said, "You're lucky, Benny."

"I know, Frankie," Ben stated. "Now enough about him. Is that it?"

"I think so."

"Work good?"

"Yeah."

"Your sisters or brother phone you recently?" he went on.

I shook my head.

"Good. So now, do you have any fuckin' clue how unbelievably hot it is to see you and that body of yours, with all that crazy-beautiful hair all over my gut and thighs, takin' my cock with your mouth?"

My body jerked, even as I felt a spasm between my legs.

"No," I whispered.

"Thought I was gonna come just you touchin' the tip with your lips. You took all of me…*fuck*."

With that, his expression changed to the one I was used to when we were naked, and I felt my legs shift restlessly.

"I—" I started, but his face dipped close and I cut myself off.

"Lick, baby," he whispered, and I felt a surge replace the spasm between my legs. "Taste me. *All* of me. Take your time. Suck. Glide. Get me wet. Nothin's off-limits. Look at me while you take me. Watch what you do to me. Or, you want, I'll get you there with you sittin' on my face while you go down on me. I got my mouth on you, you won't think of anything but that and my cock."

Oh God, I wanted that. And he was right. If his mouth was on me, I wouldn't think of anything but what he was doing, doing it with him in my mouth.

I kept shifting.

"Or you can kneel in the bed next to me and give me your pussy. I'll play with you while you suck me off."

At that, I stopped shifting and started squirming because I wanted that too.

Immediately.

My hands started moving all over Benny.

"Or," he kept going, "I'll take my feet, you kneel in front of me, and I'll do the work and fuck your face."

And at *that,* I planted a foot in the bed and rolled him.

"You make a choice?" he asked when I was on top and he was on his back.

"Shut up, Benny."

He grinned at me.

That grin was a dare.

And I was suddenly feeling like a daredevil.

I moved down his chest and found for the first time, with Benny not taking charge, I had the time to discover that I'd never had before.

And all the magnificence of him was laid out before me, so I took that time with my fingers, with my mouth, with my teeth and tongue. There was a lot of him, all of it solid silk that was unbelievably fascinating. The taste of him thrilling. The feel of his fingers in my hair, or reaching to cop a feel, titillating. The noises he made to the way *I* made *his* body shift with turned-on agitation taking me straight out of my head and making me all about what I was doing to Benny.

Making me all about giving him more.

So by the time I reached my destination, I was so ready, I actually wanted to grasp his cock, climb on, and ride it.

Instead, I positioned between his legs and took it in another part of me.

The minute I did, Ben growled.

My eyes shot from what I was doing to his face, his cock still in my mouth.

When they met his heated ones, he groaned, "Fuck, baby."

Watching him, I slid up then took him as deep as I could.

His legs cocked, his head fell back, I got a view of muscular throat and all that was Benny, and a pulse thrummed between my legs.

I took him again and felt his legs tense beside me.

He liked it.

And suddenly, so did I.

That was when I licked. I stroked. I glided. I used lips, suction, and hand. I got so into it, half the time I was watching him, half the time I was all about sucking him off, going for the groan, seeing him dig his heels in the bed, and I was getting off on this so much that I was near desperate to shove my hand between my legs to take myself there.

I should have let Benny play with my pussy.

I'd have to remember to do that next time, as in, later that night.

This was my thought when I had Ben deep, and I moaned against his cock. Then his cock was gone.

I started to look to him in surprise, but he was already on his knees. Then he was hauling me around and pushing me down so I was facing the end of my bed on all fours.

Then he was driving inside me.

Oh yes. Take two of things we'd never done, doggie-style.

"Benny," I breathed.

He didn't say a word. Hands clutching my hips, he yanked me back as he pounded into me, and it was then I felt it.

Ben wasn't guiding this. Ben wasn't in control of this. Ben wasn't enjoying himself as he brought me to climax.

Ben had lost control.

Ben was fucking me because he *needed* to fuck me.

And I'd made him do that.

Me.

Frankie.

And I'd never had that.

Not ever.

It was *phenomenal*.

I felt a rush of wet between my legs at the thought, the corresponding ripple that coursed through me, and my head shot back, but I fell down to my forearms in the bed.

My head didn't fall, though, because Ben reached over me, fisted a hand in my hair, and pulled back, forcing my neck to arch, my back to arch, and my sex to drive into his.

That was so fucking hot, I cried out, coming instantly, doing it gasping, panting, and moaning.

"That's right, Frankie," he growled, slamming inside me.

"More," I begged, still coming.

He gave me more, pounding. Then his hand released my hair, both went to my hips, and he slammed me back as he bucked inside me, grunting, then groaning through his climax.

His thrusts calmed and he started to glide, his fingers digging into my hips, beginning to roam lightly across the skin of my ass, and I shivered in front of him at the beauty of it.

After a long time, Ben pulled out but bent over me. I felt his front against my back and his arms round me. Then I was up, kneeling in front of him, one of Benny's arms wrapped around my belly, the other one under my breasts. One hand angled up, cupping me, and his mouth came to my ear.

"My Frankie, she's determined to do somethin', she goes big," he whispered there.

I was right.

He liked it.

A whole lot.

I dropped my head to his shoulder and folded my arms over his on my body.

"Kiss me, honey," he ordered.

I turned my head and tipped it back, but I didn't kiss Benny. He dropped his mouth to mine and he kissed me. He did it for a long time. And when he did it, he did it deep, wet, and sweet.

When he broke it, he lifted his lips to touch them to my nose, then shifted so he could bury his face in my neck and give me a squeeze with his arms.

He seemed fine to stay that way, silent and holding me, and I wasn't complaining.

Finally, he spoke.

"Got me so hot, didn't use a condom."

And I was so hot, I hadn't even thought of that until then.

"You seein' someone else?" I teased.

"Fuck no," he answered.

Immediate and firm.

Nice.

What wasn't nice was that this brought me to a thought that I wasn't allowed to have. Not after what I'd done, burning Benny, leaving him for months, and doing it practically in the middle of a session that would have consummated what he'd worked so hard to build between us.

Now, it was a thought I had to have because of this conversation.

And it was a question I had to ask.

But I asked it quietly. "You see someone when I was gone?"

I felt his nose slide up my neck, and in my ear he whispered, "Dry spell."

My body froze solid.

Oh my God.

A dry spell? For Benny Bianchi? As far as I could tell (and I paid attention), the last dry spell he suffered was four years ago, and that was only when a friend of a friend reported to me he had mono. And that dry spell had lasted only three weeks.

"Longest ever," he went on, still whispering.

I blinked.

Oh my *God.*

"Apparently," he kept going, "when a man finds what he wants and loses it, it's not easy to get back in the saddle, even if he never actually got *in* the saddle."

Oh God.

Benny just said that. He just told me that. He just *gave* me that.

God.

"Ben," I said softly, unable to say anything else, like expressing in a million flowery words just how huge that was and just how much it meant to me.

"We've moved on," he replied on a gentle squeeze. "And it's good where we've moved on to. So it's done."

Pure Benny. Shit happened, he got over it, and he moved on.

But the beauty for me was that, this time, I got to go with him.

So I went with him and turned from the heavy, joking, "Right, so, you got the clap?"

His voice held humor when he answered, "Nope."

"Me either."

"So we're good?" It was his turn to ask, and I knew by the weight of it that the question concerned more than what we were currently discussing.

"I'm on the Pill, baby," I told him.

"Noticed that, makin' sure," he replied on another squeeze. Then he asked, "You wanna clean up or you want me to do it?"

The idea of Benny doing it was intriguing, but I'd thoroughly explored something intriguing about Benny already and decided to partial out the goodness.

"I'll do it."

"Okay, honey."

He kissed my neck and let me go.

I scrambled off the bed, nabbed his tee, and tugged it over my head on my way to the bathroom.

I took care of business and headed back to my room, finding Ben up against the headboard, still naked, legs slightly spread and cocked. Again, top-to-toe yummy, except this time *yummier*.

I entered the bed and directly climbed on Benny.

He didn't delay in shoving his hands under his tee, sliding them over the small of my back before one went up my spine and one went down to cup my ass.

For my part, I put my hands on his chest and looked into his eyes.

"Thank you," I said softly.

He smiled and did it huge, white and blinding.

Then he asked, "Seriously?"

I was absolutely being serious. His patience, guidance, and ability to turn me on and *spur me on* when I was embarrassed and formulating plans to barricade myself in the bathroom after badly attempting head the first time, I felt, deserved heartfelt gratitude communicated *seriously*.

Therefore, my "Yes, seriously" came out clipped.

"Babe," he said, still grinning, putting pressure on his hand between my shoulder blades, pulling me down to him. When he got me where he wanted me, he stated, "You do know you're thankin' me for *you* givin' *me* really fuckin' great head."

I hadn't thought of it that way.

He kept going.

"Makin' me so hot, it was either come in your mouth or fuck you on your knees."

Shit, I'd just come and he again had me squirming.

His hand left my ass so he could wrap both arms around me and bring me even closer, trapping my hands against his chest.

"So goddamned hot." His deep, easy voice was a rumble. "So fuckin' wet when I got in there, don't know how I held it, waitin' for you to come."

I licked my lips.

His eyes watched, they flared, and they came back to mine.

"You got off on that." It was a declaration.

"Yeah."

"All of it."

"Yeah."

"Came undone when I got rough with your hair."

I did more squirming and repeated, "Yeah."

His eyes got hot, even as they went lazy, and they dropped to my mouth as he warned, "It's been good, baby, in a way I thought it was great. Now I know just what great you got in you. So prepare."

My thighs clamped on his hips as the spasm ran through me.

His arms tightened and I read what he wanted, tipping my chin and offering my mouth.

He took it again, taking his time, slow, wet, and deep. Then he broke our connection but kept me close.

"You intend to feed me?" he asked.

"Sure," I replied, grinning, taking Ben's hint that after-sex talk was over, and starting to make a move to get off him.

This move was unsuccessful since his arms kept tight hold and I looked back at him.

"You okay with me layin' it out for your dad?"

I did the best shrug I could with Benny holding me. "You're lookin' out for me."

He shook his head and repeated, "You okay with me layin' it out for your dad?"

I was nearly as close as I could get, but I found my way to get closer to him and said quietly, "Yeah, Benny, 'cause you were lookin' out for me. That was insane, totally messed up, but I wouldn't have had it in me to show him the door. I needed you to do that for me. You did it for me. So yes, honey, I'm okay with you layin' it out for my dad. And, better, I'm okay 'cause he's not the kind of man who would court a scene like that again, so it's likely I won't have to endure another one." I reached up and touched my lips to his, pulling back and finishing, "Because of you. So not only am I okay, I'll say thank you, baby."

He slid a hand out of his tee and lifted it to pull my hair away from one side of my face, his eyes watching his hand, then moving over my features.

"Benny?" I called when he didn't move, didn't speak, just let his eyes roam over me.

When I did, his gaze came to mine. "Crazy-beautiful," he whispered and my heart lurched.

He meant me. Not just the way I looked, *all of me.*

"I'm crazy-beautiful 'cause I let you deal with my dad?" I asked quietly.

"You're crazy-beautiful 'cause you're the kind of woman who has a heart who holds on and won't let her show him the door." He grinned and finished, "Lettin' me have all the fun."

"You're just crazy," I told him, but it wasn't sharp or sarcastic—it was soft, and even I had to admit, it sounded sweet.

298

"Oh yeah, I'm crazy," he whispered, his eyes again roaming my face and I tensed, knowing what he meant with that too.

He was crazy for me.

"Benny," I breathed, and he caught my gaze.

"You gotta feed your man, Frankie."

I looked into his eyes and decided to let him have that play.

I did it for Benny.

And I did it for me because my cupboards were not bare. They were bursting. I had twelve different kinds of potato chips, and I had a feast planned to make for my man to show him how much I looked forward to him being with me.

When we got to the kitchen and I shared them (steaks, sautéed mushrooms, loaded baked potatoes, steamed asparagus, Pillsbury crescent rolls, and store-bought-but-still-awesome sugar cream pie for dessert), Ben liked my plans for dinner.

But he snacked on BBQ Fritos the whole time I was preparing it, which I told him I found annoying.

I didn't.

I was in woman-falling-in-love zone.

So I was crazy too.

Sixteen

WHAT A MIRACLE SHE WAS

I grabbed my workout bag from the bench in the locker room of the company gym and hit the *Go* button on my phone.

I walked out of the locker room and then out of the gym, listening to it ring.

I got voicemail while I was waiting for the elevator.

"You got me. Now tell me why you want me," my sister Cat's voicemail greeting I knew all too well said in my ear.

When I got the beep, I spoke.

"I want you 'cause I've called you a gazillion times in the last month, and I called you *seven* gazillion times before that, and I have not heard from you, Cat. Things are happening with this family and Enzo told me he can't get a hold of you either. Seein' as somethin' went down and Dad isn't talking to me, and I'm not talkin' to him, I don't know if you've heard from him. There's stuff you need to know, but you're not returning my calls, so now I'm worried." The elevator doors whooshed open and I finished with, "Call your big sister, Cat, *please.*"

I disconnected, got in the elevator and hit the button, thinking my sister Cat took middle child syndrome to extremes.

Sure, she had a case for this, even if she brought it up every single time she got her feelings hurt, which was often. Her case being Dad had a favorite, Enzo. Ma also had a favorite, Nat. I was the oldest, so I was about responsibility, spending my time looking after my younger siblings, and not thinking about all the ways I could feel injured that Ma and Dad didn't dote on me.

Then again, all our grandparents thought I was the shit, likely because they were good, loving people who had no idea where they went wrong with Enzo and Ninette and looked to me as salvation that they eventually had some small hand in creating something that went right.

This was not, of course, the way I felt my whole life. This was what occurred to me since being with Benny and him pointing out I was a Concetti by name, but I was Frankie because I was just me.

That said, my grandfather was the ultimate Concetti. He was awesome. He adored me and it sucked he moved all the way to Arizona (a choice that took him far away from my mother, who was not his favorite person) and that we'd lost Nana Concetti, because she was awesome too.

In the Concetti-offspring-having-it-together scale, Cat was right behind me. She worked for a construction company and had for a long time, meeting her husband, Art, there. Art had even managed to hold down the same job for more than a decade, a feat when it came to anyone involved with a Concetti.

Art was very hot and he was also very hotheaded. With Cat also being the last, this meant they fought like crazy. It didn't help that they were both just shy of being not-so-healthy big drinkers. The booze came out, Cat and/ or Art could get talkative and funny, or irritable and mean, and they took both to extremes. In the end, it actually wasn't pleasant experiencing either one, because even if they were being talkative and funny, they didn't shut up so you could get a word in edgewise and that always got annoying.

Cat, like every member of my family, was prone to drama, and it was not unheard of that she could get hurt and hold a silent grudge for ages.

But this was extreme.

And I did not lie on the phone—I was worried.

Both of Enzo Junior's women had had his children, a boy and a girl, and although this usually was joyous news, it was not going well for my brother. From Enzo's point of view, they'd both tried to trap him with their pregnancies, and honestly, it sounded like one of them did. The other one I'd met and liked and she'd adored Enzo. I felt for her at the time because she thought she was in it for the long haul, this being because Enzo gave her that impression.

So one was pissed she didn't get what she wanted, ended up with a kid, and was intent on making him pay. The other one was bitter, and bitter was *way* worse.

Enzo was fucked.

Though, he'd texted pictures and the babies were adorable.

The elevator doors opened. I headed out and nearly stopped dead when I felt the vibe—a vibe that was buzzing in an unhappy way across the entire floor. I slowly walked into the space, seeing people in huddles, a few directors behind closed doors in an office, nearly all faces shocked.

Something was wrong.

I hit my assistant, Tandy's desk. When I stopped there, she jumped and looked up at me.

"Frankie," she greeted.

"What's up?" I asked quietly.

"Paul Gartner was murdered."

I stared at her, stunned, even though I had no clue who Paul Gartner was.

So I asked, "Paul Gartner?"

"Dr. Gartner. Scientist. Research and development. He was lead on Tenrix," she told me.

Tenrix was a new product to treat high blood pressure we were gearing up to launch. Just the week before, Randy had chaired a team meeting, telling us all about it.

Randy had been excited in a way that, for a guy who was not often in a good mood and all other times was a dick, made the meeting weird.

It was weirder because it didn't seem genuine. After ages of testing, the different phases of trials, the millions and millions of dollars sunk into that, all of which could be flushed down the toilet at any stage if a product didn't work, excitement that something new, cutting edge, and reportedly very successful in combating high blood pressure didn't need to be faked.

I had to admit, I didn't get a good feeling about the meeting, but I hadn't been at the company during any other product launch so I figured maybe that was always Randy's way when he had to be in a good mood about something.

That said, all the other directors and managers at the team meeting were giving each other looks after it, which didn't make me feel better. At the time, I put it down to the fact that, with the way people avoided him, the consensus of the team matched my opinion that Randy was a dick.

But the death of the man behind that new product after that weird pre-launch meeting didn't sit real great with me.

"What happened?" I asked.

"I don't know. The police are investigating. They came in and talked with Mr. Barrow and Mr. Berger. Mr. Berger kinda scares me, but he came out of the meeting with the police and did the rounds with the vice presidents and directors, looking like someone told him his dog just got run over."

As he would.

This was not only because I suspected Travis Berger was a decent guy. It also was because, when he got to where he was right now on the company food chain, he'd gone all out, talking our president and CEO, Clancy Barrow, into aggressively headhunting and claiming the top biomedical scientists in the industry. Wyler had paid a fortune in signing bonuses, stock options, and salaries in order to ascertain products currently in testing and new products to be developed would be the best they could be.

One of those scientists biting it meant we'd lost a huge investment.

What also didn't surprise me was that Berger went out and shared the news. I'd only seen Clancy Barrow in passing on a handful of occasions. He was not hands-on. He let Berger do day-to-day and pretty much everything else. Whereas Berger was visible, aggressive, driven, and hardworking, Barrow, surprisingly for someone in his position, was practically invisible, letting his executive vice president be the face of Wyler on a variety of fronts.

There was, of course, another way to look at this. That being, if something went wrong, it would be Berger who would likely take the fall, even if it wasn't on him what went wrong.

"Do they know how it happened?" I asked Tandy.

She looked uncomfortable for a second before she said, "Details aren't making the rounds, but I do know he was shot."

She also knew I was shot and I remembered what I remembered every day about fifty times a day. This being that I liked Tandy. She was funny. She wore kickass clothes. She was a hard worker and totally on the ball. But also, she was sweet.

"That's terrible," I pointed out the obvious.

"Yeah. I didn't know him, but still, it's terrible," she said, her eyes drifting across the office floor. They came back to me and she went on, "Anyway. The Tenrix stuff is on your desk. Chelsea brought the files around while you were working out."

Something about this coincidence sent a chill sliding up my spine, but I nodded, murmured, "Thanks," gave her a smile, and went to my office.

I had a million things to do, but after I dumped my workout bag, I reached right for the file on Tenrix. A lot of it I didn't get because it was about chemistry and biology and we'd been told we'd have someone (though, not Dr. Gartner, obviously) explain it to us in detail.

What I focused on were the mock-ups of the glossy brochures and pamphlets that had *Proof* stamped on them in big red letters. I read them and, in doing so, read what Tenrix promised to do.

And from knowing Randy Bierman promised the same in the team meeting, weirdly, I didn't believe a word.

My phone ringing took me out of the Tenrix file.

I stayed out of it, doing half a million of those million things I had to do, when close to five, my phone beeped.

I looked at it, picked it up, and smiled.

It was a text from Benny that said, *Thinking about you, baby. Call me when you get home from work. I'll take a break.*

It had been just over a month since the scene with Dad.

Unfortunately, that month included a lot of me traveling.

Fortunately, one of my trips was to Chicago, a territory rich in prospects and a trip whose primary purpose was to bring my rep to heel. He might have had more pharmaceutical experience than me, but he was my only rep not only not exceeding his numbers, but not making them.

I'd extended that trip, working from Benny's for three days and then having the weekend with him.

I liked this. I liked being at Benny's and playing house, falling into a pattern that included him having nights off to be with me and him also working. I didn't mind him working. I went to the pizzeria with friends and saw him, or I stayed at his house and vegged.

But it was more.

What we had was not normal. Any relationship was work, but being separated, that work was harder. I never liked leaving him or him leaving me, but each time it was getting harder.

When I was working at Benny's, it felt normal. His house felt like home. Our schedule felt natural. Like the life and times of any average couple. I liked that. I wanted that.

The same could not be said for when Ben came to see me.

When Benny came to see me, it was definitely a visit. Not him coming home. Not natural. Not normal. Not anything but good to be with Benny.

I loved being with Benny any way I could be.

Still, I wanted more.

In order not to take advantage and make Manny or Vinnie work the kitchens on their busiest nights of the week, namely weekends, in the last month, Ben had attempted a two-day visit during the week.

This did not go great. Mostly because he showed in the morning when I was at work and all I could think about was coming home to him. While I worked, he putzed the days away at my place and hung with Cal, who was living in a house with his woman *this close* to having his baby, plus three females who were planning a wedding.

Ben was a reprieve for Cal.

For me, Ben was in Brownsburg and I was at work and I didn't like that, the limited time we had, the fact that it felt like he barely got there and then he had to leave.

In other words, this wasn't working for me.

The problem with that was, I didn't need a résumé that said I jumped jobs every year. Possible employers needed to get the hint that they weren't going to dump the money and time into a hiring and training process for someone who didn't have staying power. So I felt I had at least another sixteen months with Wyler.

The other problem with that was, although Ben seemed just as disappointed to watch me leave or leave me, he hadn't mentioned our future and what it might bring, or the fact we might need to plan to bring it to normalcy. That including being together more than a few days a month and then such impossible dreams as wedding, kids, and family.

I wasn't exactly getting younger. In fact, my birthday was a few weeks away.

Ben wasn't either.

I didn't know how to bring it up. If Ben was good with what we had, after nearly fucking us up in the beginning, I wasn't big on rocking that boat.

But this didn't mean the fact that Ben hadn't even mentioned it wasn't beginning to worry me.

I did not include this in the text I sent back, which only read, *Okay, honey, I'll be leaving in a few.*

I focused on getting as much of the last half a million things I needed to do done so I could get home and call my man, have a brief conversation with him that would leave me wanting more, and then eat alone, hang at my house alone, and go to bed.

Alone.

I was closing in on feeling I'd done what I needed to do when my phone rang and I saw the time on my computer said that it was after six. In other words, I'd lost track so it wasn't the "few" I'd told Benny it would be.

He was probably worried and this was my thought when my eyes went to my cell.

My brows drew together when I saw the screen said, Keira Calling.

I grabbed the phone, took the call, and put it to my ear.

"Hey, honey."

"Mom's havin' the baby!"

My heart thumped hard in my chest and I came right out of my seat.

"Right now?" I asked.

"Yeah!" she cried, then chanted, "Ohmigod, ohmigod, ohmigod."

"Where are you?"

"At home. Kate is, like, *freaking*! Joe called. They were out pickin' up dinner and it just happened. He took her right to the hospital. We gotta get her bag. We gotta get gas 'cause Kate says she's almost out. And we gotta call *everybody*."

"Stop right there," I interrupted. "Kate's in a state and she's drivin' you?"

"*We gotta get going!*" she shrieked. "And I got, like, *seven million calls to make*."

Hurriedly, I went about turning off my computer. "Do not leave that house, Keirry. I'm comin' and I'll take you both."

"You got a two-seater," she pointed out.

"We'll take Vi's Mustang."

"Oh, right," she muttered.

I kept closing down and grabbing shit as I said, "Listen to me. Are you listening to me?"

She sounded like she was hyperventilating when she said, "I'm listening."

"Get the keys to your mom's car. Make sure she has everything she needs for her and Angela in her bag. Grab some waters, some pops, and some snacks 'cause we probably got a wait ahead of us. Make your calls. Deep breathe. I'll be there as soon as I can."

I was rushing through the mostly deserted floor on my way to the elevator when Keira replied, "It'll take you forever to get here."

"It takes a while to have a baby, honey. Just try to keep calm. I'll get there as fast as I can and we'll get to your mom and Cal."

"Okay, Frankie."

"*Mawdy's bag doesn't have nightgowns!*" I heard Kate screech from a distance through Keira's phone.

I tagged the elevator and smiled.

With Ben in Chicago, and Cal, Violet, and the girls the only friends I had close, I spent time with them. Dinners at their place, dinners at mine, dinners at Frank's Restaurant in town. They were the only things keeping me sane, being so far from Benny and everything I knew.

Doing it, I'd gotten to know the Winters–Callahan family.

And now I knew that Kate, who was normally level-headed, lost it when her mom was about to give her another sister.

"Well, get her one!" Keira yelled back.

"Keirry, honey?" I called.

"Yeah, Frankie?" she asked.

"Deep breathe. Calm. It's all gonna be great. It's gonna be amazing. Something beautiful is happening. Yeah?"

I heard the rush of breath come with her "Yeah."

"Be there soon," I promised.

"Okay. See you soon, Frankie."

"'Bye, honey."

"'Bye, Frankie."

I disconnected. The elevator opened. I dashed in, hit the button to the parking garage, and as the doors were closing, I didn't fuck around with RECENTS. I just dialed Ben's number right into the phone.

"Hey, baby," he greeted.

"Vi's delivering Angela right now," I told him.

There was a hesitation before he asked, "Come again?"

"Vi…is…delivering…*Angela right now*!" I was near on shrieking myself when I finished.

"Jesus, that's fuckin' great," Ben replied.

"Uh…yeah," I agreed. "I'm off to pick up the girls. They were driving themselves, but they were freaked. I don't want them behind the wheel."

There was another hesitation, this one weighty, before he whispered, "My Frankie."

"I don't have time for you to be sweet right now, Ben. I only have time for you to tell me you're coming down as soon as humanly possible."

There was a smile in his voice when he said, "I'm comin' down as soon as humanly possible."

"Awesome," I whispered as the doors opened.

"Be safe with you and those girls," he ordered.

"I will."

"Okay. Love you, baby."

I stopped dead on my mad dash to my Z.

"'Bye," he finished.

"Uh…'bye, Benny."

He disconnected.

I stood there, frozen.

Love you, baby.

Oh my God.

Love you, baby.

Oh my *God*!

Ben told me he'd never loved a woman.

And now he'd just told me he loved me.

What I did next, I didn't care that security probably saw me doing it on the monitors and would rightly think I was crazy.

Cal and Vi were having their baby.

And Benny Bianchi loved me.

I did a war whoop and a big feet-thrown-back cheerleader jump. In pumps. Holding my phone, my computer bag, my purse slung over my shoulder. Just like a woman in a commercial who successfully got through her stressful day as an executive and did it without getting underarm stains.

Fortunately, I landed firm on my feet.

Then I ran right to my Z.

~

I was sitting in the maternity waiting room of Hendricks Regional Health.

Next to me sat Kate, who was wired and fidgety.

Across from me sat a man who'd introduced himself as Pete Riley, Vi's father. He'd arrived not very long ago from Chicago.

Standing and swaying a sleeping baby named Jack in her arms was Keira.

The baby belonged to two other people who were there. Kate introduced them as "Colt and Feb," and I knew them because Vi talked about them as her neighbors, though I hadn't met them (until then).

I also knew them, because a while ago, they were all over the news when a serial killer had gone on a killing spree in Feb's name. Obviously, she did not want this or the attention it garnered after he'd killed a slew of people and committed suicide by cop. But still, shit happened in life and you got on with it.

In Feb's case, she got on with it by finally marrying her hot guy and high school sweetheart, namely Colt, and giving him a baby.

There was also another woman there. Her name was Cheryl. She had a lot of blonde hair, showed a lot of skin, what skin she didn't show she still hinted at since everything she was wearing was skintight, and she had a lot of attitude. I liked her immediately and wished there would be a time when I could introduce her to Nat (if I ever started speaking to her again) so she'd be inspiration to be what you were, not give a damn, but not be a skank doing it.

She had her son with her, Ethan, who had long since fallen asleep in a chair, his weight slanted sideways and resting on Colt, who had his arm around the kid.

Colt and Feb had brought an enormous bucket of KFC. Cheryl had brought "everything they had left" from Mimi's, a kickass coffee shop on Main Street in Brownsburg that I'd discovered a couple of weeks before. This meant a plethora of cookies and brownies.

Thus, the snack stash Kate and Keira brought was unnecessary.

Calls had been made and a number of people would eventually descend. Before I got a chance, Keira had called Vinnie and Theresa. The girls had also (weirdly, to my way of thinking) called Vi's dead first husband's parents, who, apparently, were tight with the new family, including Cal. Not to mention they'd called their grandfather, who wasted no time getting there, and a variety of other people, as evidenced by Colt, Feb, Jack, Cheryl, and Ethan being there.

So all was in order.

Except no word from delivery.

We did get an update, procured for us by Colt, who was a cop, since he arrived when we'd been there over an hour and hadn't had one. He'd flashed his badge and we'd found out that Vi's water had broken in Cal's truck and things went fast. Fast, as in, upon arrival, she was nearly fully dilated. A hint that things would continue to go very swiftly.

But that was hours ago.

"Is this okay?" Kate asked quietly from beside me, and I saw Keira's head whip around when Kate asked the question.

I reached out and took her hand. "Yes, honey."

"It seems to be taking a long time," she noted, her voice uncertain and shaky.

"That happens," I told her.

"On TV, people can visit a woman in labor for, like…*ages* before she goes into delivery," she informed me.

This was true and it happened not on TV as well.

I didn't tell Kate that.

I said, "Like all babies are different, all births are different. Sometimes it takes time in delivery."

"I don't like it," she whispered, and I squeezed her hand.

"It's gonna be okay," I told her, my eyes on Keira and suddenly, Feb moved, getting up quickly and going directly to Keira.

My head turned the other way when I felt movement there, and I knew why Feb went to claim her boy.

Cal, in scrubs, was coming our way.

He looked haggard and my heart skipped a beat, but he didn't even get to a full stop before he announced in a gruff voice, "Vi's good. Angie's good. Everybody healthy."

Kate shot out of her seat and, almost simultaneously with Keira, did their best to take Cal off his feet when they hit him full on. They did their best, but Cal was a big, powerful guy. He rocked but stood strong.

It was then I received one of those unexpected but precious gifts life could send your way, that being watching Cal wrap both girls in his long, strapping arms, drop his dark head, and kiss the hair on both of theirs, murmuring, "It took Angie a while to wanna join us, but now it's all good, babies."

I heard Kate's choked sob, but Keira just burrowed closer into Cal.

I stood with everyone else and we approached—but didn't get close, giving them their moment—stopping and huddling.

"You wanna see your mom and sister?" Cal asked the girls, his focus totally on them. No one else was in the universe (except, of course, Vi and his new daughter).

"Yeah," Keira said unsteadily.

"Absolutely," Kate said croakily.

Finally, his eyes came to the gathered crowd and he murmured, "Be back."

He shifted the girls, turned them and moved them in the direction from where he'd come.

I watched them go. Then I gave jubilant smiles to people I barely knew, who returned them just as jubilantly, and I went right to my purse.

I grabbed my phone and called Benny.

Only when I heard his deep, easy, sweet voice saying, "Give me good news, baby," did I start crying.

But my tears were jubilant.

⟳

Benny parked in Frankie's guest spot, shut down the Explorer, and jumped out, turning toward Frankie's apartment only to see her hustling his way, hair big, makeup heavy but sweet, wearing a bright orange sundress that showed skin and cleavage. This was paired with some sexy, high-heeled sandals. She was carrying a huge basket covered in cellophane that had a massive pink bow and looked to be filled with a gigantic mound of baby clothes, all pink. She was holding it awkwardly to the side so she could see him.

"Please tell me you didn't dress that way for work," he remarked when she was ten feet away.

She gave him a look.

It was two days after Vi had Angela. Two days too long for Frankie, who had wanted him down immediately. But Vi had had Angie on a Tuesday, so he waited for Thursday when he could push it into a long weekend with his woman.

And anyway, his folks went down first and left Brownsburg to go back to Chicago this morning so they could help out at the restaurant while Ben was away. It was also so his pop could get Theresa away from Angela because, as reported direct to Benny from Cal, "You'd think the woman pushed her out herself, she's hoggin' her so much."

This Ben read as Cal not getting enough time with his woman and girls, especially the new one.

Now it was near on six o'clock, Frankie was done with work that day, and Benny was there to stay.

For three days.

Which was not near long enough.

Still giving him a look, Frankie ordered, "Ass back in your truck. We're goin' directly to Cal and Vi's."

"No welcome to Brownsburg kiss?" he asked as she veered to the passenger side.

He in no way liked it when she didn't turn her ass right around to give him what he wanted.

Instead, she opened the back door to his truck, dumped the basket, slammed the door, and climbed right in the front seat.

He angled in the driver's seat and turned to her to tell her precisely how he felt about her non-greeting. The minute he did, she latched onto either side of his head, yanked him to her, and laid a hot, wet one on him.

She broke away but didn't let go as she whispered, "Welcome to Brownsburg, Benny."

He grinned at her and replied, "That's the way I like it, Frankie."

Something even more crazy-beautiful than the crazy-beautiful she always was lit in her eyes before she kept whispering, "She's so beautiful, you would not believe."

He knew what that crazy-beautiful was and he wondered, when she gave him their babies, how much more crazy-beautiful it would be.

"Then let me go, baby, so I can meet her," he whispered back.

She grinned and let him go.

Ben turned to the wheel, started her up, and put her in gear.

He was backing out when she declared, "By the way, that gift's from you and me."

"Good, seein' as I'm never shoppin' for a girl baby. When they have their boy, I'll kick in. Though, sayin' that, I'm not kickin' in in a way I'll go shoppin'. I'm kickin' in in a way where you call me and get my approval before you buy anything."

To that, he got silence and this silence lasted until he was at the gate to her complex.

So he called, "Frankie?"

Her voice was soft when she said, "That's a deal."

He'd stopped to make the turn on the main road so he turned his head and looked at her.

Her gaze was directed to the side, but he saw that smile on her face. He liked all her smiles, but that was the one he liked the best. It was the one that said she had a secret.

And it was a good one.

But Frankie didn't have any secrets, except the ones buried deep inside, planted by the whackjobs who were her family.

"What you thinkin', *cara*?" he asked and she looked to him.

"I'm just glad you're here, Benny."

That wasn't it, but he'd give her that play. He had a cousin to meet and he was hungry. But also, he knew she'd give it to him when she was ready.

So he just gave her a smile, checked the street, and made the turn when it was safe.

He parked in Cal and Vi's drive, got out, and made his way around to grab the basket. He held it in one arm, Frankie's hand in the other, and they headed to the front door.

Frankie knocked, but she barely quit doing it before the door was open and Cal stood there, his arm lifted. In it was cradled a little bundle with a tiny, light green cap on her head, her baby body wrapped up tight in a soft, pink blanket.

For a second, Benny couldn't move. This was because this wasn't the first time he'd seen his cousin holding a baby just like that. The last time was nearly two decades ago with Cal's little Nicky, a beautiful baby boy that Ben was pretty certain Cal had convinced himself the world revolved around. A beautiful baby boy that Cal's junkie ex-wife let drown in the bathtub.

His eyes went from Angela to Cal and he whispered, "*Cugino*."

Cal grinned a grin Ben had never seen before from him. He'd seen it though. It was the kind of grin his father aimed at his mother. The kind of grin he was starting to see from Manny.

It was the grin of a man content in the knowledge he had everything.

"Get your asses in here," Cal offered as an invitation and stepped out of the door.

Ben pulled Frankie in and was accosted directly by Keira, then Kate. Keira took the basket from him after hugging Frankie. Kate went in for hug from Francesca and Ben moved to Vi, who was lying on the couch.

"I'd get up, but I've had kind of a long day," Vi explained, lifting her arms to curl them around his shoulders as he bent into her to brush his lips against her cheek and round her with his arms for a quick, light squeeze.

"Theresa and Vinnie left and Joe practically threw Dad out. I had to intervene." Her voice lowered. "Joe doesn't know, but Dad's at a hotel by the highway, giving us some space."

"You don't have to get up for me and I won't say a word," he said in her ear and straightened, feeling her arms slip away while letting her go, all this smiling down at her as she beamed up at him.

And there was the look of a woman who had it all, lost most of it, and found herself again having everything.

He then turned to Cal. "I wanna meet my cousin."

Cal came to him and stopped two feet away. He looked down at this daughter and said, "Angie, Benny." He looked to Ben and finished, "Ben, my baby girl, Angie."

Benny waited and started chuckling when his cousin just stood there and didn't offer up the baby.

"You gonna let me hold her?" he asked through his laughter.

"You know how to hold a baby?" Cal asked back.

"Uh, yeah. Carm's had three, and at one time, they were all babies."

Cal hesitated. Ben stopped chuckling and started laughing, hearing himself joined by four women.

Kate pushed in, got close, and took control, gently taking hold of Angie and turning with her toward Benny.

"That's my baby, *baby* sister," she declared, handing Angie to Benny.

Ben wrapped both arms around her, cradling her against his chest. Her mouth was puckered and her eyes lazily opened, then closed and stayed that way when Ben settled her close.

Staring down at her, he saw Frankie was right. She was so beautiful, he couldn't believe.

"I'll get you a beer, Benny," Keira called, then asked, "Frankie, do you want Joe to open you some wine?"

"That'd be great, honey." He heard Frankie reply as he moved to an armchair and sat down.

"Joe, that'd be your cue to get Frankie some wine," Keira prompted, and Ben looked up to see Cal scowling down at him, legs planted, arms crossed on his chest.

"She's safe with me, *cugino*," he assured his cousin, fighting back a smile.

"He's that way with everybody," Kate said, going to sit at her mother's feet and promptly picking them up and putting them in her lap. "I thought he'd belt Granddad a good one when he hogged Angie."

Ben could believe this. Not because Cal was insanely protective of his brand-new daughter. Because Cal had been insanely protective of his son, he was a man who took protecting his loved ones seriously, and he'd lost Nicky when he wasn't around to keep him safe.

Ben figured anyone around Angie was going to have to deal until Cal worked that out.

"Joe, *I* could open a bottle of wine," Keira offered.

Cal's body jerked and he turned her way. "I got it, Keirry."

Ben looked from his cousin to Vi and said quietly, "You did a good job, honey."

She grinned proudly, her eyes dipping to her daughter in Ben's arms before she looked back at Benny and stated, "I know."

Ben looked meaningfully at his cousin in the kitchen with Vi's daughter and back to Vi before he repeated, "You *did a good job*, honey."

Her face got soft and her grin went sweet and she, too, repeated, "I know."

Ben smiled back before he sat back and turned his attention to the baby he held in his arms.

He felt Frankie sit on the arm of his chair and he didn't have to bother looking up because she bent over. He smelled her hair, her perfume, and felt the side of her tit press against his arm as she got close and peered at Angela.

Her head turned and her eyes caught his. "What'd I say?" she asked quietly, eyes so warm, he could feel their tenderness on his skin.

"So beautiful, I don't believe," he answered.

She smiled.

Then she bent deeper and kissed Angie's little hat. She moved and kissed Benny's jaw. After that, she sat up, turned to Vi, and asked, "What's for dinner and can I help?"

"Shanghai Salon," Vi answered. "We're bein' lazy."

"Perfect," Frankie replied.

"I'll get the menu!" Kate cried as she slid out from her mother's feet and dashed to the kitchen.

This was when Keira came in, holding a glass of wine she gave to Frankie and a bottle of beer she set on a coaster on a table beside Ben.

And this was when Cal moved to his woman and didn't sit at her feet. Like she was crystal, he lifted her in his arms, turned, sat, and adjusted her so she was ass and legs to the seat, the weight of her upper body resting against Cal's chest, his arm around her ribs.

Vi's head fell naturally so the top was tucked in Cal's neck and her eyes fell on Ben with her daughter.

Taking in Cal with Vi, holding the love he saw on that couch in his arms, Ben looked back down at Angela, wondering if she'd ever know in the miracle that was her, what a miracle she was.

He wondered it.

But he hoped not.

⟵⟶

Ben felt every muscle in his body turn to stone.

Somehow, though, he managed to get his mouth to move in order to say, low and slow, "What?"

Frankie was next to him in her kitchen. It was Saturday morning and they just got back from the bakery, a place called Hilligoss. A place Vi shared had the best donuts perhaps anywhere in the world. A place Frankie took Benny frequently when he came down to see her.

He'd had some good donuts, but Vi was right. Hilligoss was worth considering opening a second Vinnie and Benny's Pizzeria right next door.

Now, Frankie was opening a white box that contained a dozen donuts they would hoover through in the next two days, wishing they had more.

She was also talking.

"I know. Crazy. Murder. Killed in his own house. Shot right in the head."

Ben did not have a good feeling about this, mostly because he never had a good feeling about murder.

He also didn't have a good feeling about this because Frankie just told him an employee at her company had been murdered, and Frankie was a magnet for drama. It wasn't her that did anything, unless she was crazily following some goons who'd kidnapped three people a state away.

That didn't mean she didn't attract more than her fair share just by breathing.

People went their whole lives without, say, their boyfriends getting whacked. Or themselves getting shot. Or working at a place where someone took a bullet to the brain.

Frankie had all three.

And then some.

"The thing is," Frankie went on, "I've got a weird feeling."

This did not make him feel any better.

"A weird feelin' about what?" he asked as she plucked a powdered sugar, chocolate-cream-filled donut out of the box and turned to him.

"Dr. Gartner getting murdered."

"Babe, he was murdered. That'd give anyone a weird feeling."

She took a bite, chewed, and swallowed, and he reached for a glazed as she continued.

"He was lead on a big product we're launching. It doesn't go live for a while. They're designing packaging, brochures, leaflets. Organizing presales talk-ups through the reps. Shit like that. But his boss, the big cheese of research and development, gives me the heebie-jeebies."

And Ben again did not feel better.

"How does he give you the heebie-jeebies?" he asked, taking his own bite.

She moved to the coffeepot and started filling the cups they'd left there when they went to get donuts, doing this one-handed, the other hand holding her donut in the air, saying, "He's a dick."

Ben's body got tight again.

"A dick, how?"

She looked to him. "How's a dick a dick? He's just a dick."

"He a dick to you?"

"Not directly. He just spreads his dick-ness wide."

"And so he's a dick…" Benny trailed off on a prompt.

"I don't know," she said, grabbing a mug and bringing it across to him where he stood at the bar that delineated the kitchen from the dining area. She set it on the counter by him and went back to get her own. "The whole thing just gives me a weird feeling. He's all over this product, as he would be. Pharmaceutical companies dump a shitload into development, so they like the happy place of rolling it out and finally making money on it. I just get…" She shook her head, lifted her cup, took a sip, dropped it, and caught his eyes. "A weird feeling."

"You have anything to do with development and this dick guy?"

"Not really."

"Don't have anything to do with development or this dick guy," Ben ordered.

Her eyes narrowed and she stated, "I have to work with him, Ben."

"Right. I get that. But stay away from this. Stay away from talk about this man who was murdered. Put your head down. Do your job. Let whatever happened blow over."

Her eyes stayed narrowed as she replied, "I kinda was intending to do that already."

"Take the 'kinda' outta that and we're good."

"Benny!" she snapped.

"Baby, you and murder and dicks…not a good combination. It doesn't have anything to do with you. Let it play out not havin' anything to do with you."

"It can't have anything to do with me, Ben. There're rumors it was a professional hit. Obviously, the guy got into someone for money or pissed someone off he shouldn't have. I mean, it's shocking but shit happens. It has nothing to do with me."

"Keep it that way."

At that, her brows shot up. "I'm hardly gonna start my own amateur investigation."

"Good news."

"Benny!" she snapped, louder this time.

"*Cara*, this guy got murdered and he worked for your company. My brother was murdered. My woman was shot. You live in Brownsburg. I live in Chicago. Not easy for me to keep an eye on you the way a man should keep an eye on his woman, and I don't like that normally. When professional hits are carried out on your coworkers, I *really* don't like that. Cut me some slack here, yeah?"

She glared at him as she announced, "And this is yet another time you've made protectiveness annoying."

He grinned, lunged, caught her around the back of her neck, and pulled her to him so she slammed into his body.

Luckily, she'd put down her mug.

Also luckily, she tipped her head back to say something smart so he had his target and he aimed.

His tongue sweep encountered donut, coffee, and Frankie. Getting that, even though he'd fucked her before donuts and coffee, he wanted her again.

On her knees.

First, fucking her face.

After that, taking her pussy.

So he ordered, "Finish your donut. In the mood to fuck you again."

Her eyes widened, her body melted into his, but her mouth said, "So annoying."

"We could spend the day at the pool," he suggested.

"Annoying."

He grinned. "You want me to fuck you."

She glared and snapped, "Annoying!"

His hand tightened on the back of her neck and he dipped his face close to hers. "You want it."

"Benny, you're making it impossible to eat my donut," she shared.

He put his mouth to hers and whispered, "Finish it quick, baby. I want you to drop right here and take my cock in your mouth."

Again, her eyes got wide right before her lids went hooded.

Since he talked her through it, there was nothing in bed that fazed his Frankie. She was up for anything with no hang-ups.

Now, all attitude gone, sweet wonder was in its place when she asked, "Are you hard?"

"Oh yeah."

She slid a hand over his hip and he touched his tongue to her lower lip when she felt for herself.

"I can eat my donut later," she stated and proved this true, putting it on the counter.

Ben could eat his later too and knew he'd be doing that when Frankie dropped right down to her knees in front of him, opened his fly, pulled him free, didn't hesitate a second, and took him deep.

Ben's head fell back at the brilliant feel of the sweet pull when she slid him out and the sweeter glide when she took him back in.

He looked down and watched her work and that didn't last very long before he slid his fingers into either side of her hair, pulling it back, and then taking over.

She held on to his hips as he watched and fucked her face. He did it slow at first, but after he got her first moan vibrating against his cock, he went faster. Finally, he watched her body start moving with his rhythm, coming up and down on her knees like she was riding him with her pussy with each stroke, and he knew she was liking this near as much as he was when he saw her hand move toward her panties.

That was when he pulled out, reached down, yanked her up, and pushed her against the kitchen counter, facing it.

"Baby," she breathed.

He yanked up the skirt of her dress and tore her panties down to her thighs. She spread her legs and tipped her ass.

Fuck, Frankie. Ready. Wanting it. Probably so wet she was drenched.

He drove in.

Totally soaked.

Fuck.

Frankie.

He kept thrusting into her wet, tight pussy, bending over her to put a hand on the counter and press his chest into her back, face in her neck, smelling and feeling her hair, fucking her cunt, hearing her gasp and whimper, everything that was his world centered on his woman.

She tipped high and pressed up into his chest, her hips into his, moaning, "Benny."

He slid a hand over her belly, down, and found her clit.

"Benny," she gasped, her body jerking, one hand moving to cover his on the counter and curl over the top of it.

He bent his knees and powered deep.

Her neck twisted and her back arched as her cunt tightened around his cock and she cried out when she came.

He took his finger from her clit, wrapped his arm around her belly, held her steady, and drove in deeper.

She whimpered through it, clutching him tight with her pussy until she took him there. He shoved his face deeper into her neck and exploded on a grunt against her skin.

He kept taking her, gliding his hand back down her belly and in, cupping her, feeling his cock slide in and out slowly, how wet she was, how deep she was breathing. Fuck, he couldn't even see her face and everything he had from her was crazy-beautiful.

She slid a hand down his forearm, his wrist, then covered his hand between her legs, holding there lightly but shifting her index finger so she could run it along his cock as he pulled it out and glided it back in.

He buried his face deeper into her neck.

Finally, he twisted his hand, taking hers from between her legs, and slid out. He straightened, put his hands to her hips, and turned her to face him. He pulled up her panties and pulled down the stretchy skirt to her sexy-as-fuck, threw-it-on-like-it-was-nothing, straight-from-the-pages-of-a-magazine tight black dress.

He righted himself while brushing his lips against hers, her hands curling into the waistband of his jeans as he did.

Finally, he lifted his head and said, "You can finish your donut now."

Her eyes were still hooded and sated from her climax.

But still, pure Frankie, she whispered, "Annoying."

⁓

"Don't court that either, Frankie."

Lying on top of him on her couch, she lifted her head from his chest and looked down at him.

They had been winding down after dinner, about to watch a movie, discussing which one to watch as Benny shuffled through Netflix, and somehow they got to the fact that Frankie had not heard from Cat since before the shooting.

"Ben, she can disappear, but she's never *disappeared*. I'm worried."

"Francesca, the last time I saw Cat and Art was at Vinnie's wake. Before that, every time I saw them, they were half a step away from bein' functional alcoholics. They were hammered at Vinnie's wake, and watchin' them, I figured they took that half a step but took out the functional part. They tried to leave with Art havin' the keys to the car. Pop intervened. Art lost his mind and Manny and I had to step in, get 'em into a taxi."

Her eyes had grown wide while he talked, and when he was done, she asked, "Really?"

"Yeah," he answered.

"How'd I miss that?"

"I don't know. Maybe it was because your man had a hit carried out on him. He was dead at thirty-two. You were understandably beside yourself, grieving. And your sister, who should have been at your side holdin' your hand, was downing vodka tonics like they were gonna outlaw vodka the next day."

"Oh, yeah," she whispered. "That's probably how I missed it."

He shook his head and muttered, "Unbelievable."

"What?" she asked.

"You nearly imploded us, thinkin' you were gonna bail on me, and you hold tight to anything you got, no matter that it's not good for you."

"She's my sister, Benny, and Dad's havin' a baby any day now. Enzo's already had two. Enzo says she's not answering his calls either. And Nat says she hasn't heard from her in longer than I haven't heard from her."

He felt his brows snap together. "You're talkin' to Nat?"

Her head tipped to the side. "Not exactly. I'm keepin' tabs on her through Enzo."

"Thought she was dead to you," Ben noted.

Frankie bit her lip for a moment before she said, "She's dead to me, but she isn't actually *dead*."

Jesus.

Frankie.

"Leave it at that," he ordered.

"I can't," she returned, her voice rising.

He tightened his arms around her and pulled her up his chest so they were face-to-face.

"I get it," he said quietly. "You didn't have a lot to hold on to growin' up. It would stand to reason you not growin' up with anything solid that you'd hold on to anything you can get. But you gotta learn when to cut shit that is not healthy for you loose."

Her face softened and her tone lightened as she slid a hand up to curl it around his jaw and said, "Ben, I'm seein' things clearer now, but I am who I am. And I need you to see that's how I am. I also need you to see that how I am is okay now. It's better. Because now I *do* have something solid, so when the unhealthy part comes, I can deal."

She dug her fingers in on her emphasized "do," but Benny felt her words in his gut in a way he liked.

So he let it go.

Mostly.

"So, let me guess, you've talked to Chrissy," he noted.

"Yes," she admitted.

"How many times?"

Her eyes got squinty. "Twelve thousand seventy-three."

He fought a grin, gave her a squeeze, and repeated, "How many times?"

Her eyes slid to the side before coming back to his. "Seven."

"She doin' okay?" he asked.

"Things are not great with Dad because she's a little freaked he wasn't there for me and she's giving him another daughter, so it would stand to reason he won't be there for my baby sister. But pregnancy-wise, she's good."

"Holdin' on to anything you can in a way that you even grab on to new shit that's gonna do your head in."

She rolled her eyes and muttered, "Whatever."

When they rolled back, he held her gaze and made his point even clearer when he asked, "How's Sal?"

She pressed her lips together.

"He still in touch?" Ben pushed.

She unpressed her lips to answer, "Actually, he phoned a while back, but it was the day Dad came calling, so I got lost in that and my newfound ability to give amazing blowjobs, so I forgot to mention it to you."

Ben felt his body shake under hers at her comment about blowjobs, but it didn't deter him from their conversation.

"And?" he prompted.

"And, well…the last time I was up there, I called so I could chat with Gina, maybe set up lunch with her. Gina answered, but she answered from Tuscany. They were in Italy on vacation."

Ben did not like that.

"You hidin' that shit from me?"

"No," she returned immediately. "It was just that she wasn't around for me to have lunch with, so since there was nothing to get into it with you about, I decided to avoid the hassle. If she'd have been around, I would have told you."

If he was her, he'd also take that play so he relaxed.

"We're eventually gonna have to have that conversation," he noted.

Her eyes again slid to the side as she murmured, "We're eventually gonna have to have a lot of conversations."

"What does that mean?" he asked.

Her eyes took their time coming back and he didn't think she was giving it all to him when she declared, "My birthday is in three weeks."

"Yeah, and you need to have your ass at my house when it comes."

Her eyes got big again and she asked, "Really?"

"Meant to tell you, you gotta come up. Not me comin' down. So do what you gotta do at work to make that happen."

Her gaze grew alert and her head tipped to the side. "Why?"

"Benny and Frankie livin' together in relative harmony, it comes to birthdays, Valentine's day, anniversaries, and Christmas, you don't ask questions."

Her body relaxed into his and a smile lit her eyes before she said softly, "I can do that."

"Benny and Frankie livin' together in relative harmony, it comes to those days, we're together. No work. No nothing. No excuses. You gotta travel for work, you plan trips around those days. And for that part, I'll add Easter, Thanksgiving, and the Fourth of July."

Her lips curved up as she stated, "I've finally stumbled on a time when I don't mind you bein' bossy."

He grinned through his, "Shut up, Frankie."

She dropped her head to touch her mouth to his and pulled back, declaring on a complete lie, "I'm back to a time when I mind you bein' bossy."

He grinned again and asked, "What we gonna watch?'

"You pick," she offered.

"I pick, you can't bitch."

Her brows shot up. "What's the point of givin' up my pick if I can't bitch about yours?'

Ben looked to the ceiling and sighed.

"All right, I won't bitch," she gave in and he looked back to her. "You want popcorn?"

"Yeah."

"You queue up the movie, I'll make the corn."

"Deal."

She smiled down at him, then dropped her head again but went low, touching her lips to his throat. Then she pushed up with her hands in the couch and angled off him.

After watching her ass in her tight skirt moving to the kitchen, he turned his attention to the TV, thinking that that conversation didn't go too great. She didn't back down from keeping people who treated her like shit in her life and maneuvered him so he'd let her.

At least he got her to agree to important holidays spent together.

It was something.

And with Frankie, he'd take it.

Then again, with Frankie, he'd take anything.

"I hate this," Frankie whispered into his chest.

"Yeah, baby," Benny whispered into the top of her hair.

He felt her draw in a deep breath and let it go. After that, she tipped her head back to look at him.

"You'll call me when you get home?"

"Yeah."

"Okay, Benny."

She lifted up in her heels and pressed her mouth to his.

He slanted his head, took it, and took his time doing it. He memorized her taste, the smell of her, the feel of her in his arms. Only when he had it etched deep so it could keep him going for weeks of being away from her did he let her go.

She gave him a squeeze, a smile she didn't mean, and pulled out of his arms.

She bent and got her computer bag from the sidewalk where she'd dropped it, and Ben stood in front of her house and watched her walk to her Z.

She waved before she got in.

She waved as she reversed out.

And she waved as she drove away.

Ben watched her, doing it the whole time smiling.

And he watched until her car disappeared.

He moved only to walk down the sidewalk to look around her unit, then he stood there, eyes on the straight Indiana street that led to corn country one way and right into the heart of a city the other.

He did this no longer smiling.

And he thought this shit had to end—Frankie leaving him or him leaving Frankie. He was done with it three months ago.

But he knew it couldn't end. She was good at what she did, she liked her job, and he loved her. He couldn't fuck that for her.

So he had to be patient and wait for her to get to the time when she felt she could come to him and end this long-distance thing.

That didn't mean he had to like it.

And he didn't.

Seventeen

ELECTRIC

*B*en slammed the door on his truck and moved to the trailer that was removed from the noise and activity of the construction site.

He went up the two steps, pounded the side of his fist on the door twice, and heard a woman call, "Come in!"

He went in and saw a narrow space that was surprisingly tidy. Plans tacked to walls. Filing cabinets. A drafting board. A desk with a computer and phone that was covered in papers with a very pretty, dark-haired woman behind it wearing a dark blue polo with MCCANDLESS CONSTRUCTION stitched in white over her heart.

Her head lifted, her attractive face holding an expression that was not unwelcoming, but it was distracted.

Until she caught sight of him.

That was when Catarina Concetti Lugar declared, "We are not doin' this."

Not a good start.

Benny ignored that and walked further into the office, deciding to try to get them on track, even as he didn't hold much hope he'd succeed, and he did this by greeting, "Hey, Cat."

She did not greet him back. She ordered, "Ben, I'm at work. Just go."

He shook his head and told her, "Your sister is worried about you. It's her birthday tomorrow. She's comin' up tonight, I've been makin' calls, calls you haven't returned, so I thought I'd extend the invitation face-to-face. I'd like you and Art to come to the pizzeria for Frankie's birthday party tomorrow night. More, it would make Frankie happy you were there."

"I ignored your calls because me and Art aren't gettin' anywhere near that pizzeria," she retorted.

And now it was getting worse.

"You wanna explain that to me?" he invited.

"Not really," she refused.

"Do it anyway," he ordered, holding her eyes.

She stared at him before she looked out the window, huffed out an annoyed breath, and gave him back her eyes. "My sister was shot," she announced.

"I know. I was the one who carried her through the forest after that shit happened."

"Yeah, I know. Frankie, up in the shit of another Bianchi," she fired back.

Ben felt his skin start to itch, pissed that another of the Concettis brought that shit up. At the same time, he was wondering how in the fuck they couldn't get their heads out of their asses and see *why* their sister would want to be part of a good, decent, loving family. Even so, she wasn't the kind of woman to go about getting that with how they thought she was doing it. They had to know her better than that.

Then again, since they had their heads up their asses, and when they didn't, they were all about themselves, he shouldn't be surprised.

When he got control and spoke, he had to force his mouth to move but, in doing that, not to yell.

"I'm not feelin' a lot of love for explainin' anything to you, seein' as your sister was in a hospital bed for a week and a half and you didn't even call. Then she was recuperating at my house and you didn't come 'round. But Francesca is worried about you. It's her birthday. I want her to quit worryin' and have what's important to her on her special day. Not sure I agree with what's important to her, seein' as the majority of you Concettis treat her like shit, but it is so I'm here."

Her face started to get red, even as ice formed in her gaze as he spoke, and she didn't hesitate to reply when he was done.

"Concettis treat her like shit?" she asked. "How 'bout the Bianchis?"

"You spoke to your sister, you'd know that's done and we're all movin' on."

"Yeah, you're here and word is she's in your bed. I know how *you're* movin' on."

"Known me decades, Cat. Honest to God, do you think I'm gonna sink low enough to field that one?" Ben clipped.

She glared at him, not like Nat, much like Frankie, except a lot less cute because he didn't love her, and more, he'd never really liked her.

"You know," she started, "your big sister's boyfriend gets whacked in a mob war, then she gets shot, then it's all over everywhere that her dead boyfriend's brother is up in her shit and then it's everywhere they get hooked up, a girl's gotta make a decision. She continues to get caught up in that ridiculous drama that ain't real healthy, or she cuts herself off and tries to make a decent life. Me and Art talked about it a lot. He's tight with his folks, his brothers. He didn't get it. Why I wanted to cut ties. Until Frankie got shot and *you* were involved. Frankie involved with another Bianchi. Then he got it. Totally messed up. Totally unhealthy."

She flipped her hand in the air and didn't shut up, she kept on yapping.

"Art and me got marriage counseling so we'd quit fightin' all the freakin' time. Art and me found out in marriage counseling that it might be a good idea not to drink so freakin' much. Art and me quit the booze, and now Art and me are in a good place so we're tryin' to make a baby. We got a good thing goin', had it goin' for a while. We don't want anything to fuck that up. More, we bring a kid into this world, we don't want that kid to be involved in fucked-up shit."

Benny couldn't believe his ears.

"You quit the booze?" he asked.

"Yep. We've been dry now for nearly a year."

"Congratulations, Cat," he murmured.

"Yeah, hold a party for *that*," she returned.

"Cat—"

She shook her head and lifted a hand to him, palm his way. "No. My sister got *shot*. Before that, her boyfriend was in the *mob*. Now, after years of watchin' the Bianchis like she was on the verge of beggin' you to adopt her, she went from one to the other to get her in."

"That's not what she's doin'," Ben said, his voice tight.

"No?" she asked, sarcasm easy to read. "She's gorgeous. I know it. She's sweet. She's funny. I see why you want a piece of that. Totally. I love her to bits, my big sis. Only one who gave a shit about me *my...entire...life*. Until I met Art. But she's messed up, Benny. Took me a while, but I finally woke my ass up and saw I needed to get out of the crazy that was my family draggin' me down. I love her. I know the way you're lookin' at me you don't believe that, but I *love her*. That doesn't mean she's any good for me. It was a hard decision to make, but I gotta look out *for me*. And you can take this as my good turn to you, you need to get outta that shit before she chews you up and spits you out like Ninette chews up every man who even looks at her."

"Your sister is not Ninette," Ben bit out.

"Who lives with one brother and then hooks up with the other one?" she retorted, shaking her head. "No one does that."

"Vinnie died seven years ago."

"He's still your brother."

"He quit bein' my brother when he joined the mob."

At that, she snapped her mouth shut.

Yeah.

She got him.

"Life sucks, Cat, for everyone, not just you," he told her something she should know. "Shit happens and you make decisions that can make it suck even more. From what you're sayin', I see you took a look at your life and decided to make good changes. But what you're doin', slammin' the door on Frankie, means you won't see she's doin' the same thing. Makin' good changes to her life. And you didn't ask, but what she did when she got shot was crazy. Crazy-stupid and crazy-brave. She helped save a woman's life. You got a screw loose if you'd turn your back on a woman who'd take a bullet to do somethin' like that. But I know it's loose 'cause she's had your back your entire life. Took you as you came, made no judgments when you were three steps away from bein' a full-blown drunk, a mean one half the time, and she never shut the door in *your* face."

He saw by her expression that he'd scored with that one, but he still took a step back, shaking his head and lifting, then dropping his hands.

"That's your decision, it's your life. I came by, we had our words. I leave, you continue your life. I'm happy for you. You're tryin' to make a good one for the family you wanna build. But that doesn't mean what you're sayin' isn't complete bullshit. The thing is, you sit there knowin' it. You cast judgment for the decisions Francesca has made in her life, sittin' there knowin' you let your sister lie in a hospital bed with a hole in her without showin' your face and givin' some love. And still, you did that to her, Frankie calls *you* because she's worried about *you*. What's that say about her, Cat? And more, you can take this as *my* good turn to *you*, what's it say about *you*?"

He knew he scored another point when the red went out of her face and it got pale.

He also didn't give a fuck. He was done.

"Dinner's at seven," he ground out. "You're there, you're welcome. You're not, I do not share blood with you so I do not have to put up with your shit. You don't show, Frankie won't cut ties. But seein' as I'm in love with her and she'll be the mother of my kids one day, you'll have to work to get *me* to let you in our door, because, straight-up, Cat, I don't need my woman or my kids around that kind of fucked-up shit."

He left it at that, turned, and walked out, deciding he wouldn't share this visit with Frankie. Cat and Art showed the next night, then he'd get the goodness of her gratitude that he went out of his way to get her sister back. If not, she didn't need to know.

And anyway, he didn't need to give more headspace to Cat, seeing as not fun as that visit was, the next one he was going to make he knew was going to be a fuckuva lot worse.

⟜⟶

Ben looked around the huge-ass house Gina was leading him through, thinking that she'd had the whole fucking place redecorated since the last time he'd been there.

Since he lost track of when that was, he shouldn't be surprised. It was more than eight years. It was more like fifteen.

She now had marble floors. Acres of them.

Things must be good in the mob business. He'd never be able to give Frankie acres of marble floors. That said, she'd never want them, and if she did, she'd work to get them for herself.

"It really is nice, you showin', Benny," Gina murmured, and he looked at her.

She held some weight, not much, but she no longer had the slender, built figure she'd had a couple of decades ago. That didn't mean she wasn't dressed well, she was. She'd always dressed well. Slightly over-the-top with jewelry and bright colors, but she wasn't the stereotypical mob wife you saw in the movies.

But she was beyond middle age and her face didn't have a line on it that he could see. And she dyed her hair so there wasn't a strand of gray.

She took care of herself. Then again, she could. She had the money and she had the time.

Wouldn't matter if she didn't, Sal was devoted to his wife. Doted on her. Never was a time back in the day when they were around where he wasn't affectionate or didn't look at her like she jumpstarted the world every morning.

That didn't mean he didn't fuck around. He did. Always. Even now. Word flew through the family, regardless if you didn't want to hear that shit, and Ben knew Sal had two women on the side, both kept, both thirty years younger than Gina.

Gina probably knew too and kept her tongue. It was a thing with men like Sal, and the women with them had to put up with it. It was his way to show how big his balls were and that they still worked.

It was also as whacked as everything else Sal did.

"It's good to see you, Gina," he muttered in order to be nice, even if he didn't mean it. He liked her, but that didn't mean she didn't bring up bad memories.

She turned her head to look over her shoulder at him and he knew she knew he was lying through his teeth by the sad look in her eyes.

Her husband fucked around on her and did seriously fucked-up shit for a living, which meant every day anything could happen, and that "anything" could include him being incarcerated or assassinated. When you lived a life like that, family was important, and not the kind who were all in danger of the same thing.

He couldn't say he didn't feel for her. She was a good woman. But he couldn't help her by biting the bullet and giving her the big family that would make the shit in her life less shitty. She'd made her choice.

She looked forward again and led him out onto a patio with a pool, gazebo, and pool house. There was a huge-ass, ostentatious fountain shooting water into the deep end of the pool. There were pots filled with thriving flowers and greenery all over the place. It looked like it belonged in a resort, not in an affluent Chicago suburb that would much prefer the local mob boss hadn't bought a house there but no one would say jack for fear they'd find a horse's head in their bed the next day.

And like he was at his own personal resort, which he was, Sal Giglia was sitting at a table with an iced drink in front of him, along with a tablet, his phone to his ear.

He, too, was a good-looking man, a big man, tall, broad. He'd been built back in the day, but now he had a gut. His dark hair had silvered and he'd left it at that, but he did slick it back, even if he was doing that to sit on his patio. He dressed well—designer polos, nice slacks, custom-made Italian loafers. He looked like Tony Soprano with more hair, classic features, and an extra fifteen years.

When they came out, Sal's eyes came to Gina and Benny. He then said something in his phone, ended the call, dropped the cell on the table, and stood, face breaking into a huge smile.

Ben felt his throat prickle and fought back the urge to form his hands into fists or, the better option, turn and walk away.

"Benny, *figlio,*" Sal called as they made their way over the expensive pavers to Sal.

Figlio.

Asshole.

"Frankie's birthday, am I right?" Sal asked, eyes lighting, misunderstanding the situation and thinking Ben getting in there with crazy-beautiful Francesca Concetti meant that either he was thinking with his dick or being led around by it.

"Not exactly," Ben replied, his gaze moving to Gina and back to Sal to make his point that what he had to say, Gina shouldn't be around to hear.

Sal's huge smile faded, but only slightly, as he took hold of his woman's hand, pulled her closer, kissed her cheek, and leaned back to ask, "Get Benny a drink, would you, *cara*?"

"Of course," she replied, smiling up at her husband before turning that smile to Ben. "What can I get you, Benny?"

He shook his head, searching for words that would take the sting out of his meaning. "Thanks, but I don't have time for a drink, Gina. Frankie's comin' in tonight. After I talk with Sal, I gotta run some more errands so I can't stay."

She nodded understandingly, trying to hide the disappointment and failing miserably. She aimed another smile at her husband, then moved away.

Sal threw out an arm, inviting, "Sit."

Ben didn't want to sit. He didn't want to breathe Sal's air.

He had no choice.

So he sat, pulled the shades out of his hair and over his eyes to beat back the sun, and trained his gaze on Sal.

"Last place I wanna be," he said quietly.

At his words, Sal's mouth got tight. "Do not tell me my Gina let you into our home for you to sit on my goddamned patio and be an asshole to me."

"Last place I wanna be 'cause I'm here 'cause I need you to do somethin' for Frankie."

Sal suddenly went still.

He was listening.

Intently.

And Ben did not get that, why Sal and Gina sunk their claws into Frankie before and after Vinnie died. He could get falling in love with her, he did that himself. And these people understood loyalty. But not the healthy kind, which it seemed they gave Frankie.

They had two daughters.

It didn't make sense.

But he wasn't there to make sense of it. He was there to do something three months ago he would have told you he'd put a bullet in his own brain before he did it.

But there he was.

"Actually, two things," Ben went on.

"You gonna tell me what they are?" Sal asked.

"Yeah," Ben answered. "One, we're havin' a birthday thing for Frankie tomorrow night at the pizzeria."

Sal's brows shot up.

"You and Gina aren't invited."

Sal's brows lowered and he scowled.

"That is not disrespect," Ben said low and it was the truth. "Feels like it, but that's me respectin' my family and givin' a good night to my woman. Ma and Pop would not want you there, Frankie would want everyone to have a good time, and knowin' that they weren't, it would fuck with her. Last, it would be awkward and I do not want that for Frankie on her birthday. But Frankie will wanna see you so I made reservations at Crickets for a Champagne brunch tomorrow morning," Ben told him and finished with, "I will not be there."

Sal nodded slowly. "And the second thing?"

"Guy at Frankie's work got whacked."

Sal's brows shot up again, but Ben didn't miss that his body also got tight. Preparing. Like Benny, he knew Frankie was a magnet for drama.

"Whacked?" Sal asked.

"Professional hit, one shot to the head in his home. Nothin' stolen. Nothin' even moved. Guy came in, did him, left. He was a doctor who worked on developing drugs for her company. Police have no suspects. Cal's got a friend who's a cop in Brownsburg who asked around. Indianapolis Metropolitan PD have no clue why this guy had a hit taken out on him. Nothin' in his life leads to that kinda retaliation. They've been over everything repeatedly. He has a wife, two kids in college, nice house. No gambling. No drug use. Not a big drinker. Kids not fucked up. Wife all good. Plays golf. Belongs to a club. No shit in his past. No shady friends. Not one fuckin' thing."

"And you're tellin' me this because...?" Sal prompted.

"I'm tellin' you this because Frankie told me the guy bought it, she feels weird about it, and she feels weird about the guy's boss."

"Fuck," Sal muttered.

"Yeah," Benny agreed, knowing Sal again got him. "Her feelin' weird can die on the vine or it can flourish, and Frankie bein' Frankie, I'm wantin' to nip it in the bud before it flourishes."

"Tell her to keep out of it," Sal advised.

"Sorry, thought you knew Francesca Concetti," Benny replied, and Sal grinned.

"Reckless, that one," he muttered. "And headstrong."

"And stubborn and crazy," Benny added, and Sal's grin grew into a smile, clearly these being traits Sal admired. The troubling part of that was Ben did too. "Told her that she needed to steer clear. She promised me she'd do that and just do her job. Far's I know, she's doin' that."

"And you're here because you want me to make some inquiries, find out who whacked this guy and why."

That was why he was there.

Asking a favor from Sal.

Fuck.

"That's why I'm here," Ben confirmed.

"Consider it done," Sal replied.

Fuck.

"I give, I take," Sal went on, barely taking a breath before calling the marker.

Fucking *fuck.*

Ben stared at him through his shades and said nothing.

Sal did.

"When you two get married, Gina and I are invited."

Ben's back straightened and he leaned toward Sal, starting, "Sal—"

Sal shook his head, lifted a hand, and dropped it. "Not the reception. We'll sit in the back of the church. But I'll wanna see my Frankie happy. I'll wanna give that to my Gina. And I am not unaware you do not like me much, Benny Bianchi, but I still wanna see you happy. So does Gina. You give that to us, I'll find out everything there is to know about what's goin' on in Indy."

"That seems too easy," Ben noted suspiciously.

"That's because what I do in Indy isn't for you. It's for Frankie. But she didn't ask for it, *you* asked for it, so *you* pay."

He got that and he could pay that marker without too much headache.

Except one thing.

"My parents don't see you," Benny stated, and Sal's face went hard.

"I'm not gonna slink into a church like a snake and Gina's not doin' that shit either."

"I don't care how you walk in," Benny returned. "You just do it so my parents don't see you."

Sal held his eyes before he jerked up his chin.

Assent.

They had a deal.

Christ.

"Then we're done," Ben ended it, and Sal's face changed in a way Benny did not get, even when he did.

Sal Giglia didn't want to be done with Benny. With the Bianchis. With family.

How the man could think he could hold on to blood when his business was about taking it, Ben had no fucking clue.

He'd never figure it out and he had another stop to make. Then he had to drop what he was picking up at home before he went to get Frankie from the airport. So he didn't give that headspace either.

"We're done," Sal released him.

"Tell Gina I said 'bye," Ben murmured, rising from his chair, Sal coming with him.

"Will do," Sal replied.

Ben gave him a nod, turned, and started away.

He stopped when Sal said, "She was with the wrong brother."

He turned back, his throat prickling again, and he leveled his shades on the man.

Sal wasn't done. "Vinnie was a good man, but not for her. She was made for you. Always knew it."

Ben said nothing.

Sal did.

"She'll drive you fuckin' crazy and you'll love every minute of it."

Ben kept his silence.

"Happy for you, *figlio*," Sal finished quietly.

Since Vinnie died, Ben had spent nearly zero time with Sal, putting up with him at the hospital the night Frankie got shot only because he had no choice.

Now, he was reminded why someone like Frankie would hold on to a man like Sal. Away from him, it made no sense.

But fuck, you got anywhere near, the man was likeable. Always was.

So maybe he had a piece of the puzzle as to why his brother did the shit he did, and having that piece was a miracle.

Ben didn't tell Sal that, mostly because all the other puzzle pieces did not fit.

He only nodded again and got his ass out of there.

"Can you explain why you're gonna be here six days but you got enough luggage to be here for the rest of your life?" Benny bitched as he hauled Francesca's huge-ass suitcase up the stairs of his back stoop, along with her carry-on.

"I told you I'd carry them," Frankie replied. He twisted his neck to give her a look, so she widened her eyes at him and continued, "You wanna be a protective, take-care-of-my-woman, Italian guy, you can't bitch."

She was absolutely right.

Still, it bought him Frankie with wide eyes being cute, so he was going to bitch.

He let go of a bag to open the door, asking, "What do you have in these bags anyway?"

"You gave me no hint as to what you had planned so I had to come prepared," she answered as he shoved in through the door, hauling her bags in with him.

"So by 'prepared' you mean you came prepared to assault the White House?" he asked.

"I have clothes and shoes in those bags, not assault rifles," she shot back.

"Feels like half a ton of C4," he muttered.

"Shut up, Benny," she returned, but he heard the smile in her voice.

That made him smile as he kept moving toward the door to the hall.

Once he hit it, he said, "Shit, babe, forgot to put your Fanta in the fridge. It's in the den. I'll take these upstairs. You toss a couple cans in the fridge, and while you're at it, pop me a beer."

"Your den is not a den. It's a den-shaped dump," she replied.

"You gonna pop me a beer or what?" he returned, still smiling.

"All right," she murmured, and he heard her purse hit the table.

He hauled the bags to the foot of the stairs, left them there, and retraced his steps, timing it perfectly to hit the door to the den so he could see Frankie's hands shoot to her mouth as she shrieked, "*Oh my God! Benny!*"

He grinned as he watched her drop instantly to a closed-knees squat as a wrinkly bulldog puppy—brown body, white feet, belly, face, and ears, with little brown spots on one floppy ear, and brown emanating out the sides of his eyes—waddled her way.

Benny leaned against the jamb as she gathered the puppy in her arms and rubbed her cheek against his fur.

"Meet Churchill," he said.

She tipped her head back, gave him her eyes, and when he got them, Ben went still.

"Gus," she whispered, her voice husky, her eyes shining with tears. "His name is Gus."

Looking in those crazy-beautiful eyes that were filled with tears and love, Ben found he couldn't move.

The dog and Frankie could.

The dog squirmed. Frankie came out of her squat and moved toward him, holding the puppy close to her face, her eyes never leaving his.

She came to a stop not a foot away, and he said softly, "One day early, but couldn't leave him in there forever." His voice dipped low, "Happy birthday, baby."

He barely got the words out when he watched a tear slide down her cheek. But she didn't move.

So he asked, "You gonna kiss me?"

She rubbed the still-squirming puppy against her cheek and asked back, "Do you have any clue how awesome you are?"

"Pretty much," Benny joked.

"No you don't," she whispered, and his gut clenched.

"Come here, Frankie," he growled.

She came to him. He wrapped his arms around her (and the dog) and bent his head to take her mouth.

He didn't have to take it.

She gave it to him.

He kissed her deep.

But not long.

Because in the middle of it, using puppy tongue, Gus kissed them both.

⟿

"This okay?" Benny asked as he parked behind the pizzeria the next night.

The night of Frankie's birthday.

"Are you makin' my birthday pie?" Frankie asked back.

Ben grinned as he shut down the ignition. "Yeah."

"Then yeah," she finally answered.

He looked her way to ascertain if she was bullshitting him and saw her leaned forward, face in the visor mirror, slicking on lip gloss.

But doing it on smiling lips.

There it was. She wasn't bullshitting him.

She liked his pie enough to be perfectly happy eating it on her special day.

She'd finished with her gloss and hopped down by the time he got to her side of the SUV.

He slammed the door for her, and as he did, he took her in yet again, top to toe, doing it thinking he was looking forward to what was going to happen in a few minutes. But Frankie in that red dress with its short, tight skirt and slouchy, sleeveless top that fell off one shoulder, her hair big, her makeup set straight to "going out," her jewelry set to "seriously tricked out," and a pair of high-heeled sandals, he was more looking forward to later when he intended to feel those heels in his back.

He took her hand, guided her to the back door, and she started talking.

"You should have told me, though. I could have invited Asheeka and Jamie and some folks from my old work and tried to get Cat to give up whatever grudge she's holdin'. A grudge, no matter how deep, is no match for a Bianchi pie." He'd shoved open the door and pulled her in when her eyes came to him and she said hurriedly, "Sorry, I didn't mean that to sound like I wanted a bunch of people around. You want this to be a couple thing, I don't get enough of you, so I'm *way* down with that. You, me, your pie, and your pizzeria." She leaned into him and finished on a bright, happy smile, "Perfect."

It was going to perfect all right.

"Glad you're down with that, honey."

"Totally," she assured him, squeezing his hand.

He moved her through the bustling kitchen, giving nods to his kids as they went.

Then he moved her through the short hall that led to the dining room.

Finally, he moved her into the dining room.

When they hit it, he knew the kid he gave the order to keep an eye out for them and spread the word when they showed didn't fuck it up, because the minute he cleared the hall and pulled Frankie to his side, a cacophony of streamer poppers sounded, bits flying through the air, along with shouts of, "*Surprise!*"

That was when Ben saw that his ma had also done her job.

To one side, there was a table set up with a massive cake on it that had white frosting and a shitload of pink and purple frosting flowers that said *Happy Birthday, Frankie*, presents placed all around it. They'd closed the restaurant for the night so the floor had been arranged so there were two long, rectangular tables with red-and-white-checkered tablecloths taking up the space. Each table had several huge bouquets of balloons floating up from them down their lengths and big bouquets of flowers in the middle.

His eyes went through the smiling crowd and he saw Asheeka there with her date. Frankie's friend Jamie was there with her boyfriend. Manny was there with Sela. His ma and pop obviously were there. Asheeka had gotten the word out to Frankie's friends from her old work, including her ex-boss, and they were all there. As were Frankie's best friends from high school, and old lady Zambino and her bowling posse.

Last, he was surprised to note, Cat was there, looking anywhere but at Benny or Frankie, and her husband, Art, was standing beside her.

"Hello, girl, you alive in there?" Asheeka called, and when she did, it hit Benny that Frankie stood unmoving at his side.

He looked down at her and saw her staring at the crowd, face set firm to stunned.

"Babe," he said, pulling her by her hand his way, and her head tipped back to look at him.

That was when his chest warmed, because her face was still set to stunned, but her gaze was filled with so much wonder and tenderness, seeing that look in her crazy-beautiful eyes, it was a wonder he could breathe.

"How're you gonna top this next year, Benny Bianchi?" she asked quietly.

"I'm awesome so I'll figure it out," he answered.

Her eyes got bright again, but this time, no tear fell.

This was because she threw herself in his arms and laid a hot, wet one on him.

They went at it to catcalls, shouts of encouragement, offers to get them a room, and his mother yelling, "Thank God Father Frances couldn't make it!" before he broke it off and said softly, "Gotta start makin' pies, baby."

She held his eyes and held on to him tight when she replied, "All right, Benny."

He winked at her, gave her a squeeze, and turned her from his arms and toward her crew.

When he did, she threw her arms straight in the air and shouted, "Birthdays rock!"

Two seconds later, she was engulfed by friends and family.

Benny watched it, grinning.

Then he went into the kitchen to start making pies.

⌒

"Oh my God!" Frankie yelled. "I love these!"

Benny, sitting beside Frankie, where she was at the head of the table, figured she did love the present she just opened, seeing as she instantly yanked off the bracelets she had on and shoved on the bracelets whoever just gave her.

She jiggled them in his face. "Aren't they gorgeous, honey?" she asked.

"Gorgeous," he muttered, smiling at her and not looking at the bracelets at all.

She gave him a look, dropped her hand, leaned into him, and hissed, "Don't be sweet."

He looked down the length of the table that was filled with empty cake plates, wrapping paper, used streamers and confetti from the second (and third) round of streamer poppers, and people who loved Francesca Concetti.

Then he looked back at her and asked, "Seriously?"

"If you're in the mood to be sweet...*er*," she went on, "maybe you can get one of the kids to bring out more Chianti. I'm dry."

"I'll go to the bar," he murmured, but she caught his wrist as he made a move.

"I'm not done with presents, you can't leave. If you do, whose face am I gonna jiggle bracelets in and who am I gonna force to smell my candles?"

Benny got off on seeing his baby happy.

He did not get off on having jewelry jiggled in his face or courting a headache because he had to sniff another candle.

He looked across the table at Art and said, "Art'll stand in."

"Great," Art muttered, eyes rolling to the ceiling.

Benny ignored him, got out of his seat, bent to Frankie, and said in her ear, "Wine for my woman."

He pulled back, she gave him a big smile, and he went to the bar to tell the bartender to set the tables up with more wine.

He was heading back when he saw movement out of the corner of his eye. Asheeka was there, so he stopped.

"Yo, babe," he greeted.

"Hey, Benny," she replied, coming to a stop next to him. "Great pizza, as usual."

"We kinda got practice at that here."

She nodded her head, her lips curved up.

"*Ohmigod! I love this lotion! It's the best evah!*" Frankie shrieked, and Ben and Asheeka looked her way to see she was forcing a bottle of lotion under Art's nose.

Art's face did not communicate he much liked the smell, but at least the guy was game and was sniffing it.

"That girl isn't half breathin'," Asheeka said softly, and Benny turned to look at her just as her hand caught his. "Got my gratitude, Benny."

"Not sure what to say to that since I'm the one who gets to enjoy a Francesca Concetti who's breathin' easy."

"You got it anyway."

He tightened his hand in hers and said quietly, "Appreciated, Asheeka."

She squeezed his hand back, let him go, and moved to the table just as Cat vacated her seat, a seat that was strategically far away from Frankie.

Art had thrown himself right in, and the way he did, it reminded Ben that he was a good guy, when he wasn't hammered.

Cat, so far, had not thrown herself into anything. She wasn't hanging back, sulking and making a point. She was hanging back like she wasn't sure how to get close anymore.

Now, she was making her way toward Benny.

Shit.

"Ben," she greeted.

"Cat, glad you came," he replied.

"Me too," she said. "Been so long, thought the delight of a Bianchi pie was a dream. Now I know it's better than I remembered."

She stopped next to him as one of the kids who worked the floor passed them with two bottles of wine in each hand.

When the server was gone, Ben, eyes to the tables, noted, "Keepin' a distance from your sister."

"Been a bitch," she whispered, and Benny looked down to her, surprised again.

"Rectified that tonight, Cat," he reminded her.

"She got shot and I did somethin' selfish and stupid, and now I show at her birthday party for free pizza and cake?" she told the table where her eyes were aimed.

"Sortin' out your life isn't stupid," he remarked.

"Doin' it bein' a bitch is," she returned.

"Better late than never," he pointed out.

"That's bullshit and you know it," she retorted.

"Frankie givin' you crap?" he asked.

She turned her gaze to him because she knew the answer. Frankie was giving her sister space, mostly because Cat was taking it. But she wasn't giving her crap.

"Trust me, she'll take you as you come," he said. "She's just glad you're here. She gives you that gift, Cat, just roll with it."

She heaved a sigh, looked back at the table, took a few moments, then asked, "It true, Dad's latest bitch havin' his baby?"

"Any day now," Ben affirmed.

"Shit," she muttered.

"You're gettin' a sister," he told her.

She kept muttering. "Jesus."

"I'm not Enzo Senior's biggest fan, Cat, but his woman seems solid."

"They always are," she said to the table, and Ben didn't doubt that.

Another question that would go unanswered in his lifetime was how good women got hooked up with dicks all the time.

He decided not to reply and looked back at the table to see old lady Zambino sitting in his chair, leaned into Frankie's space, and Benny couldn't tell by his woman's expression if she was about to laugh, cry, or shout.

"Thinkin' I should get back," he said.

"Yeah," Cat replied.

Ben made a move, but stopped and turned back when she called his name.

"Thanks for havin' the balls to come and get in my face," she said.

"You still got her love, and you'll always have her love. You fuck up again, I'll do it again."

For the first time that night, he saw her smile. "I'm thinkin' I'll do my best to avoid that."

"That'd be my call."

She rolled her eyes.

He heard Frankie burst out laughing and turned back to the table to see she had her hand wrapped around the back of Mrs. Zambino's head, she'd pressed their foreheads together, and she was giggling herself sick, her entire body shaking with it.

Mrs. Zambino wasn't giggling.

She was yelling. "Francesca Concetti, you're ruining my hair!"

Frankie did not let go.

She just kept giggling.

Ben left her to it for three beats before he made his approach to unlatch his woman from his neighbor so Mrs. Zambino wouldn't unsheathe the talons or take him off her Christmas gift list.

Frankie's chocolate-filled snowballs were his favorite.

But Mrs. Zambino's homemade cookies cut out like poinsettia leaves and filled with green-colored creamy frosting were a close second.

Ben lay in his bed, back to the headboard, sheet to his waist, and just managed to avoid a traumatic injury when Gus made to jump right on his dick. Frankie had scooped him up and put him on the bed before she skipped to the bathroom to clean up after Benny'd fucked her. And Benny was making a mental note to see to it that she did not do that again.

He pulled the dog up his chest and got a wet jaw for his effort. Still, he kept the dog where he was and scratched his head. This got him puppy breath right in the face because Gus started panting happily.

Ben continued to keep him where he was and give him scratches as Frankie, now in a sweet, short nightie, skipped out of the bathroom, made a beeline to the bed, and hopped in, landing on her knees. She bounced across the bed to him and tossed out a thigh, ending up straddling him.

Once positioned, she pulled Gus right out of his arms, lifted him up in front of her face, and cooed, "Who's Mommy's special little boy?"

She was being cute and dorky, which was also cute, but Ben had frozen.

This was because Frankie had *skipped* out of the bathroom, *hopped* into bed, and *bounced* across it.

Frankie, after hours with family, friends, food, presents, and unlimited wine. After digging her heels in his back hard and riding his cock harder.

And there she was.

Electric.

"Is Gus Mommy's special little boy?" she asked, and he had to jerk himself out of his freeze to lift his hands and rest them on her hips.

347

"Babe, don't talk to him like that," he ordered, trying to ignore the warmth in his gut at the happiness written all over the woman astride his hips.

She looked down at him and curled Gus into her chest. "Why?"

"'Cause he's an English bulldog," Ben explained.

"And?" she prompted as Gus made a successful escape attempt, which meant he successfully landed dead weight on Ben's chest, something that made Benny grunt.

Frankie scooted the puppy to Ben's gut and gave him scratches there, her eyes on Ben, waiting for an answer.

Benny got his breath back and continued to explain.

"He's a male English bulldog. In other words, he's a badass breed. A chick baby talks him, his ears might start bleedin'."

She grinned. "His ears won't start bleedin'."

"Don't look at me when you coo at him and that shit happens."

She rolled her eyes, rolled them back, and declared, "Just so you know, you being annoying is not gonna kill my buzz. I mean, you got Cat there, *and* Art, *and* old lady Zambino, who was still so pissed I bailed on you, she hadn't talked to me in months, but she showed too."

He tipped his head to the side and asked, "You work that out with Mrs. Zambino?"

She nodded but said, "She busted my chops about how I went off half-cocked and didn't walk across the street to," she lifted her hands and did air quotation marks, "'get some wisdom.' But I had your pie and a ton of wine in me, so she couldn't kill my buzz either."

He took in her shining eyes, squeezed her hips with his hands, and asked quietly, "Happy?"

"Yes and no," she answered.

He felt his head jerk with surprise. "What's the no part?"

"You kicked this birthday's ass. I mean, Ben…" She scooped up Gus and cuddled him to her chest again. "You closed the *entire* restaurant. Cake. Flowers. *Balloons.* A surprise party. A sisterly reunion." She cuddled Gus closer, finishing, "And a freakin' puppy."

"And there's a part of that that doesn't make you happy?" he pushed when she explained no further.

"Yeah, seein' as it's gonna be practically impossible to one-up you on your birthday and I have barely a month to plan."

At that, Benny burst out laughing, did an ab crunch, and confiscated the dog. He also put an arm around his woman, twisted, leaned to the side, and put the dog on the floor. Then he lay back, taking Frankie with him the way he wanted her, with one arm still around her, the other hand in her hair, holding her close.

"My birthday's easy, baby. You, a couple sweet nighties, and a bottle of chocolate sauce."

Her eyes got big and she asked, "Chocolate sauce?"

"Yep."

"That'll be sticky," she declared, but in a tone that said it might be sticky, but it was far from out of the question.

"That's the point, Francesca. You get sticky, I make you unsticky."

Her hips rolled against his.

It was after two in the morning, after wine, food, cake, friends, presents, and she was ready to go again.

Electric.

He ran a hand over her ass. "I get greedy and make a mess, I got a big shower."

"Mm," she murmured, eyes dropping to his mouth.

"You gotta hold that thought, *tesorina*. I gotta put the dog in the kennel and I won't be in the mood to leave this bed to do it after I do you."

"Okay, honey," she whispered, then leaned in and touched her mouth to his.

He gave her ass a squeeze before he let her go. She swung off him and he got out of bed, found the dog, scooped him up, and headed to the door.

"Ben?" she called when he was almost there.

He turned back and saw her and her hair and her body sitting on one hip, legs curled under her, eyes on him.

"Yeah, Frankie?"

"I'll give you nighties and chocolate sauce, all you want," she told him. "But I'm still gonna find a way to give you more so you'll remember it forever in a way that never fails to make you smile and feel allover happy, like I'm gonna remember tonight."

Jesus, seriously?

She was giving him that when he was a room away from her?

"Don't be sweet when I'm naked, got a puppy in my arms, and I'm a room away from you."

It was then she gave him all the gratitude he needed.

She smiled that smile. That smile that said she had a secret and it was a really good one.

Then she urged, "Hurry."

Ben turned and moved into the hall knowing Frankie didn't have any secrets. What she wanted to whisper in his ear wasn't words.

It was moans.

And he liked hearing them.

So he didn't waste any time.

Eighteen

THIS WAS FAMILY

I was there and I didn't even know why I was there. It was the last place I should be.

I should be in my car driving home to get ready for Cal and Vi's rehearsal dinner and the hour-long drive to get to the lakeside resort where I needed to be.

But unless I hit crazy traffic, I had time. Not much, but I had it. And I didn't want to hit the scene while they were rehearsing. They didn't need hangers-on for one. I wasn't in the wedding party, though Ben was as Cal's best man. For another, I had enough to do that I didn't need to be hanging around waiting for them to finish.

That wasn't true. I had everything sorted, and chilling at a lakeside resort was hardly torture.

The thing I needed to do I shouldn't be doing.

That was why I was there, using my employee ID to get into our production facility. It was a twenty-minute drive away from our main offices, and although I'd had a tour during my employee initiation, there was absolutely no reason for me to be there.

And if Ben knew I was there, and why, he'd lose his mind. So there was not only no reason for me to be there, I *shouldn't* be there.

But that morning, something happened and I just couldn't seem to stop myself.

This something was Randy Bierman showing up in my office. No knock. No warning. No eyebrows-raised, do-you-have-a-moment, nonverbal inquiry. He just walked right in, crossed his arms on his chest, and stared down at me where I was sitting at my desk.

It was then that all that was Randy hit me.

He was tall and lanky and probably about ten years older than me. He had brown hair that wasn't light or dark but did have a subtle cast of red to it that wasn't unattractive. Neither were his features. He wasn't take-your-breath-away good-looking, but if I was single and he bought me a drink at the bar, I'd have time for him.

That was, I would until it became clear two seconds later when he'd no doubt show he was a huge dick.

I'd been on the phone with my rep in Charlotte and was nowhere near finished talking to her, but I couldn't keep talking to her with him staring at me. It was uncomfortable, he was creeping me out, and I couldn't focus on what she was saying.

So I ended up telling her something came up and I had to go.

The instant I put my phone in the receiver, Randy stated, "Your rep in Chicago, his numbers are way too low. Markedly lower than the numbers of the rep who was there before you started."

I had no idea why he barged into my office to share this with me, seeing as I already knew it. I also didn't much like the "before you started" part, like the problem was me, not my rep. Further, I had a huge team who, besides the Chicago guy, was not only making their numbers, but exceeding them *and* the numbers they'd made prior to me being employed there. So his insinuation was not only not nice, it was ridiculous.

Further, he was research and development. I was sales. Why he was walking into my office to have a word with me about my Chicago rep was beyond me. It wasn't like it was none of his business. It was like I had a boss that was on his level, so if he had concerns, he should take them to my boss, not waltz into my office, scowl me off the phone, and give me information I already had.

My only choice of reply was, "I'm aware of that."

"You've been here for quite some time now, Francesca, and he's been with us for some months, and his numbers are not improving," he noted.

God.

What a dick.

"That hasn't escaped my attention," I shared.

"Is he going to be able to support Tenrix?" Randy asked immediately.

I felt a chill glide up my spine at the mention of Tenrix.

"Of course," I answered.

"He's not supporting our current product catalog so it stands to reason he won't do much better with Tenrix, and Wyler has a lot riding on that product doing well."

More information I knew.

"I'm also aware of that, Randy," I returned.

"I prefer those under me to call me Mr. Bierman," he shot back instantly.

I blinked, then stared, mostly because I'd been working with him for ages, and although I had the occasion to address him directly only a handful of times, I'd always called him Randy and he'd never breathed a word.

But more than that, that was totally an outrageous thing to say.

"And I prefer that my team refer to their colleagues by their given names." My boss, Lloyd Gaster, was suddenly there and my eyes flew out my wall of windows to Tandy.

She was sitting at her desk, looking over her shoulder into my office, giving me wide eyes and a stretched out "eek" mouth, so I knew she'd heard Randy being a dick and went to Lloyd to tell on him for me.

Totally liked Tandy.

Randy turned to Lloyd. "Did I invite you to this meeting?"

"We're having a meeting?" I asked fake innocently, giving my attention back to the men in my office, and Randy turned his glower back to me.

"I should hope not," Lloyd put in. "A director having a meeting about sales and the performance of a member of my team with another member of my team without my knowledge wouldn't make me very happy."

I tried not to smile a gloating smile as Randy turned his bad mood back to Lloyd.

"It probably wouldn't make Travis very happy either," Lloyd continued before Randy could say anything. "He tends to like it when we follow the chain of responsibility. I do believe he's also pretty keen on not shoving the hierarchy down anyone's throats, say, by making them address you formally."

"She has an underperforming rep," Randy clipped out.

"Frankie and I are both very aware of what's happening in Chicago. We're keeping our eye on it. Taking measures. Hoping for improvement. But if there isn't any, we'll be quite capable of making difficult decisions and carrying them out."

"That's good to hear," Randy returned curtly.

"I'm glad you're pleased," Lloyd murmured, then his focus on Randy intensified and he stated in a much louder voice, "In the future, if you have concerns about what's happening in my department, I'll ask you to bring them to me, as, should I have concerns about how *you* and *your team* are performing, I'd bring them to you."

Randy didn't reply to that. He just gave Lloyd a dark look, turned it on me, and prowled out.

When he was gone, Lloyd walked to my desk and said quietly, "Sorry, Frankie. That guy's an ass."

I pressed my lips together in order not to agree verbally. I managed that (barely), but I couldn't stop myself from nodding.

"He gives you any more trouble, let me know. Okay?"

"Okay, Lloyd," I agreed.

He smiled at me, then moved out the door, and Tandy, totally being the shit, waited the exact right amount of time before she wandered into my office with a file I didn't need.

"Oh my God," she hissed before putting the file I didn't need on my desk and sitting across from me. "Randy Bierman is *such* a *dick*."

It probably wasn't good to talk that way in an office setting, but since she was entirely correct, and our head honcho had just called him an ass, I said not one word to refute her.

"What's up his butt today?" she asked.

"What was up it yesterday?" I asked back.

"Well, yesterday, Miranda requested to be transferred to someone else." I stared at her.

Miranda was Randy Bierman's assistant.

"She said she didn't even care if it was a demotion or she had to work on another floor or something," Tandy went on. "She's d…o…n…e, *done*."

"That's news," I noted, though I didn't note it was news she should have shared with me yesterday.

It probably also wasn't a good thing to encourage office gossip, but since I was always on the receiving end, not the giving end, I encouraged away. But I liked my gossip fresh, not day-old stale.

"She went to Mr. Berger to make the request."

This time, I blinked, hard, and asked, "Seriously?"

"Yeah, she went in, had a chat with him, and he came out looking big-time angry. He had a chat with Mr. Bierman, then Mr. Bierman took off and didn't come back. Miranda was at her desk after that, but she hasn't been there today. Jennie says she's moving to production. One of the scientists' assistants is going on maternity leave and Miranda is going to take over for her while she's gone until they can find her a new place to be. That new place to be, according to Jennie who got it from Miranda, is guaranteed."

My eyes drifted to the glass wall as I murmured, "That's very weird."

"Yeah, you want a transfer, you don't talk to the VP. You go to HR," Tandy agreed.

You absolutely did.

But more, if you didn't like your boss and a transfer was not to be had, other things were done. Like getting to the bottom of the issue and fixing it, or trying to. Or, say, telling the employee you're sorry they can't get along with someone and telling them to move on.

Not going out of your way to find them a slot while you went out of your way to transfer them permanently within a day.

That smacked of something bigger, hinting that Miranda had leverage. I didn't want to be intrigued. I wanted to stay out of it. But I was Frankie Concetti. I was intrigued.

"Miranda told me he's totally tripped out about Tenrix," she declared, and my eyes shot back to her, another chill going down my spine.

"Tripped out how?"

"Lloyd is an awesome dude but when I heard Mr. Bierman going at you, I didn't hesitate to walk to his office and give him a heads up. This is because pretty much everyone knows yesterday Bierman went after Heath, and his reps aren't doin' as well as yours. Lloyd blew a gasket when Heath told him but Heath told him when it was over. So he was all over making a statement when Bierman went after you."

Heath was my colleague in sales, his territory the west side of the US. And although his reps weren't turning in the numbers mine were, his numbers far from sucked.

More gossip that was not fresh.

I'd have to have a word about that with Tandy.

Before I could, Tandy kept going.

"Bierman acts like the only product we have or ever will have is Tenrix. I don't know, I've never been around when we launched, but he seems Tenrix-crazy to me."

I'd never been around during a launch either, but he did seem Tenrix-crazy.

Absolutely.

We were launching a brand-new product in six months. He should have plenty of other things to do rather than walk across an office floor to give me shit about one under-performing rep.

"Frankie?" Tandy called, and I realized I was looking at her but not focused on her.

I was focused on the weirdness.

Weirdness that wasn't just about a jacked up co-worker who made people's lives a misery. Every office had at least one of those.

No, the weirdness I was focused on included a jacked up co-worker who was "tripping out" about a new product, assistants going to VPs for transfers (and getting them), and scientists being shot in the head for no apparent reason.

"You okay after he was such a dick?" she asked.

"Takes a lot more than a guy like Randy Bierman to get to me, honey," I answered.

She grinned, popped out of her seat, and said, "Yeah." She tipped her head to the side, still grinning. "Anyway, my turn to go down to the coffee cart for lattes. I'll be right back."

Without another word she took off to get us lattes, our daily lattes another reason Tandy was the shit.

But I couldn't get any of that out of my head. Not after Tandy left. Not all day.

The thing was, I didn't know what was in my head.

It wasn't like I'd never worked with a dick. Hell, my first boss was a total jerk and every single one of his salesmen made Randy Bierman look like an amateur.

Then again, no one at the car dealership had ended up dead.

Not able to get it out of my head, instead of going home, getting ready, and getting on the road, I went to Wyler Production. I used my employee ID to gain access. Then I went to the observation deck to stare down at the mammoth space, with its sterile machinery and people wondering around doing stuff wearing white jackets, white hairnets, white gloves, and goggles. I did my staring gig like the space could talk to me.

What I wanted it to say or what I'd do with the information, I had no clue.

What I had was a wild hair, and I should have learned long ago when I got one of those to pluck it, throw it in the toilet, and flush.

Instead, I was there, the last place I should be, and this became even more apparent when I heard, "Frankie?"

I turned and started when I saw Travis Berger walking my way.

Shit.

"Hey, Travis," I called fake casually.

He looked to me, the production floor, then back to me before he stopped a few feet away.

"There a reason you're here?" he asked.

No there was not.

I thought fast but spoke slow.

"Brainstorming."

His brows drew together. "Sorry?"

I thought faster and immediately commenced bullshitting.

"I have…well, I'm concerned about the performance of a member of my team. Lloyd and I've discussed it, and I've had a variety of conversations with him but nothing's working. His numbers were better before I was managing him so I know he has it in him. I'm just…well," I threw a hand out to the production floor, "thinking maybe he's too far away from home. Not his home, of course, he lives elsewhere," I babbled. "The home of Wyler. Maybe if I brought him down here, gave him another tour, reminded him of what we do and how cool it is." I tipped my head toward the floor and finished lamely, "I don't know."

Berger studied me and I tried not to squirm.

Finally, he said, "Chicago."

Very on the pulse, Travis Berger, to know that kind of detail.

Then again, that was why he made the big bucks.

"Chicago," I confirmed.

"You're being very patient," he noted.

I shrugged. "Our business is drugs but those drugs are made to help people. Our employees are also people. So I think, as a company who's in the business of helping people, we should exhaust every option before decisions need to become more extreme in a way that will negatively affect lives."

"Yes," he said, turning toward the windows. "I agree, however irritating these endeavors can be."

I was glad he wasn't looking at me because I felt my eyes get wide, seeing as I had a feeling he was referring to the person whose antics had me standing right there.

"Well!" I said too loudly, and he turned immediately to me. "I have a rehearsal dinner to get to. I better get going."

He nodded, not cracking a smile or even a grin when he said, "Enjoy it, Frankie."

"Thanks, Travis, I will. Uh…later."

He nodded again and looked back at the production floor.

I got my ass out of there.

I did it thinking that whatever was happening was none of my business.

I sold pharmaceuticals. I was not in human resources and I was not investigating a murder.

So, Randy Bierman took asshole to extremes and someone on his team got whacked.

It had nothing to do with me.

And yet, I couldn't shake the thought that, even if it didn't, it still did.

Dusk was forming by the time I hit the lakeside resort where Vi and Cal were holding their wedding.

During one of the many times I went over to Cal and Violet's place to drink wine, shoot the shit, and be a casual observer while Vi, Kate, and Keira discussed wedding plans, Vi had shown me brochures. But as I got out of my Z, left my bag to grab later, tucked my clutch under my arm, and made my way toward the stately-but-welcoming, flower-festooned, red brick building with its white columns in the front, I saw that this was a case of pictures not doing it justice.

The rehearsal dinner was in one of the private rooms inside. The wedding was going to be outside by the lake.

And taking in the graceful building, I knew it was going to be amazing.

I walked in and found signage that directed me to the Lakeview Lounge, where the dinner was going to be.

I was a couple of minutes late but had texted Benny when I left my place, then proceeded to drive like a crazy lady to get there on time so I wasn't more late than my ill-advised side trip and crazier-than-normal Friday traffic threatened I would be.

I saw the double doors to the room were opened. I walked through and stopped.

I did this mostly because the back of the room was made up of windows, which had a fabulous view of a flawless green lawn that had pots and flower beds filled with vibrant color and greenery, and beyond that, a massive, tranquil lake, one of many in Indiana.

I also did this because there were three intimately arranged six-seater tables, all with white tablecloths, candles, and exquisite bouquets made of downy-green hydrangea, creamy roses, and spikes of purple iris.

Oh yeah, just with a glance at the rehearsal dinner setup, I knew the girls did good. I also knew this wedding was going to be amazing. Then again, even if they'd decorated in neon and asked everyone to wear '80s outfits, it would be amazing simply because of the people involved and what this wedding meant.

The end to Cal's years of grief.

The same for Violet and her girls.

I scanned the room and spotted Benny, his suit-jacketed back to me, Cal on one side wearing dark gray suit trousers and an open-necked, black, tailored shirt. Vi was to Ben's other side and when I saw her, I smiled.

Cal and Vi, I found, were much like Benny and me in the squabbling department, and this occasion, joyous as it should be, was not immune to said squabbling.

Since Vi had shared during one of my shooting-the-shit times at her place, I knew that Cal wanted his band on her finger and he wanted that done yesterday. He didn't give a shit about how that happened, he just wanted it to happen. Pronto.

Vi, on the other hand, was not about to make her second star appearance at a wedding wearing a maternity gown, something she'd done at age eighteen during her first big event.

"Been there, done that. This time I'm livin' the dream," she'd told me.

Because Cal loved her like crazy and wanted her to have what she wanted, he gave in, but only slightly. That was to say he wanted the wedding as soon as she could pull it off after she had their baby.

Thus commenced more squabbling because Vi didn't want a maternity wedding part two, but she also didn't want to be carrying baby weight at her dream wedding.

I was actually there during one of these squabbles, to which Cal remarked, "I don't give a fuck if you got an extra pound or two."

"It'll be more like forty," Vi retorted.

"Okay, I don't give a fuck if you got an extra pound or forty," Cal returned.

"I do!" Vi snapped. "Wedding pictures last an eternity."

"Yeah. And we'll look at them and remember a coupla weeks before we got hitched, you gave me my baby girl. How's that bad?"

You couldn't really fault that logic, and Vi agreed because she gave him a look but said nothing further.

Therefore, Vi, who had gained thirty-five pounds with Angie, had spent the last six weeks doing what she could to work it off.

Luckily, she was active by nature and went back to the side business she had within a couple of weeks of having Angie. She worked at the garden center in Brownsburg but also maintained a few personal clients' lawns and gardens. So although the weight didn't melt off dramatically, she'd taken off fifteen pounds and planned ahead, ordering a wedding dress that was two sizes too big.

At her last fitting on Monday, it had had to be taken in.

And now, she was standing there wearing a purple, strapless cocktail dress with a ruched bodice and a flirty skirt that fell just past her knees, which had a long, green, satin ribbon as a belt, the same adorning the flippy hem. She had on spiked-heeled, strappy green sandals and her fabulous, thick, dark hair was arranged away from her face and fastened in a side ponytail that was a burst of soft curls.

She was smiling at something Benny was saying.

She looked amazing.

She also looked completely happy.

Which made me completely happy.

I quit looking at her, and eyes to the prize (that being Ben's broad shoulders in his suit jacket), I headed their way.

Cal's gaze came to me when I was five feet away, Vi's smile a couple of feet later. Ben noticed and started turning when I was right there.

So when I slid my arms around his middle, I got his back, his side, and full face. This meant I could roll up on the toes of my own strappy sandals and press my mouth against his.

I smelled his aftershave, felt his strength, and therefore couldn't stop myself from touching the tip of my tongue to his lips before I pulled away.

"Hey, baby," I whispered.

"Hey," he whispered back, then twisted further and brought me around so I was at his side, doing this with his eyes dropping to my dress.

I was not wearing a graceful-yet-flirty dress like Vi.

My dress was coral, short, skintight, had one long, tight sleeve and one exposed shoulder and arm. I'd toned down the jewelry (even so, my thin rhinestone hoops nearly brushed my shoulders) and went big with my hair. My sandals were copper. My makeup dark but dewy.

I had the process down so vamping it up prior to driving there didn't take forever.

Still, from the look in Ben's eyes and his arm tightening around my waist, I knew he appreciated my efforts.

I pressed closer to him and turned my attention to Vi and Cal. "Hey, guys. How did the rehearsal go?"

"We're all set," Vi said. "Tomorrow, five o'clock go time."

I grinned and replied, "Awesome."

I barely said that word before I watched Cal move in and touch his mouth to Vi's, muttering, "Gonna check on Angie."

"Honey, she's sleeping and she's with Mimi. She's fine," Vi told him.

He didn't move back, but he did focus more intently on her face as he repeated, "Gonna check on Angie."

Vi searched his face for about two seconds before she whispered, "Okay, baby."

He touched his mouth to hers again, slid his eyes through Benny and me, giving us a chin lift, and took off.

"How's that goin'?" Ben asked when Cal was gone and Vi, who had followed Cal's departure with her eyes, looked at Benny.

"I think when Angie gets past Nicky's age when he lost him, he might calm down," Vi answered, knowing what he meant, that Cal was crazy-watchful over Angie. "Though, he's Joe. He takes protectiveness to extremes on a normal day, so maybe he won't. He hasn't had the pleasure of watching a child he created blossom into something beautiful, smart, and strong. It's like he's a new parent. So I let him have that because it isn't unhealthy, but it is all kinds of beautiful."

She grinned a small grin with that, but it slightly faded when she went on.

"I didn't have his tragedy in my history and I was the same with Kate. So was Tim, even if we were teenagers. So I'm not too worried about it."

Tim was Violet's husband who was killed several years ago. And Vi was right. Cal didn't get to advance from the new parent stage to know that things were all going to be okay as he watched his baby mature.

He'd get there.

Or he wouldn't and Angie would have an overprotective father on her hands who met boyfriends on his porch with a gun stuffed in the waistband of his jeans.

There were worse things, as I well knew.

And it struck me on this thought what Mrs. Zambino had said months ago.

I felt warmth gather around my heart because I knew when Angela Callahan grew up, she'd look in the mirror and see what Cal and Vi taught her to see.

Nothing but beauty.

I had that happy thought and studied Violet, noting, "You seem pretty calm." I said this, but I thought she didn't seem calm so much as she seemed utterly serene. "If it was the night before my wedding, I'd probably be a wreck."

"Well, I have two daughters who show signs of being wedding planner savants and one of them is Kate. She could be the president's secretary and be cool during another missile crisis," Vi replied, and I giggled as I heard Ben's low chuckle. "They're all over this and have everything in hand." She smiled. "So I can be calm, kick back, and just enjoy my perfect wedding."

I loved that for her so I told her that.

"That's wonderful, Vi," I said softly.

"I know." She was talking softly too. "I'm one lucky lady."

With all she'd been through, she wasn't right, even as she was.

Her story of being a child bride with baby, happening into that situation to marry the man of her dreams, losing him, being stalked by the man who was responsible for his death, and ending that mess running through a forest with me, she'd earned this.

The hard way.

Kate rounded her mom, eyes to me, stopping and murmuring, "Hey, Frankie."

"Hey, honey."

She grinned at me and looked at her mother. "Mawdy, where's Joe? It's time to sit down to eat."

"He's with Mimi and Angie," Vi answered, and Kate nodded understandingly.

"I'll go tell him it's time," she said.

"I'll help Keira get everyone to their seats," Vi offered.

"Thanks," Kate muttered, gave Ben and me another grin, and took off.

"Excuse me," Vi said.

"Sure," I replied.

Ben just moved out of her way as she started drifting toward her guests.

Then he moved to shift me front to front, both arms around me.

I looked up at him.

"How's Gus?"

He smiled, even as he shook his head. "Gus is fine. Gus is with Mrs. Zambino. *I'm* fine too, in case you're wondering. Was fine before, but I'm a lot more fine, seein' you in that dress."

His eyes had dropped to my chest so I gave him a squeeze to get his attention back.

"You can't blame me for worrying about my baby. You gave me a present and then kept it."

He didn't stop smiling as he returned, "You travel half the time, live in a rental, and have nice shit. I live in big house and have shit that's just shit that he can chew on as much as he wants."

I felt my brows draw together and told him, "You shouldn't let him chew, Ben."

"You stop a puppy from chewing," he told me.

"I would, if he actually lived with me."

He pulled me closer and dipped his head toward mine, saying low, deep, and easy, "He's assurance *my* baby will keep comin' back to me."

"Like that wasn't gonna happen already," I whispered my reply.

His gaze dropped to my mouth before his lips touched there, then he pulled back and offered, "Want a drink before we sit down?"

I nodded.

"Bellini or somethin' else?" he asked.

"I'd love a Bellini."

"Then you'll get one," he said on a squeeze.

That made me feel warm and happy, even though Benny had been demonstrating regularly, in fact constantly, that whatever I wanted was mine. Like a puppy. He'd even shown that he could give me things I didn't know I wanted. Like an off-the-charts fabulous birthday party. And last, he'd shown he would do pretty much anything for me. Like set up a Champagne brunch so I could celebrate part of my birthday with Sal and Gina.

Suffice it to say, I was no longer in crazy-woman-falling-in-love mode.

I was in a much more dangerous mode. That was crazy woman *in love*.

"We're at the head table with Vi, Cal, and the girls," Ben informed me, jerking his head toward a table by the windows.

"Right. Meet you there."

"Right," he said on another squeeze and a touch of the lips to my temple. Then he let me go and took off toward the bar.

I moved to the table, having honored seating because I was Ben's date. He was the best man and Kate and Keira were Vi's maids of honor. Manny was also in Cal's wedding party, as well as Colt. Vi's bridesmaids were rounded out with her friend Cheryl. That meant Manny and Sela were there, Colt and Feb too, and Cheryl, with her date being her son.

Vi's dad was there (not her mom, they weren't tight), as were Theresa and Vinnie as the only parental figures Cal had left. Still very close with her first husband's parents, this meant Bea and Gary Winters were also there, rounding out the three tables.

Folks settled in their seats. Ben brought my drink, then took off his suit jacket to expose the deep green tailored shirt underneath. He tossed his jacket over the back of his chair. Cal showed, coming in with Kate, and I knew another friend of Vi and Feb's was there, Mimi (the lady who also owned the kickass coffee shop in Brownsburg), who was coming to the wedding but was there early to look after Angie and Colt and Feb's Jack.

I sipped my Bellini, sitting back, slightly listed to the side because Ben was leaning into me and the arm he had on the back of my chair. I smiled, chatted, giggled. Champagne and red and white wine (consumer choice, total class) were brought around, as were mushroom caps stuffed with cheesy, creamy crab meat.

It was when the appetizer plates were whisked away, glasses were refilled, and we were gabbing while waiting for our main meals when the clink of a knife against a wineglass sounded.

All eyes went to the parents' table to see Gary standing, holding up his Champagne glass.

When conversation died, his eyes to Vi and Cal, he started speaking. "I apologize. I have something to say, but I've had concerns if I should say it. In the end, I felt it needed to be said. I talked with Bea and we decided it was more appropriate tonight, in close company, than tomorrow."

He drew in a deep breath and his voice got softer, but it still carried when he went on.

And now his eyes were just on Vi.

"My beautiful flower," he started, and I didn't even know what he was going to say, but the way he started made me deep breathe in an effort not to start crying. "This day was a day I never thought would come to pass. This day was a day I never would wish to come to pass. But here we are, witnessing you closing one book and opening another that's empty. A book you get the privilege of writing, the story of the life you're about to start making. Bea and I know, to the depths of our souls, just like the extraordinary story you crafted the first time so magnificently," he tipped his head toward Kate and Keira, "this one will be no different."

"Holy crap," I whispered, and Ben's hand went from dangling off the side of my seat to wrap around my arm.

Gary's eyes went to Cal.

"This day is a day I never would wish to come to pass. But you must know, Bea and I are honored beyond imagining that you're the kind of man who would allow us to be here tonight, to share in your joyous celebration tomorrow, to keep us stitched into the fabric of your life. However, it's more, Joe Callahan. Bea and I are honored beyond imagining simply to know a man with such love in his heart, he would give it freely to our girls, strength in his mind and body to protect them, firmness in his resolve to take care of them. Regardless if this new book you're writing with Violet means Bea and I must close our book, a book that has no hope of reopening, there is no other man in the world we would wish to sit in the seat you're currently occupying. We're pleased to know you. We're pleased to have you as a part of our family. And we wish you, Vi, Kate, Keira, and little Angie have all the beauty you deserve as you write your story."

He lifted his glass as I heard Vi make a whimpering noise, but I didn't look at her as Gary kept going.

"To the soon-to-be Joe and Violet Callahan, wishing you a life story full of all the love, hope, promise, joy, and laughter you not only deserve, but you've earned."

A variety of "here here's" and "To Cal and Vi's" were shouted as we all grabbed our drinks and took a sip.

Except Violet, who got up from her chair, walked with red cheeks and shining eyes to her father-in-law, wrapped her arms around him, and shoved her face in his neck.

And I sat there thinking I loved that. I loved that emotion from Vi. I loved that she was the kind of person who could take something possibly awkward, but knowing the players, understand it would end up stunningly beautiful.

And I sat there looking around, seeing Cal give his attention to Kate and Keira, both overwhelmed with emotion from their grandfather's speech, both not his by blood but his all the same. I took in Vinnie and Theresa, who were there not only as relations but also because they'd earned their spot there, being the only real mother and father Cal had his whole life.

And then there was me. Loving one brother who was killed and, years later, loving another one because he was everything a man should be and he gave all that beauty to me.

And I sat there thinking that what was in this room was it.

This was life.

This was family.

This messy, strange, awkward, crazy conglomeration of people that totally fit when they shouldn't. That could make beauty like Gary's speech, even through the heartbreak of knowing they were there because their son was not.

This was what I'd always wanted.

And this was what I'd always had. Maybe mine was messier, stranger, more awkward, and definitely more crazy.

But this was family.

And sitting beside Benny Bianchi, surrounded by family, I knew without any doubt there was no place on the planet I'd rather be.

I stood at the panoramic window of Benny's and my cabin, staring at the dark lake.

The hotel had seventy-five rooms and a string of cabins along the lake. Benny had checked us into one for the whole weekend. So after the festivities tomorrow, Ben and I would have nearly a whole day to ourselves surrounded by beauty.

Before that, though, tomorrow, Ben, Kate, Kiera, Feb, and I were going out on the lake in Colt's boat that he'd brought down. We were going to tube and water-ski.

Cheryl and Vi were going to the hotel spa to get a massage, facial, and polish changes before having hair and makeup done.

I'd been invited to the spa, but I didn't need any of that. I'd had a mani/pedi yesterday and I could totally do my own hair and makeup.

What I needed was time with Benny and time in a speedboat on a beautiful lake with two gorgeous girls, a cool chick, and a nice guy.

Ben had walked up to the hotel from the cabin for the rehearsal so he drove me and my Z back down.

He was taking my bag into the bedroom.

I was staring at the lake, thinking I'd never felt the feeling I was feeling. I didn't know what it was because it wasn't just happy.

It was more.

I was thinking I felt like how Vi looked that night (when she wasn't crying due to Gary's speech).

Serene.

"Thinkin' that Cal didn't think it out when he demanded they get hitched so close to Angie comin' into the world," Ben called as he walked into the room. "Girls are goin' up to Chicago to spend the week with Bea and Gary. But Angie's goin' with Vi and him down to Virgin Gorda. So I'm not sure the honeymoon will be all it can be."

"Cal's determined to do something, I figure he'll make it work," I told the window.

"Yeah," Ben answered, then asked, "Fridge is full, baby. You want a drink?"

"No, I'm good."

And I was good.

Better than I'd ever been.

Two seconds later, I got even better when Ben fitted his front to my back and slid his arms around me.

I felt his face in my neck and got even better when he whispered, "My baby's quiet."

"Your baby's happy."

His arms gave me a squeeze.

"Thank you for givin' this to me, Benny Bianchi."

He heard me. He got me. And he knew what it meant to me.

I knew this when he growled, "Jesus, Frankie," into my neck, his arms going super tight.

"A while ago," I said to the lake, "you told me you love me."

His arms didn't loosen, but his lips slid up to my ear. "Yeah? When was that?"

Like he didn't remember.

Still, I told him, "The day Angie was born."

"Well, I didn't lie."

He remembered.

I closed my eyes so I could fully feel the magnificence of those words sliding through me.

"You never said it again," I noted.

"Showed it," he replied.

He did do that. Constantly.

"Yeah," I whispered, gliding my hands along his arms where he was holding me and settling them there. "Do I show it?"

"*Tesorina.*"

He said nothing more.

"I want to show it," I said so quietly I could barely even hear myself, but I felt my words trembling with the feeling behind them. "I want to know I show it. I want to know you feel it. Even when you're away from me. I want to know you wake up every morning knowing you have my love and you go to sleep every night knowing the same thing."

"Never said it, Frankie."

I opened my eyes and looked at the lake. "Well, I'm saying it now. I love you, Benny Bianchi. Even when you aren't with me, I wake up knowing how much I love you and I go to sleep knowing the same thing."

I just got out the word "thing" when I lost my view of the lake because Ben turned me in his arms. One hand slid up in my hair, the other arm crushed me to him, and he bent his head to me.

Then he kissed me, slowly, deeply, gorgeously.

But when he lifted his head, he simply said softly, "Let's go to bed."

There was no other place I'd rather be.

I didn't tell Ben that.

I just felt him let me go, take my hand, and then he led me to bed.

⌒

"Babe, I gotta get to Cal!" Benny called toward the bathroom where Frankie had been for half an age, shrugging the jacket of his tuxedo on and thanking God that Cal was as Cal was. That being a man who hated ties and, therefore, a man who not only was not wearing one to his wedding, he didn't expect the men standing up with him to wear one either.

Cal's groomsmen were wearing tuxes with deep purple shirts, the whole getup Cal and Vi had tailored specifically for each of them, all of it, including the tuxes, they could keep.

He didn't need a tux, though he didn't say no. But even deep purple, the color was dark, the material was fine, so the shirt was the shit.

Cal was wearing a black shirt with his tux. Then again, except the blue of his jeans, Cal never wore anything but black.

"Go!" Frankie called back through the closed door. "I'll take the Z up."

"Don't need two cars up there and the lot's gonna be packed. By the time you get up there, you'll have to hoof it a mile. You need to take me. You can hang with Mimi," Ben returned.

He was walking toward the bathroom to open the door but stopped suddenly when the door opened and Frankie stood there.

Her hair was done, up in a large, messy, sexy, loose arrangement at the nape, the curls and waves leading to it. Her makeup and jewelry were one step up from yesterday but probably because it was a formal wedding. She wasn't wearing any shoes.

He liked her heels but that dress didn't need shoes.

Turquoise, strapless, short, tight, it had two thick strips of black lace running diagonally across the dress; one at the hip that slanted up around her ribs, one at her ribs on the other side that slanted up over a breast and ended at the line of the top of the dress, the scalloped edge protruding past the turquoise so fucking sweet, it was like another accessory.

She was always varying nuances of crazy-beautiful.

Right then, he'd never seen anyone, not in his entire life, so fucking stunning.

"I'll just grab my shoes—" she started.

"Seriously?" he cut her off.

She ceased moving and her eyes came to him.

She read him and he knew it when she started backing away, saying, "Benny, my hair—"

"Seriously," he said it again, a statement this time, and started stalking toward her.

"We can't do this, Benny. You have to be up at the hotel."

"We'll be quick," he replied, and she ran into the wall.

She started sliding along it, but he stopped that when he made it to her and put a hand in the wall by her side.

"Even quick—" she began.

"Pull up your skirt," he ordered, taking his hand from the wall, the other one joining it, spanning her waist as the rest of him got in her space.

Her eyes had widened, but they also flashed and he knew what the second one meant.

Still, she declared, "We don't have *time*, Benny," but her voice was wispy.

"Skirt up, babe."

"Ben—"

He dropped his mouth to hers. "Now."

Her lids fell and her hands went to her skirt to yank it up.

When she had it up, his hands went to her panties to yank them down.

Then he lifted her and pressed her against the wall.

Hands on her bare ass, mouth touching hers, he told her, "Need your hands, baby."

She knew what he needed and her fingers went to his pants. Not wasting time, she had him free and took her shot to give him a firm stroke, taking in the whole length.

Jesus, Frankie.

He clenched his teeth and through them ordered, "Guide me to you."

She ran her teeth over her lower lip, catching his when she did, something that scored straight down to his dick, as she slid him through her wet and the tip of his cock caught at her pussy.

"Fuckin' ecstasy," he groaned and thrust in.

Her hands lifted so she could round his shoulders with her arms and she whispered, "No, baby, *that's* ecstasy."

She was not wrong and it got better as he banged her hard and fast against the wall, her arms and legs clamped around him, her pussy clenching tight, her lips brushing his, their breaths escalating until his was labored and broken by grunts, and hers was panting.

"Love you, Benny," she whispered against his lips, holding on tight with everything she had.

Jesus.

Frankie.

Fucking ecstasy.

He slid one arm to her upper back to hold her closer. "Love you too, *cara.*"

"It's coming," she whimpered, holding on tighter.

"Take it, honey."

She took it, gasping against his mouth.

Once she got it, he took it, fucking her harder and faster until he got it.

After he came down from the high she gave him, he slid his lips to her neck and kissed her there.

And there he said, "Maybe we should buy you some sweatshirts."

"And miss my shot at Benny Bianchi banging me against the wall? I don't think so," she said in his ear, her words breathy.

He lifted his head and grinned at her beauty, stayed inside her and kept her close, even as he murmured, "Now I really gotta go."

"Okay, honey. Find my shoes. I'll clean up and we'll hurry."

He touched his mouth to hers, slid out, and set her on her feet, holding her until he knew she was steady.

He cleaned up and zipped up. She cleaned up and yanked on her panties. He grabbed her shoes as she shoved her feet into some flip-flops.

And he held her hand as they walked out to her Z.

⟨⟩

"*Cugino*, seriously?"

They'd just been told by a member of staff that it was time to take their places at the gazebo by the lake.

Mimi was there to take Angie from Cal, but Cal told her to go on out—he was keeping his baby girl.

That was when Benny asked his question.

Cal looked at him. "She's good with me."

"Brother, you're about to get married," Benny pointed out.

"And she's gonna be with me," Cal declared.

Ben caught Manny smiling at Colt, who grinned back, then aimed his grin at his shoes.

Then Ben looked to Mimi and said, "You can go, darlin'. Thanks."

"Right," she murmured, laughter in her tone. "Have a great wedding!" she said loudly before she disappeared.

"Got the ring?" Cal asked.

"You think I'd forget somethin' like that?" Ben asked back.

"Didn't ask that. Asked if you got it," Cal returned.

"Of course I've got it."

"Brilliant. Let's get this shit over with so I can get somethin' to eat," Cal muttered, securing his daughter more firmly in the crook of his arm and heading to the door.

Ben shook his head but did it quietly laughing as he followed his cousin.

They walked through the side door and Ben saw what he saw earlier when he arrived to keep Cal and his daughter company before the wedding.

Lots of white chairs, the outside of the rows connected at the ends with green and purple ribbons, some chairs holding a trailing bunch of flowers that were cream and purple, the flowers also decorating the inside row of chairs but without the ribbons.

The inside roof of the gazebo was dripping in flowers. There were also white ribbons attached from a massive bouquet at the front of the gazebo that led out to poles stuck in the ground every third chair all the way across the space. Ben didn't know much about this shit, but the ribbons and poles were a nice touch, creating the sense of intimacy, even when they were outside, but doing it without obstructing the phenomenal view.

The judge officiating the ceremony was standing in the gazebo and a string quartet was playing "Canon in D."

Without hesitation or looking at anyone, Cal strode right up to the gazebo carrying Angela in her little purple dress with the scrunchy purple thing wrapped around her pretty, bald-save-for-a-hint-of-dark fuzzed head.

Ben stood on the step beside the gazebo opening, Manny took his place on the grass by him, Colt next, and they barely got there before Cheryl started walking down the white runner that led down the aisle. She was in a tight, strapless, green satin dress and was carrying a thin bouquet of purple irises, the length of their stems wrapped in green ribbon.

Kate and Keira came next, walking together arm in arm, wearing purple that was strapless but not tight. Their dresses had floaty skirts. Same bouquets.

He took his eyes off them and found Frankie, sitting between Sela and his ma in the front row, her body totally turned in her seat to watch the girls walk the aisle.

Taking her in from hair to heels, it was then he realized he should have waited to fuck her after she put on her shoes.

On that thought, he heard Cal make a low, rough noise and his eyes lifted from Frankie, who was now coming out of her seat to the aisle, and he stopped breathing.

On the arm of her father, holding a massive, fluffy bouquet with what he could see were cream roses, the big flowers from the table decorations last night but in white, and little violets, Vi was walking down the aisle.

Her sleeveless, ivory dress was lace from the V-neck that showed a hint of cleavage all the way down to the long train trailing behind her. She had a wide, violet ribbon wrapped around her waist and the ends mingled with her train. Her hair was up, curled and fastened in a loose bun at the side of her neck, and around the bun and radiating from it into her hair were a bunch of rhinestones and tiny, real violets.

Her hand was in the curve of her father's arm.

Her eyes were on Cal.

And her face was beaming.

Ben forced in a breath and watched Vi walk down the aisle to Pachelbel, her eyes never leaving Cal, her smile never faltering.

Cal met her at the bottom of the steps, and she shook her head at her soon-to-be husband before she leaned in and kissed their daughter's head.

Her father gave her away and Cal led her back up the steps.

Within fifteen minutes, they were married.

Once proclaimed husband and wife, even holding his daughter in his arm, Cal pulled his wife close. The kiss was long, wet, and deep to the point Benny heard laughter. He couldn't beat back his smile, and along with the crowd, Benny participated in the clapping and shouting.

The kiss only ended when Angela was done with it, communicating this by giving a loud baby shriek.

After the kiss, Cal settled his girl, then walked his wife and baby girl down the aisle, both of them stopping to smile at people, Vi to bend deep and do cheek presses, Cal to do chin lifts and allow his daughter to have her chubby baby cheek touched.

Ben moved into the aisle and took Kate on one arm, Keira on the other, and followed them.

Colt and Manny flanked Cheryl and they followed Benny and the girls.

Short, sweet, and pure beauty.

This was how Anthony Joseph Callahan made Violet Winters his wife.

Nineteen

LONG SHOT

Ben was pissed off and not because his phone just rang and it had Sal's number on the display.

Because it was his birthday, the Thursday after Cal and Vi's wedding, and Frankie was supposed to be down for the entire day, arriving that morning, leaving the next.

But she'd called the day before and said there was a work thing she couldn't get out of. This meant she was taking a late afternoon flight and he'd have her for dinner and a fuck, then she'd be gone on the first flight in the morning. A flight that left at 6:30, which meant they had to be out of the house before five to get her to her plane.

Technically, she was with him for his birthday so he couldn't get pissed at her.

That said, he clearly hadn't expressed the totality of his expectations when it came to special days.

But her work was her work, it meant something to her, and he had to stand down.

This time.

He was just wondering when the fuck the time would come when he wouldn't. They loved each other. They'd said it. They showed it. When they were apart it was okay, they kept as close as they could with the distance, but it was not near as good as when they were together.

When they were together it was dynamite.

She had to want more, didn't she?

He had no answer to that question, and was getting increasingly frustrated with Frankie not even bringing it up, which meant he was going to have to and possibly not like her answer.

On these thoughts, he pulled into his garage after going to the gym that morning. Going to the gym when he should have been going to the airport to pick up Frankie.

No, when he should have been home from the airport and having a birthday fuck with his woman in his bed.

And Sal was on his phone.

In other words, so far it'd been a fucking shitty birthday.

He grabbed his phone, took the call, nabbed his workout bag, and rolled out the car door.

"Sal," he greeted after he put the phone to his ear.

"Benny, *figlio*."

Ben clenched his teeth, wishing Sal would quit with the *figlio* crap.

"I hear Violet made a beautiful bride," he went on as Benny moved through the side garage door into his backyard.

"Yeah," Ben agreed, not about to tell him he thought it was cool that Gina and he had declined the invitation Violet had extended, knowing in that small resort gathering they would be hard for the Bianchis to avoid.

It was a kind thing to do for Cal and Vi, not giving them awkwardness, not to mention respect to his ma and pop, who didn't need that shit on a day they were over the moon happy.

"I'm hoping to see pictures," Sal muttered.

Ben said nothing. He had pictures on his phone, about three thousand of them, all taken by Frankie whose phone didn't fit in her miniscule purse, a purse she carried for the sole purpose, that Ben could see, of holding her lip gloss.

Even if he had pictures, he wouldn't be sending them to Sal.

He let himself in the back door of his house and changed the subject by asking, "There another reason you're calling?"

"Unfortunately, yes," Sal answered.

He wasn't big on the "unfortunately."

Ben dumped his workout bag on the table and went to the fridge to get a water, prompting, "That would be...?"

"Made a number of inquiries, Benny, dug deep. That's why it took so long. It would seem the job you asked about was done by out of town talent. No trail. I've got nothing."

Ben dropped his head to look at his running shoes.

He didn't know how to take this news.

On the one hand, Frankie had not mentioned the murder again and everything seemed status quo at her company.

On the other hand, she'd told him she'd had a direct run-in with the dick she worked with, something with that guy that was not status quo. He'd instigated it, Frankie didn't buy it. She was just doing her job when he'd perpetrated a surprise attack.

However, when she told him this on the Sunday after Vi and Cal's wedding, she did it acting cagey.

He'd never known Frankie to be cagey. She let it all hang out. Even when she bailed on him, the only reason he didn't have answers to why she did was because she didn't know them herself.

And because of that, he didn't have a good feeling about Frankie's cagey.

"But you know it was a hit," Ben stated.

"It was a hit," Sal confirmed.

"You just don't know why the hit was called," Benny went on.

"No, Benny, I don't know why," Sal again confirmed.

Not good.

"Would you like me to keep digging?" Sal asked into the silence, and Ben lifted his head but looked unseeing at the old calendar on his wall.

"What's your gut say?" Benny asked.

"With Frankie?" Sal asked back, then answered, "I keep digging."

That was what Benny's gut said.

Fuck.

"This another marker?" he asked.

"Job undone, Benny," Sal replied. "So no."

Ben drew breath in through his nose and moved to the door to the hall, giving a little for reasons he had no fucking clue. "I'll get Frankie to send you some wedding photos."

"Gina would like that."

Whatever.

"Gotta go," Ben told him.

"*Addio, figlio.*"

"Later."

Ben ended the call and jogged up the stairs, wondering if he should shower first and then take Gus for a walk, or release Gus from the confinement of his kennel, take him for a walk, and then shower with Gus in his bathroom, gnawing on the rug.

He had eyes to his feet and mind on his puppy—Frankie's puppy, a puppy *she* should be going with him to take out for a walk—when he moved into his bedroom.

This meant he jerked to a halt and his head snapped up when he heard Frankie say, "Happy birthday, Benny."

He stood still and stared at her in his bed, wearing a deep plum nightie that had a middle that was sheer material, so even if she was on a hip, her legs curled beside her, he could still see the thin, plum, lace ribbon of her panties that he hoped like fuck led back to a G-string.

Her hair was a big mass of curls tumbling over her shoulders and down her chest, just as he liked it.

Her makeup was heavy but classy, just as he liked it.

And even several feet away, he could smell hints of her perfume.

All of it, all of her, reclining on his bed, smiling at him with that smile of hers, just like he liked it.

"So," she said and got up to her knees, something that made his cock start to get hard in a way that he knew would break a record. This was because he saw only a small triangle of plum covering her sex and the ribbons riding the swells of her hips through the sheer, not to mention a good view of her creamy thighs spread slightly. "You kicked my birthday's ass so huge, I had to get creative…" She tipped her head to the side and her hair went with it before she continued, "And tell fibs."

She reached behind her, her arm came around, and she held in her hand a big plastic bottle of chocolate sauce.

"I came prepared," she finished, waving the bottle in the air beside her head.

Taking her in, suddenly he had a feeling this was going to be the best birthday he'd ever had.

Not to delay in getting to that part, he walked to the end of his bed, stopped to stand in front of her, and tossed his phone and the water beyond Frankie onto the bed.

As he did this, Frankie put her free hand to his chest and whispered, "Sweaty."

Ben took the bottle out of her hand and tossed it so it landed with the other shit.

She tipped her head back to catch his eyes and asked, "Not hungry?"

"How long can you stay?" he asked back, and the playful light flickered in her eyes.

"Until morning."

Disappointing.

For him, and with that light flickering, for her.

"How many nighties did you bring?" he went on.

"Five."

Now that was something.

"This one the best?" he kept going.

"I don't know," she answered. "You'll have to rate them."

He'd do that.

But first, he'd have to get better acquainted with this one.

In order to accomplish that, he bent to her, but only to lift the sheer material, find the ribbon of her panties with the tips of his fingers, and trace it over her hip to the top of the cheek of her ass and down until he encountered the portion of ribbon that disappeared in her cleft.

G-string.

Jesus.

Frankie.

She slid her hands into the sides of his tee and up over his skin at the sides of his ribs, her head tipped back, her eyes on his, not playful anymore but something he liked a fuckuva lot better.

He slid his middle finger under the string, dragged the pad down between the cheeks of her ass, and her lids lowered, her lips parted, and his dick jumped.

"I like this, baby," he murmured.

"Does it say happy birthday?" she asked.

"Fuck yeah."

"You gonna unwrap your present so you can play with it?"

His finger encountered moist, showing she was ready, and he growled, "*Fuck* yeah."

Her hands slid back and down, diving into his workout pants and cupping his ass as she tipped forward so her mouth was brushing his. "Then play, honey."

Definitely.

This birthday was going to be the fucking *best*.

He bent deeper and slid the tip of his finger through her wetness and up, gliding it inside.

Her fingers clenched into his ass and she breathed, "Benny."

He slid it deeper and asked, "What else you got planned, Frankie?"

"Well," she whispered, and he pushed in deeper, then pulled out and gave it back and again and again so her hands quit clenching his ass and dragged up his back. "I have the chocolate sauce."

"Saw that, honey."

"And Mrs. Zambino has the ingredients for the cake I'm gonna bake later."

He kept fucking her with his finger, looking into her eyes, feeling his dick begin to ache, watching her get excited, feeling it coat his finger as he said, "I'll look forward to that."

"She also has all the stuff for the dinner I'm gonna make you later. *A deux*, just you and me. I called Theresa and she and Vinnie are happy to wait to celebrate with you on the weekend."

Just you and me.

Yeah.

She was kicking birthday ass.

"Sounds good," he rumbled, continuing to thrust into her wet with his finger.

"And, of course, I bought you a present," she went on huskily.

He drove his finger in deep, got her gasp, and noted, "Thought my present was right here."

"I got you another one," she breathed.

He didn't need another one. But for her, he'd take it.

"What else, Frankie?"

She slid one hand from his back, over his stomach, and down over his hard cock, her hips moving with his finger, ready to move on, and he knew it when she begged, "Need you to fuck me, Benny."

"What else you got planned, baby?"

"What do you want, honey?"

"You gonna sit on my face while you suck me off?"

Her hips jerked and her lips whispered, "Yeah."

"You gonna ride me naked while you play with your tits and clit?"

Her hand at his cock started rubbing as she repeated a breathy, "Yeah, Benny."

He slid his finger out, rubbed it hard over her clit, and watched her eyes roll back as a moan rolled up her throat.

"You gonna let me do anything I want to you?"

"Yes, Ben."

"Then turn around, stay on your knees, face to the mattress, ass in the air, and give me that pussy," he ordered.

She did as told instantly, knees to the edge of the bed, head down, ass up, the sight of all that was her, and the flawless skin of the cheeks of her ass in that G-string nearly making him come in his pants.

He didn't.

He got the G-string down her thighs as he pulled his cock out, positioned, and drove it inside her.

Her head shot back, her dark, shining hair flying all over the place. He reached out, caught it, and pulled hard.

"Yes," she said on a clipped cry.

"What you want?" he asked, driving deep and doing it hard.

"Fuck me, Benny."

"Hard?"

"Yes."

He drove in, stayed, and ground deep.

"My baby want it rough?" he pushed.

"Please," she begged.

He tugged on her hair.

Her pussy convulsed around his cock and her hips started moving in opposite tandem to his so she was slamming that sweet, tight, slick cunt onto his dick.

Fucking ecstasy.

He dropped her hair but bent further over her to curl his fingers around her shoulder, and even as she powered back, he drove her into him, using his other hand to slap her thigh, making her jump.

"Faster, baby," he ordered, his voice thick, his dick ready to explode.

He fucked her hard as she fucked herself fast.

"Faster," he repeated on another slap to her thigh. Her head shot back, her body reared back, and he heard her cry out as he felt her come around his cock.

He drove her with his hips and hands up the bed, coming onto it on his knees, kept taking her pussy, and not long after, hands clenching her hips, his head went back on a grunt as he thrust deep and shot himself deeper.

He'd barely come down before he pulled out, flipped her to her back, and fell forward between her legs, settling some of his weight into her soft body, some of it on a forearm.

Still breathing heavy, feeling her chest rise and fall with her own breaths, he lifted a hand and trailed his thumb over her lower lip before he lifted his eyes to hers and whispered, "Gonna have to step it up."

"Wh-what?" she stammered.

"What I do for your birthday next year. Spent weeks planning, runnin' around, doin' shit, and in twenty minutes, you kicked its ass."

Her eyes warmed. She pressed her thighs tight to his sides and circled him with her arms, everything about her telling him that's what she wanted to give him and everything about Benny liked it.

"Love you, Ben," she whispered.

He liked that better.

He dipped down, touched his mouth to hers, lifted up, and whispered back, "Love you too, *cara*."

"Happy birthday," she said softly in a tone that meant it.

"Thank you, baby," he replied quietly in that same tone.

Then he kissed her.

After that, they both got dressed so they could release Gus from his kennel prison and take their puppy for a walk.

Ben walked into his kitchen to see Frankie in his tee at the counter with all sorts of shit that said "birthday cake" surrounding the bowl in front of her.

Gus was at his food dish, face stuck in it. Even with his attention on his food, he sensed Benny walking in and his tail started wagging, even if his face didn't come out of the bowl.

They'd walked Gus, come back, he ate her on the couch, then fucked her there. They took a shower, then he'd thrown on some clothes and went over to Mrs. Zambino's to get Frankie's stuff while she fed Gus. He did this because he didn't want her out of his house. He didn't want her dressed in anything but one of her nighties or one of his tees, and it was his birthday so Frankie gave him what he wanted.

Moving toward her, Benny decided he wanted something more so he took it, sliding a hand from her hip, around, down, and in. Under his tee, skin to skin, he glided it up her belly, her ribs, and cupped her breast.

She leaned back and pressed her head to his jaw, saying, "Although the challenge has been thrown, and I think I can best it, not sure how your cake will taste if I make it, you playin' with me."

"It's shit, we got chocolate sauce," he replied and heard her soft laugh.

He loved that laugh. He loved her in his tee in his kitchen making his birthday cake. He loved her in his kitchen doing anything.

He just loved Francesca Concetti.

She turned her head and tipped it back until she caught his eyes, but hers weren't filled with humor.

They were filled with worry.

What the fuck?

"I know you were upset when I told you I couldn't come. But you gave me a good surprise. I wanted to give you one too. It sucked to upset you, but—"

That was the fuck. She was worried she'd upset him.

He shut her up by dropping his head and brushing his lips against hers before he lifted away and whispered on a squeeze of her tit, "Baby, am I complaining?"

She pressed her lips together and shook her head.

"Love my people, love spending time with them, but you in that nightie waiting in my bed wet for me was the best surprise you could give me."

"Good," she said softly, then went on, "I wanted to stay the weekend, but there's a lunch meeting tomorrow I can't miss. Though, I can drive up after work so I can be at the family celebration Saturday night."

He grinned at her. "I'll take it."

She grinned back and turned to her bowl. Ben slid his hand from her tit, engaged his other one, and wrapped both arms around her belly under his tee.

"How'd you get here from the airport?" he asked.

"Mrs. Zambino picked me up," she answered. "But I have an airport pickup arranged in the morning so you don't have to get up ungodly early to take me."

"Cancel it."

She twisted her neck to look at him. "Ben, I have to leave here at 4:30."

"Cancel it, Frankie."

She held his eyes a beat, saw in them that there was no use prolonging the discussion, nodded, and looked back down to what she was doing.

"Tomorrow, probably should haul my ass over there and see if Mrs. Zambino needs anything done on her house. Payback for her helpin' you out."

"That'd be a cool thing to do," she said, measuring flour.

"Though, she probably doesn't, seein' as she doesn't hesitate to haul her ass over here and ask me to fix shit when she does."

Again she twisted her neck and looked at him. "She does?"

"Yep."

"Do you do it?"

His brows drew together at what he thought was an asinine question. "Of course."

Her face got soft and she whispered, "Pure Benny."

"Just bein' a good neighbor," he pointed out.

"Just bein' a good man," she returned, and her words and the look in her eyes that was part marvel, like she couldn't quite believe he was real, part pride, and a lot of love made his arms give her an involuntary squeeze.

"Like it when you look at me that way," he murmured.

"Get used to it," she replied.

Fuck.

Frankie.

"Love you, baby," he whispered.

"Love you back, Benny," she said quietly.

He wanted to let that moment last. He wanted more for her to be done with the cake so she could give him another nightie. But she wasn't done with the cake, she wanted to give him that, had gone out of her way to plan it, so he needed to let her give him that.

So he took them out of the moment by asking, "What kinda cake you bakin' me?"

"Chocolate maraschino cherry," she answered, and his chin jerked.

His favorite, bar none.

And no one had made it for him but his mother.

"Ma give you that recipe?"

"Yep."

That wasn't a surprise, it was a shock. Theresa Bianchi was like her husband (and then some) when it came to her cooking. Her secret family recipes were *hers*. She made them for the restaurant, but she didn't share how to make them with anyone, even family.

So he muttered, "Holy fuck."

"I know," she turned back to the counter. "She gave it right up, no begging, no bribery, no markers owed. Freaked me out."

Benny liked what this said.

Years ago, Connie had asked for that same recipe and his ma hadn't given it up. It disappointed Connie not to be able to give him what he liked on his birthday, direct from her, not getting it from his ma. But Connie was the kind of woman who didn't put up a fight. She hid her disappointment and never asked again.

Frankie asked for it, Ma handed it right over.

"She loves you," Ben noted quietly.

He watched her profile smile. "Yeah."

"She loves you for me."

Her smile stayed in place, but her face again got soft. "Yeah."

He dipped his head, used his chin to move her mass of hair away from her neck, and kissed her there.

Lifting his mouth to her ear, he said, "You makin' chocolate maraschino cherry cake, I'll want it to be good so I'll play with you after it's done."

She turned her head and caught his eyes, saying, "Deal."

He bent in, touched his mouth to hers, and copped a feel as he let her go.

"Got the groceries put away?" he asked, scanning the floor for Gus, not finding him, thus moving to the door to look down the hall. And there he was, dragging one of Ben's running shoes by the string across the foyer.

"Yeah, you just relax. Today I do all the work."

That wasn't strictly true, but she was only letting him do the work he liked to do.

He moved down the hall and saved his shoe from Gus by tossing it on the dining room table which, again, was covered in shit, but more of it since he piled everything that had to be out of Gus's way there, and everything that needed to be out of Gus's way was everything.

He carried the dog under his arm to the kitchen, held him while he warmed Frankie's coffee, warmed his own, and then sat with their puppy at the kitchen table.

Gus didn't need a shoe if Gus had Ben's chest, neck, jaw, and hands, so Benny leaned back, stretched out, and gave them to him.

"This weekend, I'm tackling the dining room."

This announcement was made by Frankie, and Ben's eyes went from the dog on his chest to his woman.

"Come again?"

"No, the office. I think I should start there because half the shit in the dining room will end up there anyway," she went on.

"Uh…come again?" Benny repeated.

She looked over her shoulder at him, stirring the batter in the bowl. "We'll have to go get some hanging files, maybe a small filing cabinet or some shelves to put expanding files. Your pick, but it has to be something other than different piles all over every surface and the floor."

"What are you talkin' about, Frankie?"

She turned to the prepared tin and started pouring in batter.

"You have a big house and use only four rooms because the rest of them are junk rooms. And half the crap I've seen in them are just that, junk. So I'm startin' with the office, movin' to the dining room, then the den, and the junk drawers in here." She stopped pouring and threw out a hand to indicate the kitchen. She started pouring again and kept talking. "When you were at work last time when I was home, I ventured into your basement. I took one look and escaped before anything attacked me. That has to be seen to too. There might be squatters down there."

Ben grinned and caught Gus trying to take a flying leap off his chest to the floor, then bent and put him on the floor, saying, "I don't have squatters down there."

She put the bowl on the counter and asked, "When's the last time someone's been down there? 1977?"

He wasn't going to tell her but that could well be. He looked at it when he viewed the house, and the place was packed to the rafters, but he couldn't say he'd been down there since, even to check to see if the shit was removed before he moved in. Mostly because he didn't need that space so he didn't bother.

"That's your project," Frankie continued. "Clean that up. The Little League stuff can go down there opening up a bedroom for a guestroom."

"Don't need a guestroom."

"Uh...yeah you do," she informed him. "Vi and Cal and the girls might be up and want to stay. Which means you should probably have a futon or something in the office."

"I'm not makin' a guestroom on the off chance Vi and Cal come up and need a place to crash. Mostly 'cause Ma would lose her mind if they crashed here and not with her."

She'd been putting the tin in the oven. When he was done talking, she closed the door, turned to him, and put her hands on her hips.

"What about when Enzo comes to town? Or my brother, Dino, and his family?"

These words made Ben go still and stare at her.

"We need a guestroom," she declared.

Fucking shit.

She said *we*.

She looked to the floor, saw Gus was dragging the rug in front of the sink to an alternate location he preferred, and walked to him, bending, picking him up, and cuddling him close as she used her bare toes to move the rug back, and she did this all while talking.

"So I'll tackle the office first. And you need a computer with Internet, Benny. You may wish to be choosy about how you communicate in this modern age, embracing only your cell phone, but you're missing out on easily accessible game times, movie times, up-to-date weather, my flight statuses, so we'll have to get on that." She leveled her eyes on him and didn't shut up. "I'm not saying you get a computer and immediately start your Facebook profile. I figure, if you tried to type in your profile information on Facebook, your fingers will catch fire. I'm just sayin', in this day and age, a house isn't a home without a computer."

A house isn't a home.

Jesus.

Jesus.

Frankie kept bossing.

"You do the basement. But while I'm sorting stuff, I'll need you around to ask questions if I find something I don't know if I should toss or keep."

She finished this, moving Gus close to her face to give him a snuggle, and the puppy showed his appreciation by licking her jaw.

Benny's voice sounded gruff when he asked, "Where'm I gonna be?"

She looked at him. "What?"

"You said you'd need me around. Where would I be?"

"I don't know, pullin' a man stunt and disappearing when shit work needs to get done you don't want to do, as evidenced by the fact you've lived in his house for a long freakin' time and you haven't done it."

"What are we doin' here, baby?" he asked quietly, and her brows shot together.

"Talkin' about makin' your house a home, Benny."

Fucking shit.

"For me or for you and me?" he pressed, and her face went blank.

That was when he knew she had no idea what it meant, all she was saying.

He had an idea of what it meant. He just hoped like fuck he was right.

So he kept pushing.

"You movin in with me?"

Her voice was breathy and her hold on Gus was close when she replied with a question.

"You askin' me?"

"Take you today, you could swing it," he answered.

"Benny," she whispered, face soft, eyes now just holding marvel and love.

A lot of love.

Christ, she was all the way across the kitchen and she had so much love shining out of her eyes, he felt it warm every inch of his body.

He took that as a yes.

And there it was. His birthday just kept getting better.

"You gonna be able to swing that?" he asked.

"I…I have a lease."

"When's it run out?"

"October."

"Then you move in in October," he declared.

"Ben, I work in Indianapolis," she said quietly.

"You travel half the time, they got no problem with you workin' from here. Ask 'em if you can have a home office in Chicago and conference in for meetings. You in my bed, my house, got no problem with clearing out that basement, gettin' a computer with Internet, and givin' you a guestroom so your fucked-up family can stay, drive us crazy, and we can celebrate when they get the fuck out."

She stared at him but said nothing.

"You think they'll go for that?" he asked.

"I think, come my one-year anniversary, which is the same month my lease runs out, if they don't, then I'll quit and find a job in Chicago."

Jesus.

Jesus.

"Come here, Frankie," he growled.

"No. I do, you're gonna get busy with me and the cake will burn."

"Come here, *cara*."

"No, I can tell by your face you're happy and I'm super happy and all that happy is gonna translate into ruined birthday cake."

"Baby. Put the dog down and *come...here*."

She bent to put Gus on the floor and came to him. When she got close, he guided her ass in his lap and rounded her with his arms. As he did this, Frankie wrapped hers around his shoulders.

When he had her where he wanted her, he said softly, "Best birthday ever."

Beauty saturated her features, more than he'd ever seen from her, and he'd spent decades seeing a lot of beauty from Francesca Concetti.

"My awesome Benny," she replied in a whisper, her arms tightening, one hand finding his neck and curling around, but her body melted into his.

"You've made me happy, *tesorina*."

"I'm glad."

"Kiss me, Frankie."

"Okay, Benny."

She put her lips to his, but it was Benny who took her mouth, leaning into her, bending her back, and drinking deep, one of his hands going down, then up her shirt and down again in her panties to cup her bare ass, both her hands diving into his hair.

He broke the kiss but didn't move far away and waited for her eyes to slowly open, giving him crazy-beauty before he said, "Love you, Francesca."

"Love you too, honey."

He grinned, held her closer, but ordered, "Now go make frosting."

She rolled her eyes, but she also pushed up, he went with her, and she climbed out of his lap.

After that, Gus under her feet, tripping her up, and her not minding, Frankie made frosting.

⁓

"Okay," Frankie said, skip-walking into his bedroom that night.

It was after the dinner she'd made him (roast beef tenderloin, boiled new potatoes, asparagus coated in oil and toasted sesame seeds, and rolls Mrs.

Zambino bought the day before from the bakery). It was after cake. It was after he told her he wanted her ass upstairs because he wanted to see another nightie. She showed him and wore it for about five minutes before he took it off so she could sit on his face and he could have his mouth on her while she used hers on him.

She'd put the nightie back on (red satin with a sheer panel around the hem and matching panties that had sheer at the ass, sweet but nowhere as sweet as the plum one) and gone back downstairs to grab his presents from where she'd hidden them.

Now she was back, hands behind her, hiding the presents from view.

She hopped on the bed, walked on her knees to him, and flopped down to a hip before one arm came out and she slapped a mostly square, thin, large wrapped package on his chest.

"That one's the goofy one," she declared. "You get the good stuff second."

He'd already had the good stuff.

She knew that so he didn't tell her. He just opened the present and he did it with her talking.

"The first one may be goofy, but it was *way* harder to find. I had to order it off the Internet since they don't sell them this time of year. I also had to find one you'd like, but they kinda don't make those things for guys. Or, not guys like you. Still, it isn't about tits and ass or muscle cars, which would be something I wouldn't want to look at, but it isn't too girlie, which is something you would toss in the trash, so I think I did all right."

The paper off, he turned it in his hands and saw a calendar for that year, its theme: photos of Lake Michigan.

There was no cellophane on it. It had been opened.

Ben held it in his hands, stared at it, and stopped breathing.

"See? Totally goofy," she stated, not sensing the change his mood was making in the room, just reaching out to pull the calendar from his hand and babbling. "Yours is, like, ten years old. Crazy. So it's kind of a joke but kind of not." She started flipping through and found what she wanted, showing him a month that had her writing in the little squares and flipping to the next, which had more of her writing. "See, I wrote all the birthdays in: Man, Sela, Vinnie Senior, Theresa, Carm, Ken, and the kids. I put Vi and Cal and all the girls in there, and Manny and Sela's wedding date."

Benny's eyes looked at the calendar and his heart started jackhammering.

"And here," she said, flipping back. "I put all my travel schedule in that I have set, all the times and flight numbers and hotel stuff and everything. You can write in the stuff that comes up."

She stopped yapping, finally looked at him, and when she did, she went visibly still.

They stared at each other a couple of beats before she said hesitantly, totally not reading him, "The other present is a lot better, Benny."

"Only one thing I want in my life," he declared.

"Wh-what?" she stammered.

"All my life, didn't have big hopes and dreams. Only one thing I wanted."

"I…" She swallowed, kept her eyes locked to him, and asked, "What was that, honey?"

"A life that meant I'd have a calendar on my kitchen wall filled in with birthdays and anniversaries and parties and practices and special occasions. All the shit that makes a good life scribbled in the blocks printed on glossy paper hangin' on a wall."

Her eyes grew bright and her breath grew shallow.

"You gonna give that to me?" he asked.

"Yes, Benny," she responded instantly.

Instantly.

Yeah.

She was going to give that to him.

And he was going to give it to her.

The…best…*fucking*…birthday…*ever.*

"No lip, no shit, come here right now, Frankie," he ordered.

She tossed the calendar aside to land on the bed and she came to him immediately.

And Ben crushed her in his arms, rolled her to her back, and found reason again to get rid of her nightie.

In the end, she slept beside him in a hot pink one with black lace.

Her second present was an expensive, handsome watch that had an inscription on the back that said, *For Benny, Love Frankie.*

It was fucking kickass.

But it wasn't better than the calendar.

Not by a long shot.

Twenty

SWINGIN' IN THE BREEZE

"You okay?"

I looked from the computer screen, on which I was obsessively watching the time change in the bottom right corner, to Tandy standing in the doorway of my office.

The answer to her question was, no, I was not okay.

It was Monday after spending the weekend with Benny for the sake of spending the weekend with Benny, as well as being there for the family celebration that consisted of him blowing out birthday candles on a pizza pie that he made and everyone on staff getting to suck back quick sips of Chianti while they worked. Ben opened presents in between making pies and getting out orders. Theresa, Vinnie, Manny, and Sela all were around, mostly being loud, giving Ben shit, and getting in the way.

I hung with Ben the entire night in the kitchen, my ass taking up counter space since I sat on one with a wineglass in my hand, and alternately gabbed with my man, gave him my own shit, and communed with what he called his "kids." I took this time to get to know them, something I liked a whole lot since they were good kids and fun to be around.

In fact, Ben ran a fun kitchen. It was work, definitely—hot work with the ovens going and the stoves on, people rushing around, always busy.

But I'd been in those kitchens when Vinnie ran them, and although he wasn't an asshole, he was a taskmaster.

It was strange knowing a father's way and then seeing his son's.

They both took what they did seriously. They both communicated that. But Ben was far more laid-back about it and the kids responded to it.

Watching him work, firm in woman-in-love mode, I fell more in love, my already immense pride at being Benny's woman growing, watching him run his kitchen. His kids liked him. He organized chaos without any apparent effort. He wasn't about shouting and bossing. He was about quiet words and direction. And every pie or dish put on the warming shelf to be taken out looked mouth-watering because I knew it was.

It wasn't like he was organizing a disaster relief effort.

Still, it was awesome.

Saturday during the day and Sunday before I left to drive home, Ben and I tackled his office. On Friday, Ben had called the cable company to have Internet jacks installed. On Saturday, we went out and bought a filing cabinet, shredder, and a desktop computer. It took us hours, but we got a system down that might (*might*) make the rest of our efforts throughout the house easier. We tossed a bunch of crap, filed some away, and in the end, the office looked more like an office and less like a dump. The kind of room you'd find in a home, not a bachelor's pad.

In other words, I thought every minute was worth the effort.

The cool thing in doing this was that I found Benny wasn't a hoarder. He just didn't bother to throw shit away when it should have been thrown away. There were no battles about keeping stuff. He also didn't get into the project for fifteen minutes, then get sick of it and try to find an excuse to escape. Except for me giving him guff about being a lazy ass and Benny grinning through it, we worked beside each other in harmony.

It was kind of fun.

Domestic bliss, Frankie and Benny style.

So now it was Monday. The Monday after being awed by Benny's kitchen prowess and gaining another promise from Benny that a life at his side would be good, seeing as I wasn't buying one with a hoarder or someone who would dump all the crap work on me and go his merry way.

It was also the Monday after I gave Benny what I considered lame birthday payback and he considered it something else entirely. And the something he considered it made me fall even deeper in love with him, because as simple as it was, it was everything to Benny and I liked that. A whole lot.

And last, it was the Monday after I gave a goof gift I expected Ben to laugh at and toss aside, and it would be me who tacked it on the wall in the kitchen and wrote stuff on it, but it was very much not.

I liked that it wasn't. Actually, I liked *why* it wasn't.

It was a gift I had a feeling changed both our lives.

Because, unexpectedly, we'd made plans to move in together.

But when I gave him that calendar, we'd made plans to spend the rest of our lives together.

I was down with that. I didn't think twice about it and I knew I didn't in a way that I never would.

This was because Benny Bianchi was always going to be a promise at the same time Benny Bianchi was the prize at the end of a crazy life.

So there was no reason to think twice about it.

And I was also never going to feel stupid about my goof gifts again.

Now it was Monday and I had a four o'clock meeting with my boss to ask if there was a possibility the company would consider letting me work from a home office in Chicago starting in October.

I was nervous because I expected the answer to this would be no, since everyone who was management worked from our head office in Indianapolis.

I liked that job. I made great money. My reps (all but one) were awesome. They did good, and in doing it, they made me look good. And I had a great assistant. I didn't want to lose any of that.

Further, job hunting sucked.

So a lot was riding on this meeting.

If they said no, I still was going to quit. I just was *really* hoping I wouldn't have to do that.

"I'm fine," I answered Tandy on a lie.

"You seem weird," she noted, walking in, eyes to me. She sat across from me and went on, "I know it's nosy, and it's cool if you don't answer, but Friday you seemed to be in a really good mood. But you went back to your guy this weekend and now you seem, well…*not* in a good mood."

She was so sweet.

It would suck if I had to lose her.

Another reason for me not to be okay.

"We're fine, Tandy," I assured her, and at least that was the truth, though it was an understatement.

"Okay," she replied, sounding like she didn't buy it.

"I just have this meeting with Lloyd on my mind," I explained. "Once I've had the meeting with him, I'll give you the full story."

She tipped her head to the side and I didn't like the look on her face when she did it.

"Should I be worried?" she asked, explaining the look.

"No," I said quickly, reaching a hand toward her and tapping it stupidly but hopefully comfortingly on my desk. "Absolutely not. It's not about you."

She suddenly looked evasive (thus, clearly the desk tapping didn't work) as she murmured, "I just thought you might have found out…" She trailed off, twisted her neck to look to my wall of window, then back to me, but she said no more.

"Found out what?" I prompted.

"Nothing. It's stupid. It's probably not anything," she stated.

"What's probably not anything?" I pushed, not getting a good feeling about her manner, which wasn't like her at all.

She drew in a breath, then rocked her ass in her chair like she was settling in and leaned toward me. When she spoke again, her voice was lower, quiet, conspiratorial.

"It wasn't a big deal. I told Lloyd and he took care of it, so I really didn't want to worry you, but Thursday, when you were taking a personal day up in Chicago, Mr. Bierman came and asked me to give him a copy of your schedule. He asked how many times you'd been up to Chicago on company business and how many days off you've taken."

Oh my God.

"Why would he do that?" I asked.

"I don't know," she answered. "And I didn't give it to him. I told him to talk to Lloyd if he had questions about your schedule. He got kind of dicky, as is his way, and Heath saw it happening. He came out and intervened. Mr. Bierman backed down and took off, but Heath told me I should report it to Lloyd and went with me when I did. When I told him, Lloyd looked really pissed off. He promised me he'd take care of it. Then he and Heath were in his office forever and it didn't look like the conversation was happy. Later, Sandy told me when Heath was in San Francisco last week, Mr. Bierman asked for the same kind of information about him."

Sandy was Heath's assistant and Sandy was like Tandy in the sweet, smart, on the ball, and very pretty department.

I also had a feeling Heath was nailing Sandy, which wouldn't be good, dipping your toe in the company pool with someone who worked under you. But if he was, she wasn't talking and, obviously, Heath wasn't. If she was talking, Tandy would tell me.

That said, they had a lot of closed-door meetings where you could see through the windows that they were smiling at each other and laughing a lot. In these times, Heath was not looking at her like he thought she arranged his flights to Seattle so well, it was worthy of a belly laugh but, instead, like he enjoyed having her in his office the same way that he would enjoy sharing a glass of wine with her later and getting a blowjob from her after that.

However, at that moment, I couldn't think about Heath and Sandy.

I could only think that I was getting pissed at Randy Bierman, resident dick.

"For freak's sake, why?" I snapped.

Tandy rubbed her lips together uncomfortably, then leaned further toward me and said, "Through the grapevine, he thinks you're both underperforming."

"We're both exceeding our numbers," I pointed out.

"I know that. Lloyd knows that. Mr. Berger knows that. But the girls have been talking and we actually think it's not about you and Heath. It's about Lloyd. He's targeting you guys to undercut Lloyd."

I felt my eyes get wide.

"What? Why? Lloyd is awesome."

This time, she scooted forward on her chair so she was leaning into my desk when she whispered to me, "A while back, after Dr. Gartner was murdered, Lloyd asked for some details about Tenrix that he couldn't find on the servers, the usual stuff that he as a director should have access to. Important stuff, I guess, though I don't know what it is. But it wasn't there. He needs it, seeing as he has to guide you and Heath in guiding your reps to sell the product so he should have access to it. Mr. Bierman told him he'd find it and give it to Lloyd. He didn't. Lloyd's asked, like, *a million* times. Before Miranda took off to production, she told Jennie who told me that she heard Mr. Bierman and Lloyd arguing in one of the back conference rooms, Lloyd telling Mr. Bierman if he didn't provide that information in twenty-four hours, he was going to Mr. Berger."

"Did he provide it?"

She nodded. "Yes, but this is where the weird comes in."

Oh shit.

More weird.

"What weird?" I asked.

"Kathleen said that the dates on the computer files were that day."

Kathleen was Lloyd's secretary, but even so, Lloyd got his email directly and confidential documents would not go through her.

"How did she know that?"

Tandy started looking uncomfortable. "She, uh…kinda looked over his shoulder and saw it."

I let that go and pushed, "This means…?"

"Frankie, those files should have been saved by Dr. Gartner, like, months ago. Some of them *years*. They were all saved *on the same day* and that day was *that day*."

Oh no.

I had a feeling I knew what that meant and there was no way it was good.

"Someone amended them?" I asked.

She shook her head. "I don't know. It didn't escape Lloyd's attention and Kathleen told me he went to Mr. Bierman about it. Mr. Bierman explained it, but, Frankie, it's fishy. Everyone thinks so."

I did too.

What I also thought was that perhaps the assistants were sticking their noses a bit too far into something that might not be real healthy.

So I advised, "You need to be careful, honey."

She looked to her knees.

"Tandy," I called and she looked back to me. "You need to be careful. I get he's a dick, he's being more than his usual dick, office politics are getting nasty, he's acting weird, and you guys are curious. But I'm not thinking any of this is good, so whatever you do, you gotta do in a way I can protect you.

Lloyd or Bierman or anyone finds out you guys are nosing around this, bottom line, it isn't any of your business and this information is probably confidential. Because of that, what you're doing will be hard to explain and might be grounds for, at best, a written warning, at worst, dismissal. It also means, if you're found out, those are serious transgressions and I can't protect you."

What I didn't tell her was that Dr. Gartner, whose files had been amended, was dead, something she knew, but she might not know what that could mean.

And what it meant was that if one had to do with the other, I *really* couldn't protect her.

"Let it play out," I said to finish it. "I'm lookin' after you when I tell you to do your job, stay safe, and let whatever's gonna happen, happen. Lloyd isn't stupid. He's been with this company for six years. He's invested. He's not Bierman's biggest fan. Let the big fish prove who has the sharpest teeth."

She rubbed her lips together in a way that didn't give me warm fuzzies. These feelings turned downright prickly when she avoided my eyes for several seconds. But I felt better when she looked back to me and nodded.

"Okay, honey, share that wisdom with Sandy and Jennie and whoever and be smart, okay?"

"Okay, Frankie."

I smiled at her.

She gave me a small, weird smile back that also didn't give me the warm fuzzies and left my office.

I looked back at my computer and saw I had seventeen minutes until my meeting.

This meant I snatched up my cell, found Benny's number, and connected.

He answered with, "Yo, *cara*, I thought your meeting wasn't until four?"

"Ben, Bierman is targeting me and my colleague Heath in an effort to make my boss look bad, and the way he's targeting me is by trying to get information on my trips to Chicago and my personal days."

Ben was silent a minute before he muttered, "Fuck."

"Uh-huh," I agreed.

"You covered on that?" he asked.

"Time off isn't accrued very quickly in your first year, but you do get some. I have three sick days and another personal day accrued so that's kosher. My reps are producing so that's kosher. And there isn't a trail to find where I was incommunicado while I was in Chicago because I was never incommunicado when I was in Chicago. That said, Bierman is moving from dick to total asshole. I don't know how total assholes act and office politics can get ugly. It's not unusual for team members to get targeted in order to take down a higher up, and those team members are the first to fall."

"So you think it's not a good idea when he's lookin' at your time in Chicago to ask to work from Chicago," Ben surmised.

"No. I think that you and I both need to be prepared for this to get ugly. And the *you* part of that is, if this gets ugly, you're gonna have to listen to me rant and put up with me regularly freaking out. Because I work my ass off for this company, and if they say no to me workin' from Chicago, so be it. But if I get targeted by an asshole with a vendetta against my boss, I am not the kind of girl who goes down without a fight."

There was a smile in his voice when he said, "That's my Frankie."

Yeah. That was what I was.

Benny's Frankie.

Suddenly, I wasn't nervous anymore.

"There's more," I told him.

"The way you say that doesn't sound like you wanna tell me you're in the mood to call me tonight after I get home from the restaurant so we can have phone sex."

At this, I made a mental note to set my alarm so I could wake up and call Benny when he got home from the restaurant so we could have phone sex.

Then I said, "No, babe, that's not the more. The more is, my assistant, in cahoots with several of the other assistants, found out there's more weird shit goin' down to add to the seriously weird shit already goin' down with Bierman."

"Stay out of it, Frankie," Ben ordered, and my back went straight.

"I am," I hissed. "But my assistant isn't and I like her. I told her to drop it, but she assured me she would in a way that didn't give me warm fuzzies."

"She puts her neck out there, that's her problem, not yours."

"Ben—" I started.

"It's not yours, Francesca," he interrupted me. "You told her to stand down. She doesn't, her decision, her consequences."

When he said the word "consequences," my stomach started to turn.

"Babe?" Benny called.

"What?" I asked.

"You with me on that?"

"She's a good gal, Benny. I like her. And what's she's uncovered is *not* good."

"So report it to your boss," Benny advised.

"If I do, he'll know she and her crew have been snooping around."

"Her consequences," Benny repeated. "If it's not good, you report it to him and let him deal with it."

"He already knows it, I think," I muttered.

"Right. Then that's good. Let it lie."

I drew in breath and looked down at the clock on my computer.

Fourteen minutes until go time.

"I gotta go," I said to Ben. "I need to mentally prepare for the possibility I'll be instigating a job search tonight, something that's on my list of favorite things to do just above having all my hair pulled out by the roots."

There was laughter in his voice when he advised, "Eyes to the prize, babe."

Yeah.

Eyes to the prize.

"Okay, honey," I said softly.

"Call me when you get out of the meeting," he ordered.

"I will."

"Good luck, *tesorina*," he said softly.

"Thanks, Ben," I whispered.

"Love you, babe."

"Right back at you."

I heard his chuckle before he said, "Later," got my "Later" in return, and we disconnected.

I was able to concentrate on replying to two whole emails before I sucked in breath, got out of my chair, and headed to Lloyd's office.

It was past five by the time I got out of Lloyd's office.

Not because we had an in-depth strategy meeting about how I could continue to do my job but from a home office. Instead, because Lloyd took our meeting as an opportunity to get briefed about absolutely everything I was doing.

He was checking up. Not because he had any issues with my performance. So he could get his ducks in a row because he was bracing for impact.

Tandy was gone by the time I got back to my office. I checked email, sorted some stuff on my desk, then I closed down, grabbed my cell, and took off. I didn't hit Go on Benny until I was in the elevator and I only did it because I'd entered the elevator alone.

"What'd he say, babe?" was his greeting.

He wanted good news for me. He also wanted my ass in Chicago.

That made me happy.

My news did not.

"He said he has no problem with it, but it's unprecedented, no one has done it, and he'd have to talk to Mr. Berger," I told him. "He also said he'd do that this week and get back to me."

"With his 'no problem,' did he really seem like he had no problem with it?"

Ben's question said Ben wasn't stupid, but I knew that already.

"He wasn't exactly doing cartwheels and congratulating me on the progression of my relationship with the man I love."

I heard the smile in his voice, even if what he said next was serious. "So you have no idea if he'll back your play."

"I only know he likes me and doesn't want to lose me. How that'll be communicated when he approaches Berger, I have no clue."

"So no answers, just a step closer to them," he muttered.

"Yeah," I answered.

"You gonna wait it out or plan ahead?"

"Tonight, I'll be trolling through online want ads while eating my Lean Cuisine."

Ben sounded surprised when he asked, "You eat Lean Cuisine?"

I grinned at my phone as the door to the elevator opened. "No, honey. I'll probably stop at Arby's."

There was a moment of silence before he murmured, "Need my baby home so I can feed her better."

Now, *that* gave me the warm fuzzies.

"Minute by minute, Benny," I said softly, walking through the parking lot to my car.

"Minute by minute, babe," he replied. "Gotta get back to the kitchen."

"Okay, Ben."

"Later, *cara*."

"Later, honey, love you."

"Back at you."

I grinned as I disconnected. Then I opened my car door, maneuvered myself in, holding my phone in one hand, purse over my shoulder and my computer bag in my other hand.

I got settled, put the key to the ignition, and looked unseeing through the windshield. But at what I saw, I focused and didn't turn the key.

This was because Tandy, Sandy and Jennie, with freaking Miranda (who was supposed to be at the production facility) and the IT geek guy, who came up and set up my computer on my first day (his name escaped me), were all standing in a huddle beside a blue Honda CR-V.

And the huddle didn't look like Tandy was letting things go.

I had half a mind to get out and go have a chat with them, but that half a mind was taken when my phone rang. I looked at it, sitting on the top of my purse in the passenger seat, and saw it said CAT CALLING.

Cat was back, though that didn't mean we had girlie chats every day about what we wore, what hot guys we'd seen, and how our men were treating us.

Still, hearing that she and Art had dried out and why, I was glad for her and I'd always be glad to have her back. The family was growing like crazy, but Cat and Art not drinking and giving a shit about their marriage, their future, and the kind of future they could give their family made me a lot more excited about the possibility of them bringing more Concetti blood into the world than the tangled webs my brother and father were weaving.

I grabbed my phone, took the call, and greeted, "Hey, babe."

"Welp, it happened. Dad's bitch popped out our little sister. Get this, her name is Domino."

I blinked at the windshield, then asked, "Domino?"

"Affirmative," she answered. "Dom…in…fuckin'…o."

Oh God. I couldn't even begin to enumerate how many ways mean kids could make fun of that name.

What were they thinking?

Cat cut into my thoughts. "You want more?"

What I wanted was to know why Chrissy hadn't called me to share the good news, and more importantly, why she hadn't consulted with me on names.

I didn't get the chance to tell Cat that.

Cat kept talking.

"Ma's latest dude dumped her and she's out fifteen thousand dollars because she bought the dress and can't get any of her deposits back on all the other shit."

My mouth dropped open and for a few seconds I didn't say a word. This was because I couldn't believe it. None of Ma's other men bailed on her pre-wedding. Post, yes. Pre, never.

I got myself together enough to ask, "He dumped her?"

"Apparently, she didn't share there were four before him and he wasn't feelin' the love for the writing he saw on that particular wall."

"Oh God," I whispered.

"She's freaked," Cat continued. "Told Nat he was the love of her life and that she can't be around him, so she's movin' back to Chicago. Nat told Enzo, who's currently holed up in a bunker somewhere to escape all the crazy bitches in his life, but now also to escape Ma. He told me about Ma. And we all know this translates to the fact she's fucked up money-wise, and needs to mooch off someone seein' as she was livin' with the guy with him footin' the bill."

Suddenly, I was wondering if Benny would move to Indianapolis, at least temporarily.

"Needless to say, I'm not takin' her calls," Cat carried on.

"Probably a good idea for a while," I muttered, meaning for about eight months.

"She could change plans and head to Indy, so this is your friendly, sisterly heads up to avoid that shit at all costs."

"She can't stay here because I'm not gonna be here in a few months," I told her.

"What?" she asked.

"I'm moving back to Chicago, shackin' up with Benny."

This brought silence that I thought I could read.

Therefore, I decided to tackle that later and start at the beginning.

"And Cat, Chrissy is not a bitch. She's really nice. I think she loves Dad and I know she's excited about that baby. So, she named her a weird name. We'll call her Minnie or somethin'."

Cat didn't reply.

"But I'm with you on Ma," I went on. "You have to focus on makin' a baby with Art that I hope you won't name Solitaire, and I'll back that play with Ma if she calls. And Ben will not ever in this lifetime let her live in his house. He's not Ma's or Dad's biggest fan so, luckily, I can throw him under that bus and he won't give a shit if I do. He takes my back on everything, but tellin' Ninette to move on along, I think he'll actually enjoy. Nat takes her on, that's her gig."

Cat said nothing.

I ignored what I was sure that meant and kept babbling.

"This is what we've got to work with, a growing family of craziness that's annoying half the time, whacked all the time, but under that, we love each other. I never really got that until recently. I know we could have had it better. We could have all made better decisions. But I think everyone on this planet can probably say the same thing. We have what we have, and if we accept it no matter how insane it can get, set boundaries to how much we can deal with, and remember that in that mix there's a whole lot of love, we'll be okay."

Cat didn't reply.

So I called, "Cat?"

"He takes your back on everything?" she asked, and I smiled at my steering wheel.

"Yeah. He's awesome like that."

And a lot of other ways besides.

I stopped smiling and started to feel different kinds of warm fuzzies when Cat's voice came at me again.

Actually, it wasn't just what she said. It was the way she sounded when she said it.

"You've been swingin' in the breeze, Frankie, for so long, it is not funny," she said quietly, but her voice was trembling. "Even with Vinnie, he let you swing in the breeze. They all thought you were behind his shit, but *he* let them think that. He should have stepped up on that, got that straight, not let you carry his burden. He didn't. That pissed me off. Then he dealt the ultimate, leavin'-you-swingin' 'cause he got whacked." She paused and I held my breath. "I'm glad you finally got someone who isn't gonna let you swing in the breeze."

This was not what I expected her to say.

Not even close.

It was a whole lot better.

And it reminded me of why I loved my sister and why it was always worth the crazy.

"Thanks, Cat."

"You're welcome, darlin'. And, just to say, my boundaries are gonna be a whole lot less flexible than yours are gonna be."

"I get that."

"And sayin' that, I'm okay with it, because I'm thinkin' that yours are gonna be flexible but Ben's are not."

She was not wrong.

"Yeah," I agreed.

I heard her take in an audible breath before she asked, "Chrissy isn't a bitch?"

"Nope."

"She seemed pretty much not there the couple times I met her," Cat noted.

"The couple times you met her, she was around one or all of us, and when that happens, no one is there but us and our big mouths."

"I see your point," she muttered.

"She's nice," I reiterated.

"You like her?"

"Yeah. I mean, we've chatted occasionally. It isn't like I've written her in my will, but she's pretty cool."

"They all are."

She was not wrong about that either.

"Well, this one has our sister so I figure she'll be around for a lifetime, one way or another," I pointed out.

"Even if she's nice, this does not make me want to jump for joy, 'cause Enzo Senior is gonna fuck that shit up and we both know it."

"A baby sister, Cat," I reminded her of what would come out of that particular craziness for her and for me, at the same time mentally hoping I could get Chrissy to text me photos. I was also thinking it was time to mend fences with Dad. And lastly, I was wondering how I'd talk Benny into not losing his mind if I did that.

"Whacked and annoying, but we love each other," Cat said. "We're totally messed up."

"I'm thinkin' so is everyone else. They just deal with it better or cut each other a lot more slack."

"Yeah," she said softly.

"Now go home, get laid, make me a niece or nephew, and call me in a month with good news."

"I'll ask Art how he feels about the name Solitaire," she joked as I turned the ignition.

"You do, I'll still love her...and you," I did not joke.

"You're a pushover," she stated, but her voice was softer and kind of husky.

"Whatever," I replied.

"And a dork," she went on, not sounding soft or husky.

"I'm hanging up now."

"And if you think I'm gettin' mushy, just to say, that's another boundary I won't cross."

"I've already hung up," I lied.

Her voice was smiling when she said, "Later, Frankie."

"Later, Cat."

I ended the call, tossed my phone to the seat beside me, and looked through the windshield.

Tandy, Sandy, Jennie, Miranda, and the IT guy were gone. So was the CR-V.

I put my car in gear while hoping that was Tandy, away from prying eyes, telling everyone to stop doing shit that could get them fired and start being cool, even as I had a feeling Tandy was doing the exact opposite.

Then I reversed out of my spot to go to Arby's, get home, and start searching want ads.

⁓

"I'm givin' up," Cheryl decreed, leaning into the bar toward me.

I didn't know what she was talking about, but I'd given up too.

On want ads.

I had also given up on waiting around my house alone the hours it would take for me to go to sleep, wake up when Benny got off work so I could phone him and listen to him saying words that would give me an orgasm.

So I'd changed into jeans and a blousy, drapey, yet still clingy tee, strapped on fabulous spike-heeled sandals, fluffed out my hair, and took myself out to J&J's Saloon, the local bar, a bar owned by Feb.

Feb was working. As was Cheryl.

This was good since I knew no one in Brownsburg but Vi, Cal, Kate, Keira, Angie, Colt, Feb, and Cheryl, plus a few more friends of Vi's (who were also friends of Feb and Cheryl) that I had met at the wedding and bonded with over Bellinis. They were all married, most of them with kids, so we had yet to do what we promised to do at the wedding, hook up for a girls' night out. So I didn't count them. And Angie didn't count either because she couldn't yet cogitate. And since Vi and Cal were still in Virgin Gorda, and Kate and Keira were not of age to go to a bar (and they were still in Chicago), this left me fortunate that Cheryl and Feb were both working that night so I didn't end up looking like a stylishly dressed barfly.

Once I got there, I wished I hadn't left it until that late in my sojourn in Brownsburg to go.

Granted, I was more the subdued lighting, fabulous décor, every-drink-served-in-a-martini-glass type of establishment kind of girl, and this was not that. It was mostly made out of wood, rough and worn with age, and undoubtedly had more than its fair share of bar fights. There were pool tables in the back, and pool tables usually heralded a joint that was not my scene.

I still liked it.

Maybe it was because I walked in, Cheryl and Feb looked my way, and both of them called out greetings, Feb's being, "Hey, babe! Cool you finally showed," and Cheryl's being, "Yo, Frankie, how's tricks?" and that felt good.

After being away from everything I knew and found familiar all my life, to walk into a bar and have the women behind it give me a smile and a greeting, it made me feel at home in Brownsburg for the first time since I'd been there.

It felt better gabbing with them both as I drank glasses of chilled white wine and people watched.

Though, now, I didn't know what Cheryl was talking about.

"You're givin' up on what?'

"Men," she decreed.

We'd been discussing the best brands of extra hold hair spray.

How did we get here?

"Uh…why?" I asked.

"'Cause, see, I've been livin' in this 'burg for, like, *ever*, and the minute I hauled my shit over the city limits was the minute that commenced a dry spell unprecedented for me. And I work in a bar. That shit's impossible."

"A dry spell?" I asked.

"Babe, a dry spell. As in, I haven't been laid in…*forever*," she shared.

Clearly, as she barely knew me outside of us being in a waiting room for a joyous event and us mingling at a wedding reception during another one, she had to get this out. And as a sister, even without years of bonding over martinis (or tequila) and discussions of the best beauty brands of anything, I had to let her.

"That sounds like it sucks," I noted, though I didn't share with her that I had possibly the world record in dry spells after Vinnie, so I knew her pain like no other.

"It does," she agreed. "And it does more, seein' as you been in this bar once, and Tanner Layne has been checkin' you out. From the moment he walked in the door, his eyes went to your ass and his eyes have been strayin' your way the last twenty minutes."

"Tanner who?" I asked.

She jerked her head along the bar and my eyes went to the other end, where a very good-looking, dark-haired man was sitting, smiling, and talking with Feb.

"Tanner Layne. Now, I'd go there," Cheryl announced. "I'd go there the last four times he's been in. I'd go there when my radar pinged when he moved to town not long ago and I'd never even met him, I just sensed his off-the-charts ability to provide quality orgasms. I'd go there right now in the bathroom or the office. But he only looks at me to order a drink. You, though…"

She trailed off so I said, "I'm taken."

"Yeah, you're you and that's *all* a' you," she replied, rounding my head with her hand, including my big hair. "And your man is way hot. But he's in Chicago. You look like you, Tanner Layne looks like him, your man is in Chicago, shit happens."

"I gave him a calendar for his birthday with my schedule written in it, family birthdays, shit like that, and he told me that's all he ever wanted. A life reflected in the busy family times written on a calendar stuck on a wall in the kitchen. He asked me if I was gonna give that to him and I said yes. So that guy is hot and Benny might be in Chicago, but that shit is also not gonna happen."

I finished my pronouncement and Cheryl stared at me but did it saying, "He said that's all he wanted out of life?"

"Yep."

"And that doesn't freak you?"

"Absolutely not."

"What do you want out of life?"

"A man who wants a calendar on the wall in his kitchen written all over with busy family times."

"Then you're sorted," she noted, her eyes lighting, her lips curling up.

"Yep," I agreed, knowing my eyes were lighting and my lips had curled up.

"'Cept you live here and he lives there," she pointed out.

"My lease is up in October and then I'll live there."

To this, her eyes got big, her mood deteriorated, and she surprisingly snapped, "What?"

"Well," I started hesitantly, uncertain of her sudden mood swing. "I'm movin' in with Ben."

"Great," she bit out. "Finally, you stroll in J&J's and I'm ready to groom you to be my wingman. Feb can't do it 'cause she's taken and has a baby, and Colt would lose his badass mind if I took her out carousin'. Vi used to do it, then she got hooked up with Cal, and he's arguably more badass than Colt and would definitely lose his mind if Vi went out carousin' with me. And I know this for fact 'cause I asked, she told him I asked, and he lost his mind. You look like you'd be a good wingman and you're the only semi-kinda-single woman I know in the 'burg that I like. Now you're leavin'?"

I felt for her. A good wingman was hard to find.

Still, I answered, "Yep."

"Freakin' awesome," she said, not meaning it. "Now how'm I gonna get laid?"

"We could go carousin' while I'm still here. You've got a coupla months."

"What you doin' Wednesday?" she asked instantly, and I grinned.

"Carousin' with you," I answered.

That was when she grinned.

Feb moving caught my eye and I looked down the bar to see that Tanner Layne was now taking a phone call.

He really was hot.

But Benny was so totally hotter.

This thought and the man's age made my eyes go to Cheryl and I asked, "Tanner Layne have kids?"

"Yep, word is two boys."

"One named Jasper?" I asked.

"No clue, seein' as he hasn't fucked my brains out so we could get down to the pillow talk of sharin' how many offspring we might bring to a Brady Bunch scenario."

I smiled at what she said but kept eyeing Tanner Layne as I muttered, "I wonder if he's Jasper's father." I said this as I hoped he was because those genes would undoubtedly be dominant and that would mean, once Cal lifted the ban, Keira would get a live one.

"Who's Jasper?' Cheryl asked, and I looked back at her.

"The boy Keira has a crush on."

She jerked up her chin high on an "Ah." Then she said, "I'll find out," and moseyed toward Feb.

I sipped my wine, and after a couple of minutes, Cheryl moseyed back.

"Jasper is the oldest," she confirmed. "His other one, Tripp, is younger. Neither have been picked up doin' stupid shit by Colt or anybody as far as Feb knows. But she's willin' to interrogate Colt about Jasper's suitability for Keirry."

"That'd be good, seein' as Cal's reluctant to give her the go-ahead to make her play with the kid because, according to Kate, he's a high school player."

"I'll get Feb on it," she said.

"Thanks," I murmured, then we both went silent since Tanner Layne was throwing some bills on the bar and he was doing a chin lift to Feb.

He walked the length of the bar, eyes on me, and when he got close, his head tilted slightly to the side, his lips tipped up, and his eyes got lazy. Then he walked right on by and out the door.

I had to admit, my nipples tingled a little, but then again, that was an automatic female response to a hot guy head tilt/lip tip.

I also had to admit it was nice to know I had it in me to be sitting on a barstool and get the hot guy head tilt/lip tip.

But mostly, it was just a pleasant thing to happen while I passed the time until I could phone Benny.

$\sim$

"You okay?"

This was Ben's greeting that night at 12:45.

"Please tell me you're close to a bed," I replied, my voice sleepy and throaty. The first because I'd just woken up and called Benny. The second because I was multitasking so I'd already engaged my vibrator.

Ben's voice was no longer concerned but something a whole lot better when he demanded, "Tell me you're serious, *cara*."

"I'm very serious, Benny."

"How far gone are you?" he asked.

"You still got work to do, honey," I answered.

"*Fuck, baby,*" he growled and there it was. That was all I had to hear. Benny got to work.

Luckily, that wasn't all Benny gave me. He gave me a whole lot more and he did it until he heard me come. Then I set my vibrator away, rolled to my side, curled up, and in my throaty, quiet, post-orgasm voice, I gave him a lot more until I heard him come.

I was silent a moment for him to come down before I whispered, "I miss you, honey."

"Comin' to you this weekend."

I blinked at my pillow. "What?"

"My turn."

"So soon?" I asked, my heart leaping, hoping he would confirm that yes, he was coming back to me and soon.

"Done with this shit. I'm down there or you're up here every weekend."

Even though I loved that I idea, it worried me.

"That's a lot for you at the restaurant."

"Two months. They'll cover me."

I knew that was a sacrifice for Benny.

But it made me happy, and not just because I'd see him more, also because he wanted to see me more and he was a man willing to make that kind of sacrifice for me.

"Cheryl is gonna have to make do with a weekday wingman," I muttered, thinking that'd work for her because she probably worked most weekends.

"What?" Ben asked.

"Nothin'," I answered.

"Cheryl's wingman?" he pushed, and I pressed my lips together because I had a feeling Ben was a man of the Colt and Cal variety. "Frankie," he prompted in a warning, not throaty, sexy, post-orgasm voice, but in a growly, sexy, getting-pissed, post-orgasm voice.

Yep, Benny was a man of the Colt and Cal variety.

So I gave it up. "Cheryl asked me to be her wingman."

"And you said yes?" Ben asked, like I told him Cheryl asked me to help her bomb the Canadian embassy.

"She needs to get laid," I explained.

"Seen her, figure she can accomplish that feat on her own," Ben returned.

"Every girl needs a good wingman, Benny," I shot back, my voice not throaty, post-orgasm anymore either, mostly because I was kind of getting pissed.

"Maybe. It's just that hers isn't gonna be you," Benny declared, and I stopped kind of getting pissed and just got that way.

"Why?"

"You and your ass, hair, legs, tits, and smile do not need to be out on your heels with fuckin' Cheryl, gettin' attention and gettin' into trouble."

"Benny Bianchi, do you think in a million years I'd do anything to jeopardize the promise of you?" I snapped.

I got silence from Benny for a moment before he asked quietly, "The promise of me?"

"Yes," I hissed. "The promise of you."

"Babe, I'm yours. How am I a promise?" he asked, tone now cautious, and my belly did a dip at the "I'm yours" business.

But still.

"Every day is a new promise, Ben," I told him sharply. "Every night I go to sleep knowin' it's a promise, every day I wake knowin' in some way it's gonna be fulfilled. And repeat. For…hopefully…*ever.*"

"Frankie," he whispered but didn't go on.

I ignored the depth of meaning behind that whisper and stated, "So don't tell me I can't go out with Cheryl. She's funny. She's edgy, but she's nice. I know Vi wouldn't let her close to her or her girls if she didn't have a heart of gold, but just sayin', Cal wouldn't either. So I've got two months left in the 'burg. The whole time I've been here it felt like I was in limbo, not at home, away from everyone I love, primarily *you*, and that really hasn't felt great. So I'm gonna go out and have fun with one of the few people I know and you aren't gonna stop me."

"Okay, baby."

I blinked again at my pillow. "Okay?"

"Yeah, go out and have fun."

"As easy as that?" I asked dubiously.

"Pretty much," he answered.

I didn't trust it.

"Does this mean you're gonna play some guy's wingman while I'm away?"

"Francesca, when do I have time to be some guy's wingman? I work, and when I'm not workin', my ass is with you."

Oh yeah.

Right.

"But, are you sayin' you can and I can't?" Ben went on.

"You're hot," I pointed out. "Girls like hot."

"You aren't butt-ugly," he returned.

I had to admit, this was true.

He kept going.

"And do you think in a million years I'd do anything to jeopardize the promise of you?"

God.

Benny.

Suddenly, I was not pissed at all.

"No," I whispered.

"I'm not Enzo," Ben declared.

"I know you're not."

"And you aren't Ninette."

"I know."

"So are you done pissin' me off after you got me off?" he asked.

"I think so," I answered. "But just to say, you started it."

"Fuck," he muttered.

"Ninette's fiancé dumped her, by the way," I told him to change the subject.

This got no response.

"She's heading up to Chicago to find someone to mooch off of," I shared.

"That will not be you and me," Ben stated firmly.

I knew it, and because I did, I smiled.

I also kept at it.

"And Chrissy had the baby."

Another non-response.

"They named her Domino."

That got a response.

It was, "Jesus."

"We'll call her Minnie."

"Puttin' my foot down right now, babe, our kids are not gonna be named stupid-ass names."

Our kids.

God.

Benny.

"I was thinkin' Solitaire," I lied.

"You'd be thinkin' wrong."

"Spade?"

"No."

"Club?"

"No."

"Monopoly?"

He chuckled through his "Fuck no."

"How about John?"

"John I'll consider."

I grinned at my pillow, and through my grin, I said softly, "Love you, Benny."

"Love you back, Frankie," he replied softly. "Now go to sleep with the promise of me, and tomorrow I'll make certain I do somethin' to fulfill it."

God.

I fucking loved Benny Bianchi.

"Okay, honey."

"'Night, Frankie."

"'Night, Benny."

I waited and he waited, then I let him off the hook and disconnected first.

After that, I brought my phone to my lips like it was him and I could touch my mouth to his as a goodnight.

In a couple of months.

Then I'd be full-on happy.

I set the phone aside, snuggled up, and fell asleep.

Twenty-One

FIRING LINE

The phone rang in Benny's back pocket. He flipped the flaps closed on the box he was sorting through in the basement, pulled his phone out, and saw it was his ma calling.

"Hey, Ma," he answered.

"Benny, we're out," she told him something that he really didn't need to know.

"She's out and she dragged my ass with her!" He heard his father shout, which meant wherever they were, everyone heard it.

"Quiet, Vinnie, yeesh," his ma shushed his pop.

"Ma," Ben called to get her attention back in hopes of getting this conversation over a lot faster.

"We're at a furniture shop and we've just seen the sweetest bed," she announced.

"*She* thinks it's sweet." He heard his father yell. "*I* think it's girlie."

"Vinnie, *quiet*," his mother snapped.

But Ben knew what this was about. He'd told them Frankie was moving in and he was doing a clear out to prepare for that event.

He'd also, now he saw was stupidly, told them Frankie wanted a guestroom.

"Ma, let Frankie pick the furniture," he ordered.

"I am," she returned smartly. "But she needs to see this bed so I need her email address 'cause I'm takin' a picture of it with my phone. I don't wanna text it to her. She's gotta see it bigger, in all its glory."

Ben gave a moment's thought to the kind of redecorating Frankie would undoubtedly instigate in his house. These thoughts included the muted colors, candles, minimal knickknacks, and photos she decorated her apartment in. Since he liked all that, he quit thinking about it.

What he did not think was that any bed his mother picked would be something Frankie would want. It was a surprise, but when it came to her home, Francesca Concetti wasn't about flash but was about taste and minimization. Theresa Bianchi decorated in bulk, with a heavy dose of Catholicism.

Still, he gave his mother her email. A bonus of having Frankie, she could deal with his ma when she got like this. He felt no guilt about that. He was going to have to put up with her whacked family, she was going to have to put up with his family's brand of whacked.

This was something, he'd noted repeatedly, that she not only had no problem doing, she actually liked doing it.

"Do you want your father to come over and help with the basement this weekend?" she asked, taking him out of his pleasant thoughts.

"Workin' on it now, Ma. And goin' to Brownsburg this weekend."

"Oh, right, of course," she muttered. "Do you want me to send your father over there now?"

Vinnie Senior popping the cap on a beer, finding a sturdy box to sit on, and bossing his ass around for two hours?

No. He didn't want that.

"I'm good," he answered.

"You sure?" she pushed, and he sighed.

"Yeah, Ma, I'm sure."

"Boy, deliver me!" his father yelled over him talking, and Ben looked at his feet and shook his head.

"Okay, you need us, call," his ma ignored his pop, and gratefully ended it.

"Later, Ma."

"'Bye, Benny."

He disconnected, shoved his phone back in his pocket, and moved to another box. He was finding the ex-owners of his house left him mostly junk. Some was good enough that he'd call the Salvation Army to pick it up. The rest he'd take to the dump.

That said, this was not going to be a day's job. It would take at least a week and he was not looking forward to it.

What he was looking forward to was not having to drive down to Frankie's every few weeks or waiting for her to come to him. He wanted this. She wanted this. He wanted her to make his house hers. So he was doing what he could so she could do that.

He got through two more boxes before his phone rang again. He pulled it out, expecting it'd be his mother having seen another piece of furniture, or God knew what, this time something she wanted him to see. This was something that could happen easily when his mother was out doing anything.

Not for the first time he was understanding Carm's play of moving all the way across the country.

But his display said, SAL CALLING.

He put his cell to his ear and greeted, "Yo, Sal."

"Where are you?" Sal barked, and Ben's back shot straight.

"In my basement," he answered, not feeling good feelings about Sal's greeting.

Sal was talking to someone else when he ordered, "Get him to put someone on her and you drive down now."

Ben took the punch to the heart those words caused and he did it moving quickly to his dog, who was lying on his back, four paws in the air, sleeping on a pile of rags Ben had tossed in the corner. Gus was out because Gus had attacked every attackable item in the basement, and there were a fair few of them, and he'd engaged in this activity for a solid hour.

Benny bent, scooped up Gus, who jumped with surprise in his arm, then immediately started wriggling, ready for play, even right out of sleep. But Ben had to ignore it for once as he headed to the stairs.

He did all this demanding, "Talk to me."

"Word's shiftin' through Indy. A man lookin' for someone to do a hit for him. Easy job. Some computer kid who works for Wyler

Pharmaceuticals. He's in a hurry this time and doesn't mind local. He's also found local."

Jesus, what the fuck was happening where Frankie worked?

"You are fuckin' shittin' me," Ben growled, making it to his kitchen.

"I'm not. Got that, but yesterday, I got more."

Fucking brilliant.

More.

"What?" Benny bit out.

"PI down there, sleazebag and middleman for a variety of shit, he's got himself a job trailin' some boy who's boinking his secretary. Guess where that boy works?"

"What the fuck?" Ben clipped, now taking the stairs to his second floor two at a time.

"This shit is not good shit, whatever this shit is. But I do not know what this shit is and I do not like that. So I'm gonna find out. I also know two hits called on two folks who work where Frankie works, this PI, who is not a good guy, Benny, he's a piece of shit, if he's involved, I'm not likin' this *at all*. I got friends down there. They'll put a man on Frankie until my boy gets down there to take over."

Ben stopped dead in his bedroom. "Why're you doin' that?"

"Why?" Sal clipped. "'Cause this is Frankie. She could be standin' in a field in the middle of the day and a dead body would drop on her."

He was not wrong.

Frankie got born into a family who bounced her around, didn't give that first shit about her, and caused her headaches to that day. Her first and only real boyfriend before Benny got involved with the mob, then was murdered. Her play for redemption with his family got her shot. Now she had a job where people were getting whacked.

Fuck.

"Why is the computer guy a target?" Ben asked.

"No fuckin' clue," Sal answered.

"You know if Frankie knows him?"

"Nope, but I do know the boy who's bangin' his secretary has a job title just like Frankie's, 'cept it says 'west' and not 'east.'"

"A close colleague," Ben muttered, making a decision. He put Gus on the floor and went to his closet. He pulled out the bag that had seen a lot of use the last months, telling Sal, "I'm gonna be on the road, headed down there in ten minutes."

"Got a boy already on his way, Benny. He'll trail her everywhere, keep an eye. You got the restaurant."

"No disrespect, Sal, and I mean it this time, but I'm not a big fan of one of your boys trailin' Frankie."

"You think she'll make him?" Sal asked, and Benny's brows shot together.

"You weren't gonna tell her this shit's goin' down?" Ben asked back.

"Fuck no, *figlio*. She knows this, she'll stick her nose in. She's in that field and that body that drops on her?" he asked, but he did it not wanting an answer. "It'd be a friend she was helping."

He had a point.

Ben tossed his bag on the bed. "That's not why I don't want one of your men on her."

"He'll take care of her, Benny."

"That'd be my job," Ben returned.

Sal was silent.

Ben wasn't.

"Explain to me your take on this."

"Got no take," Sal replied. "All I know is that it's not good and Frankie's in the firing line."

That was Benny's take.

"She's got a guy who works with her, forgot his first name but last name's Bierman," Ben told him. "He's a dick and Frankie says he's targeting her boss for a takedown."

"Another hit?"

Fucking hell, the world Sal lived in.

"Office politics, Sal."

"Oh," he muttered. "Right."

"To get to her boss, he's got his eyes on Frankie and her colleague," Ben told him. "You got a name behind the ordered hit?"

"Don't work that way, Benny. Only thing exchanged is money and the name of the guy goin' down."

"What's the name of the guy goin' down?"

"Peter Furlock."

"You got a guy on him?"

"Don't give a fuck about him."

He'd grabbed shit from his drawer and was tossing it into his bag when he told Sal, "I gotta call the cops on this, Sal."

"You cannot do that, Benito Bianchi."

Ben went solid at his tone.

"I got my name all over Indy askin' these questions," Sal stated in a cold voice. "You put the cops on this, they stick their noses in, me askin' around, one and one will make two, and that'll fuck me. Don't got a lot of business in Indy, but the business I got and the relationships I got I wanna keep. I ask around about somethin' the cops get wind of and move on, my name takes the kind of hit I don't like. I love you, *figlio*, but no one fucks me, even you."

Goddammit!

He should never have asked Sal to get involved. He knew it. Problem was, this was about Frankie, it was important, and he had no one else to ask.

"Then you put a man on that guy," Ben returned.

Sal was silent.

"Sal, put a man on that guy or we got problems," Ben said quietly. "I do not want to have problems with you for obvious reasons. And I do not want to have problems with you for Frankie."

"I'm pretty sure it hasn't escaped your attention that I'm not in the business of doin' good deeds."

"Get in it for Frankie," Benny replied.

"How in the firing line is she?" Sal asked.

"I don't know what's goin' down with these hits, Sal, but I figure from what she's told me, the PI was likely hired by Bierman. This could mean he's got the same on Frankie. The hits, I've got no clue. The PI, it fits."

"Right," Sal prompted when Benny took a breath.

"There's weird shit happening with this guy that's beyond office politics," Ben kept going. "I've never worked in an office, but it seems way over the top to hire a PI to find dirt on some random member of the team in order to take out a bigger fish. Frankie's keepin' clear, outside of cataloging all the weird shit that's happening. Her assistant is not. She's stickin' her nose in with a posse of other women who probably don't like this guy and wanna see his ass canned, but are maybe puttin' themselves in harm's way."

"Detail, Benny."

"I don't have it."

"Get it," Sal ordered. "Get down to Frankie. You take her ass, I'll take Furlock's ass. And you want me to solve this quiet-like, you keep your ass in that 'burg and you just became a Giglia foot soldier."

Ben's throat started burning and he growled, "That shit's not happening."

"In my brand-new good deeds department, Benny," Sal said on a sigh.

Benny drew in a deep breath.

Then he made another decision.

"I gotta make some calls about the restaurant. I gotta pack more shit. Then I'm on the road. In the meantime, you find out if she's got a PI on her."

"Done. You get info, call me."

"Done."

"Take your gun, Benny," Sal advised.

Fuck.

"You got a bad feeling," Ben guessed quietly.

"About Frankie? Don't know. About whatever this shit is? Yes. Definitely," Sal confirmed.

"Right. Later, Sal."

"Later, *figlio*. And Benny?"

"Yeah."

"You're a good man."

Great.

He had approval from Salvatore Giglia.

Sal disconnected.

Ben went to find a bigger bag.

"*What?*" Frankie asked on a muted scream thirty minutes later when Ben was in his SUV, heading down to the 'burg. He'd called Frankie to tell her he was coming for an extended visit.

She sounded partly freaked, mostly excited.

He liked the excited, wasn't big on the freaked, and more, wasn't big on the fact that when she found out why he was coming down, that freaked would get *freaked.*

"I'm headed your way. I'll be at your place around the time you'll be at your place and I'll explain everything when I see you."

She sounded a lot less excited and now quietly freaked when she asked, "Explain everything about what?"

"Babe, I'll tell you when I see you."

"Is everything okay?"

Absolutely not.

"I'll see you in a few hours and explain it to you then."

"Is Theresa okay?" she pushed.

"Yes," he answered.

"Vinnie?"

"Yes, honey."

"Manny and Sela?"

"Everyone's okay, Frankie," he said patiently. "There's just somethin' you need to know and somethin' I need to do."

She gave him a beat of silence before she stated, "This is weird, Benny."

"I know, baby. But I'm not sayin' anything while you're at work. A few hours, you'll have the story."

"While I'm at work?" she asked leadingly.

"Babe," he said a lot less patiently. "I'll. Explain. Everything. When I *see you.*"

"Yeesh, Ben. Come on. You're bein' mystery man. I'm gonna be curious," she replied.

Ben sighed.

"Oh shit," she muttered.

"What?"

"I'm going out with Cheryl tonight."

"Not anymore."

"Ben, honey, she's lookin' forward to this."

"She can look forward to it another night."

"I love you. I want to see you. I've been away from you not three days and I'm freakin' thrilled I'm gonna go home and you'll be there, or I'll be there and you'll be there right after me. But she's a sister. You don't tell a sister who needs to get laid you can't be her wingman, bagging on her last-minute."

"You cannot be serious," Ben stated, hoping she was not.

"I totally am." Her voice lowered when she finished, "I'm sorry, honey. Hopefully she'll hook up fast and I'll get home early."

Ben made another decision. "I'm comin' with."

"Holy crap, you can't do that," she returned immediately, sounding shocked. "I can't be a wingman with my boyfriend with me."

Ben clenched his teeth.

Then he said, "We'll talk about this later too."

She read his tone and he knew it when she replied, "Probably a good idea."

"Leave at five, babe."

"Like you're headed down here and I'll kick back and clean out my inbox," she murmured.

"Frankie?" he called.

"What?" she answered.

"The answer to 'leave at five, babe' is 'all right, honey,'" he informed her.

"Annoying," she muttered.

At that, he grinned.

Then he said, "See you soon."

"All right, honey."

At that, he chuckled.

And after he told her he loved her and got it in return, he disconnected.

Ben had just let himself into Frankie's place, minimized the devastation Gus could make by putting him in her guestroom, got a beer and was taking a tug, when he dropped his chin and the bottle and caught sight through her living room window of her Z sliding into her parking space.

He put the beer on her bar, headed to her door and through it, and the instant he came out from the recess of her front door, he saw her stop walking from her Z and start skip-running.

On heels.

Fucking Frankie.

He smiled.

She smiled back, threw herself in his arms, and banged him hard with her computer bag on his bicep.

"Oh, sorry," she whispered, her face close to his.

He said nothing.

This was because he didn't give a fuck about her bag hitting him, but he did give a fuck about the fact that her mouth was close.

So he ignored the first and took advantage of the second.

He broke the clinch, took her bag from her, then took her hand and pulled her into her apartment.

She threw her keys on the table by the door and moved in, turning the second she cleared the entryway, saying, "Well?"

"You wanna get changed?" he asked, bending to set her bag on the floor against the wall by the table.

He also saw she was wearing spike-heeled slingback pumps and another business-type dress, high neck, short sleeves, black.

Skintight.

Short.

Jesus.

"I wanna know why I got a Benny Bianchi surprise visit," she answered.

"You wanna get a beer first?"

"I already answered that question."

"You wanna let me get my beer and relax after the drive, seein' as I got here about five minutes before you?"

"Benny," she snapped.

"Not even ten seconds, baby," he said softly, moving toward the kitchen and right to his bottle of beer.

She didn't follow, just pivoted, so when he took a pull and turned to her, she was facing him.

"Well?" she repeated.

"A while ago, I did something."

Her body went still and there was a look on her face he didn't get and couldn't read. It was the first time in a long time she gave him a look he couldn't read. Especially one like this one.

One that was not good.

"What'd you do?" she asked.

"You told me that guy in your company got whacked, so I went to Sal to see if he could find out who did it and maybe find out why."

He could read her face then. Her eyes got huge and her mouth dropped open.

She snapped it shut to ask, "You went to Sal?"

"Yep."

"For a favor?"

"He and Gina are invited to our wedding."

At that, her face got soft, her eyes warmed, and the tenseness in her body loosened so much, he braced to catch her if she folded to the floor.

"Our wedding?" she asked softly.

That's when he got the reaction.

"You might wanna shack up for the rest of our lives, but I don't wanna put up with Ma's shit if we do somethin' like that," he replied. "Not to mention, I want a lifetime of catching sight of my rings on your finger. So yeah, that's where we're heading. Our wedding."

That got him love and marvel, like she couldn't believe he was real *and* she couldn't believe her luck, and he fucking loved that. Loved it.

Unfortunately, he couldn't take advantage of it in that moment.

"I think I wanna kiss you all over," she said quietly, and he grinned, preferring her to do that but needing to get this shit done first.

"You wanna know what this is all about?" he asked.

"Okay, I think I wanna kiss you all over after you tell me what this is all about," she amended, and his grin grew into a smile.

He felt it fade when he shared, "Not sure you're gonna be in that mood when I'm done, baby."

"Oh shit," she replied.

"You wanna sit down?" he offered.

"Do I need to sit down?"

"My guess? Definitely. With a beer. At least."

"Oh shit," she repeated.

"Sit down, *cara*. I'll get you your beer."

She gave him a long look, then moved to her couch. A big, overstuffed, pillowy, muted green couch that was unbelievably comfortable and would look great in his living room with her muted blue, overstuffed, pillowy armchair and ottoman. Not to mention switching out her ace square coffee table with his beaten-up rectangular one. Partly because it was ace, partly because it wasn't beaten-up, but mostly because it was bigger and would hold a lot more shit, like beer bottles and bags of chips.

He was nixing her purple wingback chair, mostly because it was purple and partly because he was keeping his recliner.

When he came to her with her opened beer, she was in that muted green couch, shoes off, legs curled underneath her.

He gave her the beer, sat down next to her, and shoved his fingers in the bend of her knee, yanking her closer and keeping his hand there.

"You know a guy named Peter Furlock?" he asked, and her brows drew together as her head tilted to the side.

"No."

"He works at Wyler Pharmaceuticals."

"Okay," she replied slowly, her gaze turning alert and her body again getting wired.

"He's a computer guy and Sal found out he's had a hit put out on him."

She gasped, her eyes going huge in a way that was still cute but he didn't like as much, and she cried, "Oh my God, Benny!"

"Yeah," he agreed.

"Did you call the cops?"

He drew in breath, held her eyes, and answered, "I can't, baby. Sal got this intel. Sal put himself and his name out there to get it. We don't know what's goin' on or who's behind it. The hit isn't interrupted by anyone but Sal, Sal is gonna be vulnerable, and Sal doesn't like to be vulnerable."

"Shit," she mumbled, getting it. Then she focused intently on him and asked slowly, "And you're okay with that?"

"I'm okay with it 'cause Sal's lookin' after this Furlock guy. He's also lookin' into this whole situation fully. And if I wasn't okay with it, then Sal wouldn't be okay with me, and I'm about two months away from bein' really fuckin' happy. I don't need that shit, but more, *we* don't need it."

She looked worried. "Do you think he'll take care of this Peter guy?"

"I think Sal would not make me live with a decision he's gotta know I didn't like very much and let this Peter guy swing."

"Okay, I…okay…" She shook her head. "I don't get it. What's going on?"

"Sal doesn't get it either. But he's goin' to and I'm gonna help."

"What?" she whispered.

"Your colleague, the guy who does the West Coast sales, he's bangin' his secretary."

Her eyes went huge again as she breathed, "How do you know that?"

He cocked his head to the side. "You know that?"

"No, I was guessing," she told him.

"Were you guessing in a way that anyone around could make that guess?" he asked.

"Probably. They're not out about it, but body language and the time they spend together screams it."

"Is that frowned on in the company?"

"Well, I was pretty good at reading my employee handbook when I started, Ben, but I didn't memorize it. That said, even if it wasn't against policy, it's still frowned on."

"If Bierman has that on your sales guy for the west, does he have leverage over him?"

Her hand lifted to her mouth, and through it, she said, "Oh my God."

That meant yes.

He studied her and decided to lay the easy fix on her.

"Frankie, baby, this sucks. I hate sayin' it to you, but the entire drive down, I've been tryin' to think about the best way to end this for you, to get you safe, and that best way is you got no choice but to quit."

Her hand dropped. "What?"

"Babe, that place is a mess, a bad one—hits-taken-out-on-people bad. You gotta get the fuck out."

"But I need a job, Benny."

"Work at the restaurant until you find one." Her eyes started to get squinty so Ben gave her knee a yank to make his point, even as he said, "Francesca, your co-workers are getting investigated by PIs for doin' the dirty with their secretaries and *hits are being taken out on them.* You got…to get…the fuck *out.*"

"It's Tenrix," she said absurdly.

"Come again?" he asked, and she scooted even closer to him, her knee on his thigh, her hand on his chest.

"Listen, Benny, what I know is, Bierman is obsessed with Tenrix, the product we're launching at the end of the year. He's gung ho on the salespeople pushing it and it hasn't even been launched. My boss is not letting him get up in our shit about it and he's also pushing him to get information that couldn't be found on the servers about the product. The information was finally handed over, but the files might have been tampered with. The lead scientist on that project was murdered, a professional hit for what seems like no reason. And now some random IT guy has a hit out on him."

"You're tellin' me this because…?" he prompted.

"I'm tellin' you this because I'm thinking that IT guy is the guy who was talking with Tandy and the other girls in the parking lot the day I told her to stand down and advise the others to do the same. They didn't look like they were discussing where they were going to have a drink after they all decided to stop sticking their noses into shit. They looked like they were discussing the shit they had their noses into."

"So she didn't stand down," Ben noted. "Like I said before, babe, her consequences."

She shook her head and got closer.

"No, Ben, what I'm sayin' is, the IT guy might be able to ascertain if the files were tampered with. And if he has access to the servers and backups, he might be able to get his hands on the original files."

"Babe, I'll say it again, this is not your problem or your business, and it would be less of your business if you quit and came home to Chicago."

"Benny," she said quietly. "You aren't gettin' me. Important files about a pharmaceutical product that's soon to be launched have been *tampered with*. The scientist heading the project is *dead*." She got even closer. "Ben, I think there's something we don't know about Tenrix, and there shouldn't be anything you don't know about a drug. In development phase, everything is strictly confidential. But once it's out there, it has to be transparent. And the only thing to hide about a drug that's imminently being rolled out is that drug is dangerous."

He stared at her. "Who would hide shit like that?"

"Bierman, the Director of Research and Development, who might get a rather hefty bonus for a successful launch of a product and who has been backing this product for years."

"Putting unknown numbers of people who take that drug at risk?" Benny asked, unable to wrap his head around someone doing something that unbelievably dickish.

"It's highly likely the side effects that are dangerous don't occur in the entirety of the subjects that took it or they wouldn't be able to hide it. It's probably that it happens very rarely and only came out in the later phases of the trials, which could mean the longer the drug is taken, that's when the adverse effect is experienced. And at this juncture, dumping Tenrix, the loss of capital on that product would be colossal."

"That makes it okay?" Ben pushed.

"No," Frankie answered. "But for someone like Bierman, it might make it worth the risk."

"The FDA has to approve that shit, Frankie."

"Yeah," she agreed. "But what did they approve?"

"Fuck," Benny whispered, getting what she was saying.

"If that drug is dangerous, Ben, I can't let it launch."

Fuck.

There it was. Frankie getting a wild hair and wanting to get involved.

"You're not stickin' your nose in this," he stated.

Her eyes got wide again, and this time, it was in a way he absolutely did not like.

"So I leave, turn my back on this, Bierman succeeds in getting Tenrix launched, and people in a couple of months of taking that drug, or a couple of years, or a couple of decades, suffer unknown consequences? Consequences that were worth quashing data and two men getting dead?"

"I thought you said your boss has his own concerns."

"Yeah, but you blow the whistle on something like this, you gotta prove there's been a foul on the play. You can't make allegations without anything concrete backing it."

"So let him find the concrete."

"What if he doesn't?"

He turned to her and shot back, "And what if *you* do?" He lifted a hand, curled it around her neck, and yanked her closer so they were near nose-to-nose. "This guy is desperate enough for this drug to go through, he's killin' people and you're already on the firing line 'cause he wants to take down your boss who's askin' questions. You get involved in a deeper way, what will he do?"

Her eyes slid to either side before coming back to his when she announced, "That's where you and Sal come in."

He dropped his hand and sat back in the couch, resting his head on the top to look at the ceiling, before he muttered, "Fuck me."

He lifted his head when he felt Frankie positioning to straddle his lap, something she set her beer aside and yanked her skirt up to do. A dirty play since he liked her there too much, he liked her skirt up around her hips more, she knew it, and she hadn't even started talking yet.

Then she started talking.

"I'd like to talk to Lloyd, but I can't. Not yet. Not this early. I'd like to talk to Colt, but I can't do that either without throwing Sal under the bus. So what I have to do is talk to Tandy, speed shit up, get just enough that it won't make it look like *seriously* nasty office politics if I go to Lloyd with my concerns about Bierman. It can't be hard to find. Nurses worked on those trials all over the country. There have to be witnesses, data, files, and not all on a computer. This drug has been in testing for ages. There has to be something."

He looked into her eyes and stated, "You do know that I carried you through a forest with you bleedin' from a gunshot wound."

"I know," she replied gently.

"So you know I kinda don't want a repeat performance of that."

Her face was soft when she said, "Sal and you'll keep me safe."

He curled his fingers around her hips and informed her, "This is not a smart play, Frankie."

She lifted her hands to hold him on either side of his neck and she returned, "This is the only play, Ben. People's health is at stake."

He stared at her, thinking she was right. If that was a possibility, it'd be a dick move to walk away and hope someone else would deal with it.

But Frankie was not that kind of person. If that was a possibility, and it sounded like it was, she'd never walk away.

So now she was walking right into that field.

But it was Ben's job, working with fucking Salvatore Giglia, to make certain a dead body didn't drop on her.

Or far fucking worse, her beautiful body dropping.

He kept staring at her, thinking he'd like to bring Cal in on this. He and Vi would be home from their honeymoon in three days.

But people were getting whacked. Cal was a new husband, new father.

He couldn't bring Cal into this.

It was Sal. Sal and Benny.

Fuck.

"I don't like this," he told her.

"It won't take long," she replied. "I think Tandy's crew has laid the groundwork." She leaned into him. "And it might turn out to be nothing. It might not be Bierman and Tenrix. It might be he's just a massive dick. It might be the hits have nothing to do with this or each other. It might just be Wyler has bad luck and attracts crazy people, and then I'll have another decision to make 'cause I won't want to work for a place like that, even from a home office in Chicago."

Ben kept staring at her, knowing that was not in the realm of possibility. The company was big, but there were too many coincidences. It had to fit together.

He just didn't want Frankie being the one to fit it together.

Even so, knowing his baby, he had no choice.

So he said, "You make no move without me knowin' about it."

She grinned, bent in, and touched her mouth to his, a light in her eyes he *did not like* and her body wired a different way.

No fear. All in. Raring to go.

Fucking Frankie.

Moving back, she said softly, "Okay."

"I gotta fill Sal in on all this shit."

She nodded and repeated, "Okay."

"I'm close for the long haul," he told her, and her head tipped to the side.

"What about the restaurant?"

"Pop and Manny are on it."

"Is that gonna be okay?" she asked.

"My other choice is…?" he asked back.

"Well…Sal," she answered, and his fingers dug into her hips.

"*I* keep you safe."

That got him another soft look before she whispered, "My Benny." Then suddenly, her head jerked and she asked, "What did you do with Gus?"

"Put him in your second bedroom when I got here."

Her eyes got huge again, this time in a way he liked, and she asked loudly, "You brought him?"

"Not gonna leave him behind for an indeterminate stay with Mrs. Zambino. He might forget who's payin' for his puppy chow."

"Oh my God!" she cried, and he lost her straddling his lap since she jumped off and ran toward the hall.

Ben let his head drop back to the couch and, again, looked at the ceiling, wondering if he'd gone insane.

He turned his head to the side and saw Frankie come in, cuddling and cooing at Gus, no shoes, skintight, sexy, don't-fuck-with-me business dress (that in about five minutes he was going to peel off of her), her mane of hair pulled back at the top, wild with curls at the bottom, and he knew he hadn't gone insane.

He'd gone and got himself pussy-whipped.

"I haven't paid a pet deposit," she announced.

"That gonna be a problem?" he asked in reply, and she gave him a huge smile.

"No, seein' as I have no qualms with them evicting me early."

He liked that answer a fuckuva lot so he ordered, "Come here, Frankie."

"Though, they do, while I instigate my heretofore unmined sleuth powers to uncover probably highly felonious acts at a major, multinational pharmaceutical company, the commute is gonna be a bitch."

"Come here, Francesca."

She again tipped her head to the side. "Has Gus been walked?"

Fuck.

He hadn't.

Ben folded out of the couch and ordered, "Go get some flip-flops."

"I can walk him in heels."

He cut his eyes to her. "You put those heels on to walk Gus, you'll find yourself ass to the hood of the first car we pass, giving your neighbors a show. You want to give your man a break from all that," he threw a hand her way, "you put on flip-flops and I might be able to control it until I get you and our dog back through the front door."

She grinned her I-have-a-secret-and-I-wanna-moan-it-in-your-ear grin and replied, "I'll get some flip-flops."

"Good call," he muttered.

She bent to put Gus to the floor, torturing Benny by giving him a direct view of her ass with her tight skirt stretching tighter, thankfully straightened, turned, and walked back toward the hall.

Gus looked at Benny, then down the hall toward Frankie and immediately started waddle-trotting after her.

She came out in flip-flops, got some plastic bags just in case, and they took Gus for a walk.

After, Ben made it all the way to her bed before he peeled off her dress.

Twenty-five minutes later, when he made her come, she moaned her secret into his ear.

It consisted of three words.

"Love you, Benny."

⟝⟞

"My turn!" Frankie announced when Ben came back from the bathroom at J&J's Saloon and approached where Cheryl and Frankie were sitting.

She laid a hard but quick one on him that obliterated any possibility of wingman status (not that it wasn't already gone since he was there), grinned into his face, then part-walked, part-strutted, and part-bounced to the back where the bathrooms were.

She did this with every male eye in the joint following her ass covered in the tight skirt of her dress, or her long legs that were bare and led into a pair of hot-as-hell heels.

So although Benny appreciated the view, it was also irritating as fuck.

"You're a new breed of badass," Cheryl noted, taking his attention to her.

"Come again?" he asked, seeing she was studying him closely.

"Not the show-up-and-demand-to-go-out-with-your-woman-to-make-sure-she-doesn't-get-into-trouble move. That's not a new breed of badass, that's the usual one. The after-she-gets-shot-let-her-stick-her-neck-out-and-do-it-with-the-Chicago-mob-at-her-back move."

Jesus Christ.

Frankie told this woman what was going down? How long was he in the goddamned bathroom?

His stomach tightening, he slid in front of her, did it holding her eyes, necessarily and intentionally getting close because there was no room, but also because he had a point to make.

"She shouldn't have told you," he said low.

"No shit?" she asked in return.

He didn't reply to that.

He ordered, "And you aren't gonna say dick to anyone."

Her eyes narrowed.

He'd been around Cheryl once before, at Vi and Cal's wedding.

Frankie called her edgy.

Benny and any other man who took one look at her would call her hard.

When she met them at J&J's, reminded of that hardness and seeing it without her in a bridesmaid gown, happy her girl was happy, Ben understood this was why she wasn't getting laid.

Men didn't like hard. They liked soft. They didn't mind attitude and there were those, like Benny, who wanted that. Some men could get off on the challenge of smoothing out sharp edges, or knowing that was what a woman gave out in the world, but when he got her home, she gave him the sweet underneath.

But Cheryl was straight-up hard. Her eyes said "you are not getting in there no matter what you try, so don't bother trying." And everything about her said she'd take what she wanted, and if you got anything out of that, she didn't give a fuck. This would mean you wouldn't get anything out of that except maybe an orgasm, but not a good one.

This woman wasn't about exploring the possibility of building a future or just having a good time and some laughs.

This woman was about riding you hard until she found it, climbing off even if you hadn't, getting dressed, and going home.

The loyalty she gained from Vi and now Frankie made him wonder what made her like that and why she didn't put out what she gave to her girls in order to at least get laid and at most find herself a man.

"You do not know me, but I am no dumbfuck," she said in a voice cold as ice, proving his thoughts true.

"I figure you aren't, I'm just remindin' you not to be."

She ignored that and stated, "But you do know your woman so you know she isn't one either. If she couldn't trust me, she wouldn't have said squat."

She was right.

But the stakes were high.

"She's playin' with fire," he pointed out.

"Then don't let her get burned," she shot back.

"And I'm doin' that by makin' sure you know to keep your mouth shut and don't do somethin' stupid like thinkin' you can help your girl by makin' this a *Laverne & Shirley* scenario."

Her eyes slid to the side.

Jesus.

"Which one are you?" he asked, and her eyes came back. "Laverne or Shirley?"

"I know a guy who's ace at surveillance," she told him, chin lifting slightly.

She was Laverne.

"There it is," he muttered, looking away and reaching for his beer.

"And you should be involved, a guy who owns a pizzeria?"

He took a pull off his beer in an effort not to allow that remark to irritate him before he reminded her, "She sleeps at my side."

"And my mom's got high blood pressure. Takes meds for it."

Benny shook his head. "Cheryl, I got a man in Chicago who got the story of what I could give him while my woman was gettin' sexed up to go out for drinks with her girl, and in doin' that, tease every guy here, none of 'em who are ever gonna get close to tappin' her ass, all of 'em wantin' to, and all of that annoying the fuck outta me. And this man has resources. Your surveillance guy might be tight, but I'm thinkin' my guy has that covered."

Suddenly, she grinned, and if he had a vagina, he would advise her to turn that grin to the room because it was almost cute, definitely playful, and showed she had a sense of humor. All of this in a way that, with her big hair, nice tits, and show of skin, would mean her dry spell would end in about the time it would take to walk back to the bathrooms or get to a car.

"I see your point," she said through her grin.

"Thrilled, babe," he muttered around his bottle of beer before he took another pull and moved to sit on Frankie's stool.

She sucked back some of her cocktail.

When she did, Benny threw her a hint. "Just sayin', might be good you troll for talent in a bar that's not the bar where you work."

She looked at him.

"Yeah. I see that. Problem is, I make some cake here, but it's the only bar close. I'm not about to get nailed for drinkin' and drivin' so I cab it when I hit the scene. And me payin' hefty cab fares means I can't buy six packets of Oreos for my boy every week 'cause that kid eats the whole damn thing the minute I take it out of the bag."

Another thing that would make her a winner if a man knew about it, she gave more of a shit about getting her kid Oreos than getting herself laid.

"Then maybe you should widen the net and not just fish in bars," Benny suggested, and her head jerked in surprise.

"Like where?"

Shit, he walked right into a discussion he did not want to be in and it was a discussion with no exit door.

"I don't know," he answered. "What kinda man you want?"

"A man who looks good, fucks better, and likes kids." She gave him her limited wish list and tipped her head to the side. "Got any friends?"

"You willin' to move to Chicago?"

"No."

"Then no."

She gave him another grin, even as she told him, "Just to say, you're crampin' my style."

He glanced through the bar that wasn't packed, but it wasn't a slow night either, then looked back to her. "Anyone here you're even remotely interested in?"

"No."

"Then let me buy you a drink and you tell me about your boy."

Her grin turned into a smile at the mention of her boy, a smile that, if she put it out there, might get her more than just laid, just as Frankie came back, asking, "I miss any action?"

Benny started to make a move to give her back her stool, but she made her move faster, sliding in in a way that forced him to shift a thigh and twist on the stool so she could press her hip and side to his crotch and chest between his legs that were up, feet on the rungs of the stool.

Much better than him standing behind her on the stool, pressed to her back.

"No action," Cheryl answered. "Night's a dud."

"Yo, babe." They all heard.

Ben was about to twist his neck to look, but he didn't when he saw something flicker over Cheryl's face when she heard the voice and her eyes shifted beyond Frankie.

It was only there a second, but he caught it, and if he wasn't mistaken, it was pain. The kind you get when you want something you can't ever have, you know it, you're resigned to it, but that doesn't make it hurt any less.

"Yo, Merry," Cheryl replied, and Ben finally looked to the good-looking, tall, dark-haired man who stopped at their sides. "Merry, this is Frankie and Benny," she went on. "Kids, this is Garrett Merrick. J&J's regular. Detective at the BPD. Decent guy, as far as I can tell, who can hold his liquor and is smart enough to laugh at my jokes."

"Jesus, Cher, you wanna share my shoe size?" Merrick asked, smiling down at her in a friendly way that said that was all it was. Friends. He had zero interest in getting in there.

"Shoe size ten," Cheryl stated, turning to look at Frankie and Benny.

"One off," Merrick muttered, and Cheryl looked back at him.

"Which direction?" she asked.

"Not sayin'." he answered.

She rolled her eyes to the ceiling. "Please, God, for all my sisters, make it one size up."

Merrick burst out laughing. So did Frankie. But Ben just chuckled and he did it feeling shit.

And he felt shit because she was a good woman. A hard one, but a good one. And now she was a good one going out of her way to be funny because she liked this guy, but knew he was not the kind of man who had an interest in taking on whatever shit made her hard. He preferred soft. She had no shot, it didn't enter his mind, and him being a regular meant she read that on him every time he showed. So she was grasping on to all she could get.

Friendship and making him laugh.

Merrick took his mind off these thoughts when he greeted them both, ordered his beer, and joined them, standing close to Cheryl, shooting the shit with her, laughing at her jokes, giving shit back, and generally torturing her not having that first clue he was doing it.

An hour later, Merrick took off, Cheryl announced she had to go home or find a place to sell a kidney in order to pay her babysitter, and Ben loaded both women into his SUV so Cheryl wouldn't have to pay for a taxi.

When he stopped in the driveway of her crackerbox house, which was crackerbox but still tidy and well cared for, he put his truck in neutral and angled out, even as Cheryl was saying her goodbyes.

He caught Frankie's eyes and said, "Walkin' her to her door. Safe inside. Be back."

That got him her look that said he'd fulfilled a promise he didn't even know he was giving as her lips said, "Okay, honey."

He grinned at her, closed the door, and rounded the hood, meeting Cheryl on the short, cement walk that led to her front door, a walk that was trimmed on each side with a thick, bushy, healthy line of what looked from the outside light to be little white flowers mixed with purple ones.

Probably not making enough cake to hire a gardener, he knew she did that and that was surprising.

It also said a lot about her that no man who would look at her would know.

"I can make it to my front door, you know," she muttered, sounding vaguely annoyed.

"Figure you can," was all the answer he gave her.

They made it to her short stoop, she opened the screen door, then the inside door, and that was when he stopped her.

"Smile," he said, and her head tipped back to look up at him.

"What?"

"You are far from hard to look at. You smile and mean it that ups significantly. You wanna get some, let a guy in. And to do that, all you gotta do is smile."

She studied him before she said, like she was talking to herself, "Definitely a different breed of badass."

He didn't comment on that.

He said, "You give what you give to your girls, the love you got for your son, your sense of humor and whatever drives you to plant little flowers along your walk to some guy, Merrick'll see you givin' it and he'll kick his own ass."

Her lips parted, her face softened, and Ben instantly bent closer to her.

"That, Cheryl. Give that right there and a guy will get lucky, and not the way you want him to think he'll be. The way he'll just be, he gets that from you."

Her face closed down and she stated, "Gave a guy that and I'll hand you the understatement of the year that the results were not pretty."

Benny figured as much.

So he straightened and shrugged. "Your call. But heads up, at our age, guys are no longer all about pussy. They want a woman they know can give them a smile like you got and the promise of what's behind it."

"I work in a bar, Ben, I know that shit's not true," she returned.

"Then you either got an eye for assholes or you aren't payin' attention. And, looks of Merrick, I'll tell you straight up, it's you not payin' attention."

She stared at him.

He ended it with, "'Night, babe," and without her reply, he walked away.

He was backing out of her driveway, arm hooked behind Frankie's seat, when she asked, "What was that about?"

"Your girl doesn't wanna get laid," he told her. "She wants to stop bein' lonely. She's got the tools to do that but she's not usin' 'em. I pointed that out to her."

Frankie was silent as Ben put his truck into drive and headed them home.

Ben thought it was done until he stopped at a light and Frankie spoke.

"Have I told you you're awesome today?"

He looked at her and grinned, replying, "Nope."

His grin died when he saw her face lit by street and dashboard lights and he heard the tone of her words, saying, "You're awesome, Benny Bianchi."

At that, Ben lifted a hand, curled it around her neck, and pulled her to him, dropping his head and taking her mouth.

The car behind them had to honk to get them to break it off.

And that was all good, since where they were going, he could fully show his appreciation, and to be able to do that thoroughly was not in the time he had at a red light.

Twenty-Two

Awesome

The next morning, sacrificing greatly for all the unknown people out there who might possibly get messed up by my company putting out a bad drug, I left Benny Bianchi in my bed and went to the office early.

I wasn't the first one in.

Travis Berger was in.

So was Randy Bierman.

I hit my office, started my day, and every time I saw movement outside my window, I looked to see who it was.

So I saw it when Heath walked in about twenty minutes after I did.

I also saw it when Sandy walked in only two minutes after Heath did.

Heath was not stupid, and yet, he still was.

I gave them time to settle, Tandy coming in while I did this, but she was not first on my list that morning.

Heath was.

"Hey, honey," I greeted Tandy, leaving my office and making a beeline to Heath's.

"Mornin', Frankie," Tandy replied.

I threw a smile at her over my shoulder and didn't miss a step.

"Hey there, Frankie," Sandy said when I got close.

"Hi, Sandy." I smiled at her but, again, didn't miss a step and went right to his office. I saw Sandy open her mouth to say something, but by that time, I had a hand lifted and was knocking on the jamb of Heath's door.

When he looked up, I asked, "Got a minute?"

Heath looked to me, out the window to Sandy, then back to me before answering, "Sure."

I walked in, closed the door behind me, and moved directly to the chairs opposite his desk. I sat in one, then asked the more truthful question.

"You got more than a minute?"

He looked to the closed door before he studied me and asked back, "Is everything okay?"

I gave him more truth. "Not even close."

He studied me more intently. "What's not okay?"

"No way to put this out there and do it delicately," I started. "So I'll just put it out there. I know you and Sandy have something going on outside this office. I know it because neither of you are very good at hiding it. I also know it because a PI is watching you and he knows it."

Heath's face had grown pale as I talked. He'd also leaned forward before I was done.

Watching him react, it hadn't escaped my attention that he was very good-looking. Sandy brown hair. Nice blue eyes. Trim and fit. Not exactly tall, but he wasn't short either. He was just too lean and too classically good-looking for my taste. I liked them darker. Rougher. Bigger. The kind of man you looked at and knew he'd order a beer but hoped he wouldn't mind drinking Champagne with you during happy occasions.

Heath probably drank martinis.

Nothing wrong with that, but I liked it that Benny ordered beer.

"I got nowhere to go with that lead in," Heath replied, "except to ask what the fuck you want."

I blinked.

Then I told him, "I don't want anything except for you to go to Lloyd, share that you and Sandy are in a relationship, thus cutting off at the knees whoever hired this PI to get the dirty on you."

"It wasn't you?" he asked.

"Why would I do that?" I asked back.

"Why would anyone do that?"

Was he serious?

"Uh…Heath, maybe you need to look around and start paying attention," I suggested.

"What?"

God, he was serious.

I leaned toward him. "I have no idea who hired him. I just know the PI was hired and what he found. That is, I don't know who hired him yet. But Randy is riding your ass just as he's riding mine, so I have my suspicions."

"Yeah, because he's a dick. Riding my ass at work because he's a dick and gets off on swinging it around is one thing. Hiring a PI because I'm banging my secretary is *insane*."

I had hoped he wasn't just banging his assistant.

Obviously, he was.

"I'm not going to Lloyd and telling him I'm nailing Sandy," he continued.

"Your call, but if you don't, whoever's behind this will, and he probably won't go to Lloyd. He'll go to Berger."

"Whoever's behind this…right," he said snidely. "You want me to go to Lloyd and get my ass fired, so when Bierman takes Lloyd down, even though you got two less years than me in your chair, it'll be you with a direct shot to Lloyd's seat."

I was seeing Heath was a dick too, he was just better at hiding it.

This wasn't surprising, he was a salesman. Not nice to say about one of my people, but they were my people so I could say it.

He kept going.

"Ambitious. Driven. A slave driver to your reps so they'll bust their asses to make you look good while you hang with your boyfriend in Chicago." When I just stared at him, stupefied and remembering how much I hated office politics, he said, "Yeah. Trey told me about it while asking me if I could swing a transfer for him into my territory."

Trey was my rep in Chicago, and I wasn't surprised about that because I already knew Trey was a dick. What I hoped was that he was only spreading that bullshit to Heath and not further.

Unfortunately, Heath wasn't done.

"You probably don't have a private dick, just makin' your play to get me to swing my ass out there. Well, fuck that, Frankie. I'll call your bluff."

"I am not aiming at Lloyd's seat, Heath. I *like* Lloyd," I informed him.

"I do too. That doesn't mean I don't want his salary and his title."

Yep. Total dick.

I ignored that and continued, "Furthermore, you tell him, that doesn't mean he'll fire you."

He leaned further across his desk to me, the look in his eyes ugly, the twist of his mouth nasty. "Maybe not, but he could tell me to end it and I *like* getting head from Sandy. She's a fucking *virtuoso* at head."

Way too much information.

I tried not to curl my lip while suggesting, "Uh…can we get back to the matter at hand?"

"That being some unknown entity has hired a PI. Seriously? Are you for real with this crap?"

Okay then. I did my best. He wanted to be a shark, when the bigger fish gobbled him whole, that was his call.

"Then don't tell Lloyd," I said. "But watch your back and brace, Heath."

"I don't go to him, you won't?" he bit out.

"Of course not," I returned sharply.

"Berger?"

"Your business isn't mine. I know it sounds weird because it *is* weird, but I'm only making it mine because I'm trying to do you a favor."

His eyes narrowed. "How do you even know this shit? Sandy and I have been cool."

Okay, maybe he wasn't that smart.

"I can't say since I don't know yet who hired the PI, just what he got," I told him, deciding not to tell him that he and Sandy have *not* been cool.

"You can't say, and you know it, but you aren't behind it?" he asked acidly, not to mention dubiously.

"If I was behind it, wouldn't I ask for something or threaten something rather than just giving you a heads up?"

"I don't know. I've never had someone do something as totally jacked as hiring a PI to follow me, so how would I know what they'd do?"

I leaned forward and said softly, "Clue in, Heath. Now. Seriously. *Clue in.* And if you don't care about Sandy, I hope you care enough to know she's sticking her nose into something that's happening around you that's obviously escaping your attention. At best, it could get her fired. At worst, no joke, it might get her dead."

His brows shot up and he clipped, "*What?*"

Definitely not as smart as I thought.

I didn't reiterate.

I told him, "I've got someone on this, and when I know the name of the PI and who hired him, I'll tell you." I thought about Sal, who was on that and who loved me, and shared, "Odds are, I'll know soon. You want, you can wait that time before whoever's behind this hits Berger with it or hits you with it to get you to do what he wants you to do. Or you can man up and sort your shit. And, just sayin', bangin' your assistant..." I shook my head and finished, "Love is never wrong. If it's not that, and it's in the workplace where she might not know that it isn't about that, it is."

"Don't need you lecturing me on ethics, Frankie, or making bizarre threats to my secretary."

I wanted to shake some sense into him, but obviously I couldn't.

"You'll see I'm doin' you a solid, Heath. If that isn't right now, I'm okay with that. I'll accept your gratitude later."

"You've lost your mind," he muttered, staring at me just as the door to his office opened.

I turned, expecting to find Sandy there.

My skin started crawling when I saw Randy Bierman there.

"Francesca, I need Heath," he stated, his meaning clear; no matter what we were talking about, I needed to get the fuck out and now.

I looked to Heath, gave him big eyes, got up, and moved out of his office.

As I passed Tandy on the way to my own office, I said, "Give it five minutes and come in. We'll go down to the coffee cart to get a latte."

Her eyes were on me. They moved to Heath's office, came back to me, and she nodded.

I walked into my office, checked my cell on my desk to see if I had any missed calls, and when I saw I didn't, I faked working for five minutes until Tandy came to my door and asked somewhat loudly, "Hey, wanna hit the coffee cart?"

I grinned at her, grabbed my wallet out of my purse, and got out of my chair. I rifled through my inbox and grabbed a random file, hoping I looked like I wasn't grabbing a random file.

I looked to Tandy. "Get your notebook and your phone, would you?"

Her head gave a slight jerk before she went to her desk and did as I requested.

We were standing alone in the elevator bay when she asked through the side of her mouth, "What was that with Heath?"

"Don't worry about Heath, honey. We'll talk in the lobby."

She looked fully at me, but she was still whispering when she asked, "Am I in trouble?"

This clearly stated she'd done something to be in trouble for, and since her work was stellar, I knew why she was worried about being in trouble.

"We'll talk in the lobby," I repeated, but I did it gently, hoping to assuage her fears.

We got to the lobby and got our lattes. When we were sitting in a comfortable waiting section that was far from the cart and not close to the reception desk, I knew I hadn't assuaged her fears because, by the time we sat down, she looked about ready to cry.

Shit.

"Tandy, do you know Peter Furlock?" I asked.

That got me pale face number two of the morning and her voice was a squeak when she answered. "Yes." She leaned toward me and rushed on, "But, Frankie—"

I cut her off. "Is he checking to see if the Tenrix documents Bierman gave Lloyd were amended?"

"He already knows that," she whispered, looking terrified. "He found the backup files and downloaded them before Mr. Bierman got someone to get to them and replace them with the tampered files."

Oh man. They were a lot further than I would have imagined.

Which must be why Peter Furlock had been targeted.

"You got his number?" I asked, and she nodded. "Call him, right now. Make sure he's at his desk."

Her eyes got huge and she asked back, "Why?"

"Just do it, honey."

She set her latte aside, gave her attention to her phone, and put it to her ear. I sipped my latte, leafed through the file on my knee I didn't see, and listened to her connect with Furlock, as well as give a lame excuse why she was calling, totally no good at cloak and dagger.

I looked back to her when she disconnected and told me. "He's there."

I nodded. "So the files on the server that people can see are the tampered ones?"

It was her turn to nod.

"And the other ones have disappeared, outside what Furlock has."

"Yes, Frankie."

"Did you take this to Lloyd?"

"Not yet," she said. "We wanna make sure all our ducks are in a row."

All their ducks.

Shit.

"What ducks?" I pressed.

She drew in breath, grabbed her latte, and took a sip, trying to look cool and casual doing it—and failing—then she looked back to me.

"Okay, Frankie, there's a lot," she said quietly.

"Tenrix is dangerous," I stated, also quietly.

She nodded again. "In five percent of test subjects who were on the product for more than three years, serious and irreparable heart conditions formed that could be traced directly back to taking Tenrix."

Shit, shit, *shit*.

"How did this get by everybody?" I asked.

"Because Bierman is just the henchman. The mastermind is Barrow."

I sucked in breath.

Clancy Barrow. CEO of Wyler Pharmaceuticals.

The top of the food chain. The number one shark.

Shit!

I leaned toward Tandy and hissed, "How do you know?"

"Okay, Frankie, okay…" she semi-chanted, then leaned toward me. "My big sis, she went to school with this girl—totally cool—her name is Roxie."

"Babe, point," I warned.

"I'm gettin' to it," she squeaked. "Roxie moved to Denver a while back. She met this guy, married him. He's a cop."

"Okay," I prompted when she stopped talking.

"But his brother owns this big investigations firm."

And there it was.

She kept going.

"And we did trials for Tenrix at a research facility in a hospital in Denver."

"So you called her, she engaged the brother-in-law, and what happened?"

"What happened was, the guy he put on it found out two, Frankie," she leaned deeper toward me, "*two* nurses on that trial got in bad car crashes. *Bad.* One lost her legs. One, such severe head trauma, she can't work anymore."

"Whistle-blowers," I whispered.

Tandy nodded. "We think so. We also know the turnover in nurses during that trial was severe. Nearly all of them went in and out the door. The investigator tracked some of those nurses down and they would *not* talk. Not at all. The investigator suspected this was because of fear, but also maybe payoffs. And Bierman may make some dough, but we figure he doesn't have the resources for that kind of operation." She paused before she finished, "But Barrow does."

I figured they figured right.

"They find evidence of the payoffs?" I asked.

Tandy shook her head. "We only could pool so much money together to pay the investigator guys, so no. We couldn't ask them to dig deeper. They're really cool guys and they offered to keep going, get us on a payment schedule. But we really couldn't do that."

Fuck.

"But Peter found something," she stated, and I again focused on her.

"What?"

"He's really clever with computer stuff. He did some of his voodoo and found out Dr. Gartner was getting payoffs. He'd put it in an account under his stepmother's name. His dad's dead so that's probably why the cops didn't catch it. I don't know how he managed that, but he never touched it and neither did she. And we all figure, because apparently he was a super guy, Gartner was playing the game, pretending he was taking payoffs, but amassing his own evidence to take to Berger or the board or whoever could do something to stop Tenrix getting out. They found out and he got killed."

I'd totally forgotten about it until that moment, but it was then I remembered the tense phone call I partially overheard Bierman having. It was before Gartner died. But it could have been anyone in this drama he was threatening.

"Miranda and Peter are working that," Tandy informed me, and I focused back on her.

"Working what?"

"She's in production now and Dr. Gartner's computer, files, *and* assistant are in production. They're looking to see if he left anything behind or if they cleaned up after him."

Jeez, they totally had it going on. The Miranda move was a ploy to get her into production.

I was impressed.

But I still didn't get it.

I looked away from her and asked, mostly to myself, "Why would Barrow be behind this?"

"Because we need a winner," Tandy answered.

I looked back at Tandy. "What?"

"They headhunted you, the best of the best to jumpstart our sales program, which the numbers were okay, but it wasn't buying anyone yachts. Before you, they headhunted Heath. He was a big hotshot rep from another company. We've had two big products that have had competing products launched in the last five years that have cut into our profit margins. And we had one major earner that went generic and now is sold over-the-counter. It's not like the company is dying, but they need a winner and none of the other products are even close to launch. Tenrix is supposed to be that winner. Most of the data is awesome. The problem is, in those few cases, it's devastating and, if not caught, could be lethal."

She and her crew had done their homework.

"Tandy," I started gently, "with all that, can you please tell me why you didn't give this to Lloyd or Berger?"

Her shoulders straightened, and when she spoke, her voice was stronger. "Because I need this job, Frankie. I have a roommate. We live in a nice place, but only because we go in on it together. Without her, it'd be tough to find somewhere to rent that's that nice, safe, and in a good part of town. I want to be able to afford to keep my part of that place and it isn't like people headhunt for assistants. I don't have the reserves to make it if I get fired. I need to work. And with things this big, you never know who's in on it. So, if we don't have everything we *have* to have to prove what we know is true, if they fire us, we have nothing to give to the newspapers to expose them."

She and her crew hadn't just done their homework, they'd thought it all through.

But my mind was whirling with what to do next.

Then I hit on it.

"I need the name and phone number of the investigator in Denver. I also need Peter to make copies of absolutely everything he has. Call him and tell him to do that, then I'll go down to IT on my way back from the gym at lunch to get it myself. You make the rounds and be cool about it, telling everyone to stand down for now. I'll let you know what we're doing next."

Her expression went suspicious as she said, "No offense, Frankie, but we've been at this a lot longer than you and you're kind of management. So I know you're cool, but with this kind of stuff, I have to *know you're cool.* I don't think it's a good idea to hand everything over to you."

I got that.

I also had to get past it.

"All right, honey, take a deep breath and keep *your* cool when I tell you something that's gonna blow your mind, freak you out, and put the fear of God in you."

Her eyes widened, but I went on.

"The reason I'm sticking my nose in is because someone close to me is keeping Peter Furlock safe. And that's because he's had a hit put out on him. Now, I'm taking this over because I have the resources to do it, I have more weight in this company than any of you, and because I want you, Sandy, Miranda, Kathleen, Peter, and whoever else to stay *alive.*"

"Oh my God, that's why you wanted me to call him," she breathed.

"That's why," I confirmed.

"Should I tell him?" she asked.

"If you want, I will. But I think he should know. He has someone shadowing him to protect him, but it doesn't hurt to stay vigilant."

"I should tell him," she whispered. "He knows me."

I nodded. "I understand that," I assured her, then I leaned toward her. "But please warn him that he does not go off the beaten path. We can't let the people who are doing this know how on to them you are or what the people who are working with me are doing."

She looked so freaked, I wanted to reach out and grab her hand, but I didn't want anyone to see me doing it.

So I didn't and just kept talking.

"Now, you gotta trust me. This is huge and what you've been doing is making someone antsy. Let's get this product safely off our catalog and do it without any more good, brave people getting harmed. Okay?"

"Okay," she whispered.

"You need a minute to get yourself together?" I asked, and she nodded. "Take it, then, babe. But do it scribbling on your notepad, right?"

"Right, notepad, good idea. Just a normal meeting with new scenery between Frankie and Tandy," she said in a near chant.

I smiled at her. "Just that, honey."

She nodded again, snatched up her notepad, and started scribbling.

I took a sip of my latte and decided on what was next.

Benny first, obviously.

Then Sal.

I looked to Tandy, who was rabidly scribbling like I was a taskmaster about to pull out my whip.

"Babe," I called, and she looked to me.

I made my voice low when I spoke again, and even if my words were clear, my tone made them clearer.

"You did good. You did right. You took initiative, even when I told you to back down. You were brave. And you're gonna save a lot of people a lot of heartache. Literally. I admire you, Tandy." Her lip started trembling so I finished gently, "Just a normal meeting, honey."

She forced a weak smile and replied, "Just another meeting, Frankie."

I grinned at her and took another sip of my latte.

That evening at 5:05, I sauntered to my car just like any other day I'd saunter to my car, except way earlier.

This was because Benny was at my place and I wanted to be with Benny.

This was also because I wanted to get the fuck out of there.

The last was partly because I'd picked up all the evidence Tandy's crew had amassed from a visibly terrified Peter Furlock. Although not nice to say, he was a man who was squat, dumpy, had thinning light brown hair, and wore thick glasses either due to weak eyes or squinting at a computer screen or a TV while playing a game all the time.

Even so, he was also building up to being a hero because he was smart and brave and doing the right thing, all this I told him in order to get him to calm down, stick with the program, and assure him my "people" had his back.

When he went back to wherever IT people holed up, he looked less terrified but still jittery.

The stuff he gave me was in my computer bag.

So I also wanted to get out of there because the place was giving me the heebie-jeebies. It felt like the walls had eyes and it didn't help that Heath disappeared at lunch and didn't come back.

This sent Sandy into a tailspin for reasons that were probably not good. She was visibly nervous. She dropped several things, including a full mug of coffee. She avoided Tandy (and thus me) like the plague. And twice, I saw her rushing to the bathroom.

She maybe didn't feel well.

But she probably went in there to freak out and/or burst into tears.

Something was up with that and it was either what I'd said to Heath or what Bierman had said.

I'd called Benny with the news, giving him the detail on Nightingale Investigations, the firm Tandy's sister's friend from Brownsburg (of all freaking places) had connections with. Ben told me he'd relay everything to Sal so I didn't have to.

This was not because he didn't want me to talk with Sal. It was because he didn't want to chance me being overheard by anyone.

Since all the evidence was on three thumb drives, no paper, I was going to hand them over to someone Sal was sending to keep them safe.

That was my plan for the night.

I was also going to cuddle with my man, play with my puppy, look forward to the time when that was my life but in Chicago, and try to forget about all this crap.

Until tomorrow.

I was at my car when my phone in my purse binged with a text. I got in the car, settled, dug out my phone, and looked at the display.

When I saw what was on it, I forced myself to act normally, seeing as they had cameras in the parking garage. And when the text faded to a dark screen, I went to my texts to read it again.

McCaffrey's. Now. Come by yourself.

It was from Heath.

One thing I knew, I was going to McCaffrey's.

The other thing I knew, I was not going alone.

I put my Bluetooth in, made the call, and pulled out of my spot as it rang.

"You headed home?" was Benny's greeting.

"No, I'm meeting you at a place called McCaffrey's where I'm giving a command performance for Heath, my colleague who disappeared at lunch after a first-thing-in-the-morning meeting with me followed immediately by one with Bierman."

"Fuck," he muttered. "Where is it?"

I gave him directions and he sounded like he was walking when he said, "Got it. Be there in a few. But do not go in without me. Do not even park in the parking lot without me. I had shit to do with Sal's boys today, so one of them took your ass on the way to work and was gonna trail you home. He can clock out when I get there, but you're not goin' in without someone at your back. Take a drive. Circle it. I'll text you when I'm there."

Seemed Ben was good at cloak-and-dagger shit.

I found that interesting.

And hot.

"Right, *capo*."

"Whatever," he said with a smile in his voice, then, "Later."

He disconnected and I did as told, though it wasn't for a few since Brownsburg was half an hour drive on a good day from McCaffrey's and it was rush hour. Since 86th Street and its environs, where McCaffrey's was located, was crazy busy, I also did it wanting to murder somebody. And I did it until my phone binged and I saw the text that said Ben was there.

That's when I went to McCaffrey's, which was a pub restaurant off 86th where a lot of folks from Wyler went after work for a couple of drinks and a plate of appetizers. I'd been there twice, always with folks from Wyler.

I parked, and when I got out, Benny was at my door.

"Got the shit on you, babe?" he asked and there it was again. He was good at this cloak-and-dagger shit. I'd left it in my computer bag on my passenger seat. It probably wasn't such a hot idea to leave evidence of all that Tandy's crew had been doing in a decades-old Z outside a pub frequented by Wyler staff.

"Right," I muttered, leaned into my car, nabbed my bag, pulled it out, and when I did, Benny took it.

I locked up. He grabbed my hand and led me into the bar.

We found Heath away from the having-a-few-and-attempting-to-hook-up crowd around the bar. Side booth, out of the way.

Obviously, he didn't want to have a beer (or in his case, by the cocktail glass in front of him, I was again guessing a martini) and share about our day among the heaving throng.

I led Benny to Heath, and when we got to his booth, Ben guided me in first.

We barely stopped sliding our asses in when Heath asked, "Who's this fucking guy?"

"My boyfriend," I answered.

He leveled his eyes on me. "I thought I told you to come alone."

"She's not alone. Get over it or not. Call it now. We leavin' or we stayin'?" Ben declared, and Heath glared at him.

Then he shrugged. "What the fuck, doesn't matter. It's gonna be all over the Internet soon anyway so everyone can see it," he muttered bizarrely, then turned, picked something up out of the seat beside him, and tossed it across the table our way.

It was a manila envelope.

"What's this?" I asked, reaching for it.

"Proof Randy Bierman is a total dick," Heath answered.

"Need more to go on there, man," Benny said.

Heath looked at me but jerked his head toward Benny. "Again, why is this guy here?"

"He's Italian. He's protective. He tends not to like me having a drink on command alone with guys who don't like me much, so he's here. Like he said, get over it," I replied, having grabbed the envelope during that exchange. I flipped open the flap and started to pull out what was inside.

I shoved it back in and I didn't even get a full look.

This was because what I saw was Heath sitting in a nice armchair, fully clothed, head thrown back, and Sandy was between his legs doing something that could not be mistaken, completely naked.

I barely got the photo shoved back in before Benny ripped the envelope out of my hand and sent it sailing back to Heath.

"You wanna explain why you're givin' my woman shit like that to look at?" he demanded to know, his voice not smooth, not easy, but rumbling and irate.

Obviously, he got a look too.

"Thought she should know she's right," Heath answered like it was all the same to him. I looked at his martini glass, which was drained, and wondered how many he'd had.

When he spoke again, I looked back to him.

"Bierman. Like you guessed. Told me to tell Sandy to keep her shit together or her consequence would be everyone across the globe knowing she has a birthmark on her ass. Also told me to end it with her. And last, he told me if my resignation wasn't on Lloyd's desk by Monday, that picture," he jerked his head to the envelope, "was going to be all over the Internet."

I did not get this.

So I asked, "Why does he want you to resign?"

"Because he's a dick," Heath answered.

The way he opened our discussion came back to me.

"Are you resigning?"

"Fuck no," he clipped, and I blinked.

He was swinging Sandy out there.

What a jerk!

"You're gonna put your woman out there?" Benny stated my thoughts, but he did it incredulously, like that idea was so foreign to him he couldn't process it, and I remembered (not that I'd ever forget) how much I love Benny Bianchi.

Benny Bianchi had a lot of my love, but he would earn more in the coming exchange.

"I'm not lettin' some twat strong-arm me into quitting my fucking job," Heath declared. "And she's not my woman."

"Your dick been in her mouth more than once?" Benny asked.

"Not that it's your business, but yeah," Heath bit out.

"Then she's your woman," Ben decreed.

I grinned and leaned into him, wrapping my hands around his bicep and murmuring, "You're so awesome."

He tipped his head to look down at me. "Babe, you wanna focus?"

I kept grinning and murmuring when I said, "Right," let him go, and looked back to Heath.

Heath was staring at us, and when he got both our attention, he announced, "I think I'm gonna throw up."

"I failed to introduce you two," I said, ignoring his remark. "Heath, this is my boyfriend, Benny Bianchi, master pizza maker, super protective Italian hot guy, and man who knows how to treat a woman." I looked up to Ben. "Ben, Heath. A man who gives all us salespeople a bad name."

"Jesus, I didn't ask you here to give me shit," Heath said.

"You didn't *ask* me here at all," I pointed out as Benny asked over me, "Why *did* you ask her here?"

Another shrug. "Colleagues and shit. She tried to do me a solid, I threw it in her face. She should know," Heath told him.

"The guy tell you he'd give you the photos if you resign?" Benny kept at him.

"No. He said I wouldn't see them on the Internet if I resigned."

"He keeps it and knows you'll fold, he pulls it out anytime he needs somethin' from you," Benny guessed.

"If I did something as weak as resign, I wouldn't be around for him to blackmail me," Heath returned.

"You'd probably go to another pharma and then who knows what he would expect from you," Benny wisely pointed out.

"Then it's good I'm gonna call his bluff," Heath fired back.

"Resign," Ben replied firmly, and Heath's eyes narrowed.

"Dude, I do not *know* you. I didn't ask you here. I do not want you here. And I sure as fuck am not gonna take career advice from you."

It was then Benny lost patience and pinned Heath with his eyes.

"Right now, two Chicago wise guys are workin' over the PI who took that picture. They'll have all he has on you probably within half an hour so he won't have it to hold over you. And word on this guy is, he's a big fan of piggybacking his clients' blackmail attempts. The next couple of days, the rest will be collected. You resign. Shit goes down. Things are explained, including why you resigned. A week, two, you'll have your job back."

Heath's head twitched when Ben started talking, and he was staring with his mouth open when Benny quit.

He pulled himself together to whisper, "Fuck me, you're in the mob?"

"Not me, not even close. But Frankie has connections, so heads up on that, I wouldn't fuck her over," Ben told him.

Heath's eyes near on bugged out of his head and I had to swallow a giggle. Since it was such a big giggle, it wasn't easy, and I almost choked on it.

But Ben wasn't done.

"She's got your back, and by that, I'm thinkin' she more has the woman you won't claim as yours back, but you get to enjoy that protection. Just resign. It'll all be good."

"How can I be assured of that?" Heath pressed.

"You can't," Ben returned. "You just gotta trust that not everyone in this world is an asshole out for themselves like you are."

I couldn't stop that giggle and Heath turned his scowl at me.

I waved a hand, forced myself to sober, and said, "Sorry, sorry. Inappropriate."

"You gonna fuck me?" he asked.

"What I'm gonna do is make sure Sandy doesn't get fucked, which means I have to do the same for you. So, no. I'm not gonna fuck you," I told him.

Heath's eyes narrowed. "You know why Bierman wants me out?"

"You aren't gonna know that," Ben took back the conversation, though I didn't know, neither did Benny. But obviously Ben had made the decision that we weren't sharing the rest with a jerk like Heath.

Heath looked to him. "Why not?"

"Your protection," Benny said.

"That's jacked," Heath bit out. "It's my ass on the line."

It was then I knew Ben was done.

I knew this when he stated, "Okay, I'm hungry. I don't wanna be here with you. I wanna be home with my woman and my dog, so this is the gig. It's lost on you but bigger shit is at play here and whatever your part in it is small. So we don't have time to jack around with you. You either trust Frankie or you don't. But I'll tell you something, you go in the office Monday morning without your resignation typed out in order to take the back of the woman who's warmin' your bed, you are not a man. You're a dick, a weasel, and a douche. That play you make is gonna be on you. And it might not fuck with your head but I cannot imagine how it wouldn't that the woman you toss right in front of the bus is gonna pay for your ambition and probably have men say shit and even do shit to her that she won't deserve. It could even put her in jeopardy because they saw that out there."

He tilted his head to the envelope on the table and kept talking.

"But I'll know, and Frankie will know, and your woman will know, and she'll live the rest of her life wishin' she not only never went down on you but never saw your face. You're willin' to do that to her, you can live with that, right. But you can, you're one serious dick, a huge-ass weasel, and a total fuckin' douche."

Ben said his piece and we were gone. He pulled me right out of the booth, the bar, and took me straight to my car.

He backed me into it and ordered, "You lead home. I'll follow."

"That was awesome," I replied.

His lips quirked, but he said, "I'm not out of your rearview."

"And *you're* awesome," I kept at it.

That got me a grin, but he asked, "Frankie, you hear me?"

"How hungry are you?" I asked back.

"I worked out after lunch so that's long gone."

This surprised me.

"Where did you work out?"

"Is this information you need before you drive home?"

"No, except for the fact that if you're really *truly* hungry, that'll be a bummer, because if you weren't, I was *so* going down on you the minute we got home."

"I could wait to eat."

I smiled up at him and did it for a long time.

"But not for three hours while you stand there bein' a goof because I'm awesome," he finished.

"I love you, Benny Bianchi," I blurted.

"Fuck," he muttered, then bent his head, laid a hot, heavy, wet, *long* one on me that ended with my arms around his shoulders, one hand in his fabulous hair, and one of his hands on my ass before he lifted his head, pulled out of my arms, turned me, smacked my ass, and said, "Get home."

He took a step back and stared pointedly at my door.

I took a deep breath to calm my heart and settle my system before I dug out my key, unlocked my door, and headed home to give my man a blowjob.

And, after that, feed him.

Twenty-Three

FUCKING FINALLY

I woke up when I felt Benny's hand moving down my belly.

"Baby," I whispered drowsily.

That was when I felt the tips of his fingers sliding into the edge of my panties, his other hand pushing under me, and his body shifting at my back so he could bury his face in my neck.

When he got it there, he growled, "Quiet, Francesca, and don't move."

I felt my vagina convulse at the same time it got wet.

Okay, it can be said that waking up with Benny Bianchi was my favorite part of the day. For a variety of reasons.

One of those reasons became apparent when his middle finger hit my clit at the same time his other hand curled around my breast and his lips slid up my neck. I knew he wasn't messing around when he put his thumb and finger to my nipple and tugged.

Hard.

This felt so good it made me push my hips into his crotch. Feeling him hard, a whimper slid out of me.

Ben nipped the skin of my neck with his teeth before he said, "Don't move, baby."

"I gotta move."

"Don't," he ordered roughly, pressing his cock into my ass.

Oh God. This was hot.

I quit moving. Ben played. He pulled and twisted. He swirled and pressed. He nipped, licked, sucked, kissed. All while I lay there trying not to move.

It wasn't easy, and with each passing second, I got wetter, more turned on, and it got more difficult.

Finally, it got so difficult, I whispered on a plea, "Benny."

"What you want?" he asked.

"Your cock, baby."

"How you want it?"

"Any way you wanna give it to me."

"Pull your panties down, Frankie."

I did what he ordered immediately, hooking my thumb into one side of my panties and yanking down. Ben gave me what I needed almost instantly. He thrust inside.

"*God*," I breathed.

Ben twisted my nipple, circled a finger at my clit, and drove deep.

"Fuck, you're wet," he groaned into my neck, pounding in hard, fast, rough, so much of all three, my body jolted with each thrust.

"Harder, Benny," I begged.

Without delay, he rolled into me, taking me to my stomach, still inside. I had to spread my legs wide and my panties stretched to the limit, biting into my thighs in a way I liked. All this so amazing, I felt a tremor rock through my entire body.

Then he yanked my hips up, even as he kept thrusting deep. He reached over me, his hand went into my hair, fisted and tugged back.

God.

Hotter.

"Up, baby," he demanded.

I pushed up to my hands and he gave my hair another tug so I knew he wanted me *up*.

I straightened and the minute I was up, he ordered, "Nightie off."

I moved my hands to the hem of my nightie and pulled it off.

I got my reward immediately as Benny's hands roamed over my skin.

I knew he was watching his hands move when he muttered into my neck, "Fuckin' beautiful," even as he kept taking me.

"Need your finger, honey," I told him.

"Had you last night, babe. Got it in me for this to last awhile. Don't want to take you there too soon."

He might have it in him, but he was driving me the good kind of crazy so I didn't have it in me.

"I'm already close," I shared.

He drove in, stayed there, but grinded up.

I liked that, being filled with him, Ben pushing deeper. I liked it so much I moaned.

His hand slid down and covered my sex as his other one glided up my breastbone to wrap light around my throat.

"Could fuck you for hours," he murmured into my skin.

It was Saturday morning, a weekend. The day after a, thankfully, uneventful Friday, the weekend that might precede work-related Armageddon, and I decided right then on our plans for the day.

"Okay, then do that now."

"Could fall asleep buried inside you."

I felt my thighs quiver.

"Wake up, first thing I do before I even open my eyes, start fuckin' you," he went on.

My hands went to his wrists and held on as my womb spasmed at his words. I figured he didn't have to move to take me there, he just had to keep talking to me.

He glided out and slid slowly back in. "Love this pussy."

Okay, maybe he needed to move.

"Ben, baby."

His hand trailed from my throat down my body. "Love this body."

"Please, Benny, fuck me."

He nipped my earlobe with his teeth, moved his mouth to my ear, and whispered, "Love my baby."

I did a top-to-toe shiver.

I was wrong. All he had to do was keep talking to me.

"Benny," I breathed.

"Down, Frankie. I'm gonna give you what you need."

I bent double, forearms to the mattress, and Ben bent over me. One hand on the bed for added leverage and power, he gave me what I needed.

When I found it, my climax pounding through me as Ben kept pounding inside me, he kept giving it to me until I started to come down. Then he pulled out, dropped to his back, yanked me over him, and caught my eyes.

"Take me there, Frankie."

I held his gaze as I quickly slid my panties off, lifted up, and straddled him. I wrapped my hand around his cock, guided him inside, and kept hold of his eyes as I rode him fast.

"Want it again?" he asked, watching me move on him, the look on his face lazy but heated.

I loved that look.

But...

Was he crazy?

"Yes," I gasped on a downward plunge.

He grinned and moved his hand so his thumb was strategically placed. It took a while, but I found it again. Driving down, riding him through my orgasm, my head thrown back, one hand at my belly and the other one cupping a breast, I felt his hands clamp tight around my hips. He yanked me down, held me down, bucked his hips up, groaned, and I knew he found it.

I collapsed on top of him, my hair flying everywhere, I knew, but I didn't care. Two orgasms first thing in the morning, I didn't care about anything.

He slid his hands from my hips to wrap his arms around me, one going higher to gather my hair at the side of my neck.

Turning his head, he whispered, "Love you, Francesca Concetti."

I felt my lips tip up and made the Herculean effort to raise my head and look into his eyes.

It was worth the effort.

Seeing those beautiful eyes happy and satisfied was worth any effort.

"Love you back, Benny Bianchi."

He kept my hair gathered at my neck, even as he extended a thumb to stroke my jaw and asked, "You want donuts?"

Oh yes, I loved Benny Bianchi.

"Absolutely," I answered.

He grinned. "Good, babe. Kiss me. Climb off me. We'll walk Gus and then we'll go to Hilligoss."

"Can you walk Gus, then go get donuts while I stay here and make coffee?" I requested, using these words to mean, *Can you walk Gus, then go get donuts while I stay here, bask in my orgasms, and maybe have a short snooze?*

I suspected Benny knew my translation, but he still asked, "You want that?"

"Yeah," I answered.

"You got it, but I get the kissing part."

I smiled at him because I got to kiss him, and also because he was Benny. He was awesome. And he was demonstrating his awesomeness this time by giving me my way, hauling himself out of bed, taking care of our dog, and getting donuts while I got to be lazy.

I was bending my head to give him the kissing part when my phone on the nightstand started ringing.

I turned my head that way as Ben ordered, "Ignore it."

Since I liked that idea better, I did as ordered.

Mid-kiss, my phone stopped ringing. Then Ben took over the kiss and it became a makeout session, where I found myself on my back with Benny mostly on me. This lasted a happy while until my phone rang again.

Ben broke the kiss, and this time it was him that looked to my phone.

"Ignore it," I repeated his order.

He looked down at me. "Two calls in five minutes on a Saturday morning?"

"I'm indisposed," I replied. "That being I've got panty marks around my thighs. My panties are fubared since they were stretched so tight, the elastic is probably broken. You're leaking out of me. And you have our dog to walk and powdered sugar, chocolate-cream-filled donuts, three of them at least, to go out and buy for me. All that being the definition of *indisposed.*"

My phone stopped ringing as Benny's brows rose, his eyes lighting with humor, giving me that, and fulfilling promise-part-three of the day and we hadn't even been awake an hour.

He did all this asking, "Fubared?"

"Fucked up beyond recognition," I explained.

"I know what it means, honey," he replied. "I just didn't know anyone outside Tango and Cash said it."

I felt my eyes get squinty. "Don't make fun of me when I'm post-orgasm. I'm happy-drained when I'm post-orgasm and I don't have any good fight in me."

Ben grinned. "You should never have given me that, baby. Knowin' that shit, from now on, I'm totally fuckin' with you post-orgasm."

My eyes got squintier before I informed him of something he should know by now, "I recover quickly."

His hand glided over my hip, back, and in to cup my ass as his face got closer to mine. "Bet I can set you back."

He so totally could.

"Gus? Donuts?" I prompted.

"Is your detail on which donuts you want me to buy your order?" he asked.

"Yep," I answered.

"They run out of those quick, Frankie."

"Wait for them to make more."

He didn't grin that time. He smiled.

Then he said, "I might be pussy-whipped, honey, but I'm not that far gone."

I felt my brows shoot up. "You're pussy-whipped?"

"Babe, I'm makin' deals with Sal, away from my home, my restaurant, watchin' your ass while you go about something undoubtedly worthwhile but makes me all kinds of uneasy, and you're surprised I'm pussy-whipped?"

He had a point, and although his words gave me a heady feeling of power, they also bothered me.

So I wrapped my arms around him and reminded him, "We're doin' this with Wyler because it's the right thing to do."

"We are. We're also doin' it because I like to fuck you, eat you, and watch you ride me, and I can get all that, and often, I keep you happy."

Suddenly, I didn't feel bothered.

I felt annoyed.

"That's it?"

"There's also the fact I like lookin' at you, seein' you smile, and doin' what I can to make you happy. It's insane, but I've learned to own the insanity because you're you. You're crazy. Fearless. Willin' to put yourself out there doin' something you know is dangerous because it's the right thing to do. And I love all of you. The insane part is that I love all of you, including that."

I screwed up my face and declared, "You're being sweet again when I'm annoyed."

He lowered his lips to mine, eyes still smiling. "You gotta learn to get over it, baby. It's gonna happen a lot."

I got over it right then because I had the happy feeling he was going to kiss me again, but he didn't because my phone rang.

This time, we both turned our heads to it.

"Fuck," Ben muttered, reaching across the bed and tagging it. He looked to the display, then to me, his face unreadable when he said, "Cat."

That could mean anything from the happy news she was carrying Art's baby to the news that she fell off the wagon, got arrested for doing something stupid, and needed someone to bail her out.

Ben knew this and that was why his face was unreadable.

I slid my phone from his hand and took the call.

When I had the cell at my ear, I said, "Love you, but you're delaying donuts."

"Frankie," she whispered.

Oh God.

At the tone of her voice, my eyes flew to Benny as I pushed up to sitting. He rolled off to let me do that, and I didn't tear my eyes away from him as I sat on a hip, pulling the covers to my chest and holding the phone tight to my ear.

"What?" I asked.

There was a moment of silence before she said, "Okay, last night was a bad night."

Hoping her bad night did not include downing shots of vodka and committing felonies, my hand snaked out and pressed into Ben's chest. The second it did, he sat up and wrapped his arms around me, pulling me into his warmth, trapping my hand between us.

"What?" I whispered, my eyes now to Ben's throat.

"Okay, the, um…slightly-better-but-still-bad news first."

Slightly better but still bad?

"Cat…"

"Davey found out that Nat was cheating on him again. They fought... really bad, Frankie. *Really* bad. He said he was done, and I guess he did it in a way where he meant it this time because she lost it. Started beating on him. He hit her back. She called the cops. He's all messed up. Even has a concussion 'cause she hit him in the head with a plate or something. He took a lot from her, Frankie, before he lost it. He hit her once to get her off him, but he's the one in jail."

I closed my eyes.

"He didn't press charges," she continued, "but she did. His mom called me. That's how I know all this. She's pissed, Frankie. She knows Davey's been eatin' shit for years and she's seriously pissed. And making matters worse, Ma's there."

Oh no.

I opened my eyes, saw Benny's face, and for the first time in a long time, seeing it didn't soothe me.

"She was out carousin', not there for the fight, got there after the police got there. She texted me a few days ago, said I was dead to her because I wasn't pickin' up her calls to help her in her hour of need. Guess that's why she's with Nat and Davey. But according to Davey's mom, she's all up in his and Nat's shit, talkin' smack about Davey. Davey's mom wants the charges dropped and Nat and Ninette outta the house, and she wants that yesterday."

"Cat, I—" I started, but she cut me off, talking quietly.

"I can't get dragged into this, Frankie. I'm late."

My heart thumped and she kept talking.

"Just a couple of days, but I'm always regular. Art and me were gonna spend our Saturday getting a pregnancy test and hopefully celebrating. All this..." She stopped speaking and I actually heard her take in a huge breath before she went on, "And there's more that happened last night so all I wanna do is skip the pregnancy test and get a bottle of vodka."

Shit.

No.

"Don't do that, honey," I urged.

"I know, but it's hard."

"Get the pregnancy test," I said, then took my own deep breath and finished, "I'll call Nat."

Ben's arms tightening around me brought my eyes to his face. He was worried. But hearing Nat's name, he was already pissed.

I shook my head.

He shook his back.

"I haven't told you the more," Cat said in my ear.

Goddammit.

I looked to Ben's ear and invited, "Sock it to me."

"Chrissy kicked Dad out last night."

"Fuck," I whispered.

"Yeah," she agreed. "He called me, looking for a place to crash. I kept my boundaries and he lost it on me, you know, like Dad can do when he doesn't get his way made easy for him."

"Yeah, I know how Dad can do that," I agreed because I so totally did.

"He said all his kids but Enzo were pains in his ass and he never wanted to hear from me again. Then he said he was goin' to Enzo."

"Oh my God," I breathed into the phone. Just the thought of Enzo *Uno* and *Due* together and the havoc they could wreak made my blood pressure spike.

"Yeah. Just uppin' stakes, leaving Chrissy with a new baby, and heading to where Enzo is fuckin' up his own life and all the lives of the people in it."

This was not good, but I was confused.

"How is Nat's deal slightly better bad news than Dad's?"

"Well, 'cause Dad told me Chrissy was fucked since she didn't work and he was shot of her. Didn't need her shit. She may have kicked him out, but that doesn't mean she isn't livin' in his house. He says he's puttin' it on the market so that means Chrissy is jobless, soon to be homeless, and has our new baby sister."

God. My dad.

"Did Dad say anything about Minnie?" I asked.

"Not a word."

Fucking Dad.

I looked from Ben's ear into his eyes and told Cat, "All right, leave it to me."

Ben went from looking slightly worried and slightly pissed to looking mostly pissed as he clipped, "Jesus, Frankie."

"What are you gonna do?" Cat asked me.

"I have no clue, but I'll figure out something."

"Sal Giglia owe you a marker?" she queried.

Not hardly.

"No," I answered.

"Too bad. I figure he has the skills to put the fear of God into anybody, even Nat, Ma, and Dad."

She was probably right.

Still, I wasn't going to sic Sal on my family. Not because they didn't deserve it. Because Benny and I already had him coming to our wedding. We didn't need him forcing us to let him pay for it and giving me away.

"Go get your pregnancy test. No vodka. And call me back after you get done celebrating."

"Frankie, you always eat this shit and—"

"Go," I said quietly but firmly. "You need to focus on what's important, Cat, and their shit isn't important. Your husband, your marriage, you building a family is important. Get that pregnancy test. I'll send good vibes your way."

She said nothing for long moments. Then she said, "Right. I'll let you give me that, but only in a way that you're up first. I'll do my thing with the test and Art. Then you call me in if you need me, Frankie."

"You're on the right path," I reminded her. "Stay on it."

"These people are fucked up and they drive me crazy. But they're my family, too, Frankie. You've spent three and a half decades sorting their shit. Now it's my turn to kick in."

I felt those words, all of them, so deep and so warm and so welcome, I closed my eyes again and turned my head.

Ben lifted a hand and curled it around the side of my neck, so I opened my eyes and looked back at him.

Not pissed anymore, or at least not totally. Back to slightly worried.

I shook my head and gave him a small smile.

This didn't change his expression in the slightest.

"We got a plan?" Cat prompted in my ear.

"This doesn't sort out soon and you can't hack it, you back off. If you agree to that," I told her, "then we have a plan."

She hesitated only a second before she said, "We got a plan."

"Good," I replied businesslike. "Now, call me later with good news."

"I hope I can, Frankie."

"I hope so too, honey."

"Don't let them make you eat more shit than you're already gonna eat," she ordered.

"I probably would," I returned, still looking in Benny's eyes. "But Ben won't let me."

"Fuckin' finally," she muttered, and that made me grin. "Later, Frankie."

"Later, Cat."

We disconnected and I barely hit the button on my phone when Ben practically barked, "*What?*"

I reached to the nightie laying half on, half draped off the bed, saying, "Concetti drama."

"You don't got enough drama goin' on right now?" he asked, making an excellent point.

He let me go so I could pull the nightie on and I looked back to him. "Benny—"

He shook his head. "Get outta bed. Clean up. Put on clothes. Fill me in while we walk Gus. Then your ass is in my truck so we can get donuts. We're doin' what *we* wanna do with our Saturday morning. After I get a donut in my baby, *then* those whackjobs you call a family can try to take their piece of you."

"But, Ben—"

"*Try*," he cut me off to say with emphasis. "I'm close while you talk to their asses, and if I get a fuckin' *hint* they're slicin' into you, I take over."

I stared at him.

Fucking finally.

Cat was right.

She was so right.

That was why I gave in, saying, "Okay, baby. Now, let's go take care of Gus."

I saw surprise start to slide through Benny's expression, but I didn't stop to watch the whole show. Gus needed out of the kennel. I needed to give him a cuddle. I also needed donuts. I further needed my man to have donuts.

Only then would I deal with my family while I had someone at my back.

Fucking finally.

I had three donuts in my belly, only two that were powdered sugar, chocolate-cream-filled.

Ben was right. They ran out of those quickly and we got the last three. I loved my man so I sacrificed one for him. The third donut in my belly was a cinnamon twist, but I ate it first.

I was staring at my phone in my hand resting on the counter. I did this until I saw Benny slide a fresh cup of coffee on the counter beside my hand. This meant I did it the whole time he was topping off our cups.

I turned my head and lifted my eyes to his.

"I have no clue what to do," I told him.

He finished taking a sip of coffee and replied, "Not surprised."

"You're not?"

"Nope."

I guessed he wouldn't be. There was so much to it, it was like a mountain that needed to be climbed without rope or those spiky things on your shoes.

"I don't only have no clue what to do, I don't even know where to start," I shared.

Ben leaned a hip against the counter. "Not surprised about that either."

"What would you do?" I asked.

"That's the reason I'm not surprised," he answered. "'Cause what I'd do is let them deal with their own shit. They made their beds, they can lie in them."

I shook my head and protested, "But Davey just fell in love with my sister and got a shitload of problems in return."

"And how is that him not makin' his bed?"

I blinked.

Benny kept talking.

"If she pulled one over on him when they first got hooked up, I could get that. But he's taken her ass back repeatedly after she let other guys tap it. That's his decision. He needed to man up about five years ago. He didn't. Now he's in custody because he's got no balls. That's his problem. What I don't get is why you or Cat would make it yours."

"He's family and he's a nice guy," I explained.

"Yeah, he's a nice guy, but he's a weak man," Ben returned. "The second part of that is not on you. It's on him. Their relationship has been cruisin' toward disaster in one form or another since they got together. Frankly, I'm relieved that when it blew up, it did it this way rather than takin' other people down with it."

"But he's been arrested!" I snapped.

Ben leaned into me. "Not. Your. Problem."

"Do you think it's that simple?" I asked.

"Absolutely," he answered.

"Then what about Chrissy and Domino?" I pushed.

He leaned back. "Babe, she hooked her star to a man old enough to be her father."

"That's judgmental," I informed him sharply, and his brows drew together.

"How?"

"You can't control who you fall in love with."

"Nope," he stated. "And love may be blind, but anybody's gotta guard against bein' stupid. He had one marriage decades ago, a string of women in between that didn't work, children he barely saw, and when he did, they fought like teenagers and got their asses kicked out. If she didn't see all the writing on that wall, again, that isn't your problem."

"A baby is mixed up in that, Ben," I reminded him.

"Yeah. And she let a man his age with his history knock her up. Again, not your problem."

I put my phone on the counter and my hands on my hips. "That baby is my sister."

He held my eyes a moment before he muttered, "That might be our problem."

"Right," I hissed.

"Though," he went on, "I haven't seen you showin' me picture after picture she texted you of your new sister, and I haven't heard you talk about all the invitations to get to know her that you couldn't accept 'cause you live too far away."

"I have a feeling Chrissy might have been more involved with bein' a new mom and dealin' with my dad," I returned sarcastically.

"I figure your feelin' is right. Still. Doesn't cancel out what I said," he retorted.

"Every human being has to have compassion and try to be understanding, and that goes double for people who share your blood," I shot back.

Suddenly, I had Benny's hand curled around the side of my neck. He used it to pull me toward him as he dipped his head down so his face was close to mine.

"And that's why I love you so fuckin' much," he declared, and when he did and the way he did, his voice not deep and easy but rough with feeling, I felt my breath catch.

He wasn't done.

"Not because you're crazy-beautiful. Not because you're fuckin' great in bed. Not because I like the way you dress, do your hair, turn yourself out to go walk the dog like most women would to go to a club. Not because you make me laugh and you don't take my shit. Not because you wanna organize my office and can make even tuna casserole taste spectacular. Because of all that and the fact you give a shit about everybody. Even people who don't deserve it. You give enough of a shit that you put yourself out there for them. You feel deep. You give everything you got. And the best part of all that, you got a lot to give and you give most of it to me."

I stared into his eyes that were burning into mine, feeling his words burrow into me, digging deep, planting themselves inside in a way that I knew I'd not only remember them forever, I'd remember how I felt right that moment for the rest of my life.

"So, you gotta wade into this shit," he continued, "do it. It's gonna piss you off and that's gonna piss me off, but I'm here for you to rant at and I'm here to make the decision when you're done takin' their shit. So, babe, you gotta wade in, make your first call. My advice, Chrissy. Nat and Davey are adults and should know by now how to sort their own shit or wallow in it. Chrissy's got a new baby and she's probably freaked."

I didn't nod, lift my phone, and call Chrissy.

I asked, "Do you know why I love you?"

The intensity of his eyes changed. It didn't fade, it kept burning strong, just the emotion behind it shifted.

"Yeah," he replied. "Because I'm awesome."

"No," I whispered. "Because you're everything a man should be."

His fingers at my neck gripped tighter as his lips murmured, "Jesus."

"For the first time in my life, the words 'I love you' aren't strong enough," I told him.

He pulled me an inch closer and ordered, "Stop talking, Frankie."

I didn't stop talking. He needed to hear what I had to say.

No.

He deserved to hear it.

"You saved me. Not just when I got shot. When I got shot and you carried me out of there and got me to a place where they could fix me and then you didn't give up on me. Instead, you gave me family. You showed me it was okay to be me. You gave me you. You gave me *everything.*"

"Shut it, Frankie."

"I lost your brother and it broke me. If I ever lost you, I wouldn't be able to go on."

I heard Benny's coffee mug hit the counter before he lifted his other hand, put it to my neck, and slid both back and into my hair as he tilted his forehead to rest on mine, his eyes now scorching with a depth of feeling he let me read.

Then he said, "Francesca, do not say that shit."

I ignored him and kept going. "I'd breathe. I'd eat. I might one day laugh again. But I wouldn't be living. There is no life for me without you."

He was done telling me to shut it and I knew this when his head slanted, his fingers dug into my scalp, and his mouth landed hard on mine. His lips opened, mine did the same, his tongue thrust inside, and I wrapped my arms tight around him, pressing close, tipping my head back to give him more. To give him everything. To use that kiss to show him every word I said was true. To make him feel it. Believe it. All in way he'd never forget it.

Because he deserved that too.

It took a long time for me to do this, which meant we made out in my kitchen until Gus attacked the wraparound tie strap dangling from my high-heeled sandals. Unfortunately, he did this in a way I couldn't ignore, mostly because his puppy teeth started digging into the flesh of my ankle.

I still held on after I broke the kiss and looked down at our dog. The cute puppy Benny gave me for my birthday, who would grow up to be a sweet dog we would walk and pet and cuddle, who would give us love, and who would probably let our kids play with him, even if it drove him crazy.

That was when I felt the tears start to wet my eyes.

The promise of Benny. Every day. Everywhere. It was always with me.

I lifted and shook my foot, saying softly, "No, baby."

Gus didn't give up until I bent my leg back to get my strap out of reach. At that, he collapsed on his ass, and panting, looked up at me.

"Shoes are off-limits," I told him, and as I did, Ben's hands slid out of my hair and down my back so he could wrap his arms around me.

Gus panted some more, then got up and waddled toward the rug I had in front of the sink. He latched on with his teeth, and jerking his head side to side, growling at it, he dragged it out of the kitchen.

"Babe," Ben called. I took in a deep breath to control the tears and looked up at him.

God, he was beautiful.

My Benny.

He took one arm from around me so he could cup my jaw in his hand.

"I'll save the rug," he offered. "You call Chrissy."

I nodded.

He didn't move.

Neither did I.

"You good?" he finally asked.

"I'm the best I've ever been," I answered.

His fingers curled deeper into my skin before he demanded, "Stop bein' so sweet. You don't, I'll have to fuck you on the kitchen floor and then we'll have to go out and buy a new rug."

"I'm done with that rug," I told him. Then to take us out of the sweet and heavy because we both needed that, I kept the information flowing, "I'm also done with your kitchen rug. When I move in, we're gettin' all new kitchen stuff. Towels, rugs, potholders. That is, after you paint it butter yellow and put in new tile. Backsplashes *and* floor."

His hand relaxed, as did his expression, and his lips tipped up. "I'm doin' all that?"

"You have linoleum," I reminded him.

"You got a problem with linoleum?"

Was he crazy?

"Uh…yeah."

His lip tip turned into a grin. "Then my baby gets new tile. But even if that rug is bein' retired, Gus doesn't need to do that by eatin' it."

I nodded my head and remarked, "We have enough on our plate that a trip to the vet would tip us over the edge."

"Yeah," Benny agreed.

I gave him a squeeze. "Okay, you get Gus. I'll call Chrissy."

He nodded before he dipped his head, and I held my breath at the exquisite feeling of Benny skimming the tip of my nose with his before he returned my squeeze and let me go.

I decided to take a fortifying sip of coffee before calling Chrissy. This also afforded me the opportunity to watch Ben walk out of the kitchen. Then I leaned over the counter to watch him get in a tug-of-war with Gus over the rug.

Ben won.

Although not surprising, Gus felt the consolation prize was attacking the hems of Benny's jeans as he walked back into the kitchen with my rug. This was cute. It was cuter when Ben bent over, grabbed Gus, brought him up, and held him, doggie nose to hot guy nose.

"No rugs. No jeans. You got chew toys, bud," he told the dog, then finished with, "Let's go get one."

He then tucked the puppy under his arm and sauntered out. I watched Ben's ass move, alternately watching Gus's booty swaying with his wagging tail, and I watched this until they disappeared down the hall.

It was a good show and a nice reprieve.

But I was me.

I could delay no further. I had loved ones to sort out.

So I put my cup down, grabbed my phone, and found Chrissy's number.

"Thought I was dead to you."

This was Nat's greeting.

Obviously, I was on my second call.

Shockingly, the first one went great.

Dad was done with Chrissy probably only because Chrissy was done with Dad.

And during the call, she had declared, "He'll sell this house before I move out and get situated over my dead body."

I took this to mean he'd sell it over his dead body, because if he tried that shit, she'd kill him.

I was learning that Chrissy was no pushover. She was smart, and even if she fell in love with the wrong guy, she was a new mom who doted on her baby, thus, she had her priorities straight.

"Anyway, Frankie, I do hair. It's not hard to find a job doin' hair," she'd told me. "And my clients are all dyin' to have me back. I mean, I didn't wanna go back to work so soon but…whatever. And my mom will watch Eva. Mom wasn't a big fan of Enzo's, but she adores Eva. It's cool you called to check in, but it'll all be okay."

Eva, by the way, was Domino. Dad had gotten to the birth certificate first and named her the name he wanted. A name Chrissy had told him (in a way she told me could not be misconstrued) that there was no way in hell she was naming her daughter Domino.

This was not the beginning of the end of them, but it definitely (and not surprisingly) was a factor.

My baby sister's middle name was Eva, which was what Chrissy called her and wanted everyone else to call her.

Eva was very pretty, but weirdly, I'd become partial to Minnie.

I didn't tell Chrissy this.

I just silently marveled at her togetherness as I told her I was there for her as best I could be while I lived in the 'burg, but I'd be around more to help out when I was back in Chicago.

She'd thanked me, told me to come around and meet Eva when I was home again, and promised to send me pictures of my new sister. After we hung up, she made good on that promise in about a nanosecond by texting me fifteen of them.

Fifteen.

Eva was adorable.

Even Benny thought so.

The easy one down, the hard one to go.

And at my sister's greeting, I realized I should have fortified myself with another donut (or two) before I got to the hard stuff.

"Nat—" I began but was cut off.

"Got enough shit swirlin' around me, don't need yours."

"Please, listen to me."

"He *hit* me," she snapped.

I had to admit, I didn't like this, even as I had to admit in knowing Nat that she probably gave him no choice.

Needing a dose of him, I looked across the counter to where Benny was lounging on the couch, feet up on my coffee table, TV on, and tuned to a game, but his eyes were on me.

And this time, I felt soothed.

"Cat told me you clocked him with a plate," I said to Nat.

"It wasn't a plate. It was a vase. And he deserved that shit."

God. My sister.

I shook my head and looked down to the counter, asking, "He deserved that because you cheated on him and he's finally done with you?"

"Okay, which part of me not needin' your shit did you not understand?" she asked sharply.

"Has it occurred to you you're cuttin' me off from discussin' this with you because you don't want me holdin' that mirror up to your face?"

"And what is it, oh wise Frankie, that you think you're gonna make me see?" she returned snottily.

I was used to Nat's snotty and I'd learned to ignore it, give it back, or get in there another way.

This was important enough for me to find another way.

So when I replied, I did it quietly.

"The image of a woman who's in love with a man she's done wrong."

Nat said nothing.

I kept going.

"Davey's a good man and he loves you. He does not deserve this, Nat. And as fucked up as it was how we were brought up, I know deep down somewhere inside you, you know at least that."

"So he can hit me?" she asked.

"Did he haul off and do that to hurt you, or did he do it because he had no choice?"

"Does it matter?"

"Well, if you live in black-and-white, no. It doesn't matter. But if you hit him in the head with a vase and gave him a concussion, then didn't let up on him and you'd lost it like I know you can lose it so he did it in self-defense, that's pretty gray. So, no. He can't hit you. But if you're whalin' on him and he's got no choice but to take it and further damage or get physical to get you off him, it sucks to say it, but he can."

My sister had no reply.

So I pushed, "Did he have a choice?"

She remained silent.

"Natalia, did he have a choice?"

"I never thought Davey would hit me."

I went still at her words and the way she said them. All but my head, which I lifted, my eyes flying to Benny, who was still watching me.

I could tell by her voice that she was hurt, probably not physically, but emotionally.

Nat didn't show a lot of emotion. She was Ninette times a thousand. The only thing she wanted was whatever she wanted and nothing dragging on that. That didn't mean she didn't have emotion. It just meant she'd learned a long time ago not to show it.

I felt for my sister. This was her consequence for being selfish and stupid, but I knew she loved Davey in her way. And being Nat, tied up in herself and only that, it would take a miracle to get her to see beyond that and to her part in this fucked-up scenario.

I had to force my lips to move when I said, "Nat, honey, please, *please*, listen. Cat and Art have cleaned up. They've been sober for a long time. They've been workin' with a marriage counselor to get strong before they make a baby. I have Benny and I'm happy. He's good to me and he's good for me. I learned not to look for Dad, and Cat learned not to act like Mom.

We're both happy. Now you need to learn from that. Sort yourself out. This is not okay what you've been doin' to Davey. And this is *really* not okay, what happened with Davey last night."

"No matter what you say, Frankie, there's no excuse for your man hittin' you."

"Is there one for a man's woman hittin' him?" I shot back.

She didn't reply.

"Okay, I know you know the answer to that is a big, fat no. So now, tell me this, is it okay for a man's wife to keep fuckin' around on him?" I asked.

"This is you givin' me shit, Frankie," she returned.

"This is shit you need, Nat," I replied.

"No, 'cause see, I got his fuckin' mother up in my shit and Ninette's up in her shit and the phone won't stop fuckin' ringin'. I gotta work tonight and I don't need more hassle. You're hassle. So you're wrong. I don't need your shit because my life is pretty fuckin' shit right now and I'm not lettin' you make it more."

I opened my mouth to speak, but the dead I got over the phone couldn't be anything other than her hanging up on me.

Still, I called, "Nat?" But I got nothing.

I closed my eyes, took the phone from my ear, and saw the call had ended.

I looked back at Benny. "She hung up on me."

"The wrong answer to say is 'good,' but that's the only one I got, babe."

"I don't know what to do next," I told him.

"Nothin'," he told me. "You tried. You gave her good wisdom, Francesca. The shit you said was right on the money. She didn't listen. You did what you could do, but she wants to wallow in her shit. The hard part starts for you now 'cause you gotta let her."

"Ninette is livin' with her and that's not gonna make anything better," I reminded him.

"Another consequence. She let her ma in, she deals."

"Maybe I should call Ma and—"

Benny interrupted me, clipping out, "Do not even think about it."

I shut my mouth. Apparently, Ninette was where Benny drew the line at my family "slicin' into me."

"Come here," he ordered.

"I need a donut."

"Right. Get you one. Get me one. Then get your ass over here."

I was standing in the kitchen in my heels, something I'd been doing awhile so I needed a break. This was the only reason I didn't give him lip. Instead, I grabbed the baker's box and walked into the living room.

Ben took the box from me, tossed it on the coffee table, and Gus honed in on it immediately. Fortunately, he was too tiny and klutzy to jump up and get a donut (or the whole box). Unfortunately, he didn't give up. I didn't want him to hurt himself so I leaned over Benny's legs to grab hold of him.

I got my hands on Gus just as Ben got his hands on me. I pulled Gus to my chest. Benny pulled my ass onto his lap.

Gus licked my jaw, then threw himself at Benny.

Ben took hold of the dog in one arm, kept hold of his woman in the other, and caught my eyes.

"Chrissy and Eva are okay. Your little sister doesn't have a ridiculous name, icing on the cake. Your other sister is a whackjob, no surprise. So, with Eva bein' called Eva, you're not battin' five hundred in this mess. I'm thinking seven fifty. Not bad."

I lifted a hand to scratch Gus's booty and settled further in Benny's lap, noting, "Eva being Eva is definitely a silver lining."

Gus threw himself on the couch, then plopped side-first into a toss pillow and started cleaning himself. Benny wrapped both arms around me and drew me nearer.

"You gonna call your dad?" he asked.

"And say what? You're a douchebag?" I asked back.

Ben smiled.

I shook my head and gave him the real answer, "No. I have nothing to say to him, and even if I did, he's less prone to listen to me than Nat was. Doesn't matter anyway. Chrissy's a fighter. If he doesn't do right by Eva financially, she'll see he does."

His arms gave me a squeeze. "That's my Frankie."

I had no reply because I was his Frankie, and anyway, I was enjoying his words and his arm squeeze enough it took all my attention.

"So, you're done dealin' with your whackjob family?" he asked.

I grinned. "I'm done dealin' with my whackjob family…" I paused, then finished on a warning he already knew, *"Today."*

That got another smile from Benny, before, "Right. Next up, choices, watch the game or make out on the couch, then watch the game."

No choice, really.

I got closer, wrapping my arms around his shoulders. "Make out on the couch, then watch the game."

His eyes dropped to my mouth and he muttered, "I like the way you think."

It was my turn to smile.

Ben slid a hand up in my hair and pulled my mouth to his.

Then he twisted and moved so my back was to the couch, he was on me, and his tongue was in my mouth.

I heard my phone start ringing.

Neither of us broke the kiss. We both ignored it.

Some time later, after making out and then watching the game, I went into the kitchen to make my man and myself a sandwich for lunch.

Before doing this, I checked my voicemail.

When I did, I learned the joyous news that my sister was having a baby.

Fucking finally.

I brought our sandwiches into the living room and enjoyed Ben's grin when I hauled out seven bags of chips, along with some beers and a jar of pickles. Then I called Cat to celebrate and give her the lowdown on the whackjobs in our family. I then told her I was done, she wasn't wading in, and from here on out, they had to sort their own shit.

Her response:

"Fucking finally."

Twenty-Four

CHRISTMAS CARD LIST

The next morning, Benny's phone ringing woke me and I knew it woke him when I heard him mutter, "Fuck."

This made me smile as I was prone to smile any day I woke up next to Benny, even if he woke cursing. I felt his heat go from my back where he was spooning me. I turned with him, opening my eyes, and saw him reaching toward the nightstand to get his phone.

He got up on a forearm on the bed, put the phone to his ear, and greeted with a "Benny."

He listened for a few seconds before he twisted his neck, his eyes coming to me, and my stomach clutched at the look in them. Then he pulled himself up to rest his back against the headboard, took the phone from his ear, hit a button on the screen, and a very attractive, deep male voice came from it.

"...investigating," the voice said. "I understand from our former clients you have copies of what they've uncovered and it's their understanding it would be safer for you to pass that on to us. I'd like to ask you to go to a restaurant called Frank's on Main Street in Brownsburg sometime today. A man named Herb will be there. You can give him the flash drives. I've got a man en route to Brownsburg. He'll meet up with Herb and get the drives. We'll take it from there."

The voice quit talking and Ben said toward the phone, "Bud, no offense, but I do not know you. You're a voice on the phone callin' early on

488

a Sunday with no warning. So I'm not givin' anythin' to some random guy at a restaurant."

"I was told that you've been informed our services were engaged," the voice replied.

Oh my God.

Was this the Nightingale guy?

My eyes flew to Benny and I saw his were on his phone.

"Listen," he said. "Again, I do not know you so I'm not sayin' dick about anything."

"You can look us up on the Internet," the voice replied. "Like I said, I'm Lee Nightingale. I own Nightingale Investigations. The man I'm sending is Luke Stark. He'll be there this afternoon. We want the drives prior to his arrival so we can sort through them and set him on task without delay."

"If you do what you do for a living and you know what's goin' down with this and you had *your* woman on the inside, would you take a phone call from a guy you don't know and do what he tells you to do?"

There was a moment's hesitation, then, "I see your point. Look us up on the Internet. You got an email address, give it to me. I'll send you one and it'll have our domain in the address."

"Not sure that makes me feel better," Benny stated, not knowing anything about email or that it would be quite the task to register and use a domain name just to pull one over on an unsuspecting, protective, Italian hot guy first thing on a Sunday morning.

"Then I'll give you this to make you feel better," Lee Nightingale returned. "We started investigating this and our clients ran out of funds. We did not like what we found so we didn't stop investigating, even after they could no longer pay for our services. We undoubtedly have more than you, perhaps enough to lay this shit open and stop a bad drug from hittin' the market. You got the evidence to tie that bow, we'd be obliged. Moreso if we could quit dickin' around, get it, and sort it before any more hits are called. And last, do all this before Salvatore Giglia and his goons get more involved and make this mess messier and possibly take indictments off the table due to mob involvement."

At that, I gasped quietly and Benny looked at me.

Nightingale knew about Sal.

When Ben caught my eyes, I said, "Maybe we should meet this Herb guy at Frank's."

"Is that Francesca Concetti?" Nightingale asked.

I looked to the phone. "Yeah."

"You're off assignment," he stated instantly (and bossily). "So is everyone else. Giglia's men took care of the hired gun on Furlock. Now you can call Giglia off. Get the drives to Herb. Tomorrow, go in. Work. We've got it from here."

Excuse me?

Some random guy on the phone "has it from here?"

I leaned toward Benny's cell and snapped, "There are a lot of people who've stuck their necks out for a long time who have a lot riding on this."

"Frankie," Ben murmured.

"They can quit stickin' their necks out," Nightingale returned.

"And that's a good thing," Benny put in.

I turned my eyes to him to see his on me and I glared.

He turned his gaze to his phone at the same time he brought it closer to his face (and further away from mine). "We'll look you up. Send an email. In it, write something that only your clients will know. We'll confirm that information with the clients, and if it jives, we'll meet this Herb guy at Frank's at one o'clock. We're keepin' copies of the drives. And we want direct lines to you and this Stark guy so we can stay informed about how shit is goin', and by that, I don't mean email."

"Luke doesn't do email," Nightingale muttered, and I saw Ben give me a smug look so I rolled my eyes. "This is my personal cell," he continued. "Text me your email address. We'll confirm with Herb that he's meeting you at Frank's."

"Right," Ben said.

"And, heads up, Herb is…" Nightingale started, paused, and went on, "Unusual."

I felt Ben tense as he asked, "Unusual how?"

"He's not young. He's not tall. He has red hair. He's loud. He's likely to say something inappropriate. And he's very much from Indiana."

"What does that mean?" I asked.

"That means don't wear red because he's from a Purdue family," Nightingale answered.

I'd been living in Indiana less than a year, and still, I totally knew what this meant.

"Red's out," I murmured.

"We good?" Ben asked Nightingale.

"Yeah," Nightingale replied. "Text the email. We'll get you Luke's information and you and your woman can stand down."

Benny was not tense at that. I could tell by his face he was cautiously relieved.

"I'll talk to Sal and do the hand-off," Ben told him.

"Right. Thanks. This'll be over soon."

"Fuckin' hope so," Ben muttered.

"It will," Nightingale's deep, attractive voice said, and it did this so firmly, I believed him.

"Right," Benny said. "Later."

"Later," Nightingale replied, and Benny touched the button to end the call.

He then touched more buttons, asking, "What's your email?" I gave him my email address and his thumb moved over his screen. He must have hit send because he looked to me. "Fire up your laptop, *cara*."

My eyes got squinty at the order. "Can I have a good-morning kiss first?"

"You can have a good-morning fuck. A long one, a happy one, a celebratory one, if we can pass this shit off to some PI from fuckin' Colorado, get Sal out of it so he won't demand we name our first son after him, and concentrate on you either gettin' the go-ahead to work from Chicago or findin' a job in Chicago so I can get home and take my baby with me." He leaned toward me in order to finish, "All of this requiring you to *fire up your laptop*."

"You're grouchy when you get woken up by some PI from Colorado," I noted.

"Yeah, seein' as this necessitates me doin' a bunch of shit I don't wanna do prior to buryin' my dick inside my woman, that happens." When I didn't move, just continued glaring at him, he went on, "And I get grouchier when she lies there givin' me the evil eye instead of gettin' her sweet ass out of bed and gettin' her laptop."

"I think I've made it relatively clear you bein' bossy isn't my favorite thing," I told him.

"It is when you're wet for me," he returned.

It sucked, but he had a point.

And it irked me, but my choices in that moment were either to have a staring contest with Benny, continue our fight, which was kind of ridiculous, or go and get my laptop.

I decided on going to get my laptop, but as I threw the covers off me (and thus Benny since I intended to climb over him because his side was closer), I did it bossing.

"I'll get my laptop and take care of the first part of the operation. You go walk Gus."

I was climbing over him but didn't make it when his hands curled under my arms. I let out a surprised noise as he flipped me to my back, covered me, and laid a hard, short kiss on me.

When he lifted his head, he asked, "Satisfied?"

Not hardly.

"That better be a promise of things to come," I replied.

"When isn't it?" he asked.

And he had another point, this one excellent.

"Stop bein' awesome when I have shit to do."

He grinned.

I scrunched my face at him.

That made him smile. Unfortunately, he did this rolling off me so I didn't get the full force of it, though, this had its benefits since I could see to my business, he could see to Gus, and then he could get down to fulfilling his promise.

I got my laptop, fired it up, and brushed my teeth. Ben pulled on jeans, his tee, and running shoes, then got our dog and the leash and took off.

I got the email. Then I called Tandy to ask her to ask her friend what colors were used in "Roxie and Hank's" wedding. I pulled on yoga pants and a cami while Tandy made her call.

Ben came back while I was making coffee. "We good?" he asked, letting Gus off the lead whereupon he waddle-galloped into the kitchen and started jumping up my calves.

I bent to pick him up, and when I had him in my arms for a squirmy cuddle, I told Benny, "Waiting for confirmation from Tandy now."

Benny nodded and headed down the hall.

I looked down at Gus and asked, "Breakfast?"

He gave my neck a puppy kiss.

I took that as a yes and was finishing up putting clean bowls of water and food down for him when my doorbell rang.

I looked that way just as I felt Benny leave the mouth of the hall and heard him ask, "Who the fuck is that?"

"No clue," I answered.

He kept heading to the door but did it looking at me. "I thought you couldn't get in the complex without a code."

"You can't," I confirmed.

Ben didn't look happy as he kept walking to the door.

He opened the baby door, which was really a supercool peephole, then I heard him mutter, "Jesus."

"What?" I called, moving to round the counter and get to the living room.

By the time I got there, the door was open and I stopped dead when I saw Sal barge in.

He did this ordering, "Call off them dogs."

I stared at him.

"Good to see you, Sal. Wanna come in? Have some coffee?" Ben asked sarcastically as he closed the door behind him.

Sal looked at me, took me in top to toe, then greeted, "Beautiful as always, *amata*." Then he turned to Benny. "Been on the road for hours, *figlio*. Not in the mood for your shit."

Ben moved out of the entryway, stopped, planted his feet, and crossed his arms on his chest. Only then did he suggest, "Maybe you open with tellin' us what got your ass on the road, we can move on from there."

"This is *my* goodwill mission," Sal stated, jerking his thumb to his chest and leaning toward Benny. "Don't need no private dicks from the Rocky Mountain state hornin' in."

Oh God.

He knew about Nightingale.

This wasn't surprising. Sal knew just about everything, and if he didn't, he had ways of finding out. What was surprising was that he seemed proprietary about his "goodwill mission."

"Sal, they been on this case longer than us and can do shit above board, not knockin' people around and whackin' 'em," Benny pointed out.

"I'm not gonna whack anybody," Sal snapped.

"What happened to the hit man?" Ben asked. "Or do I wanna know?"

Sal settled back and grinned. "He got an offer he couldn't refuse."

I started giggling.

Ben cut his eyes to me.

I pressed my lips together and stopped giggling.

Benny looked to Sal and said low, "This shit isn't funny. We're discussin' a fuckin' *hit man*."

At that, Sal looked like he was starting to get mad and that made my breath start to go funny.

"Got hundreds, maybe thousands of lives on the line this drug is bad and it goes out, Benny. I am not in the business of good deeds, but that doesn't mean I don't know this isn't decent work that needs to get done right. But that isn't all it is. This is for my Frankie. Do you think I'd do anything to get her ass in a bind?"

I thought that was very sweet and it bought Sal and Gina being on my Christmas card list (and birthday card list, and maybe, if I could swing it and not make Benny's family lose their minds, an invitation for them to our engagement party).

For some reason, Ben didn't think it was sweet.

I knew this when he demanded, "Explain that to me."

"Explain what?" Sal asked.

"Why you're up in Frankie's shit," Ben stated. "Vinnie's gone, Sal. She's no longer a member of your family."

That comment made Sal go from looking like he was about to get mad to just looking pissed.

Not good.

I made a move toward them, whispering, "Benny—" but Sal cut me off.

"She'll always be family."

"Explain that," Ben repeated.

"Family never dies," Sal returned.

"Your kind does," Ben shot back, and in normal circumstances, this exchange would not be dangerous. This exchange might even be positive in a getting-it-all-out-there (finally), healing sort of way.

That would be if one of the people involved in the exchange wasn't a mob boss.

"You don't get this," Sal clipped, his pissed-off anger sizzling in the air, "because you had what she didn't when you were growin' up. And if you don't find some way to get it, then you aren't the man for her. The man I thought you would be. She didn't have a father growin' up who gave a shit about her and *I*," he jerked his thumb to his chest again, "get that."

At this news—deep, heartbreaking sharing from Sal about something I never knew—my breath caught and I glued eyes to him that were suddenly stinging with tears as he kept talking.

"You had it all growin' up, Benito Bianchi. When you don't, you search for it and hope to Christ that search doesn't last a lifetime, leavin' you takin' your last breath and knowin' you lived a life never havin' somethin' you *need*. I get why you don't like me. I get why you wouldn't want me around Frankie. I also don't give a fuck. If I can, in some way, give her a piece of what she needs, I'm gonna do it. Gina can give her her part of that, she's gonna do it. You like it or not."

"Sal," I whispered, and his eyes sliced to me.

"You're beautiful, Francesca Concetti. You got a light inside that those parents of yours couldn't extinguish. It shines bright on Gina and me. We got girls. We understand that light. We know the privilege of havin' it. We know the kind of person you are, givin' it to us, even after what happened with Vinnie. You wanna keep givin' it to us, we'll take it. You need to take it away, we won't like it, but we'll live with it because we love you and that's what you do."

I felt a tear slide down my cheek as I stood frozen, staring at Salvatore Giglia, finally understanding after all these years why he and his wife were still on my Christmas list.

After this staring lasted a long time, huskily, I told him, "I love you too."

"I know," he replied quietly.

"I think you just got invited to my engagement party," I blurted.

Sal grinned.

Benny muttered, "Christ."

"Come here, *amata*," Sal ordered.

I went there, and when I got there, the boss of a crime family folded me in his arms.

I folded him right back.

We held on to each other for a while before Ben called, "Babe."

I kept holding on but turned wet eyes to Benny.

"I want you to have your moment, and you need more, keep takin' it, but Sal and me gotta get this Nightingale situation straight."

"Okay," I replied, and Sal pulled away but not totally. He held me tucked to his side with one arm around me and I kept one arm around him as we turned to Benny.

"Call Nightingale off," Sal demanded immediately.

"Talked to the man once. Even so, it was pretty clear he's not the taking-orders-from-a-mob-boss-or-anyone type of guy," Benny returned.

"Convince him," Sal ordered.

Ben looked to the ceiling.

I tightened my arm on Sal and he looked at me.

"Maybe we should let him do what he does, seein' as he does it for a living," I told Sal.

"And we don't know this guy. Maybe he's shit at what he does, and us turnin' this over to him means you bein' safe now becomes you bein' not so safe."

I didn't know anything about PIs, but the Nightingale Investigations website was pretty cool. It was attractive. Very male. Extremely professional. It wasn't wordy. In fact, outside of a one sentence mission statement that was an actual mission statement, not a hokey tagline, everything was bullet points.

Then again, a good website probably didn't make a good private investigator.

I pressed my lips together and looked to Benny.

Benny sighed before he said, "Right. We get the go-ahead from Frankie's girl, I'll call Nightingale. Tell him we'll do the drop, but we want to meet his man during it so we know who we're handing this shit over to."

"And tell him his man will work with my men," Sal added.

"Sal," Benny began, "not only does this guy not strike me as a take-orders type of guy, he also doesn't strike me as a take-on-random-partners-in-an-important-investigation type of guy, those partners being Mafia."

"He'll understand a good deed," Sal replied.

"Even *I* don't understand you doin' a good deed, and I just witnessed you givin' something to my woman that was straight-up good and clean," Benny returned, and my heart skipped a beat as I felt Sal's body tighten beside me.

I felt it loosen and I looked up to see him grinning a shit-eating grin as he remarked, "I think you just said somethin' nice to me, *figlio*."

"Be sure to write it in your diary," Ben muttered as my phone rang.

I disengaged from Sal and dashed to the kitchen, Gus on my heels, thinking it was a game, and nabbed my phone.

It was Tandy.

I took the call and got confirmation that Roxie and Hank had a Christmas Eve wedding, thus their colors were green and red, something Tandy's friend's sister knew since she was invited.

These were the colors Nightingale put in his email.

Nightingale was on the up-and-up.

I thanked Tandy and gave this news to Sal and Ben.

The instant I did, Sal looked to Benny and ordered, "Make the call, *figlio*."

Ben stared at Sal for long moments before he looked at me.

"You absolutely sure you don't wanna work at the pizzeria?" he asked. "Shit like this does not happen at my pizzeria."

I smiled at him.

He waited.

I kept smiling at him so he'd know that was all the answer he was going to get.

"Shit," he muttered and reached into his back pocket to get the phone.

Gus licked my foot.

I called, "Sal, you want some coffee and a day-old donut?"

Sal turned and grinned at me.

We walked into Frank's restaurant at two thirty that afternoon, the meeting pushed back so the Luke Stark guy could land at Indianapolis International

Airport, get his rental, and meet us. A change in plans I understood, from listening to Benny's side of the conversation, Lee Nightingale didn't like all that much. A change in plans we discovered, from the instant we entered the restaurant, Lee Nightingale didn't inform Herb of.

And Herb brought company.

We knew this when we walked in and heard a woman's voice call out, "Yoo-hoo! Are you Frankie and Benny?"

I looked to a back table and saw an older woman with her arm up in the air, waving at us. Sitting beside her, staring at her like she was crazy, was an older, red-haired man.

Sal was with us. He had two men stationed outside the restaurant and one in a car across the street. For some reason, he was prepared for an ambush.

I really hoped Lee Nightingale truly was on the up-and-up since I didn't want an old-fashioned café, which looked like it hadn't changed since the early '60s (not to mention its patrons), caught in the crossfire of whatever Sal's brand of protection would be.

"This doesn't give me good feelings," Sal muttered, eyes on the waving woman as we made our way to the back table, Benny leading at the same time hauling me with him since his hand was in mine, Sal following us.

Benny stopped us by the table and declared without greeting, "It was our understanding we were meeting a Luke Stark here."

"You are," the red-haired man replied. "Lee told me I was out." He jerked a thumb at the woman at his side. "But *she* wanted to come anyway." He looked to her. "Just sayin', you're explainin' this shit to Lee."

She turned narrow eyes to him and admonished, "Herb, don't say 'shit.'"

"Woman, I'm a grown man. I'll say 'shit' if I wanna say 'shit,'" he shot back.

"It's uncouth," she retorted and swung a hand toward us. "We barely know these people."

"Barely know them?" Herb returned. "We don't know them *at all*." He then looked to Benny and asked, "Do you say 'shit?'"

Benny didn't answer. Instead, he asked, "Where's Stark?"

Herb didn't answer that. He looked to Sal and asked, "Do *you* say 'shit?'"

"We're done here," Sal decreed.

Shit.

I wanted this to work. I wanted professionals to sort all this out so no one else got hurt, and I wanted it done quickly so Benny could go home, I could go with him, and we could start a normal life (or as normal as I could be).

Therefore, I quickly stuck a hand toward the woman. "Hey. I'm Frankie."

She smiled at me, took my hand, and replied, "I'm Trish. Roxie's mom. Do you know Roxie?"

"No," I told her, giving her hand a squeeze.

She looked confused, muttering, "I thought you knew Roxie."

I pulled my hand away as Herb stated, "Not everyone on the planet knows Roxie."

She turned her gaze to him. "Well, Herb, they know Lee. If they know Lee, they might know Hank, and if they know Hank, they'll know Roxie."

"Did I say we're done here, or did I go temporarily invisible?" Sal asked.

"This is Benny, my boyfriend," I swiftly told Herb and Trish. "And this is Sal, my, uh...uncle."

"Howdy!" Trish cried on a wave that took in the entire front of her body.

"Someone kill me," Herb muttered.

"This is my husband, Herb," Trish said, jerking her head to Herb. "He's in a bad mood because he doesn't wanna be here. He wants to be fishing."

"Do you wanna be here?" Herb asked Benny. "Or would you rather be fishing?"

"If by 'fishing' you mean being anywhere but here, then yeah," Benny answered.

"See?" Herb asked his wife.

She ignored him and invited, "Sit down. We'll order you some of Frank's world famous pancakes."

I leaned into Benny and murmured, "I could eat some pancakes."

He didn't even look at me as he sighed heavily, then pulled out a chair for me to plant my ass in. So I did, Benny claiming the chair next to mine.

"This is unbelievable," Sal muttered, moving to another seat.

"You're tellin' me," Herb stated. "Me and my big mouth. Tell her I got somethin' Lee wants me to do, she thinks it's about our daughter, Roxie. How Lee translates to Roxie, I *do not know*. Then she horns in, even when

I say Lee doesn't need me anymore. If God didn't frown on it, honest to Christ, I'd consider divorce."

"That's not a very nice thing to say," Trish snapped.

"Are *you* sittin' somewhere you don't wanna be with people you don't know?" Herb snapped back.

"We *do* know them. It's Frankie, Benny, and Sal," she fired back.

Herb looked at Benny. "Pay close attention. She's beautiful, your girl. So was Trish when I met her. She ain't hard on the eyes now, but she's a pain in my ass."

"Herb!" Trish cried.

"What the fuck is goin' on here?" a deep, rough voice sounded from behind us. I turned and caught sight of lean hips and a flat stomach barely disguised by a tight black t-shirt.

I looked up and up and *up* and stopped breathing.

That was because there was black-haired, kickass-mustached man standing behind me who could be nothing but a commando.

The hottest one in the universe.

And the scariest one.

He was scowling at Herb, saying, "I thought Lee relieved you of duty."

"He did. Trish wanted pancakes," Herb replied.

The commando tipped his head back and looked to the ceiling. My breath returned but only to come erratically, mostly because I could see his muscled throat and the underside of his strong jaw.

Yummy.

Then he told the ceiling, "Fuck me."

"Lucas Stark! What would your mother say?" Trish remonstrated.

He tipped his chin down and leveled his eyes on her, and at the wrathful look in them, I stopped breathing again and fought against wetting my pants.

"You Stark?" Benny asked, fortunately taking Stark's attention off Trish, and I could feel my man coming out of his chair.

"You Bianchi?" Luke Stark asked back after an affirmative nod.

Ben didn't answer, but he did put out a hand.

Stark took it.

"Elaine! Can we get menus?" Trish called.

"Comin' right up," a waitress called back.

"I take it you're Giglia," Stark said, and I looked to Sal to see him up and giving Stark the once-over.

Sal also didn't confirm his identity verbally. He just said, "At least you look serious."

I didn't know whether to moan or whimper when Stark replied inflexibly in his rough voice, "I am. *Very* serious."

It was then Stark looked to me and his features softened.

Definitely moan-worthy.

"You're Francesca," he stated and, luckily, I was.

I stuck out a hand. "Yeah. Frankie."

He took my hand, gripped it not too strong, not too light, and let it go.

He then looked to Herb. "You can go now."

"Thank God," Herb said, immediately pushing back his chair.

"What? What do you mean?' Trish asked. "We haven't had pancakes."

"We had lunch two hours ago," Herb told her.

"Well, now I'm in the mood for pancakes," she told him.

"Herb," Stark growled warningly.

"Right," Herb said, then looked to his wife. "See that guy?"

He pointed and she looked so I looked and saw he was pointing to Sal's guy outside the window.

"And that one?" Herb went on, and I looked back at him to see he was pointing across the other side of the restaurant.

I looked over my shoulder and saw he was pointing at Sal's other guy.

"Those guys are this guy's guys," Herb went on, and I looked back to see him jerking his head at Sal. "And those guys and this guy means we are now done. We're leavin'. We're not gettin' pancakes. We're getting the hell outta here." He looked to Sal. "No offense."

"None taken," Sal muttered.

Herb looked to Trish. "Let's go."

"Oh, all right," she mumbled. Pushing back and grabbing her purse, she stuck her hand out toward me. "Nice to meet you."

"You too," I replied, taking it for a goodbye squeeze.

More of the same for Benny and Sal, then she hustled around the table, got right into Commando Stark's space, patted his arm, and leaned up to kiss his cheek.

The fact Stark would allow this shocked me so deeply, I gave big eyes to Benny.

Benny didn't see my big eyes. He was looking at Herb shaking Stark's hand and was doing this not looking happy.

Herb and Trish took their leave as Elaine slapped menus on the table, asking, "Coffee?"

"All around," Benny ordered for everybody, probably to make her leave.

"Gotcha," she said and hustled away.

Stark sat in Herb's seat, back to the wall, facing us, and Benny and Sal settled back in.

"Can you assure us amateur hour is over?" Sal asked immediately.

Sal was scary, but I wasn't sure even Sal should go head-to-head with this guy. I'd mentioned his flat stomach but not his broad shoulders or the defined, bulging biceps and chest that were straining the material of his tee so much, any movement might make it tear clean free.

An intriguing thought.

"Herb and Trish are Roxie's parents," Stark told him. "Roxie is Lee's sister-in-law. She's one of the best women I've ever met, a great wife, an outstanding mother. They raised her to be that way. They're fuckin' insane, but they're good people. They aren't amateur. They're friendly. And they got nothin' to do with Lee or his business."

"I'd say that means yeah," I murmured, and Stark looked at me.

His hard face, again, softened and he said quietly, "Yeah. That means yeah."

I grinned at him.

His lips tipped up, then he looked to Benny.

Out of sheer womanly habit I took that moment to look at his hand resting on the table. There I saw a very wide, very shiny gold wedding band.

Luckily, I had the best man in the world or the sight of that band would've been devastating.

"You got somethin' for me?" he asked Benny.

"Unh-unh," Sal cut in. "Before we give you anything, we gotta get assurances you can do this right."

Stark turned cold eyes to Sal. "I only provide references to people who're payin' me."

"I only pay people who I know can get the job done right," Sal fired back, and I held my breath as Luke Stark turned his torso Sal's way. Which meant turning his full attention Sal's way. Which meant only a man like Salvatore Giglia wouldn't cower under that dark gaze.

"Then I'll tell you, Lee does this. He finds shit he doesn't like, like the possibility of a bad drug hittin' the market, the company manufacturing it burying evidence that their product is harmful, and he gets interested. He's interested. So Lee's doin' this, and when Lee does anything, he does it right."

"I'm not talkin' to Lee," Sal pushed.

"No," Stark growled, obviously losing patience. "You're talkin' to me, but when I say Lee I mean me because he put me on this. So that means it'll be me who does this shit right."

Sal opened his mouth, but I quickly spoke because I didn't think it would be healthy for anyone if Luke Stark got more impatient.

"I have a question." Stark looked to me. "Can you kick Chuck Norris's ass?"

Luke Stark smiled, white and lazy.

My heart thumped.

"I strive to be Chuck Norris," he replied.

I smiled back. "That's good enough for me." I looked to Benny. "Give him the drives, baby."

Ben obviously liked the look of Stark too because he shifted to push his hand in his pocket when Sal said, "Hang on."

That was when Ben stopped shifting and looked to Sal.

"Look at this guy," he ordered.

Sal didn't look at Stark. He scowled at Benny.

"Fuck, Sal, I don't even have to see him in action to know this guy could successfully execute a one-man coup on a small South American country," Benny stated.

I giggled.

Sal turned his scowl to me. "This is serious, Francesca."

"Does Mr. Stark look like a comedian to you, Sal?" I asked, jerking my head Stark's way.

Sal looked to Stark. "Who protects Frankie?"

Stark's brows drew together and he looked to Benny. "I thought you were her man."

"I am," Ben confirmed.

"You need assistance with that?" Stark asked.

"Fuck no."

Stark took him in, torso to hair, and said, "Didn't think so."

Nice. A compliment from a commando.

I kicked Benny's shoe with my sandal.

Ben looked to me and shook his head.

I grinned at him and looked back toward the table.

Stark turned his eyes to Sal. "Any more problems?"

"When's this gonna be done?" Sal asked.

"Depends what's on the drives. It's good, Tuesday," Stark answered, and Sal's brows shot up.

"You can say that? Tuesday?"

"I can say that. Tuesday," Stark repeated firmly.

"That soon?" Sal asked.

"We haven't been fuckin' around," Stark told him. "We got three nurses who are ready to be deposed. They got data. And we got a lock on five patients who, if they knew why their hearts were fucked up, which they will, would be callin' their attorneys. Somethin' I can assure you they'll be doin' on Tuesday."

I leaned into the table, and as I did it, Stark caught my movement and turned his dark eyes to me. Dark eyes I just noticed were blue, they were that dark.

Amazing.

"The lead scientist on the project, who's dead now, his original documents are on the drives," I shared.

"Excellent," Stark replied.

Ben shifted again to push his hand into his jeans pocket.

Elaine came with a tray full of coffee mugs and a thermal pot, all of which she put on the table.

"I know it's nearly three, but it's also Sunday and, just sayin', you'd be fools if you didn't have Frank's pancakes on Sunday," she declared.

"Blueberries in mine," Stark said, taking the drives Ben slid across the table toward him.

"You got time for blueberry pancakes?" Sal asked irritably.

"There's always time for blueberry pancakes," Stark replied casually.

I leaned into Benny and whispered, "I like this guy."

Ben looked to me and again shook his head.

I looked to Elaine. "Can I have blueberries in mine too?" I asked.

"Live it up," Elaine answered, which I guessed meant yes.

"Jesus," Sal muttered.

"No blueberries for me, but lots of syrup," Benny ordered, leaning back and hooking an arm on the back of my chair.

Job done. He could tell by looking at Stark he could trust him. Now all he had to do was keep an eye on me and feel relief. I could tell all this by the vibe he was giving me.

And it made me happy so I leaned sideways and collided with him.

He curled a hand around my shoulder.

"Christ, I'll take blueberries too," Sal said.

I looked up at Benny and grinned.

He dipped his head and touched his mouth to mine.

After I got that bit of goodness, I turned away, reached for my coffee, and looked at Stark.

"Is your wife a commando too?"

Another lip tip before, "She's a graphic designer."

"Does she design logos for commando gear?" I asked.

The lip tip tipped higher. "No."

I kept at him. "Is she the mother of a tribe of mini-commandos?"

He shook his head but a light hit his eyes, a light that hit me right in the heart and warmed it.

"So far, all girls."

At his words and the way he said them, I knew what that light meant. I knew it meant when his daughters got to certain age and looked in the mirror, they'd see pure beauty. I figured with the way he looked, his wife was probably hot too, so it wouldn't be a stretch that their girls would be beauties.

But that wasn't the beauty they'd see.

They'd see the beauty that came from looking at themselves through their father's eyes.

Behind a sip of coffee, I hid the feelings these thoughts made me feel. Feelings that, if I let them free, might mean I'd burst into tears. As I sipped, Sal's words from earlier came to me.

Then Benny's words from yesterday came to me.

And suddenly, I wanted to rush into the bathroom and look in the mirror.

But I knew what I'd see.

So, Mrs. Zambino was no dummy.

I already knew that.

What I was looking forward to was getting home to Chicago, walking across the street, and sharing with her the face I would now see.

She wouldn't be surprised.

She'd already seen it.

Repeatedly.

I stood, hand to counter, undoing the straps on my sandals after Ben and I got home, leashed up Gus, took him on a walk, then got back.

Benny unleashed Gus and then directly slanted onto the couch, reaching for the remote, laying evidence that he was possibly preparing for a delayed pancake coma.

The pancakes were good. And I liked Luke Stark even better when he wasn't being scary but was instead being casually badass and also friendly.

But for me, I was just glad all this would soon be over and we could turn our minds to better things.

Like picking tile and kitchen towels.

Once I got my shoes off, I wandered to Benny and saw him watching me. That meant he was prepared so I didn't hesitate in collapsing on top of him.

He braced for impact, took it, and wrapped his arms around me.

I shifted mine so they were on his chest and looked into his eyes. "You liked the look of Stark," I decreed.

"Not as much as you, but yeah," he replied, and I tipped my head to the side.

"What do you mean, not as much as me?"

His lips twitched before he said, "Babe, you were practically drooling."

Uh-oh. Benny caught that.

"Well…" I started, then stopped because I had no clue what to say or why Benny's lips were twitching and he wasn't flying into a possessive, Italian hot guy jealous rage.

"He liked the look of you too," Benny noted.

I felt my brows shoot up. "He did?"

"Oh yeah," Ben stated.

"How do you know?" I asked, intrigued, even though I knew I shouldn't be.

Benny weirdly didn't hesitate with his answer.

"He wanted to be sittin' at a table with Sal like he wanted someone to pull out all of his teeth. He was puttin' up with Sal because he caught sight of you and knows you might possibly be in danger. He also knows Sal's on that so you mean somethin' to Sal and Sal means somethin' to you. He didn't show him a lot of respect, but he showed him more than he normally would and he did that because of you. He thought you are what you are, beautiful and funny. Man like him doesn't go soft for some hard bitch or just anybody. He goes soft for a beautiful woman who's funny."

"But he's married."

"He's married, but he isn't dead."

"I think he's *very* married," I informed him.

"Definitely," Benny agreed. "Man wears that obvious of a wedding band because he's weak and let his wife pick the rings or because he's seriously in love with his wife. There's nothin' weak about that man."

This was true.

"Aren't you…I mean, he was attractive and you caught that I caught that. Aren't you pissed?"

"Babe, you're mine, but you aren't dead either. It's not like just because you're bangin' me you're not gonna see guys you don't like to see."

"That doesn't upset you?" I asked.

"You gonna bang 'em?" he asked back.

507

"No," I replied sharply.

That got me a grin and, "Then why would it upset me?"

"But you didn't like the idea of me being Cheryl's wingman."

"You likin' the look of a guy who's very married and doin' that sittin' next to me is one thing. You out with one of your girls, my ring not yet on your finger, for any guy to get an eyeful and maybe call up the courage to approach is another."

"I wouldn't bang any of them either," I pointed out.

"You like the idea of some woman approachin' me when you're not around?" he asked.

I saw his point so I pressed my lips together.

His eyes dropped to my mouth, and when they came back to mine, they were lit with humor.

I understood that part, but I didn't trust the earlier part and I told him why.

"So, you're cool with this so I'll be cool with you lookin' at pretty women while you're with me?"

"I'm not dead, either, babe. And I might see a pretty woman, but even if I do, I'm not doin' my job if you don't know down to your gut there's nothin' I see that's as beautiful as what I see in you."

God.

Benny.

I liked his words so much, I couldn't stop my head from dropping so my forehead was on his throat, and that was where I kept it in order to deep breathe and not burst into tears.

Ben glided a hand up my spine and curled it around the back of my neck before he murmured into the top of my hair, "See I scored with that."

"Sometimes your sweet overwhelms me," I admitted to his throat.

"Challenge accepted."

I lifted my head and looked at him again. "What?"

He looked into my eyes. "Challenge accepted, findin' ways to give you a lifetime of just that."

I could deep breathe for eternity and not stop the tears that wet my eyes at that.

"You just did it again," I whispered.

He smiled and whispered back, "Good."

I looked to his smile, then back to his eyes that were warm and tender and beautiful and also smiling and kept whispering, "And again."

He slid his hand into my hair and replied, "Babe, you feel all I see you feelin', don't put it into tears. Kiss me."

My Benny.

So wise.

That was a *much* better idea.

So I didn't cry.

I shifted up and kissed him.

Ben shifted us on the couch so he was on top and kissed me back.

Then he banged me.

After that, Ben held me close and I snoozed off my pancakes while he watched the game.

Later, we made dinner together and watched a movie.

And later, before heading to bed, I stood in the bathroom, wearing my nightie, and stared at myself in the mirror.

I saw what I always saw, but it was different.

It was a person who inspired love and loyalty and protection. It was a person who got this because she gave it back. It was the person I'd always been but never seen.

She was beautiful.

My eyes shifted from my reflection to watch Benny, wearing nothing but light blue pajama bottoms, approach me.

He watched me in the mirror as he made his approach but lost sight of me when he fitted his front to my back and wrapped his arms around my middle, burying his face in my neck.

"You okay?" he asked the skin of my neck.

I slid my hands over his arms and held him there, answering, "Yeah."

He gave me a squeeze and murmured, "Come to bed."

One more promise that day for Benny to fulfill.

"Okay, baby," I whispered.

It was then that I got to experience the second best part of the day. Or it might be tied for first. Making love with and then going to sleep beside Benny Bianchi. Hearing his deep and easy voice saying goodnight to me. Making me fall into a peaceful sleep, knowing that tomorrow, I'd wake up to Benny and all the amazing promises he would keep.

Twenty-Five

THE PROMISE

"You don't leave your office all day," Ben ordered as he drove me to work the next morning, telling me something we'd already gone over, him being bossy all the while I got ready for work. "I'll be in the lobby at noon to take you to lunch. You don't work late. I'll be at the front door waitin' for you at five. I'll keep in touch with Stark. They don't put the nails in the coffin, tomorrow we do the same thing."

"Okay, Benny," I replied, knowing he needed me to be docile and not give him lip, seeing as he'd woken up agitated. And giving me a hard, rough quickie hadn't taken the edge off that. I knew that when he took his gun with him and put it in the glove compartment before we took off so he could get me to work.

"Nose down, you work. Don't even look at Bierman if you don't have to," Ben went on like I didn't speak.

"Okay, baby."

Benny fell silent.

I looked his way.

"You doin' okay?" I asked quietly.

He glanced at me, then back at the road before he muttered, "Woke up with a shit feeling."

Fabulous.

"It's gonna be okay," I assured him, hoping I was right.

He didn't respond quickly and when he did, he only said, "Yeah." But I could tell he didn't mean it.

I said no more. Just reached out and gave his thigh a squeeze. When I would have pulled away, he nabbed my hand, laced his fingers through mine, and held it to his thigh.

Finally, I had a good life and it would be selfish to wish for more, but it wouldn't suck if I could ride to work every day with Benny Bianchi holding my hand.

Both of us were in our own heads the rest of the way, staying silent until Ben pulled up to the front of Wyler Pharmaceuticals. He let me go to put his truck into park.

I turned to him to see he was already turned to me.

He beat me to the punch when he said, "Love you, Frankie."

I smiled at him, leaned his way, and touched my mouth to his before I pulled back half an inch and replied, "Love you back, Benny."

His return smile didn't reach his eyes so I lifted my hand and touched his face before I said, "See you at lunch."

"Yeah."

"Have fun with Gus."

He shook his head, but the smile started leaking into his eyes when he replied, "Will do."

"You gonna call Cal?" I asked, thinking spending time with Cal, who was back from his honeymoon, would be a good way to keep his mind off things.

"No. If he knows I'm here, he'll wonder why this visit is extended and he'll worry. We can tell him what went down after it's done."

I nodded, experiencing more awesomeness from Benny that he didn't want to worry Cal, who was not the type of man to worry. He was the type of man to take action instead of worrying and Stark had this covered. New-daddy, new-husband Cal didn't need to get involved.

"Later," I said.

"Have a good day, baby," Ben replied.

I gave him another smile, dropped my hand from his face, grabbed my computer bag, and exited his truck.

I waved at Benny before I entered the building and saw that he and his truck didn't move, not even an inch to glide forward in preparation for leaving. I knew he wouldn't go until I got inside.

My Benny.

I went inside and direct to the elevators, smiling at the receptionist on my way. At the elevators, I looked outside to see Benny's truck sliding away.

The elevator binged I walked into it with three other people, though, I figured it was only me who took a deep breath before I did.

When I got to my floor, I did a recon through windows of offices as I walked to my own.

Clancy Barrow was not there, but then, he never was. He was often traveling, supposedly for business, but rumor had it he played a lot of golf and he had a strict business travel schedule to destinations where the best courses were.

Travis Berger was in his office.

So was Randy Bierman.

My boss wasn't in and Heath wasn't in. Heath didn't put in his resignation on Friday and I wondered if he'd do it today. Even though he was a dick, I was hoping that Stark could sort everything so his resignation only lasted twenty-four hours. The company was about to experience some serious upheaval. We needed as much stability underpinning that as we could get. Heath may be a dick, but he was good at his job.

I got settled for the day, turning on my computer and checking voicemail. Not long after, I saw Lloyd get off the elevators, and not long after that, Heath strode in.

He looked right into my office and the expression on his face was one of a man who had just sucked a lemon.

I took this to mean he was going to resign.

Well, at least Sandy wouldn't be thrown under the bus. That was one good thing.

I hoped for more to come.

Sandy did not follow Heath in two minutes later. The offices and desks filled up and Tandy got in before Sandy.

Seriously not good at this cloak-and-dagger shit, Tandy looked right to me and waved big, her face a mixture of freaked out and excited.

She didn't go to her desk. She came straight to my door and cried with more excitement than her words needed, "Hey, Frankie! I hope you had a *great* weekend."

I grinned at her. "I had a good weekend, babe."

She widened her eyes at me. "Me too! Now, my turn to get the lattes. You wanna come with?"

I looked out my windows to the office, then back to her and said quietly, "Maybe we should stick close to our desks today, honey. Benny's comin' at noon, takin' me to lunch. You can go with us and I'll buy you a latte on the way back to work."

"Oh, right, good idea," she muttered, then brighter, "You're on!"

Clearly, she was relieved about the Nightingale involvement too.

She bopped to her desk and minutes later I saw Sandy drag in.

She didn't look near as good. She looked pale, drained, and beaten. She also didn't look at anyone when she wended her way between the desks to get to hers. She certainly didn't go to Heath's door to give him an excited "good morning."

Likely, Heath had ended it. And obviously, Sandy thought that what they had was more than what it was.

Poor Sandy.

After she sat at her desk, I started to get down to work, deciding to throw myself into it in an attempt to make the day go faster. I got two minutes into this failed endeavor when my phone rang.

The number that came up had a three-oh-three area code.

Denver.

I picked it up and greeted, "Frankie Concetti."

"Babe. Eyes up. Left corner of your office over the windows," a deep voice I knew said back.

My gaze went up and I saw nothing, so I screwed my eyes up to look harder and that's when I saw a tiny red light.

"Smile. You're on camera," Luke Stark said in my ear.

Holy crap. How'd he get in to plant cameras? The facility was covered in security.

"They're all over, Frankie," Stark continued. "Stick to your floor. We got eyes on you and your crew. We also got eyes on Furlock. I got local talent at my back and they're at the ready in case somethin' goes down, which it won't, so don't let that freak you. These are just precautions."

"Uh…okay," I replied.

"The team went over what was on the drives. It's good. Wheels are in motion. Bianchi called and reported your schedule for the day. Stick to it."

"Tandy is comin' with us to lunch," I informed him.

"Good," he replied. "Travis Berger's assistant is about to schedule an urgent meeting for him tonight at six. We'll call you after that's done. You with me?"

I looked to my computer screen and mumbled, "Unh-hunh."

"Right. Be good," he said as his goodbye, and I didn't get the chance to say anything witty or sassy back because he'd disconnected.

I barely put my phone on my desk before I saw Heath, a white envelope in hand, walking out of his office, gaze to his shoes.

I looked to Sandy, who didn't even glance his way. Then, I didn't want to but I couldn't stop myself, my eyes went quickly to Bierman's office.

He was watching Heath, his expression smug.

Something about this made me feel suddenly elated.

If he was smug about Heath, he had no idea what was coming.

And that was *awesome*.

My gaze went back to Heath and I watched him look up. When he did, his eyes caught on something that made him stop dead.

I looked that way and saw Lloyd heading to my office.

He smiled at my assistant and said, "Good morning, Tandy," as he passed right by her and came to my door, where he stopped. "Hey, Frankie. Good weekend?" he asked.

"Yeah, you?"

"Yes, Frankie. Thanks." He tipped his head to the side. "You have a second to sit down with Travis and me?"

Travis and him. The big boss, my boss, and me?

This was a surprise and it took a lot to stop my eyes from going to the camera.

"Sure," I replied, rolling back my chair and grabbing my cell.

"Nothing to worry about," Lloyd said. "Travis and I just want to talk to you about your plans to move to Chicago."

Here it was. They'd made their decision.

I hoped this was good news part two of the day, but whatever it was, it was an important question about my future that needed an answer and I was about to get it.

I nodded to Lloyd and he got out of my way so I could precede him.

"We're meeting in Travis's office," he told me as he fell in step beside me.

"Lloyd," Heath called, and Lloyd and I looked his way. "After you talk with Frankie, you got a minute?"

"Of course, Heath. It shouldn't take long with Frankie," Lloyd answered.

Heath nodded and, avoiding Sandy's eyes, went back to his office.

I went with Lloyd to Travis's office.

As I walked in, I saw that Travis Berger was a man who did not have to prove how busy and important he was. He was not on the phone, his computer, reading a file, or scribbling notes when we approached. He watched us, eyes on me, face blank. There was something about this that made me respect him more. He needed my time, and somehow, him watching me come into his office for an impromptu meeting communicated that this meeting was important, I was important, and he wanted me to have his attention.

Greetings were exchanged. A seat was offered. I took it. Lloyd seated himself in the chair beside me in front of Travis's desk, then Travis asked, "Would you like Penny to get you some coffee?"

I hadn't been to the pot yet today and could use a shot of joe, but I still shook my head no.

Travis leaned back, laced his fingers, and put them to his flat midriff. His eyes did not move to Lloyd. They remained on me.

Then he started talking.

"Lloyd has told me you have something happening in your life and that means you wish to move back to Chicago."

I nodded and confirmed, "Yes."

He studied me a moment and his voice was quieter when he said, "Our choice to hire you was excellent and we've in no way regretted it, even after your delay in starting with us."

I did not think a reminder of that boded well.

He went on.

"Your supervisor respects you. The staff likes you. Your reps perform for you. However, even if it's our policy to allow employees to work at home and do this regularly, it's not our policy to allow employees to work from remote offices."

Bad news.

Shit.

"Of course," I said softly.

"I've seen your numbers myself, Frankie, and Lloyd speaks highly of you," Travis carried on. "We would be sorry to lose you. Is there any way your significant other would move to Indy?"

"He runs a family pizzeria. He's the second generation. It's been in operation for forty years." When I saw the boredom seeping into Berger's features as I told him stuff he didn't give a shit about, I got to the point. "What I'm sayin' is, no. The family business is important and I wouldn't ask him to make that move."

Berger nodded once before he stated, "At this juncture, I feel the need to point out that there's a great deal of opportunity at Wyler, Frankie. Especially for excellent performers. Thirty-five percent of our executive and management staff is female. It's obviously none of my concern, but in my position, it's part of my job to retain talent, to keep a team that's excelling intact, and sometimes to do that, I must take a position as advisor. In this position, I'd hate to see you waste those opportunities because your significant other doesn't understand the importance of your career."

I stared at him, then I glanced down at his hand and saw his wedding band.

It was not wide and shiny.

Seeing it, I wondered, with all the times I came in before eight and he was already there, looking like he'd been there awhile, and the other times I left after six and he was still there, looking like he wasn't even close to leaving, what his wife thought of him prioritizing his career over his "significant other."

Then again, no doubt he made six figures, so maybe she made herself feel better about her husband not being around by going out and buying scads of shoes.

"I intend to spend the rest of my life with him," I replied, even though that was none of his business. I added for good measure, "And I just got news my sister is having a baby. She's in Chicago. My family is growing and my plan is to build my own family with Benny. I can't be there for my sister or do that with Benny in Indy. At least, not easily."

He looked confused for a moment, as if being there for my sister or being close to my "significant other" in order to build a life together was a foreign concept to him, and I suddenly felt bad for his unknown wife.

Then he stated, "Life isn't easy, Frankie."

"With respect, Travis, I've recovered from a gunshot wound. I know that. Because of that, among other things, I also know what's important."

He studied me and he did it for a while.

Then he looked to Lloyd and asked, "Lloyd, can you give us a minute?"

I looked Lloyd's way and saw he didn't want to give us a minute. He was protective of his staff. But this was the executive vice president. He had no choice.

He nodded and said, "Of course."

He got out of his chair, then gave me an understanding look and a small smile before he left, closing the door behind him.

I looked back to Berger and he started speaking immediately.

"I respect your decision, Frankie." But he said this like he didn't respect it at all and I was suddenly wondering if I respected him. Sure, he was great at work, but life wasn't work. Not even close. "If you find that the times we can allow you to work from Chicago are not enough and you need to leave us, this will be a blow, but a woman must do what a woman must do."

I wasn't super fond of his saying "a woman must do what a woman must do," as if women were the only ones who made decisions like this, but I let that slide and simply kept my gaze to his.

Suddenly, his demeanor changed, and I didn't like it but only because I couldn't read it. He wasn't normally a readable guy. But now he seemed impenetrable.

"Now that that talk is done and we're here alone, is there something you need to tell me?"

I blinked, not understanding what I'd need to tell him. I mean, there was a lot I could tell him—Heath was being blackmailed, the CEO and his

Director of Research and Development were killing people and arranging for them to have life-altering accidents. But it wasn't *me* who was going to share those morsels.

"Uh…" I began.

He leaned toward me, unlacing his fingers and putting one hand to his desk, his eyes never leaving mine.

"If there's something crucial I need to know, obviously, Frankie, it being crucial, *I need to know it.*"

I felt my heart start beating hard and this was a strange sensation because I felt it in my throat.

That had happened to me once before.

When Daniel Hart turned his gun on me.

My phone in my hand rang and I jumped when it did.

Gratefully, to get away from Berger's intense gaze, I looked down at it and saw the three-oh-three area code.

This told me Stark not only had cameras, he had microphones.

Yeesh, these guys were good.

"Frankie," Travis called, and I looked to him. "You can call them back later."

I wondered what Stark would advise, but I needed my job until I got another one (or until October when my lease ran out and I quit) so I didn't take the call.

I had to wing it.

"Outside of the fact that I, as a businesswoman with career opportunities, will have to think long and hard of what my future will be with Wyler, I don't have anything you need to know, Travis."

My phone quit ringing.

He again studied me. This time it went on longer, like he was giving me the opportunity to make a different choice.

When I didn't, he nodded. "All right, Frankie. Thank you for your time."

"Thank you for yours, Travis," I replied, standing.

He followed me with his eyes. "I hope you make the right decision."

I knew what he thought the right decision was.

The problem was, he was wrong.

I just hoped his wife really liked shoes.

I smiled at him and got the hell out of there.

I saw Heath was in Lloyd's office as I walked back to mine. After I saw this, I saw Tandy watching me as I was walking.

She didn't wait her usual judicious amount of time. She walked in right behind me and closed the door.

"What was that all about?" she asked.

I looked to her as I sat down at my desk. "I requested a remote office in Chicago so I could move in with Benny. Travis denied my request."

Her eyes got big, then her face shut down. "You're leaving?"

I gentled my voice when I said, "Probably."

That was when her face fell. "Oh, Frankie."

I so totally liked Tandy.

"I'm sorry, honey. But I'm in love. I have a new puppy. I have a dining room table to clear off and a kitchen to buy tile for and a life to start living."

"I get you," she said quietly. "But I'll miss you."

I grinned at her and replied, "Well, when I find a new job, my assistant better be cracking or I'll be headhunting a new one."

Her lips trembled, but they did this before they smiled.

"Sucks for me because I liked my boss before you, but he didn't ever buy me a latte. Not even taking a turn," she told me.

"I'll make sure I get you a few cards so you can keep topped up."

Her smile stayed in place, then she looked out the window and back to me. "You think Heath's resigning?"

My brows went up. "You know about that?"

"Last night, Nightingale or a member of his team called all of us. Briefed us on everything. Told us the way things were going to go. Got our statements. It was cool. It felt good knowing it's gonna be over soon."

"I get you," I agreed.

"Just sucks. It's gonna be over, Bierman will stop spreading his dickishness wide so things will be good again, but you'll be gone."

Yeah. I'd miss Tandy.

"You're the freaking bomb, Tandy," I whispered.

"So are you, Frankie," she whispered back.

We looked at each other as we both battled emotion that could come out in a variety of ways. Emotion that was about change and loss and relief.

Then we both got our shit together and she went back to her desk.

The minute her ass was in her chair, my phone rang.

It was the three-oh-three number.

I answered with, "Two calls from a commando today. That's a record."

There was laughter in Luke Stark's deep, rough voice when he replied, "You did good, babe."

"Approval noted," I replied.

"And babe," he started, "nothin' in this world is more important than buildin' a life with the man you love."

My breath caught.

They *did* have microphones.

And commandos could be gushy.

Before I could call him on it, Stark disconnected.

Or maybe he disconnected because he knew I was going to give him shit.

Either way, I put my phone on my desk, got to work, and did it smiling.

At ten o'clock, my phone rang again.

It was Benny.

"Hey, honey," I greeted.

"Status," he replied, and I knew he was still agitated.

"Well, a while ago, Heath left Lloyd's office looking like he'd been whipped. Lloyd looked pissed, but I think it's because he knows I'm going to resign soon too so he's going to be down two managers rather than one."

I wasn't done with my update, but Ben cut in.

"You're gonna resign?"

I'd forgotten he wasn't in the know since he didn't have microphones, and things were so weird, I didn't call him with the news and I should have.

"Got the news direct from Berger. No Chicago office," I told him quietly.

"Fuck."

"Job search."

"Yeah."

"It'll be okay, Benny."

"You know it will, Frankie."

That made me feel better because he was right. I knew it would.

"Anything else?" he asked.

"Sandy, Heath's secretary, has spent most the morning in the bathroom, the rest of it looking like she's about to burst into tears, this being before she runs into the bathroom. Heath hasn't opened his door and has had his back to the room since he gave Lloyd his resignation. Bierman is looking smug rather than dickish, which would be annoying if I didn't know there's a possibility he'll be incarcerated by this evening. And Tandy is coming to lunch with us."

"She is?" Ben asked.

"Yep," I answered.

"Why?"

"Because I like her. I'm gonna lose her and that means I'm gonna miss her, so I want to spend time with her. And last, I want her to meet my man."

"That's acceptable."

I rolled my eyes at my computer screen before I gave him my finale.

"I think Berger knows what's going down."

"Yeah. Stark called with his update. He didn't tell me Berger didn't give the go-ahead for a Chicago office, but he did tell me he pushed for somethin' else."

It was cool Stark left it to me to give Benny that news.

I didn't share this with Benny.

I said, "I can't be sure. I mean, Bierman is up in my shit so he could be badmouthing me and Heath, but other than that, there's nothing else to tell him."

"Glad to know Heath isn't the douchebag we thought he was, but it's too bad he got down to business. Stark told me they swept Bierman's office and found his copies of the photos last night. Also told me they just got done sweepin' his house and found a bunch of other shit, includin' more copies of the photos. They got a lock on his other hiding places and no more photos. Sal got the shit the PI had. All of it will be destroyed. This means Sandy's covered and he didn't need to resign."

That made me want to laugh.

I didn't.

Instead, I gave in to my wonder.

"Man, these guys are *good.*"

"Totally could oust a government in a small South American country."

That made me laugh.

Benny let me laugh for a while before he went about finishing things.

"Okay, if you got no more, I got no more. I'll see you and Tandy in a coupla hours."

"See you then, honey."

"Later, *cara.*"

"Later, Benny."

We disconnected.

I looked to Heath and saw his back to the room. I moved my eyes to Sandy and saw her blowing her nose.

Then I looked to my computer and wished I could get a latte.

⌒

My gaze went to the bottom right corner of my computer screen.

It was 4:43.

Seventeen minutes and I could get the fuck out of there.

Lunch with Benny and Tandy went great. Before we even got in his SUV that was idling at the curb outside the front doors, Tandy saw Ben through the windows and said, "God, Frankie. You showed me pictures and I got it, but now I *get it.*"

And I got that. One look at Benny, even through a car window, any girl would get it.

She got it more as Ben charmed her during lunch.

Tandy being Tandy charmed him right back.

Benny dropped us off and the last thing he said to me was a firm, "Five, babe."

I nodded and I also did this firmly. No way I was working late that night. Not even by a minute.

The good news was that he didn't seem agitated anymore, but he did seem on guard, which was understandable.

The afternoon dragged no matter how much I tried to throw myself into work. I just wanted that day done. I wanted to go home and wait with Benny until we heard the rest of it was done. And then I wanted to get on with a life filled with promise without anything fucking it up.

I took in a deep breath and considered shutting down early just so I could get out of there without delay.

This was when my phone rang.

It was Benny.

"Hey, honey. We're in the home—"

"Do not leave your desk."

My back went straight at his tone and my eyes went out my windows to Bierman's office.

He wasn't there.

"I'm ten minutes away," Ben told me. "I'll come in and get you at your office."

"What's happening?" I whispered.

"Stark's team is there," Ben replied immediately, and I felt my heart stutter. "But they're occupied, seein' as two thugs in ski masks just cornered Furlock in a bathroom on the third floor and are haulin' his ass down the stairwell toward an SUV that's waitin' at the back utility entrance."

"Oh my God," I breathed and started doing a scan of the floor.

"Stark's team has neutralized the driver," Ben went on.

Heath at his desk.

"They've also called the cops who are en route," Ben kept going.

Sandy at hers.

"But they don't want you to move."

Lloyd at his. Kathleen at hers. Jennie at hers.

"Keep an eye on your crew," he finished.

The eye I was supposed to keep on my crew hit Tandy's desk.

She wasn't there.

My blood turned to ice.

"Tandy," I whispered.

"What?" Ben asked.

"Tandy's not at her desk."

"Fuck," he muttered. "Stark's busy, but I'll call. He's got eyes everywhere. If somethin' was goin' down with her, he'd be on it. Stay at your desk."

I looked again through the floor.

No Tandy anywhere.

"Benny—"

"Do not...*leave*...your desk, *tesorina*."

I started deep-breathing. "Furlock is gonna be okay?"

"You think Stark would let anything happen to him?"

No.

I did not.

"I'm almost there, baby. Then we're out of there and safe."

I stared at Tandy's empty desk, saying, "Okay."

"Don't move, Frankie."

He so knew me because I *so* wanted to move, search for Tandy, make sure she was okay.

I visualized rooting myself to the chair, even as I itched to jump out of it, and said, "I won't, Benny."

"Keep it together, babe. Love you."

"Love you too, honey."

He disconnected.

I deep-breathed and went about shutting down for the night.

In this time, Tandy didn't come back.

At the end of this time, my phone rang again.

It was Benny.

"Ben," I whispered as greeting.

"Stay where you are. I'll be there."

He'd already told me that.

Why was he again telling me that?

"Benny—"

"Promise me you will not move, Frankie."

Shit.

Something was going down.

And Stark was occupied.

They needed Benny.

"Ben—"

"Promise me."

"Is it Tandy?"

"Promise me."

"Benny!" I snapped.

"I need you to *promise me*."

Oh God.

God!

"I promise, Benny."

"Good, baby. Be there soon."

"Be careful, Benny."

"I will."

"Be *very* careful, Benny."

"I will, honey. Gotta go now."

He sounded normal, if impatient. Almost businesslike.

Oh God.

"Love you," I whispered.

"Love you too. See you soon."

"Yeah."

He disconnected.

I looked to Bierman's empty office.

Then to Tandy's empty desk.

Then I looked to my phone and called Sal.

He picked up in one ring. "We're on it, *amata*."

Oh God.

On what?

"What does that mean?" I asked.

"Gotta go, Francesca," he said as answer.

"Sal!" I snapped.

He disconnected.

I shot out of my chair.

Don't move, Frankie.

Tandy sometimes went to the bathroom to freshen up before leaving work because she was going out to get a drink.

I knew that night she wasn't going out to get a drink.

I couldn't see her purse because she put it in a locked drawer. She wouldn't leave for the day without telling me. Especially not early. But never.

I wanted to run to the bathroom and check it to see if Tandy was there.

I looked to Berger's office to see him on the phone. He was far away, but he appeared business as usual and I wanted to run to his office and tell him what was happening. Get his big ass out of his executive chair and make him do something human for a change.

I didn't.

I sat down in my chair, tipped my eyes to my phone, and willed it to ring.

Bierman had made a move on Furlock *at Wyler.*

Desperate.

What ends would desperate men stoop to?

Benny.

My Benny.

I heard police sirens outside, not one, many, but I didn't look out my windows.

I stared at my phone, my brain chanting, *call me, call me, call me.*

The sirens got close and stayed close. The police were outside.

I clenched my teeth.

How did Benny do it, make a myriad of promises every day and then set about keeping them? Each one. Dozens of them. Small and large. Every day.

A promise kept.

And I could hardly contain myself from moving.

Promise me.

"God," I whispered, my throat beginning to get scratchy. "*Benny.*"

I had to stay where I was. I had to keep this promise to Benny. I had to prove to him that when he needed me to do something important, I could do it. When he came back to me, I had to show him that it was okay that he put his faith in me and I kept myself safe for him.

I had to keep my promise.

On this thought, I felt the wave of shock penetrate my office and my head snapped up. Two police officers were walking into Berger's office with a member of Wyler security. Four more officers were fanning out across the space looking like they were looking for something.

No Tandy.

No Benny.

I kept my seat.

People were moving, freaking, I could hear whispering. I felt eyes on me from other staff, but I kept my gaze on the officers.

And kept my seat.

My throat closed. My eyes stung. I watched Berger move swiftly out of his office with the two policemen and the security guard, and they went directly to the stairwell. Squawky voices could be heard on police radios and two of the officers fanning out made a move toward Bierman's office.

I watched, my hand clenched around my phone.

And kept my seat.

I quit watching and looked toward the elevators. I locked my eyes there. I kept my grip on my phone.

And kept my seat.

An eternity slid by.

Then the elevators binged.

My chest tightened.

Benny walked out.

My chest loosened, but a tear dropped down my cheek.

He looked around, his eyes came to me, and he walked direct to me. Two police in Bierman's office, two of them with Heath, Ben passed them as he made it to me, walking through my door, tall, handsome, healthy.

I still kept my seat.

"Tandy?" I asked, my voice scratchy.

"Downstairs with the police," Benny replied, rounding my desk.

I still kept my seat, twisting my neck to keep my eyes on him.

He came to a stop at my side, cocked his head, his brows drawing, and he asked, "Baby?"

"I can't move," I whispered.

Tenderness softened his features before he whispered back, "Come to me, Frankie."

That was when I could move.

I shot out of chair and into his arms.

They instantly closed strong and tight around me.

"They got to her roommate," Benny told me much later.

That later was after he spoke for-fucking-ever with the police, then got me the fuck out of Wyler and took me home. When we got home, we walked our dog. Then I got into yoga pants and a tee and called to order pizza while Benny talked to Stark.

Finally, we stretched out on the couch, me on top of Benny, which was where we were now.

"The roommate called," he went on. "Told Tandy they had her and that she had to go to her car in the parking garage. Nabbed her there, put her in their car, took off, and since I was in my SUV, Stark called me and set me on them."

"How did Stark know where you could find them?"

"My question too," Benny replied. "At the time, I thought either clair-voyance or he had helicopters." I grinned at his quip and Ben kept talking, "But he knew where their base was so my guess is he predicted the route they'd take to it. A route that was on my route so Stark called me."

"And you...what?" I asked, even though I wasn't sure I wanted to know.

"I was bein' tailed by Sal and his boys, probably because he was bein' cautious 'cause he kinda likes you." That got him another grin. "They came with me and we..." He paused before he finished, "Took care of business."

"Is that all I want to know?" I asked, having been sequestered in my office while Ben talked to the police so I didn't hear the full story.

"That's all you want to know," he confirmed.

"Was it clean?" I asked.

"Good Samaritans, seein' a couple of women hustled into a warehouse and investigating," Ben answered. "I called the cops beforehand so they knew we were there. No gunplay as Sal came in heavy and hot and scared the fuckin' shit outta them. Figure the police are still scratchin' their heads that Sal and his boys just happened to be there and were playin' Good Samaritans. I figure by now they've cottoned on to who he is. But their guns, and mine, incidentally, somehow disappeared between there and gettin' the women back to Wyler. So it's all good."

Sal was definitely invited to the engagement party.

"So it's over," I remarked, and his arms gave me a squeeze.

"It's over," he said softly. "And if Bierman and Barrow already didn't buy jail time with the serious shit they were pullin', this latest move would do it. Stark said they had plans in motion to take care of the whole crew who were amateur sleuthing, including women named Kathleen, Jennie, and Miranda. Barrow was picked up on a golf course in Florida. Stark also told me that Barrow kept his shit clean, probably so if anything went wrong, Bierman would take the fall. Nightingale tied him to it though, so he's gonna be processed and sent back to Indiana to deal with his mess."

"They seem kinda like private investigator superheroes," I muttered, and it was Ben's turn to grin at me. "What I don't get is why Bierman targeted Lloyd, Heath, and me."

"Stark had that answer too, babe, seein' as Bierman and Barrow needed a team to toe the line. Not only were you, that douchebag, and your boss under fire, so was Berger and a number of other people. They were settin' up to clear house. They already had replacements they'd secretly been interviewing."

"Whoa," I whispered.

"Yeah. They knew people were already asking questions, your boss for one and Berger another one. They knew they had to put their own team in place, or at least people who weren't there before product launch who might ask questions, and they were gearin' up for that."

"Dickheads," I muttered.

"Understatement," Ben said through a grin.

It was while I was taking in Benny's grin that a loud pounding came at the door.

Ben's grin died and his eyes narrowed as he looked toward the door. "Jesus, that always the way the pizza delivery guy knocks?"

"No," I answered, thinking this also wasn't the time the pizza delivery guy would be delivering, considering if it was, he had superhuman speed.

Benny sat up, taking me with him and then taking us both to our feet. He left me standing by the couch and stalked to the door in a way that told me the pizza guy was going to get an earful.

I was about to collapse back on to the couch but didn't when I heard the door open, Ben start to say, "Yo," but was cut off when I heard Cal bark, "*What the fuck, Benny?*"

My mouth dropped open at his tone. I felt the heavy anger filling my place and I watched Cal stalk in from my entry, wondering if maybe I shouldn't have given him the gate code. He stopped and turned to Benny, who sauntered in behind him.

"Let me guess. Sal called you," Ben stated.

"Fuck yeah, he called me. Jesus, Benny. You went into an unknown situation with *Sal* as backup and me fifteen miles away, havin' no clue serious shit was goin' down?" Cal asked irately.

"As you can see, *cugino*, I'm breathing," Benny replied.

"Jesus, fuck me," Cal muttered as he turned to me. "And you. Shit's goin' down at work, you got family five miles away, nothin'?"

"Uh…Ben and Sal had it covered," I replied.

Before Cal could say a word, there was another knock on the door. I looked to Ben, who was already on his way toward it, then back to Cal, who was scowling at me and ignoring Gus, who appeared to be attempting to climb up Cal's jeans.

"You want a beer?" I asked.

Cal kept scowling at me.

I didn't know if that meant yes or no and had no chance to make a guess before I heard Vi snap, "Joe! For goodness' sake! You can't go tearing into someone's house at dinnertime."

Then Vi stormed in with Angie cradled in an arm, Kate and Keira on her heels.

"Hey, Frankie," Kate called on a smile.

"Hey, baby." I smiled back as she didn't ignore Gus when he waddle-galloped to her. She bent, picked him up, and gave him a cuddle.

"Yo, Frankie," Keira greeted.

"Hey, honey," I returned.

"I think we need more pizza," Ben muttered, coming in after the girls.

"Cool! Pizza!" Keira cried, grabbing on to Angie but not getting very far. She got her little sister out of her mother's arms only to have Joe stalk to her and pull her into his own.

He did this automatically, his attention still on Benny.

"Ben. Explanation," he growled.

Benny was on his way to the kitchen and he stayed true to his path while saying, "I'm not explainin' anything." He opened the fridge and looked to Vi, then the girls. "Vi? Girls? Drink?"

"Diet Coke," Kate ordered.

"Does Frankie have any of that diet Fanta Grape?" Keira asked.

"Is she Frankie?" Benny asked back to Keira, and I found myself smiling again.

"That for me," Keira put in her order.

"Me too," Vi called, moving toward a chair and taking a load off. She then looked up at me. "You got any games?"

"We're not playin' a fuckin' *game*," Cal bit out.

"We're not havin' an argument either," Vi returned, twisting in her seat to look at her husband. "They're fine. So now we're havin' pizza and family time." Then she turned to me. "And I have to tell you about Virgin Gorda. Oh my *God*, Frankie. You *have* to take Benny there."

"Fuck me," Cal muttered and another knock came at the door.

Benny came out of the kitchen with cans of pop while Cal stalked to the door.

"We'll have to eat pizza in waves," I noted as he handed Vi her can.

"I'm on it," he said. Giving cans to Kate and Keira, he headed to the door, hand to his back pocket probably to get out his wallet to pay the pizza guy.

"You guys want glasses?" I asked the girls, ready to head to the fridge to polish off Ben's hosting skills.

They didn't get answers in.

This was because I turned toward the entryway when I heard Sal exclaim, "Dear God, Cal, she's a beauty!"

Two seconds later, Sal walked into my living room with Angie held up to his face, Cal prowling close to his back with an expression like thunder, and Benny joining the party last, looking part-resigned, part-annoyed, and part-like he was about to burst out laughing.

"Who's a beautiful girl? Who's a pretty baby?" Sal cooed, then cuddled Angie close to his chest, looking into the room. He spied Vi, Kate, and Keira and turned back to Cal. "You did good, *figlio*, a room filled with beauties." He turned back. "Hello, girls," he greeted Kate and Keira. "I'm Uncle Sal."

"I'm Kate," Kate told him.

"I know," Sal told her.

"I'm Keira," Keira told him.

"I know that too, *bella*," Sal told her.

"You wanna give me my daughter back?" Cal butted into the conversation.

"No," Sal answered.

"That wasn't really a question," Cal pointed out.

"Take this beauty from me, I'll cut off your hand," Sal shot back.

Cal looked to his boots before he repeated, "Fuck me."

"Do I have to say, *again*, how I'd prefer you refrain from the f-word in front of my girls? *All of them?*" Vi snapped.

"Buddy, Angie doesn't even understand what I'm sayin'," Cal bit out.

"Let's not let her understand that particular part of what you're sayin' until she's about twenty-three," Vi fired back.

"Yeah." I heard Benny say at this point. "This is Benny Bianchi. Twenty minutes ago, we ordered a pizza to go to The Brendal. I need," he looked through the room, "two more. Large."

"I like pepperoni!" Keira shouted.

"Sausage!" Kate yelled.

"Don't forget the peppers," Sal put in.

That was when I flopped onto the couch and burst out laughing.

I felt Sal (and Angie) sit beside me. When I could see again through my laughter, I saw Cal sitting on the arm of Vi's chair, his hand on the back of her neck, with his eyes on Kate and Keira, who were settling in, Keira close to my side, Kate on the arm of the couch next to Sal and Angie.

And I heard Benny saying, "One half pepperoni, half sausage. The other with everything."

Keira leaned her weight into my side and whispered into my ear, "School's gonna start soon and I think I have Joe where I want him on the Jasper Layne situation."

I turned my head, looked into her beautiful face, and that was when it hit.

There I was. Safe. At home. With my man and my family.

A moment that was the beginning of the rest of my life.

It was full of promise.

Epilogue

GOT IT RIGHT

I parked at the back of the pizzeria, opened my door, threw out my foot in its high-heeled pump, and hauled my business-suited ass out of my Z.

I dashed in the back door of the restaurant, through the vacant kitchen that was nonetheless messy, and into the dining room.

They were congregated close to the front door. Vinnie, Benny, Vi, Cal with Angie, Kate, and Keira. Theresa, with her camera, was standing in front of them.

"Hey!" I called, rushing around the bar.

"Frankie!" Kate cried.

"Yay!" Keira yelled.

"Frankie! Just in time! Get in the shot," Theresa ordered.

"I can't, honey, got another interview I gotta get to. But I wanted to pop by and say 'hey,'" I said, coming around them, seeing Kate and Keira in stained white aprons, holding a pizza pie.

This was because Benny had spent the last hour, while I was at another interview, teaching them how to make it.

They were up for Thanksgiving. They'd gotten in late that morning as I was headed off to interview *numero uno*.

Theresa was hosting Thanksgiving (of course), and Carm, Ken, and the kids were arriving that evening.

So it was good Ben and I got our guest room done, because with Carm and the family in town, that meant Vi, Cal, and the girls could stay with us.

Something that made me happy.

Then again, those days, days that started with Benny in bed with me and ended the same way, I was always happy.

I gave out quick hugs and kisses, ending with the girls.

"Save me a slice," I said, smiling down at the awesome-looking pizza pie that I knew was also awesome-tasting because Benny showed them how to make it.

"We will," Kate promised.

I gave her a grin, then I went to my man.

Hand to his chest, feet up on my toes, I said in his ear, "Be back as soon as I can."

"Knock 'em dead, *cara*," he said in mine, hand on my waist when he kissed my jaw.

I kissed his, leaned back, gave him a smile, and made to rush right back out.

"Frankie! Two seconds! I want you in this shot!" Theresa called.

"I'll be in the next one!" I called back, hustling forward but smiling and waving backward.

"Frankie!" she shouted.

"Love you, Theresa!" I yelled from the kitchen and kept going.

It sucked that I had back-to-back interviews the day before Thanksgiving when family was hitting town, but the jobs were both local and they were both promising.

It wasn't that I minded being out of work for a while. It was nice. It was just that all Benny's junk was sorted, the house was clean, the guest room done, so I had nothing to do with my days. It would also be good to get back.

And anyway, I was right.

I wanted to be in that photo Theresa was taking.

But I'd get in the next one.

⟨⟩

I disconnected my call, got off the couch in the living room, and headed down the hall. Hearing Godsmack playing low in the kitchen, I got myself a diet Fanta Grape from the fridge Ben had moved in the den.

Then I walked across the hall and stood outside the baby gate at the kitchen door, which was there to keep Gus out. This was something Gus didn't like and I knew this considering he was sitting on his ass at the door, his tail wagging, his eyes aimed through the gate.

I aimed my eyes into the kitchen and saw my man in the gutted space, its walls newly painted butter yellow, laying tile.

"I'm uncertain how me wanting new towels, a floor, and backsplashes translated into you gutting the entire kitchen," I remarked, popping the tab on my Fanta.

"Is that you askin' me why I'm doin' something?"

I grinned. "Yeah."

He looked from the tile he'd just laid to me. "You get a new kitchen. Why do you wanna know why I'm givin' it to you?"

"Because I don't have a stove right now and I like havin' a stove."

Ben looked back to what he was doing, saying, "You'll have a stove in about a week."

"A week is a long time," I noted.

"A week is a week," he replied.

"True enough," I muttered, smiling. "A week is a week."

"You done bustin' my chops?" Benny asked, setting in another tile.

"Maybe."

"Whatever," he murmured, grinning at the tile, being my awesome Benny because I was a woman who busted her man's chops and he was a man who liked it.

"You wanna know what Tandy said?" I asked.

"Yeah," he answered.

"The board officially promoted Travis Berger from acting CEO to just plain CEO, seein' as he did so well with all that crap that went down after Tenrix bein' bad was outed."

"And I give a shit about that because…?" Ben queried.

I grinned at the lip of my can and replied, "Just an FYI," before I took a sip.

"What did Tandy say about the job?"

"Seein' as it pays ten grand more a year and I told her I talked my new bosses into payin' her moving expenses because she was *that good* of an assistant, she said she'd take it."

Benny's eyes came to me and I found, not for the first time, that I was right; I wasn't used to their beauty. I'd never get used to their beauty. Especially not when they looked like that—happy in a way that I knew he was happy for me.

"Good news, baby," he said softly.

"Yeah," I replied just as softly. "Team Frankie and Tandy are gonna kick ass at our new jobs in Chicago."

He smiled at me.

No. I'd never get used to getting all that goodness from Benny Bianchi.

"We'll celebrate tonight. Come in and keep me company in the kitchen," he invited on an order.

"That I can do," I told him, but only because I liked keeping him company in his kitchen. "Now, what I'm gonna do is leave you to do what you seem to have to do. I'm goin' over to bug Mrs. Zambino."

"Take Gus with you. He's makin' me feel guilty."

I looked down at Gus, who did indeed look like he was pining for his daddy, even if his daddy was only six feet away.

I looked back at Benny. "You got it, *capo*."

Ben gave me a look, but he did it with his lips twitching.

I gave him a grin and informed him, "You can turn the music back up now." Then I patted my thigh and called my dog as I moved to the front door. Gus followed me, no longer pining for Daddy. He was panting and had a doggie smile on his face, happy he was getting time with Mommy.

The music ratcheted high. I grinned as I found my cardigan, pulled it on, put the leash on Gus, and we headed out the door and across the street. I walked up Mrs. Zambino's stoop and Gus waddled up beside me.

Once there, I juggled the leash and my hold on my can of pop and knocked on the door.

She opened it two seconds later and a half second after that, demanded to know, "What are you and that mongrel doing over here?"

I took in her perfectly coifed hair and made a mental note to ask where she got her sweater so I could get the same exact one before I replied, "We've come for a visit."

"I thought Benny was puttin' in a new kitchen for you," she noted.

"He is," I confirmed.

"And why aren't you helpin' him?"

I looked down at my awesome jeans, my fabulous top, my stylish cardie, and my magnificent high-heeled boots, then I looked at her.

"Do I look like a woman who lays tile?"

"He should have help," she informed me.

"Manny's gonna come over when he does the cupboards and stuff," I informed her.

"He's doin' something *for you*, Francesca."

"Yes, and it's my job to look amazing to remind him why, thus…" I swept a hand down my front and let that speak the rest for me.

She rolled her eyes.

"Are you gonna let us in?" I asked.

"I suppose," she muttered irritably and stepped aside, but did this still muttering. "You get any of that grape soda on my furniture, you're payin' for the cleaning."

"I'll be careful, Mrs. Zambino," I said as we moved in.

We got settled in her living room. I let Gus off his leash and he went directly to Mrs. Zambino's feet and laid on them.

She said not one word about this, mostly because she might call him "the mongrel," but she adored him. I knew this because she came over in the mornings and demanded he go on her power walks with her.

She did this saying, "Someone has to keep that mongrel in shape," even though she knew Benny and/or I took him on at least three walks a day.

Instead of saying something about Gus, she pierced me with her gaze. "I see Benny hasn't put a ring on your finger."

"Not yet."

"He should see to that. Livin' together without God's sanction. Now that Manny has finally made an honest woman of his Sela, Theresa's lightin' candle after candle in hopes of savin' *your* souls."

I grinned at her because of her totally-didn't-mean-it surly words and at the reminder of Manny and Sela's awesome wedding.

I did this before I suggested, "Why don't you do me a favor and tell him to get on that?"

She looked to her knees, murmuring, "I don't want to disturb his work in your kitchen."

This meant she was happy giving me shit, but she wasn't about to give the same to Benny Bianchi. I figured this was not because she was afraid of Benny. She wasn't afraid of anything. This was because she didn't want to do anything that might make him stop fixing stuff around her house when it broke, which didn't happen frequently, but her house was old so it happened regularly.

"Mrs. Zambino," I called, and she looked back at me. I crossed my legs and held her eyes as I said straight out, "You were right."

"I'm always right," she returned, and I grinned again. "But what in particular was I right about this time?"

"Love is never wrong."

She studied me, but I could swear her eyes got soft.

"I'm lucky," I said quietly. "Havin' an old woman across the street who'll give me wisdom."

She looked toward her TV.

"Mrs. Zambino," I called again, and she looked to me. "It took a while, but you started it, so you gotta know, I look in the mirror now and see what you see."

Yes. Definitely. Her eyes were soft.

"Frankie," she whispered.

"Do you know what I see when I look at you?" I asked.

She pressed her lips together.

"Pure beauty," I said softly.

That was when I saw her eyes get bright a second before I saw her chin lift and heard her mouth say, "If you think you can get into my will by bein' sweet to me, forget it. I got enough girls fightin' over my jewelry and handbags. I'll pick a piece for you to get when I die and you'll like it."

"Of course I will, you have great taste," I told her.

"I know I do," she returned.

That was when I burst out laughing.

⌒〜

The instant the waiter left our table, I grabbed my Champagne glass, glued my eyes to Benny across from me, put my glass to my lips, and belted it back.

All of it.

Benny burst out laughing.

We were at Giuseppe's. I was wearing a phenomenal dress I knew was phenomenal because we were late for our reservation, seeing as Benny banged me against the wall about a nanosecond after he saw me in it.

We were there to celebrate our new kitchen, which was a bit crazy, seeing as I didn't want to be in a restaurant. I'd had enough of restaurants and takeaway and microwave meals the last month Benny spent working on the kitchen.

What I wanted was to use my fabulous new stove and stare into my scarily expensive, new stainless-steel fridge until it started beeping (then close the door, open it, and stare into the cavernous space again).

But Benny wanted to celebrate at Giuseppe's.

And Giuseppe's was Giuseppe's.

So who was I to say no?

Ben reached to the Champagne bottle and started to refill my glass, saying, "Glad we had a good week at the restaurant so I don't have to take out a loan to pay our check tonight."

Every week was a good week at Vinnie and Benny's Pizzeria.

But I didn't say that.

I said, "Most fortunate."

He shoved the bottle back into the bucket, then shoved his hand into his inside jacket pocket, all this saying, "Also glad business is steady so I could pay for the new kitchen I know you love but still bitched about, and so I could get you this."

That was when he set a diamond ring at the top of my place setting.

I stared at the cushion-cut diamond surrounded with little diamonds twinkling in the candlelight. A ring that was not small or understated. A ring that was about flash and impact.

A ring that was perfect for me.

Then my eyes shot to Benny, the man who was perfect for me.

His brows rose, but his eyes were locked to mine as his deep, easy voice asked, "Wanna spend the rest of your life with me?"

My breath stopped.

"Frankie?" he called.

I didn't move or speak. I just sat frozen in my chair staring at my Benny Bianchi.

"*Cara*," he whispered.

"Did you have to ask?" I whispered back, and his lips curved up.

"No."

"Will you put the ring on me?"

That was when he gave me a full-on, beautiful Benny Bianchi smile.

"Yeah."

I licked my lips and held out my hand.

Ben reached out and picked up the ring. He slid it on my finger and, swear to God, I felt an electric charge over every centimeter of skin as he glided it to the base.

When he was done, his fingers curled around the side of my hand with the pad of his thumb pressed to the diamond, but his eyes stayed on mine.

"You gonna down another glass of Champagne?" he asked.

"Absolutely."

"You wanna do that after you kiss me?"

"Most definitely."

We sat there, Ben holding my hand, his thumb pressed to the diamond he just laid on me, and neither of us moved. We just looked into each other eyes.

When this lasted awhile, Ben prompted, "You wanna do that before the waiter comes back, interrupts the most important moment in my life, and pisses me off?"

The most important moment in my life.

God.

Benny.

I moved, but Benny didn't let go of my hand and he continued not to let it go, even as I rounded the table and he shoved his chair back.

We were in Giuseppe's. This demanded decorum.

But I didn't care.

I sat in his lap, slid the fingers of my free hand in his amazing hair, while he pressed the hand he held to his chest. Once situated as close as I could get to my man, I tipped my head and kissed my brand-new fiancé.

When I was done, Ben didn't let me up. He cupped the back of my head, pressed my forehead to his, and kept hold of my eyes.

"Never loved another woman. Not in my life," he said quietly, and my breath went funny. "Waited until I got it right," he went on. His hand squeezed mine, he moved so the tip of his nose skimmed mine, and he finished, "I got it right."

God.

Benny.

"Honey," I whispered.

"Love you, Frankie," he whispered back.

"Love you too, Benny."

I watched his eyes smile, then this time, he kissed me.

When he was done, he pulled an inch away and declared, "Told Ma I was givin' you Aunt Mary's ring. Gotta be you who tells her you didn't want it."

I jerked back and snapped, "Benny!"

Then I was jerked forward, held tight in his arms, in his lap, and I listened just as I felt Benny Bianchi burst out laughing against the skin of my neck.

Oh well.

Whatever.

So Theresa would be mad at me about the ring.

She'd get over it.

I sat curled in the corner of Gina's couch in her living room, Sal in his armchair beside me.

Benny was in the kitchen helping Gina get after-dinner coffees for everybody.

This was because he was awesome.

This was also because he was doing what I'd asked him to do before we went over to Sal and Gina's for dinner.

"Proud of that boy," Sal said, and I looked to him. "Went large. My Frankie, she deserves a man who'll go big."

I had no idea what he was talking about until he reached out and touched the kickass diamond on my finger that was on the hand I had lying on the armrest close to him.

"Yeah, he's awesome," I agreed.

Sal looked from my ring to my eyes, his warm with happiness for me, and he said, "Yeah."

I had to admit, I loved it that Sal loved Benny for me.

And now it was time.

"Speaking of my ring," I started, straightening a little in the couch and turning fully to Sal.

"Frankie, *amata*, it's okay," Sal said softly.

"I—"

"Gina and I understand."

"Sal, if you'd—"

"We're just glad Benny brought you over for dinner tonight so we could have our moment to celebrate your good news with the two of you."

"Sal—"

He reached out his hand and curled it around mine. "Happy for you, Francesca."

"Can I say something?" I asked.

He steadily kept my gaze and nodded.

"I talked to Vinnie and Theresa."

"You don't—"

"Sal," I cut him off quietly. "Please let me finish."

He shut up.

"Benny talked to them with me."

When I said no more, Sal nodded.

"They understand."

"It's a joyous day for them, you and Benny, and Gina and I don't—"

I interrupted him again.

"They understand and agree that, if you want to do it, you should give me away."

Sal went still.

I went on.

"It was Benny's idea."

Sal stared at me.

Suddenly, I felt funny.

"Dad still isn't talking to me, partly because I'm not talking to him, and anyway, he really didn't earn that honor. But if that's weird to you—" I began.

That was when, suddenly, my hand was jerked, making my arm lurch painfully right before I was out of the couch, on my feet, and in Sal's tight embrace.

He still said nothing. He just kept hold of me.

So I asked, "Can I take that as a yes?"

He continued his silence, but he gave me a squeeze that took the breath right out of me.

I took that as a yes.

"Your father is a horse's ass."

This was said by Chrissy, who was sitting at the table next to me.

It was Benny's and my engagement party. A huge do that Vinnie and Theresa insisted we have since, once Sal agreed to take the honor of giving me away, he horned in and declared he was paying for the entire wedding. Benny and him got into it and the compromise was that Benny and I were going to pay for the rehearsal dinner and honeymoon.

So when there was nothing left to pay for, Theresa lost her mind and declared we were going to have a huge-ass engagement party. She then set about planning it before she got the official go-ahead from Benny and me.

Benny found this annoying.

I liked parties and having a reason to buy a fabulous dress that would make my fiancé get hard, so I absolutely didn't.

"What's this?" Cheryl asked, sitting with Chrissy, Cat, Violet, Asheeka, and me.

I tore my eyes away from Keira, who'd brought up her very handsome young boyfriend, Jasper Layne, so she could show him off at the party, and looked to Cheryl.

But Cat, holding her sleeping son, Sean, piped up first.

"Enzo Senior, our not-so-illustrious dad, bein' a moron. No surprise." She looked to me. "It's Nat who has my panties in a bunch."

Mine weren't.

I was hurt.

Genuinely.

I'd called to share the news and heal the breach. I did it, even though I had a feeling Nat wouldn't be in a good mood, mostly because she was in the middle of a divorce, living with Ninette, and things weren't going well.

Nat being Nat, she had pushed it, but Davey beat the rap, what with the amount of damage he'd sustained and Nat not even having a bruise. But even before, his mom had bailed him out, then he'd kicked Nat's ass out, changed the locks, and got a second job so he could pay for the attorney he hired to file for divorce.

She was now working as a stripper, living with a mom who never grew up, and had lost the man she loved—all that on her because she made bad decisions. All she refused to grow up and see her decisions, and change the course of her life, so she just got bitchier.

She was not feeling family love so when I'd called to heal the breach and ask her to be a bridesmaid, she told me to go fuck myself and, while I was at it, invited me to tell Benny to do the same.

I told Benny and he not only heard my words, he got a look at my face as I was saying them.

So he declared, "*Now* that bitch is dead to you and, *tesorina*, I *mean that*."

I couldn't miss the look on his face when he was saying it so I knew he meant it.

But the truth was, with that, it was up to Nat to heal the breach.

She wouldn't and that hurt.

But that was her decision too.

Ninette decided to side with Nat, mostly because she wasn't paying any rent and knew where her bread was buttered.

That didn't hurt. I'd long since learned not to let Ninette's selfishness dig deep.

I'd asked Enzo Senior to come. He didn't pick up my call so the invitation was extended on voicemail. He didn't respond and I was okay with that because I wanted Chrissy and Eva there and I wanted to have a good time without any awkwardness, so in the end, he gave me what I wanted. Enzo Junior couldn't come because he had zero money, considering how much child support he was paying. But my brother Dino and his family were there, as were Cat and hers.

As was the rest of mine, the ones who were true, even if they weren't blood.

"Suffice it to say, our family's messy," I told Cheryl.

"Whose isn't?" she asked back, and everyone knew the answer to that. Nobody's.

Somehow escaping Art and Sela, who had been looking after her, Eva trundled over to her mom and slapped her hands on her thigh, then turned to me and slapped her hands on mine. This meant I picked my baby sister up, put her in my lap, and she shouted, "Fwanquee!"

I smiled at her, dipped low, and skimmed my nose against hers.

She giggled, caught sight of Vi, squirmed in my lap, and launched herself into Vi's arms.

Something about this made me search the room, and there I found Cal talking with Sal and Vinnie. I kept looking and saw Theresa, who was with Tandy and Kate, holding Angie.

Cal's back was to them. He had a beer in hand and his lips curved up at something Sal was saying.

There you go. Cal had finally settled into happiness.

And that settled happily in my soul.

"News from the 'burg, Keirry's boy's dad is now very taken," Cheryl told me, and I looked to her.

"Yeah?"

"Colt and Feb scenario," she explained. "Apparently, he fell for a girl years ago. They broke up, now they're back together and blissfully happy."

"Cool for him," I said.

"Another one bites the dust," she replied.

I smiled at her but caught sight of Eva out of the corner of my eye, launching herself my way and moved just in time to catch her.

"I work in construction," Cat stated, cottoning on to what Cheryl did not say but still did. "Lotta guys I could introduce you to."

"I live in Indiana," Cheryl pointed out.

Cat gave Cheryl a once-over, then replied, "They find total losers. Women…" She shook her head. "You would *not* believe. I think they'd do long-distance in order to get a live one."

"Haul out your cell, bitch, and program my number," Cheryl ordered.

Violet looked to me and grinned.

I grinned back.

After doing that, my gaze wandered from Violet to across the room.

There, I saw Benny standing with Mrs. Zambino and half of her bowling posse. It looked like they were all talking at once, but Mrs. Zambino had a death grip on Benny's arm, even though it appeared she was telling off one of her minions and doing it testily.

But my man was looking at me.

I did my best to hold my active sister safe against me, even as I lifted my fingers to my lips and blew him a kiss.

He caught it and I knew this because, from all the way across the room, I saw his beautiful eyes smile.

Or maybe I didn't see it.

But I knew it happened because I felt it.

Strange how he could do that. Me sitting with my girls, surrounded by people I love, celebrating my engagement to the best man in the world, holding my baby sister against me, all of that a promise fulfilled, and he did it again.

With just a look and a feeling.

Making another promise come true.

⟿

I signed the room service bill and, staring at it, suddenly froze.

There it was. In black ink.

Francesca Bianchi.

I came unfrozen and I did this in order to smile.

Huge.

I handed the bill to the staff member with his tip. He dipped his chin and walked out the door. I opened it behind him and resecured the Do Not Disturb sign.

"Jesus, Frankie, you answered the door?" Ben growled, and I turned to watch him walk in, towel around his hips.

Eyes to the prize.

There was my prize. Mine to keep for always.

Benny.

"You were in the bathroom," I pointed out.

"Yeah, for two minutes."

"I need Champagne."

"And you couldn't wait two minutes?"

"No. And it's rude to make someone wait outside a door for two minutes, not to mention he might have walked away."

"You're in a nightie," Ben pointed out.

"I'm sure he's seen women in less," I returned, then noted, "You're in a towel."

"I'm a guy. Was he a guy?"

"Yes."

His eyes moved the length of me in my little, lacy, clingy, ivory nightie.

"Christ," he muttered, going to the Champagne.

I looked to the windows.

Vi was right.

Virgin Gorda was *awesome.*

Or at least it looked that way.

Maybe, before the end of our two-week honeymoon, Ben and I would see more of it than what we could see from our hotel room window.

Though, I wasn't holding much hope for that since we'd already been there four days and we hadn't left our room.

I heard the Champagne cork pop and looked to my husband.

He was looking at me.

"You wanna dirty a glass?" he asked, holding the bottle by its neck.

"No way," I answered.

He grinned at me.

Then he stalked me.

I retreated.

Straight to the bed.

Ben handed the menu to the waiter and looked across the table at his wife.

Big hair. Dark makeup. Beauty by candlelight.

Then he looked down at her full glass of Champagne, something she hadn't touched in all the time since the waiter put it in front of her, they looked over their menus, the waiter came back, and they ordered.

"Not gonna try to break the record for fastest single-person consumption of a bottle of Champagne tonight?" he teased.

She looked into his eyes and smiled that smile he liked so fucking much.

But this time, she *did* have a secret.

A secret she wasn't keeping.

He knew this when she replied, "No, seein' as I can't drink for a while 'cause I'm carrying your baby."

Benny went still.

She kept talking.

"When you see the waiter, can you order me a virgin Bellini?"

Benny didn't answer.

"Benny?" she called.

He didn't move or speak. He just sat frozen in his chair, staring at his Frankie.

"Honey," she whispered.

"Get over here right now," he growled.

For once, his wife didn't give him lip. She got up, rounded the table, he pushed back, and she sat right in his lap and tipped her face to his so he could take her mouth.

When he was done, he held her eyes but moved a hand to her flat belly where she was nurturing their baby.

Fuck.

Frankie.

"Happy?" she whispered.

"Absolutely."

She skimmed her nose against the tip of his before she said quietly, "Love you, Benny Bianchi."

Jesus, so fucking sweet.

"Love you too, Frankie Bianchi."

He watched her eyes smile, felt her touch her lips to his, then she slid off his lap.

He was wiping her lip gloss from his mouth when he caught sight of Elena at the hostess station, smiling at them.

Having his own place, a place where people went to have good times, he knew that feeling. He knew it was why, generation after generation, you kept that close, worked your ass off to make it thrive—so you could give it your family.

But she got the better parts and they came often. People coming to her restaurant for reasons just like this—to share the most important moments of their lives.

He lifted his chin to her, then looked back at his pregnant wife.

Ten minutes ago, she was crazy-beautiful.

Right then, right there, sitting across from him, carrying his baby, Benny knew without a doubt there was nothing in his life he could see or feel that would be more beautiful.

He would be wrong.

⟨⟩

Ben slid his hand down Frankie's side, in, and cupped her bare ass. He pulled her up so she could take his cock deeper, and when she did, he felt her breath go heavy at his ear.

"Like that, baby?" he whispered in hers, thrusting slow, but firm and deep.

"Yes, Benny."

"You want more, all you gotta do is tell me."

She squeezed the leg she had wrapped around his thigh tighter, trailed her fingers up his spine, and glided her other hand through his hair as she took his cock again and said on a soft breath, "I know, honey."

Benny smelled his wife, felt her hair on his cheek, her wet pussy clutch his cock, and listened to the noises she was making, even as he heard through the opened window the sounds of the surf pounding against the shore and his son and daughter shouting and giggling as they played in the sand with their grandparents.

And he had it again.

A moment in his life where he was in no doubt there would ever be another more beautiful.

This time, though, even as he experienced it and had no doubts about it, he still knew he would be proved wrong.

Ben walked into the huge-ass kitchen of the huge-ass house he'd bought for his family six years ago when Frankie popped out his second son and his third baby.

When he did, he stopped dead when he saw Frankie in her business suit and heels, standing with a pen in one hand, cell to her ear in the other, writing something on the calendar, saying into the phone, "Yeah. We can do that. We're free." She was silent a moment before she said, "Cool. What do you need us to bring?"

He heard her laugh and even a sound he liked hearing no matter how much he heard it, and he heard it a lot, didn't take him out of his freeze.

"We can do that. Totally. See you then." A pause before, "Yeah. You too. Later, Vi."

She disconnected, looked to him, and smiled.

"Hey, baby."

"Hey, *cara*," he said quietly, her smile and greeting finally pulling him out of the freeze.

"Vi and Cal are havin' a barbeque. We're goin' down. Two weeks."

"She pregnant again?" he asked, and that got him another smile.

"No."

He went to the coffeepot asking, "You pregnant again?"

"Not that I know of."

He poured himself a cup, muttering, "Just checking."

"I have a meeting so you have to pick Alessandra up from dance. And there are birthday cards on the counter." She tipped her head that way. "The kids have signed them and they're stamped and addressed. Could you sign them and get them in the mail today?"

He turned, leaned hips against the counter, and replied, "Got it covered," before taking a sip of coffee.

Her eyes went to the ceiling. "Are they tearin' shit up?"

"Probably."

"They gotta get ready for school."

"Seein' as that happens every day and I take them there, I know that, Frankie."

She tilted her head to the side. "You're standin' there enjoyin' a cup of coffee, Benny."

"It looks like I'm enjoyin' a cup of coffee. What I'm really doin' is a favor to the teachers, lettin' our hellions get some of their energy out before I drop 'em at school. That means they'll wreak havoc here and only 'cause mayhem there."

"Oh, that's what you're doin'," she muttered, her lips curving.

He watched her lips before he looked into her eyes and ordered, "Stop bustin' my chops, give me a kiss, and go to work."

Those eyes got squinty. "Stop bein' bossy."

He grinned at her.

Her eyes got squintier.

"Come here, baby," he demanded quietly.

She rolled her eyes and came there.

He pulled her into his arms, put his mouth to hers, hers opened, and like always, Ben didn't waste the opportunity. He drank deep.

When he lifted his head, she said softly, "Remember, we're comin' to the pizzeria for dinner."

The best nights at work, when Frankie hauled their crew to the restaurant. They always started at a table. They always ended in the kitchen, his girl helping her daddy, his boys stealing balls of mozzarella and eating them in his office, Frankie gabbing to his kids.

"I remember."

"Okay, honey."

He lifted his head and touched his lips to her forehead.

She bent in and kissed his jaw.

"Dad!" they heard Joey shouting from upstairs. "Van is gettin' into my stuff!"

"Donovan!" Benny shouted back, still holding his baby close. "Leave your brother's stuff alone!"

That was when they heard from Van, "Joey's got a big mouth!"

And that was when they heard from Joey, "It's *my* stuff!"

And that was when he felt his wife kiss his jaw again before she whispered in his ear, "Good luck with that, baby."

Benny looked down to catch her smiling.

She pulled out of his arms, grabbed her purse, computer bag, and travel mug, shouting toward the door, "Momma's leavin' and she's doin' it lovin' her babies!"

"'Bye, Momma," Alessandra, their oldest, shouted. "Love you!"

"'Bye, Mom!" Joey, their second, yelled.

"'Bye!" Van, their last, put his in, then bellowed, "*Joey!*"

She grinned at Benny and walked through the door to the garage.

It was then that Ben heard Gus bark, this always a warning that things were deteriorating.

But before he hauled his ass from the counter and walked through his huge-ass kitchen to sort out his sons, he looked toward the calendar.

Varied colors of ink. Different handwriting. Mostly Frankie's. Some of Benny's. Even some of Ales's and Joey's. All marked up. Hardly any white space at all. Alessandra's dance. Joseph's karate. Playdates for Donovan. Slumber parties for his girl. Sleepovers for his boys. Birthdays. Dinners with Man and Sela and their brood. His Ma and Pop. Chrissy and Eva. Cat and Art and their crew. And when they could expect people walking through their door to get their own meal made by Frankie.

All the shit that makes a good life scribbled in the blocks printed on glossy paper hanging on a wall.

And on their calendar, full of scribbles, proof the Bianchis lived a good life.

They'd had calendars like that for years.

And Frankie kept each one. Taking it down on January first, always when Benny was in the kitchen. Then putting the new one up and carefully sliding the old one on the shelf in the living room by the TV that held the kids' baby books and their wedding album.

Taking in his life on a calendar meant Benny was smiling at his feet as he walked out of his kitchen, down the hall to the foot of the stairs, and shouted up them, "Right! Stop screwin' around! School! Now!"

He heard pounding feet.

Then he saw Gus at the top of the stairs. Their dog woofed, reporting in that the kids were minding.

And since Dad had spoken, and even Van listened when Dad spoke, Ben stood where he was, arms crossed on his chest, waiting for his kids so he could take them to school.

~

Theresa Bianchi parked at the back of the pizzeria.

She turned to her big bag in the seat beside her, hefted it up, and looped the straps over her shoulder before she got out of the car.

She headed in the back door and went directly to her son's office.

There, she saw her handsome boy standing at his desk, phone to his ear.

Always standing, her Benny. She didn't think she'd ever seen him sitting at his desk. Even as a child, he'd always been doing something.

Now as a man, a husband, a father, a business owner, he was the same... except more. Even sitting and watching a game on TV, he seemed somehow full of energy.

Electric.

His gaze came to her and his lips curled up.

She smiled at him and walked in, taking her bag from her arm.

She opened it and pulled out the picture she'd put in the frame that morning.

She set it on its stand on his desk, which was cluttered with some papers, but mostly it was cluttered with picture frames.

Like she'd done since they opened their pizzeria, she still hung pictures of family all over the dining room. So many, from the time her kids were little through the time her kids had kids, the walls were covered in them.

Except there weren't many of Benny's family.

This was because her son didn't get into the dining room very often. But he did spend time in his office. And since he did, if he saw a photo of his family that his mother put on one of the walls in their pizzeria, he took it down and set it on his desk so it was in a place where he could see it.

So now, Theresa didn't put the photos she took of Benny and his family in the dining room.

She put them on his desk.

And she put that one on his desk. Eight-by-ten. Black-and-white. She took it at Frankie's last birthday party.

In it, Benny and Cal were standing close together at the front door. Benny had Alessandra leaning heavily against his side, tuckered out because it was late. So tired, her thick, lush lashes were sweeping her cheeks. She had her daddy's arm around her shoulders.

Cal was holding his youngest son, little Ben, in his arms. Her boy Benny's namesake was asleep. Joey, Van, and Vi and Cal's second son, Sam, were in the shot—a blur, because they were chasing each other.

Benny and Cal were looking at each other and they were grinning.

Off to the side, Frankie and Violet also stood close. Frankie was wearing her tight, short dress, with her head tipped back, laughing. Vi had Angie's hand in hers and she was looking down at her smiling daughter. Vi was also laughing.

To the other side, Kate and her husband, Tony, and Keira and her fiancé, Jasper, were standing and talking to Vinnie. They were also laughing.

Balloons festooned the entryway. Cal and Vi and their family were getting ready to leave.

It had taken them half an hour to get out the door.

But no one complained.

Family always had a lot to say, but most of it happened during goodbyes.

This was because no one liked saying them.

Once Theresa set the picture down, she lifted her eyes to her son.

He was looking at the picture in its frame. His face was soft with memories.

Then he looked at his mother and she saw his eyes warm with love.

Theresa gave him another smile as she walked silently out of his office, that warm look of love in his beautiful eyes a memory she'd forever keep.

That was her Benny.

We'll say goodbye to The 'Burg with *Hold On.*